Out of Oz

ALSO BY GREGORY MAGUIRE

Confessions of an Ugly Stepsister

Lost

Mirror Mirror

Making Mischief: A Maurice Sendak Appreciation

Matchless

The Next Queen of Heaven

OTHER BOOKS IN THE WICKED YEARS

Wicked

Son of a Witch

A Lion Among Men

Out of Oz

The Final Volume in the Wicked Years

Gregory Maguire

ILLUSTRATIONS BY DOUGLAS SMITH

HARPER LUXE

An Imprint of HarperCollinsPublishers

"Duck Variations" © 2010, Ron MacLean
"Atlantis" © 2010, Todd Hearon
Maps designed by Gregory Maguire, drawn by Douglas Smith
Illustrations by Douglas Smith

HarperCollins books may be purchased for educational, business, or sales promotional use. For information please write: Special Markets Department, HarperCollins Publishers, 10 East 53rd Street, New York, NY 10022.

FIRST HARPERLUXE EDITION

HarperLuxe™ is a trademark of HarperCollins Publishers

Library of Congress Cataloging-in-Publication Data is available upon request.

ISBN: 978-0-06-208868-0

11 12 13 14 15 ID/RRD 10 9 8 7 6 5 4 3 2 1

for Cassie Jones

Contents

The Wicked Years
A Note to Readers

Our story so far:

Wicked begins with the birth of a green-skinned child, Elphaba Thropp—later known as the Wicked Witch of the West—and portrays her unlikely college friendship with Galinda Upland and her romance with Fiyero Tigelaar. The arriviste Wizard of Oz consolidates his power in the Emerald City and throughout Oz. Under the governance of the Wicked Witch of the East, Nessarose Thropp, Munchkinland secedes from Loyal Oz. The novel closes with the Matter of Dorothy, when Elphaba is thirty-eight and her son, Liir Thropp, is fourteen.

Son of a Witch tells the story of Liir's life, revealed in flashbacks, while Elphaba's brother Shell strengthens his position in the Emerald City, particularly against Munchkinland. Orphaned at fourteen, without guidance or patronage, Liir stumbles into the military, leads a raid against Quadlings, and goes AWOL, eventually heading a protest against his uncle Shell, now the Emperor of Oz. *Son of a Witch* concludes with the arrival of a child—a green-skinned daughter—born to Liir and Candle, a Quadling. Liir is about twenty-four.

A Lion Among Men refers to the Cowardly Lion, known as Brrr. His story is told alternately with that of the ancient oracle, Yackle. Brrr muses on his part in the Matter of Dorothy, his rise and fall in society, and his plea-bargaining with Emerald City magistrates to avoid a prison sentence. Hunting for the mysterious oracle Yackle, he locates the lost Grimmerie in the bargain. At novel's end, a skirmish between rabble-rousing Munchkinlanders and the Emerald City military threatens to ignite into full-scale civil war. Caught in the crosshairs, Brrr escapes with the troupe that accompanies the Clock of the Time Dragon.

Out of Oz begins a few months after the close of *A Lion Among Men*.

Charting the Wicked
Years Chronologically

"Oh, as to time, well, no one in Oz ticks off tocks very systematically."
Each dot or upstroke represents a year . . . more or less.

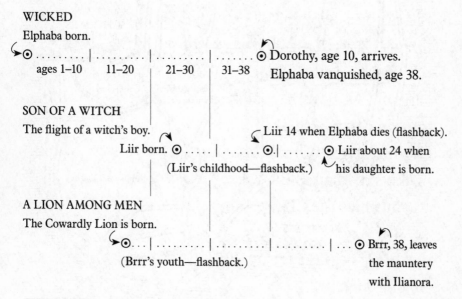

WICKED
Elphaba born.

ages 1–10   11–20   21–30   31–38   Dorothy, age 10, arrives.
Elphaba vanquished, age 38.

SON OF A WITCH
The flight of a witch's boy.   Liir 14 when Elphaba dies (flashback).
Liir born.   Liir about 24 when
(Liir's childhood—flashback.)   his daughter is born.

A LION AMONG MEN
The Cowardly Lion is born.
                                                                           Brrr, 38, leaves
(Brrr's youth—flashback.)   the mauntery
                                                                           with Ilianora.

OUT OF OZ
The story begins six months after the end of A LION AMONG MEN.
Liir is about 30; Rain is 7 or 8, give or take.

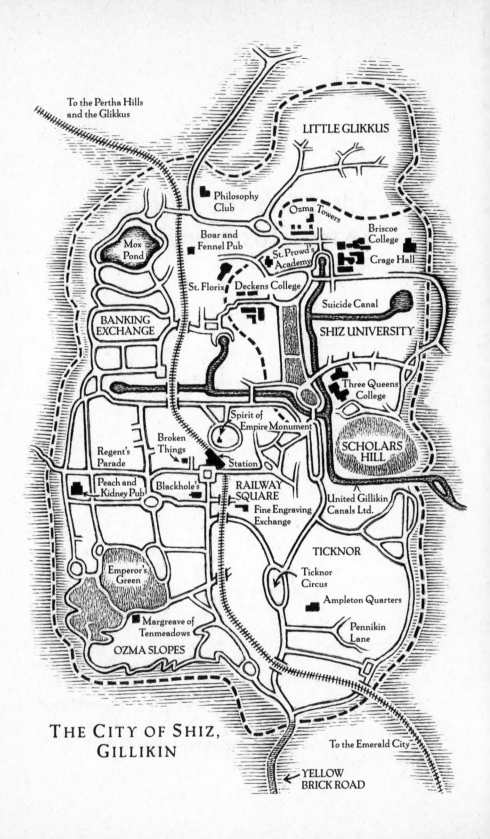

To the Pertha Hills
and the Glikkus

LITTLE GLIKKUS

Philosophy
Club

Ozma Towers

Briscoe
College

Boar and
Fennel Pub

St. Prowd's
Academy

Crage Hall

Mox
Pond

St. Florix

Deckens College

Suicide Canal

BANKING
EXCHANGE

SHIZ UNIVERSITY

Three Queens
College

Spirit of
Empire Monument

SCHOLARS
HILL

Regent's
Parade

Broken
Things

Station

Peach and
Kidney Pub

Blackhole's

RAILWAY
SQUARE

United Gillikin
Canals Ltd.

Fine Engraving
Exchange

TICKNOR

Emperor's
Green

Ticknor
Circus

Ampleton Quarters

Margreave of
Tenmeadows

Pennikin
Lane

OZMA SLOPES

THE CITY OF SHIZ,
GILLIKIN

To the Emerald City

← YELLOW
BRICK ROAD

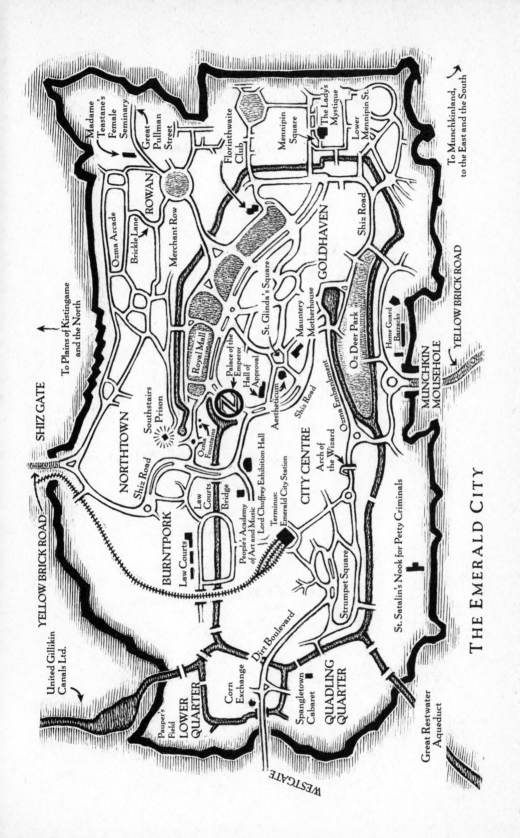

THE EMERALD CITY

Significant Families of Oz

Key

= marriage   (~) romance sans wedlock

THE HOUSE OF OZMA
——*The Emerald City*——

Ozma Initiata

(many **Ozmas** and several Ozma Regents)

Ozma the Bilious = Pastorius (the Ozma Regent)

Ozma Tippetarius

THE THROPPS OF MUNCHKINLAND
—Colwen Grounds in Munchkinland—

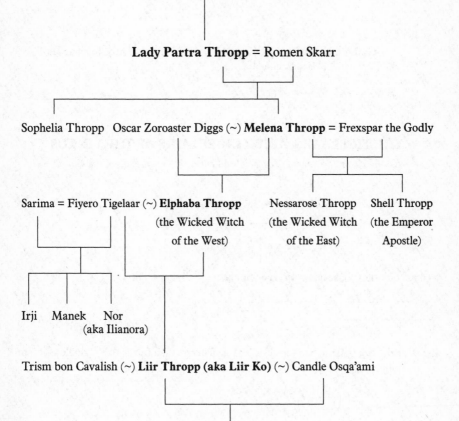

Peerless Thropp (the Eminent Thropp)

Lady Partra Thropp = Romen Skarr

Sophelia Thropp   Oscar Zoroaster Diggs (~) **Melena Thropp** = Frexspar the Godly

Sarima = Fiyero Tigelaar (~) **Elphaba Thropp**   Nessarose Thropp   Shell Thropp
(the Wicked Witch   (the Wicked Witch   (the Emperor
of the West)   of the East)   Apostle)

Irji   Manek   Nor
(aka Ilianora)

Trism bon Cavalish (~) **Liir Thropp (aka Liir Ko)** (~) Candle Osqa'ami

(Oziandra) Rain

THE UPLANDS OF GILLIKIN
——Frottica in northwest Gillikin——

Larena Upland = Highmuster Arduenna

Galinda Upland (aka Glinda) = Lord Chuffrey of Mockbeggar Hall
(Throne Minister)

THE TIGELAARS, ARJIKI CHIEFTAINS OF THE VINKUS
——Kiamo Ko on the slopes of Knobblehead Pike, the Great Kells of the Vinkus——

Marillot Tigelaar = Baxiana of Upper Fanarra

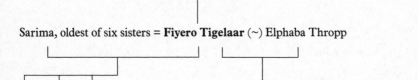

Sarima, oldest of six sisters = **Fiyero Tigelaar** (~) Elphaba Thropp

Irji   Manek   Nor   Trism bon Cavalish (~) **Liir Thropp (aka Liir Ko)** (~) Candle Osqa'ami
              (aka Ilianora)

(Oziandra) Rain

A Brief Outline of the Throne Ministers of Oz

Augmented with notes about selected incidents of interest to students of modern history.

THE OZMA YEARS

- The matrilineal House of Ozma established.

  The Ozma line descends from a Gillikinese clan. The Ozma line claims legitimacy through a purported divine relationship with Lurlina, fabled creatrix of Oz. Depending on the argument, historians recognize between forty and fifty legitimate Ozmas and their regents.

- The last Ozma, Ozma Tippetarius, is born of Ozma the Bilious.

Ozma the Bilious expires through an accident involving rat poisoning in the risotto. Her consort, Pastorius, becomes Ozma Regent during the minority of Ozma Tippetarius.

- Pastorius rules over central Oz.

The Ozma Regent renames the hamlet known as Nubbly Meadows, near the ancient burial ground of Open Tombs, as the Emerald City (EC). Declares the EC as the capital of united Oz.

- The Great Drought begins.

- By balloon, Oscar Zoroaster Diggs arrives in the Emerald City.

Diggs successfully mounts a Palace coup d'état. Pastorius is murdered, and the infant Ozma Tippetarius disappears. She is presumed slain, perhaps in Southstairs Prison (built over the Open Tombs), though an evergreen rumor claims she lies enchanted in a cave awaiting her return at Oz's darkest hour. Diggs becomes known as the Wizard of Oz.

THE WIZARDIC YEARS

- The Emerald City renovation is completed.

- The Wizard of Oz orders construction of the Yellow Brick Road.

  This serves as a highway for the armies of the EC and aids in the collection of local taxes from previously independent populations, especially in Quadling Country and on the eastern flanks of the Great Kells of the Vinkus.

- Animal Adverse laws enacted. (The "Animal Courtesy" acts.)

  Social unrest deriving from the Great Drought promotes an atmosphere of scapegoating and hysterical patriotism.

- Munchkinland secedes from Loyal Oz.

  Under the rule of Nessarose Thropp, Eminence of Munchkinland, the secession of the Free State of Munchkinland is conducted with a minimum of bloodshed. The "breadbasket of Oz" maintains an uneasy trade relationship with Loyal Oz.

- Nessarose Thropp dies.

  The arrival in Oz of a visitor, a Dorothy Gale of Canzizz (sometimes transcribed as "Canzuss" or "Kanziz"), results in the death of the Eminence. Though rumor suggests her sister, Elphaba Thropp, will return to Munchkinland to mount a more aggressive campaign against the EC than Nessarose ever did, such predictions prove baseless.

- Elphaba Thropp is vanquished.

The so-called Wicked Witch of the West, one-time agitator, now recluse, is subdued by the powerful Dorothy Gale.

- The Wizard of Oz abdicates the throne.

The Wizard has held power for almost forty years. The causes of his departure remain a matter of speculation.

THE TWIN INTERREGNUMS

- Lady Glinda Chuffrey, neé Upland, is briefly installed as Throne Minister.

The Animal Adverse laws are revoked, to little effect; Animals remain skeptical of their chances of being reintegrated into human society in Oz. Many refuse to return to Loyal Oz from Munchkinland, where they have taken refuge.

- The Scarecrow replaces Glinda as Throne Minister.

The Scarecrow, a figure of uncertain provenance, is often assumed to have been installed as Throne

Minister by Palace apparatchiks sympathetic to Shell Thropp, the youngest of the three Thropp siblings. The Scarecrow proves a weak figurehead—a straw man, figuratively as well as literally—though his elevation allows Shell Thropp to avoid having to challenge the popular Lady Glinda for the leadership. The Scarecrow's whereabouts following the end of his abbreviated realm are never revealed.

Some historians hold that the Scarecrow serving as Throne Minister is not the same Scarecrow who befriended Dorothy, though this assertion is based on circumstantial evidence.

THE EMPEROR APOSTLE

- Shell Thropp installs himself as Throne Minister of Oz.

Shell claims rights of ascendancy through an adroit manipulation of Palace power brokers. He styles himself an "Emperor Apostle" by dint of formidable piety and sacred election.

In retaliation for a sortie into Loyal Oz by a band of Munchkinlander guerrillas, Shell authorizes the invasion of Munchkinland for the purpose of appropriating Restwater, Oz's biggest lake.

[He] . . . had a magical view of the work of words, that "it is hard to conceive of a nobler magic" than the prospect of a salvation which is not just for us.

—Michael Wood, in *The London Review of Books,* on Frank Kermode's appraisal of I. A. Richards from *Bury Place Papers*

We believe the explanation we hear last. It's one of the ways in which narrative influences our perception of truth. We crave finality, an end to interpretation, not seeing that this too, the tying up of all loose ends in the last chapter, is only a storytelling ruse. The device runs contrary to experience, wouldn't you say? Time never simplifies—it unravels and complicates. Guilty parties show up everywhere. The plot does nothing but thicken.

—Michelle de Kretser, *The Hamilton Case*

Out of Oz

Prologue
Out of Oz

It would take Dorothy Gale and her relatives three days to reach the mountains by train from Kansas, the conductor told them.

No matter what the schoolteacher had said about Galileo, Copernicus, and those other spoilsports, any cockamamie theory that the world was round remained refuted by the geometrical instrument of a rattling train applied to the spare facts of a prairie. Dorothy watched eagles and hawks careering too high to cast shadows, she watched the returning larks and bluebirds, and she wondered what they knew about the shape of the world, and if they would ever tell her.

Then the Rockies began to ice up along the spring horizon beyond the shoot-'em-up town of Denver. Uncle Henry had never seen such a sight. He declared himself bewilligered at their height. "They surely do remind me of the Great Kells of Oz," agreed Dorothy, "though the Kells looked less bossy, somehow." She tried to ignore the glance Uncle Henry shared with Aunt Em.

Some of the passes being snowed over, even in early April, the train made slower progress than the time-table had promised. Aunt Em fretted that their hotel room would be given away. Uncle Henry replied with an attempt at savoir faire. "I'll wire ahead at the next opportunity, Em. Hush yourself and enjoy the nation."

What a charade, that they were accustomed to taking fancified holidays. They had little extra money for emergencies, Dorothy knew. They were spending their savings.

The train chuffed along valleys noisy with rushing waters, inched across trestles as if testing them for pur-chase. It lollygagged up slopes. One cloudy afternoon it maneuvered through so many switchbacks that the travelers lost all notion of east and west. In her seat, Dorothy hummed a little. Once she thought she saw a castle on a ridge, but it was only a tricky rock formation.

"But I never before saw a rock that looked like a castle," said Aunt Em brightly.

You never saw a castle, thought Dorothy, and tried not to be disappointed.

They worried their way through Nevada and its brownish springtime and at last came down into Californ-eye-ay through a napland of orchards and vineyards. When the train paused outside Sacramento to take on tinder, Dorothy saw a white peacock strutting along next to the tracks like a general surveying his troops. It paused at her window and fanned out its impossible stitchery. She could have sworn it was a White Peacock and that it would speak. But Toto began to yap out the open window, and the Bird kept its own counsel.

Finally the train shrugged and chuffed into San Francisco, a city so big and filthy and confounding that Uncle Henry dared to murmur, "*This* beats your old Emerald City, I'll warrant."

"Henry," said his wife. "Pursed lips are kind lips."

They found their hotel. The clerk was nice enough, a clean young man whose lips weren't so much pursed as rubied. He forgave their delay but could no longer supply them with a room only one flight up, as they'd been promised. Aunt Em refused to try Mr. Otis's hydraulic elevator so they had to climb five flights. They carried their own bags to avoid having to tip.

That night they ate Kaiser rolls they'd bought at the train station. All the next day they stayed in the hotel's penitentially severe room, as Aunt Em recovered from the taxation to her nerves caused by the swaying of railway cars. She could not tolerate being left alone in a hotel chamber on their first day, not when it felt as if the whole building was rocking and bucking as the train had done.

Dorothy was eager to go and see what she could see, but they wouldn't let her walk out alone. "A city is not a prairie," Aunt Em proclaimed through the damp washcloth laid from forehead to chin. "No place for a compromised girl without a scrap of city wits."

The spring air wafting through the open window next morning revived Aunt Em. All these flights up, it smelled of lilacs and hair oil and horse manure and hot sourdough loaves. Encouraged, the flatlanders ventured outdoors. Dorothy carried Toto in a wicker basket, for old times' sake. They strolled up to the carriage entrance of the famous Palace Hotel and pretended they were waiting for a friend so they could catch a glimpse of sinful excess. What an accomplished offhand manner they showed, sneaking sideways glances through the open doors at the potted ferns, the swags of rust-red velvet drapery, the polished doorknobs. Also the glinting necklaces and earrings and cuff links, and gentlemen's shirts starched so clean it hurt the eye to look. "Smart enough," said Aunt Em, "for suchlike who feel the need to preen in public." She was agog and dismissive at once, thought Dorothy, a considerable achievement for a plain-minded woman.

"The Palace Hotel is all very well," said Dorothy at lunch—a frankfurter and a sumptuous orange from a stall near Union Square—"but the Palace of the Emperor in the Emerald City is just as grand—"

"I shall be ill." Aunt Em, going pale. "I shall be ill, Dorothy, if after all we have mortgaged on this expedition you insist on seeing San Francisco by comparing it to some imagined otherworld. I shall be quite, quite ill."

"I mean nothing by it," said Dorothy. "Please, I'll be still. It's true I've never seen anything like most of this."

"The world is wonderful enough without your having to invent an alternative," said Uncle Henry. A tired man by now, not a well man either, and stretched to put things baldly while there was time. "Who is going to take you in marriage, Dorothy, if you've already given yourself over to delusions and visions?"

"Snares of the wicked one." Aunt Em, spitting an orange seed into the street. "We have been kind, Dorothy, and we have been patient. We have sat silent and we have spoken out. You must put the corrupting nightmare of Oz behind you. Close it behind a door and never speak of it again. Or you will find yourself locked within it. Alone. We aren't going to live forever, and you must learn to manage in the real world."

"I should imagine I'm too young to be thinking of marriage."

"You are already sixteen," snapped her aunt. "*I* was married at seventeen."

Uncle Henry's eyes glinted merrily and he mouthed across his wife's head at Dorothy: *Too young.*

Dorothy knew they had her best interests at heart. And it was true that since her delivery from Oz six years ago, she had proved a rare creature, a freak of nature. Her uncle and aunt didn't know what to make of her. When she had appeared on the horizon, crossing the prairie by foot—shoeless but clutching Toto—long enough after Uncle Henry and Aunt Em's home had been carried away that they'd built themselves a replacement—her return was reckoned a statistical impossibility. Who rides the winds in a twister and lives to tell about it? Though Kansans set store on the notion of revelation, they are skeptical when asked to accept any whole-cloth gospel not measurable by brass tacks they've walloped into the dry goods counter themselves. So upon her return, Dorothy had been greeted not as a ghost or an angel, neither blessed by the Lord nor saved by a secret pact she must have made with the Evil One. Just tetched, concluded the good folks of the district. Tetched in the big fat head.

The local schoolchildren who had often before given Dorothy a wide berth now made irrevocable their policy of shunning her. They were unanimous but wordless about it. They were after all Christians.

She'd learned to keep Oz to herself, more or less; of course things slipped out. But she didn't want to be figured as peculiar. She'd taken up singing on the way home from the schoolhouse as a way to disguise the fact that no one would walk with her. And now that she was done with school, it seemed there were no neighbors who might tolerate her company long enough to find her marriageable. So Uncle Henry and Aunt Em were making this last-ditch effort to prove that the workaday world of the Lord God Almighty was plenty rich and wonderful enough to satisfy Dorothy's curiosity for marvels. She didn't need to keep inventing impossible nonsense. *She keeps on yammering about that fever dream of Oz and she'll be an old spinster with no one to warble to but the bones of Toto.*

They rode cable cars. "Nothing like *these* in all of Oz!" said Dorothy as the cars bit their way upslope, tooth by tooth, and then plunged down.

They went to the Fisherman's Wharf. Dorothy had never seen the ocean before; nor had Uncle Henry or Aunt Em. The man who sold them hanks of fried fish wrapped in twists of newspaper remarked that this wasn't the ocean, just the bay. To see the ocean they'd need to go farther west, to the Presidio, or to Golden Gate Park.

For its prettier name, they headed to Golden Gate Park. A policeman told them that when the long swell of greenery was being laid out, the city hadn't yet expanded west past Divisadero Street, and anything beyond had been known by squatters and locals as the Outside Lands. "Oh?" said Dorothy, with brightening interest.

"That's where you'll find the ocean."

They made their way to the edge of the continent first by carriage and then on foot, but the world's edge proved disappointingly muffled in fog. The ocean was a sham. They could see no farther out into the supposed Pacific Ocean than they'd been able to look across the San Francisco Bay. And it was colder, a stiff wind tossing up briny air. The gulls keened, biblical prophets practicing jeremiad, knowing more than they would let on. Aunt Em caught a sniffle, so they couldn't stay and wait to see if the fog would lift. The clammy saltiness disagreed with her—and she with it, she did declare.

That night, as Aunt Em was repairing to her bed, Uncle Henry wheedled from his wife a permission to take Dorothy out on the town. He hired a trap to bring Dorothy into a district called Chinatown. Dorothy wanted so badly to tell Uncle Henry that *this* is what it felt like to be in Oz—this otherness, this weird but convincing reality—that she bit a bruise in the side of her mouth, trying not to speak. Toto looked wary, as if the residents on doorsills were sizing him up to see how many Chinese relatives he might feed.

After a number of false starts, Uncle Henry located a restaurant where other God-fearing white people seemed comfortable entering, and a few were even safely leaving, which was a good sign. So they went inside.

A staid woman at a counter nodded at them. Her unmoving features looked carved in beef aspic. When she slipped off her stool to show Henry to a table, Dorothy saw that she was tiny. Tiny and stout and wrapped round with shiny red silk. She only came up to Dorothy's lowest rib. To prevent her from saying *A Munchkin!* Uncle Henry said to Dorothy, with his eyes, *No.*

They ate a spicy, peculiar meal, very wet, full of moist grit. They wouldn't know how to describe any of it to Aunt Em when they went back, and they were glad she wasn't there. She would have swooned with the mystery of it. They liked it, though Uncle Henry chewed with the front of his lips clenched and the sides puckered open for air in case he changed his mind midbite.

"Where are these people from? Why are they here?" asked Dorothy in a whisper, pushing a chopstick into her basket so Toto could have something to gnaw.

"They're furriners from China, which is across the world," said Uncle Henry. "They came to build the railroad that we traveled on, and they stayed to open laundries and restaurants."

"Why didn't they ever come to Kansas?"

"They must be too smart."

They both laughed at this, turning red. Dorothy could see that Uncle Henry loved her. It wasn't his fault she seemed out of her mind.

"Uncle Henry," said Dorothy before they had finished the grassy tea, "I know you've nearly poor-housed yourself to bring me here. I know why you and Aunt Em have done it. You want to show me the world and distract me with reality. It's a good strategy and a mighty sound ambition. I shall try to repay you for your kindness to me by keeping my mouth shut about Oz."

"Your sainted Aunt Em chooses to keep mum about it, Dorothy, but she knows you've had an experience few can match. However you managed to survive from the time the twister snatched our house away until the time you returned from the wilderness—whatever you scrabbled to find and eat that might have caused this weakness in your head—you nonetheless *did* manage. No one back home expected we'd ever find your corpse, let alone meet up again with your cheery optimistic self. You're some pioneer, Dorothy. Every minute of your life is its own real miracle. Don't deny it by fastening upon the temptation of some tomfoolery."

She chose her words carefully. "It's just that it's all so clear in my mind."

"A mind is something a young lady from Kansas learns to keep private."

As they began to pile up their plates, the Munchkin Chinee—that is, the little bowing woman in her silks and satins—scurried to interrupt them, and she brought them each a pastry like a crumpled seedpod. When Uncle Henry and Dorothy looked dubious, she showed them how to crack one open. The fragments tasted like Aunt Em's biscuits, dry and without savor. Inside, how droll: a scrap of paper in each one.

Marks in a funny squarish language on one side, letters in English on the other.

By the red light of the Chinese lantern leering over their table, Uncle Henry worked to decipher his secret message. His book learning had been scant. "Mid pleasure and palaces though we may roam, Be it ever so humble, there's no place like home," he read. "John Howard Payne."

"Pain is right," said Dorothy. "Meaning no disrespect, Uncle Henry."

"He has a point, though, Dorothy. Be it ever so humble, and we have the humble part covered good enough, there's no place like home. Now you read yours."

"My mind to me a kingdom is, Such present joys therein I find, That it excels all other bliss That Earth affords or grows by kind. Sir Edward Dyer."

"Dire is right," said Uncle Henry.

The hobbled, squinch-eyed woman in red saw them through the beaded curtains toward the street, but at the lacquered door she grabbed Dorothy's sleeve. "For you," she said and handed Dorothy a tiny bamboo cage. Inside was a cricket. "For ruck. Cricket for ruck."

Why do I need luck? Dorothy thought she'd spoken to herself but the woman answered as if she'd spoken aloud. (Maybe she had. Maybe she was dotty, a dodo, like the children had called her. Dotty Dorothy. Dorothy Dodo.)

"You on journey going," said the old woman, though whether this was an observation, a prophecy, or a swift good-bye, Dorothy couldn't tell.

Distastefully Dorothy fingered the little cage. The locusts of Kansas had made her dubious about crickets. Still, the little twiglet was alive, for it bounced against its straw-colored bars. It didn't sing. "I don't believe animals should be in cages," she said to Uncle Henry.

"People neither," he answered, almost by rote. His one-note message. "Don't cage yourself in your fantasticals, girl. Before it's too late, get your mind out of Oz, or you'll be sorry."

"I take your point, Uncle Henry. I've taken it for some time now."

"You're welcome." He put his hand on his rib and breathed through the pain for a moment.

They walked down the street in silence, under a magnificently carved and painted gateway that spanned the street. Electrification had come to San Francisco and the granite of the buildings glittered as if crystals of snow were salted into the stone. It seemed a nonsense-day and a half-night at the same time.

Maybe Uncle Henry was right. Maybe there was enough in this world to make her forget Oz. But was that the right motivation for marrying a Kansas farmer, assuming she could land one?

Only, she supposed, if he was the right farmer.

At the hotel she begged Uncle Henry that they ride the lift up to their floor. "Your Auntie Em wouldn't approve, fretting for our safety," he replied. "Whether she's around to notice or not, I never behave as she'd disagree with, in honor of her."

What a set of stairs to walk up, she thought.

But when they reached the fifth floor, he winked at her and kept going. Three, four more flights. She followed wordlessly. At the top level they found a door. It opened easily enough to reveal to them a glowing cityscape. The canyons between buildings were running with light and sound. On the electric blue darkness, all around Dorothy and Uncle Henry, hung the illuminated windows of people in rooms. A museum of their living lives. Golden squares and rectangles. "Oh," she exclaimed, "no fibbing—it's better than the Emerald City! But where is the ocean? We're so high. Can we see it?"

They worked out which direction to look. This late at night there was nothing except for darkness. "That empty place without lights," said Uncle Henry. "It must be there, though you can't see it."

"Some say that about . . . other places," she replied, but not harshly. "Beyond the ocean, what's there?"

"The land of the Japanee and the Chinee. A whole society of them, all talking in that singy-song way they got."

"And the ocean." She could hardly bear it. "What's it like?"

"I never seen it yet, but tomorrow we can come back up here."

She was lost that night, when she finally managed to sleep, in the raspy claws of dreams that wouldn't declare themselves fully. The cricket chirped on one side of her and Uncle Henry wheezed in concert. As the first light weakened the blackness of sky, but long before dawn, Toto began to whine. "Hush, Auntie Em is feeling poorly after our long trip," whispered Dorothy, but Toto needed to go outside. Dorothy hunched herself into her clothes and grabbed the cricket cage, and let herself out of the room, leaving the door open a crack so she could return without disturbing her worthy relatives.

It didn't take long to find Toto a scrap of junk ground in which to do his business. Dorothy turned her head. Many of the lights were lowered now but there was a strange apprehensiveness to the street, like the setting of a stage in which a play was about to begin. The charcoal of the night decayed into a smokier shade, still dark but somehow more transparent. "Come on, we'll be in six kinds of trouble if they find us out on the street alone," said Dorothy. "Let's go up."

In the lobby she saw the elevator man asleep in a lounge chair, his head to one side and his little cap askew. In that funny high-waisted jacket he looked like a flying monkey she'd once known. How were they ever affording this, poor dear Henry and Em, late of the Kansas prairie? So frightened of her. So eager for an acceptable future. She *would* make it worth their while.

She stepped into the cage and pulled the door shut. The door was fretted, like sets of linked scissors, like the threads of an old apron if you scrub it too hard with lye. Connected to itself, but airy. There was a single control, as far as she could see. She gripped the brass handle and revolved it a full half turn, and the floor began to lift, with Dorothy and Toto and the cricket inside. She almost squealed, but she knew the merest sound might wake the elevator attendant, and she probably risked being put in jail for ambushing a lift and taking it on a joy ride.

The perforated room sailed up past the fifth floor, all the way to the ninth, which led to the roof. She remembered. She tiptoed from the elevator cabin and shouldered her way through the door, into the chill of dawn above the ocean.

In the few moments she'd been rising in the lift, the sky had lightened that much more. The effect was not so smoky, more pearlescent. The buildings at this hour seemed less defined by light. They looked like stone formations left behind after some unimaginable geologic event.

She could make out a tongue of sea beyond the buildings to the west. But no sound from this far away. No apparent motion. Only a lapidary expanse dimming and shading into the sky. No horizon line: just endlessness. Sea and sky inseparable.

Toto began to whimper and to jump around as if he wanted to leap from the ninth floor. "It's not frightening, it *isn't*," she said, though she didn't know whether she was trying to convince herself or the dog. "It's just the ocean, and another world on the other side. You know all about that. You're the best-traveled mutt in history, Toto. Stop your fussing! What *are* you fussing about?" The dog appeared to be going mad, running in circles around her and yipping in some sort of distress.

Dorothy set the cricket cage upon the stone barrier that kept people from falling off the flat roof. "You can come out," she said to the cricket. "I make my own luck, you make yours. Nobody should live in a cage. Never surrender to *that*."

The cricket emerged and rubbed some scratchy parts of itself together. Whether it leaped or whether the wind took it, Dorothy couldn't say. The cricket guest was there one moment and gone the next.

"Safe landing," she called lightly after it. "Oh, all right, Toto, stop that infernal fussing. The wind isn't going to take you, too. Once in your life was enough."

She picked up the dog and went back into the building. The elevator was where she had left it, quivering at this height. She would ride it down to the fifth floor, and go in and rest next to her uncle and aunt. She had spied something of the ocean, some little hem of it. The globe was round. She could see there was another world beyond this one. That would have to do. Meanwhile, some corn-blind farmer, walled on four sides of his life by Superior Alfalfa, was waiting for her.

She began her descent. She passed the eighth floor and the seventh. About quarter past five on the morning of April 18, 1906, the buildings of San Francisco started to shake.

I

To Call Winter upon Water

1.

One of her earliest memories. Maybe her first, it was hard to tell, time was unstable then. Swimming through grass that came up as high as her underarms. Or it may have been new grain not yet roughened by summer. Late spring, probably. Her chin stroked by paintbrush tips of green.

Sunk in the world, unable to feel anything but the magic of it. Unable to take part.

The field was as wide as the sky, while she was so low that she couldn't see over horizons of any sort. At a small clearing where (she later realized) a farmer's cart or plow might turn around, she came upon the skin of a mouse in the cropped and daisied grass.

The mouse pelt was still soft and almost warm. Supple, not leathery. As if some snake or owl had caught the creature and eaten it through a seam, blood and bones and little liver and all, but had tossed aside, nearly in one piece, the furry husk.

She had picked it up and dressed her forefinger with it, becoming Mouse. Quickening into Mouse. It had made her feel foreign to herself, and real. Realer. Then the feeling overwhelmed her and with a cry she shuddered the Mouse-shuck off her, away.

It disappeared into the grain. Immediately she loathed herself for cowardice and the loss of a magic thing, and she hunted for it until the memory had hardened into a notion of stupidity and regret.

She kept the memory and suffered the longing but never again was so real a Mouse, not for her whole life.

2.

"Please," said Miss Murth. "He won't take no for an answer. It's been an hour and a half." She laid her palm on her bosom as if, thought Glinda, it were in danger of being noticed. Her fingers fluttered. Murth's fingers were notched and rickety, like her teeth.

"There is no need to be afraid of men, Miss Murth."

"It's an imposition for you to be expected to receive visitors when you are not 'at home,' but these are trying times, Lady Glinda. You must hurry. And I can tell by the bars and braids upon his dress uniform that he is a commanding officer."

"How commanding? Don't answer that. At least he carries dress uniform into the field." She worked with a brush and then plunged an ivory comb into her hair, buttressing a heap of it at the nape of her neck. Ah, hair. "This whole thing *is* vexing. When I was young and at school, Miss Murth—"

"You're still young, Lady Glinda—"

"Compared to some. Don't interrupt. How times have changed!—that a woman of position can be importuned almost at the doors of her boudoir. And without so much as a letter of introduction."

"I know. Can I help you in any way . . . ?"

Glinda picked up a small looking glass with a handle of rather fine design. She peeked at her face, her eyes, her lips—oh, the start of vertical pleats below the join of chin to neck; before long she would look like a concertina. But what could she do? Under the circumstances. A little more powder above the eyebrows, perhaps. At least she was younger than Miss Murth, who was hugging senility. "You may give me your appraisal, Miss Murth."

"Quite acceptable, Lady Glinda. There aren't many who could wear a sprigged foxille with such confidence . . . under these circumstances."

"Considering we're wallowing in a civil war, you mean? Don't answer that. Show the unwelcome visitor to the pergola. I shall be down presently."

"In any weather, you do us proud, Lady Glinda."

Glinda said nothing more for the moment, just waved her hand. Miss Murth disappeared. Glinda continued to dally at her dressing table in order to buy time to think. Strategy had never been her strong suit. So far the time spent over her toilet had bought her precious little except for a manicure. Well, she could admire her cuticles after the chains were slapped on, if that was where this was heading.

She was affixing an earring when the door burst open and Miss Murth entered the room backward. "Sir, I protest, I do protest—Madame, I have protested—Sir, I insist!" He pushed her into a chair so hard that three top buttons of her respectable blouse popped and spun onto the floor. Several inches of Miss Murth's private neck were exposed. She grabbed a pillow to conceal herself.

Poor little me, surrounded by the retinue I deserve, thought Glinda. She nodded at Cherrystone and waved to a tufted stool. He remained standing.

"I was told you were ready to see me," said General Cherrystone.

"Well, I was almost ready to see you in the pergola, where thanks to the grapevines the light is less

accusatory." She finished putting on the second earring. "Still, we must move with the times. Miss Murth,
if you have finished composing yourself? A little air,
the window, such stifling . . . Excuse the atmosphere,
sir. Ladies in their chambers and all that."

"I was afraid I'd hear that you'd been spotted leaving through the servants' entrance and taken into custody by my men. I wanted to spare you the indignity.
I assumed that ninety minutes was enough for you to
compose yourself, and I see I was right. You remain a
captivating woman, Lady Glinda."

"When I was the Throne Minister of Oz, that would
have been a most impertinent remark. Still, I'm retired
now, so thanks a lot. To what boysy sort of escapade do
I owe the pleasure of your company?"

"Don't play the naïf; it doesn't suit you any longer.
I'm here to requisition Mockbeggar Hall."

"But of course you'll do nothing of the sort. You
have no grounds and I am certain you have no authority. You will stay for elevenses though? Do."

"I'm sure you're aware that your name has come up
for questioning in the Emerald City. For your refusal to
evacuate the premises. Some call it seditious."

She studied him before he spoke. It had been some
years since their paths had crossed, and she had once
been his boss. Had she treated him well? But what did

that matter? Here he was. With a good head of hair; she admired that in any man past fifty. Though the gloss in his locks was gone, and the color was of dirty coins. He'd shaved. A missed stand of stubble under one ear betrayed the grey. Shaved—for her? Should she feel flattered? Curious: his eyes were no more guarded than they'd once been. *That* was how he had gotten ahead, she thought—oh, mercy, a moment of clarity, how unusual and piercing, but concentrate, what was that thought again?—Cherrystone had always seemed . . . *approachable.* Sanguine. Ordinary, cheery. Those peppery, bitten smiles, the self-deprecation. The shrugs. *A pose like any other.* Beware, Galinda, she said to herself, not realizing she was addressing herself with her childhood name.

"Sedition?" she ventured. "Bizarre, but you're joking."

He spoke in even tones, as if briefing a dull-witted client. "Lady Glinda. Loyal Oz has mounted an invasion of Munchkinland. We are at war. Under the circumstances, the Emerald City magistrates have found your refusal to leave Mockbeggar Hall and Munchkinland all but treasonous. You hardly need me to explain; the Emperor's counsel has sent you petitions by diplomatic pouch, to which you have refused to respond."

"I'm not much for correspondence. I could never choose the right stationery, rainbows or butterflies."

"You make it impossible for anyone to mount a case in your favor. Even your supporters in the EC are flummoxed at your obstinacy. What's your rationale? Lord Chuffrey, rest his soul, was from the capital, while you originate in Gillikin Country. You can claim no family roots here. Ergo, your insistence at residing in a state with which we are at war is tantamount to a betrayal of Loyal Oz."

"Is that what determines one as a traitor these days? One's address?"

"It makes no difference now. It's my sad duty to inform you that you are under arrest. Still"—the good guy at work, she saw it—"you're free to make a statement on record, as we have a witness in your lady-in-waiting. What do you call yourself? A rebel? Or a loyalist?"

"I call myself well bred, which means not talking politics in society."

He gave a half-nod, though she couldn't guess if it was acknowledgment of protocol or proof that he considered her borderline berserk. Still, he continued in a dogged manner. "You understand the thinking of the EC magistrates. You must. Mockbeggar Hall is in *Munchkinland*. And you haven't been seen in the city in five years. You haven't hosted a soirée in your house in Mennipin Square in too many seasons to count."

"When one has become famous, one finds it harder to go out to the shops without being pestered by well-wishers and rabble. And really: Where would I go? The Emerald *City*? Please. I couldn't step foot outside the front door in Mennipin Square without people flocking to me. It's tiresome to have to . . . *beam* so. My face hurts."

He looked as if he thought her quite the incapable liar.

Doggedly she went on. "I prefer the quiet life now. I look after my garden . . . I train the climbing roses, deadhead the pansies." This was sounding feeble. "I like to arrange flowers."

Their eyes both drifted to a milk jug on the table between them where a fistful of listing tulips, papery and translucent with age, had dropped a few browned petals. Sad, really. Condemning. She tried again. "In truth, I've been composing my memoirs, and the country is conducive to reflection, don't you see."

"But why have you parked yourself in a country home abroad instead of in Loyal Oz, from where the Arduennas and the Uplands hail?"

"Darling Cherrystone. Lord Chuffrey's family had this house long before Munchkinland seceded—what, is it thirty years ago by now? And when I became

Throne Minister, and this place remained accessible via the east-leading branch of the Yellow Brick Road, why shouldn't I repair here? I could get back and forth to the capital with ease and safety."

"You could have relocated. There are other great houses within a few days' ride of the Palace."

"But this *house*. It's the real thing. Pallantine Revival, don't you know. Without any of those tacky so-called improvements affixed with sticky tape and safety pins . . . no, it's simply the best of its kind. You must have noticed the twice-etched pillars inlaid with strabbous onyx on either side of the south porch? In ranks of three? Genuine Parrith's, I tell you, verified by the Parrith Society. He didn't work in onyx anywhere else, not even in the Emerald City."

"In fidelity to the nation, a patriot would pick up and move house. . . ." His tone was ominous, as if he had forgotten to notice the south porch. The oaf.

"This house doesn't move. Most don't. Or are you referring to Dorothy?" she said coldly. "She moved house rather capably, as we all remember. Mercy, could she move house."

"Always clever. But, Lady Glinda, you align yourself with the wrong sort if you do not step in line."

"I didn't draw this line, or any others. And if by 'the wrong sort' you are referring to the departed Thropp sisters, Nessarose and Elphaba, well, that's tired business. They've been dead and gone, what, fifteen, sixteen years now."

"I have little time for this; I've heard what I need. You have not declared yourself unequivocally patriotic. That's now a matter of public record. But I warn you, Lady Glinda. There are borders one should not cross."

"If Elphaba observed any border, she'd go out of her way to trespass against it. Or are we talking, obliquely, about social class? Have a brandy, it's nearly noonday. Miss Murth, *are* you composed enough to decant something for us?"

Cherrystone said, "I must decline. There is much to arrange. You have been served notice of detention at home. I am taking over Mockbeggar Hall as my headquarters."

Glinda sat forward and gripped the arms of her chair, though her voice remained casual. "I would do the same were I you, I suppose. It isn't often that a boy of your humble beginnings gets to lodge in a jewel box like this. Will you be a honey, though, and do mind your bloody boots when it comes to the sofas?"

His boots shone like ice, of course.

"And where will you expect me to lodge?" she continued in a stiffer voice. "Do you intend to plunge me and my staff into some oubliette?"

"You may maintain your private apartments and you won't be disturbed. I am afraid we shall have to dismiss your staff."

She gave a laugh. "I don't do without staff. *Sir.*" Her refusing to use his military title was intended as an insult, and she watched it land.

"A skeletal company then. Two, three."

"A dozen. And the departing staff will need guarantee of safe passage through the armies that seem"—she indicated the window—"to be wreaking havoc in the hydrangeas."

"Please submit a list of those who will remain so we can have them vetted."

He crossed his long legs, as if making bivouac in some forest glade. The nerve.

"I mean now," he added.

"Oh, my goodness, military life is so brusque. I had quite forgotten. Have *you* forgotten, Commander Cherrystone, that in my station—"

"General. General Cherrystone, not Commander."

"Oh, I beg your pardon." Could he tell she was having him on? "Nonetheless, though I wish I'd maintained a private army to turf you out, I shall do as you request in return for your promise not to molest those staff who must be made redundant. I shall require, let's see. A chef, a sommelier, a butler. That's three. An ostler and a driver. That's five. And a lady-in-waiting as chaperone at home. . . ." She gestured toward the woman nearby. "Not you, Miss Murth, you are too dour."

Miss Murth wailed.

"Only kidding, Miss Murth! Though I turn serious if you shriek again."

"That's six," said Cherrystone. "More than enough. Though in actual fact you won't need an ostler or a driver."

"Surely you don't plan to confine me? To keep me from making my rounds among the poor of the parish?"

He snorted. "You're doing charity?"

"Don't sound so surprised. It's bundles of fun."

"When you wish to dispense largesse, you can rely on me to supply you a driver and a chaperone. We'll subtract two from your list of six. No ostler, no driver. That leaves you four. That sounds quite enough."

"Oh, and yes, I shall need a girl to help me bathe."

"You've forgotten how to bathe?"

"The powders, dear Sir. The unguents. The gentle persuasion of peroxide. You need study me more closely, or do you think such beauty as I pretend to is wholly of the natural order?"

He colored slightly. She had him, and carried on. "Unless you want to dispatch a young foot soldier to do the work? In the interest of military economies? Very well, if I must. Provided I get to interview the nominees and make the choice myself. I pride myself on being able to tell a healthy—"

"Five retainers, then. Submit to me their names and their points of origin. You will not be allowed to maintain Munchkinlanders, I am afraid."

"Well, we stand in agreement on that matter, for I always found old-stock Munchkins too petite to reach the sideboard. In any event one is wise to keep the sherry on an upper shelf, don't you know."

He ticked on the fingers of one hand. "A companion, a butler, a chef, a sommelier, a private maid. You may take the afternoon to write out their references. But we'll drop the sommelier, I think. I know a bit about wine. I'll take pleasure in making recommendations myself."

"I don't supply supporting documents, General Cherrystone. I am Lady Glinda." She stood up so suddenly she felt light-headed. "Your horses are eating my roses. Miss Murth, would you see the General out?"

When he'd gone, she remained at the window. Restwater, the largest of Oz's lakes, glowed keenly white in the high sun. A few storks waded in the rushes of the nearer cove. She could glimpse little sign of the fishing fleet out on the water. The fishermen had tucked their vessels up tightly somewhere, and were hoping to sit out the invasion without starving.

There was no safe place in Oz for Glinda. She knew this. The government administrators in the Emerald

City—the Emperor's men—were just waiting for her to emerge. She was too popular a figurehead to be allowed to swan about freely in the EC. Her longtime sponsorship of an institute of maunts latterly accused of printing seditious broadsides was enough reason to lock her away. Risky business, offering patronage. No, her bread was buttered good and hard on the wrong side. Better to tough it out here and manage her private obligations as best she might, for as long as she could.

3.

By noontime the next day the soldiers' horses had drunk the fountain dry. The forecourt of crushed lake abalone reeked with horse manure. "Do bring a message to the General," said Glinda, "and inform him that there's a whole lake forty feet beyond the lawns. Since this invasion is all about the appropriation of water, perhaps he'd be so kind as to lead his cavalry down to the water's edge?"

"I do not think, Lady Glinda, that he listens to me overmuch," said Miss Murth unhappily. "I would not command his attention."

"Try. We are all under pressure, Miss Murth. We must do our best. And we may be confined for some time, so I suppose I should convene a colloquy among the help. Propose a common attitude toward this intrusion, and so on. What do you think?"

"I was never good at current affairs. I preferred the arts of needlework and correspondence."

"Correspondence? To whomever would you write?"

"Well. The papers."

"So you took the papers. You never read the papers, surely?"

"I found news somewhat sullying." Miss Murth fluffed the feathers on Lady Glinda's afternoon hat; they remained droopy. But Lady Glinda wasn't going anywhere. "It wasn't a wise choice, I now see," said Miss Murth. "I might have followed politics, but I preferred the society columns. When you were in them."

"Surely I'm in them still."

Miss Murth sighed. "It's a shame about the horse droppings."

"Miss Murth. *Are* you listening?"

Miss Murth straightened her shoulders to indicate that she was indeed listening, damn it.

"You ought to follow events, Miss Murth. You remember that skirmish by Munchkinlanders into Loyal Oz last fall? Oh, don't look at me like that, it was west of here, near that strip of land that divides Kellswater and Restwater. *You* remember. Near the mauntery of Saint

Glinda, where I sometimes like to go and consider my soul, my debts, my diet, and so on? Yes?"

"Yes. With those cloistered ladies who think they're so holy."

"Miss Murth. Do try to attend. Out of the goodness of my heart I'm sharing what I have picked up."

"The skirmish. Yes. Everyone was so vexed," recalled Miss Murth, aiming at drollery and achieving condescension. "It completely upended the social season."

Damn the attitude of help; Glinda was talking this out to get it straight in her own head. "When by winter's end our Munchkinlander tenants and neighbors had retreated under the superior fire of the EC forces, they scurried back east. I hear they've been beavering about, renovating some antique fortress at the easternmost end of the lake. Where the Munchkin River debouches. So I believe General Cherrystone is stopping here to wait for reinforcements before pressing farther east. If he takes the fort at the head of the lake, he'll have access to the river, which is a virtual high road of water straight into the breadbasket of Oz, straight to Bright Lettins and to the seat of the Munchkinland government at Colwen Grounds."

"Where the Thropp family used to live, back in the day." Miss Murth sniffed.

"Indeed. Well, not Elphaba, nor her brother Shell. Oh excuse me: *Emperor.* But their great-grandfather the Eminent Thropp ruled from that house. A pretentious heap compared to Mockbeggar's understated charm! But never mind all that. It's on the strength of his bloodlines that Shell Thropp claims Colwen Grounds and, by extension, the right to rule all of Munchkinland. So he starts with Restwater, which until the secession of Munchkinland twenty-umpty years ago, or something like that, had always provided water for the Emerald City."

"If we're through reviewing current events," said Miss Murth, "the General is waiting for the list of staff. He threatens to imprison the whole lot of us if he doesn't receive it by teatime."

"Very well. Find a quill and take down this list. You can remind me of the names, if you will. Put yourself first, Miss Murth. Have you a first name?"

"Yes, in fact."

"How alarming. Next, Chef. What's he called?"

"Ig Baernaeraenaesis."

"Write Chef. Write Puggles the Butler."

"*His* real name is Po Understar."

"Oh, this is so tedious! Am I expected to remember these names? Is that the lot? Are we missing anyone? I think that's it."

"You requested a chambermaid."

"That's right, I did. Now whom should I pick? There's Mirrtle. She's a little cross-eyed but she plays a mean hand of graboge. There's the broomgirl who does the steps. I don't recall her name. And then silly Floxi-aza. No, she steals my cologne. Not Floxiaza. What do you think? Mirrtle, shall we?"

"I like Mirrtle," said Miss Murth. "One can rely on Mirrtle to keep a civil tongue to her superiors."

"Then I'll choose the broomgirl. Write down the broomgirl. What *is* her name?"

"I'll ask her," said Miss Murth. "Nobody ever uses it so I doubt she'll remember, but maybe she'll surprise us all. May I deliver this now? I don't want to appear cowering but the General seems insistent."

"I suppose I should sign it."

"I have signed it for you."

"You're a blessing in disguise." Glinda looked her over. "A very capable disguise. You may consider your-self dismissed."

4.

She was standing at a weir. Though later she realized someone must have built it, at the time it seemed just another caprice of nature. An S-shaped curve of broad flat stones, to channel the water, slow it, creating a deep pool on the upstream edge. Along that side a fretwork of bentlebranch fronds had been twisted and laced together laterally, further helping to slow the water that coursed through—when water coursed, that is. Today it was frozen.

Probably she'd been wearing boots, but she didn't remember boots, or mittens, or even a coat. What the mind chooses to collect, and what it throws away!

She leaned from the walkway over the top of the artificial thicket. She could see that the whole affair guided the stream through a channel. Good for fishing.

The surface of the stream was glassy, here and there dusted with snow. Beneath the surface of the ice some hardy reed still waved underwater with the sloweddown motion of a dream. She could almost see her face there beneath all this cold, among the hints of green, of spring.

Never one for studying herself, though, her eye had caught a flick of movement a few feet on. In a pocket in the ice of the stream, a little coppery fish was turning round and round, as if trapped. How had it gotten separated from the members of its school, who were probably all buried in the mud, lost in cold dreams till spring? Though she couldn't have known about hibernation yet.

One hand on the unstable balustrade, she ventured onto the ice. The trapped fish needed to be released. It would die in its little natural bowl. Die of loneliness if nothing else. She knew about loneliness.

A stick came to her unmittened hand somehow. She must have dropped her mittens, the better to grasp the stick. Or she'd been out without protection. It didn't matter. She bashed at the ice for some time, never thinking that the floor could capsize and she might go in the drink. Drown, or freeze, or become mighty uncomfortable some other way.

Little by little she hacked away a channel. The fish heard the vibrations and circled more vigorously, but there was no place for it to go. Finally she had opened a hole big enough for her finger.

The fish came up and nestled against her, as if her forefinger were a mother fish. The scrap of brilliance leaned there, at a slight tilt.

That's what she remembered, anyway.

She had gone on to release the fish. What had she done with it? With the stream frozen over? The rest was lost, lost to time. Like so much.

But she remembered the way the fish bellied against her finger.

This must be another very early memory. Was no one looking after her? Why was she always out alone?

And where had this taken place? Where in the world did childhood happen, anyway?

5.

Glinda finished her morning tisane and waited, but no one came to take away the tray. Oh, right, she remembered. But where was Murth when you needed her? The woman was useless. Useless and pathetic.

A light rain pattered, just strong enough to make the idea of Glinda's giving an audience in the forecourt something of a mistake. She'd rather send remarks through a factotum, but that was the problem: the factotums were getting the boot. The least she could do was give her good-byes in person.

There was nothing for it but that Glinda must poke about the wardrobe herself and locate some sort of bumbershoot.

Puggles saw her struggling with the front door and rescued her. "Let me help, Mum," he said, relieving her of the umbrella. It had a handle carved to look like a flying monkey; she hadn't noticed that. Probably Cherrystone would decide that the umbrella was grounds for her execution. Well, stuff him with a rippled rutabaga.

"Everyone's assembled, Mum," said Puggles. "As you requested. Too bad about the weather, but there you are."

She'd written some notes all by herself, but raindrops smeared the ink when she took them out of her purse. "Goodness, Puggles," she said in a low voice. "Do so many work here?"

"Until today."

"I never quite realized. Well, one rarely assembles the staff all at once."

"Once a year. The below-stairs staff party at Lurlinemas. But you don't attend."

"I send the ale and those funny little baskets from the Fairy Preenella, one for everybody."

"Yes, Mum. I know. I order them and arrange for their delivery myself."

Was he being uppity? She couldn't blame him. She should have realized the household staff was this large. There must be seventy people gathered here. "If this is the number on which we normally rely, how are we to get along with only a skeletal crew, Puggles?"

But he'd stepped back to join the paltry retinue that would not be dismissed, which had lined up behind her.

Awkward. In what degree of affection or distance ought she to address them? The situation was grave; many of them were in tears. She was glad she had worn

the watered-silk moss luncheon gown with the peek-a-
boo calf flare and the carmine collar; she'd be stunning
against Mockbeggar's rose-colored stucco and ivory
entablatures. A comfort to the staff, she hoped, her
ability to maintain her style. An example.

She plunged ahead. "Dear friends. Dear laborers in
the field, dear dusters of the furniture, and whoever
uses the loppers to keep the topiary in check. Dear all
of you. What a dreary day this is."

She was reaching for a hankie already. How revolting, how mawkish. She didn't know most of their
names. But they looked so respectable and kind, in
their common clothes. Men with hats in their hands,
women in mobcaps and aprons. Surely they were going
to leave their aprons behind? Aprons marked with
House of Chuffrey crests? Well, better not to make a
fuss over it.

"I know some of you have lodged here, lovingly
tending Mockbeggar Hall, since long before I met Lord
Chuffrey, rest his soul. For many of you—perhaps all
of you, I'm a bit wobbly on the details—this has been
your only home. Where you go to now, and what life
awaits you there, is beyond my comprehension."

One or two of the young women straightened up and
put their hankies away. Perhaps, thought Glinda, this
hasn't started well.

"I have arranged for your safe passage off the estate. The General has promised you will not be accosted, nor will your allegiance to my welfare all these years be held against you. Indeed, I have not supplied him a list of your names or your destinations." This much was true. Cherrystone hadn't asked for that. He was irritatingly fair from time to time, which made resenting him a tricky business.

"Nothing should have pleased me more than to provide you with lodging and work here until the end of my days," she said. "In the absence of that, I have had the seamstresses work overtime, hand stitching on some cotton geppling serviettes the lovely old-fashioned blessing OZSPEED. By the way, thank you, seamstresses; you must have had to stay up past midnight to manage supplying all this lot."

"Actually, we're a few short," muttered Puggles.

She paid him no mind. Having been Throne Minister for that brief period had taught her several useful skills.

"Mum," called someone; Glinda couldn't tell who it was. "Will you have us back, in time?"

"Oh, if I have my say," she replied cheerily. "Though I doubt you'll recognize me when that day comes! I'll be sun-bronzed and wizened and my elbows will be raw from the dishwater! You'll think I'm the bootblack's grandmother!"

They liked this. They laughed with unseemly vigor. Though perhaps commoners have a different sense of humor, she thought.

"Dear friends," she continued. "I cherish the dedication to your tasks, your love of Mockbeggar, your sunny good natures at least whenever I came in the room. And next? None of us knows what waits down the lane for us." She was about to refer to her own power as compromised, what with the house arrest, but caught herself. Surely they knew about it, and they wanted to remember her as being strong. She threw her shoulders back and pinched a nerve in her scapula. Ow. "As to whomever was in the habit of filching the leftover pearlfruit jelly from the sideboard in the morning room, you are forgiven. You are all forgiven any such lapses. I shall miss you. I shall miss every one of you. I hardly knew there were so many . . . so many"—but that sounded lame—"so many brave and dedicated friends. Bless you. Ozspeed indeed. And on your way out, don't hesitate to snub the new sentries at the gatehouse. Don't give them the benefit of a single word. This is your home, still. Not theirs. Never theirs."

"Burn the place down!" cried someone in the crowd, but he was hushed, as the emotion seemed misguided at best.

"Don't forget to write," she said, before she remembered that quite likely some of them couldn't write.
She'd better get off the top step before she did more
harm than good. "Farewell, and may we meet again
when Ozma returns!"

The bawling began. She had ended as poorly as
she'd begun. Of course, the common people believed
that Ozma was a deity, and they must have concluded
that Lady Glinda was referring to the Afterlife. Well,
so be it, she thought grimly, hoisting her skirts to clear
the puddle by the front door. The Afterlife will have
to do for a rendezvous destination. Though I suspect
I shall be lodged in separate quarters, a private suite,
probably. "Puggles," she murmured, "get the yard boy
to pick up the mobcaps some of that lot were trampling
into the mud as they left."

"There's no yard boy, Ma'am," said Puggles gently.
"He's off with the others."

"It's a new era, then. You do it. It looks a sight. And
then join the rest of us in the grand foyer."

The others who were to remain had retreated inside
and stood in a line with their hands clasped. Their
uniforms dripped on the checkerboard marble. Glinda
would fix each one with a dedicated personal beck.
She could do this, she could. She'd been practicing
all morning. This was important. "Miss Murth," she
began. "Ig Baernae . . ."

"Chef'll do, Mum. Even I can't say it unless I'm soused."

"Ig Baernaeraenaesis." She was glad to see his jaw drop. Puggles slid into place in the line; Glinda nodded at him. "Mister Understar. And—" She came to the chambermaid. "And you. Rain, I think it is? Very lovely name. Scrub your nails, child. Civil unrest is no excuse for lapses in personal hygiene. Dear friends . . ." But perhaps this was too familiar a note to strike now she was inside her own home. She had to live with these people.

"I'm grateful for your loyalty," she continued in a brisker tone. "As far as I know my funds have not been impounded, and you shall stay on salary as usual."

"We don't gets salary, if you please, Mum," said Chef. "We gets our home and our food."

"Yes. Well. Home and food are yours as long as I can manage it. I cannot pretend this is a pretty time for Mockbeggar Hall or for any of us. Murth, don't scowl; it's not too late to exchange you for someone out in the forecourt lingering over farewells."

Miss Murth slapped on an inauthentic expression of merriment.

"A few remarks. I am still the lady of the house. You are my staff, and according to your stations you shall maintain your customary retiring ways in my presence."

"Yes, Mum," they chorused.

"And yet, and yet." She wanted a conspiratorial chumminess without a breakdown in authority. She must step softly. "We are now bound together in some unprecedented manner, and we must come to rely on one another. *So.* I shall ask you all to refrain from fraternizing with the military who will be bunking in the servants' quarters, in tents in the meadows, in the barns and stables. I shall ask you to be no more than minimally polite and responsive to the officers who have taken up lodging in the guest quarters. If they ask for food, you must procure it. You must cook it, Chef. You need not season it and you must not poison it. Do you understand?"

"Wouldn't dream of it, Mum."

"I daresay. If they request their shirts and stockings done . . ." She looked about. She had forgotten about laundry. "Well, they will have to do it themselves, or hire a laundress. No doubt they will try to cozy up to some of you." She took a dim view of cozying these days, though soldiers probably got lonely. She didn't think Miss Murth was in danger of being meddled with, and as for the girl . . . "You, Rain," she said, "how old are you?"

Rain shrugged. "I believe she is eight, Lady Glinda," said Miss Murth.

"That should be safe enough, but even so, Rain, I'd like you to stick near to Miss Murth or to one of the rest of us. Chef, Puggles. No running about and getting into mischief. I've kept you here because you have work to do. Sweeping up. You're the broomgirl. Remember that."

"Yes, Mum." The girl's gaze lowered to the polished floor. She wasn't overly bright, to judge by appearances, thought Glinda, but then some had said that about her, in her day. And look where she'd ended up.

In virtual prison, she concluded, sorry she'd begun the train of thought. "That'll do. To your work, then. Hands to your task, eyes ever open, but keep custody of the lips. If you should hear anything useful, do tell me. Are there any questions?"

"Are we under house arrest too?" asked Puggles.

"Open up a bottle of something bubbly," she replied. "When I figure out the answer to your question, I'll let you know. You are dismissed."

She stood for a moment as the foyer emptied. Then, mounting the first flight of the broad fleckstone staircase to her apartments, her eye drifted through the doors of the banquet hall. Before she knew what she was doing she had turned and pitter-patted down the steps and marched into the room. "Officer!" she shouted. She had never raised her voice in her own home before. Ever.

A soldier snapped to and saluted her. "Where is Cherrystone?" she barked.

"Not here, Mum."

"You're not in my staff. I'm not *Mum* to you. I am Lady Glinda. I can see he is not here. Where is he, I asked you."

"That's privileged information, Mum."

She might have to throttle him. "Officer. I see charts and maps all over my banquet table. I am sure occupying armies need charts and maps. I am also sure they do not need to be held down flat by early Dixxi House spindle-thread vases. Do you know how rare these are? No more than thirty exist in all of Oz, I'll wager."

"Do not approach the table, Mum."

She approached the table and she snatched up first one porcelain vase and then the second. They were almost four hundred years old. Handworked by artisans whose skill had been lost when Dixxi House went factory. "I will not have magnificent art used as . . . as paperweights. You put your boots on all the other furniture. Use your boots."

The maps had rolled up.

"Begging your pardon, Mum, you're striding in where you've no—"

"I don't stride, young man. I never stride. I glide. Now you heard what I told you to do. Take off your boots and put them on the stupid maps."

He did as he was told. She was impressed. She still had some little authority, then. She turned and left without addressing him again.

She cradled the vases against her breast as if they were puppies, but she wasn't thinking of the vases. She had seen that one map featured a detailed drawing of Restwater, all its coves and villages, its islands, the locations of its submerged rocks. She had seen a dotted line drawn from Mockbeggar Hall to Haugaard's Keep, the garrison fortress at the east end. The marking didn't run along the north shore of Restwater, but right through the middle of it. But what army could march through a lake?

6.

Of an afternoon, Glinda had been accustomed to the occasional carriage ride. She would set out for nearby villages and take a full cream tea in someone's front parlor. She would drag along Miss Murth and a novel, and ignore one or the other, sometimes both. From favorite overlooks she sometimes watched the sun subside toward the horizon. Spring in Munchkinland usually lent a certain cheer to her days. Summer the same. She didn't suffer pangs of longing for the house in Mennipin Square until after the first frost of the autumn. And by now she had learned to endure those pangs. For the time being, those lovely fall social seasons in the Emerald City were a thing of the past.

Like, it seemed, her excursions by carriage. It only took a few days after Cherrystone's appropriation of Mockbeggar for a new pattern to set in: the carriages were always spoken for when she requested one.

Unsettling, that the activities of the house were being determined by someone else's needs instead of her own.

And what a commotion! The army had set up a sizeable village of tents and built a pair of rude temporary structures—latrines, she expected. One for officers, one for enlisted men. The farm animals were turned out of the barns—no hardship, since the weather was good—and the barns became ad hoc mess halls and, perhaps, a wood shop of some sort, as the sound of hammering went on all day and half the night.

Glinda had Puggles show her how to find the stairs to the parapet so they could peek from behind an ornamental urn and grasp something of the size of the operation.

"I should think there are a full three hundred men on the demesne, Lady Glinda," said Puggles. "Given the amount of food I hear is being conscripted from local granges and farms."

"Can that be enough force with which to prosecute an invasion?" she wondered.

"You'd have a better sense of that than I. You managed the armies of Loyal Oz for a time," he reminded her. "And word has it you yourself once hoped for reunification."

"Of course I did," she snapped. "But not through military action. Too messy by half. I hoped if we put on a ball and went lavish with the refreshment budget, the Munchkinlanders would come back into the fold. I'm speaking figuratively, Puggles, don't look at me like that."

"I wouldn't dream of it. How could we humble Munchkinlanders refuse an invitation to dance with the overlords of the Emerald City? But when that rogue missile of a Dorothy-house came down on Nessarose's holy head? The Munchkinlanders discovered that liberation from sniffy Nessarose didn't provoke them into wanting a return to domination by the EC. Can you blame them? What population signs on willingly for slavery?"

"You mean other than wives?"

"I've never married, Mum. Don't accuse me by association."

"Oh, never mind. I just think Cherrystone is going to need a vaster force if he expects to drive a division right into the heart of Munchkinland, to Bright Lettins or Colwen Grounds. Unless the Emerald City is simultaneously mounting an invasion from the north, through the Scalps. Though I can't imagine the Glikkun trolls in the mountains would let them get very far with that. Or is Cherrystone going to be content with snatching Restwater and leaving us the rest of the province?"

"I wouldn't know, Mum."

"Well, what *do* you know, Puggles? How would we find out what's going on in those barns, for instance? I can't go waltzing around as if I'm used to milking the cows of a spring evening."

"No, Mum. But I'm not allowed to wander about, either. Guards are posted, you see, beyond kitchen gardens on the barn side, beyond the forecourt on the carriage frontage, and beyond the reflecting pond and the parterre to the west."

"Is that so." She wasn't surprised.

"I do hope you're not going to contemplate some campaign, Mum."

"You flatter me with that remark."

"I have a hunch that General Cherrystone wouldn't hesitate to restrict your liberties even further than he has already done."

She began to cross the roof and head for the stairs. "I'm sure you don't believe me capable of laying gelignite sandwiches on the party platter. Anyway, I can't cook."

When she was back in her salon she wandered along all the windows to see what she could see. She had never considered herself an inquisitive woman, but being confined to a suite of only eight rooms made her restless. She was also gripped with curiosity. Why hadn't she thought to retain someone nubile? Someone who could smolder, sloe-eyed, near a vulnerable soldier? Someone who could pick up some useful information? She herself was too high, Murth was too dead, Rain hardly more than a babe in arms . . . and Glinda doubted that Chef or Puggles would attract much attention among itchy-triggered soldiers.

Was it too late to exchange Miss Murth for someone a bit younger—younger by, say, a half century? Glinda could pretend to do it out of concern for Miss Murth's health.

But then Miss Murth came tramping in, hauling six logs of oak she had split and quartered herself, and she knelt down at the hearth to arrange the fire for when the evening chill took hold. Glinda knew that unless she herself brained Miss Murth with one of these spindle-thread vases, the old fiend would probably never die. She'd collapse over Glinda's grave with dry, red eyes, and then take up a new position somewhere else.

The tedious never die; that's what makes them tedious.

Glinda remembered the death of Ama Clutch, her governess. Almost forty years ago. Glinda never wakened from any sleep, even the luscious damp sleep that follows rousting sex, without sensing a pang of obscure guilt over her governess's demise. Glinda didn't feel she wanted to take on another such debt, especially over someone as irksome as Miss Murth.

"Miss Murth," she found herself saying, "Puggles was telling me about how limited a range he is allowed to traverse these days. Does the same apply to you?"

"I suspect it does, Lady Glinda," said Murth, "but I haven't pressed myself to try. I have no place else to go, and for years I haven't had reason to leave the premises unless you require my company."

"What had you been used to *doing* when I would go to the Emerald City for six or eight months?"

"Oh . . . tidying up some. Dusting."

"I see. Have you no family?"

"I've been in your employ for twenty years, Lady Glinda. Don't you think I would have mentioned my family if I had any?"

"You may have nattered on about your kin for yonks. I never know if I'm listening."

"Well, since you're asking, no. I am the last of our line."

And I the last of mine, thought Glinda, who had had no siblings. And she and Chuffrey had never managed to conceive. How quirky, to share this common a lone-liness with a member of her staff. Whereas if Glinda had had children—even now, some child or children dashing in every direction, carrying on irresponsibly as the young do—well, what a different place Mockbeg-gar would seem.

"There are all sorts of maps and missives in the dining hall, Miss Murth, but I draw attention to myself when I enter. There's no chance you could sneak a peak at them and report to me anything you read?"

"Out of the question. We're all under supervision, not just you."

"Do you think that our Rain has the run of the grounds?" She picked at a thread on her shawl as she spoke and didn't look up. She could hear Murth settle on her heels in front of the fire and let out a worried hiss between those old well-chewed lips. "And does she have any family, do you think?"

"To the best of my awareness, she has no more family than you and I," replied Miss Murth, vaguely.

7.

The first time a dinner invitation arrived from Gen-eral Cherrystone, Glinda folded up the paper and said, "Thank you, Puggles. There will be no reply."

The second time she had Murth write a note to decline. "How shall I sign it?" asked Miss Murth. "Lady Glinda, or just Glinda?"

"The scandal of you. Sign it Lady Glinda Chuffrey of Mockbeggar Hall. And none of those twee little hearts and daisies and such."

But the next night Glinda sent *him* an invitation. "Dinner at ten, on the roof of the south porch." She had Puggles and Chef take apart the sallowwood table from the card salon, put it through the windows leg by leg, and reassemble it on the graveled flat of the porch roof. Then she arranged herself upon the balustraded area ahead of time so she wouldn't have to be seen clambering through a window like a day laborer. The stars were out and the moon was wafery. She wore her midnight blue scallopier with eyelet fenestrae and a ruched bodice the color of wet sand. Chef would serve lake garmot stuffed with snails. "Is it a mistake about the candles?" called Murth through the lace swags. "They'll drip wax all over the food."

"Don't hector me," said Glinda. "I know what I'm doing." The two precious spindle-thread vases held a bounty of prettibells and delphiniums selected for their vigor. They better not so much as drop a single petal if they knew what was good for them.

Cherrystone came up the grand staircase just at ten. She could hear the clongs of the grandmother clock strike and the clicking of his heels as he turned at the landing. The windows were wide but the sills two feet high, so he had to sit and swivel to get his long legs across. "A novel place to host a dinner guest. Perhaps you intend to push me over the rail as a divertissement," he said. "Good evening, Lady Glinda."

"General. You understand that a person of my position doesn't entertain in her private apartment, and in any case I notice that the banquet hall has been requisitioned as a strategy center. So I've improvised. We dine at my invitation, as this is my home, but we dine neither in my own apartments nor in the spaces you have appropriated. Instead, a neutral territory. Above it all, as it were. Won't you have a seat?"

He offered a bottle of wine. "Not from Mockbeggar cellars, so I apologize if it doesn't suit. It's Highmeadow blanc, a good year. I don't travel without it. I hope you approve."

"My butler is a bit stout to be climbing through windows. So this is something of an evening picnic, I'm afraid. Will you do the honors? There's a cork-pull just here."

The candles were guttering madly for the first ten minutes. Glinda took care to sip sparingly. "While I understand the intent toward courtesy in your recent notes to me, General, I can't bring myself to accept an invitation to dine in my own home. My study of etiquette provides no precedent. So I thought I should be cordial and explain this to you in person."

"Damned awkward I'm sure, but you're being a brick, as I knew you would be."

"The meal will grow cold, so please, shall we sit?" She waited for him to pull out her chair. From over his shoulder she could see the campfires of soldiers beyond the ha-ha. The distant sound of singing, more rowdy than tuneful. "How will you keep all these men occupied and out of trouble, General? You've clearly settled in for a while, and no matter what construction you're overseeing in the barns, you can't be employing more than a smattering of this large number."

"I trust they're being no bother. You let me know if they are."

"I'll let *them* know if they are." She leaned forward, taking care not to seem coquettish, which, she recognized, seemed to be her default position. "Allow me to remove the covers, will you? Since it's just the two of us?" She lifted the lids off the plated dinner of garmot, braised stalks of celery, and mashed spinach forced to look like a green rose. Oh, Chef could make magic out of whatever lingered in the larder. "I hope this meets with your approval, General."

"Please; as we're dining, I should be happy if you called me by my first name. Traper."

She shook her head as if she were being pestered by mosquitoes. "You make it all very confusing. *Traper*. A most irregular season! I am detained in my own home, I am forbidden anything but emergency staff, I am asked to house a garrison or a committee or a division or whatever you call this lot—"

"We are roughly three hundred men, which in this instance means a command made up of three brigades. One of our brigades is a cavalry unit, and the other two are foot soldiers. Messiars, as we call them."

"And Menaciers are officers in training. I know the nomenclature. I did govern the Home Guard once, as you recall. But if what you are overseeing is a command, what makes you a General instead of a Commander?"

"Long years of service, for one. I am allowed to direct as many commands as the Emperor in the Emerald City sees fit to supply me."

"Then you're waiting on more commands. I see. Traper. Please, eat; it'll go cold. There's slightly more breeze at this height than I'd anticipated."

He tucked in. "You didn't ask me here to discuss military strategy, and anyway, it would be boorish of me to bring my work to the dinner table. Tell me about yourself."

"Oh, General—"

"Traper."

"Yes. Traper. You know a woman loves nothing more than to talk about herself. But you have incarcerated me here and Lady Glinda is bored to migraines with Lady Glinda. Unable to get around as she did, or to invite old friends to spend weekends hunting or playing plunge-ball or Three-Hand Snuckett. No, I asked you here to learn about you. So I insist. I've given you your supper, and you must sing for it. Tell me about your long years in the service, as you put it, even if you must keep as confidential your present aims and designs."

Obediently the General ventured into a loose and non-specific accounting of various assignments through the years. However, he underestimated the degree to which Glinda had paid attention while she was Throne Minister. She had read everything she could get her hands on, and various details had stuck because of references to old friends and cronies. She knew Cherrystone was from Mistlemoor, a small Gillikinese hamlet a few hours north of the Shiz Gate at the Emerald City. She knew the Wizard had sent Cherrystone out to Kiamo Ko when her old friend, Elphaba, had taken up residence there, and that Cherrystone had had something to do with the death or disappearance of Fiyero's wife, Sarima, and their children, Irji and Nor. She knew he had had a hand in some nasty business in Quadling Country, where he'd been stationed for nearly a decade, and when things went hot there he was recalled to the Emerald City. A desk job for a few years, under the Emperor. But called into field service again. His final triumph? Before retirement with a pension? She wondered. And all the time she kept smiling like a barkeep, unassuming and unflappable.

"You have a family," she said.

"Oh, yes," he replied. His fork poked back and forth as if checking for poison darts hidden in the fish. "A wife and three daughters. Now mostly grown; indeed, a granddaughter at home too, who I rarely see."

"I can't imagine. It must be dreadful for you."

"I'm sure it would be." He smiled under his lowered brow. "I mean, the noise of a gabbling child and four women under one roof."

"You don't fool me. You miss them dreadfully. What are their names?"

"I choose not to talk about them. It helps me not miss them as much."

"Is that breeze causing the candle to spit wax on your plate? Thoughtless of me." She leaned back in her chair. "Miss Murth?"

Murth was sitting in an upright chair just inside the window, her hands folded in her lap. "Yes, Lady Glinda."

"I know you aren't spry enough to clamber out the window ledge with an oil lamp in a glass chimney. One that won't gutter so in this updraft. Would you call the broomgirl to do it? She is agile enough, unlike the rest of us."

"I'm happy to oblige, Lady Glinda," said Cherrystone. "Allow me."

"I wouldn't hear of it. Miss Murth?"

"I think the girl is asleep, Lady Glinda."

Glinda waited.

"But I'll wake her."

"How wonderful. The lamps on the escritoire. Both of them. Thank you."

She tried without success to bring up the subject of the construction going on in the barns, but Cherrystone affably declared that too dull to discuss over such a fine meal. What next? He complimented the local landscape. She concurred: the lake before them in the moonlight, sheer silk spangled with diamond chunks, wasn't it *divine*? Less cloyingly, they discussed the social makeup of the nearest villages. "I do trust you're paying the local farmers for all the food you're demanding from them," she ventured.

"We're at war, Lady Glinda. I try to make it look as much like a picnic as I can, but you can't have forgotten that Munchkinlanders provoked the Ozian army to invade."

"Well, nor have I forgotten that Oz was massing an army of invasion on the border for weeks and weeks before the Munchkinlanders made a raid against it."

"Defensive positioning, Lady Glinda."

"Spoiling for a fight, and the fools bit. Though had they not bit in time, you'd have come up with some other reason to invade. The Emerald City has had its eye on Restwater even since my own time in office, Traper, though I did my best to change the subject."

"Don't let's talk military strategy. Do you play an instrument, Lady Glinda?"

"I have a set of musical toothpicks I must show you someday. Ah, here she is."

Rain slung one leg over the windowsill. She was dressed in a man's cast-off nightshirt. It made her look like an urchin. Her calves were smooth and pale, the color of new cream in the moonlight. Her dark hair hadn't seen the benefit of a comb recently. Once through the window, she turned back and took the lamps Miss Murth handed her. The light on either side of her face made her look like a visitation from some chapel story of youthful piety. She was nearly pretty, but for the dirt on her face and her cross, sleepy expression.

"Where does you want 'em," she said, forgetting to make it sound like a question.

"Oh, how about one on the table and then one on that stone ledge between the windows," said Glinda.

"Then if Miss Murth comes at the General with a crossbow we shall spy her before any damage is done. Miss Murth has many hidden talents."

"Lady Glinda!" hissed Murth from inside. But Cherrystone was laughing.

"Stay, little Rain," said Glinda. "We might need something else, and you're better at getting over window ledges than we are. You can rest with your head against the wall there." In the lamplight, squatting with her back against the stone, the girl looked like a beggar outside a train station in the Pertha Hills, back in the day. Frottica, Wittica, Settica, Wiccasand Turning . . .

The light of the oil lamps glazed Cherrystone; he became a more fixed target. Glinda had reached the end of that part of the strategy she'd been able to plan ahead, and she was improvising now. But how formidable he looked. Patient, wary, courteous, buckled up inside himself. He did have utterly lovely eyes for a marauder. A sort of faded cobalt. "I sense that these are early days, Traper. Still, I would be irresponsible to the memory of Sir Chuffrey if I didn't ask what your ultimate intentions are toward Mockbeggar. I do hope you have no plans to raze it."

"That wouldn't be a decision of mine, though I think no one in the Emerald City would bother this place much. I see that it is a jewel. In these few days I've come to appreciate why you love it so."

"Were I at the helm of strategy, I should think that securing Restwater as a permanent source of potable water for the Emerald City would be enough. I'm wondering, should that happen, if you intend Mockbeggar to serve as a satellite capital of the EC, and might decide to leave the rest of the Free State of Munchkinland alone? Munchkinland covers a vast territory, and though decidedly rural, it's more evenly populated than the rest of Oz, which by comparison is either urban or hardscrabble and too remote to be habitable. The attempt to subdue all of Munchkinland would be punishing."

"You have a good head for strategy, Lady Glinda, as befits a former Throne Minister. But you retired to seek other pleasures. Like gentlewoman farming, and flower arranging. So I shouldn't fret about the future. What will happen will happen."

"Don't get me wrong. I'm too selfish to care primarily about Munchkinland. What happens to the stucco walls of Mockbeggar and to its staff also happens to me. What happens to Mockbeggar's irises and prettibells happens to me. You think me shallow, but I have been breeding prettibells for eighteen summers now. It is my passion. I have a new variety that was even written about in our local newssheet, *Restwater Dew Tell.*" This was partly true. The gardener had been doing something with that ugly little orange flower. "Rain, can you slip into my library and find a copy of the newsfold with the article on prettibells?"

The girl said, "I don't know how to find it."

"It is a printed journal. It will say 'Prettibells Galore' in the headline, or something like that. Get up when I speak to you."

She stood, but shrugged. "I don't know how to read, Mum."

"I can find it," called Miss Murth.

"She'll do it," said Glinda tartly. "Child, there is an engraving on the page just under the masthead. You do know what a prettibell looks like, don't you? A blossom like a kind of grubby little chewed sock?"

Cherrystone was laughing. "They *are* your passion. You speak with the sour affection of the convert."

"Do as I say, Rain." Glinda felt herself flushing and hoped it didn't show in the lamplight. "I tell you, Traper, you abuse my ability to entertain when you reduce me to such a staff."

"Your prettibells will likely suffer this year," he admitted. "Sorry about that. Where are they in the garden, so we can avoid them?"

He almost had her there. "I can't discuss it any longer. It's too vexing to think of them in extremis. There's a dormant polder of them out beyond the little village of Zimmerstorm. Won't you allow Puggles to escort me to check on them?" There was no such polder. But if she could get out for a day on a false pretense, she might gain a better sense of what was going on.

"It may be possible. Depending."

Rain clambered back over the sill with several papers. "Not sure which one you want, so here is the lot."

"I don't want to look at them anymore. I've become distressed by the thought of them. You may return these."

"No, wait," said Cherrystone. He took several papers from Rain and studied the headlines. Then he turned the front page so the girl could see it and said, "Do you know your letters?"

"No, sir. I don't, sir."

"Why not?"

"Never had none to teach me, sir."

"Your mother doesn't know how to read?"

"If you remember, Cherrystone," said Glinda, "you required me to dismiss almost everyone."

"You kept a girl from leaving with her mother?"

"Well. Actually, the child is an orphan. I look after her out of charity. Don't pick your fingernails, Rain."

"But you don't teach her the alphabet." Cherrystone sounded incredulous.

"I can't do everything. I have prettibells to propagate. Until recently I didn't know this girl by name, so how could I know if she could read or not? Perhaps it's time for the cheese board. Rain, clear the plates."

"I'll take them through," called Miss Murth, stifling a shadowed yawn.

"My granddaughter is learning her letters," said the General. "Letters are a kind of magic, Rain. Coming together, they spell words, and words then are a kind of spell, too."

"She doesn't want to learn to read. She wants to carry those plates to the window. Leave her be, Traper." But Glinda was now on this. Could she play the hand? She'd never been good at bluffing when the local gentry came by for a couple of rubbers of Three-Hand Snuckett.

She picked up one of the papers and pretended to look at it for the article on prettibells, and then she moved the paper up close until it almost touched her lips. A little blind, to buy her some time, while Cherrystone asked the girl, "What does this letter look like? This thing?"

Rain said, "It looks like a stick for finding water with."

"Doesn't it just. It is called Y."

"Why?"

"Indeed."

"Too too touching," said Glinda, "but I'm afraid you're wasting your time. Our broomgirl is thicker than mud on the moor. Now, Rain, unless you want to annoy me, leave the General alone. He is a busy man and he needs his cheese."

"I have the board," called Miss Murth through the lace, which was now swaying in a stiffer wind off the lake. "A nice Arjiki goat-cheese and a Munchkinlander corriale, and an aged Zimmersweet made with the ash layer. Though one corner may be the wrong color of mold; it's hard to tell in this light."

"Would you like to learn to read, Rain?" asked Cherrystone.

"Do you specialize in impossible tasks?" interrupted Glinda. "You might as well ask a rural Munchkin-wife if she would like to brush the teeth of a mature draffe. The little scold can't reach and she *won't* reach no matter how many lessons in growing taller you squander upon her."

"My granddaughter is seven and she can read," said Cherrystone. "How old are you, Rain?"

"Now you're impertinent. Rain, go with Miss Murth." The girl shrugged and slung one leg over the windowsill. Straddling it, her hair fallen back about her neck, she reviewed the diners on the roof of the porch. Looking at the girl's curious expression, with a certain thrill Glinda thought: she's learning to read already. Letters are only the half of it.

She kept the paper over her face to hide her tiny twitch of triumph. What if Rain could be taught to read? She might sidle places in the house no one else could visit. Peer at maps. Directives to the field officers. Might be risky, but still . . .

When the girl had gone, and they had demolished a good deal of the cheese and two glasses of port each, Glinda returned to the subject to clinch the deal. "Do you want to help me survive the boredom of this incarceration, Traper? Shall we enter into a little wager? I'll wager you can't teach our broomgirl to read by the end of the summer. That is, assuming your tasks will keep you here all summer."

"About our tenure here, I can make no comment. But I've had a grand time helping my daughters learn to read, when I was home on leave, and my granddaughter too. I can make of your stupid little maid a capable reader of simple texts in a month or two. By Summersend, anyway, if we're here that long. It's a deal."

She raised her glass; the edges chinked to seal the wager.

"But you must have a challenge of your own," he said. "I shall dare you to . . . oh, what is it you can't do? Is there anything?"

She hoped he wouldn't say *generate a new strain of prettibell.* "I've always had Chef, of one name or another," she said. "I suppose I could enter into the fun of it and learn to prepare a meal on my own."

"It's a deal," he said, and the glasses chinked again. "But really?" he added, as he stood to go. "Even in childhood you had a chef?"

"Mumsy was an Upland," she said, as if that explained it.

"But didn't you linger in kitchens and pick things up, as all small children do? Even I did that."

"I don't recall much of my childhood," she told him. "It's been such a full rich life ever since, I haven't felt the need to dwell on that simpler time. Life, with whatever it has brought—university one decade, the Throne Ministry of Oz the next. The cultivation of roses and prettibells one year, house arrest another—well, daily life has always seemed distracting enough. Childhood? It's a myth."

"Good night, Lady Glinda. And thank you for a very pleasant evening. I shall send for your chambergirl in the next day or two."

It was late. She dismissed Miss Murth and the girl, but not before thanking Rain for her help. Then Glinda prepared herself for bed. She didn't need to check with the little mirror to see herself smiling. She believed she had won the hand.

Though as she settled herself upon the pillows, she found herself thinking about childhood. Had she meant what she had said? Had her own childhood really evaporated as thoroughly as all that? Or had she merely forgotten to pay it any attention once she'd left it behind and headed off to school in Shiz?

8.

The third, and as far as she could figure, the last of her early memories. Though who knows the architecture of the mind, and whether the arches that open upon discrete episodes are ordered in any way sequentially?

Probably they are not.

Still, this was a memory of autumn. Either it was actual autumn or she was dressing her few memories in contrasting colors, the better to render them distinctive.

Apple trees? Yes, apples. An orchard hugging a slope. Hesitating in its ascent, the incline leveled off several times—built up manually, to accommodate carts, or maybe the hill just preferred itself like that. This was her only memory to begin with the setting first, and with her entering the place, rather than with herself central as a maypole and the situation emanating from her.

She was wandering about the contorted trunks, trees twisted in their growth by a constant upsweep of wind from the valley. (So there must have been a valley. What lay below? A house? A village? A river? Why were memories so independent? So jealous of corroborating detail?)

Windfalls jeweled the grass, the colors of russet, burgundy, limeberry, freckled yellow. Fruit hung in the boughs like Lurlinemas ornaments. Leaves twitched as if signaling to one another: *she approaches.*

Around a certain tree she came upon a wounded bird humped in the grass like an overturned spindle. At first she thought it had bruised its head in an accident, twisted its neck. She had never seen a side-beak merin before.

The eye above the treacherous beak stared at her. She felt herself being pulled into the bird's gaze, sacrificing her own centrality for a moment. She felt she was being seen and understood by the merin.

The merin is a waterbird, distant cousin to the duck and the swan, though devoid of both the duck's work ethic and the swan's narcissism. The unusual bill swivels sideways to filch morsels from other birds. When not in use the beak, on a double-hinged jaw, can swing and tuck backward into creamy neck feathers so that in flight the merin resembles a coat-knob with wings.

This merin, the color of a stag-head beetle, didn't store its beak in its ruff. It merely looked at her and opened its mouth as if to speak.

She hadn't yet known that some creatures can speak. She did not learn it now—at least not through evidence. But she could tell by the serrated stroke of remark, by the waterfowl's stuttery smoker's vowels, that the merin had something specific to say.

She tried to lift the bird but it wouldn't let her. The subsequent scratches on her forearms, chalk marks at first, slowly beaded up. Crimson stitches on an ivory bolster.

She said, "You're hurt, but hurting me back won't help you any."

It humped itself a few inches away, as much by willpower as by mortal strength, and regarded her with need and fury.

"If I can't pick you up and take you—"

But where would she have taken it? To some house, some village, some river?

She rolled an apple at it in case it liked apples. The merin knocked it away savagely.

Then—so why did she remember any of this?—she took care of it. She didn't remember how, just that she did. She found a way to feed it for a while until it had gathered its strength.

Say what you know.

I remember pulling a golden minnow or smelt from my pocket, still flapping, as if I had just rescued it from the weir, and feeding it to the merin. I remember how the fishlette flopped in the beak, dropped in the grass, and with what acumen and zip the merin retrieved it, and swallowed it whole.

But what a patently false memory this was. The rescue of an ice-bound fish happened in winter. The merin's recuperation from some unknown attack or disease clearly happened in the autumn—all those apples decorating the memory.

So—if the oldest memories could contaminate one another, could prove impossible—what good was memory at all?

Was that why she remembered nothing more?

Except that when the merin had recovered its nerve and its composure, it staggered to its bandy legs and rushed at her, clacking its beak like scissors. Until it pivoted. Like a one-legged man picking up his false leg and tucking it under his arm before hopping to bed, the merin swung its beak into place. Then the bird raised its weird puppet-head and opened its wings. She could see that one wing had been wrenched at; its feathers thinned. An ugly viscous patch glistened on the leading edge like wet shellac.

And still it somehow managed to launch itself. It battered through branches as it learned how to fly all over again, with new strength in its left wing correcting what it had lost in its right. Lopsidedly it lifted along the slopes of air that mimicked the steps of terraced orchard below. It wheeled against silver blue, heading for something beyond the scope of memory to imagine.

To climb up the invisible staircases of the sky—!

Without benefit of a mouth, which was in storage, it said to her, one way or the other, "Remember."

9.

Cherrystone was true to his word. The next morning he sent an underling to collect Rain for her first lesson in reading. It would take place in the Opaline Salon. Safe enough. Miss Murth reported that the door had been left ajar, as if for Lady Glinda or her minions to be able to check for impropriety.

"Is that so. Well, then, be a dear, Murthy, and nip down there to investigate, just in case," said Glinda.

"Lady Glinda. I do many things and I do them well, but I do not nip."

Rain returned an hour later not visibly glorified with learning. She trotted off to water the potted prettibells in the south porch, since Glinda now felt obliged to keep the damn things alive.

Chef sent word that his supplies of potatoes had been appropriated. Also three whole smoked haunches of skark and a pair of hams. Would Lady Glinda settle for a lunch of coddled eggs and new carrots?

Miss Murth had a headache and retired for the afternoon.

Glinda walked the length of her apartments. Since Mockbeggar Hall crowned a headland, it enjoyed water views from three directions. Westward Glinda could see a flock of geese. Out the front windows she spied a lone tugboat plying the waves. Easterly, several stacks of smudgy smoke unfurled from an indeterminate source.

She rang for Puggles. "They're not burning Zimmerstorm, surely?" she asked.

"I can't say for certain, Mum," he replied. "All our kitchen deliveries are now handled through an EC lout who acts mute. Perhaps he is. He is called Private Private, and he doesn't speak to us or anyone else, near as I can tell. So I can get no word out of him."

"This is intolerable." She tried to summon Cherrystone, but the guard who seemed permanently stationed in the banquet hall replied, "He's not at home, Mum."

"Of course he's not at home," she snapped. "His home is someplace else. This is my home. Where is he?"

"Privileged information, I'm afraid, Mum."

"I'm not Mum to you, laddie. Address me as Lady Glinda or Lady Chuffrey. Who are you?"

"Privileged information, Mum."

She almost hit him. But Cherrystone came swooping in, pretty as you please, through the kitchens. "I thought I heard your voice," he said, like a husband returning from an afternoon shooting grouse. She almost felt he was going to swing across the room and plant a kiss on her cheek.

"Traper. I need a word. Privately."

He shrugged. "As you know, privacy doesn't do either of our reputations any good."

"This is war, Traper. Reputations be damned."

"As you wish." He made a gesture and the Menacier skated away.

She told him she wanted to know what was burning to the east. "Oh, that? It's the cotton harvest, I'm afraid. The holdings between here and Zimmerstorm."

She gasped. "You must be mad. What has cotton ever done to you?"

"Oh, very little. Cotton is blameless, I admit."

"What is the point? Just to deprive the farmers of their cash crop? They sell to mills in Gillikin, you must know that. You'll force up the price of cotton in Loyal Oz. That's madness pure and simple."

"Maybe there was a population of boll weevils doing the nasty on that farm."

"I'll say. Are you trying to foment the farmers into attacking you here? The Battle of Mockbeggar Hall? Seriously. Traper. I want an explanation."

He raised an eyebrow. "I didn't think you'd become the Good Witch of Munchkinland, Lady Glinda. They already have a pretender to the position of Eminence squatting up there in Colwen Grounds, I'm told."

"And I have friends in the neighborhood."

"Among cotton farmers? Please."

It was a stretch; she saw that. She tried again. "Those farmers supply you and me both with dairy and grain and who knows what else. You're playing with fire, General. Rather literally, I'm afraid."

"Well." He poured himself a small portion of her brandy. Before lunch! He offered her a glass. She didn't acknowledge his offer. "The truth is, the boys are antsy. Soldiers like to be on the move, and they're going slightly stir-crazy. They need to be kept busy. A little burning of fields is a useful exercise. Gets them out and working."

She stared at him as if he were mad.

He added, "You haven't had sons, you wouldn't get it. Soldiers like to destroy as well as to build."

She was flummoxed. "If you're going to be here for months, what will you do—scorch the entire district?"

"Maybe we'll take up lowland sports. Like hip-sprung dancing, the way the old ones do in the pub in Zimmerstorm. Or darts." He was being amused by her consternation. "Or I could teach my men to speak Qua'ati, perhaps. By the way, your Rain made a creditable start at learning her letters this morning."

"I need a carriage."

"There's nothing available today."

"You'll have to locate me one. I have an appointment. I'm leaving directly after luncheon."

"I can't spare a driver."

"I'll have Puggles or Chef. They'll know how to manage a team."

She turned to leave as he was speaking. "Where is your appointment?"

"East of the cotton fields," she replied. "I haven't decided the exact destination."

Somewhat to her surprise, when she descended the stairs in her wine-colored summer cloak with the musset panels, the front doors were open and the Menacier from the banquet hall was waiting. "The name is Zackers, Lady Glinda," he said with crystalline politeness. "I have orders to accommodate you within reason, and to turn back if you cannot be reasoned with."

"I have nearly no sense of reason," she told him, "so be forewarned."

It wasn't her best carriage but it was better than nothing. Miss Murth had brought a fan, but the breeze off the lake was strong this afternoon and the horseflies mercifully few. What a treat to hear the trap clicketing along on the abalone drive, and then the softer sound it made in summer dust when they passed through the front gates of Mockbeggar and turned east along the lake road. Lady Glinda hadn't really felt imprisoned yet, but her release was more welcome than she'd anticipated.

The road rose and fell as the low hills of the Pine Barrens to the north approached the lake. This part of Oz had been farmed for hundreds of years. Some tedious old geezer at a dinner party once had told Glinda that the Munchkins of antiquity had settled here first before colonizing the breadbasket of Oz to the northeast. How anyone could deduce such a thing seemed dubious to her, though in time her eye for architecture began to assemble clues that supported his thesis. And, she had to acknowledge, the fecundity of this district would have appealed to any wandering troll or trollop.

How she'd come to love Restwater. As if she didn't see it every day from her chambers, she marveled once again. Every bend in the road, every dip after every rise, bringing new vistas of blue shattered by sunlight. Blue between the pines, one shade; blue between the birches, another. Blue in chips and fragments; blue opening up. If there were such a place as heaven, she thought, it could do worse than modeling itself on the road from Mockbeggar to Zimmerstorm.

All too soon, however, she began to smell the stench of char, and most of those blues went brown with heavy hovering smoke, a kind of industrial fog. She coughed, and Murth coughed, and their eyes stung and then ran. "Shall I turn back, for your health, Mum?" asked Private Zackers.

"Press on."

The fields were destroyed. At least—she peered through the streams in her eyes—at least the outbuildings and farmsteads seemed standing. Those visible from the road, anyway.

What had those farmers done? Where had they gone while their livelihoods were being torched?

The carriage passed a vegetable garden that for the fun of it, she guessed, had also been ravaged. A scarecrow shrugged its shoulders at the sky, presiding over ruin, as if asking the Unnamed God the reason for such wantonness.

Murth's tears were real tears. She was a fool, after all, if a dear one. For herself, Glinda felt ready to take some training with a halberd.

Before long—not soon enough—they had cleared the worst of the damage and were beginning the descent into Zimmerstorm. Its town hall steeple, its pitched roofs clad in the blue-grey tiles of the region—it all looked more or less correct. A mercy.

Glinda directed Zackers to halt the trap in the village square. "We shall take our tea, my companion and I," she told Zackers. "Your company is not required."

He stood on guard at the street door of the local tearoom anyway.

Then Lady Glinda had the most unfortunate experience of realizing—very slowly, picking up cues as if they were bug bites—that the residents of Zimmerstorm didn't fully believe the testimony of those who'd been dismissed from Mockbeggar. They harbored a suspicion that Lady Glinda was in collusion with the occupiers.

She could hardly blame them. She was Gillikinese herself, of course, and she *had* had high-ranking association with the Emerald City. And she couldn't mount an explanation in public—former Throne Ministers didn't do that. Besides, who would believe her? She just had to sit in stony silence as the cabbage-faced Munchkinlander hostess grunted and scowled and made as if to dump the tea in her lap. "A biscuit," Glinda begged.

"No biscuits," snapped the proprietress. "Your military friendsies scarfed 'em all up. For 'emselves."

"Perhaps a roundlet of toast?" wondered Miss Murth.

The toast came about twenty minutes later. It had been burnt inedible. As burnt as the cotton fields.

"Perhaps a constitutional," suggested Lady Glinda.

"That's five farthings, Mum," said Sour Peasant Woman.

Lady Glinda wasn't in the habit of carrying coin. Miss Murth had none to carry. How embarrassing to have to petition Private Zackers to pay the establishment. I won't make *that* mistake again, Glinda thought.

Still, while Zackers was settling up, Glinda and Murth got ahead of him, across the village square. A miniature escape! Oh, hilarity.

"Into the lending library, Murthy," said Glinda. "Quickly now. Move your arthritic hips or I'll run you down."

The librarian was a retired Munchkin on a stool. She recognized him though she didn't know his name. "I'm looking to borrow a book that can teach one the essentials of preparing a meal," she said. "For dining, I mean. For human dining."

"Books en't going to teach that, Lady Glinda," he said. "Mothers teach that. Closest I can help you with is a volume on animal husbandry, which has an illustrated index on slaughtering your own livestock."

"I think not," she murmured. Turning, she saw a notice board behind his desk. A scroll was posted with nails. She peered at it. A crude drawing with a handwritten announcement. She hadn't brought her reading glasses. "Miss Murth, can you decipher that message?" she asked.

Miss Murth could not. "You want something read, you should've brought Rain," she said, somewhat cruelly.

"I can read that for you, Lady Glinda," said the librarian. "It says that the Clock of the Time Dragon is coming through in the next week or so, weather and the military situation permitting."

"It looks like a chapel on wheels of some sort."

"It's an entertainment, Mum. Sort of a puppet show for adults. You en't never seen it?"

"Nor heard of it." She intended frost in her tone, but thought better of it. "My dear man, would you tell the managers of this traveling enterprise to make their way to Mockbeggar Hall? I do believe that if the soldiers had something to look forward to, we might keep them from doing any more damage than they have already done, for instance, today."

Luckily, this Munchkinlander wasn't as suspicious as the tea-wife in the shop. "Can't say them traveling clocksters will listen to me," he replied. "But I can pass on the word and see what they'll do. They operate with cheeky diplomatic immunity, far as I've heard. Cross these parts every few years, don't matter if it's Wicked Witch of the East or the old Eminent Thropp or that mean old Zombie Mombey in charge. They seem pretty fearless. I'll give 'em your message."

"You're too kind," she told him. Here came Private Zackers, looking red under the collar.

"You were nice to my sister, that time she lay in childbirth a month too long," said the librarian softly. "You put a cloth to her brow. Don't pretend you forget."

She turned away, confused by an accusation of charity. "How impertinent!" hissed Murth on her behalf.

10.

Day after day as different plantings came to flower, blossoms patterned the gardens and the meadows with a shifting palette. Now the eggy frill of late forsythia, now the fringe of fern. Now the periwinkle mycassandrum on the hillsides, until pale daisies overtook the lavender, and then wild dusteria the daisies. The leaves on the trees flexed their palms wider. Let me in, said the sun. Let me out, said the tree.

Beyond the reflecting pool, the topiary hedges thickened into rooms again, chambers of green set round with statues, plinths, benches of marble carved to look like rural twigwork. Once the daily cloudburst had passed, Glinda often grabbed a parasol and picked her way through the maze. Miss Murth had an allergy to the mites that came out of the ivy after a downpour so she stayed inside, and Glinda got herself a little privacy. The Green Parlor, as they called it, was considered an extension of her private chambers, so she had no cause to worry about some wayward soldier interrupting her meditations.

She was surprised, therefore, one afternoon about a week later, to come upon a dwarf with a hoary beard sitting upon the drum of an aesthetically collapsed column.

"I beg your pardon." Her tone was High Frost.

"No offense taken," he told her, lighting a pipe with a long stem.

"This is a private garden."

"You'd better take yourself off, then." He winked at her. The nerve. "Or should I say, All the better for a private conversation."

"Do you know who I am?"

"Glinda, or else I made a wrong turn," he answered. "Easy enough to do in a hedge maze. Especially for a dwarf."

"I'll set the dogs on you unless you leave."

He looked up over the tops of his spectacles. "That's a sour welcome considering you called for me. You don't remember we've met before? Or is it, Seen one dwarf, seen 'em all? They all look alike to me?"

"Forgive me. I'm not myself. I no longer have the staff to hand me notes of reference." She peered at him sideways. "Oh. I see. You're with that circus. That pantomime troupe. No?"

"We prefer to think of ourselves as social critics. The conscience of Oz. But we take any cash comes our way, so you can call us dancing bears or moral vivisectionists, whatever you like. Makes no difference to me."

He gave his name as Mr. Boss, which rang no bells with her.

"How did you know how to find me in the maze?" she asked.

He laughed. "Oh, knowing things; that's my line of work, missy."

"Well . . . thank you for coming, I suppose. I had thought maybe you could put on a performance or rally or sing-along, whatever, to entertain the men garrisoned here. Is that the sort of thing you do?"

"I do anything that suits me. But it can be made my while, I think."

"Well, what do you charge?"

"I'll let you know. Can you show me the setup?"

"First remind me how we came to meet the first time. For the life of me I can't recall."

He didn't comply with her request. "You must meet so many dwarfs in your line of work. Let's go."

She didn't like to be seen taking the air with a dwarf, but she supposed she had no choice. And really, she thought, what do I care what soldiers think? Bloody hell. They've spent the week burning cotton fields.

But she did care, which was annoying.

Still, she ushered Mr. Boss out of the Green Parlor. The dwarf breathed noisily and spat his tobacco into the prettibells.

In the widest open space among the farm buildings, where two stables and three barns and some carriage sheds fronted a sort of ellipse, Private Zackers showed up to refuse her further access. "I have no interest in the barns right now, Zackers," she told him. "I'm engaging a troupe of traveling players and I'm examining the barnyard as a possible venue."

"Has the General approved this?" asked Zackers.

She made a disagreeable face. "I'm not submitting to him for reimbursement, Zackers; there's nothing to approve. I'm supplying my uninvited guests with a little weekend entertainment. I am the lady of Mockbeggar

Hall, after all." She turned to the dwarf. "What do you think?"

"Some can sit in the upper windows and get a balcony view," he said. "Shall we say sunset tomorrow?"

"How will I reach you in case plans need to be changed?"

"You won't need to reach me."

He was confident. As well he might be: Cherrystone had no objection. "I saw posters mounted on various kiosks in Zimmerstorm and Haventhur," he said. "I'd been wondering what it was all about. Bring it on."

So, ten days after the burning of the first cotton field, Glinda left Miss Murth and Chef and Rain behind. They could keep an eye on the silver if nothing else. She accepted the arm Puggles extended to her because the cobbles were uneven. Cherrystone had arranged a chair for her—one of the precious bon Scavella chairs from the Hall of Painted Arches!—but she pretended not to be outraged.

Men surrounded her in jostling, good-natured mumble. The ones nearer the appointed arena had brought cloaks upon which to sit, but most of the fellows stood, arms about one another's shoulders, or leaned against the various walls. Several hay carts provided mezzanine seating, while other fellows appeared in the hay doors under the peaks of the barn roofs. From a height sometimes known as the gods they swung their heels and hooted at their buddies.

General Cherrystone hauled out a camp chair for himself. He sat some distance away from her, as was correct. She nodded, acknowledging him briefly before turning her attention to nothing of interest in her purse.

Just as the sun was slotting between two hills to the east, raging the lake with ruddy copper, she heard the sound of wheels on stone from around the edge of the farthest barn. This was the signal, apparently, for soldiers to light some torches. Within a few moments the last of day became the first of night, a magic as peculiar and welcome as any other.

A wheeled monstrosity of some sort emerged. Nothing less than a small building erected on a dray. Between the shafts, where one might expect a team of horses or donkeys, a lion strained, head down, mane over his eyes. The temple of entertainment was accompanied by a number of young men in tangerine tunics, black scarfs covering their noses and mouths. A slim white-haired woman in a golden veil struck a set of chimes with a mallet. She looked spiky and consumptive. The dwarf drew up the rear, banging a drum almost as big as he was.

Glinda hoped she wasn't going to ask to be converted. She didn't have much to be converted from. She began to wish she'd sat farther back. Now where had she met that dwarf before? She'd been racking her brains for a day and had turned up no clue. She supposed, not for the first time, that she didn't have a whole lot of brains to rack. Or was she at the age already when memory begins to fail? She couldn't remember.

The lion muttered something to the veiled woman. So it was a Lion, then. Curious. Most respectable Animals wouldn't be seen doing menial labor like pulling a cart, but perhaps this was a sort of penance. Glinda knew that Animals in Munchkinland fared no better than Animals in Loyal Oz; you rarely saw a professional Animal on the shores of Restwater. But then her social circuit was circumscribed by her position; who knew what Animals might be getting up to in the back of beyond? All kinds of unsavory mischief. She preferred not to contemplate it; life at Mockbeggar these days was vexing enough.

She turned her attention to the performance. Things were starting up.

The jittery-totteriness of it. A sort of omphalos made of wood, capped by the semblance of a dragon. Its countenance was lurid, its eyes glowed red, like embers. Clever and banal. Long struts carved of sallowwood flexed to suggest the limbs of a bat. When the dragon shifted its wings to reveal a clock-face, the sound of leathery creases shifting was like wet laundry on the line, flumping in a stiff wind.

So this was the Clock of the Time Dragon. Ready for all manner of foldiddy-doodle.

Then the facade of the great structure along the length of the cart, the long side, began to separate into segments. It folded back cunningly, the best of tiktok play. Small stagelets receded or nested against each other. Protrusions locked into recesses. The whole thing was a set of shutters collapsing against one another like a sentient puzzle.

All this clockwork commotion revealed a central arena, cloaked from view by a curtain as broad as two bed linens hemmed together. The drape must be stiffened with wooden braces. The surface of the cloth was painted with a fanciful map of Oz. More iconography than geography. The Emerald City glowed in the middle through some apparatus of backlighting; a loose approximation of the four main counties fanned out to the margins. Gillikin to the north, Quadling Country to the south, the Vinkus to the west, and Munchkinland—the Free State of Munchkinland, for her pains!—to the east.

She was sitting close enough to peer at the margins of the map. The outlying colonies and satrapies of Ugabu and the Glikkus. A few arrows pointing, variously, away, off margin, to countries across the band of deserts that isolated the giant Oz as competently as a ring of seas might, were seas anything other than a mystical notion of everlastingness.

Some sort of music began. She was dimly aware that the boys in their sunset robes had picked up nose whistles and cymberines, tympani and strikes. Someone drew a bow across a squash-bellied violastrum. Someone lit a muskwax-taper that smelled of rose blossoms. To a man, the soldiers squatted, relaxing on their haunches; this was well done enough to be convincing before it had even begun.

Cherrystone, she saw, was lighting a cigarette.

The dwarf gave a bow at the close of the prelude. The curtain rose on a lighted stage as the yard appreciably darkened by three or four degrees of violet.

A couple of figures strutted lazily onstage. What were they called again? Homunculards. Puppets on strings. Marionettes, that was it. They were meant to resemble the Messiars and Menaciers squatting in the barnyard of Mockbeggar Hall, no doubt. They were hale and fit, and their ash limbs had been carved to exaggerate military physique. Waists tapered to pencil points, while biceps and buttocks and pectorals were all globular as oranges. Faces were blank but rosy-cheeked, and one chin had a sticking plaster across it, suggesting a soldier so young he was still learning how to shave.

The two soldiers sauntered across the stage, looking hither and yon. Lights came up further to reveal the painted backdrop, which seemed to be a field of corn or wheat or cotton. A rough fence, a scarecrow, a few squiggles of bird painted in the sky across fat clouds in summersweet blue.

What craft the handlers showed! The puppet soldiers were bored. They whistled (how did they do that?). They kicked an imaginary stone back and forth. Funny how in the telling of it, thought Glinda, in the arc of the leading foot and the posture of the defense, the presence of the implied stone seemed as real, or even realer, than the puppet fellows themselves.

The puppets soon tired of kick-the-pebble. They approached the front of the stage and looked out at the audience, but it was clear they weren't peering at real soldiers in the gloaming. One of the carved Menaciers put a palm to his eyebrows as if shielding it from sun while he scanned the horizon. The other knelt down and dipped his hand a little below stage level, and the audience heard the sound of water swishing about. The puppet guard was meant to be on the shores of Restwater.

From offstage a melody started up, a saucy two-step in the key of squeezebox. The soldiers looked at each other and then off to one side. On came a line of dancing girls with high-stepping legs, bare to the knee and venturing quite a bit of thigh. In the porphyrous barnyard, General Cherrystone's soldiers roared and applauded the arrival of this squadron of hoofers. Well, they were cheery, Glinda had to agree. And so smart! Eight or nine dancers. Their dresses, sequinned and glittery, were made of silvery blue tulle netting stitched from the hip of the first dancer on the left all along to the last dancer on the right. Their kicks were so uniform they were no doubt managed by a single lever or pulley of some sort. Offstage, some of the musicians were hooting out in falsetto as if the dancers were cat-calling the men, "Heee!" and "What ho!" and "Oooh la la!" and "Oz you like it!"

Then, through some sleight of theater that Glinda couldn't work out, they'd turned back-to-front somehow. The vixens put their hands to the floor and their legs in the air, and their skirts fell down over their bosoms and heads, revealing pink panties that looked, from here, like real silk. Their costumed behinds faced the audience. Each one of the girls had a bull's-eye painted on her smalls.

The soldiers in the barnyard roared their approval. Glinda noticed that the two puppet Menaciers had disappeared. Well, who needed male puppets when females were available?

You could no longer make out the heads of the dancers, nor even their legs. The blue netting seemed to be rising and thickening; there was more and more of it, until all that was left were nine pink behinds bobbing in a sea of blue.

Thank mercy she had left Miss Murth at home, she thought, as—oh sweet Ozma—the dancers somehow dropped their drawers. The pink sleeves slid under the waves, and on each of the nine bobbing unclefted arses a different letter was painted.

R-E-S-T-W-A-T-E-R.

The articulate rumps quickly disappeared beneath the blue waves of the lake. The audience booed good-naturedly. But Glinda noticed that the smell of roses had given over to a smell of smoke.

From wing to wing, across the back of the stage, some long slit in the floor must have opened, for the dancing girl puppets and then their drowning lengths of blue skirt drained within the aperture. Their disappearance revealed one of the soldiers from earlier. His face had been smudged with coal dust, his clothes as well. He carried in his hand a torch. The fire was made of orange flannel lit from within; a spring-wound fan made the flames dance to the same melody that the girls had jigged to.

Oh, thought Glinda suddenly, as the smell of smoke intensified. Oh dear.

The aperture opened again and up from beneath the stage rose a stiffened flat. It was in the shape of a hill, the same shape as the hill on the backdrop, and very soon it stood in front of the backdrop, blocking the view of Highsummer crops. The hill was denuded of crop, and blackened. The scarecrow was a scorched skeleton with hollows for eyes.

The second soldier came on, and the two companions returned to the shore of Restwater. Somehow while the audience had been distracted by the rising dead hill, a segment of the stage had slid forward, like the broad bowed front of a shallow drawer. From the recesses flashed scraps and humps of the costumes of the dancing girls, now clearly signifying the waves of Restwater. Then—oh, horrid to see!—from the surface of the tulle-water emerged the head of the Time Dragon itself. Its eyes glowed red; its scissoring jaws seethed with smoke.

The two soldiers waded in the water, one on either side of the puppet Dragon, and they clasped their arms around its neck. They fell to kissing the creature as if it were one of the dancing girls, and as its smile turned into a leer, it sank beneath the waves, dragging the two soldiers with them. They couldn't pull away. They courted the dragon with affection until they drowned.

"Enough!" barked Cherrystone in the dark, but he hadn't needed to say this. The lights were going down and the music fading upon a weird, unresolved chord.

The barnyard fell silent. The dwarf came around from the back of the Clock and gave a little skip and a bow and a flick of his teck-fur cap.

Glinda stood and applauded. She was the only one until she turned and made a motion with her hands. Then the men joined in, grumblingly and none too effusive.

Improvising, she walked over to Cherrystone and pretended she couldn't read his ire. "Would you care to join the troupe of entertainers back at the house for a light refreshment before they go on their way?"

He didn't answer. He began barking orders to his men.

She couldn't resist fluting after him, "I'll take that as regrets, but do feel free to change your mind if you're so inclined." Then she cocked her head at Mr. Boss and indicated Mockbeggar Hall's forecourt.

11.

My, but Cherrystone needed to sort out his men. They seemed bothered by the turn toward tragedy that the episode had taken. Clever little dramaturg, thought

Glinda, sneaking a glance at Mr. Boss and his associates as they dragged the Clock of the Time Dragon across the forecourt of Mockbeggar.

Puggles had rushed ahead to light a few lanterns and arrange for a beverage. But Mr. Boss said, "There's no time. We have to get out quickly before your General Mayhem arrives to put us under lock and key."

"But you're my guests," said Glinda.

"Fat distance that'll get us, when you're in durance vile yourself." He turned to the Lion. "Brrr, guard the gateway, will you? If you can manage to look menacing, you might hold off the law for a valuable few moments."

"Menacing isn't my strong suit," said the Lion. "How about vexed? Or inconvenienced."

Glinda recognized the voice, dimly. Not the famous Cowardly Lion? Doing menial labor for a bunch of—shudder—theater people? She had made him a Namory once, hadn't she? "Sir Brrr?" she ventured.

"The same," he replied, "though I drop the honorific when I'm touring." He seemed pleased to be recognized. "Lady Glinda. A pleasure."

"To your station, 'fraidycat," snapped the dwarf. Brrr padded away. The brittle woman in the veils went with him, one hand upon his rolling spine. In the lamplight he looked quite the golden statue of a Lion, regal and paralyzed, and his consort like some sort of penitent. The lads in orange were still strapping up the Clock and securing it.

"I have been trying to think of where we met," said Glinda. "I ought to have kept better notes."

"You ever intend to write your memoirs," the dwarf said, "you're going to have to make up an awful lot. Maybe this will remind you."

He motioned to the young men to stand back. They looked singularly strong, stupid, and driven. Ah, for a stupid young man, she thought, losing the thread for a moment. Lord Chuffrey had been many wonderful things, but stupid he was not, which made him a little less fun than she'd have liked.

The dwarf approached the Clock. She couldn't tell if he pressed some hidden mechanism or if the Clock somehow registered his intentions. Or maybe he was merely responding to *its* intentions; it seemed weirdly spirited. "The next moment," he murmured, "always the next moment unpacks itself with a degree of surprise. Come on, now."

The section of front paneling—from which the lake of blue tulle had swelled—slid open once more. There was no sign of the dragon head, the drowned Menaciers, the rustling waves. The dwarf reached in and put his thwarty hands on something and pulled it out. She recognized it at once, and her memory snapped into place.

Elphaba's book of spells. Glinda had had it once, after Elphaba had died; and then the dwarf had come along, and Glinda had given it to him for safekeeping.

"How did you persuade me to give it to you?" Her voice was nearly at a whisper. "I can't remember. You must have put a spell on me."

"Nonsense. I don't do magic, except the obvious kind. Fanfares and mistaken identities, chorus lines and alto soliloquies. A little painting on black velvet. I merely told you that I knew you had the book of spells, that I knew what was in it, and that I knew your fears about it. I'm the keeper of the Grimmerie. That's my job. If not to hoard it under my own protection, then to lodge it where it will do the least harm."

He held it out to her. "That's why I've come. It's your turn. This is your payment for our service tonight. You will take it again. It's time."

She drew back, looked to make sure that Cherrystone wasn't approaching from the barns or the house itself. "You're a mad little huskin of a man, Mr. Boss. This is the least safe place for the Grimmerie. I am incarcerated here."

"You will use it," he said, "and you must use it."

"I don't respond to threats or prophecies."

"Prophecy is dying, Lady Glinda. So I'm going on a hunch. Our best thinking is all we have left."

"My best thinking wouldn't boil an egg," she told him.

"Look it up. This thing is as good a cookbook as any you're likely to find. Come on, sister. Didn't Elphaba trust you once to try? It's your turn."

"I don't mention her name," said Glinda. Not coldly, but in deference.

"Shall I leave you the Lion to help you protect the book?"

"I am not allowed pets."

Brrr, circling the court and sniffing for trouble, gave a low growl.

"Sorry. I'm flustered. I meant to say staff. I have a skeletal crew on hand to look after me, but I think you need the Lion's services more than I do."

"His services aren't much to speak of," said the dwarf. The boys laughed a little nastily. They were Menaciers themselves, she saw, just in a different uniform, serving a different commander. She wanted nothing to do with any of them.

"When I saw you once before," she told Mr. Boss, "you were on your own. You didn't have this extravagance of tiktok mechanics at your heels."

"Once in a while I park the Clock in secrecy when the times require it. That instance, as I recall, I was making a little pilgrimage on foot. I told you that I knew you had the Grimmerie, and what was in it. I told you things about Elphaba that no one could know. That's how I convinced you to relieve yourself of the Grimmerie then, before Shell Thropp had acceded to the Throne and approached you, intending to impound the book. I trust he did make that effort?"

She nodded. The dwarf had predicted events quite cannily. Thanks to him, she'd had nothing to show Shell, not in the palace treasury nor in her private library, not in Mennipin Square nor in Mockbeggar Hall. She'd been clean of this dangerous volume.

And now, Cherrystone breathing down her throat every day, she was expected to take it back again? To hide it in plain sight?

"Are you working to set me up for execution?" she hissed.

"I never talk about the end game." He winked at her. "I've lived so long without death that I've stopped believing in it."

From the shadows of the great Parrith onyx pillars with strabbous inlay, the Lion spoke. "Things are settling down now. Campfires being lit, men sorted out. We don't have much time."

"Please," said Mr. Boss to her. "And I don't say please often."

Glinda kept her hands tucked under her arms. She looked up at the dark windows of Mockbeggar. If she took this book, she wanted to make certain that Miss Murth and Puggles and Chef were ignorant of it. She didn't want to put them under any more danger than necessary.

There was no sign of a shape at the windows. Or was there? Perhaps a little thumbnail of darkness at a lower pane. Surely Rain was off and asleep?

The spooky woman in the veil hesitated, but then left the Lion's side to approach Glinda. The lamplight etched shadows from her veil along the sides of her face, but Glinda could make out her strong thin nose and full lips and a shock of white hair, odd in one who seemed otherwise so young. A wasting ailment, perhaps. Her skin was dark, like a woman from the Vinkus. "We do not play at intrigue," she said to Glinda. "We work to avoid it wherever we can. But I ask you. Do this for Elphaba. Do this for Fiyero."

Glinda reared back. "What license have you to take their names to me!"

She replied, "The right of the wounded, for whom propriety is a luxury. I beg you. In their names. Take the book."

"Listen to Missy Flitter-foot of the Prairies," said Mr. Boss to Glinda. "Before they tear us limb from limb."

The Lion shook his mane. "Ilianora. Gentlemen. Mr. Boss. They're beginning to marshal their forces. I can hear them coming."

She didn't know why she took the Grimmerie from the dwarf, but Brrr was already settling himself between the shafts of the Clock, and the lads in tunics were putting shoulders to the carriage. The one they called Ilianora drew her veil down upon her forehead. "If they catch us up, and tear the Clock apart with their fingers, they won't find its heart," she said to Glinda, and put two dusky fingers upon Glinda's pale hand. "Much depends on you now." Then she turned, a corkscrew twist of white sleeves and ripples, and hurried after the Clock as it passed through the gates of the forecourt and into the dark, heading not toward Zimmerstorm and the Munchkin strongholds, but west along the road leading toward Loyal Oz.

The dwarf was walking away backward, hissing at Glinda. "We won't go far. Into a tuck between low hills in the Pine Barrens. Just until we're sure everything is copacetic."

"You have no reason to look after me."

"Don't flatter yourself. We want to make sure the book doesn't come to harm." Then on his bandy legs he stumped to catch up with his companions.

She was alone for a moment, alone with the Grimmerie in the guttering light of lanterns. It weighed against her breast and clavicle like the child she had never had. It was nearly warm to touch. It *was* warm to touch. The tooled binding seemed to relax in her hold.

Nonsense.

She flung herself inside and up the grand staircase. She was huffing by the time she reached the top, and she could hear soldiers returning to their posts in the banquet hall and the reception rooms. She heard the crystal chink of stopper against bottleneck; brandy was being decanted. Disagreements about the Clock's presentation were being aired. She achieved her private suite, however, without molestation.

A single candle glowed in a sconce. Miss Murth sat ramrod straight, looking directly ahead. The girl was on the floor, her head in Miss Murth's lap. Murth was stroking her hair.

"You fool. You should be abed. I can manage my own nightgown," snapped Glinda.

"The girl couldn't sleep and I didn't dare let her wander about alone."

"So where did the two of you wander to? The ramparts?"

Miss Murth pursed her lip. "The girl was curious. But I did not care for the entertainment. It did not seem suitable."

"Suitable for whom? I'm disappointed in you both. Take yourselves off somewhere else to sulk. I didn't write the script. Go on, I'm in no mood to talk."

Miss Murth arose. She didn't glance at the Grimmerie, which Glinda felt was glowing against her bosom like a red-hot breastplate. "You will bring us to ruin, Lady Glinda," she said in a low voice. "Come along, girl."

The sleepy child stood and yawned. As much to herself as to Glinda or Murth, she murmured, "My favorite was the Lion."

12.

Whatever happened, Glinda was pretty sure she wouldn't be subject to a midnight inquisition, so she just stuffed the Grimmerie under her pillow. Then she humped herself into bed and blew her own candle out, and failed to sleep till nearly dawn.

What to do about the book? Cherrystone had already scoured her apartments, but he was no fool. He might work out that the performance of such a seditious little one-act was a diversionary tactic. That some transaction had occurred in the forecourt. He could come storming in here at dawn and tear the place apart. What to do? Where to turn?

And why was she the point person? Was it simply too obvious for words—that she was known to be more capricious than clever? That no one would think to look for an instrument of parlous magic in her presence? That she was a silly, dispensable figure whose moment had passed? She couldn't dispute any of this. And she still couldn't sleep.

Her thoughts returned to Elphaba Thropp. It was more than fifteen years since they had parted ways. What an uncommon friendship they had had—not quite fulfilling. Yet nothing had ever taken its place. Years later, when that boy Liir had shown up at Glinda's house in the Emerald City, she had known him at once for Elphaba's son, though he seemed in some doubt on that matter. (Children.) He had had Elphaba's broom, after all, and her cape. More to the point, he had had her *look:* that look both haunted and thereby abstract, but at the same time focused. A look like a spark on a dry winter's day, that staticky crackle and flash that leaps across the air from finger to the iron housing of the servant's bell.

What would Liir do, were he handed the Grimmerie? What would Elphaba?

She drifted to sleep at last as the summer dawn began. Birds insisted on their dim pointless melodies. She didn't believe she dreamed of Elphaba; she didn't have the kind of aggravated imagination that loitered in dreams. Maybe she dreamed of a door opening, and Elphaba coming back from the Afterlife. To settle Glinda's consternation; to save her. Or maybe this wasn't a dream, just a foundational longing. Still, when she rose to a clamor of soldiers practicing in formation outside, she found that she had an inkling about what to do. Like a bit of advice from Elphaba, in her dream! But that was fanciful.

Miss Murth was drawing the bath. "I fear a slight headache," called Glinda. "I will do without tea until later. Leave me alone."

"Very good, Mum," said Miss Murth in a voice of superiority and disdain. She slammed the door on the way out.

Glinda approached the wardrobe and removed the Grimmerie. She sat it on a towel on her dressing table. The volume was as long as her forearm and almost as wide, covered in green morocco and gussied up with semiprecious stones and silvergilt. No title upon its spine. The pages were rough cut, she could see, and when she ran her finger across the deckle edges she believed she felt a curious charge. Or perhaps she simply wasn't fully awake yet.

She opened the book. This is to say, she prised up the cover and a certain portion of pages. The book wouldn't allow her to select any old page. It seemed to know what she was looking for, and sure enough, she found it. The facing page was blank, but the inscribed page read, in majuscule so ornate as to look like lace, *On Concealment.*

A knock on the door. Without thinking Glinda murmured, "Come in." Murth approached with tea on a tray. "I said I would wait," said Glinda.

"But it's noon, Mum," said Miss Murth. "And you haven't taken your bath yet? It'll be glacial cold by now."

"Leave the tea," said Glinda, frightened. She hadn't felt more than a minute go by as she was trying to scrutinize the spell. Apparently she had lost a morning.

"I have news, Lady Glinda," said Miss Murth.

"Later," said Glinda, flustered. "I mean it, Murth. I'll ring for you presently. Good-bye."

Miss Murth departed. Glinda was almost there. She had to concentrate.

She stood. Her back was sore from hunching over. She had been studying this one page for several hours! Mercy. Had she learned to concentrate at last? Perhaps she was ready to take some correspondence classes in, oh, table gooseball. Or poem writing. Or the foreign service.

She put the fingers of both hands spread out upon the tabletop—that seemed to be part of it, to stabilize herself. It was almost as if the book wanted her to succeed, wanted to be concealed; there was a sort of sharpening of focus upon each word as she spoke it, though she scarcely knew what the words meant. "Debooey geekum, eska skadilly sloggi," she recited. "Gungula vexus, vexanda talib en prochinka chorr." She didn't think herself at all convincing, but the book didn't seem to notice.

She reached the last syllables—and the book shuddered and jumped, as if someone had kicked the table from beneath. She put one knuckle between her teeth to keep herself from shrieking in surprise. Success! Or sabotage. Anyway, something. Something was happening.

The Grimmerie began to change shape. She couldn't have said how. It was shrinking and growing at the same time, and the balsam-needle color of its spine seemed to be burning off. The book flexed and retracted. It took several moments before it returned to seeming lifeless, like most books. It was thick and square and yellow—the size, shape, and color of a bad cake. A kind of papery cover, a shiny scarf cut to order, was folded into the front and back boards and jacketed around the spine of the volume.

Glinda picked up the Grimmerie and shook it. It made no sound except the riffling of pages, which fluttered in a respectably bookish way. There was no warmth or life in it. She studied the cover as if she were Cherrystone looking for the Grimmerie. The author's name was unintelligible gibberish. Big squarish letters above it, though, which must indicate the book's title, said *Gone with the Wind*.

She humped it into a shelf next to her favorite books, *A Girl's First Guide to Coquettery* and *The Little Mercenary: A Novel of Manners*. It looked quite at home. It certainly didn't look like the Grimmerie.

She rang for tea. She was famished.

Tea arrived with bad news. Miss Murth looked at her balefully. Chef had been dismissed. Forcibly. "No," said Glinda.

"While you were busy reading your *book*," replied Miss Murth with spite.

"Where are the others? Rain? Puggles?"

"Rain is off at her reading lesson with the General. Puggles is trying to stake tomatoes upon the roof. Chef left him with several pages of instructions before he was carted away."

Glinda dressed in haste and hurried downstairs, but she cast a last look at the bookshelf before she did. *Gone with the Wind* sat smugly in its place. What a good title for a hidden book, she thought. The Grimmerie has a sense of humor.

Any sense of accomplishment she felt at the successful completion of a spell soon evaporated in the granite presence of General Cherrystone. She paused at the door to the library, where Rain was sitting at a table, her bare legs swinging and her finger tracing letters in the pollen that had sifted through the windows and settled yellowly on the tabletop. Where the *hell* is that maid, thought Glinda madly, before remembering, of course, that the maid had gone wherever Chef had been sent.

Cherrystone lifted a finger to his lips. She fell silent but quivering at the doorway.

"That was decent work today, my little scholar," he told the girl. "You're becoming very good at your standing-up letters. Next time we'll begin on the letters shaped like circles, or parts of circles. Don't forget to practice."

The child fled so fast that her dirty little soles flicked themselves at Glinda. Oh, standards, she thought. Then she pulled herself together.

"I have a bone to pick with you," she said.

"Lady Glinda." He didn't rise as she came into the room. The absolute nerve of him! Leaving her standing as if she were a . . . a servant.

She pulled out a chair so hard it scraped the parquetry. "Miss Murth tells me you've dismissed Chef. You have no right to meddle with my people."

"You've brought this upon yourself, Lady Glinda, by your endorsement of that provocative display last night."

"Don't be stupid. I'm not an impresario. This was no command performance. I didn't know what entertainment that troupe was going to provide. I merely invited them. You welcomed the notion, yourself. Furthermore I have no idea what you mean by provocative. I thought the repertoire slight, coarse, and pointless."

"I'm afraid there have had to be repercussions."

"Are you setting me up as a collaborationist of some sort? That's nonsense. I have retired to the country to write my memoirs."

"And to learn to cook. I know. How is it going?"

"How am I to learn without Chef?"

"I'm sure, like your chambermaid learning to read, you've picked up some basics. It's merely a matter of putting them together."

"Cherrystone. This is intolerable. I want Chef reinstated at once."

"I'm afraid that isn't possible. For one thing . . ." He paused, putting his hands flat on the tabletop, spreading them apart, as if smoothing a bedsheet, then bringing them together so their thumbs touched. "For one thing, he's in no condition to take up cooking at the moment."

Glinda gaped. "You—you—"

"He met with an accident."

"I thought you dismissed him."

"I did. I dismissed him. And then somehow he walked into Restwater without removing his heavy clothes, and he seemed to drown. Not unlike the set piece that concluded the little performance you so enjoyed last night, though without the involvement of any tiktok dragon."

She stood. "I don't believe it. A man who teaches a child to read doesn't turn around and condemn an innocent man to death. You're lying. I want him back."

"The subject is closed. But in any instance, I'm afraid I am moving more men into the house. I'm going to require the use of the chambers on the piano level and in the servants' quarters, both backstairs and up top. You'll have to ask your people to clear out."

"Impossible. Where will they sleep?"

"You have room in your private apartment. I will have my men move bedding and cots into one of your salons."

"Are you insane? Traper? I can't have Puggles in my apartments. He is my butler. A man!"

"You were married for some time, Lady Glinda. Surely you know how to close the door against ill-timed attentions. That's a skill every wife learns."

She was badly frightened. She needed to find out if Chef was really drowned. Ig, his name. Ig Baernaerae-naesis. "The time has come for me to ask how long you intend to loiter in my home, General."

"That, my dear, is privileged information. Private Zackers!" he called suddenly. Zackers came through the swinging pantry door. "Some sparkling cider-tea for Lady Glinda, and one for me."

"I will tell you this," she said. "You may not release another member of my staff. You may have nothing to do with any of them beyond your lessons with the girl. If anyone is to be dismissed from now on, I'll make the decision and I'll alert you by note. Is that clear?"

"Surely you'll stay for a glass of refreshment? Zackers isn't Chef, of course, but he's learning his way around the larder, much as you are."

She didn't reply, but swept away. In her rooms, she wept momentarily, feeling foolish. She rang for Murth and asked her to find out more about Chef, but neither Murth nor Puggles was allowed outside of the house anymore. "I didn't hear 'drowned,'" insisted Miss Murth. "I only heard 'let go.' But he couldn't swim."

After lunch the Menaciers began moving soldiers' trunks and sleeping rolls into the gilt-ceilinged guest chambers. Zackers oversaw the setting up of cots in Glinda's retiring parlor. Three of them, one for

Puggles, one for Murth, one for Rain. "I can't sleep in the same room as Puggles," begged Miss Murth. "I am an unmarried woman."

Glinda didn't answer. She told Puggles to find Rain. Glinda would see her at once, in the privacy of her boudoir.

13.

"I need something of you, Rain," said Glinda.

The girl didn't answer. She doesn't speak often, noted Glinda, not for the first time. Maybe learning to read will change that.

"We are being asked to keep from walking about in the gardens for a while," she said. "But you're young and can run and dash about, and no one much notices. Can you find out something for me?"

Rain looked up sideways at her mistress. Despite years of Glinda's watching her own diet and performing knee-bends in the privacy of her chambers, she suddenly felt fat. Fat and squat and old. And she feared she smelled of caramelized carrots. But enough about me, she said to herself, and shook her curls, which were due for a bleaching in a solution of lemon juice and extract of milkflower. Later. *Concentrate.*

"Are you up for this, Rain?"

The girl shrugged. Her hair was dirty and her calves were dirty, but prettying the child up wouldn't do her any good, Glinda thought. She was safer looking a little revolting. That snarled cloud of unbrushed brown hair! "What do you want me to lookit?" Rain finally said.

"I want you to find out what they are building in the barns. Can you do that?"

Rain shrugged again. "They're always hammering inside there, and the doors are shut."

"You're small. You can stick to the shadows." Glinda fixed the girl with as fierce a glare as she could manage. "Your name is Rain, isn't it? Rain slips in the cracks and slides through the seams. You can do it? Can't you?"

"I don't know."

"You better try, or I might have to cancel your reading lessons."

The girl looked up sharply, more keenly than before. "Not that, Mum."

"I trust the General is treating you well?"

"He teaches me good enough," said the girl. "I knows a passel of letters now."

Glinda pursed her lips. She didn't believe in putting children in danger, nor of frightening them overmuch. "He's permitted to teach you no more than letters," she finally said. "If he tries to teach you anything else, you come let me know. Is that understood?"

The girl shrugged again. Her shrugs were a caution against committing herself, Glinda saw. She wanted to reach out and press her palms on those insouciant shoulders. *Do you hear me?*

"Yes, Mum." The voice was smaller, but more honest.

"That'll do, then. Off you go. Remember, Rain. Tiptoe. Tiptoe, whisper, glide. But if they see you, you are just playing. Can you act as though you're just playing?"

"He's teaching me to read off my letters," said Rain. "Nobody never teached me to play."

14.

While she was waiting for Rain's report, Glinda had another thought. (A flurry of thoughts! A squall of them!) Perhaps the Grimmerie could supply a spell that would send Cherrystone and his men packing. After all, if she could use a spell to conceal the book itself, maybe her talents at magic had improved through time.

But, like any fool girl in any fool tale, she'd been bested by the magic. Now that the Grimmerie was disguised as a novel, she had no access to its spells. She could open the squat volume and turn its pages easy as you please, but the spells therein were hidden from view behind hedges of dense print. Why did people write such fat books? Where was the magic in that? Perhaps she needed spectacles, as she couldn't really make out the prose, though perhaps she also needed to try a little harder, which she wasn't inclined to do.

She replaced the book on the shelf. What *had* she done? She'd hidden the Grimmerie so well through that concealing spell that it might never again come in handy as a book of magic. Eventually Glinda would flail and fail and die, and fly off to the arms of Lurlina, or be absorbed like condensation into the cloudy dubiousness of the Unnamed God, and Miss Murth would find the damn thing and read it to distract herself from Glinda's death, and then she would dump the book in the bin, or give it to a church jumble sale.

15.

Glinda was trying to master the art of peeling a hard-boiled egg. The little grey-brown flecks of shell kept driving themselves under her fingernails, which she was beginning to see were too long for kitchen work. Rain popped up next to the table in the make-shift scullery they had sorted out in Glinda's bathing chamber.

"Goodness, child, you startled me." An egg rolled off the table onto the floor and cracked its own shell quite efficiently.

"I did the thing you wanted me to do."

Glinda looked this way and that. She didn't dare risk incriminating Puggles or Murthy. But they weren't to be seen. "Very good of you. What did you find out?"

Rain smirked a little. "It was hard to see because it was so dark."

"I'm sure you found a way."

"I waited till the men goed to lunch and then I opened the hay door up top."

Glinda waited.

Oh, the girl required another compliment. Glinda wanted to hit her. "How cunning of you. Go on."

"It's hard to say what I saw. It was upsy-wrongedy houses, sort of like."

"I see," said Glinda, though she did not.

"Like the houses in Zimmerstorm, but on their heads."

"Were the upsy-wrongedy roofs made of blue tile, as in Zimmerstorm?"

"No. Strokes of wood all hammered close together, going like this." Rain pushed her hands away from her belly as if describing a long melon in the air.

"Wouldn't the upsy-wrongedy houses fall over if they were trying to balance on their narrow roof-beams?"

"They all had leggses. Like spiders, sort of. Wooden leggses."

"How many of these houses?"

"You din't tell me to counts 'em."

"A lot?"

"They were too big to be a lot. They took up the whole space nearly, between the lofts for straw up high and the stalls below."

Glinda went to a table and looked at the implements. She selected a knife and a loaf of bread. She cut off the heels and a good deal of the crusts and made the loaf into a statue of a house, as well as she could. "So. It was like this?"

"Yes but turned over." Rain reached out and up-ended it. "And the spider leggses all up and down here and here. But this end was more pointy."

"Oh. Oh yes, of course. I see now." Glinda plucked a paring knife and quickly made of the upside-down house a sort of tugboat. "Like this. And if the spider legs were knocked away, it would look like a boat."

"Boats don't have such pointy bottoms."

"Some do. You've probably never seen a boat out of the lake, that's all." She put the knife down softly. "They're building boats. They're going to take a flotilla up the lake and attack Haugaard's Keep by water. Of course. It makes sense." She thought of the map she had seen, and the dotted line up the middle of Restwater. In the center of the lake the invaders would be beyond the reach of any local ambush brigade mounted by Zimmerstorm or Haventhur to the north, or Bigelow or Sedney to the south. Though the progress of such vessels, if they were indeed as large as Rain suggested, would be clearly visible, and allow impromptu navies up and down the lake to row out to attack them. What was Cherrystone playing at?

"You've done very well, Rain," said Glinda. She hesitated a moment, and then—something she had resisted doing for years—she put her hand on Rain's shoulder. "You deserve a reward. What would you like?"

"Do you got anything I can read?"

"Nothing suitable, I'm afraid. Besides, I hear from the General that you're at early stages yet. But perhaps you'll learn."

"I'll learn," said Rain. "Meanwhile, if you en't got no bookses, give me two slices of boat and some butter spread on 'em." She twisted her hands and grinned at Glinda. It was the first time in, what, seven years.

16.

For what was Glinda waiting? To be rescued? To have a tantrum? To be inspired to act? To warble an anthem of protest to an incredulous shoreline? She did a little crochet work, a sunny pillow with a motto. OZMA BEFORE US. She watched the thunderheads of Highsummer massing to the west, and she fled if they threatened to let loose. She studied the long lake, which curved between the foothills of the Great Kells on the far southern side and the lower slopes of the Pine Barrens on the northern. The placement of Mockbeggar on its little promontory gave her limited advantage; as the lake curved subtly to the southeast, it narrowed and disappeared between opposing banks. Same to the northwest. Due to the angle, she couldn't glimpse Haugaard's Keep even had she the eyes of a hawk. Unless she had the wings of a hawk too, of course.

Her household wobbled on. Systems seemed maintained not so much through stamina as through an inertia borne of fear. Nothing more came to light about Chef. Puggles did what he could with the odd breast of fallowhen, with parsleyfruit and wristwrencher beans, with eggs and cheese and a militant sort of pastry pot pie that refused to yield to a knife. Miss Murth lived on tea and she smelled of tea and she began to resemble a tall stalk of ambulatory celery, and she trembled when she talked, which was less often than usual. What Rain ate was a mystery to Glinda, mostly.

One day when the cloudburst began earlier than usual, the girl showed up fresh from her lesson. She hunted for *O*s and *Z*s all over Glinda's parlor, in the gnarly filigrees of preposterously carved furniture. She all but capered with the fun of it. "I know *Oz*, now," she said, and in the carving of the lintel she found that common ideogram, a *Z* circled with an *O*. "Usually letters don't hide inside each other," she told Glinda firmly.

"No, that's true. In Oz, I suppose, something is always hiding, though."

The girl turned and as if by magnetism walked directly over to the little bookshelf beside the window. She tugged the yellow book out. It might as well have been her primer. "What's this book? I can't read these words yet."

"It's called, um, *The Wind Blew Away*. Or something."

"Is it about the big wind that blew Dorothy here?"

"Where did you hear about Dorothy?"

"Miss Murth told me the story."

"Never listen to Miss Murth. She's too old to be valid. Now put that book back."

I must seem too old to be valid, too, thought Glinda, as Rain ignored her. The girl opened the cover and ran her hand along the page. "What's hidden here?"

Glinda felt a chill. "What nonsense you speak. What do you mean?"

"This book. It's like a creature. It's alive." She turned to Glinda. "Can you feel it? It gots a heart, almost. It's warm. It's purring."

"Do you come in here and touch this book when I'm not looking?"

"No. I never seen it before. But it was sort of shimmery."

Glinda snatched it away. She had never noticed a shimmer to the book and she didn't see one now. But Rain was on to something. The Grimmerie had a kind of urgent low heat to it. A kind of soundless hum.

She found herself saying, nearly whispering, "What page would you like to look at?"

Rain paused. Glinda held the book down to her like a tray of canapés. From under those horrid flea-bitten bangs of hers, Rain looked up at Glinda. Then with a hand scratched by thorns and ignorant of soap, she cracked the code of the disguise charm without even trying. The Grimmerie took on its original aspect—broader, darker, more opaque; handwritten, on this page, in inks of silver and iodine blue. A narrow design seemed to be contorting around the margins, writhing. Glinda felt faint. "How did you do that?"

The thunder made a menacing comment, but it was comfortably distant. Rain turned to a page about two-thirds through.

"You can't read this. Can you?"

Rain peered. "Everything's hitched up and kicking."

"Yes yes, but can you read it?"

Rain shook her head. "Can you?"

How mortifying. Glinda looked. A heading of some sort was squeezing like a bellows; at full extension it seemed to suggest *To Call Winter upon Water.*

"It's about dressing warmly enough. Sort of," she said. She slapped the book closed. "Why did you open to that page?"

Rain murmured, "I was remembering something once. About a goldfish."

Suddenly Glinda was tired of Rain. Tired, and a little scared of her. "Would you run tell Miss Murth it's time for my tea? And no touching this book unless I ask you to. Do you understand?"

Rain was out the door, on to the next thing in her stunted little life. "Sure," she called, disingenuously no doubt.

Glinda carried the volume to her escritoire. She opened it again, but now she couldn't even fan the pages. The book fell open to the page it preferred. *To Call Winter upon Water.* How had Rain called this spell up out of the book?

I chose to be the patron of arts festivals over dabbling in the science of charms, she thought. But there's no help for it now. I am stuck here with a book of magic that won't let me go.

She read a little bit of the charm, as best she could, and then sat back, exhausted. Thought about the Grimmerie, and its wily ways. Perhaps she shouldn't read too much into Rain's capacity to hone in on the tome. She *was* learning to read, after all. Secrets are revealed as you are ready to understand them. It seems capricious and mean-spirited of the Grimmerie to hold back, to yield and then to tease with a single page— but then the world is the same way, isn't it? The world rarely shrieks its meaning at you. It whispers, in private languages and obscure modalities, in arcane and quixotic imagery, through symbol systems in which every element has multiple meanings determined by juxtaposition.

How does anyone learn to read? she thought. How did I?

By the time Miss Murth arrived with tea, Glinda had worked through a good deal of the spell, though she didn't understand its possible uses. She closed the volume gently, drawing no attention to it, in case Miss Murth was in one of her beaky prowly moods. But Murth had other things on her mind. "The storm has moved on toward Sedney," she said, "and the General has called for the barn doors to be open. They are breaking down the front of two of the barns, Mum. They are bringing out the boats."

"You know they're boats?" Glinda felt a little cheapened.

"You think you're the only one pays attention to Rain," said Murth.

17.

The vessels rolled out on an ancient technology: clean-hewn logs set parallel. At once Glinda saw the serviceability of Mockbeggar in a new light. The appeal to Cherrystone of her country house wasn't the formal aspect of the great house. A Pallantine masterpiece meant nothing to the armed forces. It was the barns. They were tall enough to have served as incubators for these four massive ships. Sequestered, men had worked through the daily downpours and on through the night.

Even more important, the grade from the barnyard to lake would accommodate a launch. A clear access presented itself across the drive, through the wildflower meadow and down the pastures, neatly avoiding the ha-ha and (mercifully) Virus Skepticle's bentlebranch folly in honor of freshwater mermaids.

Glinda considered herself in the mirror, then drew a lace shoulderette from the wardrobe and freshened her lashes. A parasol to suggest idle ambling. She wished she had lap dogs so she could seem to be taking them for a walk, but ever since that monstrous Toto had nipped her heel and torn the hem of her favorite pink reception gown she had gone off the cussed creatures.

Puggles was making an effort to concoct some sort of soup. "I weren't raised to this grade of domestic work, Mum," he said, wiping his brow and nearly clocking himself through the clumsy application of a meat mallet.

"You're doing admirably. I shall take notes one day. But Puggles, did Miss Murth tell you? The builders have unveiled their constructions."

"She did."

"How will they avoid being attacked? The ships, I mean?"

"Lower your voice, Mum, there's soldiers every-where now." He pounded harder as he spoke, to drown out his whisper. "It's hard to get word through the cordon of guards, but I have it on pretty solid authority that the farmers and fishermen of the area already have worked out for themselves what was going on here. I think some of the Munchkinlander beached fleet might be readying to venture out again after their nice long rest." He winked at her. "Suicidal, I know . . ."

"There'll be cannon on board Cherrystone's war-ships, no doubt."

"Cannons are good for hammering at the stone walls of fortresses, Mum, but they're less good for swiping at your little lake heron or your quick minnow. If you take my meaning."

"Well." She chose her words carefully. "If you hear more about the wildlife on the lake this season, do let me know."

"I'm no longer permitted outside the house, Mum," he told her. "I'm not likely to hear more."

She moved on, worried for the local Munchkins. Cherrystone was too smart to display these lummoxy floating wooden castles without being prepared to deal with any attack on them. Still, Glinda was infected with a sense of excitement as she descended the great stairs. She admired the well-made thing, whatever it was: a slipcover, a compliment, a man-o'-war.

She ignored the muddy boots lined up on the floor, just plowed through the banquet hall and the kitchens as if she'd been used to taking charge there for years. "Zackers. Hat off in the presence of a lady," she barked at him, who whirled around from where he was rooting through a bin of biscuits. Feeling a warm breeze from an open door, she continued on through a larder and a maze of pantries, and found an exit into an herb garden. How useful, now that she knew what herbs were for. But she had no time to pause and take notes.

From the ground the four ships were even larger than they'd looked from her windows. Bowl-bellied wooden narwhals. Men with their shirts off were swarming up ladders on all sides, caulking and scraping and wielding brushes to apply some sort of gleaming oil. It made the fresh wood glow like skin.

She located Cherrystone near a commissaire or clerk who was taking notes. She bearded the General. "Traper, you are to be congratulated. This is an installation of most magnificent hue and heft. I can't think where you got all the lumber."

"There's a mill or two in the Pine Barrens. You pay enough, you can find the help you need."

"Pay with cash, or with threat of violence?" But she smiled as she said it, and he grinned back, replying, "Oh, the coin of the realm appears to be good cheer, as I understand it. We imported white oak for the ribbing, but the local fir stock is suitable for cladding and masts. Amazing how generous the locals are, if you put it to them persuasively enough."

"I don't know sail-lacing, so this is deepest arcana to me. However, Restwater being Oz's largest lake, I believe I'd have noticed vessels of such magnificent profile if they'd ever sailed by me before. They don't look like riverboats, yet the masts are lower than I would imagine useful to help propel such a capacious hold."

"Oh, it's a manly art, is shipbuilding," said the General. "I can't pretend to follow a word of it. I have a hard time lacing my own boots."

Glinda caught herself from making a remark about not lacing her own stays. "We all know the EC wants to divert the lake for its private use, in the capital and in the mill towns and factory hamlets springing up between the Emerald City and Shiz. And so I realize these ships are intended to attack Haugaard's Keep. But I can't understand why you'd take four weeks and some to build them, giving the local farmers a chance to plan their resistance and fortify the lake, when you could've marched your army along through the villages and circled Restwater six times over by now."

"Straight through a gauntlet of pint-size guerrillas? No, thanks. But too terribly dry, this business of strategy," he said, as if in agreement. "I'd love to chat more. Shall we dine again? I can wax hysterical about the cost of labor in wartime, and you can catch me up on your successes in the field of cuisine."

"Are you inviting me to a reception upon the virgin decks of your commanding vessel?"

He blushed. She hadn't known she could make him blush. "I'm afraid it'll be some time before the accoutrements are fitted, the paint applied and dried, and so on. It's why I had the ships brought out into the sunlight, so this work could proceed apace."

"But the daily thunderstorms?"

"Spittle and eyewash. Won't slow us down."

She almost asked permission to take a promenade around the boats, but remembering herself, she started out at a pace. He caught up with her and took her by the arm, but gently, as a husband might, and escorted her about the graveled yard. She commented, "I trust you'll be putting my barn fronts back together. One bad storm and the places would collapse like houses of cards."

He didn't answer, just pointed out admirable bits of carving on the figureheads. "You have some very talented, very bored soldiers," she said. "Surely that's not a portrait of me?"

"No, it's meant to be Ozma."

"Dreadfully royalist of you. Positively seditious. I'd expect it to be the Emperor."

"Some of the men are simple. But if you want to get good work out of them, you have to allow them their prejudices."

"Tell that to the Munchkins." But she was trying to be slick as boiled sweeties. "What will you call these fine dames of the lake?"

"We'll slap their names upon them when they're waterworthy."

"I can't wait that long. I might die in my sleep tonight, of impatience."

"Oh, don't do that, Glinda."

He had used her name without the honorific. She smiled a little less winningly, more inscrutably, reeling him in. "No, do tell. Traper."

"Can't you guess what the Emperor's four lake ambassadors would be called?"

She blinked at him, grateful she'd taken time to darken her lashes.

He said, "The *Vinkus, Gillikin,* and *Quadling Country.*"

"I see," she said. "And the lead vessel . . . the *Emerald City*."

"Oh, no," he replied. "*Munchkinland*. In anticipation of the reannexation, whenever we achieve that happy marriage, and make Oz whole again."

18.

In truth, she'd begun looking over Chef's shoulder—before he disappeared. A bit sullenly, she now peered in at the efforts of Puggles. She was starting to know just enough to be dangerous in the kitchen. She watched things being ladled out of cast-iron gorgeholds and dumped into porcelain kettles or copper skillets. She understood how a single squeeze of lemon could salvage a crime against cuisine, and how a misplaced spray of orange balsam could sabotage a masterpiece. About things like salt and sugar and blanched pepper she became more confused, as they all looked more or less snowy.

She had no time to waste, though.

"Grab a sheet of paper, Miss Murth. The pen is on the blotter. Date: 18th Highsummer comma, 11 of the clock. Dear Traper comma, Unable to wait for a kind offer to dine on the deck of the Emperor's good ship *Munchkinland* comma, I propose instead—"

"Dear *Traper?*" Miss Murth's outrage was controlled and magnificent.

"—that you join me for a meal in the knot garden. Stop. The prettibells are perfection and the roses aren't too shabby either. Stop. I'll cook. Underline the *I'll* twice. Tomorrow night at eight question mark? Are you keeping up, Murthy?"

"Shall I sign it, *Love and kissies, your little Glinda?*"

"Don't be absurd. I'll sign it myself."

"I've already signed it."

Glinda snatched the paper and read *Cordially, Lady Glinda, Arduenna of the Uplands.*

"Exactly how I would have signed it. You have perfected my signature after all this time."

"I aim to serve," said Murth, aiming herself out the door.

"Miss Murth," said Glinda.

Murth turned.

"Would you kindly try not to be so cheerless. It's unsociable and it taxes the nerves. I do know what I'm about. I'm not the idiot you take me for."

Miss Murth attempted a kind of curtsey that had gone out of fashion four decades earlier. Her knees clacked like ivory dominoes dropped on a plate.

Glinda in the kitchen. "Zackers."

"Mum."

She gave up on insisting on *Lady Glinda*. "In the absence of Ig Baernaeraenaesis, otherwise known as Chef, I'm attempting to put together a little meal. Do you know where the cookery books are kept?"

Zackers found a shelf under a window seat. Some parish committee's collection: *Munchkinlander Aunties Share Secrets of the Sauce*. And Glinda liked this one, printed in large type with droll and useful drawings: *Avoid Prosecution for Poisoning: Cooking by the Book*. Particularly well thumbed was Widow Chumish's famous volume, *Food You Can Actually Stomach*. She grabbed all three and told Zackers she would send down a list of ingredients.

She was almost excited. The dishes, the pans, the wooden spoons! The heat of the stove would rosy up her cheeks and curl her hair. She hoped it wouldn't also steam off the highlights. She had found more than one frizzle of grey nestled among the gold and wrenched it out, but now it was either dye the traitorous locks or resign herself to mid-age baldness.

Glinda with Rain. The Grimmerie lay on the games table, sweetly dull in its disguise. Glinda sat before it, and Rain stood at her side.

"Your interest in reading seems to inspire this book's playfulness," said Glinda. "I wonder if you could open this book to any page?"

The girl didn't understand. *Lurline,* but she was a slow train to Traum!

"Now watch me." Glinda banged open the cover. The merciless slabs of dense print on every page looked like torture. No pictures, no diagrams, very little white space on which to rest the eye and let the mind wander. Glinda riffled the pages to make the book's point, whatever it was. "Now you do it." She closed the book and pushed it toward Rain.

The girl paused, then opened the volume. It transformed under her hands, becoming the Grimmerie, proffering the page with the spell: *To Call Winter upon Water.*

"But you see, I don't want to call winter upon water," said Glinda, as if she were talking to a simpleton. She wasn't sure if she was addressing Rain or the Grimmerie. "I'm looking for a recipe for starched muttock, maybe, or grip of lamb with a crawberry chutney to lend a sort of alto chromatic to the gaminess of the enterprise. A genteelly quibbling complement." Or did she mean compliment? She had no idea what she was talking about. She couldn't speak gourmandese. She just wanted to see Rain handle the Grimmerie.

The book, however, had its own notions. While Rain could slip the pages a little from the gentle steppe of parallel deckled edges, she couldn't move them to reveal more than an inch or two. The pages husband their secrets; the book was only interested in suggesting how *To Call Winter upon Water.*

"Well, it prefers its opinions, I see." The mistress of Mockbeggar sighed. "Personally I hate uppity books. Don't you?"

"I never got to no book yet. Books is still all secrets." Disgruntled, the girl slumped in her seat and, forgetting her place, leaned against Glinda. "The mister says that letters are the key, but even when you know the whole family, there's so many combinations you can make. And they break their word."

"Yes. Well. You'll get there." Against her better judgment she couldn't help putting her hand on the girl's hip. "I don't remember learning to read, but clearly I did, because I can."

"What does that bit say?" Rain pointed.

"Well, this is hard, even for me." She couldn't serve winter on a bed of water to Cherrystone, however often the Grimmerie recommended it. She closed the book, and it slid back into the casing of its casual disguise.

"Secrets. Pfaaah." The girl was vexed. "Look at that Oz, what I showed you previous." She traced her finger against the inlay of the table, along the *Z* whose termini and angles met the encircling *O* at four points of the oval: ⊘. "It looks like a person trapped in an egg. Bent back, on her knees. Can't stand up straight. Can't get out. Why don't the *O* let her out?"

"That's Oz for you," said Glinda. "All about crimping. And I don't mean piecrust." Perhaps a lambkin pie with a summer salad of peas and potatoes?

Glinda with Miss Murth, later in the day. "Please take down this message. Eighteenth Highsummer four hours beyond noon. Zackers colon: I need the following colon: four little thingies of lamb eight potatoes the yellow jacket kind blue peppercorn four ripe pears peeled two cloves a dish of clover mayonnaise about sixty peas all the same size and a sharp small knife stop. Oh, and some bickory root. Read that back to me."

Murth did. "How shall I sign it for you?"

"I really need these things. Sign it *Mum*."

"I'll do no such thing."

Murth took so long writing out the signature that Glinda knew she was adding a paragraph of specifics she'd cribbed from Cranston's *Encyclopedium of Gentry*. The honorary degrees, the citations of merit in the cause of charities from Madame Teastane's Female Academy to Crage Hall at Shiz. The whole nine yards of it. "Oh, Miss Murth. Are you so jealous as all that?"

"My job is to protect you, Lady Glinda, even if you are losing your mind."

———

The kitchen, next day. Zackers served as sous chef and personal bodyguard. Twice he saved Glinda from immolation. His pimples hadn't improved, but he wasn't a bad sort. His grandparents had been Munchkinlanders from Far Applerue, he told her, but they'd migrated to Tenniken in Gillikin after the Wicked Witch of the East had risen to be the de facto governor. They had smelt secession in the winds, he told Glinda, and they didn't like it.

"Oh, who would," agreed Glinda absently. "Especially if it smells like this poaching liqueur."

"You might try removing the trotters. Here's a pincers. Or shall I?"

That seemed to help. "But aren't you conflicted, Zackers? A soldier of Loyal Oz, going to war against Munchkinlanders who might have been friends and neighbors of your grandparents?"

"If they were friends and neighbors of the wrinklies, they won't be up to throwing pitchforks at me. They'll be belted into their rockers like my old kin."

"The principle of it, I mean."

"Munchkinland belongs to Oz." Adamant. "A lot of Munchkins remain Loyal Ozians despite that Mombey, arriviste Eminence in Colwen Grounds. A fair lot of Munchkins quietly think Oz isn't Oz when it's severed like this."

"What is it then? If it's not really Oz without Munch-kinland?"

He replied, "It's spoiled. Like this reduction. I think we better start over." He would say no more about himself, and became curt. But the second batch turned out less disagreeable.

In the late afternoon, she directed Puggles to set up a table for two in the rose garden.

"I'm not allowed in the rose garden, Mum."

"But who will serve? I can't be expected to cook a meal and then haul it to the table like a milkmaid."

"Were I you, I should take it up with that buttery-boy Zackers. You seem to be chummy enough with him. Lady Glinda."

Puggles didn't know she had a strategy, but she didn't dare whisper about it. She only said, "This is in-tolerable. You can't be tethered like a cow, Puggles. I shall protest. Meantime, give Zackers instruction in the correct layout of a summer table." But she didn't pro-test; she had to whip up the cream and egg yolk for the crawberry fool. And she had to study the Grimmerie.

At seven, as a half-moon appeared opposite the sunset and the lake went hazy and golden with midges, she dressed. Miss Murth saw to Glinda's hair and perked into compliance the bows that ran from her peplum to the end of her diaphanous train. "The pearl pendants, I think, will do. A jaunty little tiara would be putting on airs. This is alfresco, after all. If I'm in the mood I shall adorn my hair with a rose or two."

"The thorns will scrape your scalp and you'll bleed into the dessert."

"It could only help. I'm ready to descend. Will you carry my parasol?"

"You've not been paying attention, *Mum*. We're not allowed out of the house anymore."

"No? I'll take it up with Traper if the moment arrives. Don't wait up, Miss Murth. I can see myself to bed."

"I'm sure you can." Miss Murth pursed her lips so hard they looked broken.

The General arrived on time in a suit of ivory sartorials Glinda hadn't seen before. Crimson braid. He was as vain as she; he'd checked the colors of the prettibells, or he'd had Zackers check. She felt eclipsed in her ash satin with the double-backed sparstitch in chrome and salmon.

Zackers had done the job as Puggles had directed. The table was laid correctly enough, and an occasional table had been arranged to one side for the parking of domed serving dishes and beakers of wine. Next to it, eyes trained forward, stood Zackers. He was all in black like a maître d' in a midrange lunchery in Bankers' Court in Shiz. His pimples matched the roses nicely too.

He pulled out the chairs and poured the wine. He offered Lady Glinda a fan, as the humidity had risen during the day and there was no breeze off the water. She felt more gluey than dewy after her afternoon imprisoned in the furnace of ovens and hobs. But Cherrystone looked sticky, too, which was some comfort.

Betraying their convention, she plunged into a discussion of government policy. "Traper. With my staff ever more circumscribed—we'll get to that—I feel the need of understanding the larger picture. I've been thinking about this campaign of the Emperor to annex Restwater for Loyal Oz. It was being bruited about even during the Wizard's time, don't deny it, and my own ministers used to try to get me to consider military action. But in the years since I left off being Throne Minister—"

"—and took up cooking. Delicious," he muttered, through a mouthful of penance. She knew it. The gum-rubber little cutlets lay drowned in puddles of grainy sauce that tasted, somehow, violent.

"—I have rather lost the thread of the rationale of this conquest. The western Vinkus isn't arable due to the aridity of the plains, I know, and the slope of the Great Kells in the Eastern Vinkus makes plowing impossible. Quadling Country is a stew of mud and marshgrass. My own dear Gillikin Country—though forested, lightly hilled, with such a soft climate—features soil more conducive to manufacturing than to farming. So much iron in it. But three-quarters of the grain we all require annually grows in Munchkinland. Why would Loyal Oz want to annex Restwater? Doesn't it threaten the agricultural base of the source of Oz's food supply? What if Munchkinland embargoes its sale of wheat and other crops? The EC would starve. And the rich farmers of Munchkinland might see their bank balances dip, but they wouldn't go hungry. They have what they need. They can hold out."

"Glinda, you're the sweetest peach in the fruit bowl, but I don't believe you understand the aquifers in Oz and their effect on riparian systems." Cherrystone took several lettuce leaves with his fingers and dumped them on the tablecloth. He mounded up one leaf higher than the other. "Look. The Great Kells of the Vinkus over here, right? And the lower Madeleines over here. Emerald City between them." (He put a radish, with its single-fringe dome, in the middle.) "And the three great rivers? Let's see." Several of the longer green beans.

"The Vinkus, like so. The Gillikin River. Munchkin River. More or less. Do you see?"

"Yes, and that little woggle-bug on the radish is the emperor of all it can survey. Traper, I did attend primary school." Did his knee touch hers under the table? In the act of leaning forward as if captivated, she grazed his knee glancingly and then shifted her leg away, just in case. "Go on."

"The Gillikin River, though long, is shallow. The river water leaches easily into the landscape. Gillikin is the Oz of which the poet speaks—'land of green abandon, land of endless leaf.' The river makes Gillikin into the kind of pretty picture of Oz that I expect to think of on my deathbed."

"How absurd. I shall be thinking of my portfolio, and if I've adequately kept dividends from grasping hands. Go on."

"The Munchkin River is the longest, but the Munchkins have hundreds of years of experience in irrigation by canal and aqueduct. You've seen them?"

"Of course I have. Don't patronize me. Cross-ditching, they call it."

He raised an eyebrow. Score for her. "The point is, Munchkinlanders use their water wisely—upstream. They bleed it all along its length. So the Munchkin River, like the Gillikin, gives little more than lip service to Restwater as it debouches therein. And the EC to the north long ago overwhelmed the United Gillikin Canal Company's capacity to supply it. Here's my main point, Glinda. Your lovely lake called Restwater is replenished daily by the water that courses down from the snowy peaks and wintry ice packs of the Great Kells. Every single peak of which looms solidly in Loyal Oz. The shortest but the healthiest, the fiercest, the *wettest* of the rivers of Oz is the Vinkus. And as it runs between banks of hard fleckstone ten thousand years old, it doesn't leach into and make fertile the parched land. Indeed, the flat through which it passes is known as the Disappointments. The land is poor and affords farmers little more than a sullen, resentful crop of whatever is planted."

"I always thought the Disappointments was the name of some sort of old-age hostelry."

He wasn't amused. "No, the mighty Vinkus River, all that runoff of the Great Kells, pours without subtraction into Restwater. I'm sure you've circumnavigated this broad lake and seen the Vinkus tumbling over those rounded stones—the Giant's Toes, they call it—delivering Oz's best water to the Free State of Munchkinland. Our enemy."

He picked up the Vinkus River and took a chomp. "We have every reason to claim Restwater. For one thing, the Munchkins don't use it for their farming. For another, the water in it is ours. Damn, this is a good meal, Glinda. You're going to qualify as a chef before I get your parlor maid to crack the code of the written language, I fear."

"I meant to ask. How is she doing?"

"She's a spiky little thing, she is. I don't know how much she has upstairs, frankly. She's too quiet for me to guess. But she does attend. Maybe it's just lack of other diversion."

"Well, she used to be allowed to run in the meadows leading up to the Pine Barrens when she was released from duties. You've cut down the range of all of us, Traper."

"I'm afraid I'm going to be cutting it some more."

"Have another cutlet. How do you like the wine?"

"I'm going to have to move a few men into part of your suite."

"You're joking."

"No. I'm afraid they're up there shifting furniture as we speak."

"Traper. Really. We can't tolerate this abuse. Will you have me snuggling in the same bed with Puggles and Miss Murth?"

"You could release one of them. You may have to."

"You haven't tried the mashed bickory root."

He took a long sip of his wine. "I wish we didn't have to fuss over this, Glinda. It isn't to my liking, you know. The mission has other ambitions that take priority over mine and yours. But I had accepted the assignment hoping that our paths might cross, and in an agreeable way."

"You have a wife and children."

"Grown children," he said.

As if that made a difference. But then how would she know? "By crowding me into tenement conditions in my own home, you expect to win my affection? I fear the bickory root is overmashed, by the way; I'd avoid it. Or oversomething."

"Oversalted," he proposed. "Well, winning hearts comes second. My commission from the Emperor comes first, and I'm required to carry out his instructions completely."

"How is Shell, anyway? And *who* is he, these days. Do you know, I've rarely met him? Elphaba didn't mention him much when we were together at Shiz— he's four or five years her junior, I believe, and who remembers their families when they go up to college? As a former Throne Minister I did attend his installation, as was only fitting. But Chuffrey had a spoiled spleen or something, and I had to rush off, so in fact we didn't speak. Shell hasn't been one to come seeking advice of former Throne Ministers. Doesn't so much as send me a greeting card at Lurlinemas."

"Oh, he's a deeply devout unionist. Lurlinism and paganism are as one to him. Do you know there's almost no public celebration of Lurlinemas in the Emerald City anymore?"

"Another reason to keep to my country villa. Is the wine too warm?"

"Ah, it's nice." He drained his glass. "But yes, it's a little warm."

"Would you like some ice in your refill?"

"If you don't mind."

She got up. "Zackers, allow me. And if you don't mind, I have some private business with the General. If you would repair to the portico, I'll signal when we need you."

Zackers stood his ground. "I don't think I can see you from there, Lady Glinda. The rosebushes are too high."

"I know, aren't they wonderful? A banner year for roses."

She raised an eyebrow at Cherrystone, who dismissed Zackers with a flutter of fingers. "And how are your prettibells faring in this lush warm weather?" the General continued.

Glinda almost replied, *My what?* but she caught herself. "Goodness, what with entertaining myself through cookery education, I have hardly a moment to check on them. There are some over there in the weeds. Aren't they special."

"You cook as if by magic," he said.

"Don't I wish." She reached for the wine, a rather smoothly turned-over mountain antimerguese imported from the Ugubezi. "I picked up all my best recipes through my sisters in séance."

"You're joking."

She smiled over her shoulder. A roll of evening thunder unsettled itself some distance away. She made slow work of pouring the wine, and her whisper was so low she could hardly hear herself. "Traversa psammyad, unicular artica articasta," she muttered.

"What's that?" he said.

"Reciting ingredients in my head, that's how I train myself. How *do* you manage to teach my girl anything? She's too silent to rattle off her alphabet." *Traversa psammyad, unicular artica articasta.* She circled her palm over the pale wine in the goblet. Had she ever learned anything from Miss Grayling back in Shiz?

Cherrystone mused aloud. "I wonder why the girl wants to learn to read. A domestic won't have any prospects. Particularly as she has no family. Is that what I understand?"

She squared her shoulders. *Traversa psammyad . . .*

A little ice forming a coin on the surface of the wine. She swirled faster. The ice packed itself into a white lump, split in two. Two white lumps a little larger than lumps of sugar.

"Your wine, sir." She handed it to him as if she were the domestic. She was so proud of herself she was glowing. Cherrystone misread the expression.

"Either you've slipped a love potion in here, or you've poisoned it."

"Neither. And to show you, I'll sip myself. To your health." Scandalously she took a sip of the newly chilled wine. Heavenly. She returned him the glass and she lowered her gaze to her plate. The food was heinous, mushy and parched by turns. But the ice was perfect. She had learned to cook.

At the end of the meal, most of the crawberry fool having been abandonded in its dishes, Cherrystone escorted her through the rose garden and around the corner of the south porch. There they discovered Puggles in a broken heap on the gravel. He seemed to be dead.

19.

But he wasn't dead. After Zackers and a few others had carried him into the reception room, where men on cots had leapt up to provide him a bed, Glinda saw that he was still breathing. "You have a physician among your men," she said to Cherrystone. "If not, there's a doctor in Haventhur who will come to Mockbeggar, assuming you promise her safe passage here and back again. Though I hardly know if I can rely on your word."

"I assure you, Lady Glinda, whatever happened will prove to have been an accident." In front of his men he returned to formality in addressing her. But she hardly cared about that now. She put her hand on Puggles's forehead as if feeling a servant were part of her routine. She had no idea what to think about how his forehead felt, though. It felt like a parsnip, which until this week she had never felt, either.

She refused an escort upstairs and took her leave of Cherrystone without ceremony. The evening had ended badly—horribly, for poor Puggles—but not without some small reward. She had used a spell to draw winter upon the water. A baby step, to be sure. But that wine had been nicely chilled by her work.

Her step hastened as she realized that if men had been in her private chambers rearranging her furniture, someone might have removed the books from her shelves. Luckily, soldiers seemed uninterested in books. The little library had been lifted intact and installed in her bedroom.

Miss Murth and Rain were huddled together on a settee. Miss Murth's face had been wet but was now dry as if permanently. Her grim strength had an aspect of fleckstone about it.

"This is a furniture warehouse," said Glinda. One could get about the room by climbing on top of the wardrobe, dressers, chairs. A cat would love this room, leap up and never descend again. But there was hardly enough floor space to do her daily kick-ups to keep her bottom pert. "We can't live like this. Murthy, what happened?"

"You weren't gone half an hour, Lady Glinda, before they beefed their way through the door. General's orders, they said. They locked us in this room till they'd cleared out. Puggles tried to stop them, but they'd have none of it. There were almost a dozen of them, and all young men, showing no respect for a man of his age. They took him up the stairs to the parapet to get him out of the way. I don't know what happened next. They told me he broke away and fell over the balustrade. Dreadful liars, the lot of them. What will become of us?"

"You will have to sleep on the settee. Rain, can you settle down?"

But Rain had become a cat. She had climbed up a chest of drawers and crossed on top of the escritoire and scrabbled aboard the wardrobe. "I can sleep up here!" she crowed. For her, this was fun. Well, Glinda thought, perhaps it felt to her like having a family. Which is less fun than is generally acknowledged in the popular press.

"You'll do no such thing. Get down from there. You'll be the next one to bash your skull."

Murth fussed. "Oh, Mum, is that what happened to Puggles?"

"He's alive, at least he was when I left him. I don't know his condition. I think they're sending for Dame Doctor Vutters."

Rain said, "Did your supper get all et up?"

"How kind of you to remember." Under the circumstances, Glinda was touched. "It was as well received as I might have hoped for."

Murth set her straight. "She means, is there any left. We didn't get a meal, what with the invasion of the furniture snatchers."

"I'll see to it at once." The queen of the kitchen now, she sallied forth from her room. But in her large salon she was stopped by four soldiers in dress habillard. They carried rapiers, ceremonial but sharp. None of them was Zackers.

"Curfew, Lady Glinda," said one. "Apologies from the General."

"But I'm peckish. I'm off to collect myself a little pick-me-up."

"We're here to be of service."

"Nonsense. What, are you going to remove the night soil as well? Sing us to sleep if we have a bad dream? Boys. Out of my way."

"Orders, Lady Glinda. We'll dispatch to the commissary for what you need. Will bread and cheese do?"

"Rye brisks. And milk. I have a child, don't you know." And how odd to make that statement. "I have a lady companion as well. So a bottle of savorsuckle brandy while you're at it."

Returning to her room, she felt defeated. When the door closed behind her, Rain and Miss Murth glanced up with eyes like sunken puddings. (For the rest of Glinda's life, would everything look like spoiled food? A sad commentary.) She had nothing to say. But thunder outside the house, nearer this time, said it for her. "Let's open the curtains and raise a window. The air is stuffy in here with the three of us. At least two of us ought to have bathed more recently, had we known we'd be lodging together."

She directed Miss Murth to the sash, and in doing so realized that they'd been crowded into a room with windows that looked only in one direction—east. Glinda had always preferred sleeping in a room served by the sunrise, but now that she was exiled from other chambers, she had no view of the front gardens, and none of Restwater except the distances toward Haugaard's Keep. A flotilla sailing in from the Gillikin River and western Restwater could be approaching the boathouses and she'd never see them till they passed—or arrived.

"Thunder, but no sign of rain," said Miss Murth. "The night is cloudless."

"This is what fun is like," said Rain, almost to herself.

"Get in your nightdress," snapped Glinda.

"It's in my trunk. Up in the attics, where I sleeps."

"You'll have to borrow something of mine. Miss Murth, find her a camisole. Something."

After a light supper that was rather like a picnic— they all sat on Glinda's bed and got crumbs everywhere—they made their good nights and Miss Murth blew out the candle.

"Miss Murth. Are there evening prayers for a child?"

"Lady Glinda," said Murthy through the dark, "you never assigned me the task of raising this child. Give her whatever childhood prayers you remember. My own prayers are private ones."

"I know, you're praying for my immediate death, by my own hand, food poisoning myself. Very well. Rain, here is what we said in the Pertha Hills, when my mother would tuck me in."

The memory, like ice forming, was slow to arrive. In the end, Glinda said,

> Sweet and sure the lilacs bloom,
> And the heather, and the broom.
> Every mouse and mole rejoices
> When the sparrows raise their voices.

"That's not a prayer, that's a nursery rhyme, and you've got it all wrong," snapped Murthy.

"God bless us, every one. Except you," said Glinda.

20.

The weather remained clear but stifling. Glinda and Miss Murth were allowed to sit in the parlor daily and play cards in the presence of four armed men. Rain was called once or twice for her lessons.

"Can you read enough to find out what's happening?" Glinda whispered before Rain left. "Snoop a bit?"

Rain rolled her eyes and didn't answer.

On the third night of the intolerable situation, Rain waited until lights were out. Then she interrupted Glinda's continuing attempt at devotional doggerel by saying, "The teaching man was called away while we was doing our letter writing and no one else was in the room. Somefin was happening so I creeped to the door and then snucked out. I went round by the barns. No one saw me."

"Entirely too dangerous. Don't do that again or I'll slap you. What did you see?"

"That weren't no thunder we hear at nights. It's dragons in the dairy barns up the slope."

Glinda sat straight up in the dark.

"It's true. They got dragons for them boats I think. I heard Cherrystone yelling at someone for treating one of 'em beasties wrong. The lad got his foot crushed and they had to cut it off. Dame Doctor Vutters is living there now, like us. In the shed with the mattocks and grub hoes and stuff. It's her surgery."

"Dragons!" Miss Murth sounded as if she would have wept had she been less desiccated. "Lurline preserve us!"

"They're big as houses," said the girl, "and they glint gold even in the shadows. But they stink and they spit and strike out like catses." She pounced a forearm and made the cry of a shrike.

Glinda plumped her pillows up in the dark. "It's beginning to make sense. Why we've been crowded into a room that faces only east. And why they burned down the fields around here. They don't want news of the dragons getting out to the Munchkinlanders."

"And why Cherrystone was so angry after that puppet show, with the dragon in the lake!" said Murth excitedly.

"I thought you weren't watching. You were supposed to be minding the girl."

"We peeked. So put us in prison."

"We're already there." Glinda bit her lip. "I assume they're flying dragons—I've never seen a dragon, so I don't know if there are other varieties. Do they have wings, Rain?"

"Like great sloppy tents. When they stretches 'em, they goes to the ceilings of the barns! They disturb the pigeons, who poop on 'em. Then they eats the pigeons."

"Perhaps this makes sense of the vessel designs as well," added Murth. "Those stumpy masts, and the odd twin prows. They may not be entirely sailboats, but boats to be pulled by dragons in harness. The dragon may slot between the double-breasted prow."

"How ingenious."

Glinda knew she had to get to the Grimmerie again, but she didn't dare do it with Miss Murth hovering about. Rain was taciturn to the world, but Miss Murth might gabble if cornered. "Rain," said Glinda, "I think we'd better cancel your reading lessons now. The point has been made. You are not incapable of learning your letters."

Rain's mouth made an *O*. "But I'm nearly read-ing, real reading! Cherrystone keeps bringing me old papers and training me up on them, and I'm getting the hang of it."

It was as if the ice Glinda could form in a glass of wine had begun to cloud the blood in her veins. "What pages are those?"

"I can't say. Old magicks, I think, but I can't get 'em yet."

So he knew who she was. Pure peril now and no mistake.

"Not another word," said Glinda, "it's sleepytime. If you blather any more I shall subject you to more nursery verses."

The room fell silent, and soon Murth was snoring, and Rain's breath had silenced to below the level of hearing. But Glinda did not sleep.

The next day she requested an audience with Cher-rystone. He didn't reply until late in the day, and said he'd be up to see her at sunset. Through the interme-diary, she asked for permission to allow Rain and Miss Murth to take the air in the herb garden—which she knew was sufficiently hidden from both barns and lakeside not to alarm the Menaciers—so that she and Cherrystone could have some privacy in her room. This he allowed, said his emissary.

He arrived on time, looking more worn than before.

"You've finally beaten my resistance," she told him. "Here I am, General, entertaining you in all but the very bed in which I sleep."

"I apologize for the inconvenience." He had grown more courtly and more distant. "How may I be of service?"

"I need to know about Puggles."

He looked confused.

"Po Understar. Puggles. My butler."

"Oh, yes. Well, he is hanging on. He's recovered consciousness, somewhat, but not his language."

"What does Dame Doctor Vutters say?"

"A broken spine."

And to think he might have left with the others had she not required a butler.

"General, I would like to talk with the doctor, and to see the patient."

"I've dismissed the doctor. She's done all that can be done, she says."

"Where is Puggles?"

"He's been made a chamber in a closet under one of the staircases."

Glinda stood and began to walk toward the door. Cherrystone stood and said, "I can't allow this."

"Then stop me forcibly. You ought to enjoy that." She brushed past him, angry, alert, sensitized to her earlobes and toes. He didn't touch her.

She swept past the Menaciers in the next room with their rapiers raised. "Gentlemen," she said. Behind her, Cherrystone must be signaling that she be allowed to pass.

She hadn't known there was a cupboard under the west staircase. It reeked of rising damp. Mouse droppings dotted the unpainted floor. Puggles was swathed in a crude overshirt and his knees were exposed. He didn't move to cover them when he saw her. He did see her—she was sure of that, by the tracking of his eyes—but he couldn't move his hands. Or he no longer cared about whether he was exposing his knees to his superior.

"Oh, Puggles," she whispered. She sat right on his bed and took his fingers in hers. Clammy and lifeless, but not cold. "Can you tell me anything about what happened? Can you talk?"

He blinked. The skin at his lower eyelids pouched, shadowy grey.

"I know you were behaving in proper service. I shall see you are tended to as you deserve, to the best of my ability. I want you to know that." She swallowed. "Po. Po Understar. Do you understand?"

There was no way of knowing if he did. She sat there, stroking the top of his hand, and then left him. Her escort returned her to her room. At least she was alone for a moment, for Murth and Rain were still enjoying the herb garden. She should have gone to join them, but ten minutes of solitude was bliss itself.

She took up the Grimmerie and hoped, with the success of her little exercise in ice generation, that it might relent and allow her access to other pages, other spells, but as usual it kept its own counsel. She wanted to throw it out the window, but knew better.

After lunch, when Glinda was having a little lie-down with the shades drawn, Rain flapping a palmetto fan to keep the flies away and provide some breeze, a knock came at the door. One of the Menaciers handed Miss Murth a letter from Cherrystone to Lady Glinda. "I'll look at it later, Murth," said Glinda, and she drifted off into a troubled rest. For a moment, or ten, she was back in Shiz, darting up some alley of flowering quinces, racing Elphaba to the fountain at the back of the quad. Elphaba was glowing with the effort—glowing emerald!—and Glinda, in her dream, was almost absent to herself, caught up in admiring her friend. It happened so seldom, vacating the prison of one's limited apprehensions. Even dreams seemed ego-heavy, she thought as she was waking. But oh, to see Elphaba, even in dreams, is both reward and punishment, for it reminds me of my loss.

"Where's Murth? I mean Miss Murth?" she asked Rain.

"Dunno."

Thunder came up—real thunder, not dragon cry—and the long delayed cloudburst pummeled the house. Rain leaped to help Glinda slam the windows closed. She hoped someone downstairs would remember to shutter the windows to protect the parquetry, but with Murth called away and Puggles incapacitated, the floor would probably be drenched and need refitting in the fall. Damn damn damn.

They played cards. The rain continued.

As long as Miss Murth was taking her time, they checked the Grimmerie. Again Rain could open it while Glinda could not, but as usual they could turn to no other page than the one that the Grimmerie seemed inclined to let them see.

By teatime Glinda suffered the throes of a snit gunning to become a rage. "I am expected to do everything around here?" she said to Rain.

"I'm a parrot," said Rain from the top of the wardrobe. "Tweetle twee."

When the fellow arrived with afternoon tea, Glinda accosted him. "Where is Miss Murth? Find her and tell her to stop gallivanting. She can't be outside; she's not allowed. Furthermore, it's bucketing barrels out there." She paused. Perhaps Miss Murth was tending to Puggles. Was there a tenderness between them?

No. Impossible. Not Murth. She wasn't capable of that fine a feeling, and she wouldn't inspire it in anyone else, either.

"Is Miss Murth with Puggles?" she snapped.

"I'm just doing your tea, Mum," he said.

"Are you all imbecilic? Is that a requirement of enlisted men? It's *Lady Glinda*!" She was losing it, big time. "Get me Murth!"

At sundown, when the rain had finally passed over and the heat returned as if the drenching had never happened, Zackers appeared. He had his cap twisted in his hands as if he was paying a social call.

"What is it, Zackers?"

"You asked about Murth, Mum, and the General doesn't understand."

"What are you chattering about?"

"The note that the General sent you just after lunch, Mum."

"There was a note," said Rain helpfully, leaping from wardrobe to the bed like a demented bandit monkey.

The bedclothes flew up. "Isn't it still over there, under the what-chit?"

A paper folded beneath the decanter of sherry. Glinda hurried to look.

> Lady Glinda,
> I regret the further inconvenience. In pursuance of your request to be allowed to name what member in your service might be released due to mounting pressures upon the household, I would like your recommendation. I would suggest the girl, as she must be of less service to you than your lady-in-waiting. I could use her somehow.
> Cordially,
> General Traper L. Cherrystone,
> Hx. Red., Advanced

"This makes no sense to me. I did not receive it. I was napping."

Zackers looked distinctly uncomfortable. "The General acted upon your suggestion."

"I made no suggestion. I was napping, I tell you."

He handed her a folded page of her own stationery.

> General:
> Under the circumstances, I shall release Miss Murth.

Lady Glinda of Mockbeggar Hall

Arduenna of the Uplands,

Dame Chuffrey,

Throne Minister Emerita,

Honorary Chair of Charities,

Patron of Saint Glinda's in the Shale Shallows,

    etc., etc.

Murth had brought Glinda's signature to too fine a facsimile.

21.

She went to shove past Zackers as she had done past Cherrystone, but he blocked her way. "En't allowed, Mum," he said. "Quarantine."

"Quarantine? What are you on about?"

"That's what I'm told. You're confined to your room. Meals will be supplied."

"What's been done with Miss Murth?"

"I've got my orders." Suddenly his pimples seemed a disguise; he was a man holding on to the scabby shield of youth to use it to his advantage. "You'd be wise to return to your room, Lady Glinda."

She fixed as spirited and venomous a look upon him as she could, but even within a moment she softened it.

"Zackers. I don't want to make trouble for you. Send for your commanding officer and we'll sort this out."

"The General has given orders not to be disturbed."

So she went into the room and closed the door. Rain had been jumping on the bed, and sat down *flump* with her legs outstretched. "Where's Miss Murth gone off to?"

"Never you mind about that." She went to the window and threw up the sash. Was there any way to escape? Her own windowsill extended to join a sort of stone rim or lintel, some three inches wide, that ran around the building, connecting all the windows on this level. She could not hope to get a purchase on a ledge that narrow.

She looked down. A nine-foot drop onto the flat roof of the ballroom below. Even if one could leap or lower one's self down under cover of darkness, the ballroom was twenty-two feet high, she knew—she'd had the room redone last year. The ballroom stretched out in its own wing, and its windows on three sides opened onto terraces, so fevered dancers could cool themselves by taking the evening air. This meant there were no useful trees growing up near the building, no climbing cypress or espaliered ivy to serve as an escape route.

"I were a bird, I could just wing the air down," said Rain, as if reading her thoughts.

"You won't move an inch from my side unless I say so. Not one inch. Do you hear me?"

Rain fell asleep almost at once. Perhaps, thought Glinda somewhat guiltily, perhaps she never slept in anyone's encircling arms before. They spent the night holding each other.

By morning it was clear that evacuation orders had been given. Breakfast was nothing but tea and slightly stale bread. If they sat very still at the open window, they could hear the sound of the ships being rolled to the launching point. How could they have been kitted out so quickly? Glinda supposed that, under a firm enough manager, three hundred men with time on their hands could achieve quite a lot.

At noon on this day of lancing summer light, Glinda began to hear the sound of the dragons. Their cry was at once serrated and tuneful. Glissandi of violoncello interrupted by the yowls of cats in heat. Now that Glinda was really and truly imprisoned, her aggressors clearly felt no more need for secrecy. The dragon trainers led the fearsome creatures around the east edge of the house, below the ballroom. A military parade of sorts. Six of them. Perhaps one each to haul the four warships, and an extra dragon at the front and another to the rear, as sentries.

Fearsome? She thought she might never dream of anything else again. Each one of the foul creatures was ridden
by a soldier in leather chaps. Each soldier, equipped with
a whip and dirk, looked terrified. Each leaned forward,
wrapped obscenely around the neck of his mount, whispering to it. Dragonmasters. She had heard tell of such.

But the creatures themselves. Rain had told only the
glamour part of it. Yes, there were scales that burned
in the sun, imbrications of bronze and bruise-purple
gold. But a lizardy dankness obtained as well, the
stench of the bog. Their skulls were shaped less like
horses than like some strange elongated insect. And
eyes! She remembered the glowing eyes of the Clock
of the Time Dragon. Like genuine eyes, those had
gleamed with life, but these actual dragon eyes looked
polished, blank, black, deadly. They reflected all, they
gave nothing away. "Pull back, lest one of them see
you," said Glinda, but Rain behaved as if she were at
the parade of a traveling zoo. Glinda had to hold Rain's
hands to keep her from clapping.

"Let's try the book one more time, shall we?" she
said when the dragons had passed. Before they could
pull it out, Zackers opened the door without knocking
and Cherrystone strode in.

"I'm taking my leave," he told her. "Zackers will
stay behind to see to your needs. I apologize for the

inconveniences, but you can see why we couldn't allow you the run of your house and the service of your aides."

"Why do you not kill me, and save yourself the trouble of abusing my staff?" she said, putting Rain behind her and holding her in place with clamped hands. Nonetheless, she felt Rain peering around her hip.

"Depending on how the matter unfolds, you may yet come in use. Not to me—to your country. Your liberated staff will have spread the word that you are detained against your wishes. All of western Munchkinland knows that you are locked up here. Should we decide to sue for peace, you are advantageously placed as a loyal Ozian with strong affections for Munchkinland. A former Throne Minister with personal ties to the rebel province. Munchkinlanders would accept you as an emissary of the Emperor. We have arranged it for you to be ready to serve."

"What have you done with Murth?"

He inched forward. In the heat of the impending battle was he going to kiss her at last? But he had in mind something more of a sneer. "Why should you care?" he said. "You don't even know her first name."

She sputtered and thought of slapping him, but that would be too drawing-room farce. He said, "I want to take the girl with me."

"I think the phrase is, over my dead body. And since you intend to keep me alive, you may as well go off on your capers. Your days of being a tutor are through, anyway; you've got your army to manage. Though I suppose now they've become a navy."

"I'll take up the matter when I have completed the mission of the hour. Good afternoon, Lady Glinda."

"May you freeze in hell."

He gave the briefest of bows, not so much from the waist as from the chin, and turned to leave.

And the Grimmerie proved as recalcitrant as ever.

They watched the first of the ships roll into view on the water. Glinda had to admit there was something terrific about the sight. The ships were painted red and gold, from this distance looking like wooden cousins of the dragons. Their sails puffed out; the wind was strong and apparently from the right quarter. Behind the stubby masts Glinda and Rain tracked the movement of those stubby masts against the hills, which helped them mark the acceleration of two, then three ships. The fourth would be coming along.

From this distance the dragons resembled immense overheated ducks.

There would be no stopping a fleet with six dragons. Haugaard's Keep was lost. But Rain didn't need to be lost. There was still time.

"Quick," said Glinda. "How is your head for heights?"

"I'm gooder than a bird in any tree, Mum."

It was too late to insist on *Auntie* or anything like that. "Can you balance yourself here without falling?"

Rain looked out the window at the three-inch ledge. "If there's no big wind to scrape me down."

"Blessings on you. There, that's a prayer, best I can do. I'll give you a leg up." She helped Rain out the lower sash. Thank Ozma the windows were tall; Rain could almost stand up straight before she'd scrambled out. She fit her naked feet (still dirty, Glinda saw) this way and that, a dancer's pose, until she was erect and balanced.

"Anyone's walking in the rose garden'll see up my frock."

"Never mind about that. Do you think you can safely inch beyond the edge of this window? Not far— only a bit at a time to see how it feels."

"Oh, I'm a spider on a wall. It's easy florins, this one."

"Now listen to me, Rain. I want you to inch—if you feel you can—until you're about halfway between this window and the next one. No farther. Have you anything on which to cling?"

"My fingernails."

"That'll have to do."

"What does I do when I gets there?"

"Just wait for further instructions. I am going to scream a little bit, but I don't want you to be startled. I am only acting."

"Acting?"

"Like the puppets in that play. I'm not really screaming. It's like—it's like singing."

"I didn't know you sung, Mum. Songs, like?"

"Oh, I have lots of little talents. Cooking is the least of them."

"That's what I heard."

"Don't be snarky. Are you ready? You won't be startled and lose your grip?"

"Spiders don't fall off the wall when they hear a singer."

"I may have to double the octave to get some attention."

"I'm watching the fleet. Sing away."

"Here I go." Please, Lurlina, please. Or the Unnamed God. Anyone who might be paying attention. *Elphaba.*

She reeled her voice out. It wasn't very convincing. "That was it?" called Rain.

"That was my warm-up. Here comes the real thing."

She was gratified that when she let loose, two of the dragons turned their heads. But she couldn't watch them. Zackers was unlocking the door. "Glory and gumption, Lady Glinda? Are you all right?"

She wheezed, holding her side. "The girl! She's trying to escape! Out the window! Oh, Cherrystone will have my head!

"Also yours," she added, in a more normal voice, as Zackers rushed to the open window.

"Holy Saint Florix," said Zackers. "Get in here, girl, before I whup you. You'll break every little riblet in your skinny little frame. Take my hand."

"Oh, oh," screamed Glinda, beginning to enjoy the role.

"Don't worry, Mum; I've almost got her. She's quite the little scorpion, en't she?"

Glinda walked backward, screeching, the way she'd seen opera singers do onstage—only of course their sound was musical, while she was working to deliver something convincingly atonal. In midscreech, she stopped dead. Zackers, his head and torso leaning out the window, turned at the sudden silence. She lifted her skirts and rushed him like a bull, kicked his damn boots off her good carpet, and tumbled him out the window. For Puggles, she thought.

"Nicely managed, Rain," she said. "You can come in now."

"I like it out here," said Rain.

"You heard me." She didn't want to look down. She had appreciated Zackers, for a few days anyway, and she hoped he wasn't dead. But he was moaning and cursing. It was only nine feet after all.

But too high to climb up, even if his ankle wasn't broken, which it looked to be, the way his foot was improperly hinged. And he could never leap to the ground.

"How clumsy of me," she called down to the roof. "I must take a refresher course in deportment to restore my glide." Zackers's reply wasn't suitable for Rain's hearing, and Glinda hustled her away. But not before picking up the Grimmerie.

The house was empty of soldiers, as far as she could tell; they had all evacuated onto the ships except, she supposed, a skeleton crew holding Mockbeggar hostage. Knowing an unencumbered view would be essential, she hurried Rain up the dusty steps to the parapet. Ah!—free from this summer bondage for a few moments at least.

"You need to help me with this one, Rain," she told the girl.

"I'm ready, Mum."

Glinda taught her the words. They stood facing the fleet—*The Vinkus,* the *Quadling Country,* the *Gillikin,* the *Munchkinland*—its four powerhouse dragons yoked between prows, as Murth—Murth!—had imagined, and the two extra dragons paddling along in the rear like a pair of proud snarling parents.

"Traversa psammyad, unicular artica articasta," said Glinda. "That's the start of it. Can you memorize this quickly? We have so little time."

Rain nodded. Her eyes were like iron, hard and true.

They held hands and leaned across the parapet. The wind was blowing from behind them; maybe it would carry their words far enough. "Traversa psammyad, unicular artica articasta," they chanted in unison. Glinda taught her the rest, line by line. Rain drank it in like fizzy wine and remembered it faultlessly.

"A wand would help, but I haven't had a wand in years," said Glinda. "Wands go wandering. We'll have to do without."

She stretched out her left arm, Rain her right. They delivered the spell to bring winter upon the water.

It was unclear whether it was working at first, for the strong wind continued to blow, the sails to billow and flap, audible even at this distance. Glinda held her breath and trained her gaze on the foothills of the Great Kells. It seemed as if the masts were making slower progress against them. Slower, slower still. Then the masts shivered and creaked, and one of them split because the soldiers-turned-sailors didn't yet know their progress had stopped, that the sails had needed to be brought about or cut.

The four boats and the six dragons were pinned in an island of ice that had come up from the water below and congealed around webbed feet and submerged hulls. The dragons were enraged and crashing their wings. Shrieking.

"They sound like you, Mum," said Rain.

"We haven't time to watch them drown, or burn their way loose, or turn around to catch us. We're cooked any way you look at it. Let's go."

22.

Safe enough to set one of the barns on fire, one that stood away from the house. And anyway, it had been more or less eviscerated; she saw that the soldiers had appropriated a good many of the posts and beams from the hayloft. A security measure, bringing the structure down, she could say. The clouds of black smoke would alarm residents of Haventhur and Bigelow and the rest, and ready them for whatever punishment Cherrystone and the forces of the Emerald City might still manage to loose against them.

Glinda had never saddled up a carriage, but Rain had spent her childhood in the barns. While the girl wasn't big enough to handle the tackle, she knew what was needed, and she could demonstrate how it hooked and snaggled together. In the time it would have taken them to walk to Zimmerstorm on their hands and knees, Glinda had readied the lightest of carriages. So they set out along the coast road, heading west—away from the wreckage on the water.

As it happened, they didn't need to go very far. Four miles out—away from the burning barn, the ships frozen in the summer lake, the panicked and furious dragons, and General Cherrystone—waited the Lion and that high-strung veiled woman with the pretty white hair. She was pacing and he was lolling, but when the Lion saw the carriage he drew himself to his hind legs and smoothed his mane.

"How did you know I would come here?" asked Glinda.

"You forget for whom we work," said the woman. "The Clock tells us things that may happen. Not what should happen, mind, or what will happen. But what might."

"*Anything* might happen," said Glinda.

"The secret of why prophecy is so popular," agreed the woman. "Good for business."

"I brought you back the book," said Glinda. "It's too fussy for me to have. I thought so the first time I had it, and I think so again."

The Lion said, "We'll take it. You're safer without it now, in case there are reprisals. But from the hill where the Clock is hidden—we have a good view of the lake. We saw what you were able to do with the Grimmerie. You used it well." He grinned at her. "Nice piece of work, sister."

Glinda remembered the play. "Have the sailing Menaciers all drowned?"

"It's not over yet," said the woman. "But they saw the Clock's performance, and the fear of their own drowning will undo them usefully. You've pinched exactly the right nerve. The alarm has been given, and the dragons have been slowed or made ill."

"A dragon with a head cold. Nasty thought."

"You never knew a dragon to live in an icy realm, did you? Cold is perishing pain to them, one hears tell."

Glinda took the Grimmerie from where it had lain like an old farmer's manual on the floor of the carriage. It had shed its disguise while they clattered on the road, and it looked like itself. Perhaps a bit more tattered. Could a book that old continue to age?

"You've done a great service," said the Lion, taking it from her. "Some wouldn't have thought you capable."

"Well, I learned to cook. At my age," she told him. "What's next? Arts therapy? Anyway, I've had quite a time of it this summer, and who knows what eases on down any road. Come, Rain. A quick good-bye, and off you go."

"Good-bye," said Rain to the Lion, and then to the woman.

"Not to them," said Glinda. "To me."

She turned eyes that were saucerly upon Glinda. "Mum?"

"He was too interested in you," she said in as bland a voice as she could manage. "It's become too dangerous. You are better off with them."

"We don't have those instructions from Mr. Boss," said the Lion. He growled low in the back of his throat.

"Mr. Boss is not the only one who gives instructions," she told him. "I am a Throne Minister Emerita. As I remember it, Sir Brrr, I am the one who conferred a Namory upon you. Many years ago."

"Oh, yes," he said, pussying about with his lapel. "Very nice and all that, but Lady Glinda."

"I gets to go with the Lion?" Rain was unskilled at the control of elation. It cut Glinda like onion juice in a fingertip newly slit with a paring knife. Or worse.

"You do," said Glinda. "Off with you then."

Rain clambered down and ran to the Lion. He backed away with his paws out. The veiled woman with him just laughed. "You've faced worse, Brrr. Come. Let's see what the dwarf has to say about this."

"You do know who she is—her name is Rain—" said Glinda, but her voice was failing her, and she didn't know if they heard. They were moving away, turning, cutting up through the scrappy barrens of pine.

Just when it was too much, when Glinda thought she might sob, Rain suddenly twisted about. "But en't you coming?" she called.

"Can't possibly."

"Why not?" The girl sounded petulant, as if suddenly she decided the whole world ought to go her way, all the time.

"Zackers is stuck on the roof. I have to fling some sandwiches down at him so he won't starve. And there's Puggles. He can't move, Rain. Now that I know how to make soup, I have to make some soup and spoon it into his mouth until I can find somebody to care for him, to make him better if it can happen."

"And there's Murth," said the girl ruminatively.

Glinda didn't believe there was Murth any longer. "You take care of one another. Come and see me sometime if you are passing through."

Rain had already turned back around and was chattering to the Lion. The woman lifted the girl up on the Lion's back—he was down on all fours again—and Rain squealed with glee. She grabbed his mane by two fistfuls and her little naked feet came up as her knees went down. Her head went back in joy. Blinding joy. She looked like a girl in the best of times. She looked like a girl broken out of the prison egg. But she didn't look back.

II

The Patchwork
Conscience of Oz

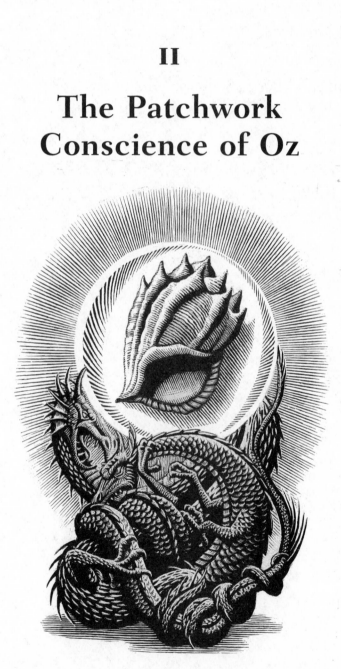

1.

The Lion backed up as the dwarf turned a red no beet would ever manage. "I sent you to collect a library book, and you come back with a child?"

Uh-oh, thought Brrr. Bad move. He arched his backbone—a bit of alley cat attitude that no one could be fooled by, but it made him feel better. He hadn't seen the dwarf this seriously off his nut before.

To Ilianora, the dwarf added, "Look, Little Nanny Ninnykins, I always thought you were simple, but I see I was wrong. You're demented. Take her back where you got her."

To Brrr's surprise, Ilianora gave Mr. Boss no quarter. "You're interested in the future," she said to him. "Any child is a head start on the future, no matter who they are."

"So we should maybe kidnap a whole orphanage? Listen, I won't stand for this. Send her packing."

"Don't get your little knickers in a twist," the Lion said mildly. "We can take care of her. Principles of child governance—how hard could it be?"

"You couldn't govern a coffee grinder. You're too big a sissy to run a nursery school."

"On the contrary. Cowardice is a virtue when it comes to protecting the young and frail. If I can be as scared as a child is of, oh, bumblebees or something, I can better remember to keep us both safely away from them."

"I en't scared of no bumblebees," inserted Rain.

The dwarf ignored her, and snapped at the Lion, "You sure put the pussy in pussycat. You couldn't even stand up to Lady Glinda when she foisted this hoyden on you."

Well, there is truth in that, thought Brrr.

Ilianora said to the child, "When did you last have something to eat?"

"I *am* hungerful," admitted the girl. "Lady Glinda en't all that good a cook."

Brrr let the child slip off his back. The dwarf fumed and spat but the Lion stood his ground. "We've got bigger problems than kindercare," he said. "Have you forgotten that the fleet that the Clock showed us has been attacked? Someone will be wondering who did it, and putting it all together."

"It gots stuck in the middle of the water," said Rain.

Ilianora, rooting about in a satchel, located some shreds of ham and bread. A pot of mustard and a spoon. The dwarf took the Grimmerie off into the underbrush of the pine barren, probably to return it to the Clock. In a clearing upslope, the assistants pitched quoits, ponying about and paying no mind.

"Why should he be so aggravated about a kid tagging along?" Brrr asked his wife. "He's already saddled with us. What's one more, and a little one at that?"

"Let me first see to some supper for the child, Brrr."

When she had finished her meal, Rain looked about her with brightening interest. "Here's where you live?" she asked.

"Until Mr. Boss gives us the word to press on." Ilianora removed her veil and shook it out. Her white braid was coiled upon her head in a henge of black pins.

The Lion said, "I do hope we'll get going soon. There'll be a marksman or even a posse on our trail by dawn, I bet. Anyway, this place gives me gooseflesh." He had never liked the forest, any forest. That sense of lostness. How a horizon so quickly gets knotted up in the fractal digression of branches. Though this stand of junk trees was thinner than some.

Sotto voce, Brrr to his all-too-human wife: "I don't want to be the only timid one at the table, but *don't* you agree we should light out before that General sends hit men to find the Grimmerie? And to mow us down while they're at it? We could move faster on our own, you and me. With the girl, of course. Since her welcome to our own little tribe has been, shall we say, a little thin."

Ilianora bit her upper lip, considering. "I've felt we should all keep together, but now that we've obeyed the Clock, delivering the Grimmerie to Lady Glinda and collecting it from her again, you might be right. Though where would we go?"

"You need to find your brother."

"I don't need to do that." She lived and breathed, Brrr knew, with a high tolerance for detachment—like a lake jellyfish floating in a glass casket, oblivious of japing crowds.

He'd been with her for six months now. In that time she'd learned—or remembered—how to laugh. Gulpily. Bitten-off retorts, like poorly suppressed hiccups. She'd seemed to grow younger through the winter. He didn't want to see her lose any ground. "*Shall* we skive off?" asked the Lion again, in a lower voice.

She shrugged. She'd know what was to come next when she knew it, thought Brrr. And though no magistrate had recorded their union—any cross-species romance revolted Mice and Munchkinlanders alike— he and Ilianora enjoyed a marriage just the same, and he'd stick by her side either in or out of the shadow of the Clock.

The dwarf was waddling back. Not for nothing was he called Mr. Boss. "You lot of layabouts, this is no picnic. We've got problems to see to. Up, up, off your furry rump, Sir Brrr. Miss Fiddlefuck of the Fairies. Hey, you noisy boysters, shape up—we're hotfooting it back to the lookout bluff, where we can see down the lake, and catch the news on the wind."

Brrr raised his eyebrows to the child, and she understood; she galloped toward him and sprang onto the Lion's back. "Don't get used to me," he found himself saying over his shoulder. "I'm no one's defender. I'm not reliable." Her finger dug into the rolls of skin at the nape of his neck and she nuzzled her face in his mane. This made her cough. He wished he'd given himself a shampoo more recently, but conveniences were in short supply in the Pine Barrens. Another reason to detest the place.

They'd stashed the Clock at the dead end of an old logging road; above this, the hills mounded to a lookout. Brrr didn't wait for Ilianora, the dwarf, his boys. He vaulted ahead, passing the Clock, breasting the hill.

The sun was just beginning to set. The stripe of glare down the lake, too bright to see at first, pinned the flotilla within it. Then the Lion's sight steadied, and Rain's must have too. The girl murmured, "Holy Ozma."

They saw four ships and six impossible dragons encased in a floating belt of ice, a flat island of white. Ice had run up the ratlines and shrouds and stiffened the sails into glass. Men had shucked their uniforms in the summer heat and jumped onto the floe. In little but braies and singlets they were hacking with axes. Here and there campfires had been set, as if to puncture the ice with melt-holes. The dragons bellowed!—you could hear it even at this distance. One or two had worked a wing loose. The military were staying clear of the twisting, snakelike heads, which snarled and snapped in rage at everything and nothing.

"They din't do nothin'," said Rain. "T'ent their fault, them beasties."

"Fell in with the wrong crowd," said Brrr, "and they'll pay. Mind who you choose for friends, Rain."

"Friends," snorted the girl, skeptical of the concept, maybe.

Out from Sedney and Bigelow to the south, from Haventhur and Zimmerstorm to the north, Munchkin boats were emerging. Shabby little barks such as had been snugged into port or tucked under screens of pine branches proved trim and ready for this opportunity for sabotage. Twelve, fifteen, twenty vessels. Compared to the mighty ships Cherrystone's men had built, these were laughable toyfloats. Powered by forearm and sail and cheery, puffing steampipes. Here came a bark shaped like a gilded swan—that must be from one of the ancestral piles farther up the lake.

"High holy hysteria," said Mr. Boss, arriving with the others in time to see the Munchkinlanders take revenge for the burning of their crops.

The dragons were making so much noise, down below, that the soldiers seemed slow to comprehend the net of lake midges drawing around them.

"Brrr, turn around, take the girl away from this," said Ilianora suddenly.

"This is the world in which she has been born," barked the dwarf. "Better to know early. Take a good look, girlie."

Ilianora came up beside Brrr and reached for one of Rain's hands; Rain shrugged her away. She didn't take her eyes off the lake.

"The local riffraff is ready with muskets of some sort," said Brrr, as punches of thready smoke also bloomed out around the raggle-taggle peasant fleet. It wasn't long before columns of cloud smeared the air from the gunnels of *The Vinkus,* the *Munchkinland,* the *Gillikin,* the *Quadling Country.* A hearty response from professional artillery.

Perhaps the kickback of Cherrystone's cannon began to shatter the ice. The rocking worked some play into the frozen girdle, and the navy Menaciers seemed encouraged. But soon it became clear that the Munchkinlanders were united in a simple strategy. *Spare the ships; attack the creatures.* The slaughter of one dragon, then a second and third simultaneously, made all the onlookers, even Mr. Boss, catch his breath. The great dragon-heads fell to one side, old sunflowers listing. The dragon-wings burst into thin flame, translucent first, then oranged, rouged; they fell to ash within minutes.

"Ow," said Brrr. "You're hurting me, Rain."

The fourth dragon died. The fifth broke loose in the commotion, at last, and rose above the fray so high that the company on the bluff drew back, ready to scatter should its eye fall upon them. But it dove upon one of Cherrystone's ships to snap the stubbed mast. Then it whirled about and attacked the gilt-tipped swan boat. It caught the silly hooped neck of the prow and rose in the air with it, dashing it upon one of the frozen ships. Brrr couldn't see if the swan's navigator or skipper had dived to safety.

The liberated dragon dropped from the air again. At first they thought it was attacking another ship, but the dragon was heaving in a death throe. In the muck of ice floes and floundering vessels, it overfreighted one of Cherrystone's vessels to the starboard side, and the ship upended with a sound of suction and shattering, stove through.

The sixth and final dragon managed to rip free, now that the spell was losing its grip. Into the sky it racked its way. Taking no notice of floating armies or vengeful ambushers, it staggered in the sunset light. Crazed perhaps. It turned to the south, heaving over Bigelow and the foothills of the Great Kells. Heading for the Disappointments, maybe, or the murk of the badlands. None of its band would follow it into Quadling Country. It had no living mates left.

2.

After soaking a puck of congealed tadmuck and mashing it up, the company of the Clock of the Time Dragon disported itself about a small fire of coals to cook their penance and eat it. They were silent at first. The smoke kept the jiggering mosquitoes off, but the light drew the moths. Cross-legged on the ground, Rain cupped her chin in her hands. Her eyes followed the mauve wings. As if she'd never seen moths before, Brrr thought. Or perhaps she was contemplating the kinship possibilities between moth and dragon.

"Not to ruin anyone's digestion," said Brrr at last, "but we're probably marked enemies of the administration lording it up in the Emerald City. Ilianora and I were talking and—well, don't you think we should scram while we can?"

"I don't work by committee, never did," snapped Mr. Boss. "I want your sympathy, you faggoty cat, I'll ask for it. You can go foul your knickers for all I care."

"What's the matter? Some mountain goat nibble at your testicles?"

Ilianora shot Brrr a look and indicated the child. But Rain continued oblivious to anything but the flutter of moth and flame, and Brrr kept at the dwarf. "What is it? You don't like anyone else making a decision? Such as our taking on the girl when Lady Glinda suggested it?"

Mr. Boss had been kind to Ilianora for the past year. She had always before been able to cozen the dwarf from his tempers. Now, when she sat down near him and put a hand on his knee, he swatted it away. "You want somebody more functional than Sissyboy Lion, help yourself to one of the lads. I'm not interested in you."

Behind the dwarf's back, Brrr mouthed singsong-ingly to his wife, *You're i-in trou-ble.*

"We'll only keep the girl till we can find somewhere safe for her to stay," she said to the dwarf. "We more or less promised Lady Glinda. In exchange for releasing the book back to us."

Mr. Boss flicked a piece of ratty bark into the fire, taking out one of the moths. Rain gasped, quietly.

"We got your precious book," said Brrr, trying not to sound panicky. "The girl is a bonus. What're we waiting around for?"

"I don't know. How the hell should I know?" Mr. Boss's tone was darker than usual.

"Ask the Clock?" suggested Ilianora, as if that thought might not have occurred to him.

"I can't."

Brrr had only been with the company of the Clock for the past six months. Still, he'd heard that the Clock decided for itself when it needed a rest. When this hap-pened, the company would sometimes disband for a while. Maybe it was time. The Lion asked, "What, is the thing on strike again? Holding out on us?"

Mr. Boss shifted this way and that without answer-ing. Off to one side, to the plinks from a silver guitar and a set of jingle-tongs, the bawd came through clearly. The seven lads were improvising more lewd verses to their nightly lay of the endless lay. Some evenings the boys sang of themselves taking their pleasures in a whorehouse, sometimes in a female seminary, sometimes in front of an audience of kings and bishops. The boys were equally godlike in endurance and readiness, the girls indistinguishably gorgeous except for variations in hair color. Hardly lullabye material, but soon enough Rain slumped in the Lion's forearms and noodled herself toward sleep.

"Now," said the Lion, "I don't mean to rush you, but assassins are no doubt starting out to find us, the Clock, and the book. They'll have put it all together, given we showed them an excerpt of what to expect. Do you want to tell us what's going on?"

Mr. Boss sighed, and a single golden tear slid out of his eye and lost itself in his bottlebrush mustache. Brrr didn't trust the tear of a dwarf any more than he trusted the Unnamed God to appear in the clearing and settle the universal contest of good versus evil. Or even good versus bad taste.

Ilianora extended their chieftain the benefit of the doubt. "What's upset you? It surely can't be the child?"

The dwarf sunk his chin farther into his chest, as if he'd rather speak to his lap. "I hoped getting the book back from Lady Glinda would refresh the Clock's executive function, but I don't believe it has done so."

Ilianora and Brrr exchanged glances, and waited.

"*You* always see the entertainment message of the Clock," explained Mr. Boss. "That's all anyone ever sees. The audience side with the stages, the apertures and balconies and suchlike. But there's a difference between public demonstration and private revelation. Around the corner? Not the side with the storage cabinets, but the back end of the cart? Where the placard says HE DREAMS YOU UP AND SWALLOWS YOU DOWN? That advertisement hides from everyone's view a private stage you never saw because I never mentioned it. To anyone. When I'm alone I go sneak a look there. I watch for direction every few days. Even if the Clock prefers to show no opinion about what might happen, always before this it has quivered with secrecy. It's been like a child trying to keep perfectly still. Can't be done. No one can play dead dead enough, not even a Clock. Until now. It gave me one more tirade while you were gone, today. Then—it died. It's mastered the art of being dead. Or comatose."

"What did the Clock say?" asked Ilianora.

"It said keep away from any grubby underage girlykins who have no business mucking with history." He tossed his brow toward Rain but couldn't bring himself to look at her. "And then it collapsed."

The lads were settling down into their usual mound. They always slept apart from management. Rain was lost into a dream of her own.

"Perhaps the Clock needs the Grimmerie to function properly?" suggested Brrr. "Like a kind of yeast, or a key? Maybe now that we have it back . . . ?"

"More often than not, the book has been clear of the Clock, and still the Clock told me whatever it needed me to know. The Clock and the book are separate systems, though sharing a cousinly interest in influence."

"Then maybe the Clock *doesn't* like having the Grimmerie back," said Brrr. "Maybe you should hot-potato it back to Lady Glinda's lap." He wouldn't relish being delegated for *that* mission, not in the current climate.

"Right. And maybe the stars are really the toenail cuttings of the Unnamed God. Don't talk about that which you don't bloody get, Sir Pussykit."

So even history can get tired too, thought Brrr. How many futures has the Clock told in its time? It's been humping around Oz for what, thirty, forty, fifty years now? And the dwarf slaving in attendance to it except during the periods when the Clock was hidden in some crevice of Oz, and the dwarf could go out and live something of a life? "Well, if you can't start it up with a hand crank, maybe it wants to be dead," said Brrr. "Ever think of that?"

The dwarf only groaned. "The Clock isn't just a font of prophecy. It's—a kind of conscience, I think."

"It won't be the first conscience ever nodded off. I'm joining it. Good night."

But the Lion's rest was pestered by the calls of hootch-owls and the slither of pelican beetles under dried pine needles. He was worried that the dwarf seemed immobilized by the Clock's paralysis. He was worried they shouldn't be sleeping here, but should be on the road already, getting away. He could hear marksmen in every scrape and shudder of forest.

Always some itch that worrying couldn't scratch. Brrr slipped sideways in and out of the kind of sleep that masquerades neatly as the actual moment—is he a Lion aware of being almost asleep in a summery pine forest, or is he dreaming of that same reality?

Apparitions of his past detached from the fretwork of chronology and drifted into consciousness, out again. The Lion swam in that underwater wonderland where action and consequence lose their grip on each other.

Look who's here on conscience's catwalk: striking poses between wakefulness and dream.

The nobleman who'd thought up for the Lion an agent's assignment. The man who had smelled of licorice and tobacco. Avaric, Margreave of Tenmeadows.

His thin pumpkin-colored mustache and goatee, that bearing few Animals could imitate. Damn the confidence of the titled!

Avaric gave way to Jemmsy, the first human Brrr could remember meeting—a humble soldier of the Wizard of Oz. The Lion's first friend, so his first betrayal. What made Brrr think he could care for a little girl, even for a while? Doing damage—that was the Lion's métier.

Jemmsy flew apart into ashes. In the Lion's hypnogogic paralysis, Jemmsy resembled the swarm of Ozmists, said to be fragments of ghost who haunted the Great Gillikin Forest. What had they asked? "Tell us if the Wizard is still ruling Oz." And Cubbins, the boy-sheriff of the Northern Bears, had asked them a return question: "Tell us if Ozma is alive."

Why didn't hooded phantasms in their sepulchral moan ever ask, "Tell us if salted butter is better than unsalted in a recipe for a Shiz mincemeat pasty?" Prophetic questions and answers only cared about rules—powers, thrones, pushiness.

Cubbins faded away into a pattern of sedges and paisleys. Brrr was nearly asleep, and then a thought of the ancient oracle known as Yackle intruded upon the artsiness of the mind yielding to dream.

She was so robust in his thoughts that he sat bolt upright. That cunning fiend! In his mind she was more demanding than ever. "Take care of the girl," she'd hectored him not six months ago. "I need you to stand for her, if she needs standing for." She'd been talking about the child of Liir and Candle. None other than Elphaba's granddaughter. But was this girl who showed up—Rain—the right one? The Clock seemed leery of her, according to the dwarf. And Brrr couldn't be sure. He lay down again. Behind his closed eyelids, as the girl stretched and rubbed against his spine and rolled over, he tried to imagine her as green, though in daylight she seemed the same filmy milkweed color of so many Munchkinlanders and Gillikinese.

Clocks are color-blind, thought Brrr. Let the Clock recover its spring and go back to being the conscience of Oz. It can sort out Rain's reality. I'm too tired.

All his previous disasters danced attendance upon him now, a big lousy finish. That nightly inquisition, as character relievedly dissolves into oblivion: *Who are you really?* The Lion had a wife with whom he didn't sleep, not only for the problem of incompatible proportions but because Ilianora was stitched into a finalizing virginity. The Lion had fixated on many humans and Animals alike, and loved only one, Muhlama H'aekeem, an Ivory Tiger. *That* had gone nowhere in a hurry. Had he sired litters? No. His part in the Matter of Dorothy and the death of the Wicked Witch of the West was puzzling to all, himself included—was he an enemy of the state? Or a hero of the nation? Or just an empty space in the world wearing an acceptably impressive mane—that was how he accounted for himself, up and down and be done with it.

So maybe he wasn't capable, he concluded, of fulfilling Yackle's request of him. "Take care of the girl." Why should he? Elphaba had done him no favors, unless you believed those who said he'd been a Lion cub in Shiz, and she and her friends had rescued him from some unsavory experiment in a lab. No way to prove it, of course.

But here was Rain, in her sleep, rudely scratching herself between her buttocks. The Lion could feel the girl's spindly arm. His spine and hers, back to back.

But *why* wasn't he capable? Come on. Lady Glinda had looked after Rain without drawing attention to the matter. And face it, Lady Glinda was hardly Old Mother Glee from the operettas. If Glinda could manage, couldn't Brrr? With Ilianora's help? With or without the dwarf's help, the Clock's advice?

But the Clock had gone somnolent, Brrr remembered. A conscience in a coma.

But but but. The endless clockwork spin of self-doubt.

He had come to no conclusion in his roundabout reflections. Sleep rescued him temporarily from the obligation to fret about it any longer.

3.

The new others were still asleep. Rain picked her way around them: the white-haired woman with the hard-soft face, the goldeny Lion, the little mean man. Also the seven acolytes of the Clock, who were tickling one another in their sleep, she thought.

She didn't miss Glinda. She didn't miss Puggles. She half expected Miss Murth to be lurking under the pines with a face flannel at the ready, but when Murthy didn't show up Rain pushed on. She was intent on climbing back up to the lookout to see what could still be seen of the dragons in the water.

Her mind for a path was clever enough. The light rowed like slanted oars along the way, showing her how to go. It felt good to be out in the world. Not dangerous at all, no matter what Miss Murth had kept saying, especially lately.

Ah, the lake. At this hour its surface steamed black-silver. Green glowed on the hills. Green painted the southern coves like a skin of algae. She noticed smoke above Zimmerstorm, though she was too young to wonder if it signified the remains of a town burned in reprisal. She couldn't see the mansard roofs of Mockbeggar Hall, and she didn't think to look for them.

The dragons were gone. The ice was gone. The ruins of one ship drifted like a broken island. Two of the ships were yoked and listing. The fourth ship was gone, maybe sunk entirely, or paddled to port somewhere out of sight.

She was sorry for the ships but sorrier for the dragons. She bet no one had asked them if they was interested in swimming boats around. She had helped to ice them in—somehow she knew that. She didn't know the word *ashamed,* or even the notion, but she felt punky and wished it hadn't happened. Lady Glinda was in trouble and there weren't no other way; but still.

The bits of timber on water looked like broken letters.

This reminded her of the word man. Cherrystone. Once he had found a book with big letters—whether it was for children or for blindish adults she didn't know—and he had sat it on his knee facing her. She hunched on the floor. He'd taken out his littlish silvery dagger and had used it as a pointer. What's that? The *E.* What's that? The *I?* No, the other one. The *L.* Right? Right. And this? The, um, the one like an *E.* The *F! E-L-F?* Can you spell it so far?

She could, but for some reason she'd shaken her head. She hadn't wanted this to go too fast.

Now she saw a big stick and went to pick it up so she could scrape letters into the pine needles. How to spell *sorry*? The stick wiggled off and she chased it. She knew it had become a snake, but maybe it would hold still and be a stick for her. Maybe it could spell better than she could. "Wait."

It hustled away, but slower, she thought; it was considering her plea. Then it paused and turned its needle head. It was allover green except where it wanted to be brown. Its eye—she could only see one—was a tight shiny opaque black lentil.

She said, "Did you wriggle up from the water this morning? Do you know what happened down there? Is those dragons friends of yours? Is any of them okay?"

The snake lowered its head, perhaps in mourning.

"One of 'em flied away. Did you see that part?"

The snake didn't move, but Rain thought it maybe looked a little interested.

"Oh, it did. I en't got any notion where it flied itself off to. Out beyond the shores over that way."

The snake seemed to be trying to turn a different color, to blend in with the bit of lichen on one side and a scrap of stone on the other, but it was slow work. She squatted down to watch it go. "Whoa-ey. I din't know snakes could shift to green and back agin."

The creature's lidless eyes were baleful and patient. "A lot could go green if they tried harder," it said. "Keep it in mind." Rain reared back, never having met a talking Snake before, nor heard of one even. She thought they were only storylike. The Snake finished its conversion to camouflage, and she couldn't see it anymore.

She missed the Snake but she appreciated the advice. "Right-o," she said to where it had been. "Oh and— sorry."

4.

Rain told them about the ships all ruined, and the dragons, dead or fled. The companions looked at Mr. Boss. He just shrugged.

"Assuming most of the soldiers survived and regrouped on shore, Cherrystone's first order of business will be to find us," said Brrr. Patient as a marmoreal Lion. Though he was finding it hard not to scream. "The Clock predicted a watery rout, remember? And Cherrystone might guess we had a mighty charm for making it come true. We really can't hang around waiting for the Clock to stamp our hall slip."

"Hey, the Lion's right. We've been romping back and forth across hostile ground for the better part of a year now." This from a boy with a chestnut mop. Brrr had never heard him speak before. "With that watery zoo in flames last night, we're going to be everyone's first target of revenge."

The towhead said, "And how. Thankth to the bloody Clock'th little prophethy to the military. That wath a collathal *fucking* mithtake, that wath."

Yet another virgin opinion: "It's time we decided which way—"

The dwarf interrupted the boy. "When *you* start to think about deciding, it's time for you to decide to leave."

"Maybe we will," groused a fourth fellow. "Being wanted in military sabotage is different from being a hand servant to Fate."

"And you can't risk bossing Fate around," spat the dwarf. "You're going to second-guess me, get out. I mean it."

The speaker, a kid shaggy with corkscrews of cobalt black, lost a measure of his resolve. He backed up a step, as if to give the dwarf room to back down too.

"I'm not stopping you," said Mr. Boss, "nor you other fellows. We've managed for years either to negotiate a kind of diplomatic immunity or to squelch out of any cowpie we happen to step into. Our stretch of luck might be over, though. Get used to it or get another hobby."

"But luck, what is luck, up next to Fate—" The boys couldn't wriggle out of the propaganda snarled around their hearts.

"Save yourselves. Last one to leave, put out the moon. You too, daughter." The dwarf pointed a gnarled forefinger at Ilianora. "Nothing's holding you here."

"I'm not going anywhere," she responded. "Yet."

The lads were packed up and ready to leave within the hour. Abandoning their orange camisoles, they hoisted rucksacks on their backs and tied civilian kerchiefs at their necks. They figured to strike out north across the Pine Barrens, avoiding militias of either stripe.

Brrr thought it best. These boys hadn't signed on to become agents provocateurs in some accidental war. Most of the lads had wanted merely to see the world and to claim their importance as acolytes of history. Or to postpone indenture in some family grocery or gravel-and-sand concern.

"You're next," said the dwarf. "Out. Vamoose. Scrammylegs."

"Not without you," said Ilianora. "Mr. Boss, you're not yourself."

"I'm not going anywhere with that ruinous child," said Mr. Boss.

"If we leave, you're not going anywhere, period," observed Brrr. "You just dismissed your backup labor force, and I'm the only one left who can drag that Clock. Unless you're ready to walk away from it."

"Curses," bellowed the dwarf, and demonstrated some.

"Hush," said Ilianora. "If they've really decided to hunt us down, you'll only pinpoint our location for them."

The dwarf went and sat under the wagon.

"I'm all packed," said the Lion to his spouse. "Nothing holding us, I think. Since we seem to be dismissed."

"He rescued me," said Ilianora. "I can't just leave him over this slight difference of opinion."

"Why en't you ask the Clock?" suggested Rain. "If you talked nice to it? What's its name, anyway?"

Ilianora gave the wrinkled wince that, in her, passed for a grin. "Oswald. But I think of it as Oswalda."

Rain went to look at it. "It en't *very* breathy," she admitted, but she walked about it, giving it the benefit of the doubt. From beneath, the dwarf pitched stones at her scraped ankles.

Brrr saw the dragon as a cutthroat charm, a vulgar but effective contrivance of tiktok ingenuity designed to remind gullible audiences of the archaic folk belief known as the Time Dragon. Though himself reared without such nonsense—because self-reared—the Lion had learned of Oz's origin legends well enough. The snot-fired underground creature, asleep in some unreachable cavern, dreaming the universe from its beginning. A fiery fatalism.

And not the only type of fatalism to grip Oz. Other more phlegmatic theories proposed existence as the result of some unholy combustion of oils and embers. Even today, some peasants credited their filthy lot to the dilettantism of Lurline, the Fairy Queen, trying her hand at creating a world. And eggheads smart enough to suffer gout or glaucoma argued that life was a benighted experiment in ethics or cruelty invented by the Unnamed God. But the dragon story was older—so old in folk knowledge that the dragon had no name. Oswald was a *nom de théâtre:* deep fate is always run from behind the curtain, from which we are asked to divert our attention.

Today the dragon of the Clock was inert. A clapped-out heap of oxidizing technology. Could it be a disguise? Oswald had so often seemed a half-creature, sinister in its apparent sense of impulse, decided in its attitude toward wrong and right. The dragon's head had ro-tated like the headlamp of some pedicycle rollicking down the college lanes of Shiz. The jaws snapped in four different positions. None of them smiling. When did conscience smile?

"It looks deaded out," concluded Rain, cheerfully enough.

"Rain, a little less noise," suggested the Lion. No sense in salting the dwarf's wounds.

"Why en't we hunting in the Grimmerie for words to wake 'm up?"

"Couldn't hurt," said Brrr. "I vote yes."

"Suddenly we're a democratic synod? That's what having children does for you? Remind me to neuter myself with a grapefruit spoon." But with what Ilianora had been through, that remark was thoughtless, and despite his distress the dwarf caught himself. "Oh, all right. But I'm not promising to play by any suggestion a stupid book makes, magic or not."

He got the Grimmerie out of a drawer that opened with a pop, as if it had been eager to deliver the book to Rain. "Reading never did much for me, in my line of work," he grumphed.

Ilianora spread her shawl on the needled ground, and Mr. Boss dumped the book upon it. "I don't like to touch the Grimmerie," said the woman, but Rain knelt down before the tome. She put her hands on the cover as if she'd like to hug the thing, and opened the great lid of it.

"It feels hummy. Like moss with sugarbees in it," she said.

"And you look like clot without the cream." The dwarf snorted. "Find what you need to find and close the damn thing up again. It makes me nervous. This book isn't for the likes of us to examine. We're just the keepers."

"Maybe the world is changing," said the Lion, "and it's up to us now."

The dwarf stifled himself as Rain turned the versos. Today each page seemed made of a different sort of paper. Different colors and weights, sieved and pressed with a variety of trash: rag content and straw, string and fuse. To Brrr's eye the hand-lettered words seemed overly hooked and pronged, a foreign language if not, indeed, a foreign alphabet. Though his spectacles needed updating. Sometimes the marginalia designs appeared engaged and in motion, flat little theater pieces performing for themselves. On other pages a single portrait without caption stared out, its eyes moving as the page lifted, wavered, settled, was covered by the next. "How do we even know what we're looking for?" asked the Lion.

"When we find it," said Rain. Simple enough.

Brrr saw it before she did. They had come upon a page that seemed sheathed in ice or glass, across which embossed patterns of frost and snowflake were wheeling, interleaving the way, presumably, the cogs of the Clock did when the Clock was in fettle. The paper glinted with sparkles as of light on snow. Rain said, "Is this calling winter upon water?"

"Who knows?" said Brrr. "No text I can recognize, unless the snowflakes are their own prose. The book has stopped riffling itself, though. Seems to be the destination page, anyway."

The girl agreed; she clasped her hands over the page eagerly as if to warm herself on a winter's afternoon. "Where is my mittens?" she murmured, almost to herself.

The snowflake patterns pulled apart like theater curtains, revealing a dark blue background that filled the whole page, like a night sky during Lurlinemas. Stars shone in midnight ink. "If this is an advertisement for classes in faith formation, honeyclams, I'm taking a match to the whole damn thing," whispered Mr. Boss.

"Shut up," said Brrr politely.

A single dot of white began to grow larger, as if nearing from a great distance across the heavens. It looked like a sort of snow globe, of the type Brrr had seen in the shops at holidays. An ice bubble, maybe? A perfect crystal drop. Hovering. It swelled almost to the margins of the page. When it stopped, they could see that the globe was clear, and a hunched figure imprisoned within.

"The *Z* in the *O*," said Rain.

They couldn't quite tell who it was.

"It's meant to be Lady Glinda," said Mr. Boss, despite himself. "People said she used to come and go by bubble. Though it was really a White Pfenix."

"No, it's meant to be Elphaba, only you can't see she's green," said Ilianora, "not behind that icy white window. It reminds me of her crystal globe at Kiamo Ko."

"It's neither." The Lion didn't know why he felt so decisive about it. "It's Yackle. Old Mother Yackle, the senile sage of the mauntery. She's the one who took up lodging within these very pages, if you recall. And the glass ball—maybe that's what's become of Shadowpuppet—Malky, the glass cat. It has swallowed her up as if she were a bird. Well, she had those wings, remember."

The figure—it was surely a she—pointed out at them as if she could see them from the book. One finger at Brrr, one at Ilianora, one at the dwarf, and one at Rain. With her other hand she collected four upright fingers and bunched them together like asparagus spears tied with string. She gripped them, indicating—quite cleary—*together. Together.*

Then she raised her right hand and pointed over their shoulders. South. She made a shooing motion with her hand, a farmwife annoyed by chickens. Go! *Go. Together. South.*

Flee.

Hurry!

"She could get a job at Ticknor Circus doing charades," admitted the dwarf. "She's pretty good, though who's to say she's not some dybbuk tempting us to our doom?"

The snowflakes began to close in, obscuring the figure. The Grimmerie became stiff, the pages blocked. Nothing to do but close the damn book before the ground around it began to ice up and the Grimmerie froze to the earth.

"I'm going south," said Brrr. "With Ilianora and with Rain. I'll haul the Clock if you choose to come along, Mr. Boss. If you can't bring yourself to join us, well, it's been jolly when it hasn't been a total nightmare."

The dwarf pulled at his hands, all but whimpering, "The Clock said no girl."

"Haven't you ever known a Clock to tell the wrong time?" Though Brrr stopped there.

"All right. I'm beat." The dwarf walked up to Rain; their faces were almost the same height. He waggled a finger. "But hey? Little funny kid? You're not to touch this book again. I don't like that look of entitlement on your smug face."

"It's called reading," she retorted.

Whatever else they griped about—whoever the image had meant to remind them of, and they argued over it—they'd come to agreement about this much, at least: better to be caught on the road headed for other mischief than to be found squatting in a cul-de-sac like mice in a tin bucket. Since the battle for Restwater might be joined again at Haugaard's Keep, to the east, then they'd head around the western tip of the lake, until they could follow the book's advice and turn south.

Now the Lion discovered that the boys had been letting him do all the work since the day he arrived a half a year ago, back when the autumn came upon them to the sound of gunpowder explosions and the odd bugle bravocatory. The harness strained against his shoulders no less than it had last week.

The dwarf walked on one side of the wagon, Rain on the other.

Some lives are like steps and stairs, every period an achievement built on a previous success.

Other lives hum with the arc of the swift spear. Only ever one thing, that dedicated life, from start to finish, but how magnificently concentrated its journey. The trajectory seems so true as to be proof of predestination.

Still other lives are more like the progress of a child scrabbling over boulders at a lakeside—now up, now down, always the destination blocked from view. Now a wrenched ankle, now a spilled sandwich, now a fish-hook in the face.

And that would be my method of locomotion, the Lion concluded. Not diplomas earned, but friendships bungled. Campaigns aborted. Errors in judgment and public humiliations. Not for nothing does the assignment of hauling the Clock of the Time Dragon between the shafts of a wooden cart seem a sort of vacation. A Lion in Oz glows in the gloom: hustlers and harlots, here's your mark! But adjacent to the Time Dragon, however slackened it might be, a Lion could enjoy being overshadowed.

5.

Deciding on a destination always makes the weather improve, or seem to improve. Though the sun remained brutal and the winds weak, and the humidity

felt heaped on like a sodden coat, the uncompanion-
able companions stepped sprightly. The farther they
got from Mockbeggar Hall, the better off they'd be.
The pines gave way to long gravelly stretches, like
dried-up streambeds, perhaps evidence of a flow that
had once moved from Kellswater into Restwater. The
companions camped by day if they could find shade;
by night they trod, wordless and lost but not, Brrr
thought, in despair. Or not yet, anyway. As soon as
the moon sank they stopped and rested too. No matter
how hot it was, Rain slept against Brrr as if she were
his kit.

Some days later, on the horizon, the first of the great
oakhair trees began to lift their frondish heads. Brrr
remembered this terrain from last fall. At noontime,
they came within sight of the mauntery where Brrr
had interviewed Yackle, and she him.

It sat and sulked by itself on its flat, like an armoire
set out on a lawn. It looked deserted, but Brrr didn't
propose going nearer to satisfy his curiosity. Neither
did anyone else. They kept to one side of the establishment, pushing south, deeper into the oakhair forest.

Ilianora carried the scythe the boys had sometimes
wielded and she knocked down what bracken she could.
If shadier, the woods were stiller, too. More spiders.

Brrr hated spiders, but Rain scurried sideways to peer through each fretted oculus.

"What are you looking for?" he heard Ilianora ask her once.

"I don't know," the girl said. "The spider world. The world the spider sees. The other world."

"Little goose." Ilianora takes such a fond tone when trashing the dreams of the young, Brrr observed. "Little monkey. Little moron. There is no other world. This world is enough."

"Of course no one asks me my opinion about other worlds," growled Mr. Boss. "I who actually have traveled a good deal wider than some."

"Well?" Rain rarely addressed the dwarf. "What would you say?"

He glowered at the girl, as if she were responsible for the Clock having suffered its rigor mortis. "Ah, what I could say, were I free to spill the beans."

"Don't fill her head with nonsense," snapped Ilianora. "It's unkind."

"What about that Dorothy?" asked Rain. "En't she from the other world?"

"Who told you anything about *her*?" asked the dwarf.

"Murthy did. When Lady Glinda was busy twisting her hair with that hot fork."

"I knew it," said Brrr, shaking his natural curls.

"Wherever she was from, Dorothy was a stooge of the Wizard," said Ilianora. "She did his bidding, from what I heard. She killed Auntie Witch—"

She paused. Brrr rarely heard her mention Elphaba Thropp. He knew his wife well enough to guess that the phrase *Auntie Witch,* rising to her own lips, had startled her. He swished his tail in his wife's face to amuse her. She blinked at him in a noncommittal way.

"Dorothy could have come from anywhere," he drawled. "There's a lot of Oz untraveled by the likes of Ozians. More outback than city centre in Oz, no? And beyond the sands, Fliaan and Ix, and other murky badlands too impossible to imagine."

"That's not what Murth says," protested Rain. "She says Dorothy was from the *Other Land.* You can't get there by a cart. Just by magic."

"It's a one-way ticket, honey," said Mr. Boss. "Trust me on this one." He turned his pocket out as if looking for a chit for the return voyage: nothing.

"Dorothy went back, though."

"Hah. They probably topped her and tumbled her in some hole. And made up another story. Just like they did to Ozma. People will believe anything if it's impossible enough."

"Don't," said Brrr. "Let Rain learn the world the same way we all did."

"The scientific method of child rearing? Analysis by trial and terror?" The dwarf cracked his knuckles. "Move aside, Lion. I'm going for a walk. I can't sit here and listen to you corrupt a child with the limits of logic. You're all boobs and bobbycats."

He humped himself straight through the big spider-web that Rain had been examining. Then he turned around and said, "Look, little wastrel girl. I'm on *the other side*. And what's the news? It stinks over here, too."

The Lion whispered to his spouse, "Is he going to hold against Rain until she's old enough to jab him one between the eyes?"

"Who likes being cut out of the future?" she replied. "The Clock is giving no opinions—so how does he learn his way?"

"The same as the rest of us. Dread, shame, and luck."

When he came back, forty minutes later, Mr. Boss had a wife in tow. His own wife. An unregenerate Munchkinlander whom Brrr believed he'd met before. The woman, like many of her kind, was compact, half as wide as she was tall, slightly bowed of leg, a face like a dented saucepan. Some sort of weed in her hands—she'd been collecting herbs, maybe. She stumped forward into the clearing with the confidence of a woodcutter.

It took him a moment to place her. "Sister Apothecaire. As I live and breathe. I thought you'd taken a vow of chastity?"

"I accidentally left it behind in the mauntery when you carried me off in that cart six months ago. Oh well. Whoever finds it can keep it; I'm through with it. Anyway, mind your own beeswax."

Ilianora turned to look. "It's good to see you so recovered."

"From my fall down the stairs? Or from my life as a maunt? Never mind. Now I appreciate that you were kind to carry me and my cracked noggin away from the mauntery before the EC forces arrived. Being a Munchkinlander, I might've been taken hostage. As I remember, I was rather cranky at the time, though. With some relief you passed me over to a team of women wheelers on their way to the EC for a championship tournament. I stayed with them for a few weeks, as they rehearsed their moves in a farmer's meadow northwest of here," explained Sister Apothecaire. "After a while, I realized even sports competitions are essentially political in nature. Who needs it. Besides, as a Munchkinlander I was too short to keep up with the team. So I found an abandoned woodman's lean-to and made do."

"Did you give no thought to returning to your roots in Munchkinland?" asked Ilianora. "Or repairing to the motherchapel in the Emerald City?"

"The motherhouse? Don't make me laugh. *They've* been co-opted by the Emperor's religious diktats for years. I'm not bowing to fix the sandal of the Emperor Apostle, no sirree. I may be short but I'm not that short. As to Munchkinland, I don't have many relatives left in Center Munch. They were all ruined by the effects of that twister that passed through when I was a child. The one that carried that little fiend of the winds, Dorothy. So I'm an orphan spinster apostate, and this morning I woke up all alone, until I met Mr. Boss, who has improved my prospects."

"I have no intention of improving anyone's prospects," said the dwarf, "my own included. That's why I married you. Someone to share a similarly sour outlook, or even degrade it some. This lot is entirely too rosy now. They're going to break into song any moment. They've even taken on a child to raise."

"Ha," said Ilianora. "No one raises that girl. We're escorting her to safety. That's all."

At this Rain looked neither right nor left. She just kept studying the bole of a tree in which a squirrel might live, or an owl, or a chipmunk. Something secret, animal, magical. Unrelated.

"The curse of parenthood. As if the world can be safe." The dwarf almost smiled at his traveling companions. "Anyway, you all can come back to our little hovel-in-the-hellebore and we'll serve you an omelet. Her specialty is plover's eggs and scallions."

"It was all I was ever able to find," confessed Sister Apothecaire. "I'm neither a hunter nor a gatherer, it seems. I'm more of a pantry parasite. Though I can bake a captivating muffin, given the right ingredients."

They accepted the invitation. "Congratulations," said Brrr to the dwarf as they walked along. "If I had a cigar, I'd give it to you to smoke in honor of your impending nuptial experience."

"Oh, we've already consummated our union," he replied.

Brrr raised an eyebrow.

"I'm a dwarf on a lonely road and I've been giving my life to this fool contraption as if there was something in it for me. She's a Munchkinlander maunt who has been celibate since before her first milk tooth came in. Put it this way: we were ready."

Well, thought the Lion. Bested at that game, too. By a dwarf, no less.

They approached the cottage in the woods, a ragged-roofed thing covered in old oakhair leaves. "Are you going to stay here?" asked Brrr. "Taking up the life of a retired husband? Collecting scallions instead of being bishop of the book, dragoman of the dragon?"

"Of course not. After a hundred years of service, or whatever it's been—it's felt that long anyway—I want to see this escapade to its natural end. Wifey can wait for me or come along, makes no difference to me. Ours is not a very strong marriage. Still, I love her, in my way."

Mr. Boss grinned at his four-square bride. "What's your name before you became Sister Apothecaire?"

She squinted, and put a finger to her lips. "I forget. In faith classes, they called me Little Daffodil."

"Little Daffy. I like it. Well, come on, Little Daffy; let's break out the best linen and tap a keg of springwater for our guests. It's a wedding party, after all."

Rain was skeptical about the newcomer. Her hard little face was like an old rye loaf left out in the sun. But in general the girl didn't care for people, so her specific apprehensions of Little Daffy came and went, uncataloged, evanescent.

Brrr murmured to Ilianora, "Maybe this is our opportunity to peel off. Who would have guessed it?

After all this time, our confirmed bachelor takes a wife."

"Perhaps, the Clock being somnolent, he needed something else to nag him, and a wife serves that function handily," said Ilianora, coming as close as she ever did to joking. Still, there was something to it.

After a slap-up supper Mr. Boss readied himself to get back on the road. Little Daffy went inside to tie on a fresh apron. Brrr admitted to being dubious about taking on another liability.

"*You* saddled us with a child, and you're second-guessing me about picking up a wife?" The dwarf raised his fists at the Lion. "I've had it with you. Come on. Last one standing. It's time to settle this."

"I merely mean that your ladyfriend should be told about the danger we're in," said Brrr. He wasn't going to fight a dwarf. He had no chance against that pipsqueak barbarian.

Ilianora said, "Listen, you louts, I'll just lay out the details and let Little Daffy decide for herself." She called Little Daffy from the cottage and made short work of it. "One. We're probably wanted for aiding in the sabotage of the Emperor's fleet of ships on Restwater. Two. They'll guess we have the Grimmerie with us, since the damage done was substantial. Three. The Clock is broken, and we can't rely on its advice. Four, the Grimmerie won't open for us anymore, once it gave us its advice to go south. So we're on our own."

"South?" That was the only part that made Little Daffy blink. "The mud people? Munchkinlanders don't venture into the clammy zone. Offends our sense of rectitude, both moral and hygienic. Why not west? I know some decent Scrowfolk who would hide us a while."

"The advice was south," said Brrr, "and that's where we're headed."

"The advice was also to keep miles away from wretched girl-children," interrupted Mr. Boss, "so this enterprise already starts off on a bad footing."

"I'm going south, with the Clock or without it," said Brrr, "so if you want to stay with the Clock and you want me to pull it for you, the matter's settled. Little Daffy, join us or not, but make up your mind now."

6.

The Munchkin woman decided in favor of adventure, to see if her marriage would hold. Before she left the woodcutter's shed, she buried a spoon in the soil beside the doorsill. She explained: an old Munchkinlander custom before travel was undertaken. If you ever make it home, there'll be something to eat with, even if the only thing left to eat is dirt.

"Lady Glinda could cook dirt," said Rain.

Highsummer turned into Goldmonth, though Brrr insisted that up north the season was known as Tattersummer, for the fringing of the leaves by insects. Little Daffy countered that in Munchkinland these late summer days were called Harvest Helltime, as farmers struggled to get crops in before thunderstorms or the occasional dustbillow. "Munchkinland is losing acres of good soil to the desert every year," she clucked. "If the EC really intends to polka on down and set up housekeeping, they'll need a good broom."

Rain listened to pictures more than people. Spoons in the ground, thunderstorms, dustbillows. The use of a good broom. The complexity of the world's menace was daunting, but perhaps she'd learn to read it as she had learned her letters. First step of reading, after all, is looking.

Eight-foot spiderwebs toward the southern edge of the oakhair forest. The Lion squealed whenever he stumbled into them, but Rain loved them. If she found them before they were battered by her companions, she looked through them, to see what she could see.

It was, indeed, like peering through a window. From one side, she was a human-ish enough girl looking in to the spider world. She saw spiders with short eyelashy legs and spiders with thoraxes like lozenges. Spider-mites with bodies so small you couldn't even make them out, but who sported legs that could span a skillet.

Hello, little capery-leg. And how do you do today?

What Rain didn't see, and she kept looking, was groups of spiders. Did spiders have attachments? Other than to their webs? She watched each silvery gumdrop sink on its strings, but when the spider climbed back up, nobody else was ever home. Any guests who blundered into their threaded nets became supper, which seemed unsociable.

Spiders had nerve, and speed, and art of a sort, but they had no friends. They didn't go get married just like that.

From the other side of the web, being a spider, Rain peered back at the humans, to see in pictures what she could see.

For instance. The dwarf had called Ilianora "daughter" one time too many, so Little Daffy wondered if the veiled woman actually was his child. Ilianora was miffed. "Mr. *Boss*? Are you joking? My father was a prince, for all the good it did him."

Everything looked like something. So what did this look like now? Mr. Boss looked like he'd been stung by a flying scorpion. His lips were blown out and bitten back.

Little Daffy looked suddenly ravished with interest by her fingernails.

As a spider, Rain thought Mr. Boss and Little Daffy looked like tiny little matching grandparents, sour as mutual crab apples. They looked like they were playing at living. Or was this living? Rain wasn't sure. She stayed out of the dwarf's way as much as she could.

She heard Brrr and Ilianora talk quietly, out of range of the dwarf and the Munchkin, but not out of the range of a spider's attention. Ilianora proposed that, given the Clock's new reticence, being married was a legitimate diversion for a dwarf at loose ends. Surely?

"That attitude toward marriage makes of our union a slight mockery, don't you think?" Brrr purred Ilianora up the side of her neck. "Anyway, they're at it like a tomcat and the parish whore. Every night. It's embarrassing."

"He's got to do something. He's not the type to take up knitting by a fireside, is he?"

Rain turned her head. The dwarf was pitching a penknife into a tree trunk at forty feet. His face was sweaty, his raveling beard in need of a shampoo. He didn't look as if he would favor doing piecework.

"At least he's stopped fussing so much over Rain," continued Ilianora. "The book's told us *what* to do—stick together, head south—but not why. You and I aren't captives, though. If you have any other ambitions once we ditch the Grimmerie somewhere safe, spell them out."

Do I care what they do? wondered Rain, and couldn't think of an answer.

"I can't go back to the Emerald City unless I'm willing to hand over the Grimmerie to them," said Brrr. "Otherwise I'll be thrown in Southstairs, and it won't be pretty. You've told me how unpretty it would be, in no uncertain terms."

"I don't want to talk about Southstairs." Ilianora's face turned a shade of stubbornness no spider had ever seen before. "I was asking you about your ambitions. No interest in your companions on the Yellow Brick Road? That Scarecrow, the Tin Woodman?"

"The Scarecrow has all but disappeared. I suppose straw succumbs to mold and weevils. And last I heard, the Tin Woodman is still a labor agitator in Shiz. Wish he could organize our mechanical conscience here. Fat chance of that. Really, that Matter of Dorothy was a sorry passage, let me tell you. In a generally sorry life."

"Mine hardly prettier. After prison, to slip from doing resistance work into writing fanciful stories for a while. The dilettante's gavotte, I think one would call it."

Rain saw their faces screw up more complicated, pancakes trying to become soufflés. Faces bloated, contorted, deflated, endlessly in disguise. Tiresome but curious.

"That General Cherrystone at Mockbeggar Hall?" Brrr spoke in a softer voice; he didn't know spiders have good hearing. "Cherrystone was the one who kidnapped you when you weren't that much older than Rain is now. He didn't recognize you all grown up, I know. But do you feel—in that vault of your heart— the yearning for vengeance?"

Ilianora held her tongue for what seemed to Rain like a couple of years, but finally she spoke. "We took a risk walking into Mockbeggar Hall carrying the Grimmerie right under Cherrystone's nose. I believed Mr. Boss when he said the book was only on tempo- rary loan to Lady Glinda. Getting it safely out of there, away from Cherrystone's hands, seemed the more cru- cial objective. If the day arrives when I'm ready to take vengeance on him for slaughter—of my family—well, I suspect I'll know it. It'll come clear to me, privately, all in good time."

Secret knowledge, thought Rain. My head hurts.

"As for now," continued Ilianora, "let history have its way: I'm only a bystander. A dandelion, a spider, nothing more."

"We aren't aimless. We have a goal," the Lion reminded her. "We're keeping the Grimmerie out of the hands of the Emperor of Oz. We're heading south, as the book advised. And, incidentally, whether Mr. Boss likes it or not, we're rescuing the girl."

At this they both looked up at her, and Rain found the spiderweb too thin between them. It had become a gunsight that focused her in its crosshairs. Their look of affection was brazen. To break the spell of their myopia, to divert them, she brayed, "I want to keep reading but we got no books. You write stories? Write me some words I can practice on."

"I don't write anymore," said Ilianora in one of those voices. "Ask someone else."

"Who's to ask?" Rain felt fussed and hot. "The world en't gonna write nothing for me. No words in the clouds. No printed page among these dead leaves. Can a spider write letters in a web?"

"What nonsense," said the dwarf from his distance, pitching his knife through the web a few feet above her head, severing a prominent girder so it collapsed like shucked stockings. "That would be some spider."

7.

They didn't dawdle but they moved without haste. The Lion had concluded that attention must still be centered upon the battle for Restwater, since goons with guns hadn't shown up yet. A few days on, as they entered the hardscrabble terrain known as the Disappointments, they spotted the next oddkin, the latest of Oz's free-range lunatiktoks. "It was ever thus," the dwarf averred.

"No, war is driving the entire country nuts," replied the Lion.

The creature seemed to be a woman, sitting in the only tree on this wide stony plain. She held an umbrella for shade and protection from the rains. Evidence of a cookfire in one direction, a latrine in the other. The place was open enough to appear attractive to lightning. Perhaps she wanted to go out in a blaze of glory.

She scrambled down when they approached and stood her ground. She wore what had once been a rather fine dress of white duck with cerulean blue piping, though the skirt had gone grey and brown. That's a useful camouflage, thought Brrr. A starched blue bib rode against her bosom. Her shoes were torn open at the toe. "Hail," she said, and stuck her arm out in a salute, and chopped it once or twice. Her eyes wobbled like puddings not fully set.

The hair piled up on her head reminded Rain of a bird's nest; the girl half expected a beaky face to peer out from above. She all but clapped with joy.

"Let me guess. You are the Queen of the Disappointments," said the dwarf. "Well, given our recent history, we must be your loyal subjects." He spat, but not too rudely.

She looked left and right as if someone might be listening. She appeared familiar to Brrr, but he imagined that most loopy individuals seem recognizable. They mirror the less resolved aspects of ourselves back at us, and the shock of recognition—of ourselves in their eyes—is a cruel dig.

"Are you all right?" asked Ilianora. Ever the tender hand, especially for a female in trouble, Brrr knew.

The woman cawed and flapped her arms. They saw she had stitched some sort of a blanket of feathers to her white serge sleeves.

"Wingses!" said Rain happily.

"She's so far round the bend, she's back home already," muttered Mr. Boss.

"Hush, husband," said Little Daffy. "Hold your snickering; she's dehydrated. In need of salts, powder of cinnabar, a tiny dose. Also a brew of yellowroot and garlic to take care of the conjunctivitis." She dove her hands into her waistband, inspecting the contents of pockets sewn on the inside of her skirt. She had, after all, been a professional apothecaire. "Heat up some water in the pot, Ilianora, and I'll shave up a few herbs and hairy tubers for the poor Bird Woman."

The woman wasn't much frightened by them. After several sips of something red and cloudy that Mr. Boss offered from his private flask, she blinked and rubbed dust out of her eyes as if she were just coming up to room temperature. When she opened her mouth, it was not to twitter but to speak more or less like a fellow citizen. "God damn fuckheads," she said. "Give me some more of that juice."

"That's the ticket," said Mr. Boss, obliging.

She lifted her chin at the Clock. "What's that thing, then? A portable guillotine?"

"That's as good a word for it as any," said the dwarf. "A cabinet of marvels, once upon a better time."

The Bird Woman looked it up and down and walked around it on her toes. That accounts for the condition of the boots, Brrr thought.

"No. I know what this is. I've heard tell of it. Never thought it would feature in my path. It's the Clock of the Time Dragon, isn't it? What are you doing dragging it out here in Forsaken Acres?" She ruffled her wings as she stepped about, like a marabou stork.

"Brought it here to die," he said. "And what are you doing here?"

"Oh, more or less the same thing," she replied. "Isn't that the general ambition of living things?"

"Hush, there's a child," said Ilianora.

The Bird Woman peered at her. "So there is. How grotesque." She put out a hand and rubbed the side of the Clock. "I figured this sort of entertainment went out once they started doing girlie shows in Ticknor Circus."

Mr. Boss made a point of humphing. "This isn't a sort of anything. It's sui generis."

She took on the expression of a crazed docent. "You're small and barky but you don't know everything. This Clock is the latest and maybe the most famous of a long line of tiktok extravaganzas. They used to circulate several hundred years ago in the hamlets of Gillikin, telling stories of the Unnamed God. Such contrivances specialized in the conversion stories of the Saints. Saint Mettorix of Mount Runcible, who was martyred when a coven of witches flew overhead and dropped frozen cantaloupes onto his scalp. Saint Aelphaba of the Waterfall, you probably have heard of her. Hidden from sight for decades, emergent at last, in some versions. Also Saint Glinda."

"I know the tale of Saint Glinda, thank you for nothing," said Little Daffy. "I spent my professional life in the mauntery of Saint Glinda in the Shale Shallows."

"A sordid little tale of grace through glamour," said the Bird Woman dismissively. "Then, little by little, as unionism rooted more deeply in the provinces, the tiktok trade became secular, pretending toward prophecy and secret-spilling."

"We specialized in history and prophecy in conjunction with civic conscience." Mr. Boss sounds like a traveling salesman, thought Brrr.

"Charlatanism," insisted the Bird Woman. "And sometimes dangerous. The masters of traveling companies used to send their acolytes ahead to sniff out local gossip, so the puppets could be seen to imitate the bellyaches of real life."

"I never needed to do that," said Mr. Boss. "Different organizing principle entirely. Real magic, if you don't mind. The rough stuff."

"You only carried on all these years because there was a tradition to hide behind," said the harridan. "You're the last one and you stick out like a sore behind. People have got to be asking why. Especially in times like this."

"Doesn't matter what people say. Anyway, you're right about one thing: this famous Clock has had it. The tok is divorced from the tik."

"It's not dead yet," she said.

"I didn't come for a second opinion," said the dwarf. "What are you, a witch doctor?"

"I know a thing or two about spells, as it happens."

"Who are you?"

"I used to have a name, and it used to be Grayce Graeling. But without a social circle, a name quickly becomes moot, I realized. So never mind about me."

"How do you know about spells?" asked Ilianora. "Seems to be a dying art in Oz."

"What do you expect, with the Emperor wanting to husband all the magic in his own treasury?" chirped the Bird Woman. "It's not going to work, of course. Magic doesn't follow those rules. It carves its own channels. But why don't you fire this thing up and show me what you've got?"

"I told you, it's paralyzed. Maybe dead," said Mr. Boss.

"Can you fly?" asked Rain.

"It isn't dead. I should know. I could tell you a thing or two about spells. I taught magic once, I was on the faculty at Shiz several yonks ago. I was never very skilled, mind you, but I was a devoted teacher to my girls, and I picked up more than anyone credited."

"The entire former faculty of Shiz seems to retire to the suburbs," observed Brrr. "Did you know a Professor Lenx? And Mister Mikko?"

"I knew how to lace up a boot from across a room," she said. "I knew how to produce crumpets and tea in fifteen seconds, for when a trustee arrived unexpectedly in one's chambers. I knew that Elphaba Thropp, once upon a while."

"Oh, sure you did," said Mr. Boss. "Seems like everyone in Oz knew her. Can't walk across the street without running into someone from the alumnae association. By the math of it, there were seventy thousand people who entered Shiz that year with her."

"How high can you fly?" asked Rain.

"She wasn't so special," said the Bird Woman, picking a nit from her feathers and looking at it with something like avarice. She didn't eat it, just flicked it off her thumb. "She was an ordinary girl with a talent for mischief and more serious complexion issues than sick bay knew what to do with. What happened to her in the end was a crime."

"What happens to all of us in the end is a crime," said Mr. Boss. "Take it up with the authorities."

"I tell you, this instrument isn't quite done," she insisted. "Or maybe it's just responding to me and my long dormant talents. Open it up. I haven't had an entertainment in months."

"What are you doing here? Did you fly here?" asked Rain.

The dwarf shrugged his shoulders and turned to Ilianora. "Well, Miss Mistress of the Mysteries, unstrap the belts, like the good old times. I'll wind up some cranks and see if she responds."

"Do you live in a nest?" Rain asked.

"Hush, child, don't ask personal questions," said the Lion.

"That's the only kind I have," said Rain.

"I know you," said the Bird Woman to Brrr.

"I had a feeling you would," he replied.

"You worked for the Emperor. You scab."

"I was in a bit of a legal squeeze. That's all over now."

Hunching down before the stage, she paid Brrr no further attention. Rain went and squatted next to her, and tried to angle her elbows out to mimic the Bird Woman. "Can you lay an egg?"

"Any eggs get laid around here, let the dragon do it," said Mr. Boss, huffing. "Well, what do you know. Some phantom juice left in the gears, after all. You aren't as flighty as you seem, Queen Birdbrain."

"I could paint stationery with butterflies and lilac sprays and shit like that," said the Bird Woman, "without picking up a paintbrush. I wasn't good at controlling the flow of watercolors, though. They tended to puddle."

"Don't we all. Grab your privates and say your prayers, folks. Here she goes." The dwarf went round to release some final clasps and rebalance the counter-weights. "What do you say," he called, "if it comes to life and tells us to give the girl to the hermit lady as a present? We'll call it magic, eh?"

Rain looked around. Her expression was intense and occluded. "He doesn't mean it," said the Lion, without conviction.

A wobble, a spasm, the sound of a pendulum wide of its arc and striking the casing. The shutters folded back, courtesy of magnets on tracks. Brrr and Ilianora exchanged glances. This should cheer up the dwarf.

"If today's matinee has anything about the Emperor in it, I'm walking out, and I want a full refund," declared the woman who had been Grayce Graeling.

"Shhh," said Rain.

The dragon at the top of the cabinet moved one of his wings in a stiff way, as if arthritis had set in. His head rolled. One eye had become loose in its socket, for the look was cross-eyed and almost comical. Little Daffy began to giggle, but Ilianora put her hand on the woman's wrist. The dwarf wouldn't like to hear laughter. The Clock wasn't a device for comedy.

The main stage whitened with a camphorous fog. A backdrop unrolled but got stuck halfway down. Hanging in midair against another scrim, one of rushes and cattails, the scene was of a tiled floor in some loggia.

Brrr muttered to Ilianora, "Should someone go forward and give it a tug?" but she shook her head.

On an invisible track a cradle came forward, rocking. An ornate ⓩ was carved on its headboard. Over it stood a puppet of a roundish man with a pair of oily mustaches ornamentally twirled in bygone fashion. He took out a handkerchief and blew his nose, possibly signaling grief. The sound that came was less nasal than industrial, like a train whistle. He didn't notice. He was just a puppet on rusty wires.

He was moving, he was turning this way and that, but he was just a puppet. He had no life. Brrr could tell that Rain was disappointed.

Down from the fly space dropped a cutout of a hot-air balloon with a smooth-cheeked charlatan grinning and waving a cigar. "It's the arrival of the Wizard," said Brrr. "I'd know any cartoon of him, for in real life he was hardly more than a cartoon."

Ilianora turned her back.

"The mustached marionette below must be Pastorius, the Ozma Regent," decided Brrr.

"Who's that?" asked Rain.

"The father of Ozma, the infant queen of Oz when the Wizard arrived. She was just a baby, see, and her father was to rule in her place until she grew old enough to take the throne. Shhh, and watch."

The Ozma Regent picked up his motherless infant. He carried the bundle of swaddle to stage right.

Out from the wings hobbled a creature dressed in a cloak all of sticks, small sticks bound together with thread. Her head was carved from a rutabaga and the stain had darkened, so she looked like a creature made entirely of wood. She wore a pale red scarf pulled over her head and tied at the nape of her twiggy hair. She lurched and grinned—her teeth were made of old piano keys, four times too large for her face, and yellowed, foxed with age—but the grip with which she yanked the baby from the father was fierce. She backed up off the stage in a crude motion. A duck walking backward: impossible.

"Some local wet nurse to lend a helping—" began Brrr, not liking the menace of this twig witch. Everyone who tries to help a child is a kidnapper in the last analysis, he thought.

Pastorius turned and made as if to mop his brow in relief, but the Wizard pointed his cigar at the Ozma Regent and cocked his thumb. A little tiny noise of firecracker went off, no louder than an urchin lad's Celebration Day bombcrack candy. The Regent fell over dead. The cords that had moved the puppet ruler were severed, so he rolled with more than just theatrical gravity. The Wizard put his cigar in his mouth and puffed genuine smoke, but it smelled like bacon. A spark caught on a curtain.

The Lion didn't care to preserve any theater of the dramatic arts. Still, the Clock was the hidey-home of the Grimmerie, and he couldn't stand by and watch *that* go up in flames. He leaped up and put out the fire by sucking his own tail for a few seconds and applying the wet mass against the nascent flame. The smell was filthy.

"Show's over folks," he said over his shoulder. "There's nothing to see here. Exit to the left, through the gift shop, and please, not a word to the late afternoon crowd. Don't spoil it for them."

Ilianora turned back. "Did that end as unpersuasively as it began?"

"Pretty much," said the Lion.

"What did it say about the Bird Woman?"

"That was the funny part," said Brrr. "It didn't seem to know she was here."

"Like any old spouse," said Mr. Boss, coming around from behind. "It's unresponsive. It's just going through the motions. I bet it showed some tired revelation from decades ago. I hate revivals. What was it about?"

"The fall of the House of Ozma," insisted the Bird Woman. "Our sorry history. The Wizard arrived just as Pastorius was packing the infant Ozma away for safekeeping to some old hag. The Wizard did the Ozma Regent in with some sort of firearm. That part is history, the murder of the Regent, I mean. The rest is apocrypha. My guess is that the Wizard probably slaughtered the baby too. Fie, fie on the myth that she's hidden, sleeping in some cave to return in our darkest hour. How dark does the hour have to get? Bunk. Bunk and hokum and sweet opiate for suffering fools. The Wizard was too canny to let a baby get away under the tinderwood fingertips of some rural wet nurse."

"Did you ever meet the Wizard?" asked the dwarf. "That brigand?"

"I never had the *pleasure*." The Bird Woman spat out the word as if it were an insect found swimming in her iced lemon-fresher.

"He came to Oz looking for the Grimmerie," said the dwarf. "This book has a mighty broad reputation, to attract miscreants like that from beyond the margins of the known world."

"And we lost our royal family in the bargain," cawed the hermit. "That book has a lot to answer for, and so does whoever stowed it in Oz. To get it safely removed from some other paradise. Not in my backyard, is that the saying? But it got dumped here. And you're its minder. You should be ashamed."

Mr. Boss didn't like this line of contempt. "But the Clock said nothing about *you*?" He stroked his beard with both hands. "The Clock is charmed to respond to the stimuli of the audience of the moment. It makes no sense for it to present a repeat performance. It's never done that before."

"It was fun," said Rain, "but not as good as the dragon in the lake last time."

"How long have you been out of touch?" asked the woman. "Do you know what's going on in the Emerald City?"

"We're clueless," said Brrr. "Surprise us with the truth."

"The Emperor of Oz—you know about him? No?"

"Of course. Shell Thropp. The younger brother of Elphaba and Nessarose. What about him?"

"He's issued a proclamation. Your magic dragon couldn't reveal that to you? Ha. Oh yes, the Emperor has called in to the palace all implements of magic the length and breadth of Oz. Every magic whittling knife, every charmed teapot that never runs dry. Every codex of ancient spells, every gazing ball, every enchanted pickle-fork. He has forbidden magic in Oz."

"He can't do that," said Brrr, thinking about what he knew of the law—which wasn't much.

"He can't do that," said Mr. Boss, whose tone implied he meant that the ambition was beyond any emperor, of Oz or other-Oz. "He might as well ask people to part with their ancestors, or the glint in their eyes. Or their skepticism. It's not gonna happen."

"Nonetheless, he has done it." The Bird Woman began to look twitchy, her eyes went more hooded. "No doubt he'll send out agents to round up those who taught in college, long ago. For debriefing. And though I spent a stint as an organist at chapel, I'm as much at risk as you are." She began to shriek like a demented mongoose.

"Stop that," said Ilianora. "What difference does it make if you taught magic once, or if you accompanied a choir? You're here, among friends. We wouldn't report you even if we were headed north into his receiving parlors. But we're going south. We have our own reason to stay out of the way of the Emperor and his forces."

"He'll find you, wherever you go."

"Oh, we can get pretty damn lost," said Mr. Boss. "Trust me."

"He has no governance over *me*," said Little Daffy. "I'm a Munchkinlander."

"I'm not anything," said Rain. "Yet. I'll be a crow. Can I climb up in your tree with you? Can you teach me to fly?"

The deranged woman finally looked at the girl. "What are you flailing at me for?"

"No one gits me anything to read, and I got to practice my letters," said Rain.

Something of the teacher she had once been made the Bird Woman glare at them all, as if they'd confessed to abusing the child with castor oil. "I have a pen and a pot of ink. I shall write you your name so you know it when you see it on a writ of arrest. Get away from this lot, child. They're headed for a cliff edge at quite the gallop."

"Oh, look who's telling the future now," scoffed the dwarf. "You going to take her off our hands?"

"Nothing doing," said Brrr, "if you want to keep *having* hands, Mr. Boss."

The Bird Woman was as good as her word. She wrote a number of words for Rain: the names of Brrr, and Ilianora; of Little Daffy and Mr. Boss; of Rain, too.

"Anyone else important in your life?"

Rain shook her head.

"What about Lady Glinda?" asked Ilianora, but Rain showed no sign of hearing.

The Bird Woman wrote, finally, *Grayce Graeling.*

"That was me before I was a bird," she told them. "So if they ask you if you ever met me, you can say no."

"Is that g-r-a-y or g-r-e-y?" said Brrr, whose spectacles were in his other weskit.

"The orthographics have it several ways," she said. "I vary it for reasons of disguise. Now I prefer Graeling, using both vowels, because it sounds more like a bird."

"They all sound the same," said Rain. Grayce Graeling regarded Rain as if she were a conveniently placed spittoon, but she wrote out some extra words on a piece of paper so that Rain could practice reading. "Is this a magic spell?" the girl asked her.

"Don't let me get sappy on you, but when you get right down to it, every collection of letters is a magic spell, even if it's a moronic proclamation by the Emperor. Words have their impact, girl. Mind your manners. I may not know how to fly but I know how to read, and that's almost the same thing."

"I know *that*," Rain declared, sourly, grabbing the paper. "I seen some books before."

"Even if it's broken, I'd keep that Clock out of sight, were I you," warned Grayce Graeling. "The Emperor doesn't want anyone else to have any toys. You're courting trouble."

"Nosy crow. None of your business," said Mr. Boss.

The Bird Woman began to scale her tree. "Mind what I say. I have a friend or two in high places." She pointed to some birds flailing against the blue, way up there.

"Are you coming with us too?" asked Rain, who thought she'd discovered the Company's new everyday trick, collecting lunatics. Behind Grayce Graeling, the other travelers made X-ing gestures at Rain with their hands.

8.

"Why din't she come along? She coulda taught us to fly," groused Rain.

"The book said us four," said Brrr. "Remember? Four fingers, to the south?"

"Then what about her?" Rain pointed over her shoulder at Little Daffy.

"The book meant me too," said Little Daffy. "I was hidden there in that spook-lady's gesture, probably. The figure you described in the *O.* I was small, the thumb. You couldn't see me in the prophecy, but I was there."

"The blind, the lame, the halt, the criminally berserk," said Mr. Boss. "You have to stop somewhere or you don't have friends, you have a nation."

The next day, meandering across the Disappointments, they kept looking back to make sure the Bird Woman wasn't pacing after them. "Is them her friends?" Rain asked, over and over, of any local wren or raven, until the others stopped answering and the girl fell silent.

They paused for supper when the heat of the day finally began to lift a little. As the adult females organized a meal, the Lion rested his sore muscles and slept quickly, deftly, for a few minutes. Then he told them, "I emerge from my snooze remembering who the Bird Woman is. Or was."

"Ozma herself, that's it," said Little Daffy. "A hundred years old but holding the line nicely. Am I right? Ya think?"

"She was the archivist in Shiz who helped me look at Madame Morrible's papers," said Brrr. "A gibbertyflibbet if ever I saw one, the kind of person who enters a café with such fluster and alarm one would think she'd never been out in a public space before. Frankly, I doubt she possesses enough talent at spells to have had to bother going dotty at the Emperor's prohibition of magic."

The dwarf lit his pipe and drew on it, releasing an odor of cherry tobacco cut with heart-of-waxroot. "Never underestimate the capacity of a magician to go dotty. Occupational hazard."

"Maybe news has gotten out somehow. News that the Grimmerie has emerged from hiding. Makes me nervous, this impounding of sorcerers' tools. If the Emperor has lowered a moratorium on items of magic, on the practicing of spells—if Shell has called for a surrender of instruments and such—perhaps he's trying to coax the Grimmerie in by default."

"Or make its presence in a barren landscape glow and shriek, so he can find it more easily," said Mr. Boss. "I take your point. Our instruction to move south may prove to have been sound. We'll keep going.

"But not tonight," he said to Rain, who hopped up and was ready to run ahead. She was happy with her scrap of paper. Ilianora had shown her how to fold it into a paper missile, and Rain had spent the afternoon launching it and chasing it, finding it and trying to read it, launching it and chasing it again. "Settle down, you ragamunchkin. There's no moon this time of month, so no night travel. We'll take our rest in the cool and move again in the morning."

"Read me what's on the back," Rain asked of Ilianora.

Brrr watched his common-trust wife unfold the chevron of paper. The Bird Woman's handwriting was on one side, but the other side had print upon it. It was a page ripped from a book. A normal book. Without its own shifting editorial policy toward each specific audience.

"What do you know," said Ilianora. "A scrap of an old tale. One of the fabliaux, one of the long-ago tales. They tell them at harvest festivals and bedtimes. This is one of the stories of Lurline, the Fairy Queen, and her bosom companion, Preenella."

"One of them?"

"Oh, there are dozens. I think." She squinted; the light from the fire wasn't strong. "I think this is the one where they meet what's-his-name."

Brrr felt uncomfortable when confronted with the lore of childhood. It always made him want to sass someone, or fart like a pricklehog. He knew why: as a cub, he'd never had someone to tell him stories of Lurline, Preenella, and Skellybones Fur-Cloak, or whatever his name was. Not, Brrr supposed, that he'd missed much. While Ilianora tried to remember the full tale—the page apparently only gave some segment of the narrative— Brrr watched Rain attend, with yawns and solemn fierce eyes. She probably hasn't had much of a childhood either, he thought. But there was still time. She was a fledgling.

By the time Ilianora was done, the fire had died down, and the dwarf and his Munchkin wife had cozied off for privacy. Rain took herself a few feet into the dark, to have a last pee. Ilianora murmured to Brrr, "What did you think of my storytelling?"

The Lion whispered, "Did you make that up?"

She nodded, shyly. "Most of it. Not the characters— not the famous ones, Lurline and Preenella and old Skellybones. But the rest."

He looked in Rain's direction, out of caution. "You have a knack."

She laughed. "You weren't listening, were you?"

"It took me back," he said, and that was true enough.

Rain returned and settled down, pulling the hemp-wool blanket to her chin. This beastly hot summer wouldn't last forever, said the night; perhaps the stars will turn into snowflakes and fall before dawn. It happens one night or another, eclipsing another summer night of youth. Snow on the blooms.

A few bugs beezled along, chirring their wings and sounding their sirens. An owl made a remark from miles off, but no one replied, except Rain, who murmured, "Lion?"

For some reason he loved, loved when she called him Lion. Loved it. When she avoided reminding him he was Brrr, the creature with the sad history of being known as Cowardly—Cowardly his professional name, just about—but chose to say simply: *Lion.* His head reared back a few inches (these days his eyes didn't always like the distance they had to take to focus on someone speaking). "What do you want, girl?"

"Is Lurline real in the world? And those others?"

It was almost a question about the sleep-world, he thought; she'd drifted far enough along. Still, he loved her too much to lie to her. What did one say? He tried to catch Ilianora's eye for help, but she had put on her veil and was in her own distance.

He would lower his voice in case, as he paused, she'd already slipped off to sleep. But when he said, "Well? What do you think?" she murmured something he couldn't quite hear. He thought she might have said, "I can wait to find out." Then again, she may have said something else.

In time, she would probably know the answer more richly than he ever would. The thought afforded him comfort, and on that he rested all night.

9.

The Kells began to loom up before them. The Lion said, "I'm not going to drag this caboose up the sides of those bluffs. Get yourself another workhorse, Mr. Boss. The book's advice seemed to suggest we go south."

"To get around them, we'll have to head a little east, then," said the dwarf. "It'll take us into the southeast margins of Munchkinland, but we'll meet up with the lower branch of the Yellow Brick Road eventually and then we can plunge to the south."

"When precisely will we have gone south enough?" asked Ilianora. "Or are we now wandering to take in the views?"

"We're putting as much distance as we can between us and the menace of the Emperor," said the dwarf. "The EC never cared for Quadling Country except for the swamp rubies. And the taxes, when they could be collected. But given a war with Munchkinland, they'll be letting the Quadling muckfolk lie fallow. A brief holiday from imperial oppression. We'll be safer there. Can hide like pinworms in a sow's bowels, like the book told us."

Rain said, "The book didn't suggest anything."

They looked at her.

"It was the *person* in the book," she explained. "And en't it possible she weren't saying 'go south' but only 'get back'? Like, um, 'get back from this book, it's too dangerous?'"

"Oh, the Clock already told us who's dangerous," said Mr. Boss. "Keep your mouth shut. What makes you think you can read better than we can?"

They settled into a better pace, but a certain germ of doubt attended their progress.

As the weather finally cooled off, Rain was working on her letters. Little by little she figured out how to form them into words. She wrote comments by placing broken twigs on the ground. RAIN HERE. And TODAY. And WHO. And SORRY. She made words with pebbles on the beds of streams, big words that someone with an eye for stony language might see one day. WATER RISE she wrote, and WATER FALL. Rather expressing the obvious, thought Brrr, but he was as proud of her as if she'd been translating Ugabumish or inventing river charms.

The occasional farmstead gave way to the occasional hamlet, with its own chapel and grange, its antiquated shrines to Lurlina, its stables and inns and the unexpected tearoom. They passed farmers and tinkers on the rutted tracks. By stature they were Munchkins ("Munchkinoid," suggested the dwarf, who was one to talk), but they seemed equable and not especially xenophobic. Little Daffy splinted someone's shabby forearm, dosed someone with rickets, and pulled a tooth from the wobbly head of an old crone. Everyone nearly gagged, but the grandmammy smiled with a bloody gap the size of an orange when the job was done, and she invited them home for tooth soup. An offer they declined.

News of the troubles to the north was thin. One farmer asserted that the whole lake of Restwater had fallen to the invaders. "Any word of Lady Glinda?" asked Brrr.

The man was startled. "Haven't heard of her since the turtles' anniversary swim meet. Is she still alive?"

"Well, that's what I was wondering."

"Scratch my behind with a bear claw. I got no possible idea if it's so or no. Why would she be dead? Other than, you know, death?"

On they trudged. The month being Yellowtime, their hours rounded golden, when the sun was out. But hours can't dawdle—they only seem to. The leaves began to fall and the branches to show their arteries against the clouds.

Finally they reached the Yellow Brick Road. It was ill tended, here; the occasional blown tree or stream overrunning its banks made passage slow. The stretch was clearly untraveled. That night they camped in a copse of white birches whose peeling bark revealed eyes that seemed to be trying to memorize them.

"Can trees see?" asked Rain.

"Some say the trees are houses of spirits," said Little Daffy. "I mean, stupid people say it, but even so."

"I don't mean tree-spirits," said Rain. "I mean the trees. Can they see us?"

"They weep leaves upon the world every autumn," said Little Daffy. "Proof enough they know damn well what's going on around here."

After Rain's eyes had closed and her breathing softened, Brrr intoned to Ilianora, "Do you think everything is right with our Rain?"

She raised an eyebrow, meaning, In what context do you ask?

"I've known few human children. That Dorothy Gale just about completes the list. So I have no premise on which to worry. But doesn't Rain seem—well—odd? Perhaps she is a girl severed from too much."

Ilianora shut her eyes. "She's young even for her age, that's all. She still lives in the magical universe. She'll outgrow it, to the tune of pain and suffering. We all do. Don't worry so much. Look at how she touches the trees tonight, as if they had spirits she knew about and we didn't. That's not weird; that's what being a child is. I was such a girl, when I was alive."

"Don't talk like that."

"Oh, I'm alive enough now." Her eyes opened, and they were filled with whatever passed for love in that woman. "I am alive. But I'm not that girl. I'm a woman grown from a life broken in the middle. I'm not even a cousin of that girl I was so long ago. I see her life like an illustrated weekly story I read long ago, and it is pictures of that that I carry in my head. Her life in Kiamo Ko. Her life with her father, long ago—that famous Fiyero Tigelaar, prince of the Arjikis. Her life with her mother, Sarima, and her father's erstwhile lover, Elphaba Thropp. It's a child's story in my head, no more real than Preenella and the skeleton hermit in the everlasting cloak of pine boughs. I'm not sad; don't shift; leave me be. We were talking about Rain."

For her sake, he returned to the earlier subject. "I don't fault her interest in the natural world. What I notice is her . . . her distance from us."

"She's here curled up against your haunches. To get her any closer you'd have to swallow her whole."

"You know what I mean. She seems to float in a life next to ours, but with limited contact."

Ilianora sighed. "We agreed to take her to safety, not to perfect her. What would you have us do? Sing rounds? Practice our sums as we march?"

"I don't know stories. Maybe you could tell her more? I wish we could get *through* a little more. She loves us, perhaps, but from too great a distance."

"She'll have to cross the distance herself. Trust me on that, Brrr. I know about it. Either she'll choose to visit us when there is enough of her present to visit, or day by day she'll learn to survive without needing what you need and I need."

"I think it's called a knot in the psyche."

"It's called grief so deep that she can't see it as such. Maybe she never will. Maybe that would be a blessing for her in the long run. If she can't learn to love us, would that keep us from loving her? Brrr?"

Never, he thought. Never. He didn't have to mouth the word to his wife; she knew what he meant by the way he tucked his chin over the crown of Rain's head.

10.

A day of mixed clouds and sudden fiercenesses of light. Breezy but warm, and aromatic, both spicy-rank and spicy-balm. The road passed through open meadows interspersed with dense patches of black starsnaps and spruces, where clusters of wild pearlfruit glistened in caves of foliage. Rain paid no attention to the clacking of nonsense rhyme that Ilianora had taken up. Rain heard it but didn't hear it.

> Little Ferny Shuttlefoot
> Made a mutton pasty.
> Sliced it quick and gulped it quick
> And perished rather hasty.

and

> Reginald Mouch sat on a couch.
> A ladybug bit him and he said ouch.

It smiled at him. He started to laugh
And bit that ladybug back. In half.

"What's up with you today, all this mayhem?" said Mr. Boss to Ilianora. "Awful passel of nastiness in children's rhymes. Toughens up the little simpletons, I guess."

"A lot of biting too," said the Lion, showing his teeth. He was proud that Ilianora was taking up the challenge to force-feed childhood lore to Rain.

"I remember a counting-out rhyme," said Little Daffy, and proved it.

One Munchkinlander went out for a stroll,
Two girls from Gillikin danced with a troll.
Three little Glikkun girls chewed on their
    pinkies.
Four little Winkie boys showed us their
    winkies.
Five Ugabumish girls started their blood.
Six little Quadlings went home to eat mud.
Now who wins the prize for being most pretty?
The girl from the Emerald, Emerald City.
One Ozma, two Ozma, three Ozma.

"And on until you miss a step," said Little Daffy.
"Which you rarely do," said the dwarf.

"There's a skipping game to that," said Little Daffy. "We used to play it in Center Munch." She found a stick of last night's kindling saved for tonight, and with the charred end she drew squares and circles on the yellow pavement. She labeled them with numbers.

"No one learned me numbers yet," said Rain.

"It's easy." The Munchkinlander skipped and huffed to the ninth circle. Whinging, Rain tried to follow, but she was stopped at the seventh circle by the explosion into the eighth of a small whirlwind of feathers and beaks. A Wren with a grandmotherly frown had landed onto the bricks in front of them. She was flustered and out of breath.

"No time for nursery games," panted the Wren. "Unless you fly, me duckies, you'll have enough time to skip stones in the Afterlife."

"Sassy thing," said the dwarf. "Are you available to stay for supper? We'll serve roast Wren."

"I cain't spend precious moments in foolflummery. I been hunting a while." She was having a hard time talking while catching her breath; her voice came out whistley. "The crazy bird lady asked me to find you. I followed the words I saw on the ground. You're in danger, the blessed lot of you. A thumping great crew of the Emperor's nasty-men is on your tail and no mistake. Oh, all is lost! Unless it ain't."

It took them a while to piece together the silly creature's message. The soldiers were armed and mounted. They'd interviewed the Bird Woman of the Disappointments, and wrung from her the information that the company of the Clock had passed that way, all jollylike and worms for brekkie.

"I wonder what wardrobe I should plan for prison?" drawled Brrr.

"Begging your pardon, sir, you'll not get the privilege of prison, I bet," said the Wren. "Not to judge by them fiercish faces. Why do you *loiter* so? Fly, I tell you!"

"I have short legs. I never move fast," said Little Daffy. "Maybe we should split up?"

"It was a nice marriage while it lasted," said Mr. Boss. "I never thought it would come to this, but life is full of pleasant shocks."

"I didn't mean you and I split up, oaf."

Ilianora roused to alarm earliest. "Perhaps it's a sign we should ditch the Clock and take the book; we can move faster on our own." The Lion flashed her a warning look; however dizzy this Wren, they oughtn't reveal to her that they had any books. But it was too late now.

"If you got the singular volume they're after, pity upon you," said the Wren. "Grayce Graeling thought you might. But the longer you sit here and mull it over, the easier a job to round you up. Those horsemen on their way are all done up in silver plate, bright as icicles, armed with saw-ribbed swords and quivers of skilligant arrows."

The dwarf had heard enough. "On we go, then. When you return to that Bird Woman, tell her we thanked her for the warning."

"There ain't a whole lot of her left to thank," said the Wren. "Ozspeed, you little egglings. Wind under your wings and all that. I'll sing out to alert what remains of the Conference of the Birds that I saw you safe, once upon a time, and I left you safe. What happens next belongs to your decisions, and to luck. Is that girl who I guesses she is?"

"Don't go," said Rain. Brrr and Ilianora looked at each other. Even in the face of mortal danger parents are attentive to the smallest improvements in the capacities of their children.

"I'll sing you cover best I can," said the Wren kindly. "If you're looking for Liir, he's well hid. But what a sight for sore eyes you'd provide him, on some happy day! Meanwhile, I've done me best, and now you do yours."

11.

Having finally been roused to worry, they made up for lost time.

"We're history," said Little Daffy. "Even without

the Clock, we can't move faster than soldiers on horseback. Not with a child."

"I can run faster than you can," said Rain.

"I know. We're both three feet tall but I'm two feet stout."

"We're not ditching the Clock," said Mr. Boss. "That's a nonstarter."

They were hurrying along; their chatter was nervous chatter. "Why armor, at this time of year?" asked the Lion.

Little Daffy spoke up. "Against some sort of spell, hammered metal can afford a minimal protection. Or it can at least slow down a spell's effectiveness."

"You're not a witch, except in the boudoir. Are you? You witch," huffed her husband, almost admiringly.

"It's no secret that some professional people can manage a bit of magic in their own line of work. Sister Doctor and I used to sew sheets of hammered tin into our clothes when we worked among the Yunamata, for instance. The mineral prophylactic. Only common sense."

"Can you do us something useful? A pair of seven-league boots for each of us, to settle us more deeply into the safer mess of Quadling jungle?"

"I'll need two pair," said Brrr. "Though I'd also accept a seven-league settee."

"Bring me an ingrown toenail and I'll trim it without my sewing scissors," huffed Little Daffy. "That's about the size of what I can do, people. Anyway, even the most powerful enchanter doesn't have the power to do *anything* he or she might want. Only certain things. No one can point a finger at a dozen horsemen and turn them, poof, into a dozen doughnuts. No one can, as a single campaign, magically remove the Emperor from his throne, nor bring Elphaba back from the dead. Magic powers are limited to start with, and more limited by the history and aptitudes of the person attempting a spell."

"Look," cried Rain. Brrr turned, aware that for once she was paying more attention than the rest of them.

Across the open meadows through which they were hurrying, they saw a clot of horsemen emerge from around a stand of larches, miles back. With a zealotry of spear and sawtooth sword. If the companions could see the horsemen, they could be seen too. It could be mere moments before the kettledrumming of horses at gallop.

"We're lost," cried the dwarf. "Brrr, take the girl onto your back; you can cover the ground faster."

"Anything to get rid of her, eh?" roared the Lion. He turned once, three times, five in desperate circles. The cart turned with him. He was tempted by the moral acceptability of a personal escape for himself in the service of guarding a human girl—but then he set his pace forward again. "I'm not leaving the book to the Emperor," he growled, "nor the rest of you to the Emperor's spears."

"We should fly," cried Rain, "din't the Wren say we should fly?"

"Now isn't the time to discuss figurative language," ventured Little Daffy, "not when our livers are about to be diced in situ." She pulled herself up onto the Clock, where Rain and the dwarf were already riding.

Rain gave out as much of a curse as she could, given that her fund of vocabulary remained on the spare side. She crab-walked up the side of the Clock and put her foot upon one of the long wrought-iron hands on the time face. "I seen a real dragon that could fly. This one knows about it as good as I do," she cried. Using the leathery flaps of the wings to scurry higher, she eventually thumped the dragon on its reticulated proboscis. "Fly, you stupid worm, and do the work you was made to do!"

Maybe she'd hit a secret lever or a magic nerve still potentially alert while the rest of the Clock remained paralyzed. The great wings shook. Browned leaves and the husks of forest insects dusted out upon them. The creak, when the sallowwood ribs attained their fullest extension, was like the snap of an umbrella when it catches. The batlike wingspan reached twenty-eight or thirty feet from tip to tip.

"Pretty, en't it," said the dwarf. "If they didn't see us before, they'll see us now. We're a whole dragon-cloud on their horizon, soon as they look to their left."

A cry of discovery. The avalanching sound of horses' hooves. As Brrr strained to pull even harder, he noticed that the wind had swung round. It had been blowing from the north, bringing with it the cool of Gillikin summer farmland, but now from the west the wind picked up with a sudden, drier emphasis. As if it meant business.

The wings of the dragon caught the wind and billowed, to the extent that aging leather, softened by time, can billow. The wagon moved faster as if loaned spirit by the weather. "Whoa!" cried Ilianora. She scooped herself onto a running board.

Rain perched forward like a gargoyle on a chapel parapet. She hopped up and down on the shoulders of the dragon, looking forward, not scared at all, as the Clock accelerated.

If it starts to fly, thought Brrr, I'll be hanging from the hasps of this cart like a kitten sagging out of the mouth of its mother. He couldn't stop to disengage from the harness, though. There was no time. The Clock hurried on.

Brrr didn't think the dragon could outpace military steeds, but maybe the horses had been ridden hard. By the time the Lion had either to pause or else risk a coronary, the assemblage had mounted a slight slope of the Yellow Brick Road and descended the other side. The gravity hurried them all the faster, into a copse that promised, just beyond, a deeper forest. Affording a small window of time to strategize before their predators were upon them.

The dragon's wings folded so suddenly that Rain tumbled forward to the pavement. She didn't complain about the scratches on her dirty limbs, the little blood. She had that look a child has only a few times in its life, when the child has bettered her betters. The expression isn't smug, though adults often take it for smugness. It's something else. Maybe relief at having confirmed through personal experience the long-held suspicion of our species, that the enchanted world of childhood is merely a mask for something else, a more subtle and paradoxical magic.

As if Rain's enthusiasm had called it into being, they soon came to an opportunity. A fork in Yellow Brick Road. A high section running along a ridge, a lower road, perhaps an older line that had been superseded by later engineers. Mr. Boss selected the descending road, as it looked more brambly. Sure enough, the scrub trees and snarled hedges snapped back into place after the Clock pushed through, providing the companions deeper cover, hiding evidence of the choice they'd made. At least for the time being.

That night the dwarf said to Rain, "You made the dragon fly. Could've tickled me in the tickle zone with a tickle wheel. A good job, that. I guess you can stay."

"I already stayed," said Rain.

12.

They couldn't imagine giving their pursuers the slip so easily, but it seemed so. A good thing too: another day or two, and the forest had petered out entirely. Pale meadows rounded beside them like billowing sheets being flapped dry by two laundresses. Here and there a rill wandered past them, and the company could pause to rinse a cup or soak a sore heel. They didn't pause for long

The little girl, thought Brrr, seems more thrilled than frightened by the urgency. Though he offered to carry Rain on his back, she preferred to walk and she didn't tire. She often sprang ahead as he imagined his own cub might have done, had he been sprightly enough to father a cub. He had to resist the urge to cuff her, not out of annoyance but love. She seemed not to appreciate the stress beneath which her companions lumbered.

And then he thought, Oh, sweet Ozma. She *doesn't* understand it. Deep down, she doesn't get it. She is younger than her years. Is she simple? She doesn't know that the world is made up of accidents jackknifed into every moment, waiting to spring out. Of poison saturating one mushroom and not another. Of pox and pestilence accordion-pleated in the drawing room drapes, ready to spread when the drapes are drawn of a chilly evening. Of disaster stitched in the seam of every delight. The fire ant in the sugar bowl. The serpent in the raspberries, as the old stories had it. She doesn't know enough to worry. She hasn't been educated enough to fret.

The General had been teaching her how to read her letters, but she hadn't learned how to read the world.

The old branch line of the Yellow Brick Road began to peter out. Local scavengers with building projects of their own had dug up the looser bricks in such a patchwork fashion that traveling the road became difficult. Around here, the meadowgrass to either side grew more serrated. It scratched against them, as if each frond were rimmed with salt crystals. Then, at last, the white meadows dipped into the first stand of something more like jungle than forest.

They didn't expect to find the going easy, as the Clock was tall and the growth was dense, but nor did they expect that the swift change in climate would surprise them with a huge increase in native population. Not forty feet under the canopy of marsh-jungle they were deafened by the jaw-jaw of life. Cawing birds and scolding monkeys. Ten thousand industrious insects chewing, sawing, fighting, digging, dragging, battling, zizzing by. The vines pulled away like spun-sugar candy. The Clock drove in deeper. The noise itself was a kind of camouflage, and welcome.

The first afternoon in the badlands, Little Daffy identified a plant whose small quilted leaves, when snapped open, oozed with an unguent that repelled mosquitoes. The need was urgent enough that the adult companions ventured out to harvest a goodly supply. For her safety, though, Rain was shoveled into the body of the Clock. Protected from mosquitoes there, and also from getting lost. She could tend to wander, thoughtlessly, and a jungle was no place for *that*.

Rain hadn't often been in such an enclosed space. The great gears made of carved wood rose like clock faces, while those of hammered iron lay horizontal. The wooden ones smiled, but some of their teeth were splintered or missing. The iron gears looked more treacherous, as if they would stop for no mouse or magician, but chew up history any way they liked.

The dust-silted interior of the Clock was all-business—a different world from the gilded scrollwork of the outside. The air was drier in here, less punitive. Greenish banyan light seeped in where a board had warped or a shutter failed to hang true. She felt like a new seed in the green light of undergrowth, or a fish in scummy shallows.

Almost lackadaisically a twiglet of moss, sort of brown and green both, began poking through a crack at the bottom of one of the shutters. Thinner than a pencil, more like a pipette. It was joined by another, and then a third and a fourth. The sensate tentacles stiffly carved out half circles in the dust, reaching in, probing. Rain didn't know what they were, but they were animated and curious.

There was room for them; they could come in. But try as she might, she couldn't budge the shutter door. She was trapped in here until her companions opened the door from the outside.

If anything happens to the Clock's minders, she finally thought (and this was perhaps the first time Rain had ever thought conditionally), I'll be locked up here tight as Lady Glinda in her housey house.

She couldn't hear any noise from outside. No chittering of mob monkeys. No appreciations of one's own remarkable plumage by the teenage birds. Instead she sensed a kind of hush, a seasoned thickness of sound.

Oh, but those little crab-fingered fingerlings really wanted to get in! Now some were trying to claw up through an old knothole whose bole had aged and didn't sit true in the plank. Six or eight of those strands poked up. If she could only knock the bole out, they could swarm in, maybe. She hit it tentatively with her hand but she couldn't focus her force enough to make a difference. She saw that the back side of the wagon, through the screen of meshing gears and flywheels and pendulums, was also being explored for entrance by a host of twitching finger-limbs. But here came the dwarf opening her door, and the spiderlets melted away.

"Free and clear," he said, "we've done ravaging the forest for medicinal help."

"Did you see them twiggy spider folks? Where's they get to?"

"What're you on about? All we saw were buzz-bugs the size of luncheon plates." The dwarf and Little Daffy and Ilianora insisted that the Clock hadn't been besieged by anything. The Lion, who had kept an eye on the Clock even while scavenging, told Rain she was inventing things. "It sounds nasty," he told her. "Like giant bedbugs. You're trying to terrorize me. It isn't hard to do, I realize, but just stop it. You know how I despise spiders."

"I didn't make 'em up." Rain described their legs or fingers as best she could, but none of the party had seen a single creature like that, let along a posse of them. Little Daffy gave Rain a tonic to calm her nerves, but the girl threw up. She didn't want her nerves either calmed or inflamed. She wanted the spiders to come back and tell her what the spider world was like.

Near sunset a human creature came slinking through the jungley-woods. He was neither a northern soldier, tall and armored, nor a Munchkinlander outcast. He looked more like a local drunk. His coloring was dark and his clothing brief. Knitting needles pinned the lanky hair piled on his head. On his back he carried a basket filled with mushrooms of a certain heft and texture and stink.

At first he spoke to them in a language they didn't understand, but he made an effort to remember another tongue, and tried again. He was a scavenger plying his trade, and he could offer the more potent of wild mushrooms for sale. *Very very good specimens very very rare.* Little Daffy looked interested, as she knew the medicinal properties of his stock, but Mr. Boss cut her off and said they had no use for recreational fungi.

The native never told them his name, but he recognized at once that the company must be the prey of the Emperor's soldiers, of whom he had heard the gossip. Rain wondered from whom: Parrots? Monkeys? Spiders?

Haltingly, Heart-of-Mushroom told them, "Your soldiers? They looking for you still. But emergency make them to divert from their task. They are not to give up too quick-like. They to return. Risky if you to go on, but more deeper riskiness if you to stay put."

"Well, that's a nice menu to choose from," said Mr. Boss. "And you look as if you wouldn't hesitate to turn us in."

"I to sell mushrooms, not people," he replied, taking no offense. He flicked open his loincloth and urinated on the ground between them. Was this a gesture of disdain, or a proof of nonaggression, or merely sign of a full bladder? Brrr thought, Well, if I ever get back to high society, there's a new trick to try out in a crowd.

The man said, "Emperor's men not welcome in Quadling Country. Heart-of-Mushroom not to sell information to bad men." He took a mushroom from his basket, scrubbed it against the hair in his armpit, and took a bite. When he offered it around, everyone professed to be full.

The Lion said, "Would it be better for us to leave the Yellow Brick Road and cut across country?"

The Quadling shook his head. "You are safer on the road of yellow brick. The trees and vines and clinging growth only thicken as you go south. Also jungle leopard to make short meal of you."

"I can take on a jungle leopard," said Brrr.

The mushroom vendor snorted and took another nibble. "Also forest harpie and small vicious deadly jungle dormouse."

"Well, then," said Brrr. "I take your point."

"But even if you not to believe me, you to think of your baggage," he concluded. "Quadling Country is wet to the shin." He looked at the dwarf and then at the Munchkinlander. "Or to the waist. You to be bogged down in mud. Easy for soldiers to catch and kill. But yellow road is built dry and high. You to move deeper from your enemies that way. Faster away from the north."

"But they'll follow the Yellow Brick Road toward Qhoyre, surely," said Brrr. "They'll move faster than we can. I'm surprised they haven't caught up with us yet. What was the emergency that diverted them?"

"They stumble upon rogue dragon," said Heart-of-Mushroom. "Not ticky-toy thing like yours. Real one. They stop to try to capture it but cannot to manage it. It fly away. So now they to take up hunt for you again."

"They saw a dragon close up, and I en't seen nothing but spiders?" Rain was incensed.

"But if we stay on this road—they'll be following us," persisted Brrr.

"No road goes only one way. When engineers to build the only dry access *into* Quadling homeland, they also build only dry access *out* of Quadling homeland. So when EC soldiers betray Quadling hosts and kill and steal and burn their bridges? EC soldiers walking away on Yellow Brick Road make easy target for Quadling dart and Quadling arrow." He spat out a mushroom bug and cursed in Qua'ati. "Quadlings not to kissy kiss EC soldiers any more."

"What's to stop your countrymen from shooting at *us*?" said the Lion. "I'm from Gillikin originally, and my wife is from the Vinkus. Little Daffy is a Munchkinlander, and Mr. Boss—"

"I'm undeclared," said Mr. Boss.

"We're a walking gallery of the enemies of the Quadlings. And you'd send us down Slaughter Alley? Hardly sociable," finished Brrr.

"Not so," said the Quadling. "You have your rafiqi, and Quadlings to give you safe passage." He bowed just a little to Rain. "She is Quadling, no?"

Brrr looked at the girl. He hadn't thought of her as positioned anywhere in Oz, ethnically speaking. But Brrr could see what the mushroom peddler meant. Rain's face was somewhat heart shaped, a little flatter than those of her companions. Her lips fuller. You couldn't say that her skin was as ruddy as Heart-of-Mushroom's, but now, in this light, maybe. . . .

Brrr caught the eye of Mr. Boss. "So the Clock told you to beware of a little girl. Did it. I think the Clock was just jealous. We got ourselves an ambassador."

The itinerant vendor spoke to Rain in Qua'ati. She didn't notice he was addressing her.

"Not to mind," he told them. "My people to see what I can see. She is to promise you safe passage on the Road." He nibbled another portion of his wares and smiled balefully. "Qhoyre is big city where you can to lose yourself. Such a small band of soldiers will not dare to follow you into Qhoyre. You to be safe there."

"Safe from soldiers," said Mister Boss. "How about invisible spiders?"

They tried to explain what Rain claimed to have seen. "Maybe the Emperor has trained bloodhound spiders through the magic he denies everyone else?" asked Ilianora.

"Invisible spiders," said the Lion. "*Did* I mention that even visible spiders cause me angina of the psyche?"

They never learned what Heart-of-Mushroom thought about invisible spiders, for at their very mention he paled. In a moment he'd melted away back into the forest, for all practical purposes having gone invisible himself.

"Another one who didn't come along," said Rain. "We isn't too friendified, is we."

13.

The Quadling's terror at spiders that only Rain had seen made the adults more squeamish than ever. Rain, however, experienced a sort of gingery buckling sensation inside. People couldn't see the spiders and they couldn't see inside of her—they hadn't been able to figure out that she'd been telling the truth.

An apprenhension of isolation—that sudden realization of the privacy of one's most crucial experiences— usually happens first when a child is much younger than Rain was now. The sensation is often alarming.

Alone as a goose in a gale, as the saying has it. Rain felt anything but alarmed, though. The invisible world—the world of her instincts—though solitary, was real.

They heard her singing that night, a rhyme of her own devising.

> Spidery spiders in the wood
> No one knows you very good.
> No one can and no one should.

14.

The deeper they penetrated into Quadling homelands, the more signs they saw of Quadling activity. Rushes laid out on the margins of the Yellow Brick Road to dry in the sun. Donkey dung and human feces. A broken harness for a water buffalo. Meanwhile, no alarums of horse hooves sounded behind them. The Yellow Brick Road south of Gillikin and Munchkinland might be Slaughter Alley, but not for a band of irregulars accompanied by a child with evident Quadling blood.

They made sure to keep Rain front and center, on the Clock's most prominent seat. No one much believed in the spidery figments, but neither did they believe in taking chances with Quadling poison-tipped arrows.

"I'd like to know what our intention is, when we arrive in Qhoyre," Ilianora said as they made an evening meal of poached garmot and swamp tomato. They sat right in the middle of the road, their cooking fire banked up upon the brick. "We're about to have obeyed the advice mimed out of the Grimmerie. We'll have stuck together and gotten south. But what next? And why? We're going to take a flat there? Start a plantantion to harvest mildew? Set up a circus? Learn Qua'ati?"

"Tut tut, my little Minxy-Mouth of the Marshgrass." The dwarf fingered out a fishbone. Marriage had eased his nerves somewhat. "No one knows where home is until it's too late to escape it. We'll know what to do when we know what to do."

"Qhoyre can't be anyone's home," argued Ilianora. "Otherwise so many Quadlings wouldn't have migrated into the northern cities."

"What is the world *after* Qhoyre?" asked Rain, who seldom listened to their discussions.

Mr. Boss shrugged. "The Road peters out, as I understand it, but Quadling Country squelches on."

"Oh, even Quadling Country ends, eventually," said Little Daffy. "At least according to the lessons in map reading we got in petty nursery. The province meets up with the ring of desert that surrounds all of Oz."

"But what's after the desert?" asked Rain.

"More desert," said the Munchkinlander. "Oz is it, sweetheart."

"To hear Ozians speak, other places don't exist," said Mr. Boss. "There's no place to the north, like Quox, for instance, except as a supply of fine brandy and the source of a certain plummy accent. Ev, to the south over the sands, doesn't really exist—it wouldn't dare. But oh, we do like our Ev tobacco if a shipment gets through."

Rain scowled. She didn't understand irony. The dwarf, more respectful of Rain now that she was their de facto rafiqi, took pity and explained. "Oz isn't surrounded by sands. It's enislanded in its own self-importance."

"Hey, Oz is bigger than Ev or Quox or Fliaan," said Brrr in mock effrontery. "Those dinky sinkholes are hickabilly city-states founded by desert tribes-people."

"Who cares what's outside of Oz?" agreed the dwarf. "No one goes there. Oz loves itself enough not to care about provincial outposts."

"But after the deserts?" said Rain.

"Ah, the innocent stupidity of kids," said the dwarf. "You might as well ask what is behind the stars, for all we'll ever know. The sands aren't deadly,

that's just the public relations put out by edge com-
munities. Not that I'm proposing we keep dropping
south to become nomads in bed linens. The deserts
aren't hospitable. It's where dragons come from, for
one thing."

"She wants to know where we're headed, that's all,"
said Ilianora. "I'm with her on this."

"Headed to tomorrow. Equally impossible to tell
what's on the other side of that, but we'll find out when
we get there," said the dwarf. "Everyone, stop your
beefing. You're giving me cramps."

The tomorrows began to blur. In a climate that
seemed to know nothing but one season of growth,
maturity, decay, all happening simultaneously, per-
petually, even time seemed to lose its coherence. The
company grew quieter but their unhappinesses didn't
subside. The cost of wandering without a named destination was proving steep.

Eventually the Yellow Brick Road petered out—
brick by brick, almost—but the tramped track remained wide enough to accommodate the Clock of
the Time Dragon. The signs of human enterprise
grew more numerous. The companions began to spot
Quadlings in trees, in flatboats, even on the mud-
rutted road. The natives gave the company of the

Clock a wide berth but a respectful one. Brrr observed that Quadlings, the butt of ethnic smears all over Oz, seemed in their own homeland to be more capable of courtesy to strangers than Munchkinlanders or Gillikinese.

Ilianora put her veil back upon her brow despite the steamy everlastingness of jungle summer.

There was no good way to avoid Qhoyre. The provincial capital had colonized all the dry land making up the isthmus-among-the-reeds upon which it squatted. And *squatted* was the word. Brrr, who had lived in the Emerald City and in Shiz, knew capital cities to be places of pomp and self-approval. Qhoyre looked mostly like a collection of hangars for the drying of rice. Indeed, Brrr reasoned, that was probably how the city began.

At ground level, the stuccoed administration buildings showcased an extravagance of softstone carvings both profane and devotional. Above them, ornament was abandoned for louvers, weathered out of plumb, and perforated screens of raffia or stone. Shabby, genteel. The hulks of Rice House and Ruby House and the Bureau of Tariffs and Marsh Law—titles carved not in Qua'ati but in Ozish even Rain could now read— loomed beside soapbone shops that wobbled on stilts above household pork-pen and pissery. But government house and grocery alike featured spavinned roofbeams. To swale away monsoon-burst, Brrr later figured out. Sensible in that climate, though the first impression was of a dignified old city in its dotage.

The Quadlings swarmed about the companions without evident panic. "They never heard of the Clock," said Mr. Boss under his breath. "How bizarre. They don't *want* a glimpse of the future from us. We could retire here, no?"

"No," said Ilianora, spooked by the crowds.

To Brrr's eye the Quadlings seemed louche and convivial. They'd survived all attempts by unionist ministers to convert them, preferring their own ob-scure dalliance with fetishes, radishes, and the odd augury by kittlestones. Stalls on the edge of market squares might be shrines or chapels, or then again they might be the tipping place for one's household refuse. Little Daffy, with her Munchkinlander's lust for a good scrub, was appalled. "It's not even the nakedness behind those loincloths," she said. "It's that you can see they haven't even washed well back there." With aggressive cleanliness she took to pumicing her own face on the hour.

When the company paused for the night in a blame-less nook, natives emerged from alleys and mews-ways to bring rattan trays of steaming red rice and fresh fruit and stinking vegetables. They set their offerings before Rain as if she were their local girl made good, and skittered away. "Monkey people," said Little Daffy.

Rain showed no particular interest in this population to whom, Brrr conceded, she did bear some resemblance. She tried to make friends with the myriad hairless white dogs who cowered everywhere, under open staircases of cedar and rope. Rain put out rice and then fruit, and they would venture forth to sniff at the offering, but scurry back. She tried with some of the brown vegetables, the ones like voluted woody asparagus, and they also turned up their snouts at that. Then she arranged some of the asparagus into a few words— FOR YOU. EAT. So they did.

"How does she do that?" asked the dwarf of Brrr. "Have you any idea?"

"I'm the muscle in this outfit, you're the brains," replied the Lion. "As long as they don't come and eat us, I don't care how she does it. *Are* they dogs?"

"Or rats. Or weasels."

The torpor of the climate induced a lethargy that the companions didn't mind indulging; they'd been moving about for some time now. Easier to have your meals delivered than to press on with no assurance of decent foraging ahead. "We'll know when it's time to go," said Mr. Boss, from the hammock he had strung between the post of a bat house and a nearby wrinkleroot tree. "Climb up here and get cozy with me, wife."

"It's the middle of the afternoon and that's a see-through hammock," protested Little Daffy.

"They don't mind." And it was true; the Quadlings acted on their impulses when so inclined, without shame or secrecy. Interestingly, Rain seemed not to notice, either. The innocence of that child, thought Brrr, was troubling when it wasn't refreshing.

The dwarf and Little Daffy didn't budge from the vicinity where they'd stodged the Clock. "We have to guard the book," they reminded Ilianora languidly. "You're feeling antsy about our prospects, you go find someone to talk to."

Brrr's wife held out as long as she could, but finally she wrapped her shawl so tightly around herself that only her eyes showed, and she began to explore the town on her own. She was looking for someone who could translate Qua'ati for them. She found an old woman in a tobacco shop whose feet had been chewed off by an alligator but who could hobble about on sticks. Ilianora persuaded her to come back to the Clock. The nearly deaf old woman agreed to answer what of their questions she could in exchange for a salve that Little Daffy swore would regenerate her feet—but not for a year, which would give them plenty of time to get far away from her.

"Anyway, she's not going to run after us protesting, is she," murmured Little Daffy to the others, sotto voce.

Her name, as near as they could make it out, was Chalotin. A bitter orange rind of a woman passing herself off as a seer. Brrr, who not long ago had spent some intense hours with old Yackle, could tell the difference between chalk and chocolate. Chalotin was rather thin chalk.

Still, for an old broad she pivoted about on impressively flexible haunches. She ran pinkish fingertips over her perfect ancient teeth as she told them what she knew.

Yes, she said, though the Emperor's forces got no love no more, no more, they still made a preemptory show of authority every now and then. The only way they ever arrived was the High Parade, the route the company of the Clock had taken—what was left of the Yellow Brick Road. Quadlings let them pass as long as they marched in dress uniform rather than field garb. They never came in the rainy season, though. Or never yet.

"So they *could* tromp in any day," confirmed Brrr in a soft roar, that she could hear him.

Yes, her shrugging expression implied. Wouldn't put it past 'em.

"Where do they set up?"

"One of the government houses." Warming to her subject, she told them that the EC had once kept a firmer grip on Quadling Country, dating all the way back to the days of the Wizard, when the extension of the Yellow Brick Road first allowed swamp engineers to come in and cull the mud flats of their rubies.

"Emeralds from the northeast, rubies from the south," said Mr. Boss. "No wonder the Emerald City got so powerful, filching from all over. I suppose there are diamonds in hidden caves in the Vinkus?" He looked at Ilianora hopefully. "We could all maybe get filthy stinking rich back at your place?"

Chalotin didn't care about rubies except to say that in the act of diving for them, the swamp miners from the EC had upset the crops of vegetable pearls harvested out near Ovvels. It had taken three decades for the agrarian economy to begin to recover, she said, and she predicted it would take three decades more before the natives of Quadling Country could rise to the level of poverty they'd once enjoyed.

"We are no longer friendly to our overlords," she finished, spitting, but smiling nicely too. "We are polite but we don't let them to stay. Not after the burning of the bridge at Bengda. That massacre. Not after attack by flying dragons."

"Dragons," said Rain, looking up. "Have you seen a flying dragon?"

Chalotin made a gesture to ward off the notion. "When the EC to set flying dragons upon us, oh, years ago, a full five miles of swamp burn south of Ovvels. That much Chalotin know for herself, back when Chalotin could both to walk and to swim. But no dragons since then, no no."

"So why aren't your patriotic fellow citizens tossing *us* out on our arses?" asked Mr. Boss.

She replied that the presence of such a young rafiqi required of the Quadlings basic hospitality and even assistance. She indicated Rain when she spoke, but Rain had lost interest and was crawling around in the dirt, pretending to be one of those white hairless dogs.

"How do we get out of here then?" said Ilianora. "We don't want to be cornered in Qhoyre if the Emperor is about to send a brigade in after us."

Chalotin explained that the Yellow Brick Road only went as far south as here because beyond Qhoyre, arcing first to the southwest and then toward the north, a fairly dry and passable berm already existed. Whether it was a natural feature of the land or the remains of ancient earthworks, no one knew, but if the companions left Qhoyre by the road near the Mango Altar they'd be safe and dry.

"Though if the rains to start, to be careful not to step off the high road," said Chalotin. "Chalotin not to believe that your dragony cart is also boat."

"Where will that *take* us, though? An endless circle around Quadling Country?" asked Ilianora. "I'm done with circling!"

Chalotin had had enough. She insisted that Little Daffy supply the salve that would regenerate her missing feet, and when the Munchkinlander came out with a small pot of something rather like cold cream, Chalotin took a portion on her finger and swallowed it. She grimaced but pronounced it useful, if not as a medicinal unguent then as a dip for fennel.

From off her shoulder she pulled a belted sack. Rain wriggled closer to look at it. A lake shell of some sort, larger than anything Rain had ever seen on the shores of Restwater. "What's that, with all its points?" asked Rain, indicating the reticulated spine of it.

"Deep magic, you buy?" asked Chalotin. "Cheapy cheap for you."

"What kind of magic?" asked the girl.

"You can't buy magic," protested the dwarf, and then, in a softer voice, added, "Of course, you can't buy feet, either."

"The Emperor is calling in all magic tools and torques," said Brrr, thinking he might wheedle the shell out of the old biddy without having to fling coin at her. Nice to supply Rain with her first toy. "That contingent arrives from the EC and finds you with something powerful, you'll need more than new feet to get away safely."

"How magic could it be, anyway, if you can't summon up your own feet?" said Little Daffy, playing along.

"It makes noise," Chalotin told them, and showed them how to blow it like a horn. "The tip has to be broken first. But Chalotin say: this shell not to sing its voice. This shell to listen to. Conch to talk to you. Conch to tell you what it know."

"No magic. No buy," said Mr. Boss. "No good. No deal."

"Well, we have no coin of the traditional sort," said Brrr, hoping to force a negotiation of some sort.

"What does the shell say?" asked Rain, nearly breathless with hope. But the old woman scurried backward and shook her head. Without another word she headed down the lane, galumphing along as well as she could on her stumps.

"Wait," called Mr. Boss. "One more thing."

Chalotin turned but didn't stop moving away.

"What are these white critters? Are they puppies?"

"They to be albinoid otters," she replied. "Smart to avoid them. They to overrun Qhoyre for long long time. When the rice terraces burn, the otters they to lose their protective coloring. Before that no one realize they color from their diet. Now they safer among pale stone buildings than in green-purple swamp. So they to overrun Qhoyre and to mess in the silk farms and to eat the worms. Bad fall of letter-sticks. Bad tumble of dominoes."

"What color are they usually?"

"Rice otters? Green of course. To swim in paddies and marsh." Chalotin crab-walked away then, and Brrr joined the others in discussing how quickly they might get out of Qhoyre, while they still had their own feet attached. Teasing and tempting the nearer rice otters, Rain wandered about, disappearing for a time and appearing again, a child with her own shadowy concerns among the green shadows of a busy neighborhood.

"But what are you doing with that?" asked Little Daffy at dinner, when Rain showed up with the shell. She checked her purse to make sure Rain hadn't stolen any farthings. "Did you steal any of my cash?"

She shook her head. "Stole the shell," she replied.

Little Daffy and Ilianora lit into Rain, but good. Had she learned nothing about honor, about moral competence? What was she thinking?

"You told her you could grow her some new *feet*," said Rain. The equivalency of the crimes was debatable, but the girl effectively shut up her elders anyway.

The company left the capital of Quadling Country the next day, doing a favor for their hosts without meaning to. In the early morning, before everyone was awake, Rain had tried to blow a sound from the conch. She couldn't hear what noise it might have made, but some several hundred white otters congregated around the Clock. The pack followed the companions past the Mango Altar and out along the high dusty road into deepening jungle. The stink was horrific, but at least the pack lagged about a half mile behind them. It was like being dogged by a murky white afghan whose segments came apart and rejoined at will. Neither Rain nor the adults were sure whether to be pleased or alarmed, but they could hear the sound of humans cheering from the squat cityscape behind them.

"Is that why the book sent us south?" muttered Ilianora. "So we could liberate a foreign capital of its pests?"

"We could look at the book agin," said Rain, slyly enough. "If you en't sure it was telling us to go south, let's see. Mebbe now it'll say go north, or go to the desert."

But the Grimmerie wouldn't open for them this time. Perhaps, thought Brrr, it had heard Rain's suggestion that Yackle was warning them to get away from it. It was sulking. Anyway, keeping its own counsel, much as any unread book does.

Maybe we *would* be better off without it?

Then Brrr thought, maybe Chalotin set Rain up to steal that shell. If all magic totems are forbidden, Chalotin herself might be safer to be shy of a powerful item.

Oooh, but what a narcotic, paranoia.

15.

Rain had never taken into account creatures en masse. To her, the companions of the Clock retained a stubborn and incomprehensible separateness. But the otters conjoined like individual autumn leaves into a single pile.

She remembered the original lonely fish against her finger, the mouse in the field that was her oldest memory—maybe these were instances of aberration. Single creatures in their single lives.

One rice otter, maybe a little bit smaller than its mates, had a slightly rosier cast. (She couldn't tell genders even when they were fucking; they seemed entirely too limber to be limited to a single gender. She found herself thinking of the rosier one as *it*.) Since she could identify it in the horde, she cared for it more than the others.

Miles beyond Qhoyre, miles beyond the ruins of Bengda on Waterslip, the rains began. A throng of pilgrims huddling under palmetto leaves, on their way back to Qhoyre from some ceremony in the swamplands, said in kitchen Ozish that the high city of Ovvels was only a day or two away. The companions would find succor there for the rest of the rainy season if they pressed on, said the pilgrims. Though the pilgrims might have softened their promise of a welcome if they'd known about the white river of otters following like a scourge behind.

High city? In this lowland swamp? What could that mean?

They found out. The track on which the companions had traipsed from Qhoyre slowly raised itself on gravel-banked shoulders. The ramp proved so slight an incline that Brrr hardly felt the strain, even though the wheels sucked into the mud. On either side of the highway—a literal highway—grew a town much smaller than Qhoyre, and more real, in a way. Ancient suppletrees, knitting their elbows together, supported small huts from which walkways were slung. A village of treehouses. Every roof was palmettoed, every window netted with gauzlin. Even in the drenching, some people were fishing from their front doors with strings let down into the swamp.

"Bird people!" cried Rain, though in many ways they proved to be more like fish people.

The main track on which the companions had arrived leveled out on top of a thick wall built of granite blocks. Twenty, twenty-four feet high, and just as wide. "Quadling know-how isn't up to this job. The flatboat to haul such heavy stone has never been built. This wall was here long before the town," said Mr. Boss.

"But the stones must have been cut by masons, and laid by engineers, time out of mind," said the Lion. "If the Quadlings didn't build this, some earlier population did." Rain ran her hand over marks left in the surface by ancient adzes and chisels.

The characteristic hospitality of Quadlings asserted itself. Some kind of mayoral commission dragged itself together to negotiate lodging for the itinerants. The side of the wall that slanted northeast had been fitted with ledges and steps leading to cells and stalls. Maybe dug out by later generations. The company could take their choice of rooms. The floors might be muddy, but there were shelves on which the companions could dryly sleep.

It was a simple enough matter to drag the Clock into a barnlike warehouse in which it just fit, to cover the thing with banyan leaves until the rain moved over. The natives were fascinated by it, but Mr. Boss said, "Go away. No looky look."

Rain was beginning to call the rosy-chinned otter Tay, after a Qua'ati word *te,* meaning "friend." Rain and Tay slept in a cell with the Lion and Ilianora. Mr. Boss and Little Daffy took a chamber beyond that. Rain would rather have been in a tree.

She instructed the other otters to sleep outside. They didn't mind. She couldn't tell Brrr how she had done this. She didn't know. The otters weren't talking Animals.

On the outer wall of the defensive rampart, if that's what it was, the Quadlings had painted illustrations of huge glowing fish. Gold and blue, ingesting each other, smiling at each other in passing, eliminating one another cloacally. "Is these fish as big as life?" Rain asked Ilianora. "Any fish so big en't fitting in any rice paddy."

"These fish look like giant ancestors dating back to the dawn of the gods. It's art. Pay it no mind. It's all fabrications and lies. I have no patience for lies of any kind, especially the lies of art."

"What about the Clock?" asked Rain. "And what it says, or won't say?"

Ilianora wouldn't answer.

Rain loved the great staring ovoids. She was living in a wall of fish that were swimming toward her from the past. She hadn't thought about the past much—not even her own past—but now her memory of the fish in the ice pocket accrued some meaning. It had wanted to get back to its gods or its grandparents. It had had someplace to swim to.

Wouldn't that be nice, to be a fish. And have someplace to swim to.

16.

It took a while for the companions to realize that the monsoons weren't necessarily annual events. A monsoon began when it began, and it lasted as long as it wanted. Until this one was over there was no hope to move on. Endless, endless rain. The company of the Clock of the Time Dragon spent almost a year in Ovvels waiting for a spell clear enough for the high road to dry.

A whole year in which no battalion of pursuers from the Emerald City swam up to the long island of the high road.

A year in which no foot-free seer from Qhoyre managed to stump up the ramp to demand her money back or to reclaim her purloined shell.

A year in which no news of the battle between Loyal Oz and Munchkinland seeped into the backwashes of soggy Quadling Country.

It was, therefore, a year of quiet. Mercy to some—including Rain—and hard luck on others. She learned to watch her companions more closely, even if she kept her distance.

Mr. Boss declared he'd had decades learning how to kick back when the opportunity presented itself. He could busy himself, thank you very much. Out of balsa bark he whittled figurines handicapped by oversize genitalia. To Rain they seemed more dead than mud, and when he wasn't looking she stole them and sent them flying through the air, to swim a while and eventually drown.

She liked stealing things, though most of what she stole she threw away. To rescue it, to liberate it. The glossy pink shell, with its spiraled belt of spikes and its silky silvered mouth, was an exception. She kept waiting for it to talk to her.

When Mr. Boss protested that his little people were disappearing, Little Daffy replied, "I think they're disgusting, but don't look at me." The Munchkinlander whiled away the hours trying to teach such advanced medicine as she could to the local fish doctors, though with limited resources her efforts were lacking in smack. The Quadlings took to the Munchkinlander as if she were a kind of toy grandmother. Rain heard Brrr mutter that Little Daffy was having too much fun and wouldn't want to move on when and if the sun ever returned.

"You think I'm just a rural squash," the Munch-kinlander snapped at the Lion. "You think I'm drunk on exotica. You think I'm going native. Maybe you've heard that when I helped my old colleague and nem-esis, Sister Doctor, tend to that ailing Scrow poten-tate, Princess Nastoya, I fell in love with the Scrow. Well, it's true. I could've stayed there. But I had my calling."

"I'm your calling now, honeybag," said Mr. Boss. "Don't you forget it."

"You kidnapped me," she told him. "But bygones be gone, as they say."

Little Daffy gave up running a rural clinic and took to playing a kind of strip canasta with a bordello of Quadling maidens possessed both of loose clothing and morals. When Mr. Boss tried to peer in the shutters at them, she called him a perv and slammed them shut. Then the giggles! The dwarf sulked for a week, fouler than usual.

"Get away from that window or you'll go blind," he growled at Rain, who was just passing, minding her own business.

She didn't answer him, just slid on by. Watching. Adults were more broken than animals, she thought. She missed the birds of the sky, the big birds: in the jungle, only sodden little feather-fluffs hopped from branch to dripping branch under the jungle canopy.

Every now and then she went to look at the Clock, to see if it had wakened up. She was the only one to visit it as far as she knew, but the thing stayed frozen, dead as one of the dwarf's ugly carvings.

For Brrr's part, the months of inaction made him consider that the one thing that had characterized his life since infancy was his constant motion. No matter how much he'd enjoyed life among the great and the good in Shiz or the Emerald City, he wasn't a house Lion at heart. He was a roving beast. Maybe his life-long tendency to take umbrage at minor slights was a symptom of his chronic eagerness to get going somewhere else. He only ever needed a good reason.

He wouldn't leave Ilianora, though. He could tell this waiting was hard on her too. Waiting for what? The book—they had kept trying to open it—offered no further advice. Meanwhile, Ilianora's veil, which for so long had stayed down, was raised again, in more ways than one. She lived in a new silence, and slept with her back to him. They'd never been lovers, of course, not in the physical sense. But they'd been lovers as most of us manage, loving through expressions and gestures and the palm set softly upon the bruise at the necessary moment. Lovers by inclination rather than by lust. Lovers, that is, by love.

So Brrr was cross, too. Everyone was more or less cross except for Rain.

The Quadling children tried to make friends with Rain, but she felt unsure of their intentions. Anyway, they didn't like the otters, who bit children when provoked. Though Tay never so much as nibbled at Rain. Except a little. And it hardly hurt.

Alone most of the day, Rain was turning into a little monkey on the vines and trestle-passes of the supplewood trees. Tay scurried along behind her like a kind of white trailing sock. Brrr watched her with cautious eyes. She was growing, their Rain. Her limbs liked this damp climate. Ilianora had had to sacrifice another veil to make a longer tunic for the girl, lest she flash her private parts by accident and invite a disaster.

Just in time, before a couple of marriages broke irreparably, the sun returned. Steamy yellow and obscure white. It hurt their eyes. With it arrived new generations of biting bug who were impervious to the few remaining sachets of unguent the companions had harvested more than a year earlier. It would be time to get moving before long. "What're we *waiting* for?" asked Ilianora.

"For a sign of some sort," said Mr. Boss.

"You're not over that yet? The Clock is broken. There are no signs." Her tone was aggrieved in a cosmic way. The dwarf rolled his eyes.

The painted fish looked now as if they were swimming in light instead of streaked green air. Early one morning Rain caught sight of an etiolated matron touching up one of the fishes with some blue paint ground up in a gourd. She was dabbing with her fingers and singing to herself. This old flamingo had never seen a big fish like that, but still she had the temerity to instruct it to swim for another year?

Strange. Another lie, thought Rain.

"We don't have a prophecy from the Time Dragon, we get no reading from the Grimmerie," said Mr. Boss one day. "The sun is our alarmus. We're off and away with the piskies. Let's unshroud the Clock and oil the axles and it's hey, hey, for the open road. The book don't like it, let it give us some better advice." He got no argument, except from Little Daffy, who had to be encouraged to swaddle her breasts again. "I'm going to miss the old damp hole in the wall," she said, sweeping it out with that Munchkinlander frenzy for housecleaning. "If we ever retire, darling Mr. Boss, perhaps we can come back here for our sunset years?"

He didn't answer. He was cheery for once, swarming as high up the Clock as he could, though he was no match for Rain.

All of Ovvels gathered to see them drag the Clock out of its tomb. However feeble the Qua'ati that the companions had managed to learn in a year, it served well enough for good-byes. A berdache of some sort, a smeary-eyed young man with pinkened lips, made a speech hearkening back to some time when another troupe of northerners had come through and lived with them for a while. Before his day, but it was local lore. "They to try convince us to believe in something they say is not there," he said, "the god who is unnamed."

"*Missionaries,*" said Little Daffy, who had put her own past behind her with dizzying alacrity. But "Couldn't you just puke?" had to do for social comment, and after that she kept her mouth shut.

"We did not to kill them," said the berdache. "Minister come to educate and steal our souls for his god who won't to name itself. Rude man. Man of moldy thought. But he has girl with him we do not forget." He smiled at Rain as if she were that girl, and he wasn't discussing something that happened a hundred thousand years ago in folk memory but this very week. "He has little green girl with him. His oldest girl. She to sing for him, when we to harvest vegetable pearl. She sing the pearl off the vine. I am not there but she is like you." He nodded to Rain.

The others bowed to Rain. She put her shell up to her head and turned away, as if she preferred its windy noise over their attention.

Brrr said, "How can you know our Rain is like that girl if none of you were alive back then?"

The man shrugged. He indicated to Ilianora that he would accept the gift of her scarf. She didn't hand it over. Sighing, he answered Brrr as best he could anyway. "Some Quadlings to have sense to see the present, to know the present," he finished. "We to see your young rafiqi girl and we to know she is the one they talk about."

"I to see myself into a loony bin in about one minute," said Mr. Boss. "Let's go."

Brrr wondered what they saw when they looked at Rain, and why they waved at her so affectionately when for a year she hadn't given them the time of day. Of any day.

"Aren't you going to show us the Clock?" asked the berdache. "Before you go?"

"It doesn't show truth to pagans," said Mr. Boss. "Why would you believe it when you can't believe in a god you can't see?"

"We housed you and fed you through months of rains. You won't deny us a look at the future. Quadlings, when they're able, can sometimes see the present, but this Clock tells the truth of all things."

"I never said that," swore the dwarf, stamping.

"You never did," agreed the berdache, batting his eyelids. "But I can see the present, and I know that is what you think."

The companions were in a bind. They couldn't leave without paying the Quadlings of Qhoyre *something* for a year's lodging and board. Cursing up a head of steam, the dwarf made valiant effort to rev the old girl up. Put on a little demonstration. All things being equal and buyer beware, and so on.

"Come on," said Rain on her haunches, bouncing up and down like the monkeys she played with. "Come on!"

The Clock obeyed nobody's deepest wishes. Mr. Boss couldn't get a shutter to open, a crank to turn, a single puppet to appear and blow a kiss at the assembled crowd. "It's done for," he declared. His furrowed expression showed him to be sincere. The Quadlings had no choice but to offer him their condolences on the death of the future.

"It died just like that god who slid off the world and lost his name," said the berdache. "Never to mind. Is pretty dragon anyway."

"The Unnamed God isn't a person," said Little Daffy, out of some final spasm of feeling for her religious past.

"And fate isn't limited to a tiktok dragon's sense of theatrics," added the Lion.

"Nor the spell of any magic book," offered Ilianora.

The Quadlings began to bow and wave the companions off. They didn't want philosophics. They'd wanted a bite at the future, and were willing to live without it the way their ancestors had done. The berdache walked them a little way out of town, on the northern ramp off the elevated road. "Perhaps the world is to heal," he said. "The vegetable pearls healthier this spring than I ever to see them. Perhaps the rice otters to learn their old way and go green as before, now there are pearls to help harvest."

"Too much mystery for an old fraying hairdo like mine," muttered the dwarf, disconsolate. "So long, chumpo."

"Lord Chumpo," said the berdache, rushing to give out embraces. Ilianora turned her head and beckoned Rain to walk with her. But Rain was getting too big to order around. Her head was higher than Ilianora's elbow now—almost as high as her breast.

17.

Their spirits lifted as they left Ovvels behind. Such was the power of the sun that even under the jungle canopy a year's worth of monsoon drippage burned off in a matter of days. The companions didn't find the passage tough, only slow, as they had to clear undergrowth every quarter mile.

Brrr had hoped, once they began to move again, that Ilianora's mood would improve, but she continued to seem vexed. It took him a few days of watching her watch the girl before he was able to frame his thought.

The girl was growing up. Their Rain. That's what was agitating Ilianora.

Growing up, and growing beyond them.

Rain had not been theirs, not for a moment. Brrr could still read with a parental eye how the world could present itself to a young girl like Rain. And how Rain might respond, this girl who seemed, increasingly, to be interested in learning to read everything except how human beings talked to one another.

"She's all right," said Brrr, splashing through the lily pads, the floating beehives. And Rain was all right. But Ilianora—he had to face it—was not.

That night, he thought another, more common thought. Maybe it's that time of Ilianora's life. Maybe it hurts Ilianora to admit that Rain isn't her daughter.

That there will be no daughter now. Not even if Ilianora could unstitch the seam and find a human male as another husband. The vegetable pearls were not growing for Ilianora.

18.

They'd been told they'd leave the mucklands behind soon enough, and the road would climb some sandy slopes, and eventually debouche into the Sleeve of Ghastille. This broad and fertile valley led northeast, marking the border between the Vinkus and Quadling Country. The berdache of Ovvels had insisted that the companions would find few inhabitants in the valley, but they must beware nonetheless.

"If it's so fertile, why is it uninhabited?" Mr. Boss had demanded. The answers had been incoherent. The natural landscape between the Great Kells to the west and the Quadling Kells to the east proved low and dry and well drained. Surely it seemed an ideal route for the Yellow Brick Road? Back in the day when it was being laid out? And why had any human travelers to the Thousand Year Grasslands to the west chosen to brave the inhospitable track over Kumbricia's Pass rather than this lower and more welcoming approach?

It didn't take long for the companions to see why. The pass was a set of gentle crescents around foothills that abutted the horizon from east and west. From slope to slope, at this time of year anyway, an ocean of carmine red flowers took their breath away. Poppies.

"I know about poppies," said Mr. Boss. "Grim business, even for me, who likes a tidy profit if I can turn one."

"*I* know about poppies," agreed his wife. "All kinds of useful applications that you can rarely take advantage of because of side effects. We were forbidden to use them in the surgery when we could even get them, which was seldom."

Brrr felt their effect at once. The odor was of scorched cinnamon, savagely beguiling. In the freshening light and the wind that swept west from the swamplands and the grasslands, the air pushed the pollen heavily ahead of them. It inflected the day no less than fog or rain or brutal heat might have done. The travelers struggled through the endless carpet. Were anyone to try to follow them after all this time, too bad: the tracks of the cart were swallowed up as the blossoms closed ranks.

Rain hunted daily for high-flying birds. Remembering the Wren? But even eagles and rocs seemed to give this valley a pass.

At night Brrr slept fitfully, with dreams of things he would rather not remember. Appetites long suppressed, for one—and healthily so, he remonstrated himself upon awakening. Chief among them an appetite for shame.

They were all affected. They pushed to get through the sweep of bloody blossom at as swift a clip as they could manage. But the Sleeve ran vaguely uphill, and the labor of hauling the Clock seemed harder than before. Or had Brrr grown soft again during nearly a full year of downpour?

The new anxiety came to a head on the third afternoon of wading through thigh-high blossoms. Rain had been caught stealing some sugar brittle from the Clock's supplies, and the dwarf went overboard railing at her. Brrr lunged to the girl's defense. "*You're* so noble? Tricking people for decades about fate with this diabolical dragon routine? Give her a break. When's she ever learned about right and wrong?"

"Not from you," replied the dwarf. "You great big shameless Cowardly Lion."

"Nor from your wife," replied Brrr, "tricking that old seer in Qhoyre into thinking her feet would grow back."

"You're hardly one to talk about conscience," began the Munchkinlander.

"Stop," said Ilianora in a low, deadened sort of voice. They did, but only because she hadn't spoken for a while. "Prophecy is dead, and conscience is dead too."

They kept walking, making whiskery sounds of passage in the verdure.

She continued, dry as a sphinx in the Sour Sands. "That berdache believed that any Unnamed God must be a dead god. But it's conscience that's dead. Maybe the dragon really w-was . . . was the conscience of Oz. But it's dead. Oz is broken in parts—Loyal Oz divided from Munchkinland, and who knows what polders and provinces might splinter off next? There isn't any full Oz anymore, and no conscience, either. That's why the dragon died. Just about the time those other real dragons threatened to attack Munchkinland. We're broke. We're broke and we can't be fixed."

"Nonsense," said Brrr, trying to hurry a little to her side, but he was so tired, and the heavy cart of dead conscience dragged at him.

"And what's left then?" The Lion's wife tried to stifle a gasp of remorse. "We're all schemers and liars, thieves and scoundrels. To our own private good cause. There's no primary conscience to call us up."

It was Little Daffy who replied—she who had toed the line of unionism the most faithfully all those years in the mauntery.

"If there's no good conscience to trust," she declared, "no Lurline, no Ozma, no Unnamed God, no standard of goodness, then we have to manage for ourselves. Maybe there's no central girl in some hall in the Emerald City, all bronzed and verdigrised, all windswept hair and upthrust naked breast, lots of bright honor carved in her blind and focused eyes. No conscience like that, no reliable regula of goodness. So it's up to us, each of us a part. A patchwork conscience. If we all make our own mistakes, from Rain stealing stuff to the rest of us lying to ourselves and each other—well, we can all make amends, too. No one of us the final arbiter, but each of us capable of adding our little bit. We're the patchwork conscience of Oz, us lot. As long as the Unnamed God refuses to take off the mask and come for a visit. As long as the dragon has croaked on us."

No one seconded the notion. No one objected. They staggered on. Wilting, aggrieved, conscience-stricken, dulled.

19.

They read the solar compass, the play of shadows on staggered sets of slope. It shouldn't take more than fifteen or twenty hours to cross the Sleeve of Ghastille, they guessed. Still, every day they could manage no more than a few miles before exhaustion set in. Brrr was aware that sunlight was good for the eradication of mange, but he needed to rest under the cart. In the shadows. Outside, in the bright light, the red of poppies burned against his retinas through his closed eyelids. A siege of coral light, a siege of fire.

Even Little Daffy, with her familiarity with amelioratives and strikems, purges and preventicks, seemed dazed with the effect. "Consolidated airborne precipitate. How *do* these blossoms manage?" she moaned, and rolled down on the ground next to her husband, exposing her bosom to the glow. The liberty of Quadling mores had rooted in her in a big way.

Ilianora, however, became ever more shrouded in her veils. Only her eyes showed.

The Sleeve was ahead of them and behind them, a river of mocking full-lipped smiles lapping a third of the way up the foothills on either side of them. Had anyone been able to look overhead, they would have thought the sky was red, too, probably; red, or by that trick of compensation that human eyes manage briefly, perhaps green.

The companions had decided to try traveling under the red stars at night, when the effect of the vegetation was less oppressive. During the day they napped or lay down with handkerchiefs over their eyes, stoned. Ilianora, perhaps because she kept her veils over her nose and mouth, became the de facto lookout, and even she found her attention hard to marshal. "You should take some water," she would murmur, to no one in particular, and then get some for herself when no one replied. On one such occasion she rounded the corner of the Clock and walked into a loosened shutter.

The main doors of the Clock had swung open. Rain was lying on the stage, a hand draped over the edge as if she were dabbling her fingers in a brook.

Then Rain sat up, and her eyes were wide and staring, but not at Ilianora. The child's expression was equal parts horror and fascination. Rain seemed in a spell of delusion, beginning to reach out to invisible creatures on the ground, to pet something, to lift them up, then to recoil her fingertips as if they'd been bitten or burned.

The poppies near the wagon stirred, roiled, as of a wind along the ground, though there was no sign of any creature among their hairy twists of stem.

Ilianora's voice issued, more steam than volume, the way that one attempts to scream in a dream but can't get louder.

She tried to stagger forward herself, to help the girl in whatever new disaster this was. Her own limbs seemed locked, frozen, her mind slowed. Her carapaced form was hindered by the winding sheets of her veils.

Her utterance sounded hollow, and Brrr only snored on. The girl began to thrash. "Oh," said Ilianora. It was the sound someone makes finding a common word in a surprising context. "Oh, hmmm."

Before Rain could fall from the stage, though, or suffer a mental collapse right before Ilianora's eyes, the poppies around the Clock of the Time Dragon whipped into frenzy. This time Ilianora could see the cause. As if swimming underneath the toxic tide, a school of rice otters approached through the greeny algae of poppy stem and leaves. The warm light silting through red petals turned their short fur greenish. Something happened that only Ilianora among the companions witnessed, unless Rain was watching too, behind her blanked-out eyes. A battle between the otters and an invisible foe. Ilianora couldn't see the event, only its effects, as otters thrashed something silly, or the field of poppies thrashed itself. A blood that was not the stain of poppy dye ran from the mouths of otters.

Something was massacred in fifteen minutes, while Brrr hummed in his sleep and Little Daffy waved an inebriated fly from the canyon of her cleavage. Ilianora trembled as if in a gale. The petals ripped and shredded and blew about them. Eventually Rain began to soften, her paralysis to collapse, and she fell weeping on the stage floor.

But Ilianora couldn't make herself move to comfort the girl. It was too horrible. She was frozen too.

By the time night fell, Ilianora was huddled against Brrr as he pulled himself up to a crouch. Little Daffy made some gloppy soup with a garnish of poppy pollen sprinkled on top. Mr. Boss was energized by the fact that the doors of the Clock had swung open, though once he refastened them they went right back into their old paralysis. Still, the fact they could still open seemed to be a useful kick in the butt. As he set to doing something of a tune-up, he whistled as he worked. Tunelessly.

"What happened?" asked Ilianora when the meal was done, and Brrr was cleaning the bowls with his tongue.

"Something was following us," said Rain. "I don't know what it was."

"What did it look like? Soldiers?" asked Little Daffy.

"No. More like, um, spiders," said Rain. "But more up-and-down than spread out. Their legs not so wide and curved like umbrella ribs, but more straight. Like what Murthy used to call a side table."

Brrr said, "You had a dream of being attacked by a matched set of occasional tables? That reminds me of my setting up my first digs in Ampleton Quarters, back in the Shiz days. Green in judgment and all that. A case of nerves about being unpracticed at both sex and society was nothing compared to fretting that the wall hangings and the upholstery didn't see eye to eye." He knew he sounded berserk. He was trying to make light of Rain's experience, whatever it had been.

"They wasn't tables. They was beasties of some sort."

"I suppose you took their names down, Rain, and all became quite cozy," said Little Daffy. "You and your little party animals."

"What did they want?" asked Mr. Boss. "You? Or the book?"

"I don't know. I didn't call 'em to me, but they came. They been following for a while I guess but I forgot to tell you."

"Call me superior, but frankly I don't think it's likely you can see things we can't," said Little Daffy. "What were we saying earlier about conscience? In my day a girl who told tales would get a right smart spanking on her fanny."

"You wasn't looking. You was sunning."

Ilianora roused herself. "Rain's not pulling a fast one. I saw it happen. I saw *something* happen. Something came at the Clock, though whether it was for her or for the Grimmerie I don't know."

"They was the things that came to scrabble into the Clock the day I got locked in for safety," said Rain. "The spiderish things from the jungle's edge."

The group fell silent. Brrr twitched his tail around exploratively, to see if it landed on something. No doubt he would scream like a schoolgirl if he touched . . . it. "Are they still here?" As baritone a voice as he could manage.

"They is all gone." Rain began to cry a little. "I don't know if they was good or bad or just hungry for something, but they is all gone. The rice otters got 'em."

It was only then that they realized the rice otters had disappeared too. Hurried back to their swamp at last. All except for the one Rain had called Tay. It curled up on her lap and made itself at home, like a kitten. But its albino period was done. It looked like a mossy kitten entirely incapable of ripping a predator to shreds.

Brrr was consoled at the sight. He turned his attention to Ilianora, who continued to seem shattered at having witnessed an attack by an invisible foe.

Anyone would be spooked by such a thing, he knew, but Ilianora—who shielded herself from notice by her veils—had been the one unlucky witness. She had withstood the opiate of the blossoms better than any of them. Why?

Well, she was sealed up, for one thing—actually and symbolically. That must be it. But having been protected by the suture, she was still vulnerable. The variety of despair brought on by panic and dread. She'd seen too much torture in her childhood. How well would she survive a genuine attack, one that had to be seen, that couldn't be denied or filed away as delusion or fancy?

20.

The clouds skirted the bright moon in a well-behaved manner, so the companions pressed on through the Sleeve of Ghastille all night. They were eager to escape whatever the lure of poppies called up. Brrr, if he had put a name to it, would have said *impatience with Ilianora.*

Ilianora would have said *panic,* though panic had been dogging her footsteps since long before they entered the valley of the poppies.

Little Daffy regretted leaving such abundance of raw poppy material behind, but she went along grudgingly, making allowances for future needs.

Mr. Boss wanted his Clock to start working again.

Hugging Tay like a rag doll, Rain fell more silent than usual. She stayed closer to Brrr than to the others. He was the biggest even if the most squeamish.

Another day or two, another week, it was hard to tell, but things were improving. Maybe they were all just drying out after the wet year. Eventually other growth began to appear among the poppies—a stand of ferns here by the streamside, a clot of sunflowers. Then a few trees, the sort that can find a scrabblehold in sandy soil. The sound of birds up in the greeny shadows. Real birds at their private lessons, then flying high and free against outrageous blue.

The sandy road began to lead along a series of ridges. Brrr had to step carefully lest the ground begin to slide. Though not quite dunes, the slopes were certainly unstable.

Worrying about the apparent conspiracy of the world against the girl, whether Rain knew it or not, Ilianora was a mess of nerves. So Brrr wasn't surprised when she lost it big-time one afternoon nearing sunset. Mr. Boss was just loosening the Lion from his tethers as the Clock perched on a sedge-grass knoll. Little Daffy was snipping some wild runner beans into a salad. Suddenly Tay set up a careering lollop as if bit by a staghead beetle. The rice otter went plunging over the edge of the rise. Ilianora followed it with her eyes—more spiders?—to see Rain walking through grass forty, fifty feet down the steepening slope, toward a fell tiger of some sort who was emerging from the shadows of a copse of birches and terrikins.

"Brrr!" cried Ilianora, for she couldn't sprint that fast, and the Lion could. Brrr was slow to twig, though. "Brrr! She has no fear!"

The Lion slewed about. He let out a roar more iconic than anything else, and he powered his haunches to cover the ground between Rain and the interloper. The dwarf fell back as leathern straps snapped. Probably half-rotted from a year in Quadling Country. The cart inched as if to see for itself, and a curvet of sandhill gave under the rim of the forward wheel. The Clock went plunging down the slope after the Lion; after Rain.

Into this bowl of poppies, the last gasp of their color and prominence, Brrr pounded to the rescue, endangering the Clock. It was a false alarm—or false enough. The stalking creature was a Tiger with Spice Leopard markings. He knew her by the affectionate disregard that rose in her eyes as she turned at the sound of his approach; he knew her for his first love, Muhlama H'aekeem.

21.

"You always were rash. I wasn't going to snack on her," said Muhlama. She neither flinched nor flushed at seeing him again. As if he hadn't been chased from her tribe by her chieftain father bent on vengeance—oh, all those years ago, twenty was it? As if Brrr had merely stepped out for an evening constitutional.

She was a matron Ivory Tiger now. Not given over to fat as some might have done, but sleek still. Markings about her cheeks had gone a silver that verged on purple. "I never took you for a pack Lion," she added as Little Daffy and Mr. Boss, like stout grasshoppers, came hopping down the hill toward the Clock, which lay on its side, the dragon snout collapsed into its own poppy cushions, laid to rest.

"Get back, Rain," growled Brrr. "Go to Ilianora. She's having a fit up there."

"I just wanted to . . ." Rain put out her hand, palm down, indicating something to Muhlama, but Brrr had no patience. He roared at Rain and she backed up, not so much horrified as, perhaps, embarrassed for him.

"I never thought I'd see you do that," said Muhlama as the girl retreated. "Roar, I mean. Didn't quite seem in your makeup. She's only a human cub, of course. But that was relatively convincing. Have you gone on the stage?"

He couldn't chitchat. "Were you going to harm her?"

"Why would I want to do that? Of course not. I've been looking for her. For you all. The aerial reconnaissance team finally located you after what, a year? I've been sent here to swim in the Field of Lost Dreams and drag you out by the scruff of your necks, if I needed to. You've been a long time making your way."

"It's quite a passage, this Sleeve of Ghastille."

"You're almost through. Two miles on there's real grass. Let's decamp there."

"I have to see to the Clock."

"Not much left of that, it looks like."

They both soft-footed it over to the heap of split canvas and detritus. One wheel was spinning slowly like a roulette. Mr. Boss was pale, and Little Daffy was trying to fling her arms around him, but he was having none of it. "We're over, we're history," he was saying. "Conscience dead, history buried."

Rain sat down in the shadow of the wreck and draped one of the leather wings over her head, a tent of sorts. Ilianora stared at Brrr with fierce eyes as if something were all his fault. Well, he was used to that, but not in a while, and not from her.

"How bad is it?" he asked the dwarf. Mr. Boss was blubbering. So the Lion looked for himself.

The wheels on the right side had buckled so that the left side, the most prominent of the stage areas, was exposed to view like a corpse. The Clock's last revelation? Brrr felt prurient to peer at it, but peer he did. They all did.

The shutters were flung wide. The proscenium had split at the top and its segments overlapped like misaligned front teeth. The red velvet curtain, fallen from its rings, draped off the front of the stage, a lolling tongue.

In the mouth of the Clock, its main stage, lay some composite material, papier-mâché perhaps, made up to look like stones. On one side of the stage they resembled boulders having avalanched down a cliffside, but on the other side they seemed more carved, as if to imitate the rusticated facades of great stone buildings.

The place didn't look much like the Emerald City, nor like Shiz. Nothing like Qhoyre.

No, this looked like a foreign city-state. Maybe someplace in Ix or Fliaan, if those places even existed. Brrr had his doubts.

Or an imagined place. As if such places existed, either.

Bits and pieces of puppets lay strewn about, spilled into an effectively ropey sort of red, almost like poppy juice. No figure resembled anyone even marginally familiar. No stripe-stockinged witch crushed under a farmhouse. No corpse of baby Ozma bundled upside down into an open sewer. No costume, even, that anyone could identify—no Messiars or Menaciers from the military of Loyal Oz's Home Guard, no cunning Munchkinlander folk getup for delighting tourists, no glamour gowns from palace balls. In their rictus, the puppets looked only like carved bits of wood and painted plasticine. The strings that held them in place lay snapped atop them. Dead, they convinced nothing about Death, except via the corollary that Life, perhaps, had always been made from scrap materials, and always would be.

"It's an earthquake," said Mr. Boss at last. He turned to Brrr. "You did this to it. You killed it."

"She called out," said the Lion. His use of the pronoun for his wife was the cruelest remark he had ever made, but he couldn't help himself. "The girl comes before the Clock. As you should have known this last year, and some."

"I told you we shouldn't take her on!" The dwarf staggered about in a circle, beating his forehead with his fists. "The Clock saw the danger, and warned me against her!"

"I don't cause earthquakes," said Rain.

"Looks a heap of damaged goods to me," said Muhlama.

Little Daffy found the Grimmerie a few feet away, lying where it had been pitched. Hidden in the shadow of the dragon's ripped wing, as if the last act of the failing tiktokery had been to protect the magic book.

The Clock might be sprung at last, its mechanism despoiled after a century of charm, but the book remained closed to prying fingers.

"Let's right the old lady, anyway, and see if we can cobble together a repair," said Brrr. He wept a little, as if the dragon had been a companion too, and dissected one of its wings to remove a sallowwood humerus. With his little knife the dwarf fashioned enough of a substitute axle to manage.

They dragged the dead Clock through the last few miles of the Sleeve of Ghastille. In a shadowy meadow where the brook widened out, they paused to breathe the air less thick with poppy dust.

Brrr noticed it was autumn again. More than a year had passed since they had taken Rain from Lady Glinda. The twisted bows of pretzel puzzle trees were raging with hornets doing their anxious final dance. The leaves were falling, red and gold. They fell into the open mouth of the theater. When the sun began to set over the Great Kells and its light struck the stage, the earthquake event glowed as if it had been further plagued by a conflagration.

After a pick-me-up supper had been prepared and mostly ignored, and they were sitting around a small fire of their own, the company of the Clock without, it seemed, the Clock to cohere them, Brrr asked of Muhlama, "On whose agency have you been trying to rope us in? You weren't a team player when last we met, as I recall."

"Still not," she said, yawning. "I've turned my back on my tribe, as you did on yours, Sir Brrr. But I never took up with humans. Yes, I've heard all about your later . . . accomplishments." She had lost none of her power of condescension, he saw, almost affectionately. She continued. "I have no money on the matter of governments either way. I owe no loyalty to the grandees of the Emerald City or to the pipsqueaks of Munchkinland." Little Daffy glowered at her in defense of her people, but Muhlama was impervious to a Munchkin glower.

"Someone sent you," prompted Brrr.

"Someone asked me to come," she agreed. "Someone said you might be in danger. I thought it might be amusing to watch. I had owed you something, after all."

She had. Brrr's dalliance with her had given her the alibi to leave the line of succession of the Spice Tiger camp. To escape the destiny of leadership her father, Uyodor H'aekeem, had required of her. Brrr saw that much more clearly now, since he too hadn't been above using others as pawns for his own ambitions. "I was happy to help," he said. "Way back then."

"I made you happy to help," she admitted. She flicked her tail in a way that reminded him of her seduction, the sordor of it, the ardor of it. But her tail was a commentary on Animal relations, not a come-on. "You freed me from my own prison. These years later, the moment arrived for me to try to do the same for you." She looked sideways at Ilianora, who appeared as if carved out of ivory, staring at the flames, and added drily, "If that's your wife, perhaps I didn't come soon enough."

"Tell us what you know," he said. "Has the invasion by Loyal Oz been successful? Has Haugaard's Keep fallen? Is the Emperor still blathering on his throne? It's been a year since we've lost touch with the news."

She limned it in quickly. "The Munchkinlanders defended their positions for as long as they could, but eventually they had to abandon the lake. All but the eastern fort. For a while it's looked as if Loyal Oz will keep Restwater, requiring a retrocession of that edge of Munchkinland. Perhaps, folks said, to avoid further incursions, the Munchkinland Eminence would settle the matter, accepting the loss of the lake in exchange for political integrity of the rest of Munchkinland."

"The EC only ever wanted water," said the Lion.

"Not true. They also need the grain supplied by the breadbasket of Oz, in central Munchkinland," Muhlama argued. "They need enough of a détente that commerce can begin again. There's been a certain amount of unrest and deprivation in the Emerald City while Oz is engaged in this civil war."

"So what's the problem?" asked Brrr. "They sue for peace."

"The Emperor," said Muhlama, and yawned. "Shell Thropp. You remember him? I see you do. The younger brother of those sister witches, Elphaba and Nessarose. He has declared himself divine. He has promoted himself god."

"Nice work if you can get it," said Mr. Boss, his first comment in hours.

"The Munchkinlanders had enough of godliness after their years under the yoke of Nessarose," replied the Ivory Tiger. "They're commonsense when it comes to commerce, but they get their backs up when it comes to dogma. They won't negotiate with a god. Who could? So just as it seemed a peace might be brokered, the Emperor had to go do a pious makeover and provoke the humble Munchkinlanders, who never ever shall be slaves. It's not money. It's some dim little ember of self-respect that won't die out in the stout breasts of Munchkinlanders."

"I'm not that stout," said Little Daffy. "I'd say pleasingly plump."

"The plumper, the pleasinglier," said Mr. Boss, laying his head thereupon.

"Who is leading this Munchkinlander resistance to a brokered settlement?" asked Brrr. "When Nessarose was killed by that house of Dorothy . . ."

"I remember that," said Little Daffy. "I was there that day."

Brrr continued. ". . . the first response upon liberation was to revoke the rights of the Eminences of Munchkinland and centralize control. No? I remember someone named Hipp, or Nipp, who named himself Prime Minister."

"I didn't read history, ancient or modern," said Muhlama. "I'm a creature of the hills and shadows. As you ever knew. But the Eminenceship is not entirely dead. Titles never die, they just go somnolent. Some crone or crony of the old Wizard of Oz has emerged to claim authority, if I have it right. Someone named Mombey. A kind of witch."

"Hasn't the Emperor called in all magic utensils, hasn't he forebade the casting of spells? I thought the time of witches was done," said Brrr.

"It's never done," said the Tigress. "Besides, you're forgetting the Emperor doesn't have the rights to legislate about magic in Munchkinland. That's part of what they're fighting against."

"I'm going to bed," said Ilianora, and she crept into the shadows of the useless Clock, pulling the ratty leather wing over her head like a blanket. "Come, Rain, settle with me. There's no need to hear gossip about government. It'll only give you gas."

"It's my belief that Munchkinlanders will launch a counterinvasion," said Muhlama. "Won't that be fun? Overrunning the EC with pudgy little ferret people? They have a dynamic military commander who has managed to hold on to Haugaard's Keep, after all. A steeltrap farmgirl now goes by the name of General Jinjuria. She calls herself the Foill of Munchkinland."

"A stage name for a commanding officer," said the Lion. "It's all stage stuff now, isn't it?"

"Get me my wrap, I don't need the second act," she replied.

The dwarf and the Munchkinlander retired on the other side of the Clock. Rain and Tay crept in among the earthquake ruins, and no one stopped them. Muhlama and Brrr stayed awake, side by side, looking not at each other but at the horizon to the east, where creatures with names like Mombey and Jinjuria were providing some background static to the story of the Cats' rendezvous.

22.

Under stars at first, then under a waterstain of vaporous cloud, high up. They didn't talk anymore, not till morning.

Ilianora gave the Tiger ample distance, and offered her no coffee.

"I'm no threat to you, Brrr. I'm joining no mission," said Muhlama. "I'm bringing you out to your counterparts where they wait, and then going my own way. Ever was a rogue Tigress. But I confess to a little curiosity about that Matter of Dorothy. When I heard you were involved, I admit I was surprised. You didn't seem to have it in you to get so deep into a mess like that."

"Yes, well, life, it does broaden you. It was just after I left you."

"I left you," she reminded him. "But let's not monkey with nuance. Tell me about that creature. The things that are said about her! A holy fool, say some. A saint. A termagant. A pawn of someone's larger campaign. She brought down the Wicked Witch of the West, for all her clumsiness—maybe *through* her clumsiness, for all I know. You were there. What happened?"

"I was nearby," said the Lion. "I wasn't present, no matter what the papers said. No one was there but Dorothy and the Witch. No one saw what happened. Liir and I were locked in the scullery, and I had managed to break through the door. . . ."

"My hero," she purred, meanly.

"But I didn't get up to the parapet on time. The Witch was gone, and Dorothy descended, blasted and incoherent about what had happened. She was never coherent about very much, come to think of it."

"Spoken like someone trying to distance himself from the inconvenience of a prior sympathy. But I never understood about the shoes. Magic shoes. *Shoes*, of all things? Why not magic braces? Or underwear?"

"I didn't write the script. Don't ask me."

"The Witch's reputation is ripe for a comeback," said Muhlama. "At least in Munchkinland it is. That peculiar creature, Elphaba Thropp, had positioned herself in opposition to the stony faith that ran in her family. Her minister father, her totalitarian sister—and now her brother is god himself! Never underestimate the mood swings of the crowd. Dorothy's gone from being thought a heroine to being tagged as an assassin, and Elphaba from Wicked Witch to martyred champion. At least in some circles."

"The pendulum will swing."

"Ah, but is there such a thing as a pendulum anymore?" They looked at the collapsed Clock, which Mr. Boss continued to try to clean and organize as if by dint of polish and spit he could persuade it to revive. But it was the preparing of a corpse, no more than that. Everyone could see it.

"You haven't said to whom we're headed," said Brrr. "Is it Lady Glinda? Is she released from house arrest?"

"I don't follow the columns," said Muhlama. "Anyway, I'm not talking." She glanced over at Tay, the rice otter, who lay unrepentantly greenly in Rain's arms. "You never know who is a squealer."

Brrr had to agree. "So enough is enough," said Muhlama. "I've done my work, I need to get on."

"But get on where?" he asked her, as they righted the husk of the Clock. The broken dragon head cantilevered forward, eyeless and insensate. "Where are you going? And alone? Or is there a companion?"

"You're so coy."

"Stay with me, now," said Ilianora to Rain. "Keep close." But the girl paid her no more attention than she ever had.

"I'm causing trouble," said Muhlama to Brrr, tossing her head toward Ilianora. "Pity."

"Only so much I can do," replied the Lion, equivocating.

That night Brrr asked of the companions, "*Are* we going our separate ways?" Muhlama, having said she would deliver them to their party in the morning, had taken herself off for a hike, to give the companions privacy to confer. "I mean, there can be no company of the Clock of the Time Dragon anymore, can there, if there is no Clock?"

"It's resting. It's called Time Out," said the dwarf, back to his old belligerence.

"The Lion has a point. Your primary charge was security for the Grimmerie, wasn't it?" said Little Daffy to her husband. "To hear you tell it, the Clock was invented as a wheeled cabinet for safekeeping. Distraction to the masses on the one hand, a magic vault on the other. No one would fault us if we ditched the scabby thing now. We sure could move ahead faster without it. The book is still intact."

"You don't need me to carry a book," continued Brrr. "I was a helpful donkey in the shafts of the cart, sure, but I'm not a house pet."

"Brrr, you do what you like," said Ilianora to her husband. "It makes no difference to me. You *are* no house pet. Go with Muhlama, or not."

"I'm not going with her," said Brrr, though he didn't know if it was *go with* in the adolescent sense, or *go with* as in the future intentional. And he also didn't know if he was telling the truth. Ilianora's suffering charged the conversation with horseradish. If he couldn't know what his wife felt or meant anymore, how could he understand his own changing aspirations?

"I'll see the girl to the next juncture," decided Ilianora, "and I'll carry the book that far too. I can't care for her anymore." Because caring for Rain would hurt—that much was evident. Too much of the young wounded Nor was still, after all this time, alive in the elegant veiled adult. Alive and dead at once. Like the dragon, whose wings flopped in the grass as if with spirit, but nothing like the spirit it had once, magically, possessed.

Midmorning came, a series of brief squalls. Cool, without monsoon steam—glorious. Acorns thrown

from trees; the last of some wild plums. Native woodland, nothing magnificent—but at least northern.
On the lip of a promontory ahead of them, Muhlama
pointed out the arches of some ancient helm that had
probably guarded the environs of Restwater from any
predation ascending through the Sleeve of Ghastille.
"That's where you're headed," the Ivory Tiger told
them. "There's something of a roof left still. You can
shelter from the rain there, should it come down stronger, and meet your maties. Then my job is done, and
I'm off."

Brrr didn't comment. He just pulled the hobbledy-
hoy cart, maybe for the last time. Up a road packed
with ancient grey cobbles, a road fringed with drying
nettles and slipweed knot. He thought of the toddler's
game, building a church with the fingers of two hands.
The guardhouse raised its ribs like the fingers of one
of those hands, cupped against the air. Built like that?
Or had the fingers of an opposite hand collapsed down
the slope years earlier? Yes, he could see ancient slates
cladding a shed dependence. He could smell a kitchen
fire, a roasting haunch of venison, or maybe loin chops
of mountain grite. For a moment when the wind died
down he heard the sound of a stringed instrument.

The approach to the ruined keep rose to a point
slightly higher than the fingertips of the broken arches.

Then the path descended in a gentle S-shaped curve. Muhlama led the way, pacing elegantly, her whiskers twitching to sniff out trouble. But the stiffness in her shoulders relaxed. No danger here apparently except the danger that new circumstance presents to old allegiance. "I've done what I said," she called. "Oley oley in-free. Wherever you are, come out, come out. They're here."

Brrr was released from his shafts, slipped from buckles and leathers, by the time a low wooden door opened and their hosts emerged. He didn't recognize the Quadling woman with a domingon in her hands, though he guessed her to be the one called Candle. He knew Liir, though. Coming behind her, his palms on her shoulders. Liir at thirty or thirty-two, maybe. Fuller in the shoulders, higher in the brow, a great mane of dark hair even a Lion could admire. A habit of youthful quiet and temerity aged into something almost like courage. But what would the Lion know about courage?

"The book," announced Muhlama, "and the girl who comes with it, as a kind of bonus."

The humans looked at one another. Curiosity and wariness shaded into something not yet like recognition, not yet like wonder. A mathematically perfect pivot, equal amounts of hope on one side and, on the other, alarm that the hope might be unfounded, that this revelation might yet be a mocking lie.

Brrr let them have their human moment. He kissed his good-bye to Muhlama—a final one, a temporary one? He didn't know. He realized that Ilianora would soon be relieved of responsibility for Rain. Perhaps her distress would lift, once Rain's parents took in the fact of their daughter. He wouldn't abandon Ilianora in any pain, whether he could help that pain or not. If, in time, he couldn't help it—if, in time, he realized that his not being able to help was making it worse—well, he would reconsider.

But not yet. For now, he'd stay by her side, through the next round, whatever it might be. Together he and Ilianora, the dwarf and the Munchkinlander, had delivered Rain to her home, or such home as she might hope to have. Rain was safe, or safe enough.

Now Brrr was left to shield the other bruised girl, the stillborn one huddled inside the veiled woman, for as long as he could. If he could. There wasn't now, nor would there ever be, any shortage of girl children whose safety he would need to worry about, either in or out of Oz.

III

The Chancel
of the Ladyfish

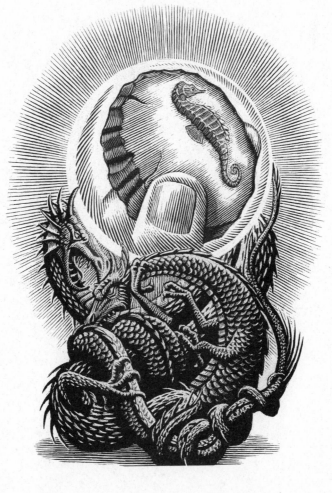

1.

The outlaws had been told by a Swift that Muhlama would be heading a delegation of exiles, but not who would be among them.

Liir gripped his wife by the hand. Hold back this instant longer, Candle. We've been waiting for all these years. Don't scatter her into the clouds, like the little wren she resembles.

She was here. She had come back. (She'd been brought back. She'd been brought in.) There would be time enough to study her. Time had begun again.

He could feel his wife strain to break free, to surround the child with scary, pent-up love. His forearm would be bulging as he staked Candle immobile. Don't rush the girl.

Our girl.

He tried to advise Candle by the theatrical turn of his own head. Look at Brrr instead. That old Cowardly Lion, as he'd come to be known. There he stands, dropped to all fours like an animal, naked but for a kind of painter's blue serge smock with a bow at the back. And rolling his boulderlike head from the girl to her parents, back and forth. The Lion could look at her. He'd earned the privilege. Liir and Candle would have to wait another moment. Now that there were extra moments.

Brrr had gone silvery about the whiskers. He must be nearing forty, surely? So was it age, exhaustion, or nerves that made the Lion's left rear leg quiver? His mane was full and nicely aerated though even his jowls were bejowled. He'd developed not only a paunch but also a bit of an overbite. However, both tokens of age disappeared when the Lion reared to his hind legs. As if he'd suddenly remembered he was a Namory of Royal Oz. He looked ready to curtsey, but he extended his front paw to Liir.

The Cowardly Lion said, "A lifetime or two ago, somebody you may remember as Dorothy Gale once browbeat me to look after you. I paid little attention. Later, a ripe old fiend named Yackle asked me to protect this child if I could. I tolerated her request without imagining I could oblige her. Yet here I am—surprise, surprise. Presenting my consort, Ilianora, and my young friend who goes by the name of Rain. I've un-wittingly obeyed both bossy females and done you two services on the same day." Dropping the sarcasm, he said more huskily, "Would that I could have been of greater service, Liir son of Elphaba."

Liir hooted. "Don't take *that* tone to me. It sounds like you've wandered out of some pantomime about Great Moments of Chivalric Oz. 'Liir son of Elphaba'? I call myself Liir Ko now." Nonetheless, he fell into the Lion's embrace. The musk of the Lion's mane was rank; it smelled like young foxes and incontinent humans. "You old pussy," he murmured. "I never liked you much, and damn it, now I'll be in your debt the rest of my life."

"A rare thing, for me to have any advantage," replied Brrr. "I'm sure I'll squander it." The dwarf nodded in agreement, character assassination at work.

Liir pulled back to say, "This is Candle Osqa'ami." He beckoned his wife forward. She nodded from the waist; but her eyes never left the girl, who was twist-ing her ragged tresses around her forearm as if in an agony to tear off her own head. A small greeny-white creature, a ferret or a rotten mink maybe, writhed at the girl's ankles as a hungry cat might do.

Finally Liir turned to the woman the Lion had in-troduced as his consort. Only now was she folding the veil back off her forehead, pulling its drapes away from her cheekbones. The cry Liir gave made everyone start except for Rain, who seemed oblivious.

Nor held up her hand, holding Liir back. "Food first, and water," said Nor, in a voice that was and wasn't the voice Liir remembered from childhood. "Our histories have waited this long; they can wait till the washing up. Candle Osqa'ami, show me a chore, and I'll help you with what needs doing. I'm south any appetite for overwrought reunions." As she passed Liir, she trained her eyes forward, but the fingers of her left hand reached out to graze his elbow and his hip.

Candle didn't budge, just flapped a hand toward the crumbling narthex as if to let the busybody find whatever she would in there. "We'll follow right along," said Liir. Nor drifted into the building alone.

Candle dropped to her knees, so Liir dropped too. Candle clapped three times. The girl looked at Candle with mild curiosity, maybe aversion. Candle clapped again, twice, and this time their daughter clapped back. Once. Feebly. It was a start.

"Oziandra Osqa'ami," said Candle.

"Commonly called Rain," remarked the dwarf, to whom no one had been paying attention. "And as we old ones remember from those decades of the Great

Drought, Rain rarely comes when she's called. Even when she's called by the name she knows. Rain."

"Oziandra Rain," said Candle.

"Child," said Liir. He didn't know the significance of that Quadling clapping. He just lifted his hands, palms out, as he might to a sniffing hound or a hurt wolf-cub. Safe, open. No stone, no knife.

The dwarf cuffed Rain on the crown of her head. "Go to them, bratling, or we'll never get a bite to eat. After all that poppy-dust in the nostrils I'm stranded on the famished side of peckish." So Rain stepped forward, out of everyone's shadows—out of the shadows of the last eight years. And Liir looked at her.

In the sloping light of evening Liir couldn't tell if he was noting a condition of facial structure or an expression. Or was it a lack of expression? The girl's eyes seemed cloaked. She had Candle's high cheekbones and hazelnut jaw, but she was urchin-thin and dusty as a rebel. She held a translucent porcelain something tucked into an elbow. A shell, he saw. Far the largest shell he'd ever laid eyes on.

"You're nice but that's nicer," he said, pointing at it. "May I see it?"

"*You're* taking liberties before you have a license," observed the dwarf, but the Munchkinlander dame cuffed him good and proper. Then the small square couple followed Nor into the keep. Even Brrr started to pad away, but the girl whimpered, so the Lion sat down halfway. He set to grooming himself with a desultory air.

"It's awfully pretty," Liir said of the shell. His heart was beating as if he were in a court of law—a court of recriminations and, maybe, pardons. "Can you hear anything in it?" He inched forward on his knees, only a scosh.

The girl put the thing up to her ear and listened. Then she turned away to ramble after her companions through the shattered archway of the porch and into the open-roofed ruin of the building. The verdant creature—perhaps an otter?—scampered after her. Candle's face had fallen but her weeping remained silent, at least for now.

"I think that went pretty well," said the Lion.

"Is the child all right?" asked Liir. His eyes followed her as she crossed a patch of gloaming light, the sort that gilds every feature at the last minute. She looked normal as a copper farthing. Not a sign of green in her skin, not at this hour, not in this sunset attention. "Is she all right, do you think?"

"Begging pardon, it's been a long day. It's been a long year," said Brrr, "and believe me, I'm no expert. But I'd say she's right as rain."

2.

Liir caught Candle's hand as they hurried up the sandy steps to their sanctuary. "She'll need to adjust," he said. "We have to give her time."

"We've given her all those years. I have no more moments to spare."

Their daughter had gone ahead wispily, surlily perhaps. Liir tried to see this hideout anew, as if through Rain's eyes, realizing that he had no notion of what she'd ever seen before. Stowed away in Lady Glinda's entourage as she'd been. And who knows what else she'd witnessed on the road.

The place where he and Candle had washed up— how improbable it seemed. Perched high over the pass that led from the Sleeve of Ghastille toward central Oz. A nameless hill, so far as they knew—in sillier moods Liir sometimes referred to it as Mountain Objection. Travelers watching their footing below would have no reason to lift their eyes; in any case, the spot was camouflaged by overgrowth.

The place may have been established as a guard keep or a pilgrim's destination. But when Liir and Candle had found it—they were hunting for a cave in which to hunker down, out of sight—it'd been abandoned for decades. Longer, maybe. For some community of cliff dwellers time out of mind, this outpost had been home. Home, or maybe an inn for passersby, for the underground warren was supplied with small cells and the remains of bedsteads and mattresses.

The ruin aboveground, through which Liir and Candle now walked, looked designed for some public function. At this stage in its collapse, the wall facing southwest was gone. The pavers of the great formal floor lay open to the sky. All that was left of the outside wall were the stumps of a line of columns. Like a lower jaw full of bad teeth. Ivory, grey, eroded. The opposite wall, hugging the hill that rose behind it, featured columns leading to the ribs of a missing roof and a dais of some sort.

In the few unionist chapels Liir had ever bothered to visit, the lectern had always stood at the far end of a rectangle, opposite the vestibule and porch. Here totemic sculptures and a sort of throne were inset against the hill wall, in the long side of the box, rather than tucked into the far apse. The carvings between the intact columns faced the broken columns and the sky and valley beyond, as if visitors on giant birds might swoop in for an audience.

Now he and Candle caught up with Rain. She'd paused at the altarpiece or whatever it was, and there she stood, tracing her hands over the surface.

At first Liir was puzzled. After an initial glance at the graven images, years ago, he'd ignored them except as hooks for bleeding a wild lamb or muttock, ledges for drying berries and onions. But Rain had set her pink shell in a niche, just so. The supports of the ledge were carved like shells too. He'd never noticed.

The shelf capped a panel of carved marble. Like a blind person, Rain was feeling the sculpture with a curiosity and openness she hadn't shown to her mother or father.

A type of fish-woman, perhaps a lake mermaid of some sort. Her lower half tapered into a scaley tale and fins. From each of her hips flared a pair of spinnerets. Her arms and breasts were naked. Her face, set in profile against a dial or plate of some sort, gave the effect of a head on a coin. Liir didn't know who she was—maybe some fishy variant of Lurline, maybe the invention of a bored unionist monk with a chisel and an appetite for breasts. But the creature looked in equal measure both beneficent and ferocious.

Rain's hands touching the stern blank eye, the weatherworn stone breasts, the imbrications of those stony scales—his daughter made Liir see that the carving had character. He hadn't noticed.

Still so much to see, so much to take in, and he was thirty or thereabouts—halfway through his life, assuming the Emperor's assassins didn't find him out at last and cut his life short.

Candle couldn't hold back any longer. She wrenched away from Liir and moved forward to kneel beside Rain. He could see the similar shapes of their skulls, but the girl's shoulders were tight, as if wound onto her spinal column like a wing nut, whereas Candle had tended toward a sexy fullness of form the past few years.

"I like this one," said Candle in her soft, bruised voice. Her hand reached out to touch a star-shaped protrusion humping along with others in a welter of runes. For all Liir knew, this row of roughs was only the pattern-block of an anonymous instructor of ancient carving. He didn't care. He had an aversion to magic, implied or actual.

"Me too," said Rain, "but this better." She chose from a protected cubby a small freestanding stone Liir had never noticed. He neared to look over her shoulder. About the size of a breviary, the display side was polished smooth as milk pudding. In it was carved something impossibly small and delicate. Liir couldn't imagine the human hand that might manage such particularity, nor the instrument that such a hand might use. A relief of a vaguely animal-shaped creature. A sort of snouted feather, a legless head of a pony erect on a curved spine or tail. An inch high, no more. "What is it?" asked Rain.

"I don't know," said Candle.

"Pure fancy, I suspect," said Liir, trying out the pedagogical function of fatherliness. "Nothing living can stand upright without at least two legs."

"A tree can. What's this?" The girl pointed to another shape carved into the lintel, a protrusion too peculiar for Liir to compare to anything else.

"An accident of the artist's adze? Or maybe it was once something remarkable, but wind and rain took away its character over time. So now it's just a mystery."

"Wind and rain?"

"They blow from the west, clear cross the hall, or from the south. Sometimes—once a year—a storm with tiny teeth of salty sand, which rub at these carvings."

"I never knowed of storms that could change off the face of a creature." Rain looked surprised at the idea of the ravage of the world. "How many storms was it?"

"Hundreds of years of storms," Candle answered her. "More years than I could count. We've only been here a handful of years, and the damage was done when we arrived. Nothing's changed since we got here, but the sand comes and settles. I brush it off with feathers when the great wind subsides."

Rain made her fingers like feathers, brushing, brushing. "What is this place?"

"It's your home," said Candle, and extended her hand to touch Rain's hand—to cover it as Rain had covered the star shape.

This was a venture too bold. "I got no *home*," said Rain, and pulled away and walked into the dark doorway that led to the stairs and the catacomb apartments in which Candle and Liir had hid, and lived, through the time it had taken seven rainstorms to deposit seven skins of sand upon the evaporating stone.

3.

Just before they'd met Muhlama yesterday, Ilianora had cried out to the Lion that Rain had no fear. Rain had heard this, and she knew it was wrong. She had plenty of fear, all right. For instance, she didn't trust these two new people in their hilltop hideaway. The man was possessed by something aggravated, something with the intensity of hornets. He tried to disguise it, but she could see. The woman was no calmer, even though she looked like a Quadling, and Rain's exposure to Quadlings in Ovvels had led her to consider them kindly and placid. Up till now.

I'll have no part of this, she thought, though she knew she had little choice.

She found Brrr downstairs, pacing in and out of stone doorways, checking out the lodgings. "Time was I might have expected the sheets turned down and a chocolate bourbonette placed upon the pillow," he said. "But since there are no sheets or pillows, I suppose hoping for a chocolate bourbonette is a waste of energy. Rain, where should we sleep?"

"Far away from here."

"Tiss toss, somebody's cross. What's gotten under your skin?"

"En't nothing under my skin but my underskin." She threw herself down on the floor, purposefully hard so she could bang her coccyx and try out a cuss. Tay twisted its head at her, confused.

Brrr had learned enough not to take the bait. He said nothing.

"How long are we here? When are we going?"

"I don't know. I don't yet really understand where we've arrived. Shall we go help with food, and see what we can learn?"

"I can't learn anything."

Brrr decided to consider morbid self-loathing something of an advance in the consolidation of Rain's character. "Well, if you're enjoying a little hissy-mood, why don't you come along and find more to disapprove of upstairs?"

"You can leave me here to die." She stretched out on her back and put an arm over her head. She made an unconvincing corpse, though Brrr knew that with enough practice—sixty, seventy years on—she'd get it right.

"Well, I'm going to sleep here. I think this room is kind of cozy. I like how a little natural light comes in through that slit. I bet you can see stars on a cloudless night, inching by." She didn't look. "But while there's work to be done for supper, it's cowardly to shirk down here. So now I'm going above. You can do as you like."

"I *know* that."

He had to suppress a smile. A vexed Rain was slightly more coherent: there was more of her on display. He knew she'd follow eventually.

Back outside, in a summer kitchen beyond the nave of the sacred fishy lady, Liir and Candle were scrubbing some turnips. A rusty kettle hanging on a hook bubbled, a rich onion broth. Ilianora—Brrr couldn't yet think of her as Nor, which was how Liir addressed her—was mashing carrots with a pestle. Little Daffy and Mr. Boss were collecting from the compartments of the Clock anything that might be of use. Scissors, forks, banged-up pewter plates. Dried herbs. Candle's eyes went wide and delighted at the sight of oregano and pumperfleck.

Brrr was no better at dicing cubes of salted grite than he was at the preparation of radish roses. His arthritic paws were devoid of opposable anythings. Settling to take some of the evening wind onto his jowls, he closed his eyes to listen to the murmur of human malcontent. It was comfortingly so like his own.

When Rain cried out, because splashed by moiling soup—so she'd emerged, no surprise there—Brrr opened his eyes. They focused to pick out a statue of an iron goose framed in a collapsing archway of unpruned peony hedge.

The bush was past its prime. Like the rest of us, he guessed. Then the statue kinked a leg and spoke.

"None of my business, of course, but have you paid *any* attention to the question of whether or not your dinner guests are being followed?" He appeared to be addressing the peonies, since one could not tell on whom his glazed eye was fixing.

"We'll get to that," said Liir to the Goose. "We'll talk after we eat. If you're so concerned, launch yourself and take a loop around once or twice. Settle your mind about it."

"Couldn't be bothered to exercise myself. The moment your incarceration arrives, I take to wing with a song in my breast and the old heave-ho."

"Ever the optimist," Candle said to the newcomers, shrugging. "This is Iskinaary. Liir's familiar."

"Not as familiar as all that," protested the Goose.

"I never knew a Bird to shelter with humans," said Brrr.

"I never knew a Lion to mind his own business," snapped the Goose.

"Don't let the Goose vex you," said Liir. "We haven't had company for so long, he's forgotten how to be cordial."

"*You've* forgotten how to be suspicious," complained the Goose. "These vagabonds come creaking like the Walking Dust of St. Satalin's Graveyard and you don't worry it's the opening salvo of an ambush attempt?"

"Muhlama has promised to stalk the perimeter tonight before she slinks away in the morning," soothed Liir. "No need to ginger up the atmosphere, Iskinaary. This feast has been postponed for too long. You were there when the little girl was born. You can manage to be glad she's back. No?"

"This is all my fault. I saw the Clock from the air, we sent Muhlama to investigate since she was passing through. I'm sorry I opened my mouth. But the girl is trouble, Liir, and dragging trouble in her wake. Mark my words. And I'm not crazy about the otter." At Liir's lowered brow, the Goose hurried on, "Not that I mind, of course. I love trouble. The spice of life and proud progenetrix of all progress, yes yes. Don't mind *me*."

"I think someone's being sentimental," suggested Liir. "We've never had reason to see how a Goose gets sentimental before. High emotion is nothing to be ashamed of, you know."

"We have a Cowardly Lion and a Sentimental Goose, is that it? No thank you," said Iskinaary. "I'm not interested in the position." He curled his neck like the hoop of an iron rail marking out the edge of an ornamental border and he nipped viciously at his breast. "I'll dine alone on my own nits, thank you."

The humans sat cross-legged on a blanket. Under the circumstances Little Daffy offered a brief grace in a general sense, addressed to Sender. The slop was good as well as plentiful. Brrr ate with his tongue rather than a spoon. He was getting too old to fuss with a spoon at every meal. Rain sulked and wouldn't touch a bite.

When they were done, Candle suggested that she and Rain might take a knife to the peonies and cut some to arrange on the shell altar. Tay slunk after, docile as an old family collie. After they'd wandered away, Liir ventured softly, "Before they come back, in case it's upsetting to Candle, can anyone tell me about Rain?"

"She's a bothersome girl, more trouble than she's worth," said Mr. Boss. He'd hardly spoken since they arrived. Well, observed Brrr, ever since the Clock took its tumble, Mr. Boss has gone very silent indeed.

Liir's fixation on the girl seemed to annoy the dwarf, who continued, "What you see when you look at Rain is all there is. You can't get milk from a salamander. I want to know what's going on down *there*." He swept his hand skyward to the north and east. "We've spent a year with Quadlings who wouldn't know a current event if it rolled over and squashed their granny. I can see you've removed yourself from the cocktail party circuit, but you must hear something in your aerie up here, if you have an assortment of winged foreign correspondents. What's the news out of Oz?"

"Since when?" asked Liir.

"When we left Munchkinland more than a year ago," replied Mr. Boss, "Lady Glinda was confined to Mockbeggar Hall. Her country estate on Restwater, as you may know. An army of Loyal Oz had gotten halfway up the lake, heading inland, but its armada was destroyed by a spot of magic. A dragon escaped and flew south, we think, and that's the last we heard for certain."

Some bad memory there, thought Brrr, seeing Liir pale at the mention of the beast. Evenly enough, though, Liir replied, "We've seen or heard no sign of any dragon."

The dwarf snorted. "Yes, Lord Limp in the Lap, but what about the armies bucking about Restwater?"

"We came here to get out of the path of armies."

The Goose suddenly snapped to life again and hissed at Liir. "You've invited them to stay the night and you're suddenly above gossip? Has the arrival of that child mischiefed your mind? Listen, little man," he told the dwarf, "the last we heard, General Cherrystone had taken the lake, even storming Haugaard's Keep. The Munchkinlanders cleverly vacated their stronghold so they could isolate and contain Cherrystone once he took it. They have him holed up there. He retains lake access but he can't move farther inland toward Bright Lettins, the new capital. Some fortresses are harder to quit than they are to breach."

The dwarf said, "Smart. And . . . ?"

The Goose went on. "Tit for tat, the Munchkinlanders have formed an alliance with the Glikkuns to their north, and appropriated the emerald mines in the Scalps. Easy enough to defend those mountain passes. And the Glikkuns have cut the rail line into Loyal Oz. You can hardly be surprised. They've been taken advantage of by the Emerald City for decades. It's all stupefyingly predictable. The Glikkuns, those trolls, are natural allies to the stumpy Munchkinlander folk."

"You should talk," said Little Daffy. "You're not any taller than I am."

"Who's leading the Munchkinland government?" asked Brrr, to keep the conversation civil, and also to find out.

The Goose gargled and hootled. "Liir himself would be eligible for Eminence in Munchkinland, should he ever claim the seat. His aunt, the so-called Wicked Witch of the East, having been the last Eminent Thropp."

Liir shrugged. "Not interested in the job. Anyway, I've changed my name to Liir Ko, so maybe I'm not eligible."

"Since the Emperor of Oz, Shell Thropp, was Nessarose's younger brother," said the Goose, "it's on the basis of a blood claim to the position of Eminence of Munchkinland that the Emperor validates *his* invasion. You'd pass muster too, Liir."

"But names," said Brrr. "Who's holding Munchkinland together?"

"To the north, the Glikkun alliance is managed by a mangy old troll-woman named Sakkali Oafish," replied Iskinaary.

Brrr closed his eyes. He remembered Sakkali Oafish. The Massacre at Traum, for which he'd earned his sobriquet as the Cowardly Lion. The one thing about a social indignity was that, like several of the nastier rashes, it was never completely cured, and could flare up at a moment's notice.

"In Munchkinland proper," the Goose continued, "the mastermind is an old witch named Mombey."

"That's not a Munchkinlander name," scoffed Little Daffy.

"She's Gillikinese originally. But as you may have noticed, the Munchkinlander that might serve, won't." Again Iskinaary indicated Liir. "And the one that would serve, namely the Emperor, isn't welcome. So Mombey's holding things together somehow. Her chief military strategist, who's kept Cherrystone boxed up in Haugaard's Keep all year, is a saucy young warrior princess named Jinjuria. General Jinjuria, she calls herself."

"Yes, Muhlama told us about her. Well, Munchkinland was ever a stomping ground for strong women," said Little Daffy. "Nessarose Thropp, this Mombey, this General Jinjuria. You got to hand it to them."

"Yes, they're just as bitter and conniving as men," said Iskinaary. "They might've offered a position to one of the many Animals who took refuge inside their borders all those years ago, back during the Wizard's pogroms. But *noooooo*. When women share power, they share power with women."

"And you have a problem with that?" Little Daffy picked up a small sharp stone and tossed it up and down.

The dwarf intervened. "Come on, Husky Honey, remember we're guests. Not nice to stone our hosts."

"This is hardly news," said Iskinaary, "but Nessarose was no fainting sweetheart, once she took the chair. The way I hear tell it, Elphaba Thropp had her own permanent case of broom rage too. Don't murder the messenger. I'm just answering the question you posed."

Once again Brrr broke in. "Is Lady Glinda free?"

"The latest gossip," said the Goose, "is that she was charged with treason against Loyal Oz. For somehow arranging the assault on the armada. As if she could manage that!—she who can't manage to thread a needle. But if she's been taken from Mockbeggar I couldn't say. My circle of informants doesn't stoop to information of such particularity."

"It en't all her fault." They hadn't seen Rain and Candle come back, arms full of satiny white peonies glowing in the fading light. The girl said, "Me and Lady Glinda—we did it together."

"Keep marching in the direction you're going, little girl," said Iskinaary, "and you'll hit the banks of Restwater again. If you apologize to General Cherrystone nicely, maybe he'll only slap you in prison for the rest of your life instead of killing you outright."

Ilianora gasped, and Liir bellowed, "Iskinaary! Mind yourself."

"Somebody's got to tell that girl the truth," snapped the Goose. "Or eventually she'll put herself in the same kind of danger she's putting you." He craned his neck and looked, just for an instant, regal—at least regal for a Goose. He kick-stepped his way across the stones to where Candle and Rain had paused and he stood before them. From Brrr's vantage point, his graphite feathers made a sort of silhouette against the white blossoms drooping from Rain's arms. The Goose all but honked at the girl. "I have no reason to like you, Miss Oziandra Rain, but neither will I let a damaged child waltz into peril because her companions are congenitally foolish."

"Well, I don't like you either," said Rain, pelting the Goose with her heap of blooms. Unfazed, he poked his bill among them to enjoy the ants crawling in the sweetness. Brrr had to admire his composure.

Candle hid a small smile of her own by raising her armful of blooms up to her nose.

4.

Under their common blanket Liir comforted Candle that evening. "You hover too close, you'll scare her away," he murmured. "She feels safe with the Lion. There, there. Hush, don't let them hear you."

"You always said I could see the present," said Candle, when she could speak. "But I can see nothing about her—my own daughter."

Liir smoothed his hand over her silky flank. "Maybe that's not so surprising. Maybe all parents are blindest to their own offspring."

"It isn't right. It isn't natural."

"Hush. They'll hear you. Remember—the morning is always brightest after the moonless night."

Eventually she fell asleep, if only, he guessed, to escape his platitudes. But it was the best he could do.

Even at this slight elevation, Highsummer was passing more quickly than in the valley. The dawn revealed a new ruddiness to the greenery. "I want to have a better look at that Clock," Liir told the dwarf after breakfast. "You're the chargé d'affaires about that, right?"

"You could call me the timekeeper," said Mr. Boss, "only I seem to have lost track of the time. Sure, come along. There's little to be lost or gained in the Clock's prophecies anymore."

They stumped down the stone path to where they'd left the Clock the night before. The assemblage look weather-beaten with age. Which it had every right to look, after all these years.

"I always thought this Clock was apocryphal," said Liir.

"It is apocryphal. That's the point." The dwarf seemed to be tilting into a sour mood.

"I never expected to see it," said Liir. "Somehow it's smaller than I imagined."

"Most of us are. You too, bub."

Liir had more than his share of personal flaws, but rushing to take offense wasn't one of them. "How's this thing work, anyway?"

"It doesn't. That's the crisis."

The stage curtains yawned open like a fresh wound. "Is this supposed to simulate something?"

"Ruin," said the dwarf. "Of the Clock, or of my life. Makes little difference. Perhaps its time has come. Even a thing can die, I guess. Though I never thought about that before this year."

"Maybe someone could fix it up?"

"Some magician, you mean?" The dwarf glanced up at Liir. "I know your mother is said to have been

Elphaba. The Wicked Witch of the West. Great stage name, that. But I doubt you inherited the talent."

"I have no capacity. I wasn't volunteering for the job. I was just wondering."

"The magic of the Clock doesn't originate in Oz, so it can't be amended here." The dwarf kicked at the hub of a wheel. The drawer with the Grimmerie in it sprung open. "I suspect you were looking for this little number, once upon a time."

"The Grimmerie?" guessed Liir.

"The same."

"Yes, I was. Once, anyway. Maybe twice . . . I hunted through Kiamo Ko for it, but it'd either been hidden or taken away."

"It's made the rounds, this great book. It was given to Sarima, your father's wife; then to Elphaba; then to Glinda, more than once. When it's not being used it's come back to me. But the Clock can't keep it safe anymore, and I can't determine through the Clock who should have it. So it's yours now. Happy birthday and no happy returns. I don't want it. You're as deserving a candidate as any. Besides, I hear your daughter can read it some."

"But—whoever brought it to Oz—whoever magicked the Clock—might want it back."

"Whoever." The dwarf snarled.

"I mean, *your* boss."

"*My* liege and master?" Mr. Boss made a rude gesture. "He cast me away in this land with a job to do and a Clock by which to count the hours of my service. He hasn't come back. If the Clock is done counting my shift, so am I. The book is yours, bub."

"What if I don't want it either?"

"Try to get rid of it and see what happens." Mr. Boss grinned, nastily. "I wouldn't like to be an enemy of that thing. I've managed to stay neutral, but even so."

"Yeah. I've tried to stay neutral too. It isn't always possible."

They paused, in a stalemate about something neither could name.

"Well. Are you going to pick it up?" asked the dwarf.

"And what if I don't? I came here with Candle to protect her, to protect myself. I'm not Elphaba. Never could be. I know my limitations. I don't deserve anything this powerful. I can't use it and I can't protect it."

"If you don't take it, sir," said the dwarf, "I shall give it to your daughter."

So Liir had no choice. A moment that comes, sooner or later, to all parents.

5.

Rain saw Liir carry the Grimmerie into the chancel. She was uneasy about the great book now she knew that Lady Glinda had gotten into trouble by read- ing it. Yet Rain still felt the book's subtle allure. Her mouth watered. She was eager not to do magic but to read. She'd had too little reading. What few things that General Cherrystone had taught her were languishing in her head, pollywogs that could never grow up into frogs.

"What you going to do with that?" she asked, as casually as she could.

"I don't think this is a good thing for you to look at. It's powerful stuff, from all I've heard."

"I'm powerful stuff."

He grinned and shook his head. Without having words to express it, Rain knew that a smile tends to avert or disguise the natural tension that pools around people trying to be in the same place at once. But Liir's smile would have no effect on her. She would see to that. "Where you going to stow it?"

"I don't know. No place seems safe enough."

"I'll hold it for you."

"That would be like giving you a boa constrictor for a pet. No father would do that."

"You're not my father." The words just slipped out—they weren't antagonistic, just commentary.

"Actually, I am. Though I surely can see how you might doubt it." As if he was afraid the book would open up of its own accord, he set it on the ground and sat on it. She hoped it would bite him on his behind. "If you could look in this book, what would you be looking for?"

"Words," she said, cannily, honestly.

"Which ones? Magic ones?"

She didn't feel like saying that all words were magic, though she thought so. But she wasn't skilled at indirection. She was more arrow than hummingbird. "I want to read the burning words," she said at last.

She couldn't think of Liir as her father, she couldn't.

Liir looked at her with sudden sharpness. "What do you mean, the burning words?"

She shrugged at that and she would have wandered off to make a point about how free of him she was. But there was the book. He was sitting on it. She wanted to see where he would put it. In case.

Was he still waiting for her to speak?

She couldn't force a remark any more than she could force a smile, any more than she'd been able to force herself to read before she'd been taught the rubrics. She waited, squatting on her haunches, casting sideways looks at the Grimmerie in case it began to leak language out onto the stones.

"You want to read the burning words," prompted Liir.

"Don't you?"

He blinked. Another language she didn't get, how people blink. How they make their eyes go wet. "Where do you find the burning words?" he asked her.

She thought of the armada scorching the ice. Something was being spelled out there; fire moved in such a way, and smoke issued from fire, as if to hide what was being spelled inside the heat. Oh, but all that was too fussy a thought. She took up a bug that didn't mind the chilly air and studied it on her forefinger instead.

She could tell this man wanted her to soothe him somehow. Burning words in his head? She didn't know what they might be, and it wasn't her job to put them out. She only saw charred letters in a lake. The alphabetic remains of ships.

"What are you going to be when you grow up?" asked Liir.

She thought and thought about that. She felt her calves begin to ache; she felt the tickle of the bug's legs against her fingers. Someday, presumably, she wouldn't have these legs or these fingers, but the legs and fingers of someone who stood as tall as this man could. She twisted in her thinking, trying to be honest since she didn't believe she could be smart, and she gave the answer to the insect rather than to the man who claimed to be her father. She wouldn't think of Liir as her father.

What would she be when she grew up? She whispered the answer. "Gone."

6.

Gone, when she grew up. A terrible thought. But in a way she was gone already, right now. Her form had come back to them but her spirit was balking.

Candle mourned that Rain wasn't bothering with her much. Liir asked himself: What mother wouldn't? But it seemed as if, instead of Liir's and Candle's warmth melting Rain's resistance, it worked the other way around. The child's aloofness was contagious. Candle and Liir were learning to weather a mutual pain separately, independently. No matter the closeness of the marriage bed, the history between them.

Maybe to distract himself from his other worries, Liir tried to fasten on his half-sister. He and Nor shared a father, presumably, though Liir had never met that distant figure, Fiyero. But Nor was also floating at some distance away from Liir. The great reunion that he'd dreamed of for years was a sham. Kidnapping, prison, escape, disappearance? You'd never know it by her self-effacing manner. She might as well just have come home after shopping for biscuits.

He didn't want to crowd his sister any more than he wanted to crowd his daughter. He watched Nor move about with a woodenness that sometimes seemed like grace, and sometimes not. Maybe this was her normal way? He wouldn't know. He hadn't seen her since she'd been abducted. Back when she'd been a girl roughly the age that Rain was now.

Never confident about women, Liir scrutinized his sister—with equal parts interest, patience, and suspicion—to see in what way might she turn out to be damaged.

As if he were writing a catalog on the subject of human misery.

Another way to avoid admitting how it had settled in too close, like lice.

The opportunity to engage Nor without threatening her arose naturally enough. Every couple of weeks Liir was in the habit of descending from the mount to a wildwood garden. He collected mushrooms, fiddleheads, frostflower pods, and lettuce. It was half a morning's hike. The next time he needed to thin the lettuce or lose it, he bundled up a few baskets, some stakes, a trowel, and he asked Nor to come along.

They strolled equably enough, chatting about the landscape and the moods of the climate. From time to time they fell into silence. A bird hopped on a blighted oak limb. A few chipmunks, at the business of growing their hoards, scampered like shadows of something overhead. The wind sawed through the thickery. You could hear the autumn inching in.

"Looks as if this has been a productive yard for generations," said Nor, indicating the ancient stone tablets tilting at the end of the sunnier furrows.

"Behold: here lies the last person to tell the truth."

She blinked at him.

"Sorry. Graveyard humor. But if those stones ever said anything like that, they stopped saying it long ago."

Nor nodded. "They look like teeth. And your hermitage, or whatever it once was—it looks like a mouth too. A big open jaw swallowing the wind."

"Swallowing the poppy trade, probably," said Liir. Nor raised an eyebrow. "You don't know about the poppy trade?"

"I don't know much. Even though we swam through the bloody sea of them."

"Sometimes the Yunamata venture south as far as here to harvest the poppy pods. The takings are useful for their groggy rituals, and the illegitimate opiate market is always eager to barter. Your little Munch-kinlander apothecaire knows all about that, I'm sure. Some of the harvest seeps through the black market for smoking in certain parlors in Shiz and the EC, I'm told."

"You're not an habitué?"

"I haven't been into a parlor of any sort since I grew facial hair."

Nor bent to pick the lettuce, which was near to bolting. "Situated where it is, maybe your private stronghold used to be a countinghouse for the poppy merchants. Or maybe the defense headquarters against such a trade."

"Whoever might tell us is probably long ago buried in the lettuces. It's all guesswork."

"But the trade has dropped off?"

"Seems so. Certainly the EC authorities don't ap-prove; they're afraid the opiates will get to the con-scripted soldiers and erode morale. You didn't see sign of anyone marking out a little meadow for harvesting?"

"Not a soul."

They worked in companionable silence. Liir staked the stems of frostflower so they would winter over.

They were best cut down in the early spring. Finished with the lettuce, Nor put her hand on the small of her back and stretched. She dropped the heap of curled green pages into her shawl, and turned her attention to some radishes, but she gave up when one after another pulled up mealy. "What next?" she asked.

Liir leaned back on his heels. "I have something to show you." She waited. He pulled from his tunic a folded bit of paper. "I found this at Kiamo Ko. Can you bear to look at it?"

She came over to squat next to him. The browning paper, creased into softness, showed a faded drawing of a young girl. Hardly more than an infant, though with a certain crude spark in the eye. A personality. The letters in childlike hesitancy said

Nor by Fiyero.

This is me Nor
by my father F
before he left

It took her a half an hour to compose herself. Liir left his arm slung around her as if around the shoulder of a drinking mate—not too close. Not imprisoning. Just there. When she was ready, she tapped the page

twice with a forefinger and said, "I found that drawing before you did. It was in the Witch's room at the
castle. My father had drawn me for his mistress, and
she had kept it. She who seemed impervious to sentimentality had kept it all those years. When I came
across it—I must have been rooting through her room
one day, bored, as children will be—I wrote the caption and put the page back where it was, so the Witch
would know she could keep the paper but she couldn't
keep my father from me, not in my memory."

"How much do you remember about those times?
With your mother and brothers and me and the Witch?
And those other aunts of yours? Back in Kiamo Ko?"

"I was hardly a teenager when I was abducted," she
said. "And so of course I remember almost all of it. Or
I thought I did. But I'd forgotten this."

"Do you remember they took me too?—but Cherrystone decided I wasn't worth the labor of hauling
overland? He left me tied up in a sack and hanging from
a tree. I had to gnaw through the burlap, which took
the better part of a day . . . then I fell twelve feet and
almost killed myself. And by the time I came around,
you were gone. You were all gone. I made my way home
to the castle and waited for the Witch to come back—
she was in Munchkinland, I think. That was just when
her sister, Nessarose, orchestrated the Munchkinlander

schism, and they seceded from Loyal Oz." He'd been talking too fast. He slowed down. "What happened to you when they took you?"

"What I do remember I don't want to talk about." She'd been with her mother and her older brother, Irji. And those aunts. Gruesome. Maybe Nor was right: maybe Liir didn't really want to know. After all. Nor had been the only one to survive.

"Do you know that I talked my way into Southstairs Prison to find you?" he asked her. "After the Wizard abdicated and Lady Glinda came to be Throne Minister? My guide was none other than Shell Thropp. Shell Thropp, the Witch's brother. My uncle, though I didn't know it yet. A cad of the first order, and now he's the Emperor."

"We've just learned he's divine. Being related to him, does that make you a saint?"

Liir bowed his head, though not in piety. "When I finally got into the prison, you had just escaped from Southstairs. A few days earlier. I was that close to finding you. They said you'd hidden yourself between the corpses of some Horned Hogs and been carried out in a pudding of putrescent Animal flesh." He tried to laugh. *"Really?"*

"I don't care to think about it." The way she spoke told Liir it was all too true.

"It sounds as if you were so close to Cherrystone at Mockbeggar Hall. Didn't you want to take revenge on him? After all, at the Wizard's instructions he abducted and murdered your family. Or had them murdered. Much later, once I went AWOL from the service of the Emerald City Messiars, he began to have me hunted too. He attacked the mauntery called Saint Glinda in the Shale Shallows because we were said to be there. He—"

"We? You and Candle?"

"Me and Trism. My bosom companion. We'd torched the stable of flying dragons that were being used to terrify the Scrow and the Yunamata, so Cherrystone was out for our blood. And when Cherrystone caught up with Trism at last he probably beat the bloody hell out of him. Listen, at Mockbeggar Hall, didn't you want to put a stiletto through Cherrystone's throat? I would have. Wanted to, at least."

She went back to the lettuces and began to arrange them in ranks of size, as if that mattered. Her voice was flat and unconcerned when she spoke again. "I've spent all my adult life either fighting the excesses of the Emerald City hegemony or trying not to fret myself into paralysis. One can only do what one can do, Liir. Today I can harvest a little lettuce. Tonight you and your wife and your child and my unlikely husband and your Goose and my colleagues, Mr. Boss and Little Daffy, will have some lettuce to eat. One day perhaps I will not find lettuce in my hands, but a knife. Maybe General Cherrystone will have come to eat lettuce but will dine on the blade that cuts the lettuce. If I only think about that, I can think about nothing else, and then I might as well lie down under these stones and join the others who can't think anymore, either."

In a steely but warm voice, she added, "I might ask the same of you, Liir. Cherrystone's zeal to find you, because you might lead him to the Grimmerie, has broken you apart from your own daughter no less fiercely than I was broken apart from my mother—and from my father. From our father. You might've spent these years of *your* strong youth hunting him down."

"I might've done," he agreed. "But if I'd been unsuccessful, Rain would've had no father to come home to, sooner or later. A fate we fatherless understand, you and I."

"We do," she said. "We understand lettuces, and we understand that. We don't understand Cherrystone. But we don't need to. Maybe."

They walked back to the hostel slowly, without talking, that final *maybe* like a heavy boulder slung between them, on a yoke laid across both their backs.

7.

About the darkness recently apparent in his wife's eyes, the Lion was puzzled. He knew Ilianora hadn't been prepared to find her brother. She hadn't been looking for Liir. Maybe having found him, then, had slapped awake an old buried ache for others who'd been slaughtered.

This was a sore that Brrr couldn't lick clean no matter how he tried. Maybe if Rain had taken to Nor . . . maybe his wife would have softened a little more . . but no. Rain never took to anyone.

Except, a little bit, to him. Which was damn awkward under the circumstances. With her parents and her aunt moping around for scraps of attention. The girl wasn't capable though. Or she just wasn't interested in them.

What were they all waiting for in this Chancel of the Ladyfish, as Highsummer turned to Harvest'our, and Harvest'our gave way to Masque? Were they all glued to Rain, as if she might give them a sign? Were the companions of the Clock to linger indefinitely? The question became moot when the snow blew in, and they were more or less ice-bound. They were no longer quite guests, these months along. But neither were they at home.

The Lion listened as Liir and Candle talked to each other in the coded abbreviations that couples develop. He couldn't make much of Candle—a cipher, that one. But he remembered Liir from ages ago, that time when Brrr had arrived, with Dorothy and the shambolic others, at the castle of the Wicked Witch of the West. The flying monkeys! They'd given him the creeps. The loopy old Nanny who had nonetheless seemed the sanest of the lot. The mysterious way Dorothy had vanquished the Witch while the Lion and Liir were trapped in a larder. Then the beginning of their long journey back to the Emerald City.

All the time Liir had been the least of them, a stringy, cave-chested marionette of a kid. The thinnest fleck of hair on the upper lip, the cracking voice, the sidelong glances at Dorothy, as if he couldn't believe his luck but still didn't know if it was good luck or bad.

The Lion hadn't expected to meet up with the lad ever again. Now it was—what?—fifteen or twenty years later. The boy-turned-man still projected something imprecise. But his back was strong and his love for Candle was tender, and he regarded Rain as a jewel so precious he couldn't touch her. That was Rain's fault, to set herself like that, but it was her father's fault too, to accept her terms. *I* never would, thought Brrr, with the smugness of the perfect parent, or dog handler, or litigator.

One day during a thaw, when Candle mentioned a hankering for a hare to roast, Liir braved the slippery paths to check his traps. The Lion decided to go along. They all but slid into the carcass of the decrepit Clock, its open stage gaping. They looked over the wrecked set. Snow upon fallen buildings.

"It's acting out the death of a civilization," said the Lion.

Liir peered with interest. "It looks like an earthquake. Growing up in the Great Kells, I saw my share. Those slides of scree when the mountains shake their shoulders. The circular felt tents of the Arjiki nomads collapse, and the herders just put them up again."

"Mr. Boss imagines the magician of the Grimmerie went to be a hermit in some cave in the Great Kells and an earthquake slammed boulders over the entrance. He's either dead or trapped for good. Though I think if he's that magnificent a wizard he could magick open a mountain."

"Yes, Elphaba mentioned hearing about a magician in the outback. Before her time. Like everyone else, he's no doubt waiting for his cue to return in Oz's bleakest hour, et cetera."

They strolled around the corner of the Clock, looking for a way into its secrets, and for a way into each
other's. He never calls her his mother, thought the
Lion. Only *Elphaba.*

He never comments on Elphaba, thought Liir. What
did the Lion really think of her? Lunatic recluse or dangerous insurrectionist? Or mad scientist lady making
flying monkeys with magic stitchery?

But who cares what Brrr thought, when Elphaba
was dead and gone, dead and gone. "What time does it
tell?" asked Liir.

"It's not a real Clock. The time on it is fixed. It's
always a minute short of midnight." They poked
through the broken drawers and cracked shutters.
Spools of orange thread, scissors, pots of evil glop
whose drips obscured their handwritten labels. "Did
the dwarf used to sit up all night preparing for the next
day's revelations?" asked Liir.

"No. The magic of it was beyond the dwarf. He was
only the custodian."

"Not the custodian of much, now. It would make
useful firewood this winter."

"I think he'd kill you before he'd let you tear it
apart."

"I call that an unhealthy affection for the theater."
Liir swallowed. "Speaking of affections, healthy or

otherwise, do you think there's any chance you're going to release my daughter into our care?"

The Lion gave him a sharp look. "We brought her here, didn't we?"

"Oh, yes. And all due gratitude. Medals for courage, bravocatories on the bugle. All that. But it's been several months now, and Candle frets that Rain continues to sleep in your room. You've planted yourself like a big furry hedge between a daughter and her parents."

"I don't tell her where to sleep. Neither do I tell her what to say or think or feel."

"Candle will go mad if Rain doesn't open up to us some."

"You can't be surprised. There was always going to be some collateral damage. Don't be disingenuous. I mean, you *did* let her go, after all. What kind of parents would do that?"

Liir's eyes were agate hard and dry. "I believe you've never been a father. So you don't understand. Any parent whose child was in danger would do the same."

"I know what *justification* means. Believe me. Had a fair amount of time nursing wounds of my own and trying out different explanations for all my behavior. In the end, you know what? I'm the only one responsible for what I chose to do."

Liir sat on a boulder and kicked at some snow.

"You don't have to explain yourself to me," said the Lion. "You had your reasons. Just don't go accusing me of, I don't know, whatever you might call it."

"Alienation of affections."

Brrr observed how readily the phrase came to his old friend's lips. The Lion growled low, warningly.

Liir relented. Head sunk in his hands, he began to tell the Lion the story of Rain's birth nearly a decade ago. He and a friend had been trapped in a siege at a mauntery in the Shale Shallows—

"I know. Your bucko companion. Trism bon Cavalish," supplied Brrr. Liir's head whipped up. "I was doing some state work for the EC before I got mixed up with the crew of the Clock," admitted the Lion. "An old maunt named Yackle told me about your handsome sweetheart."

"That part of the story is over." Liir went on to tell how he'd escaped the mauntery by broom. Flying by night above Cherrystone's forces. Leaving Trism to make his way by land, if he could, to the secret haunt where Candle, pregnant with Rain, was waiting for Liir. By the time Liir arrived six weeks later, after the Conference of the Birds, Candle admitted to him that Trism had indeed shown up. Briefly. But she wouldn't say what had happened. *Something* had happened. Affection, lust, attack, revulsion, envy—she never clarified it, and Liir had stopped asking. Husbands manage their silences like stock portfolios. He'd left again, to escort the corpse of a dead princess toward an elephants' graveyard. By the time he'd returned, Candle had given birth to Rain just as Cherrystone's men had sniffed out Apple Press Farm. They were closing in, but Candle had slipped the noose, hoping to draw them off the scent of her child and of Liir. She had left the infant for Liir to discover. It had worked.

"How had the forces found the place you'd been hidden?" asked the Lion.

"They must have used Trism, one way or the other. Maybe they tracked him there. Or after he left, they caught him and beat the information out of him. Either way, he betrayed us, and betrayed our daughter. Intentionally or through stupidity. Neither excuse is forgivable."

"What happened then?"

The Messiars from the EC had intercepted Candle. Turned out she'd been cradling and crooning to a bundle of washing, not a child. Thinking her simple, they'd let her go. Some advantages to being a filthy Quadling! Candle had taken herself to the mauntery to rest up from the unhealed bleeding that had followed childbirth. Not knowing any of this yet, Liir had headed west, into the wilderness, with the child in his arms. He'd followed the Vinkus tribe from which he'd recently parted.

"I know the Scrow," pointed out the Lion. "With their elephant chief, Princess Nastoya. I was with you the day you met them, on our way back from killing the Witch at Kiamo Ko."

"Even *you've* bought into the propaganda? You were *there*." Liir spat. "You didn't kill any witch! You and I were locked in the scullery."

"Figure of speech. We were talking about the Scrow."

Relenting, Liir continued. Through his years of tending the dying Princess, the new chieftain, a fellow named Shem Ottokos, had learned something about the magic of disguises. Liir had meant to apply to the Scrow for sanctuary, and Ottokos had agreed to extend it. But only if Rain could be suitably hidden so as to bring no trouble to the Scrow or to herself should she ever be found.

"Hidden how?" asked the Lion.

"You haven't understood? You've been traipsing around with my daughter for who knows how long, and you're that clueless?"

"I know she walks a bit askew from the rest of us," said Brrr, as gently as he could. He knew what he knew, by now, but wanted to hear it spoken.

"She was born green," said Liir. "That's like being born with a bull's-eye painted on your forehead. Ottokos did his best, but he couldn't manage the spell to conceal her stamp of bloodline. Iskinaary, who kept a watch on the comings and goings around the Scrow camp, spotted a caravansary approaching with some EC personnel. So I lit out with the child in the opposite direction—by now Rain was about a year old, maybe— and I circled overland back toward Apple Press Farm. Back toward Munchkinland. I didn't really know where to go, where we could be safe—"

"Welcome to Oz, where nowhere is safe," said the Lion.

"I stopped at the mauntery in the Shale Shallows and was reunited with Candle. We were beside ourselves with fear for our green Rain. We were young. I mean, I was twenty-four, roughly, but a young twenty-four. A stupid twenty-four. We set out without a destination, just to keep moving. A chance encounter with—with a snake charmer on the road—it provided us our only hope, and we arranged to have Rain disguised as a pale human of uncertain lineage. Then, as we approached Munchkinland's border, I thought of Lady Glinda, who had helped me several times before. We presented our-selves at Mockbeggar Hall, and Lady Glinda deigned to see me. She took a good look at Rain, and persuaded us that the safest place to hide the girl would be in her own household. Among the staff. So hidden that Rain herself wouldn't know about her origins, and couldn't give herself away."

So that was how it had happened. Lady Glinda, the protector of Elphaba's granddaughter. Well, it sort of figured.

"That was the best thing to do for a young child, I suppose." The Lion's tone was supercilious; he could hear it himself, and couldn't help it.

"Hey. She's still alive," said Liir. "It's almost ten years later, and she's still alive. Candle was apprehended and let go, and I've been an outlaw since I was a teen, but Rain—Rain was safe."

The Lion said, "They were never looking for her. They wanted the Grimmerie. They still want it. The highest secrets of magic that Oz has ever held are contained in that wretched book. They couldn't care a twig about a stupid angry little girl. And you made her that way, by giving her up. You squandered her childhood."

"What gives you the right of superiority? So you walked her home from school. Kudos. We're grateful, or haven't we mentioned it? But note that she is alive to be walked, Sir Brrr."

Liir had a capacity for cold rage, Brrr observed, just like Elphaba's own. But Brrr hadn't come here to be woodshedded. "How alive, exactly? She's more like an otter in human shape than she is like a girl. Look, I mean, really. Lady *Glinda*? She couldn't raise a child. She couldn't raise an asparagus fern."

"Well, you can yield Rain back to us and give us a second chance. Stop circling about her with your big furry mane, keeping her chained to your heel."

"She's been abandoned one time too many," snapped Brrr. "Listen, I don't mutter about you behind your back. And I don't lock any doors. She can walk your way any time she wants. She's a child and she'll come to trust who she can, in her own good time. I don't have anything to do with that. But I'm not leaving her alone with you here till she's ready."

They were all but shouting at each other. They stood en garde, panting, though their concern for the child's welfare was mutual. "You've been so thoughtful," said Liir, seething. "Hauling Rain off with the Grimmerie. When the Emperor of Oz has been seeking it on and off all these years. *That's* a really secure situation for a child?"

"Don't think the irony hasn't escaped me. With the Emperor calling in all magical totems. Isolating us for easier location. You think I've enjoyed becoming a sitting duck just to tend to your daughter?"

Liir was nonplussed. The book was a huge part of the problem. "How much longer can the Grimmerie be kept out of the Emperor's hands, especially now that its charmed vault has come to its untimely end?"

Brrr shrugged. At least Liir's tone was more moderate. The Lion paced around the fourth corner of the Clock. Liir followed. They looked up at the clock face just as a small bird, a Wren, came pock-pocking down out of the sky. She landed without the mildest sense of alarm upon the dragon's snout. The man and the Lion looked up at it, and their jaws dropped, for several reasons.

The Lion was agog because the clock face, which had read one minute to midnight since the first moment he'd seen the Clock two years earlier, now read midnight.

"We meet again," said the Wren to the Lion; it was the humble bird who had warned them to flee the Emperor's soldiers on the Yellow Brick Road.

As for Liir, he didn't dare believe he recognized the bird. Wrens, after all, look rather alike, at least to human eyes. But as the Wren spoke, Liir knew her to be Dosey, whom he'd last seen a decade ago after the Conference of the Birds had swum the skies over the Emerald City crying *Elphaba lives! Elphaba lives!*

Dosey said, "Mercy fritters, but I've been winging your way for a week! Begging pardon, gents, but your Goose just told me you were having a bit of a chinwag down this way. I thought you'd want to hear what I have to say. The message comes direct from General Kynot. I translate from High Eagle. 'Apparently a few months ago, the impossible happened. She's back.'"

"She's back?" said Liir.

"Elphaba?" said the Lion, his blood hurrying at once, so he could get himself out of the way.

"If you please, sir, not Elphaba. Dorothy," replied the Wren. "Dorothy Gale."

8.

At the Chancel of the Ladyfish, the dwarf snarled at Liir and the Lion. "I don't believe in Dorothy. Wasn't that all a ruse? Some tricky business to divert the crowd while the Wizard was being turfed out of the Palace?"

"She was real enough to me," said Liir.

"And to me," said the Lion. "Haven't I got the emotional scars to prove it?"

"Assuming a Dorothy," ventured Nor, "I doubt she's back. Her supposed return sounds like just another variation on the theme of the legendary Ozma. 'Beautiful heroine disappears, but she'll return in our darkest hour, amen.' Hah. That sort of bluff only postpones and displaces our need to reform. Listen: nobody ever comes back to save us. We're on our own."

"Dorothy wasn't as beautiful as all that," said the Lion, "so I doubt she'd be convincing as everyone's favorite martyr mounting a comeback tour. I bet it isn't her. Probably some out-of-work male escort doing a send-up. In our modern times nobody can tell the difference anymore."

"Let's assume it *is* Dorothy," said Liir. "For the sake of conversation. Once upon a time I almost had a crush on her, after all. How did she get back? What's she doing here? Where is she?"

"What's said, sir, is that she arrived about a half a year ago," said Dosey. "Up in the Glikkus. The Scalps jostled up and down. Tremors were felt all over Oz. Some called it an earthquake, others the Great Heave-Ho. A Glikkun village known as High Mercy were flattened, just about to pebbles, they say. And when they's cleared away the rubble they finds this female character in a squarish conveyance of some sort. Its dented walls are only open iron curlicues, but the frillwork has kept the creature from being crushed until herself could be dug out."

Rain looked up. "We had our earthquake too. The Clock did. Remember? All them buildings fallen, after the Clock rolled down the hill into the poppy pasture?"

They had remembered. Mr. Boss was looking uneasy.

"Did our Clock cause Dorothy's earthquake?" asked Rain.

"Don't speak about what you don't know," snapped Mr. Boss.

"We all did that, we'd be mute forever," Liir said softly, in her defense, and a silence followed until Candle brokered a return to the subject.

"So what happened?" she asked. "Was anyone else hurt?"

"Almost total good luck for them Glikkuns," warbled the Wren. "The entire village were out larking in some high meadow. It were a holiday, seems, and nobody bothering in the local emerald mine. Which was great good fortune, don't you know, as those mines collapsed whole and entire. But a cow tied up to a tree came to a sorry end."

"So what did they do with this Dorothy?" asked Nor. "Where is she now?"

"Since she came to 'em caged in a sort of cell, all imprisoned already, they blamed her for the wreck of their homes. Then the pox and parcel of 'em up and moved into the village next door, which had seen no damage to speak of. They brought her with them. None could say whether she was concussed or whether she'd arrived two worms short of a breakfast, if you catch my drift." Dosey looked around brightly for an opinion about Dorothy's capacities. No one spoke.

"Anyroad," she continued, "they tended to her for months until she recovered somewhat of her memory. Apparently she'd been hauling about some little dog, but it had gone missing. Either got itself crushed in the rubble or took its chance to make a getaway through the bars while Dorothy was trapped inside. By the time herself was sound enough to remember her name, the snows had come. The pass down into Munchkinland is closed until spring—gotta get through snow season and most of mud season before anyone can go cross-country. But 'em Glikkuns has alerted Colwen Grounds, and they mean to send her down there. For legal processing and what-have-you."

"So Dorothy is back in Oz." Liir could hardly believe it.

"Word has it that when she finally realized she was in Oz, she said, 'I suppose that cow was a sacred cow, beloved of the nation and so on,' and then wasn't she all over crying like she cain't warm to the pleasures of travel."

"If the Glikkuns had aligned with the Gillikinese instead of Munchkinlanders, she'd be on her way to the Emerald City for a high royal celebration," said the

Lion. "A return to old times! Music, parades, the whole foldiddly fuss."

"Instead, she'll be sent from High Mercy to Colwen Grounds for repatriation into Munchkinland, is my guess," surmised Mr. Boss.

"Begging your pardon, but there en't much of High Mercy left," said Dosey. "She's jailed in the town next door. Little Mercy."

Little Daffy sniffed. "Who cares about that Dorothy anymore? Nothing more than a bother, always dropping in when she's not invited."

"I doesn't pretend to know how any humans think, nor government officials neither," replied the Wren. "But I'm told they're going to hold her accountable this time."

"For arriving on a landslide and squishing a cow?" Little Daffy laughed.

"Hey, cows have feelings too, I'm told," interrupted the Lion.

"No, no," said Dosey. "It weren't no special cow with virtues or such. That Dorothy is going to stand trial for the death of Nessarose Thropp and her sister, Elphaba. That's why I come all this way to find you. Liir and Lion especially. General Kynot thought you should know."

"We live in the hamlet of No Mercy," snapped the dwarf. "What do we care about what happens to her?"

"I don't get it," said Liir. "Didn't the Munchkin-landers consider Nessarose something of a dictator? Sure, she was the one to call for secession! So she's the mother of Munchkinland. But then they went sour on her because of her tyrannical piety. *They're* the ones who called her the Wicked Witch of the East, after all. Now suddenly they're missing her enough to bring her unlucky assailant to trial?"

"I en't prepared to comment on the matter," said Dosey. "I'm just doing the job given me by the General. You can choose to come and defend this Dorothy or not. There. I've delivered my message as was asked of me. I'll be happy to accept nest for the night, and I'll be off in the morning."

"You've wasted your time, Dosey Dimwit," insisted the dwarf. "We have no interest in this matter."

"She's convicted of the murder of Nessarose, she'll be hanged."

"Good. One less illegal immigrant to feed."

"I agree with Liir. This doesn't add up," said the Lion. "Why would they bother?"

"You can't be so thick." Nor's voice was cross. "It's a public relations stunt. Don't you see? They're doing the scapegoating thing again. Probably some Munch-kinlanders are wavering about the high cost in blood and treasury of defending their country. Nothing recommits the public to the cause than a good public mocking of the enemy."

Nor seems to have a better sense of political gesture than the rest of us, thought Liir.

She went on. "Munchkinlanders stoop this low, they're courting danger. We've been talking all winter about the need to keep out of the gunsights of the Emperor of Oz. But you know, certain individuals among us are in as much danger from Munchkinland." Her eyes passed toward Rain meaningfully, flitted away. "If Elphaba were still alive," Nor pressed on, "her presence would negate the Emperor's claim to Munchkinland. Though he's her brother, she'd take precedence, by age and by dint of her gender."

"And so does her issue," said the Lion wearily. "Even if you're male, Liir. And your issue even more than you—when she reaches her majority."

Now they all looked at Rain. She squirmed under their attention. She had an even stronger right to be ruler of Munchkinland than her great-uncle Shell, Emperor of Oz, did. The Emperor must know this too, if rumor of Rain's birth had been beaten out of Trism bon Cavalish. What chance the Munchkinlanders were also factoring in some advantage in locating Rain? The Munchkinlanders had just as much interest in finding her too—maybe more.

Her presence there would pull the rug out from under Shell's claims.

The girl might be in no less danger now than she'd been in during the past decade.

"She's not safe unless she flies," said Dosey, voicing what they were all thinking. "And you must fly with her, of course. You're her flock."

"Ah, we've got wing-cramp," said the dwarf. "We're ready for a cunning little bedsit with a coal fire. You bring unwelcome gossip, little birdy-on-the-breeze. Always crying panic. Go find yourself a perch somewhere else."

Candle rarely spoke before all of them, and her voice was deferential. Her fingers knotted on the tabletop before her. "Dosey is as welcome to stay here as you are, Mr. Boss."

Liir interceded. "Dosey, let's go outside, for a moment, while Candle prepares you a perch."

Iskinaary apparently took Liir's attention to Dosey otherwise. He hissed in that aggressive way Geese have, lunging at the Wren as if to wrench her legs off. The Goose was rewarded by a wet little plop of bird spatter on his bill while Dosey escaped, squawking, "Heavens ahead a'us! En't we all confederates and veterans of Kynot's Conference?"

Out in the air again, Liir tried to wipe the smile off his face. "Envy runs in every direction that air and

light do," he told Dosey. "Never thought I'd see that
old Goose go after another Bird."

"I can see 'e's your familiar, as ever was," replied
the Wren. "Not one to stick my beak in where I'm not
wanted, I'm not. I'll take myself downslope. I can see
to my own needs."

"That would be a disgrace." Liir wished there were
a way to embrace a Bird; he put his finger out, and the
Wren hopped upon it. "It's been ten years since the
Conference where I met General Kynot and Iskinaary
and all you others. How is he, the crusty old salt?"

"The Eagle is ready, steady, and stalwart as ever, if
afflicted with wing-nits, sadly. Cain't fly as high as he
once did. But he sends his regards."

"Where is he located?"

"That's confidential, begging your pardon, sir. He
don't command a mighty following anymore, mind.
But we Birds is always suspect of treachery by every
party, given our freedom to wander the skies. So we
keeps certain facts close to our breast-feathers as we
can do. Pays to be circumspect."

"Ought we, up here in our own aerie, to be cautious
about any particular Bird population?"

"Cain't say for certain. Birds of unlike feather rarely
flock together—that was the great success of Kynot's
Conference. We various clans and congregations, we

don't much attach to one another. Nor do we go in for argy-bargy. I'd say we mostly minds our own affairs."

"But you've gone out of your way to find us and tell us about Dorothy."

"I'm nothing special," said Dosey. "But I had my reasons."

Liir cocked an eyebrow.

"I'm a bit stout in the bosom, or where my bosom would be if I had a bosom," said Dosey. "And my hearing en't all that particular, and there's silver in my wing and a rasp in my morning song. But when the word was going around about this Dorothy, and that you and the Lion would want to know in case she needed some defending, I volunteered for the mission."

"Strong feeling for a human being you never met."

"It en't that Dorothy. She can hang on a gibbet," said Dosey, cheerfully enough. "It were you, sir. Begging your pardon and all that. I've had my own clutches in my time, and when the current nestlings call to me, they have to chirp so many *greats* before the *granny* that they run out of breath. So I know what it's like when an egg rolls out of the nest. Your child were just about to be born when we was flying together, and I had a scared feeling that the Emperor might swoop like a serpent upon your nest, in revenge. I wanted to see for myself, sir. I'm glad you've got her tight under your wing now."

"You're a mother many times over," said Liir. "You've only observed her a moment here or there, I know. But what do you make of her?"

Dosey's bill was made of chitinous horn. The only way Liir could identify a smile was by the way her downy cheeks puffed out, tiny grey berries at the corners of her beak. "Boy broomist, listen to me. She's the ugliest little duckling I ever seen, but as I lives and breathes, she's got flight in her, too."

9.

Once the Wren departed, next morning, the claws came out.

"We have no reason to trust that Dosey," said Mr. Boss. "She could've been lying through that common little beak of hers. How do we know Dorothy's really returned? Far more likely she was killed as dead as Ozma was murdered before her."

"Utter rot," said Liir. "Dosey put herself in considerable danger, making a solo flight at this winterish time of year, just to find us. She has no reason to lie. The Birds are aligned neither to Munchkinland nor to Loyal Oz."

"But Liir," said his wife. "We can't fly like Dosey over the border, not during wartime. We can't forge into Munchkinland as if we're off to market day. Who knows how fiercely those margins are now guarded? So you maintain a holdover affection for Dorothy. Fine. But whoever this Dorothy turns out to be these days, surely she won't want your child put in danger?"

Liir saw the wisdom of this, but not the charity.

Brrr cleared his throat. "Dorothy has nothing to do with a civil war between Loyal Ozians and Munchkins. She's a political prisoner no less than Nor was at her age. If Rain were in the same situation, wouldn't we go through hell trying to rescue her?"

"For you, there's a bruised child behind every campaign isn't there," said the dwarf. "I'm just saying."

"She'll be a matron by now," argued Brrr, "and in any case, she asked me to look after Liir. Doesn't she deserve the same? What friends has she in Oz, if not us?"

"It's a diversion," insisted the dwarf.

"From what? Saving your own skin? I'm all for rolling out," said Brrr.

So was Nor. There was a reason the Lion and Nor had struck sparks as a couple. Brrr saw it more clearly now. Nor was no homebody, and Brrr would rather be on the prowl, too. At this late date, with arthritis in his hips and a permanent case of halitosis, Brrr was discovering a certain quality of Lion about himself he'd never identified before.

It came down to a vote. They all elected to leave except Mr. Boss, who was tired of endless commuting. Rain wasn't asked her opinion.

Iskinaary, who since Dosey's visit had begun to shadow Liir about eight feet behind, like a shawled wife of an Arjiki chieftain except more garrulous, said, "Let's go. What are we waiting for? If this good weather lapses, we'll be snowed in as deep as Dorothy. All winter long."

On the eighth day of cold sunny weather, a thaw of sorts, when the cobbles were dry of snow but the ground still hard enough not to be mud, they harnessed Brrr up to the shafts of the dead Clock. Liir wrapped the Grimmerie in what remained of Elphaba's old black cape and carried it under his arm.

Rain shunned Nor's outstretched hand, cradling her shell instead. Tay rode on Rain's shoulder. Little Daffy shouted, "Come on, you," as Mr. Boss pretended to have died of a stroke, but he got up and stumped after them.

They'd gone a third of the way down the slope, when Rain suddenly said, "Wait, but we forgot the broom-flower."

"What's she croaking about?" asked the dwarf.

Liir put his hand to his mouth—sweet Ozma, in the stress of the moment and the presence of the

Grimmerie, he had left it behind—but Rain bolted back up the hill. A few moments later she had returned balancing Elphaba's broom over her shoulder.

"Where'd you get that flea-ridden thing?" asked Little Daffy.

"Stuck in the level chink in the stones running below the Ladyfish," said Candle in a low voice. "How did she find it there? I thought we hid it well enough."

"The Fishlady tolded me it was there, and not to forget it," said Rain. "Almost I did, but then I 'membered."

Whatever accompanied them down the hill—a mood, a spirit, an apprehension, a spookiness, a sense both of mission and of menace—made them all fall silent for quite some time. Iskinaary was the first to break out of it by singing a ditty straight out of the beer hall

> The night is dark, my hinny, my hen
> Romance in the air, my dove, my duck;
> The less I see of you, my dear,
> The more I bless my blessed luck.
> Come near for a kiss, come near for a cluck,
> I'll climb aboard and blindly—

until they all told him to shut up.

Liir and Candle had made the trip through the passes north of the Sleeve of Ghastille so long ago that they hardly recognized the way back. Six, seven years ago, was it? And at a different time of year. Now, as the ragged travelers abandoned their hideaway, a cold wind gripped and pulled at their cloaks and manes and shawls. Liir looked back, squinting, at where the Chancel of the Ladyfish tucked itself against the slope. He nudged Candle to see. It was hidden to view, even though they knew where it was.

Mr. Boss insisted he wasn't going to take the Clock into Munchkinland again. He didn't trust those squirrely little people, except of course his wife. Who knew if General Cherrystone had put out a bulletin of arrest on the basis of the Clock's having predicted some disaster involving the dragons in Restwater? The dwarf would rather take his chances in Loyal Oz, he said.

So the companions turned their heads west, toward the Disappointments and the oakhair forest. Maybe they were postponing the moment they would have to separate. That moment would come, soon enough, near one of the great lakes or the other. No one was certain about relative distances across the terrain, but in Oz you tended to show up where you needed to get, sooner or later.

The little detour, the loop west, would be their coda, at least for the time being. Who knew how much time they had left together? (Who ever knows?) Without naming it as such, they all felt the tug of their imminent separation. At least, all the adults did. What Rain thought, or Tay, or for that matter the Time Dragon hunched in paralysis up there, couldn't be guessed at.

They lurched through upland meadows and past escarpments of scrappy trees, through lowland growths of protected firs, along streambeds partially glazed with ice. The warm snap had returned to the air a sense of the rot of pine needles and mud, but the air eddied with the sourness of ice, too.

They were walking into a trap.

Or they were walking home at last.

They didn't know—who does?—where they were going.

But the world was specifically magnificent this week, in this place. Behold the diseased forest east of the Great Kells, called by some the Disappointments. Largely unpopulated due to barren soil—only scrub could grow in the wind off the Kells, and only tenacious and bitter farmers bothered to hang on. The few unpainted homesteads were scrappy, the sheds for the farmer's goats identical to those for the farmer's children. The companions avoided human settlements as they could, preferring to pitch camp amidst the deer droppings and rabbit tracks in the scrapey woods.

A rainstorm blew in then and parked over their heads. Their passage slowed down due to the mud, and they couldn't build a fire. The little girl shivered but didn't complain. Four or five days in, they came to a dolmen on which someone had painted destinations. One side was scrawled with VINKUS RIVER FORD, TO THE WEST, with an arrow pointing left. The other side read MUNCHKINLAND AND RESTWATER LAKE. Brrr was for turning east, but Liir stopped him.

"We're not more than a day or two from Apple Press Farm in the other direction," he told them. "Where Rain was born. We still have two months before Dorothy can travel down from the Glikkus to be put on trial. Let's take a couple of days at the farm. At the least, we'll have a roof over our heads. We can dry out. Warm up the child. Maybe something survived in the root garden after all these years."

"I didn't pack for a nostalgia tour," said Mr. Boss, but Liir insisted. Candle agreed that they might enjoy a night or two with a fire in a hearth before proceeding cross-country toward Munchkinland. Since it was only a brief interruption of their progress, the company turned about, keeping the Great Kells to their left.

The massed fortress of basalt and evergreen and snow looked inhospitable but breathtaking.

That night the rain let up for a spell. The company took turns singing around a campfire and telling stories. Nor told the tale of the Four Improbable Handshakes. Candle sang in Qua'ati, something long and inexpressibly boring, though everyone smiled and swayed as if entranced. (Except Rain.) Iskinaary barracked a raft of Goose begats, and Mr. Boss finally riled himself out of his somnolence to provide a few short poems of questionable virtue.

> A certain young scholar of Shiz
> Right before a philosophy quiz
> Guzzled splits of champagne
> So that he could declaim
> "I drink, and therefore I is."

And

> A sweet cultivated young Winkie
> Could do civilized things with her pinkie
> Which excited young men
> Who cried, "Do me again!"
> Though the pinkie emerged somewhat stinky.

"That'll do," said Nor, Candle, and Little Daffy, all at once.

Even Liir, without a whole lot of confidence in his tone, tried to dredge up some scrap of song he had sung when he was in the service. He could only get a bit of the one called, he thought, "The Return of His Excellency Ojo."

> Sing O! for the warrior phantom phaeton
> Carrying Ojo over the mountain
> His saturnine sword was the scimitar moon
> Soon, thundered Ojo, vengeance soon!

This went on too long and no one could tell what Ojo was trying to achieve, and Liir said that was pretty much standard operating procedure for the military. But then Little Daffy recalled something from her own childhood.

> Jack, Jack, Pumpkinhead

"How does it go now?" She tried again.

> Jack, Jack, Pumpkinhead
> Woke to life in a pumpkin bed
> Made his breakfast of pumpkin bread

Fell and squashed his pumpkin head
Went to the farmer and the farmer said
Pumpkins smash but can't be dead
Plant your brains in the pumpkin bed
Grow yourself a brand-new head.
That's what he said he said he said
'Cause the farmer liked his pumpkin bread.

Rain admired that one and clapped her hands.

"*That's* a nursery ditty from a soundly agrarian society," said the Lion, "no doubt about it."

"Do you have a song to sing?" Candle asked of Rain.

"I knew about a fish once that was locked in a apple-shaped room in the ice. But I don't know what happened to it."

They waited in case she might remember; they waited with that affectionate and bothersome patience with which elders heap expectation on the shoulders of the young. When Rain spoke again, though, she seemed not to be aware of their appetite for anything more about the fish. She said, "I don't know what happens to us." She said it as a question.

"Oh well," said Candle. "None of us knows that."

"What happens to us is a joke, and don't pretend otherwise," said the dwarf.

"What happens to us is sleep," said Liir firmly. "Time to go have a pee, Rain. I'll walk you a little way out."

Tay didn't let Rain go anywhere without scampering after her, no matter how asleep it had seemed to be. It woke itself up when Rain moved, and it followed Rain and her father to a blind of scattercoin, where Liir turned his head just far enough to simulate modesty, but not far enough to allow Rain to escape his peripheral vision.

They wandered about for three more days, slogging through mud and sluicing through rain that sometimes preferred to be snow. Between low tired hills, through unnamed valleys formed by streams threading down from the Kells for ten thousand years. "You ought to know if we're closing in on the farm," said Liir to Candle as they blundered along shallow slopes. Their ankles all ached from the slant. "You can see the present."

"This isn't the present anymore," said Candle. "Apple Press Farm is in our past now, and one hill looks much the same as another."

Finally they discovered the right arrangment of slopes and dips, and they began to drive down ancient agricultural tracks kept clear by animal passage.

They came upon a tapering winter meadow. A thwart-hipped woman with a basket and a set of rusting loppers was moving about the weird beautiful verdant green glowing wetly in the thin snow and the thinning rain.

"As I live and breathe," said Little Daffy.

The woman turned, straightened up, her hand on her hip. "So the prodigal turncoat returns to the nunnery," she said. "It's hallelujah time; get the bacon out of the larder and trim off the moldy bits."

"Nice to see you too, Sister Doctor," said Little Daffy. "What are you doing here?"

"Double the work I'd be doing if you hadn't scarpered," said Sister Doctor. "If you've come home for forgiveness, you're going to have to fill out quite a bill of penitence first. Who are your traveling companions?" She took a pair of spectacles from her apron pocket and reared back a little to see the Clock at the meadow gate. "Not that thing again? And the Lion— Sir Brrr, I remember, I'm not that gaga yet—and the dwarf too. So you've joined a cult, Sister Apothecaire."

"It's Little Daffy now," said the Munchkinlander. "I've left the mauntery."

"I suppose you have." Sister Doctor snapped the spectacles closed so fiercely that one lens popped out and lost itself in the snow. Rain and Tay dug it out for her. "Are you here to sing a few pagan carols and pass the basket? You'll get neither coin nor comfort from us."

"I always admired your largesse," said Little Daffy. "But what *are* you doing here?"

"Trying to keep the community together, that's what. When the army of Loyal Oz advanced on the mauntery two years ago, we had no choice but to flee. It didn't go unnoticed that you absented yourself at the first opportunity. We assumed you must have hurried back to your homeland." She said *homeland* as if she were saying *bog*.

"I went back to release our guests from their locked chambers," said Little Daffy, "and I apologize to no one for that. I fell on the stairs, and by the time I came around, your dust on the horizon had already settled. Thanks for the show of sorority. *Sister*."

"Well, let bygones be bygones and all that," said Sister Doctor with a new briskness. "In a panic, missteps are taken. Have you come to rejoin your community?"

"I didn't know you were here."

"Where else would we be? The mauntery was burned to the ground."

"Sister Doctor. The mauntery is made of stone."

"Well, I mean the roofs and floors. The furniture, such as it was. There's nothing to return to without a massive rebuilding effort. And our divine Emperor of Oz isn't about to channel funds into the repair of a missionary outpost that he ordered to be torched. So we've crowded in here."

"How did you come to find this place?"

"It always belonged to the mauntery," replied the maunt. "Back in the days of the Superior Maunt, as you may remember, some skilled artisans among us used this outclave as a place to hide a printing press. We circulated broadsides anonymously, warning against the increasing theocracy of the Emperor. Ha! If we only knew. And him divine, can you credit it. Not a smart career move for a bunch of unmarried women trying to live out of the limelight. And with Lady Glinda our sponsor, no less. Oh, a great vexation for her too, I'll wager, unless she swanned her way through it."

Brrr looked at Little Daffy to see how she was taking the news of her former community. The little bundle from Munchkinland seemed at home, having this discussion with an associate who had been both a comrade and an adversary. The Lion said, "News of the old gang is all very well, but we're sore and soggy here and more than a bit peckish. I hope you're going to invite us in."

At this Sister Doctor seemed to recover her sense of stature. "Well, we have less than we ever had, but of what we have, we share willingly. I wonder if winter broccoli appeals?"

"A hot bath would appeal more," said Liir.

Sister Doctor took out her spectacles again, wiped the rain off them, and peered at him through the intact lens. "I thought I recognized that voice. It's Liir, isn't it—the one they say is Elphaba's son. Oh, now the soup *is* on the boil. What are you doing with this lot?"

"Hoping for supper, maybe."

"I'll get you something, something for all of you." She threw her implements together in her basket and looked over her shoulder. "It isn't safe to come into the farm, though. Let me organize something and I'll be back."

"Why not safe?" asked Mr. Boss. "We can defend ourselves against maunts in the wilderness."

"Eat first; we'll talk later. Just hunker down here, and come no farther."

"Well, we're not going to push down the barricades, but I say, we have a child with the chills. A hot posset would be most—"

"That's an order," said Sister Doctor. Little Daffy put her hand on the dwarf's arm, and he fell silent, although he growled like a bratweiler. "Build a fire, that won't hurt," added the maunt. "There's a mess of drying firewood stacked up a half mile on, near where the orchard peters out."

They walked through the apple orchard—candelabrum of branches sporting sprigs of snow, not all that unlike apple blossom—and Liir remembered the instance of magic he'd witnessed here. Using the power of her music and her own musky capacity, Candle had called up the voices of the dead to help the Princess Nastoya lose her human disguise and to revert to her Elephant nature, and so finally to die the way she wanted and needed.

Now, to return to this orchard . . . ! Another season, another crackling moment in his life. Rewarding, not morose. He reached for Candle's hand, and she squeezed his in return. Maybe everything would be all right. Sooner or later.

He recalled an outdoor oven some distance from the farmhouse and sheds. They built a fire. The grate was hooded and the flue hooked, so the fire could burn in the intermittent rain. They rinsed some of the broccoli that Sister Doctor had left behind. They munched on woody florets, hoping for better. Rain sat closest and grew less grey. In an hour the maunt was back with a donkey on which were saddled baskets and bags with bottles of claret, a ham, ropes of onions and twists of sourswift. A tablecloth, once unbundled, revealed six loaves of onion bread and a caramel cake burned on the bottom. "Heaven," said the Lion. "Don't suppose you brought any port, or some cigars?"

"Maunts go through cigars like termites through doorsills. We have none to spare."

"Thought you might say that."

Beneath the saddlebags, Sister Doctor had piled four or five pelts and two woolen blankets. The rain had faltered again, but the shadows blued up in a frosty way. Liir was about to renew the request for indoor lodging, but Sister Doctor anticipated his request.

"You can't be allowed to stay, I'm afraid," she told them. "I was distracted by seeing Sister Apothecaire— Little Daffy as she styles herself now. I didn't really take in the measure of the difficulty until I realized you had Liir with you. It's too dangerous for you to come into the house. No one must know you are here."

"You have stool pigeons among the maunts?" asked the Lion. "So much for your professed neutrality."

"I'm protecting my sisters as much as I'm trying to protect you. We've been visited three times in the past two years by emissaries from the EC military to check and see who's been through. I can't vouch that every voice among our sorority is equally devoted to neutrality—how could I? How could I plead knowledge into all of their souls? Nor can I attest that they'd stand up to harsh questioning if the investigators sniffed out that we were hiding something. Better for all that you should move on."

"What are they looking for?" asked Liir, and "When were they last here?" asked his half-sister, at the same time.

"You've eluded them for so long that some believe you are dead," said Sister Doctor to Liir. "But they don't believe you brought the Grimmerie into the Afterlife with you. So they're convinced they'll find it sooner or later. You may have heard that the invasion of Munchkinland is stalled. General Cherrystone's army has taken Restwater, but the struggle around Haugaard's Keep is a standoff. The Munchkinlanders can't reclaim the lake; nor can the EC forces advance as far as Colwen Grounds to finish their reannexation of Munchkinland. The Munchkinland farms won't sell bread or grain to Loyal Oz until the invading forces yield Restwater and retreat."

"Never yield," hissed Little Daffy, almost to herself.

"Oh, don't look at me like that, Sister Apothecaire, Munchkinland won't starve. But with no one to sell bread to, much of their unharvested grain just rots in the fields. The EC meanwhile hankers for bread but has plenty of water to drink. The term on a game board is called stalemate, I think."

"How does this figure in surveillance of maunts?" asked the Lion.

"Isn't it plain as the nose on your plain face? The EC once again ramps up its campaign to find the Grimmerie. In the hopes that it might reveal secrets of how to unleash a mightier force against central Munchkinland, and strike a blow at the heart of the government at Colwen Grounds. Finishing the job.

"In short," she said, "if you lot thought you were out of danger, you're sadly mistaken. Whoever travels with Liir Thropp courts danger, by association."

"And you've given us broccoli, bread, and wine," said Little Daffy. "Sister, thank you."

"I maintain my vows." She passed the strawberry compote for spooning upon the more burnt bits of caramel cake.

They told her what they'd heard about the legendary Dorothy making a comeback tour. Sister Doctor hadn't been apprised of this, but she wasn't much interested. "We haven't had a reprisal of the Great Drought for some time now, but if it should come as soon as next summer, punishing the fields with blight, the Munchkinlanders have little left in their coffers to buy supplies from Loyal Oz, and trading agreements are suspended anyway. The uneasy balance settled upon now seems more or less peaceful—only a few soldiers die a week on one side or the other, in this skirmish or that—but one doesn't know who will give out first, Loyal Oz or Munchkinland."

"You've become callous," remarked Little Daffy. " 'Only a few soldiers die a week?' Time was you and I would go out on the battlefield and tend to the sick, and care about it."

"Don't hector me. I care as much as I can, but I don't spend energy caring about things I cannot resolve. I tend to my maunts and keep us out of harm's way. Right now I'm feeding the hungry and harboring enemies of the state. I can't do all that and work in international diplomacy too. Pass me the butter pot."

The Lion said, "Look, we have a little girl here. Surely she deserves a roof over her head for one night? We've been on the road a week or more."

"Don't think I haven't guessed who she is," said Sister Doctor. "I'm trying to protect you all. Have you no sense? Or do you really not believe me?" She sighed, and then slipped off the starched yoke of her religious garb, and without evidence of humility or shame she let the bib of her garment slip down almost to her nipple.

The scar on her shoulder was rippled, a plum color, like congealed tadmuck. Glossy and hideous. "Do you remember how Mother Yackle went blind? These men don't come to play parlor games. I am trying in as calm a voice as I can to tell you that you're in danger at Apple Press Farm. They know from that fellow Trism that you were here once, Liir and Candle, and they suspect this will be one of the places you might return. They've turned the house inside out three times thinking they might yet find the Grimmerie on the premises. We've had to put it to rights as best we could, over and over again. Thank the Unnamed God for Sister Sawblade, that's what I say."

She dressed herself again and concluded her sermon. "Even the house might be bugged. Do you know what I mean? We have a weird infestation of woggle-bugs. I'm told there is some thought they can be communicated with—don't ask me how. My capacity for comprehending mystery doesn't extend to science, only to faith. But I can't be sure they aren't capable somehow of alerting the next contingent of investigators that you were in residence, were I to make a mistake of mercy and let you in. You see," she finished, "you can't stay. For our sake, but also for your own good. Tonight, all right, to the barn, but *quietly*. For the sake of a croupy child. After dark. I'll take Sister Manure off muckout detail. But tomorrow you'll be on your way. No one will be the wiser, no one but me and the donkey. And I can stand anything."

"She can," said Little Daffy miserably, when she had gone. "I don't like the old bitch anymore, but she's a tough little biscuit, and she means what she says. Anyone else in Oz would crack under torture before she did."

10.

Before dawn. At the sound of maunts beginning their devotional song, Sister Doctor nipped in with a cornucopia of supplies the travelers could use during the next stage of their journey. She refused to advise them which way to go or what to do. "I don't want to know if you have the Grimmerie with you," she told them. "However, I do believe it's time to lose the Clock. You'd move faster without it, and what good is it doing you now?"

Liir pondered the question as they slipped away, unheeded, from Apple Press Farm. Here he had learned to love a woman—to love this wife, this mother of their child—and even more, he had learned to love at all. He had felt a pang at coming near, had been afraid, however stiff his face and controlled his upper lip, that he would mourn for the lost simpleton he'd once been. He needn't have worried. Leaving Apple Press Farm, his mind returned to the present and the future as they headed north into drier air.

Iskinaary had kept silent while on the farm. Liir remembered only after they'd left it that the Goose, too, had been there before. Falling into step with the Bird, Liir asked him what he had concluded about the maunt's revelations.

"I could have finished off an entire generation of woggle-bugs in an afternoon's work," said the Goose. "I should have thought that might be apparent, but did anyone ask me for help? Noooooo. Just a silly Goose, old Iskinaary."

"You can be some help now, and take to the wing," said Liir. "Do a little scouting for us. Sister Doctor's caution seemed well founded. Some pots can take years to come to the boil, but when they do, the scalding is ferocious."

"I'll do that," said the Goose. "For you. For you and Candle. Oh, and for the girl too, I suppose. By extension. Though I wish she would show a little more oomph. I don't mean to be cruel, but she's a bit slow out of the eggshell, isn't she?"

"I'd go do that surveillance right now before you get an additional thrust to your liftoff by a boot in the behind," said Liir, and Iskinaary obliged.

And then Liir thought: How are we ever going to protect her?

They walked single file. The farther from Apple Press Farm, the farther apart from one another they straggled. Even Tay kept a little distance from Rain. It was as if they had all taken in the message that there would be no safe harbor for them, not while the world was at war—so, presumably, not ever.

Liir tried to remember being Rain's age—eight, nine, ten. Whatever it was. He had been in Kiamo Ko at that age, playing with Nor, surely? Or had Nor already been taken away by Cherrystone and his men? In any case, he'd been alone in his life, as alone as Rain seemed to be. He'd lived with his mother, with the Wicked Witch of the West (which might be the name of any mother, all mothers, he realized), but he'd lived apart, not unlike the way Rain kept apart from him and Candle. Of course Elphaba had shown little interest in him. Or if she had shown some kind of interest, he'd been too dull to read it as such—the way, presumably, Rain was too dull to recognize Liir's love, even passion, for her.

What a mystery we are to ourselves, even as we go on, learning more, sorting it out a little.

The further on we go, the more meaning there is, but the less articulable. You live your life, and the older you get—the more specificity you harvest—the more precious becomes every ounce and spasm. Your life and times don't drain of meaning because they become more contradictory, ornamented by paradox, inexplicable. Rather the opposite, maybe. The less explicable, the more meaning. The less like a mathematics equation (a sum game); the more like music (significant secret).

Would he ever know anything about Rain? Or would he have to accept that he would live in a world adjacent to hers, with her tantalizingly nearby, but a mystery always, growing into her own inviolable individuality?

Maybe it had been better, he caught himself thinking, if he *had* kept her close to his side, for even if she'd been ripped from his arms at the age of six, she would have known six good years of close fatherly affection—

No, he couldn't think that; he couldn't bear to. Even in an alternate history. He couldn't tolerate the thought of her being taken from him. Even though he'd given her away.

There she loped, scuffing up snow, head down between her shoulders. He could walk the rest of his life. He would never catch up to her.

Iskinaary returned. "She was more right than she knew, that old crow," he told Liir. "Menaciers four miles along, and on the very path we're trudging.

We'll have to turn off. There's a parallel track a mile to the west that looks less traveled; we should divert across country to it at once."

They began to turn the Clock.

"We're adjusting further and further off our goal," complained Mr. Boss, but Brrr was hauling the cart, not him. And the Lion never minded veering off any track that led straight into the sights of marksmen.

"Later we'll compensate and arc back eastward. If we continue to believe we should try to steal across the border into Munchkinland and be present to defend Dorothy," said Brrr. "Though perhaps she won't need our help. She seems to come equipped with all kinds of fatal architecture attached to her. First a farmhouse, and now this giant wrought-iron birdcage or whatever it is she was trapped in. The girl does wreak havoc on the physical universe. Why is that?"

"Shhh," said Liir. "The soldiers may have fanned out since Iskinaary saw them half an hour ago."

"I doubt they have," said the Goose. "They were playing cards. Five Hand Slut, if I could read the markings, though I don't have the eye of an eagle. They didn't look in any particular hurry, but I'll go take another gander. If you hear a gunshot and a strangulated cry for 'peace among all nations! peace in our time,' find my corpse and turn me into a Goose-feather bolster, and use me to suffocate one of our foes." He looked proud at the thought. "We have so many."

Liir said, "Are you going to continue to plan your own memorial service or are you going to go on a reconnaissance mission for us?"

"That Dosey has made you all military again. If I were a different sort of Goose I'd find it kind of sexy," said Iskinaary, and took off.

For the next ten days or so Iskinaary became their early warning system. Not until he came back from his rounds and sounded the all clear would they advance another three or four miles.

Liir hauled the Grimmerie on his back. When he tried to put it in a drawer in the Clock, or on a shelf, the drawer wouldn't open or the shelf broke. The shutters wouldn't latch, due to new swelling in the jambs. Even in its paralysis the Clock managed to have an opinion. The Clock didn't want the Grimmerie anymore.

A winning tribe of pygmy warthogs came through one day, snuffling around the wheels of the conveyance and peeing all over the place. Tay hissed and leapt upon the dragon's dead snout, and the Lion went upright even in his shafts, spooked. The wagon rocked and tilted and looked about to smash to one side till Nor whipped off her shawl. She gave the warthogs a cotton lashing at which they merely laughed before continuing to rootle on through the undergrowth.

Another afternoon, the companions surprised a bear doing something downright pornographic with a bee-less hive of honey. Brrr almost said "Cubbins?" in case it was his old friend—but a Gillikin Bear wouldn't have wandered this far south, and since this bear showed no capacity for shame he couldn't be a talking Bear.

Nor took off her shawl again and wrapped it around Rain's head, making a blinder for her eyes so she wouldn't too closely examine the inappropriate.

"Really, that's disgusting," said Little Daffy. *"Wildlife."*

"Disgusting? Inventive." Mr. Boss had perked up for the first time in weeks, and he nudged his wife. "Maybe if we ever get to a trading post we can invest in a pot of honey, honey, and have a honeymoon."

The Goose had become a bard of advice. "Good spot to camp," he would report, or "Long slope ahead; we'll have to take it slow." Or "Rainclouds on the horizon; better stop the afternoon here where the fir branches will give us cover." Or even "Skarks passing behind us, let's pick up the speed in case they decide they want Lion steaks for supper."

Day after day. The winter waned, but reluctantly, with glacial speed. Finally, the beginning of woodland blossom, those brave early ground-level markers like filarettes and snowdrops.

One afternoon Iskinaary reported that they were nearing the edge of a great lake. At first the companions imagined they might have veered back toward the east. But Iskinaary said he could see no sign of habitation, no coracles or villages. Just barren cliffs around flat black water bereft of whitecaps. Devoid even of avian populations. "Kellswater, then," said the dwarf. "Uck. I've seen it once or twice before. It gives me the creeps."

"Why?" asked Rain, whose experience of lakes had only involved Restwater.

"It's a dead lake, dead as doormats. Nothing swims in it. Neither fish nor frog. Nothing living floats upon it, not a water skeetle or a lily pad."

"We should make a swift detour," said Nor. "That time the Munchkinlander rebels forced the EC Messiars back into Kellswater, the soldiers didn't so much drown as—as melt. Kellswater possesses some of the properties of acid. Cold acid. It pulled their skin from their bones even as they thrashed, we were told."

"Well, that puts the tin hat on our hopes to practice our synchronized swimming," said Brrr. "Oh well.

No matter what they say about me in the columns, I never fancied prancing about the beach in a singlet and a cache-sex."

"How could a lake be dead?" asked Rain. "Or how could it be alive, either?"

Little Daffy said, "Someone in the tribe of the Scrow told me that legend suggests Kumbricia the demon-goddess lives there. Or died there. Or something. Maybe she only has a summer home. I don't remember."

"Who is Kumbricia?"

"Stop," said Candle. "Children don't need to know stories like that."

"Yes, they do," said the Goose. "Kumbricia, little gosling, is the opposite number to Lurline, in the oldest tales of Oz. She is the hex, she is the curse, she's always implicated when things go wrong. . . ."

"She's there when the shoelace snaps as you're trying to outrun the horsemen of the plains," said Nor.

"She's what breathes the pox on the wheezy child for whom the poultice, oddly, won't work," said Little Daffy.

"She is the itch where you can't quite reach," said Mr. Boss.

"*Stop,*" said Candle. "I mean it."

"Not before my turn," said the Lion. "Kumbricia is the way the whole world arches its eyebrow at you before it smacks you down. Where *is* she, you ask? Not in the lake. Not in the pox. Not in the shoelace or the horse hooves. She's in the interference of effects, nothing more than that. In the crossroads of possibility, giggling through her nose at us."

"You'll slice open the child with that nonsense!" Candle yelled at them. They almost laughed to hear her raise her high ribbony voice, but the expression on her face stopped them.

Apologetically, even though he hadn't joined in, Liir said, "But then, on the other hand, there's Lurlina. The soul of . . . of grace . . grace, and—"

Mr. Boss wasn't daunted by Candle. "No one believes in Lurline. A goddess of goodness? Forget it. She's been taking a cigarette break since the year dot. She's as gone as the Unnamed God. Pretty enough in the stories, to be sure, but once she finished breathing green into every corner of Oz, she vanished. No return in the second act, I'm afraid."

"I hate you all," said Candle. She grabbed Rain's hand and Rain tried to pull away, but this time Candle wouldn't let her.

"What you hate is the world," said Mr. Boss placidly. "We're just as blameless in talking about it as the pox is blameless, or the shoelace. What you hate is that your child is stuck here. Well, get used to it. The only exit is the final one."

"To the bosom of Lurline," muttered Little Daffy.

"And a scratchy bosom it is, I bet," said the dwarf.

Liir opened his mouth again but found he couldn't say anything more. There was no apology for the way the world worked. Only accommodation to it, while at the same time committing—somehow—not to give up. Not to give up on Rain, and her chances—whatever they might be. In fact, not to give up on anyone.

"I want to see the dead lake," said Rain.

"Can't hurt you if you don't go near it," said the dwarf.

But they'd been walking as they talked, and suddenly Kellswater opened up before them. The greyness of it under a fine blue sky seemed to deaden the entire district. The forest wouldn't grow within a hundred yards of it. The margins of sand and tumbles of rock were desolate. No yellow pipers, no reeds, no bouncing sand-sprites. No breeze, no reflections. A scent of salt and iron, perhaps.

"I know a lot of families that would pay good cash to send their kids to a summer camp pitched on this shore," murmured Mr. Boss.

"Enough, you," said Little Daffy. "Do stop. It's too hideous. Somehow."

Iskinaary took wing again and circled about. They waited safely back on a limestone promontory some twenty feet above the lake. The Goose rose, banked, rose again. When he returned, he seemed shaken. "One senses almost a magnetic pull," he told them. "On a sunny day I usually can ride the updrafts over a body of water, but this water works to the contrary. Let's not linger here."

"Which way looks safest?" asked Liir.

"Northeast," replied Iskinaary. "Keeping the lake on our left. We'll come upon the oakhair forest that spans the divide between Kellswater and Restwater. That's as far as we go together. If the forest isn't filled with border patrols, those heading for a rescue mission might slip eastward here and find themselves back in Munchkinland, back near the banks of Restwater. With another big push. Shall we?"

They should, yes. They would. As they turned about to leave Kellswater behind, however, a couple of stray warthogs who must have been following them these past few days came charging up the slope from the underbrush.

The warthogs of Kumbricia: innocently troublesome, like all aspects of the world.

They darted beneath the cart and between the legs of the Lion, spooking him badly but spooking Tay worse. They caught the otter for a moment, pinned him to the ground on the edge of the bluff, and played with him prettily as they readied to gore him. Brrr twisted in

his shafts. The others screamed and waved their arms.
Rain dashed forward, between the grunting terrors,
and thwacked one of them over the forehead with her
shell. It didn't break, but blood gushed forth from an
eye socket of that creature.

The rice otter broke free and dove for Rain's leg,
snaking up her thigh onto her shoulders. The second
hog charged Rain. The Lion was nearest and the first
to arrive in defense. Shooting his claws, he raked half
the pelt off the warthog, which grunted in fury and
surprise. Rain fell back into the arms of Candle and
Liir. As the Lion twisted about to check for the first
warthog, in case it was readying for another feint, the
Clock on the wagon overbalanced. The replacement
axle, carved from the sallowwood dragon wing, buckled at last. A wheel caved inward. The snout of the
dragon reared up at the sky as if trying, one final time,
to escape its tethered post upon this theater of doom. Its
broken wings flapped, but there was no wind to catch,
not in this open air tomb-land. Slowly, and then faster
the Clock hurtled down the slope toward Kellswater.
Wheels and shaft, temple of fate adorned with a clock
face at midnight and dragon up top—and the Lion still
laced to it.

The dwarf managed a partial rescue. Dragged down
the bluff, still he managed to pull his dirk from some

inner pouch and slash the leather harness. On sands that shifted, conspiring with gravity to drag them to their wet grave, Brrr scrabbled for a purchase. The Lion escaped, the dwarf leapt clear, but the Clock careered off the bluff. Brrr turned in time to watch the wheels, the carriage, the theater, and finally the Time Dragon disappear into oily deeps. The last thing they saw was its red red eye, until black liquid blinked out whatever final vision it might have enjoyed.

"Ladyfish got 'm at last," murmured Rain.

And when the Lion had caught his breath—some hours later—he thought: maybe that's why the Clock told the dwarf to avoid taking on a girl child as an associate. It could see in that decision the chance of its own destruction. When we disobeyed it—it shut down. It wouldn't accept the Grimmerie anymore. For the Clock, then, it was only a matter of time.

11.

That was the end of the company of the Clock of the Time Dragon. Four days later they prepared for a parting of ways.

The dwarf expressed no preferences. Cross-country to Munchkinland or north, deeper into Loyal Oz—it made no difference now. The Clock was extinct and the Grimmerie deeded to Liir. "Come to Munchkinland," suggested the Lion. "Without the Clock to slow us down or the book to guard, what harm might come to us? If we need to outrun a border patrol, I can easily carry you and Little Daffy on my back." He held back from saying, "Your stint as a kindergarten supervisor is over." He owed his life to the dwarf.

In any event, Munchkinland would be safer for the Lion, who in Loyal Oz might still be considered AWOL from his mission to locate the Grimmerie. Brrr intended to light out to Bright Lettins or to Colwen Grounds or wherever the trial of Dorothy would be staged. He had always thought Dorothy a bit of a blockhead, but not a malicious one. Maybe he could help her. It would be good to help someone. He was beginning to accept that he couldn't do as much for his own wife as he'd have liked. He couldn't remove from her history, by force of either comfort or magic, the fact that she'd spent some of her girlhood in prison. He couldn't repair her. But he could, just possibly, do for Dorothy what he couldn't do for Nor.

Whom he now would leave behind. But not, they both promised each other, for good.

Little Daffy, for her part, was eager to return to her home after all these years. She'd emigrated as a child, entering the mauntery after a stint at a home for incurables in the Emerald City, but she was returning a married woman in this time of trial. She was ready to stand at the ramparts of her homeland and spit in the eye of any gangly Emerald City Messiar who might deserve it. As long as she had a ladder to stand upon, for the height.

She kept her husband close to her side. What would he do, who would he turn out to be, now that the Grimmerie was traded to Liir, and the Clock of the Time Dragon was history? Maybe he'd find her Munchkin cousins affable, and he'd adjust to domestic life. Maybe when the troubles were over, they'd settle in her childhood home of Center Munch or even in Far Applerue, nearer the Glikkus. Perhaps Mr. Boss would find he had an affinity with the troll-people of the Glikkus, who didn't farm but mined emeralds for their livelihood. Little Daffy didn't know. The Clock wasn't there to advise them. They would have to make it up as they went along.

She was glad, however, she'd collected in a few private pockets a little bit of the poppy dust from the great red flourish in the Sleeve of Ghastille. She was finding that, used in moderation, it came in handy at moving her poor aggrieved husband ahead.

The companions made their good-byes in a grove of oakhair trees. Long strands of new growth, acorns forming at the tips, dropped a kind of silent rain among them. An outdoor room laced with harp strings. As the companions stood there, reluctant to take their leave of one another, a breeze scurried along the floor of the forest. It strummed the strings of the oakhair fronds, a soft and jangled music, an orchestral evocation of the mood that had settled upon them.

"You'll be better off the farther away from the fighting you get," the Lion told Liir. "But, taking a leaf from Sister Doctor, don't tell me where you're going. It'll be safer for you if we don't know."

"I don't know myself," said Liir. "I have an idea or two, but time will have to tell. We wish we could come with you to the defense of Dorothy. But it's too dangerous."

"No joke," replied the Lion. "If you show yourself in Bright Lettins, the Munchkinlanders might impress you to take the Eminenceship of Munchkinland whether you want to do it or not. You'd give Munchkinland an edge. Your investiture would render void the claim that the Emperor Shell is making upon Munchkinland. It wouldn't be safe for you, and certainly not safe for Rain."

"We aren't done keeping her hidden," agreed Liir.

"We'll never be done with that," added Candle. "I think that will be our curse."

Nor knelt down before the Lion and spoke as if to her knees, not her husband. "I don't want you to go, but it's for the best. You do the work at the trial that I would do if I could. The public statement is beyond me, in any venue. And I may be useful yet in helping take care of Rain. If Liir and Candle are ever recognized, if they're accosted in any way, I'll be able to stand in for Rain. She is my niece, after all."

"I know," said Brrr. "She is closer to you than I am."

"That's not what I mean," said Nor, "and furthermore it isn't true. No one is closer to me than you are. But she's in greater peril. She will be grown one day. She may be safe sooner than we think. We'll meet up again."

Liir took his sister's hand as he disagreed with her. "Dear friends. While the country is at war, no living citizen is safe. If we choose to find one another again— and we may never have that choice—let's agree to use the Chancel of the Ladyfish as a mail drop. We can leave notes for one another on paper weighed down by Rain's favorite stone—that one with the tiny carving of the question mark sporting the head of a horse. Agreed?"

They all nodded. In this treacherous land, the chapel seemed as safe a rendezvous point as any other.

"It's time to go," said Liir.

"Check anytime a Goose flies overhead," said Iski-naary to the Lion. "If I lose my bowels in your direction, it's not personal." He ducked his head under a wing, pretending to work at a nit, to save face in the face of strong feeling.

Rain wouldn't come forward to say good-bye to Little Daffy or to Mr. Boss. And she wouldn't look at Brrr. But she seemed to understand that there was a need to move on, even if she didn't understand why. She put her grandmother's broom on the ground. She set her shell on the ground next to it. She walked forward to the Cowardly Lion. She didn't stretch her arms for a hug—how does a girl hug a Lion? Her arms lay straight at her side, as if she were a member of a military guard on duty. She sloped forward and she fell woodenly against the Lion's cheek and mane and brow. She didn't cry, but leaned upright against his face as he cried for both of them.

IV

The Judgment of Dorothy

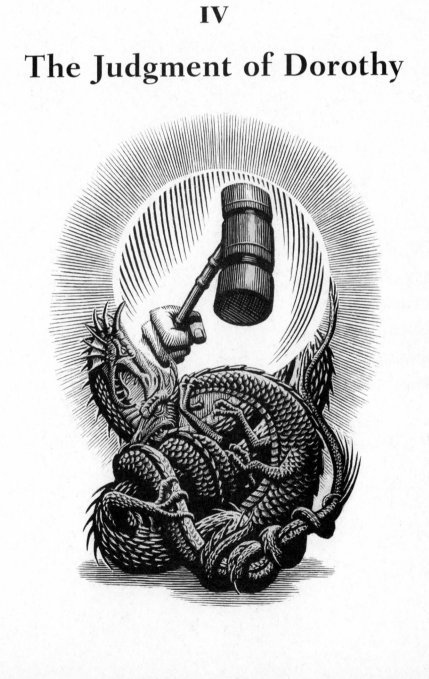

1.

By night the Lion and his pair of comrades crossed into Munchkinland without incident. They'd skirted to the north, avoiding Haugaard's Keep and those aggrieved lake villages. Restwater and the Pine Barrens were behind them. It felt pretty damn good to be pacing a well-maintained stretch of the Yellow Brick Road. The Free State of Munchkinland might be nearing insolvency, but trust little farming people to keep their blue roofing tiles scrubbed clean of birdshit and their tomatoes staked as if they were prize philanthriums.

"The Munchkinlanders," said Little Daffy, "call this season of the year Seedtime."

"I can see why," said Brrr. It seemed to belie the anxiety of wartime, to spit in its face, this bounty of Munchkinland. Mile after mile of pasture rilled with green fringe. Paddocks dizzy with birdsong and cloudy with bugs. Meadows patrolled by farmers, by the occasional tiktok contrivance on its wheels and pulleys and traction belts. "A Gillikin abomination in Munchkinlander fields is my partisan sentiment," said Little Daffy.

"Machinery in exchange for grain. It's called free trade," said Brrr.

"Call me old-fashioned, but I prefer the traditional scarecrow. Any chance we're going to run into your friend? Might he be heading to rescue Dorothy too?"

"Doubtful. He had the brains to make a clean break of the matter. Me, I'm too much of a coward."

"Mmm," said Mr. Boss, which was as opinionated as he got these days.

"No wonder this part of Munchkinland is known as the Corn Basket," said the Lion. He had only ever seen the scrappier bits, the hardscrabble places that Animals had retreated to a generation or two ago, when Loyal Oz kicked them out of the law and commerce and the tonier echelons of the banks and colleges. Now he saw Animals in the fields, more than he'd expected. True, they were labor rather than management. But it was still work. "Do they comb off anything in the way of sharing the profits?"

"I couldn't possibly say," puffed Little Daffy. "I left Munchkinland years ago, before the infusion of new labor. Why? Are you looking for a farmhand position after we scope out this business about the trial of Dorothy?"

Well, he wasn't. He'd done his share of farmwork on pocket handkerchief farms to the south. Barely subsistence enterprises. He'd hauled manure and brought in spattery little crops. He'd been paid in last winter's carrots and he'd been loaned a flea-infused blanket to sleep under. No one had talked to him for seven years, and that had been fine with him. But had central Munchkinland always been so prosperous? He hadn't noticed. Too distracted by self-loathing.

With every mile Little Daffy grew more cocky. She'd been born, she told them, up near the terminus of the Yellow Brick Road—Center Munch. From a family of farmers, of course. One of four or five siblings whose names she couldn't now recall. She'd only traveled the Yellow Brick Road once before, when she was a teenager starting as a student nurse in Bright Lettins. "It was hardly more than a hamlet back then," she said, "at the head of a tributary of the Munchkin River. I can't wait to see it gussied up as a capital city."

"It won't look like the EC, anyway," said the Lion. "This place is so different from Loyal Oz. I wonder that Munchkinlanders were ever willing to be ruled by the Emerald City."

Little Daffy replied, "Nessarose Thropp rose to prominence by exploiting a provincial identity that Munchkinlanders had always felt, but suppressed. We never trusted Loyal Ozians even before the secession. We're not like you."

"Well, I'm an Animal," said Brrr, "but I take your point."

"I'm not like me anymore, either," said the dwarf.

"And it's not just the height thing," said Little Daffy. "Lots of Munchkinlanders are tall as other Ozians."

"Lots of us are taller inside our trousers than outside," said her husband.

"Shut up, you," said Little Daffy, but lovingly. At least he was verbal.

A few days later they approached the new capital over a series of low bridges spanning irrigation canals. Something of the feel of a holiday park for families, thought Brrr. Bright Lettins wasn't gleaming and garish, like the Emerald City, nor ancient and stuffed with character, like Shiz, the capital of Gillikin. But it ornamented the landscape with its own brand of Munchkin confidence. From this approach, the effect at a distance was of a huddle of children's building blocks: roofs of scalloped tile, blue or plum. Entering the city, the travelers found buildings made of stone-covered stucco painted in shades of grey and sand. Many structures were joined by arches over the street, creating a series of outdoor chambers, squares funneling into allées debouching into piazzas. Pleasing, welcoming.

And clean? Gutters ran under iron grills next to the coping in the streets, carrying away ordure of every variety. Windows clearer than mountain ice. The buildings ran to three and a half stories, by diktat apparently, though since they were Munchkin stories they weren't very high.

"Where do taller people and Animals stay?" asked Brrr.

"Not here," was the answer they got from chatelaine and inn master alike. After a while someone directed them to an Animal hostelry in a shabbier neighborhood. Reportedly the only place where Animals and humans could find rooms under the same roof, with a sign outside that read A STABLE HOME. The entrance for taller people and Animals was supplied at a side door marked OTHERS. "Well, I've been waiting almost four decades to decide who and what I am, and I've finally stumbled upon the answer," said Brrr. "I'm an Other. But how are we going to pay?"

Little Daffy dug from some hidey-purse under her aprons a clutch of folded notes. "Whoa, have you been peddling poppy dust behind our backs?" asked Brrr when he caught sight of the wad.

"Before I left the mauntery several years ago, I dashed to its treasury," she said. "I guessed that Sister Petty Cash abandoned her stash as she and the others were fleeing for their lives. I've never had the need to spend it yet."

"Isn't that theft?"

"I consider it back wages for thirty years of sacrifice."

"I'm not complaining."

The innkeeper was a dejected widow fallen on hard times. Taking in lodgers out of need. She resented them from the start. But rent was rent. "Your old fellow needs a rest," she said to Little Daffy as she glanced over at where Mr. Boss was propped against a wall. "*He's* not from around here. Sick, is he?"

"He's a dwarf. He comes like that," said Little Daffy. "It's been a long trip. We'll be grateful to take our key and find our room."

"You two are just up the stairs. Next to my room, so I can keep an eye on you should you get up to anything."

"What's your name so I can call it out during wild sex?" asked Mr. Boss. Grumpiness made him come to life.

"You won't need my name. I'm in business only until the troubles are over. I don't leave the establishment untended. Now I'll thank you to avoid monkey business while in this hostel."

"I'll call you Dame Hostile," said Mr. Boss, grinning to show his tobacco-stained smile.

"I'll be happy to help you sweep up. I can remove splinters, bake a little," said Little Daffy hastily. "We'll be ideal guests, believe me."

"You," said the chatelaine to the Lion, "your room is out back. Down the alley. Don't brush your mane in the public rooms, I have allergies."

Ah, little has changed for the Animals, thought Brrr. His room, though separate and sparely fitted, was clean enough.

The next day, market day in Bright Lettins. The central district was packed dense with stalls and shoppers. Plenty indeed—mounds of baby squash, punnets of spring berries like pucklegem and queen's beads. Lettuces so new and tender you could hold the leaves up to the light and see through them. Despite the abundance, however, the haggling was fierce. Voices raised on both sides, vendor and housewife. "No spare coin to be had in *this* crowd," murmured Little Daffy. One furious merchant upended a cart of his own pricey white asparagus tips and let his pig eat them rather than sell them for the pittance that had been proferred. The pig sported the only satisfied smirk Brrr saw all morning.

The newcomers settled for elevenses at a café, hoping to overhear something useful. Farmers muttered over the weather, the prices, the progress of the war. Words were said about General Jinjuria, the peasant warrior, and about Mombey, the head of the government. Little Daffy ordered tea and beer and river prawns in tarragon. They ate in silence, listening for all they were worth.

"They'll never starve us out," said one old bearded fellow with a prosthetic ear made of tin. "They can siphon all the water they want from our precious Restwater, but as long as our farms are upstream of the lake, we'll not go short of water and so we won't go short of food."

"We should dam the Munchkin River and dry out the lake," said the waitress, settling down with her own beer.

"We couldn't drain that lake any way shy of a miracle. It's fed by runoff of the Great Kells," someone argued. "That's part of the rationale for the EC requisitioning the water in the first place."

"How is this Jinjuria holding the EC forces at Haugaard's Keep?" asked Brrr. The Munchkinlander locals glanced at one another. Maybe, thought Brrr,

Animals don't talk across café tables to humans they didn't know socially.

"The Lion asked you a question," said Little Daffy. "Nicely."

The old man looked suspicious of their ignorance. He stroked his taffy-colored beard, combing it with his fingers. "Jinjuria, she could have held on to Haugaard's Keep, you know that. It's almost impregnable. Slit-ted windows high up, and a pair of moated entrances. With their superior numbers the EC Messiars swarmed up the lakeside of the keep, see, and General Jinjuria's forces put on a handsome show of repelling them—but only as a lure. Soon as the assailants had gained the ramparts on ladders and arrow-slung ropes, Jinjuria set in motion the quick retreat she'd planned. The bulk of our forces that had held Haugaard's Keep retreated on the land side, burning the wooden decking on the moat entrance as they went. Not everyone made it out, of course, and the heads of our patriot martyrs were bowled down into the moat for several weeks afterward and bobbed there like muskmelons. But Jinjuria's strat-egy worked. She boxed up the Emerald City high com-mand, General Cherrystone as they call him, and the cream of his forces too. She can't starve him out, as she can't prevent supplies from arriving on the lakeside, by flotillas of this sort or that. But she can prevent him from leaving by land. And if he left by lake—well, that would be a retreat, pure and simple. No, she's got him cornered, like a cat playing with a larder mouse."

"Brilliant." Little Daffy's eyes glowed with pride.

"It's a stalemate, no pretending otherwise," said the garrulous one among the locals. "Where have you lot been, that this is all news to you?"

"Doing missionary work," said Little Daffy quickly, before Brrr could falter or fudge. "Is Mombey here?"

"Said to be in residence at Colwen Grounds."

"And Dorothy?" asked Brrr. "Is she expected soon?"

They didn't know what Brrr was talking about. "Dorothy? *Her?* We won't see the likes of Dorothy again. Not in this lifetime."

"She shows up here for a pint, I charge her triple," promised the waitress, and bit the farthing Little Daffy was paying with. "She has a lot to answer for, knocking off our lady governor like she did."

The old farmer chided the waitress. "You're not old enough to remember Nessarose Thropp. That Dorothy may have played fast and loose with government figures, but there was quite a bit of singing and dancing back in the day. Folks fell to their knees in thanksgiving for their release from bondage."

"Munchkinlanders don't have too far to fall," said the waitress, swishing a rag at a table. "Who can even tell when we're on our knees?"

"Well, *she* fell from a great distance, that girl," insisted the farmer. "Wearing a wooden house around her as some sort of defense. A weird cleverness in that child."

"She wasn't all that clever," said Brrr, realizing too late that neither was he.

"You have a point of view? Listen—you're not that Lion? The Cowardly Lion, they called him? One of Dorothy's lackeys? Say it en't so."

"Not so, I'm afraid," said Brrr.

"You have no right to any opinion then." The other farmers dropped their chins over their steins and frowned across the froth. The atmosphere had a tang to it, like saltpetre. "I think it was you. Wasn't it? Got her out of here safely before she could be asked to account for herself?"

"That would be my brother," said Brrr. "My twin brother, I'm afraid. A luckless sort, but there you have it." For the first and perhaps the last time in his life, he was glad to have an identical twin he'd never met. "Finish that prawn, Mr. Boss, and we'll be on our way."

2.

"Why don't the Munchkinlanders sue for peace?" asked the Lion of his cronies. "Sure, they've lost Restwater, and it's an insult and an outrage. But if their agriculture carries on nicely enough upstream, why not make the best of a bad situation and call for an armistice? Give up the lake and get their lives back to normal?"

They asked around, they gossiped, they eavesdropped. It turned out that supplying the EC with water all those years had been fiscally advantageous to Munchkinland, and the government of the Free State was as reluctant to part with the income stream as with the territory itself.

The deeper question—why do populations squabble for dominance?—remained unanswered. Native pride, the patriotism of different peoples, seemed jejune to the Lion. Mawkish, embarrassing. Though since he'd grown up without any pride of his own—neither a family tribe nor that pestery, myopic little fuse of self-admiration—he no longer expected to understand what motivated others.

But was it even true that Dorothy had come back to Oz? No one in Bright Lettins seemed to have heard about it. Maybe the rumor of her return had been planted to stir things up, to try to flush the Grimmerie into the open somehow. Or maybe strategists had hoped to flush *Liir* into the open. In which case, what a relief to have left the great book behind with Liir and his family.

Maybe Dorothy had taken ill and died before a show trial could commence. Or maybe she was being held incognito until her public humiliation could do the most good, at least in terms of lifting homeland morale.

The Lion and his friends took to wandering the streets after their morning coffee and cheddar-and-onion butty, ambling and window-shopping and keeping their ears open. Brrr was surprised to see little in the way of a police force. "Is the absence of a civic constabulary a sign of self-confidence?"

"I bet the Munchkinland defense is all occupied in the apron of land around Haugaard's Keep," said Little Daffy. "But who cares? We're not here to bring down the nation or to save it. We're just here to help Dorothy if we can. Look, a distress sale at that milliner's shop." She came out sporting a bonnet of uncertain charm.

The dwarf snorted. "*We're* looking for Dorothy. *You're* looking like you're wearing a failed dessert."

"I love you too," said Little Daffy, clearly glad to see him returning to form. "Let's go back to our room and play Tickle My Fancy."

"The loud version," agreed Mr. Boss, cheerily enough. "Give Dame Hostile a little entertainment through the keyhole."

"I'll catch you up later," said the Lion.

He was perusing the goods in a pushcart and being ignored by the merchant when a sudden cloudburst forced him under a nearby portico. Waiting out the rain in a throng of Munchkins, he heard the swell of their comments include the words *La Mombey*. Brrr didn't need to push to the front of the crowd. He could see over their heads. One of a pair of horses pulling a brougham had cast a shoe, and a farrier was sent for. Without fanfare the door to the carriage opened. An attendant in Munchkinlander formal couture, cobalt serge and silver buttons, held up a parasol as a woman alighted.

Could this be Mombey? The murmur at ground level suggested so. She was tall and striking, nowhere near as old as Brrr had imagined. Her full shimmery-coppery silk garment draped, uncinched, from the fabric yoke at her shoulders. Her pale hand looked linen smooth. She pivoted to study the street with a languid air, her face impassive, cut almost too prettily, as if a wax model for a bronze casting of Lurline, or maybe the Spirit of Munchkinlander Assiduity. She gave a half-curtsey toward the citizens crowded under the arcade, and retired into a private home whose astounded owners, standing on either side of the door, appeared ready to explode with honor and subservience.

The Munchkinlanders resumed gabbling in appreciation of their leader. Brrr listened for some reference to Dorothy, but he heard only about Mombey; her behavior discreet, intelligent, warm, reserved. Her military sense subtle and her clothes sense impeccable. *We'll win out over the EC in the end. She has talents she hasn't yet used.*

"What exactly do you mean, 'talents she hasn't yet used'?" asked the Lion. But by now he knew that while Munchkinlanders tolerated talking Animals in their capital city, they rarely wanted to exchange more than pleasantries.

He waited along with the rest of the crowd. When an hour had passed and the rain let up, he left his post and returned to A Stable Home.

The disgruntled chatelaine was dusting the ferns and sneezing. To his report, the old woman said, "Mombey makes her way west from time to time, to discuss military strategy with General Jinjuria. We're quite used to having Her Eminence pass through and we think nothing of it. We are now the capital city of Munchkinland, after all."

"What was meant by the rumor 'talents'?" asked Brrr.

"Oh, she's got more than a touch of magic skill." The old woman flapped her rag out the window. Most of the dust blew back in and landed on the top of the credenza.

"I didn't know Munchkinlanders approved of magic."

"I don't approve of discussing politics with Animals. You want another opinion, try the Reading Room down by Clericle Corners. A bit of a pong but what do you expect."

Brrr decided he would and was glad he did. At the end of a long reading table, peering out of one eye through a handheld lens, sat an elderly Ape whom Brrr had once known. Mister Mikko. A former professor at Shiz, now sporting a fiercely unconvincing set of false teeth. Which he bared at Brrr when Brrr approached, and then had to pick up and jam back into his mouth because they fell out on the table.

"I'm joining no Benevolent Societies for Stray Cats today, sir," the Ape barked at Brrr. "How dare you approach me in this sanctuary of repose."

"You don't recognize me?"

"I couldn't recognize my own grandmother if she bit me on my blue behind. My cataracts have baby cataracts of their own." Still, Mister Mikko squinted, fitting his monocle under his brow. "Upon my word. It's the Lion who helped me lose half of my savings. Have you come to pay it back, with interest?"

"Take it up with the banks at Shiz. The harm done you originated there."

"You stiffed me of a higher rate of interest than the banks allowed, and you got in trouble for it. Don't think

I didn't hear about the scandal. We may be at war with Loyal Oz, but that doesn't stop the financial news from getting through. I follow the papers, sir!"

"Well, if my pot of gold ever turns up at the end of the rainbow, you'll get the first scoop."

"I don't want a scoop of whatever is in the pot at the end of *your* rainbow." Still, Mister Mikko folded the paper and closed his arms around his chest. "I'm surprised you'd show your face to me, after that larceny."

"I've paid my debt to society, and I'll make it up to you if I ever get the chance. How is Professor Lenx?" Mister Mikko had lodged with a Boar, another professor retired from Shiz during the enactment of the Animal Adverse laws.

"He passed away, poor sod. I couldn't keep the house up on my own. Didn't have the heart, and what's more, couldn't afford the help. Thank you very much for *that*. So I abandoned the old place at Stonespar End and I moved here, where I live in a disgusting hotel for elderly Animals. It's a good thing I lost my sense of smell a long time ago, believe me. No, don't sit down, I didn't invite you."

"This isn't the Emerald City under the Animal Adverse laws. I can sit where I like." Brrr looked about to see if their conversation was annoying anyone, but the only other patron was a White Parrot who had fallen asleep clinging to the windowsill.

"Don't mind him," said the Ape. "He's both deaf and asleep. We can't disturb him even if we shouted *fire* into his ear."

"I don't trust anyone anymore," replied the Lion.

"Welcome to the club." But the Ape relented a little; he clearly was lonely after the death of his companion. "Not that paranoia seems an inappropriate response to a government that relies on secrecy to protect itself. Rather it seems quite sane. Oh, yes. I lectured in Oz history, so you see I know whereof I speak. Surely you remember."

"No, I was never a student of yours. I was your fiscal agent."

"Time runs together. How recently did you fleece me?"

"How recently did Professor Lenx die?" This was cruel of Brrr, but he had to move the conversation on.

Mister Mikko removed his monocle and looked coldly out the window. "I never can remember," he said, quite evidently lying: probably he could remember every hour of his life since. "My area was the early and middle Ozma realms. I never was good at Modern History. Why are you interrupting my meditations with your prattle?"

For all his meekness and tendency to isolationism, the Lion had never entirely trusted sentient Animals.

He would have to speak carefully and try to avoid attitude. "I'm told that the Eminence herself has arrived in town today—Mombey, I mean," in case Mister Mikko's short-term memory was faulty and he was imagining Nessarose Thropp.

"I'm not a nincompoop," barked the Ape. "I know who Mombey is. She has the right to come and go as she pleases. What is your *problem*?"

"I've been trying to find out if she's here to convene a legal investigation. A court case, I mean."

"You're afraid you're being brought up on charges of embezzlement? Where's the party? Sign me up as a witness for the prosecution."

"No." He supposed there was nothing for it. "I'm told that the girl from the Other Land has returned."

"Ozma?" The Ape snorted his teeth onto the table again, and a good deal of saliva too. "You *are* imbecilic. Ozma Tippetarius was flung into an infant's grave eleventy-seven years ago. She decides to come back to life after all this time, she'll be in a wheelchair. She can have my teeth as tribute."

"Not Ozma. Dorothy."

The Ape snorted again. "You'll have to remind me about Dorothy. Was she one of those idiotic Gillikinese scholarship girls from Settica or Frottica? It was all the rage for about ten years, sending milkmaids off to college. A bad plan all around."

"Dorothy from Kanzass. The one whose house flattened Nessarose and released the Munchkinlanders from tyranny."

"Oh yes. So they could rise and embrace another tyranny: our good queen Mombey."

"Look, Mister Mikko. I'm only asking if you know anything about the return of Dorothy. I heard that she was going to be put on trial, and I wondered if Mombey's arrival in Bright Lettins means Dorothy is about to be brought in too. If you're not interested in current affairs, well, don't let me bother your nap." The Lion stood up to leave.

"Oh, don't mind me, you young fool," snapped the Ape. "I'm less interested in the return of Dorothy than I am in the return of my missing bank deposits. But let me put my ancient ear to the thin walls of my single room and catch what's squawking, and I'll be back here tomorrow to tell you what I have heard."

The next day, a brighter day on the unpleasant side of warm, Brrr met Mister Mikko again. After spending the fee to enter, and finding the Reading Room as sparsely used as the day before, he learned from Mister Mikko that the Ape had had no luck scaring up any information about Dorothy. "I didn't expect to," said the Ape, "but in good faith I did ask."

"You didn't ask," said the Lion. "You just wanted me to have to spend money to find out you were useless. Thanks a lot."

"Nothing like old friends when you need 'em, is there."

The Lion supposed he deserved this. He had, after all, bilked the Ape of some part of his portfolio. Before Brrr could think of a parting comment that would suggest even a shred of remorse, the White Parrot opened its eyes and said, "Well, you didn't involve me in the question, but in fact, good sir, I've done a little investigation of my own."

"Oh, my," said the Lion.

"You've got keen instincts," observed the Parrot. "Yes, Mombey is in town, and yes indeed, to open a court proceeding against Dorothy. It'll all come out in the town squares tomorrow. I know this from a few Pigeons who live on the rough in a gutter outside a printery. The bills are being run up for posting on kiosks and newsboards. One has to wonder how you knew."

"A little bird told me," said the Lion.

3.

DOROTHY: ASSASSIN OF PATRIOTS read one broadside.

INCOMING! said another. SHE'S BACK.

THE TRIAL OF OUR TIMES read a third.

"Tell me about it," said Mister Mikko. He summarized for the Lion. "The proceedings will start in five days. That gives magistrates for the defense and for the prosecution a chance to prepare their cases. It looks like Mombey herself picked the barristers."

Brrr had had his brushes in court before, and always on the wrong end of the law. But that was back in the Emerald City. Were things done differently in whatever passed for Munchkin justice? Mister Mikko set Brrr straight.

"Generally disputes in Munchkinland are settled on a case-by-case basis. The tradition of reliance on precedent isn't deeply rooted in Munchkinland, given the rural and piecemeal settlement of the county. Most cases are decided behind closed doors, the traveling magistrate serving as confessor and adjudicator both. I'll wager he pockets the fine, too. It's my belief that jurisprudence in Munchkinland doesn't exist at all except to reinforce the prejudices of the top dog. Which despite the metaphor is never an Animal, at least in Munchkinland."

"I didn't know you had a Dog in this fight," said Brrr.

"Ha-ha. Well, pay attention. This trial will be more formal. No executive sessions here, this one will be open to the public—you can't be surprised at that."

"Are there jurors? Witnesses?"

Mister Mikko elaborated. For a so-called open trial, a five-member jury was usually empaneled at its own cost. In this instance, it seemed Mombey was going to present the case herself, in an initial declamation, and then turn the proceedings over to a celebrity magistrate appointed to the position for this trial only. The barristers pleading the cases for the prosecution and for the defense would post their requests for witnesses on a billboard on the door of the Grange Central. Potential witnesses only had to show up in time to get a seat. Generally they could nominate themselves of their own free will, or refuse to testify if they weren't in the mood. But rules could vary case by case, so who knew.

"Nipp," Brrr told Little Daffy back at the inn. "He's the appointed magistrate. Does that name ring a bell?"

"Not to me," said Little Daffy. "But don't forget I was cloistered for all those years."

"I know of him," said Mr. Boss. "He was the first governor of Munchkinland after Nessarose Thropp was murdered in cold blood by that prim little Miss Dorothy, bless her little soul." He was in a good mood.

"You're not opinionated, I see," said Brrr, though he was glad Mr. Boss seemed to be coming back around some.

The trial was designated for Densloe Den, a little salon theater, but for fears of crowding was soon shifted to a venue called Neale House. A former armory now used for the spring cattle fair. Above its arches on three sides ran a gallery. The Neale could sit a large number of visitors, but on the first day the interest seemed slim, so Little Daffy, Mr. Boss, and Brrr easily got tickets to attend the instructions to the jury. The room wasn't a quarter full. They could have had front row seats, though Brrr by dint of his size was required to recline on the floor to one side. He couldn't have fit a single thigh in a folding chair scaled for Munchkinlanders, not for money nor love.

The day's newsfolds, left on the seats of chairs, presented potted biographies of the trial's dramatis personae. Brrr only had time to read about the magistrate. Nipp had begun his career as a kind of concierge at Colwen Grounds, serving Nessarose Thropp up until the day she was squished. Apparently because he'd held the keys to the actual house, Nipp had stepped in as emergency Prime Minister until the Munchkinlanders' appetite to be governed by an Eminence reasserted itself. Mombey had emerged from a prior anonymity—the argument for her elevation wasn't rehearsed here. Whereupon Nipp had retired with honors that included a fancy cake, a sash, and a lifetime supply of ammonia salts, which apparently had some symbolic significance no one at the city desk of the press had bothered to identify.

Brrr had hardly finished the bio when Nipp entered the chamber. Among the taller of Munchkinlanders, he wore a conical hat whose brim was sprightly with felt balls. He flung the hat onto the top of a coat stand, to a spatter of applause. That he could land it like a horseshoe, Brrr deduced, was proof of his capacity to serve with a steady hand. Then Nipp took the bench. It was supplied with the traditional gavel, the bell, a slate on which messages could be scrawled for private viewing in case the magistrate didn't want to be overheard, and a small pile of ham sandwiches under a net to keep off the flies. Behind him two grammar school students were ready with fans made of blue ostrich plumes in case it became too warm.

"Citizens of Munchkinland," Nipp began, in a voice quavery with age but strengthening by the sentence, "we are here to keep our big mouths shut and to listen. To listen to what is presented. Anyone in Neale House who makes a fuss or disrupts our attention to the proceedings shall be taken out and fined, or shot, or put in the stocks. Which this time of year are very uncomfortable what with mosquito season just beginning. Are there any questions?—then let us continue. I predict this trial will last a week—perhaps two. Those who can't tolerate the heat should stay at home. Babies are not allowed. If there is a fire don't everyone scream

'Fire!' all at once—it's terribly muddling and only makes people nervous. Should I feel the need to call additional witnesses I shall do so and I hereforth declare that for this trial there is no right of resistance—if you're in the room, you're considered fair game for service. Furthermore if you're not in the room and you are required you shall be apprehended by deputized mobs and escorted here whether you like it or not. Tell your friends and neighbors. If you are wanted and you're on holiday up at Mossmere or someplace, you shall be sent to prison when you return for taking a holiday thoughtlessly. Are there any questions—speak up—no questions—I see—then let us begin by my presenting the barristers and the jurors."

"This isn't going to take two weeks," whispered Brrr to Little Daffy, who was sitting in a chair on the end of her aisle.

Nipp introduced the envoy for the prosecution, a part-time barrister whose regular job was being a professional mourner. Dame Fegg. She emerged from a curtained doorway dressed in something that looked to Brrr as if it had been cut down from a choir robe—about five minutes earlier, without benefit of a seamstress. She was still putting pins in her hair as she came through. A no-nonsense middle-aged farm frau with pockets beneath her eyes deep enough to hold tokens for an EC omnibus. "Yoiks," muttered Brrr.

The envoy for the defense was introduced next, a certain Temper Bailey, who turned out to be a brown Fever Owl. "They couldn't spring for a human?" muttered Little Daffy. "Guess this is what is called an open-and-shut case."

"Animals still draw lower salaries, I bet," replied Brrr.

The Owl flew to a perch and rotated his head on his neck, all the way round. Not an unusual gesture for an Owl, but unsettling in a court of law; accusatory, somehow, of them all, even the spectators. Temper Bailey then nodded to Dame Fegg, but she was applying some sort of liquid paint to her nails and didn't return the obeisance.

Only when the jurors had been seated did the magistrate seem to notice that the room was sparsely populated. He stood on his toes and regarded the audience with disdain, as if it were they who were skiving off. "The Eminence suggests this is a trial of interest to all Munchkinlanders," said Nipp. "I need hardly mention that without the unprovoked invasion by Dorothy a generation ago, we wouldn't be in the position of defending Restwater from the Emerald City. The Eminence of that day, Miss Nessarose Thropp, would

484 · OUT OF OZ

likely still be ensconced in Colwen Grounds. Or else she and her consort would have brought forth a new Eminence to take her place."

A rude titter, quickly suppressed. Enough of the crowd was old enough to recall that Nessarose had not been thronged with suitors. She had died without benefit of spouse or spawn.

"When are we going to see Dorothy?" asked Temper Bailey. Brrr would have guessed that the defense might have had a chance to question his client before opening ceremonies, but it seemed the government was running this trial on the cheap.

Nipp made his first ruling, not with a gavel but with a bell. "I am dismissing all parties until tomorrow morning. Come back with your relatives and friends. Tell them that La Mombey herself will be here to introduce the accused. If this hall isn't filled to capacity word will get back to the Emerald City that Munchkinlanders have lost all public spirit. Do as I say, in the name of justice."

"I should think he meant 'in the name of public relations,'" said Brrr.

"I heard that, you," said Nipp. "I'll brook no backtalk from the floor, especially from an Animal. Dismissed."

As might have been expected, the next day saw the gallery nearly full. Munchkins en masse. Perhaps

Nipp's refusing to bring out Dorothy for the introductory session had whetted appetites. At any rate, it was a good time of the summer for a trial. Harvest was still six weeks out. Among a bunch of farm people come to town for the fun, Brrr and Little Daffy and Mr. Boss, brandishing their tickets, took their places. Little Daffy was equipped with a sack of muffins and fruit and a thermos of potato brandy in case things got dull. A couple of teenage scowlawags nearby played a game of Hangman using the word *DOROTHY* as the clue.

Nipp marched in followed by Dame Fegg and Temper Bailey. The Owl had been slip-covered with a tunic not unlike Dame Fegg's. It made him look like a tea cosy with an owl head. He winced at the laughter of the crowd. Everyone settled down when Nipp clapped the gavel on its stand and introduced the Eminence of Munchkinland, La Mombey. "And rise, you dolts. This isn't one of your talent shows!"

The crowd obliged as a pair of Chimpanzees in livery swung open the double doors at the back of the bench. The Eminence flooded into the room in another tidal barrage of silks, these flowered, white petals against maroon. Brrr studied her face. It seemed different. Less chiseled, more delicate, even fragile. And the hair on her head, in a chignon so crisp it might have been a crown, looked darker, spikier. But he didn't dare mutter in her presence. She looked full of sorrowful dignity. He found himself lowering his head just for a moment in the presence of something he couldn't name. Self-possession, if nothing else.

"We are Munchkinlanders," she told the crowd. Her voice was like honey coating the knife. "We are hospitable to all, even those who arrive on our home-land to spite us and murder us. I ask you to extend the courtesy of our traditions to the accused, Dorothy Gale. I beg to remind you that there is no statute of limitations where crimes against the heart are con-cerned. If we must convict the accused, let us convict her justly. If we choose to decide she is not guilty of the charges of murder, let us not harbor thoughts of malfeasance when she is liberated." Mombey turned to the five jurors, who stood to one side. They were all unrepentently human. "You five are the eyes and ears of Munchkinland, and you must be the heart and soul of justice. Bring Dorothy to trial with merciful dispatch. Whatever you recommend to the magistrate will be taken under deepest consideration, but it is his conclusion that we will follow. You are here as advi-sors only. And the public is here not to second-guess the proceedings but to witness them, so that they can tell their children and their grandchildren that justice is alive in Oz.

"For his services to our country, today I elevate our former Prime Minister to the peerage. Henceforth he shall be Lord Nipp of Dragon Cupboard. Let the constabulary bring forth the alien."

La Mombey retired behind the doors through which she'd emerged, as if to be seen in the same room as the accused would constitute an affront to her dignity. Only when the Chimpanzees had closed the double doors with a click did Brrr notice a trapdoor to one side. The Chimpanzees put their overknuckled paws to the ring, and together they pulled it up. Then they retreated to the far side of the pen. The Lion leaned forward to catch a glimpse of Dorothy again, after all this time.

4.

As she emerged, clumsily, reaching for a hand to help her up the ladder, though there was no one to stretch out such a hand, the Lion realized he'd been thinking of Dorothy as about ten years old. Just about the age Rain was now, more or less. A few other assumptions followed, nearly simultaneously.

His affection for Rain was related to his memory of Dorothy.

He hadn't ever done much for Dorothy except provide a few laughs and some companionship on the road.

He'd done no better for Rain, yet he felt more implicated in Rain's future than he had in Dorothy's. Was this age and maturity on his part? Or sentimentality?

Or was it that Rain was less competent than Dorothy had been at that age? Needed him more?

The crime for which Dorothy was being charged had occurred fifteen, eighteen, twenty years ago. She ought to be a mature woman now, able as needed to explain away or to apologize for the accidents of her youth.

In her maturity, will she recognize me?

He held his breath, but his tail thumped on the floor. Agitation, pleasure, and the curiosity that sometimes killed the likes of him and his kin.

5.

Dorothy's head rose farther out of the square in the flooring. She was facing the magistrate, who glared upon her as if he hadn't seen her before. Maybe she'd been kept sequestered from *everyone* involved in this trial. Six times Temper Bailey rotated his head on his stem.

"This is like climbing into the hayloft back in Kansas." Yes, it was Dorothy's voice, her real voice, misguidedly cheerful as always. Brrr felt the muffin lurch up his throat. "Still, you'd never see a Kansan owl dressed up in a petticoat!"

Something stronger than a titter rippled through the hall. Temper Bailey blinked balefully. "Mind your manners," said Lord Nipp. "That's your representation."

"What a hoot," Dorothy replied. "Meaning no disrespect, of course."

She turned to look at the crowd seated on the floor and in the galleries. Brrr knew himself to be in shadow, as he had crouched down by the wainscoting below where strong sunlight was heaving in through the windows. He doubted that she could see him, at least not at first, and that gave him a chance to study her.

Either she'd become stunted by her experience in Oz a generation ago or some perverse magic was at work. Yes, she was quite recognizably Dorothy. Those cocoa-bright eyes. The way she led with her shoulders and clavicle. Surely she ought to be middle-aged by now? But she seemed merely a few years older than he remembered her. Taller but hardly leaner. Her baby fat had only begun to reorient itself into incipient womanliness. Her face remained eager and unshuttered even after her latest travails. Proof of Dorothy.

Lord Nipp banged a gavel, as if to remind himself he was in charge. "Identify yourself. Name, age, origin, and your designs upon us."

"Well, that's easy enough," said Dorothy. As if she couldn't decide who to love first, she turned this way and that, toward Temper Bailey, who inched away on his perch, and then to Lord Nipp, and finally to Dame Fegg. "I'm Dorothy Gale, if you please, from the state of Kansas. The thirty-fourth state in the union, a free state now and proud of it. No slavery to speak of." She made a clumsy curtsey to a family of Pigs in the second row, one of the few groups of Animals present. "We're still working out a few wrinkles."

"Answer the questions," said Nipp.

"Oh yes. Well, I'm sixteen at my last birthday, you know."

Nipp scribbled a few marks upon a pad and frowned. "And your intention in returning to Oz after your long absence?"

"Goodness, there was no *intention* involved. After what I'd been through, do you think I'd choose to return? I'd have to be mad . . . well, never mind. The truth is I seem to have no control over my whereabouts. Makes me dangerous to let out on the streets, says Uncle Henry. Or said Uncle Henry." She teared up a little. "I don't know if he's still alive."

"What are you cawing about?" asked Dame Fegg. "You haven't answered the first question posed by the magistrate."

"I have no designs in Oz," said the girl. "Uncle Henry and Aunt Em and I had gone to San Francisco, see, for various family reasons. My mental fitness for marriage among them, to be blunt. We ate funny food and saw sights till we felt like gagging. And then, one morning, oh my word! I took a trip to the roof of my hotel and the whole building began to shake and buckle, and I could hear stones falling and people screaming. For a moment the elevator stopped and everything became dark, and I could detect a bad smell, though maybe that was Toto. My dog. Then the elevator began to move again, sliding faster and faster, and I thought I would smash to my death at the bottom of the chute! It was much the scariest thing that ever happened to me since the twister. The noise grew louder, the air grew thick with powder; a moment later, while in the elevator, I lost my mind for my dog had got away. . . ."

Brrr had to concede it. She was dotty as ever, but blistering buckets, how people listened to her. They were nearly swaying in time with her rhetoric.

"The earth began to quake, for goodness' sake; I knew I'd made a big mistake when the cage began to shake. . . ."

"A little restraint in the theatrics," said the magistrate.

"When I came to," she continued, less sonorously, "I found myself in the elevator cage half buried in a landslide. When people dug me out I assumed they would be San Franciscans. But just my luck. Imagine: a tribe of little people! Again! At first I thought I'd discovered yet another tiresome country, but eventually someone called Sakkali Oafish told me I was in Oz. So you see, your honor, I had no designs at all, except to have a nice holiday and maybe buy some lace for my hope chest, in the off chance any fellow ever gets interested in me." She looked with big eyes across the room again. "I don't think my prospects for a husband are terribly strong, not at this particular point in time."

"First things first," said Lord Nipp. "Dorothy Gale, you are charged with crimes against Munchkinland. Crimes of the most grievous sort because they conflate aggression against the state with assault against individuals. You are charged with the murder of Nessarose Thropp, the onetime Eminent Thropp and de facto governor of Munchkinland. Also with the murder of her sister, Elphaba Thropp of Kiamo Ko, though originally of Munchkinland."

"Well, that's a pretty big plate of sauerkraut, if you ask me," said Dorothy. "I never murdered a soul. Do you think I was *navigating* that house from Kansas, back in the day?"

"It is my first duty to make sure you understand the seriousness of the charges brought against you. If convicted, you could be put to death."

The girl opened her eyes wider than usual. "Everyone in Oz is far too nice to do a nasty thing like that to an accidental immigrant."

"I must ask you to restrict your remarks to answering the questions. I don't know what experience of legal proceedings you might have gained in your tenure in Kanziz—quite a bit, I would suspect, as you seem to career about wreaking mayhem—but here in Oz we maintain a certain decorum in court. This goes for those unwrapping sandwiches in the gallery. If you must arrive with lunch, make sure it is wrapped in cloth so it doesn't make so much noise when you bring it out!"

"I understand the charges," said Dorothy, "but I'm sure when I explain the circumstances you'll see that this is all a dreadful misunderstanding. And certainly there will be witnesses to testify in my defense? You've arranged for character witnesses, at the least? I did have some friends here, once upon a time."

"We've had to pull this trial together rather quickly."

"Then perhaps we should postpone this little charade until we've all gotten ourselves prepared adequately."

Dorothy could still say the most inappropriate things and get away with them, thought Brrr.

"The job is put to us by the Eminent Mombey. These are desperate times for Munchkinland. We will perform our duties as best we can under the circumstances."

"Are you saying there's no one here who remembers me?" Dorothy turned and looked out at the crowd again, shading her eyes against the sloping sunlight. "Can you call for a show of hands, Lord Nipp?"

"You don't get to decide how we proceed. You're the accused."

"I should like to request that Dorothy's idea be acted upon," ventured Temper Bailey. "Before we proceed, may we see if anyone present has direct knowledge of the Matter of Dorothy?"

"Very well," said the magistrate. "If among us there is anyone who has ever laid eyes on this Dorothy Gale before today, you are ordered to rise."

This was why they had come to Munchkinland, after all. His heart not quite in his throat—somewhere south of the esophagus, it felt—the Lion stood up. A murmur of Munchkinlanders caused Dorothy to turn toward his side of the chamber.

"Oh, I don't believe it!" she cried. "I knew someone would come. I had hoped it would be the Scarecrow, but even so."

"Approach the bench," said Nipp.

Brrr did, trying not to sashay. It was still sometimes a problem in public. "I am Brrr. I come with several other names. Popularly known as the Cowardly Lion in some circles, I'm afraid, but there's nothing I can do about that. When in Gillikin I'm sometimes addressed as Sir Brrr, Namory of Traum."

"That's Loyal Oz," said Nipp. "Cuts no mustard here, Lion."

"I was elevated by Lady Glinda when she was Throne Minister," said the Lion. "I don't require the honorific. I'm just trying to be sure you don't accuse me of concealing pertinent facts. I'm probably wanted for sedition by the Emerald City for having jumped bail after a spot of legal trouble on that side of the border."

"We have no extradition treaties, so you're safe here as far as that goes," said Nipp. "Not that you deserve to be harbored, necessarily."

The Lion turned to Dorothy. They were only six feet apart now. She was too mature to throw her arms around him. Indeed, she looked a little frightened. "Up until now I had hoped this might all be a dream," she said. "But you are just like yourself, and yet different than you were. Put on a little weight? I think you have."

"You're a sight for sore eyes yourself," he told her.

"Save your chatter for after hours," advised the magistrate. "Anyone else?"

Brrr oughtn't to have been surprised to see Little Daffy approach the bench. She had murmured something once about having seen Dorothy. "I suppose I have an obligation to make myself known to you. I am called Little Daffy. My name originally was Daffodil Sully, but I was known for some years as Sister Apothecaire, a unionist maunt housed at the Cloister of Saint Glinda in the Shale Shallows, in the southern corner of Gillikin."

"And how do you know the accused?" asked the magistrate.

Little Daffy looked sideways at Dorothy Gale. "I can't say I know her. I'm merely answering your call to identify myself as someone who has crossed paths with her before. I was present in Center Munch on the day when Dorothy first arrived in Oz. The day that her house tumbled out of the sky and killed Nessarose."

The mumble in the room grew louder. It was one thing to have an Animal or an illegal immigrant questioned by a magistrate. But a Munchkinlander present at the death of Nessarose Thropp! Brrr wasn't sure if the susurrus suggested admiration, disbelief, or alarm. Little Daffy gave a curt nod to Dorothy and said, "When it comes time to discuss what happened that day, I'll put my bootblack on my brogans, same as anyone else."

Nipp sent them back to their seats but ordered their continued attendance through the duration of the trial. They'd be called to testify in time. Probably not today, he suspected. There were other matters to get through first.

The rest of the afternoon was spent in a recital of previous cases that had been heard in Bright Lettins. Dame Fegg had enjoyed quite a career of prosecution. Each description of her most famous wins was met with bursts of applause. The matters at hand involved hexed chickens, tax evasion, one or two cases of lechery. Interesting enough, but they didn't seem pertinent to the task of trying Dorothy for murder. Temper Bailey, on the other hand, had never won a case.

After catching Little Daffy's eye and signaling that he should be roused if something interesting began to happen, the Lion put his head on his paws and slept. He didn't waken until the magistrate concluded proceedings for the day with a loud bang of the gavel. "You didn't miss anything. The good stuff starts tomorrow," said Little Daffy.

"Oh, Brrr," said Dorothy over her shoulder, as she was prodded toward the trapdoor by the Chimpanzees. "It makes such a difference to me that you would come to my defense."

"If you knew my record of accomplishments in the years since I last saw you," said the Lion, "you wouldn't feel so cheery. But I'll do what I can, Dorothy. I never understood you for a single moment, but in the choice between wishing you ill and wishing you well, I wish you well."

"I should think so," said Dorothy, and she opened her mouth as if to say more, but the Chimpanzees slammed down the trapdoor, narrowly missing the crown of her head.

6.

By the time Brrr and Little Daffy arrived the next morning, the room was full to bursting. After Lord Nipp entered and called Dorothy from the musty holding pen below, Dame Fegg minced forward and said, "Since we've concluded the opening statements, may I begin to question the witness, Your Honor?"

"One moment," said Lord Nipp. He fished out a paper from beneath his robes. "Dorothy Gale, you claim to be sixteen years old, and you certainly look and sound like a child of that age, if rather big by local standards. Can you tell us how old you were when you first arrived in Oz and murdered Nessarose Thropp?"

"I take exception to that definition of my actions," said Dorothy, "but letting that go for a moment, I will tell you: it was 1900 when the twister came through our parts. I was ten years old."

"And you say you are sixteen now. That's six years older. Yet by my figuring, and believe me I have counted it frontward and backward since I left here yesterday, it is about eighteen years since you spent a few months in Oz."

The girl looked flummoxed. She counted on her fingers for a moment. "I didn't go far in school. Eventually the teacher said I was too fanciful and sent me back to the farm. But here, I can do these sums. . . ."

"Nessarose Thropp and her sister Elphaba have been dead for eighteen years," said Nipp sternly, as if this were proof enough of Dorothy's guilt.

"But how odd. How irregular! The last time I was in Oz I *was* ten years old. Big for my age, but even so. And this time around I am sixteen. That is six years older, you're right about that. And you tell me that those witch sisters have both been gone for about *eighteen years*? How can this be?"

"Maybe time moves slower in Kansas," said the magistrate.

"Time *crawls* in Kansas. But some say Kansas is a state of mind." She sat up and pushed her bosom forward as if she'd just remembered she wasn't a little girl anymore. "It's uncanny. Perhaps I've become mentally unfit."

Dame Fegg delivered a moue in the direction of the jurors to make sure they caught Dorothy's admission.

The accused brightened up. "We can work this out. I just need to know how you count time in Oz. What year did I first arrive?"

The court waited for her to explain. A fly drove itself insanely around an upper windowpane.

"You arrived the year that you arrived," said Lord Nipp evenly, patiently, the way a parent responds *because* to some child's question of *why?*

"Yes. But what was the year named? I mean, at home I was born in 1890 and I was ten years old when the cyclone came and drove the farmhouse from Kansas to Oz, so that was 1900. Was it the year 1900 in Oz? The year I made my first visit? And so what is this year called? I mean, if anything ought to be universal, time ought to be."

The magistrate said, "I'm not here to be your tutor, Miss Gale. Nonetheless, I'll tell you that you seem to be relying on a system of naming years that is unfamiliar to us. In Oz we have no universal method of notching time or assigning arbitrary numbers to year-spans. I'm told that the Quadlings live quite comfortably without any system at all, since the climate there more or less precludes seasonal variation. The Gillikinese and the Emerald City refer to the passage of time in terms of the reigns of the various Ozmas or, since the Wizard first arrived, the various reigns of the Throne Ministers. The first, the seventh, the twelfth year of the Emperor Shell's reign, and so on. Here in Munchkinland the length and disposition of our months vary according to cycles of the moon. In years of a jackal moon, for instance, we skip the month of Masque, out of some old superstition no one remembers. In years when the sun casts no shadow on Seeding Day, we add seven weeks of agricultural season called the Corn Time. If it rains too much in the spring we just skip over Guestlight. So, our years being irregularly shaped, they don't line up for easy counting. No one tries to do it."

"Besides," added Little Daffy, speaking from the sidelines, "if I might add a word, arithmetic has its own cultural moods. In the mauntery, for instance, any span of years more than six we counted as a decade. It doesn't always mean ten years. It just meant 'looks about like ten years, sooner or later.'"

"To say nothing of the fact," added Brrr, as long as this was turning into a colloquy, "that when nothing seems to be happening, you can't tell if time is stuck a little. Six years might go by—call it a decade or call it the blink of an eye—but until something else happens to make you pay attention, it doesn't matter what you call it. If there's no reason to notch the memory, why waste time counting dead time?"

The magistrate said, "I didn't ask for opinions from the floor."

Dorothy looked withered and testy. "So *I* say I was here six years ago, and now I'm sixteen. *You* say it was about eighteen years ago, depending on the moon, the province, and whether anyone remembered to notice that time was passing. According to you I could be twenty-eight. In Kansas that's downright grandmotherly."

Clearing his throat, Temper Bailey ventured his first remark. "Time is fascinating, sure, but why are we spending time on this?"

"If I'm twenty-eight," said Dorothy, "then I've reached my majority and I can serve as my own attorney. I want to call for a recess. I'm going out to try my first whiskey smash. Uncle Henry says they're great. Anyone want to join me?" She held out a forearm to the Owl so he might perch there.

"It's hardly past breakfast, and the court hasn't adjourned for the day," said Nipp. "Not to mention that you are under arrest."

"Oh, right." Still, Dorothy's shoulders squared a little straighter on her spine.

"I shall begin," said Dame Fegg, and Nipp nodded his assent. "I would like to start with a question about your life of crime *prior* to your first arrival in Oz, Dorothy Gale."

"Oh, do call me Dorothy," said the defendant. "Everyone does."

"In your home territory, Dorothy Gale, is killing witches something one might have trained for in grammar school? Or taken up as an extracurricular hobby?"

"Goodness, Dame Fegg—is that how I should address you?—they didn't teach much in grammar school. Some simple sums. Our letters and how to form them on a slate. A little Virgil. The Christian principles of government. Also how to share. In any case, there are no witches in Kansas, nor as far as I could tell in San Francisco either, though frankly I don't believe I got to the bottom of what was going on there. It sure wasn't like Kansas, though there felt like some kind of magic at work. In any case, I wouldn't have killed anyone, witches or no. Uncle Henry says we're makeshift Quakers. We don't believe in violence except of course at hog-killing time, because as the waiter said to me in the San Francisco hotel, there is nothing like a nice hot sausage slapped between warm buns first thing in the morning." The Sow in the second row turned grey and put her hooves over the ears of her littlest Piglet. "He was 'tremely agreeable you know but I do believe he wasn't my type. Uncle Henry said I didn't have a type as far as he knew and in any case by the looks of things I wasn't going to find a fellow for myself, suitable or otherwise, in San Francisco."

Dame Fegg had stopped as if calcified at Dorothy's reply. Her mouth opened once or twice and when she made a note her hand was trembling. "Dorothy Gale, I must remind you to answer only the question I ask. Otherwise we could be here for a year. However we count it."

"Oh, yes, Dame Fegg. *Answer only the question.* That's what my teacher in Kansas used to say. That's why I had to take my lessons sitting on a bench outside the school building. I could lean my books and my slate on the windowsill. If I started talking too much, the teacher would come over to the sill and close the window. So if I couldn't hear him I just would look around at Kansas, which is maybe what first gave me a yen to travel. I mean you'd have to stand on your head to make Kansas novel, and even that only works for a while. Have you ever traveled, Dame Fegg?"

"Not to Kanziz," said the prosecutor, in a voice that made it into a kind of joke, as if she were saying *haven't gone out of my mind—yet.* The crowd tittered, not knowing if that was allowed, but Nipp hid his mouth behind his hand too, so maybe it was all right.

"I'd like to be the first to invite you to visit," said Dorothy. "I would have to be your chaperone, of course, because a little woman like yourself might be considered a child, and then you couldn't get a whiskey smash either. Not that you could get one in Kansas under any circumstances. It's a dry state. Dry, dry, dry."

Dame Fegg pounced on those words as if Dorothy were casting a spell. "When you first came from Kanziz, Dorothy Gale, we were recovering from a drought that had plagued most of Oz for as long as we could remember. In a great wind you arrive, you with your suspicious name of Gale, which suggests windstorms and rain. You succeed in a matter of months in doing away with both of the Thropp sisters, who with their magic capacities might have further united and strengthened Munchkinland. In their absence, however determined our own population to govern itself, Munchkinland has not thrived. The annual rainfall has improved only slightly, and the armies of Loyal Oz have invaded our fair province and requisitioned Oz's largest basin of potable water, the lake called Restwater. You have a great deal to answer for."

"Well, let me start by saying we know drought in Kansas, believe me. I—"

"You may start by being quiet," said Nipp. "Dame Fegg, at the moment please confine your questions to the matter of the murders. We may not number our years in Oz as they do in this place called Kanziz, but we number our days as precious, and we don't want to be here until our grandchildren have grandchildren. And you, missy, keep your answers short and to the point. You are brought up on most serious charges indeed."

"Got it," said Dorothy.

"Briefly, I beg you, briefly," said Dame Fegg, "describe your arrival in Center Munch for us, however many years ago we pretend it was or wasn't. I would like you to answer for us particularly how you knew that Nessarose, the Eminent Thropp and governor of Munchkinland, would be present that day, and how you organized an assassination of such cunning and precision, and also when and how you decided to proceed with your march on the Emerald City."

Chastised and trying to please, Dorothy recounted what she could of her first arrival in Oz, either six or eighteen years ago. Off to the side, Brrr remembered quite a bit of what she'd told him, the Scarecrow, and the Tin Woodman. As far as he recalled she'd gotten the facts of her alibi down straight, if alibi it was. In the safety of her family's farmhouse, the child Dorothy had taken refuge from a storm. Through some sort of catastrophe of nature, aided perhaps by a deep magic, the house had been lifted into the air, whirled through dark agency across the uncrossable sands that surround Oz, and deposited in Center Munch. Right on top of Nessarose Thropp. Apparently Dorothy hadn't been taught about Oz in her schooling on national geographics, though perhaps that was part of the curriculum she missed by being exiled to the bench outside the closed window. She had never been able to ask about Oz even after she returned to Kansas because the teacher, frightened out of his mind by the twister coming so near, had taken off for Chicago.

"Taken off for Shiz?" asked Dame Fegg, scratching her ear.

"Chicago," said Dorothy, but trying not to run on at the mouth she just mimed a cityscape with huge buildings. "Chi-caaaaa-go."

Dorothy continued her narrative. It was a grisly tale. After landing, she'd learned that a good part of the town of Center Munch and outliers had gathered that morning for some sort of religious festival. Young students had been receiving prizes. Experiencing a sudden darkness, they all dove into the shrubbery and nearby homes. They heard a weird whistling followed by a shattering crash at which precise moment all their eyes were closed in terror. When they emerged from hiding, they found that a house had stove in the grandstand erected for the occasion. Dorothy stood in the center of the town square, not far from the start of the Yellow Brick Road. It took the astounded citizens of Center Munch a few moments to realize that Nessarose Thropp, alone of them, had refused to move an inch, even under the signs of the imminent attack.

"How like her," murmured Dame Fegg. "Proof of her character." Though Brrr had remembered it being said that her standing her ground had been proof of her noxious superiority. Once she had learned to stand on her own two feet, that is.

"At any rate," continued Dorothy, "you may call it murder now, but at the time no one clapped me in chains. They celebrated their release from a wicked fiend. Or that's how they said it to me. The Wicked Witch of the East had claimed for herself all powers of deciding right and wrong." Dorothy straightened up. "I was hailed as a liberator, and soon Glinda arrived to set me on the road to the Emerald City to accept my reward."

"Maybe she intended you to be imprisoned there, in Southstairs," said Dame Fegg. "Getting a dangerous criminal out of commission is the first duty of a public figure."

"It wasn't like that," said Dorothy. "There was singing and dancing, and someone brought out sweet bricks of bread spread with a hideous sticky cream jam of some sort. I had never meant to kill a witch—I hadn't even known witches existed, except in storybooks, and not the kind of storybooks we were allowed to read in Kansas, believe me. It was all so sudden, you see."

"There are a great many holes in your testimony," said Dame Fegg. "For your house to crash exactly upon the place our Eminent Thropp stood, killing her and her alone—it beggars credulity. It smacks of a conspiracy in high places. I suspect someone in the Emerald City was involved."

"When I landed, they didn't call it an impossible coincidence," said Dorothy in about as cold a voice as Brrr had ever heard her use. "They called it a miracle."

"I put it to the judge and the jury that with malice aforethought the defendant conspired to alight in a most deadly manner," said Dame Fegg. "She wreaks havoc wherever she goes, both last time and this. The poor cow." Though it was unclear whether she meant Dorothy or the Glikkun milk cow she squashed upon arrival this time.

Brrr saw Little Daffy's arm waving right in front of his nose. "Ladies and gentlemen, may I add a word?" She popped out of her chair and approached the magistrate's desk.

"If it's pertinent, go ahead," said Nipp.

"I was there at Center Munch. I was about the age then that Dorothy is now, or says she is, I mean. I was sixteen or eighteen years old. It was the end of our year of studies of the writings of the unionist fathers. I can speak to what actually happened and to the sentiment at the time."

Nipp nodded, and Dame Fegg seemed wary, but she waved her quill at Little Daffy to proceed. Temper Bailey hopped on one leg, looking interested for the first time.

"Of course I was young," said Little Daffy. "But none of us had ever seen anything like the arrival of Dorothy before. She wore that preposterous costume and carried that inarticulate puppy—"

"Oh, please don't mention Toto or I just might cry," said Dorothy.

"—and I verify that it seemed to all of us as if she might be a sorceress or a saint, arriving out of nowhere in some sort of portable house, to liberate Munchkinland from a tyrant of sorts."

"The tyranny of Nessarose being primarily religious?" asked Dame Fegg.

"Yes. That's right."

"And yet you went on to spend your life in a mauntery. So your illustration of Nessarose Thropp as a bigoted dominatrix of some sort is a bit lacking in smack."

"It's true I was dressed up as a sunflower or a daisy, or maybe even a daffodil," replied Little Daffy. "It was a pageant of sorts. And as a young person of course I was susceptible to the special pleading of startling atmospherics. But my memory isn't at fault here. Dorothy was greeted by wild regaling. The death of Nessarose was viewed as an accident. And I insist, a happy accident. I stand up to tell this because it is so."

"Very nice, very sweet. Testimony of a daffodil. You may stand down," said Nipp.

"And it wasn't just me," said Little Daffy. "Lady Glinda arrived soon thereafter."

"That'll do," said Nipp.

"May I pose a question?" The Owl seemed entirely too timid, thought Brrr, though perhaps that was a courtroom strategy of legal counsel who happened to be Animal.

"If you must," said Nipp. Dame Fegg curled her lip.

The Owl said, "Did you like being a sunflower on display for Nessarose Thropp?"

"I adored it," said Little Daffy. "I wore a kind of snood on which were sewn big flat yellow petals cut out of felt. We stood in ranks and had our own lines to sing when Nessarose walked by in those glamourous shoes she had. It was a children's song called 'Lessons of the Garden.' "

"What was your line to sing? Can you recall it?"

"Out of order. Inappropriate," said Nipp. "Besides, no one cares."

"I do," said Dorothy. "I love to sing."

"If it pleases the court," said Little Daffy, "and I won't do the whole thing—I just had a single stanza. Correcting for pitch, as back in those days I was a soprano and now I'm a beery contralto, it went like this."

"Oh, please," said Dame Fegg. Brrr bared a canine at her. Just one.

"Go on, and perhaps I can become a sort of musical anthropologist, collecting melodies. I'll call it 'Songs of the Munchkinland,'" said Dorothy, clapping her hands.

Little Daffy sang,

Little sorry sunflower seed,
I know exactly what you need.
The love of the Unnamed God is pure,
As good for you as rich manure.

"Or maybe not," said Dorothy.

"*That* took up a few valuable moments of my life," said Nipp to Temper Bailey witheringly.

"I've established the innocent nature of Little Daffy and proven she isn't lying to protect the accused," said Temper Bailey.

"I was a maunt," said Little Daffy. "I took vows not to lie."

"You also presumably took vows of commitment, and you seem to have thrown *those* over when they got inconvenient," snapped Dame Fegg, indicating Mr. Boss, who was holding his wife's hand. "I recommend that we count as inadmissible anything the little Munchkinlander dandelion sings."

"She's as tall as you are. I'll snap your legs, you," said Mr. Boss, "and then you'll see who is little," and so he was tossed out of court for rudeness.

"I don't believe we can consider the testimony of a witness so young and impressionable as Little Daffy evidently was," said Nipp. "Please strike her remarks from the record." But since he'd neglected to appoint a court reporter no one moved to obey.

"I'm as young today as she was then," said Dorothy. "If she was too young then to be taken seriously, you can't try me now. I'm a minor."

"You're a middle-aged woman by our count, even if you look like a big lummox," snapped Nipp. "We're not taking that up again. Over to you, Dame Fegg. And let's hurry this up. We're going to break at lunchtime and reconvene tomorrow, and I'm uncommonly ready for lunch."

Dame Fegg spent the next ninety minutes grilling Dorothy on her knowledge of Munchkinland. The prosecutor seemed to be trying to trick Dorothy into giving away some scrap of privileged information about the geography and politics of Oz, but either Dorothy was a canny defendant or she genuinely remained, even now, largely clueless about how Oz was organized. She floundered along, Dame Fegg darted and carped, Nipp groaned and made noises with his implements. Whenever deference was shown to Temper Bailey, his questions couldn't seem to provoke Dorothy into proving her innocence. By the time Nipp sounded the bell and closed the proceedings for the day, the whole exercise seemed pretty much a waste of time to Brrr. Still, as the crowd of spectators filed out of the courtroom, the buzz was loud, argumentative, laughing. It was going over well as an entertainment, anyway. And so maybe it would be a successful trial, depending on whose measure of success you chose to adopt.

7.

At a café, in the shade of aromatic fruit trees unruffled in the breezeless evening, they discussed the day's proceedings with Mister Mikko, who had been persuaded to leave the Reading Room behind and dare the public agora.

"I still wonder what this trial is intended to achieve," said Little Daffy. "It's one thing to build up a villain to help concentrate a sense of national purpose and struggle. But I should think the divine Emperor of Oz and his chief commanding officer, General Cherrystone, already qualify as enemies of the Free State of Munchkinland. Finding out whether Dorothy is now sixteen or sixty-one doesn't seem worth the public fuss. What good does it do anyone to persecute this poor girl?"

"The Free State of Munchkinland can't get at Shell, more's the pity, and their engagement with Cherrystone seems at a permanent standstill," observed Mister Mikko. "This exercise against Dorothy is meant to siphon off national frustration. Give the Munchkinlanders a sense of achievement."

Brrr said, "So this isn't going to be a fair trial? Is that what you're saying?"

"Of course it isn't. The very premise of the accusations is bizarre. Conflating the deaths of both sisters! Though Elphaba Thropp was born in Munchkinland, she maintained no political association with her sister Nessarose, and Elphaba ignored the opportunity to seize power once her sister was dead. And a Munchkinlander court prosecuting anyone for the murder of the Wicked Witch of the *West?* Absurd. The west is deep in Loyal Oz. The premise is prejudicial and proves that what's wanted here isn't a trial but a conviction."

"I'm with you," said Mr. Boss. "Nothing cheers folks up like a public beheading."

"I'm no student of history," said Little Daffy, "but I don't like the way this has all lined up. Mombey and General Jinjuria, two strong defenders of Munchkinland, concentrating the attention of the country upon a legal assault of another female? The real enemies of Munchkinland are the man in the Emerald City and his chief officer at Restwater."

"Total bitch gripe," agreed Mr. Boss. "You've never seen that before? And you lived with maunts for several decades? What were you, blind?"

"She has a point," said Mister Mikko, who after all had taught history back in his day. "Shell in his emerald towers, and Cherrystone holed up in Haugaard's Keep . . . two powerful men in Oz, after the forty-year history of the Wizard's oppression that beleaguered my parents' generation, and their parents', too. It's been sixty years since Pastorius was deposed, and so maybe sixty-five, is it, since the last Ozma died? A lot of rule by men in a land with a long tradition of matriarchy."

Little Daffy said, "That's it exactly. If Munchkinlanders needed to take against someone to prove their strength, you'd think they'd nominate someone who stood in for the Emperor of Oz a little more keenly. This Dorothy seems a pale substitute."

"She's what turned up," said Mr. Boss. "You're not going to rear back and change her gender for the sake of a more satisfying trial."

"But Little Daffy *has a point,*" insisted Mister Mikko. "Since Ozma the Bilious died leaving her husband the Ozma Regent and the baby, Ozma Tippetarius, there's been only one female minister of Loyal Oz as we know: Lady Glinda. And she ruled well but all too briefly."

Brrr said, "But what's the point of the prosecution of Dorothy?"

Mister Mikko responded with a tone of gentle irony. "The fight to retake Restwater won't be won in the court of public opinion."

"Then what is really going on here?" asked Brrr. "It seems important to figure out, if only to find a way to defend the hapless Dorothy."

They sat, confounded, fiddling with the silverware until the dwarf said, "I often thought the displays of the Clock of the Time Dragon were intended to divert the attention of the public from the Clock's real mission: to serve as the secret vault that housed the Grimmerie. I wonder if this trial isn't so much a public relations exercise as a diversion. Is something going on elsewhere on the war front that La Mombey doesn't want us to be noticing? The Clock might have given us a clue. Damn its rotted soul."

On their way back to the dubious comforts of A Stable Home, they passed a beer garden. Over their pints, little lager louts were singing something clangorous. The words were slurred.

> Ding dong, the bitch will swing
> Like a clapper on a string
> Back and forth until the bitch is dead!

"What has gotten into my countrymen?" said Little Daffy.

"Don't dawdle and gawk, you'll only draw attention," said Brrr, his old irritable-bowel thing threatening to flare up. "Eyes front, move along."

"It's just that the melody is so jolly," said Little Daffy. "True, we used to hold singing festivals, but the texts weren't so rabid."

"Climate of the times," said Mr. Boss. They hurried past.

When the court convened in the morning, the room was full to capacity. Lord Nipp instructed the Chimps to wave large rush fans. The casement windows were cranked open to their fullest, and more spectators gathered outside. There, the sight lines being poor and the sun hot, a pretty penny was to be made passing among the crowd selling cups of lemon barley. Mister Mikko, who was waiting outside, would later report that the atmosphere seemed a cross between a state funeral and a harvest festival, morbid and giddy at once.

Since yesterday Dorothy had been allowed a change of clothes, but the selection offered her hadn't been the kindest. She seemed to be wearing a dirndl of some sort, cut for someone with the proportions of a Baboon. The sleeves were so long they could have been tied together in a bow. She looked like a child in her father's nightshirt.

Dame Fegg dove into questioning at a gallop today, returning to the subject of Dorothy's prior arrival in Oz. "You say that Glinda Chuffrey gave you Nessarose's enchanted shoes and advised you to tiptoe out of town?" asked Dame Fegg. "She has a great deal to answer for herself, that Glinda. Those shoes should have belonged to the treasure-house of Munchkinland."

"I can't speak to Glinda's motives," said the defendant. "She simply told me that the Wizard of Oz could help me, and that the Yellow Brick Road would lead me to him. For all I knew she was in the tourist business and wanted me to see the sights."

"She gave you no armed guard, no escort, no inkling that Munchkinland was devolved from Loyal Oz?"

"I don't think so. But it seems such a long time ago, and of course everything was so new. And I did love those shoes. Maybe I wasn't paying enough attention."

"Maybe, Miss Dorothy, you have *never paid enough attention.*"

The crowd chortled quietly at this line, as if it were the end of a scene of some parlor farce on a stage at Shiz. But Brrr thought Dame Fegg had made a mistake. Hitherto she had not addressed Dorothy as "Miss." Having started now, she wouldn't be able to retreat, and that accorded the girl a little more dignity than she seemed to deserve, given her ridiculous getup.

"Dame Fegg," piped up Dorothy, "if you were suddenly, magically carried off to my home of Kansas, how long do you think it would take you to pick up on our ways?"

"That calls for speculation," said Dame Fegg.

"You're not asking the questions, Miss Dorothy," said Lord Nipp. Aha, thought Brrr, there it is: she *has* graduated to Miss Dorothy. In her zanily earnest way, she's commanding the respect of her enemies despite themselves. Brrr would never call it charisma but oh, Dorothy had charm of a sort, for sure.

Dame Fegg proceeded to grill the girl about the Yellow Brick Road Irregulars, as in popular lore they had become known. Having spent his life timid enough over every living thing, and a few gloomy stationary things as well, Brrr had his concerns about being tarred by association with Dorothy. But he was a Lion, after all. A Lion among Munchkins. And thanks to good dental hygiene he had all of his natural teeth. So he straightened up and tossed his head to make of his mane a more impressive quiff, to make himself look stouthearted, even if it was all public relations.

"And the Scarecrow was so dear and so helpful," said Dorothy, "and then the Tin Woodman such a sweetheart. And the Lion, when he showed up, a total mess." She smiled at him as if she weren't out to ruin his reputation, that is if he had had a reputation he cared about. "If I ever get you back to San Francisco with me, I think you would all fit in there just fine."

"At what point did you let them in on your secret background as a regicidal maniac?" asked Dame Fegg.

"I object. Leading the witness," said Temper Bailey, who most of the time looked as if he were napping on his perch.

"They called her a witch, that Nessarose," explained Dorothy. "It took me a while to cotton on to the fact that she was governor as well."

"In your single-minded campaign to deprive both Munchkinland and Loyal Oz of its entire bank of leaders, you collected a mob of collaborators," pushed Dame Fegg.

"May I speak?" said Brrr, and stood. He was roughly ten times the girth and weight of either Lord Nipp or Dame Fegg, so they couldn't object, though Dame Fegg focused her pious squinty bloodshot eyes on him with contempt. "Dorothy didn't entice me with plans of sedition or the overthrow of any government. Truth to tell, I was rather at loose ends at that stage in my life. I wanted to put behind me the shame of some poor choices and some dead-end experiences—"

"Please, spare us the melodrama," said Lord Nipp. "We're a court of law, not a guidance counsellorship."

"We went to the Emerald City, Your Lordship, to see if we could find a way to help Dorothy return home," said Brrr. "As I heard it told, no one in Munchkinland had had any bright ideas about *that*."

"That's true enough," said Dorothy. "But at least no one put me under arrest, that time."

"And then the Wizard of Oz, so called, enlisted you in the assassination of Nessarose's sister," said Dame Fegg.

"Well now, that much I can't deny," said Dorothy. "The Wizard said the Wicked Witch of the West was tremendously evil and needed to be stopped. I was young and didn't think to ask 'stopped from what?' He said she deserved to die. He wouldn't entertain my request for help until I'd killed her."

"Now we're getting somewhere." Dame Fegg was steely with purpose.

"I had no choice but to head to the west," said Dorothy. "But I had no intention of doing the Wizard's dirty work for him. Doesn't that count for something? It was either leave town or take on a job as a chambermaid in one of the seedier neighborhoods of the EC."

"Nonsense," said Fegg. "There's always choice."

"No, I'm not explaining it correctly. I mean, for myself, I had no choice. For it had dawned on me how dreadful the accidental squashery of Nessarose Thropp had been. I wanted to apologize to the closest survivor for my inadvertent part in her sister's demise. That's why I went west. That, and for no other reason."

"You expect us to believe that?" Fegg looked offended. "The Wizard, by your own admission, asks you to kill the Wicked Witch of the West, and you carry out his plans with cunning and immediacy, and then you claim you had no culpability in the matter? It's preposterous." She gave a sneer that could have won her an acting award.

"Hey now, wait," said Dorothy. "The coincidence of the Wizard's aims and my experiences at Kiamo Ko, the Witch's castle, is no proof of my guilt."

Coincidence again, thought Brrr. Not proof, but not helpful, either.

Temper Bailey spoke up again. "Let's hear more from the Lion. He was on that mission too, was he not?"

Nipp turned a cold eye on Brrr and nodded.

The Lion thought: If this does end poorly, what happens to Dorothy—? To me?

He said, "I wasn't present at Dorothy's commission from the Wizard. I can't confirm what he said to her. I do concur that the Wizard asked *me* to kill the Witch too, and about their private meetings with the Wizard, both the Scarecrow and the Tin Woodman reported the same. We proceeded to the west not to fulfill the Wizard's request but to lend succor to our companion on the road, who we all could see was young and innocent if not a few sequins short of a diadem, if you know what I mean."

Dorothy pulled a face at that.

"And what can you tell us about the murder of Elphaba Thropp?" asked Temper Bailey.

"I can tell you precious little about her death; I don't answer to its being called a murder," said the Lion. "I was locked in a kitchen larder with the Witch's son, Liir, and by the time we'd escaped the room and dashed up the tower stairs to the parapet of the castle, Dorothy was already descending the stairs, weeping her eyes out."

"I cried so hard," said Dorothy, "I looked like I'd thrown that bucket of water over myself."

"And so the question is," said Brrr, "what happened up there? *Did* Dorothy kill the Witch? Either on purpose or by accident? All any of us know about the matter is that the Witch is done with. She's gone. But was she killed?"

The room fell silent. Dame Fegg turned to Dorothy and so did Temper Bailey. Several hundred Munchkinlanders paused in their knitting or their munching of small round breakfast pastries. The Chimpanzees held their fans still.

"I shall remind you that you are under oath to answer honestly," murmured Lord Nipp, almost as if afraid to break the spell of the question.

Dorothy put her face in her hands, a sloppy gesture given the length of her sleeves. When she lifted her teary cheeks, her upper lip was creamy with mucus; it looked as if she had applied a depilatory unguent. "I believe in taking responsibility for what happens," she admitted. "I believed it six years ago, and that's why I went to Kiamo Ko, to confess my part in the death of Nessarose Thropp. And I confess my part in the death of Elphaba Thropp too, to the extent I can be sure that it happened. But when I threw a bucket of water at the Witch, to save her from burning to death in her black skirts, what happened was a huge plume of smoke and a sizzle, as of fatback on a griddle, and the Witch collapsed amid the drapes of her skirts and the billows of smoke. The acrid stench and the burning in my eyes made me turn away, and I vomited in terror and surprise, and when I looked back—well, she was gone."

"Killed," said Fegg.

"Gone," said Dorothy.

"Is that the same thing?"

"Who can say?"

"Very good question," said Temper Bailey. "Who can say? Were there witnesses?"

"Only Toto, and he used to be the strong silent type," said Dorothy.

"Oh, now, let's not start that sniffling again," scoffed Fegg.

"The Witch's old Nanny finally made it up the stairs, and she swept me away while she cleaned up," said Dorothy. "I never went up there again, and I never examined the scene of the death. I was a witness at her disappearance—and, sure, maybe it was a death. But wouldn't there have been a corpse?"

"Of course there was a corpse," snorted Dame Fegg. "You've proven yourself to be an unreliable witness any number of times. In your glee and relief you just didn't check, or you're pretending not to have checked."

The room seemed to rock a little; maybe it was the heat, or maybe that Dorothy carried personal earthquakes with her to deploy at will. Brrr sat up straight. Temper Bailey emitted a series of small *who-who-whos,* but whether that was a stutter or an admission in Owlish that he was not wise enough for this particular job was hard to say.

"Before you kill again," said Dame Fegg, "I will see you put to death."

Lord Nipp had to pound his gavel repeatedly. When silence returned at last, he called a halt in the proceedings for two days. He made the suggestion that Animals should be invited to hear the final assessments and the judgment of Dorothy, and Munchkinlander farmers should roundly encourage their lodgers and farmhands to show some civic spirit and witness the conclusion of the trial. After all, a cow had been killed in the Glikkus. There was such a thing as solidarity.

8.

Why the adjournment? From the point of view of the prosecution, it seemed to Brrr a clumsy move. The hiatus might allow that rumor—that Elphaba was somehow still alive—to gain weight and sway public opinion in Dorothy's favor. Mister Mikko agreed and concluded that Nipp *must* have a sound reason for delaying. Might they be trying to dig up a witness, somewhere, someone who could confirm Elphaba's death by revealing anything about the disposition of her corpse?

"Preposterous," said Brrr. Who could it be? Back on that dreadful day, neither he nor Liir had been allowed up the stairs to the parapet where Elphaba had died. The only human souls who might give testimony about the scene of that tragedy were Dorothy herself and the Witch's old Nanny, who had gone up after Dorothy had come down but who had refused Liir access. Brrr had assumed it was out of kindness; Liir had, after all, been a mere fourteen years old. And a young fourteen at that.

Could Elphaba's old Nanny have been capable of a deceit of any magnitude? Concealing the Witch? . . . Brrr thought not. Even then Nanny had been stunningly unmoored from reality. Were she still alive, she'd be over a hundred years old now. At any rate, Kiamo Ko was a thousand-some miles away any route you took. They wouldn't be putting Nanny or her ghost on the witness stand.

Then, he wondered, what about Chistery? The chief of the flying monkeys? As far as Brrr knew, Chistery was an anomaly in Oz. He'd begun life as an animal incapable of language, and yet he had managed to learn it, thanks to Elphaba's ministrations and maybe to her magic. Brrr had no idea how old Chistery would be now, nor how long snow monkeys generally lived. He asked Mister Mikko his opinion, but the Ape bared his false dentures at Brrr and refused to get into a discussion about it. "I don't even know my own expected life span," he snapped; "how could I possibly be conversant on the life span of an invented line like a flying monkey?"

Even if he were alive, Chistery would likely be too old to fly all those miles to speak in confirmation of the Witch's death, decided Brrr. And an Animal's testimony would carry only so much weight.

The evening before the trial was set to reopen, Mr. Boss said, "In the absence of any other clue about why Nippy Nipp Nipp adjourned for two days, I've been wondering if emissaries of La Mombey have been working to get information out of Dorothy now that she's been threatened with execution."

"Information about what?" asked his wife.

"Isn't it obvious?" he said. "La Mombey must be as interested in locating the Grimmerie as the Emperor is. Maybe she thinks that only something as powerful as that book could have drawn Dorothy back to Oz, and that Dorothy knows something about its location. A threat of death might loosen her tongue."

"Dorothy's is one tongue that doesn't need any more loosing," said the Munchkinlander. But Brrr wondered if Mr. Boss had a point.

They made the mistake of walking back to their lodgings through the piazza outside Neale House. Flares had been set up so that the tradesmen could hammer together a kiosk of some sort. "They're going to sell souvenirs that say THE JUDGMENT OF DOROTHY! Headbands or armbands," guessed Little Daffy.

"They're building her a little house she can ride back to Kansas," said Mr. Boss.

They stopped joking then, as someone strung up a rope, and someone else tested the trapdoor. "They wouldn't," said Little Daffy, dabbing her eyes. "My own folk, coarsened so?"

At A Stable Home, she ventured to ask Dame Hostile, "Do you think Lord Nipp will order Dorothy to be hanged?"

"She'll swing like a bell, ding dong, they say," replied the widow. "And by the way, I'm giving notice to you lot. When you booked in, you concealed your association with that Dorothy. So I want you to clear out tomorrow. I don't need this house to get a reputation for attracting lowlife."

"But I'm a Munchkinlander!" cried Little Daffy.

"That's pretty low," said the dwarf, "though I'm not one to talk."

"I'm retiring," said the chatelaine. "I can't talk to you anymore."

"We didn't do anything to you," said Little Daffy. "I know my manners. We clean up after ourselves. Look, I'll bake you a coffee bread for the morning." She was almost beside herself, to be treated this way by her own kind.

The only response from upstairs was a slammed door.

Brrr had had enough. He repaired to his chamber, from where he could hear the distant sound of hammering and cheering half the night, as the laborers tested and retested their equipment.

Regardless of the reasons for the postponement, when the trial reconvened Neale House was even more crowded the next day. A thousand Munchkinlanders surrounded the building and spilled into the square by the front doors. The Animals that Munchkin farmers had cajoled or browbeat into joining them were largely of the junior variety—kits, cubs, pups in training harness. They were escorted by Ewes and Dames, in hooded expressions and the occasional going-to-town bonnet. The human factor in the crowd snickered and occasionally nickered. Even a jaded old Goat with a beard on her chin and a wen on her rump commanded little respect in a crowd of beer-barrel farmers.

"So far in this picture-pretty town, my size and presence has seemed more than enough to allow me to pass through any crowd," murmured Brrr to the dwarf and his wife. "But the Munchkinlanders seem to be gigantic in menace, or is that just me?"

Mister Mikko said, "I'm turning back. This atmosphere reminds me too much of the crowds that gathered to hear about the Wizard's Animal Adverse laws. I can wait till tonight to hear what develops. And if I happen to die today of hexus of the plexus or bonkus of the konkus, don't think I go unwillingly. It's been a long rocky life, with plenty of possibility but too much human ugliness."

The room was filled to the rafters, literally, since Munchkinlanders sat straddling the beams. The atmosphere had gone grave. Nipp cleared his throat and took sips of water and cleared his throat again before harrumphing, "Due to circumstances on the international front, I've been required to speed up the trial. In the absence of further witnesses this morning, I'm going to ask the advocates to present their final arguments. I will then charge the jury with making a judgment of Dorothy Gale: guilty as charged or innocent of some or all charges. I retain to myself the privilege of listening to the jury's advice and determining if it is sound. May I remind you all that the final arbitration of justice remains in the hands of the magistrate. Me. Dame Fegg, you may begin."

The prosecutor, clearly, had been briefed about the change in calendar. She'd come cloaked in some sort of dark academic robe that set off her iron braids, this morning coiled and pinned to each temple with treacherous-looking hair swizzlers. In a voice rounded with theatrical tones, perhaps the better to carry out the windows, she called Dorothy to the chair for a final time.

The defendant emerged from belowstairs in the usual manner. No one lent a hand, but at least for her final turn on the stand she'd been allowed to appear in her own clothes, an ensemble that had no origin in Oz—a blue velvet skirt with shiny black jet piping at the hem that, at intervals, looped waistward in hand-stitched arabesques. Cut to the midcalf and girdled with a wide stomacher, it cinched a white linen blouse with mutton sleeves. A toque filigreed with spiky feathers and fake linen roses in blue and silver perched at a drunken angle upon her head. She clutched her gloved hands repeatedly as if in her distress she were about to burst into song.

"Lord Nipp," began Dame Fegg. "Counsel Bailey. Ladies and gentlemen of the jury. Ladies and gentlemen of the gallery and beyond. Indeed, ladies and gentlemen of history: I address you all."

Dorothy gave a little cough. "Yes, Miss Dorothy, I address you too," said Dame Fegg in exaggerated courtesy, the first nasty giggle of the morning. Brrr rolled his eyes at Little Daffy and Mr. Boss.

"This trial has not taken so long that we need to review point by point what's been put before us already. I shall therefore make a cursory summary for the sake of the record. I put it to the jury that Dorothy Gale is guilty as charged of the murder of Nessarose Thropp and Elphaba Thropp. Whether she is also guilty of the murder of that cow in the Glikkus is not our concern this morning."

"No one said it was a talking Cow," said Dorothy. "But I've kind of noticed you don't always pay attention to that distinction."

"Ooooh," said the humans in the crowd, as if this were a point in a debating tourney. Brrr couldn't tell if they approved, generally, or if Dorothy was hitting too close to home. The Animals, he noticed, were silent, even stiff in their composure.

"I believe we've established that, some eighteen years ago, the collapse of Miss Dorothy's domicile upon Nessarose, the Eminent Thropp and governor of Munchkinland, indisputably resulted in her death. Though known at the time as the Wicked Witch of the East, Nessarose is honored for her role in launching Munchkinland independence. Therefore Dorothy Gale is guilty of slaying the mother of our country. Our dear Munchkinland."

"Here comes the dump," murmured Mr. Boss to Brrr. "I can smell it."

Dame Fegg left the circular plinth from which she had conducted most of her examination. "We are a small people," she said. "Before most of us were born, the Ozma Regent, Pastorius, began the job of strangling our native independence by renaming Nubbly Meadows in southern Gillikin as the Emerald City. Pastorius planned the early stages of what would become the Yellow Brick Road. His work, however innocently meant, was ready for exploitation by the Wizard of Oz. Until Nessarose Thropp inherited the mantle of Eminence that was rejected by her sister Elphaba, we were in thrall to the powers of what is now called Loyal Oz. So the recent history of Munchkinland—the history into which many of us were born—casts us most often as the handmaiden of the rich, the laborer in the field, the servant under the stairs, the midget comedy troupe."

The room had gone fully silent, humans and Animals alike.

"Small, yes," said Dame Fegg, reclaiming her dais now for emphasis and striking a pose, "small, but not insignificant. We accept from our forebears the stewardship of our dear Munchkinland. The bones of our ancestors herringbone the soil we plow. The land they tilled, the views they cherished, are ours. We shall never allow any invader, either Dorothy Gale or the Emerald City Messiars at Haugaard's Keep, to abuse our liberty and to confiscate our sacred trust of land. From the slopes of the Scalps to the north, where the Glikkuns still dig for emeralds . . ." She paused to drag out a handkerchief, giving Mr. Boss a chance to mutter, "Technically the Glikkus isn't Munchkinland; this lot is as blind to native borders as anyone else." She continued, ". . . to the brave little hamlets perched on the edge of the great desert to the east—to the lonely, sere sweeps of the Hardings and the Cloth Hills that divide us from soggy Quadling Country, and over, yes, to Restwater! to Restwater, damn it! which shall *not* remain in the greedy grasp of the invaders, but shall return rightfully to those who cherish it most!"

A cheer went up. "This could turn into a riot," muttered Mr. Boss to his companions. "I always enjoy a good riot."

"We came to do a job, and we'll see it through," said Brrr, hoping he meant it. He glanced at Little Daffy to see how she was faring. She nodded that she was firm.

"And on up to the Madeleines," continued Dame Fegg. "That rank of soft mountains to our west, dividing us from Gillikin. The longest stretch of unprotected border of Munchkinland, an easy bolster, nothing more, along whose slopes the clouds roll toward us, furnishing us with the rain that makes us the Corn Basket of Oz, nothing less. Productive Munchkinland, that part most of us know best—the soft rolling lavender fields, the farmsteads lit with cheery lamplight of an evening, the harvest festivals, the local traditions of long tables set out on village greens. The beer—yes, let us defend our right to brew hops!"

Another big cheer at this.

"All of it—all of our way of life, treasured bequest of those who went before—all of it threatened by invaders. I give you Miss Dorothy," she said, playing to the crowd rather than the jury. "Miss Dorothy Gale, a young woman unreliable in her memories of how she came first to Oz to commit regicide against the ruling family of our motherland, our Munchkinland."

Later, Brrr swore he heard someone from behind a door sound a note on a pitch pipe, but perhaps cynicism was getting the better of him. Someone in the crowd began to sing what the Lion had come to know as Munchkinland's anthem.

> Munchkinland, our motherland,
> No other land is home.
> We cherish best this land so blessed
> As pretty as a poem.
> We'll never rest when from the west
> By rude oppressors we're oppressed.
> We proudly stand with Munchkinland,
> Our treasure chest, our humble nest,
> Our motherland, no other land
> Is home.

Brrr cast a glance to the front. Even Temper Bailey was singing—to keep mum was probably considered sedition. The cheering that followed could probably be heard all the way to Kanziz. Not good, the Lion thought. He wouldn't have been surprised to see those Chimps come out with tankards of ale to sozzle the mood further.

Dame Fegg wiped her eyes. "And so, from the heartland of Oz, from the capital city of our Free State of Munchkinland, do I put it to the jury one final time. Dorothy Gale's testimony about her youth and innocence in her prior sojourn in Oz can't be considered admissible, as that very youth made her an unreliable witness to the events of the times. Nonetheless, in this country everyone must pay for what crimes they commit, and nobody can adequately defend Dorothy against the crime of murder of Elphaba Thropp. By extension one deduces that the accused's aims were coherent, her capacity to assassinate our leaders honed to surgical precision, and her disguise as gullible sweetheart on a walking tour entirely convincing to those morons with whom she came in touch."

"I object," called Little Daffy. Mr. Boss looked at her sideways with a clenched lower lip, dubious but approving. His little Munchkinlander spitfire. "I may have been young and dressed as a daffodil, but I was no moron."

"You aren't counsel. You have no right to object," said Lord Nipp.

"I should think that's exactly the kind of right we are trying to defend in Munchkinland," said Little Daffy. Brrr found he wasn't so surprised at her brass. Purportedly she had spent a decade or so chafing under the direction of her former colleague Sister Doctor. She's not shy, our Little Daffy.

"Counsel Bailey," said Lord Nipp. "Have you any-thing to add?"

The Owl had come to court in native dress, which is to say naked. This was a risky gambit, Brrr thought, but who knows? It set him apart from the Munch-kinlander prosecutor, who had returned to her stool and was blowing her nose with sentiment and force. Temper Bailey flew to a perch provided him halfway between the jury and Dorothy, who was sitting up-right, back ramrod straight, eyes open too wide.

"I assert that my client, Miss Dorothy Gale from abroad somewhere, must be innocent of the charges of murder and assassination," said Temper Bailey. "For one thing, while it is true that her arrival coincided with the death of Nessarose Thropp, there's no way to prove that Nessarose didn't look up into the heav-ens at the sight of a small house lurching through the clouds and have a heart attack from terror, falling down dead on the platform just before the house of Dorothy landed. I took advantage of our unscheduled recess to fly to Center Munch and search the coronor's records. While Nessarose was conclusively determined to be dead, the cause of death is not mentioned."

"Well, I doubt coroners are trained to identify the cause of every possible fatality in this universe," said Lord Nipp. "Cause of death: Collapse of Real Estate? Please. Point dismissed."

"Nonetheless, we must deal with the facts legally as we find them," said Temper Bailey. "In any case, if we accept Counsel Fegg's conclusion that Dorothy Gale is an unreliable witness to her own actions, we must also therefore strike from the record Dorothy's observation that the Wicked Witch of the West, Elphaba Thropp, actually died."

"Preposterous," said Dame Fegg. "All of Oz knows that she died at the hands of this witch."

"If you please, I am not a witch," said Dorothy. She mimed tying a bonnet under her chin "I've been trying to make this point for some time, but you people here never seem to *put on your listening caps.*"

"I propose to the jury," said Temper Bailey, "that of the charges brought against the defendant, we must strike them both off the chart of crimes."

"Wait; we can get the coroner in here to testify what he saw," said Lord Nipp.

"The coroner is dead, my Lord. So all we have are his records. May I close by saying that we've heard no conclusive evidence that the defendant committed the crimes with which she is charged? Here in loyal Munchkinland, even as we struggled against the encroachments of the Emerald City barbarians to our west, we must remember that what we are defending is not only the golden treasury of our arable fields and our native customs. We are defending our own honor, too. And we will not convict someone for whom there is no evidence of wrongdoing."

"Now I've heard everything," snapped Dame Fegg. "I suppose as a coda you're going to propose that due to the contradiction in time schemes, that the defendant before us is not even the actual Dorothy Gale who was here eighteen years ago, but an impostor?"

"Oh, I'm me, all right," said Dorothy earnestly.

"I haven't given you the floor," said Lord Nipp.

"Oh, but Your Reasonableness, may I have a word? Please?"

Brrr could see that Nipp was inclined to say no, but the crowd wanted to hear Dorothy speak. They rhubarbed away in an insistent manner. Maybe the magistrate was stuck between his formal obligations and his own curiosity. If so, his curiosity won. He waved her forward.

Dorothy stood up for the first time. She towered over the Munchkinlanders, even Lord Nipp on his stool. "When I first came to Oz however many years ago we count it, I was merely ten," she said. "I don't know if in Munchkinland a child of ten can be convicted of murder, but I believe in fairness, and I think you do too. When the twister lifted my house from its foundations, and I went whirling off in the skies, I was as helpless as a flea on the hide of a dog. I knew nothing of Munchkinland or anything about Oz, and I don't see how I can be convicted of murder of a Wicked Witch whose presence I wasn't even aware of until her corpse was pointed out to me by Lady Glinda."

This was, perhaps, not a sound association for Dorothy to make, thought Brrr; Lady Glinda seemed to be persona non grata both in Loyal Oz and in Munchkinland. You couldn't win.

"I've been fed newspapers in my jail cell—and a very comfortable jail cell it is, I might add. I have seen this trial referred to over and over as 'The Judgment of Dorothy.' With all due respect to my estimable hosts, today I would like to interpret that phrase as 'Dorothy's Judgment on the Matter.' And so before you deliver your verdict, dear honorable jury and magistrate, I would like to deliver mine."

"Entirely out of order," said Nipp, sorry he'd let this cat out of the bag, but the crowd was straining to hear what Dorothy would say next.

"When I first came to Oz as an untraveled farm-girl," she went on, "everything seemed magical to me. It took some getting used to, the presence of witches and wizards, and talking Animals, to say nothing of a Scarecrow who could walk and a man hammered with tin. It made Kansas look very tame. When I got home a few months later, thanks to the magic shoes that had caused so many problems, everything appeared pale by comparison. I thought maybe I'd somehow made the whole thing up. But then Uncle Henry and Auntie Em showed me a whole new house with a real indoor washroom instead of an outhouse, bought with insurance, and I hadn't made *that* up. Plumbing is uniquely persuasive. So I decided my trip to Oz had been real, even if no one in Kansas believed in you."

She looked at them. "Yes. No one believed in Munchkinland. They thought I was being fanciful or perhaps tetched in the head. But *I* never stopped believing in you. I never stopped believing in the Yellow Brick Road, and the Emerald City, and that frightening old humbug, the Wizard of Oz."

She paused. She wasn't quite as good as Dame Fegg, thought Brrr, but she had strengths of her own. "Here I stand now, before the very people I pledged never to forget, only to be accused by them of murders I didn't intend to commit. I'm older now, as we've discussed. And I've traveled a little bit since I was ten. Uncle Henry took me by train all across the great mountains in my land to the city by the bay—to San Francisco—and for all that I have seen, the Rocky Mountains that, no offense intended, rival the magnificent Scalps in stature and purity—the great fertile plains of Nebraska—the ocean beyond the bay—I haven't seen anything that could deflect my memories of Munchkinland and Oz. Not yet, not ever. My judgment of you is that you are a kind people and a fair people, and you will do what is right. You will make for me more memories of charity and justice that I can carry home, if I can ever reckon how to manage the return trip."

She curtseyed at Lord Nipp and again at Dame Fegg, and then she curtseyed a third time, not to the jury but to the crowd in Neale House. A small spattering of applause, quickly repressed.

"Mmm, she's good," murmured Mr. Boss. "This should be rich."

"I shall liberate the jury to its deliberations," began Nipp, but then Dame Fegg stood up.

"There is a matter I meant to follow and I have just remembered," she said. "May I be allowed to ask a question?" Nipp nodded. "I wonder if Miss Dorothy could describe for those of us who know nothing about Sanfran Tsitsko, or however it is said, the sea you mentioned once or twice. What sea is this?"

"Oh, goodness," said Dorothy. "It's called the Pacific Ocean. It is as wide as the sky, and as broad."

"Poetic license is inadmissible in court," said Dame Fegg. "Nothing could be as wide as the sky. The sky goes to both sides of us, you see, whereas a landscape to be viewed can only go in one direction."

"You're right, in a manner of speaking," said Dorothy, "but you see, this sea is so broad that you can't view the other side. It's said to stretch as far as Asia, and to take many, many days to cross by boat. Once you are out in a sailing vessel or a steamer, you lose sight of the land, of California and all, and there's nothing around you but water. The sea is as wide as the sky, exactly so, for the water, I am told, stretches under you and the sky above, in precisely identical proportions. . . ."

"That'll do," said Dame Fegg. Munchkinlanders were vomiting into their lunch sacks. "You describe a mystical sea that bears no resemblance to reality. I hold you are criminally insane."

"Just because you've never seen an ocean doesn't mean it doesn't exist," said Dorothy. "The same way that, when I go home, *if* I get home, your existence is not obliterated just because none of my family has ever been to Munchkinland."

Dame Fegg said, "I have heard enough, Lord Nipp. I think you can send the jury out."

"The presence or absence of an ocean of the mind has no bearing on this case!" hooted Temper Bailey.

"Are there any final remarks?" asked Nipp, picking up his gavel. He pointed at Brrr, who shrank back. But Little Daffy stood up and approached the table.

"I want to thank you for hearing my testimony, sir," she said. "As the only Munchkinlander present who witnessed the arrival of Dorothy, I'm grateful to have been welcomed into the proceedings. It's a custom of Center Munch to conclude a disagreement or a negotiation with a sweet, to show that honorable people can agree to disagree and still be courteous. So I have baked a little present for you." No one could argue with Little Daffy; none of the Munchkinlanders from Bright Lettins knew the customs of Center Munch. She pulled from a basket on her arm a checkered cloth and unfolded it. "Please, in the name of those Munchkinlanders who remember Nessarose Thropp, accept this offering in the spirit in which I give it."

Nipp took a little pastry between thumb and forefinger. Dame Fegg did the same. Temper Bailey, using his claws on his perch, declined an offering. "May I approach the defendant?" asked Little Daffy. "It's the custom. 'With special zest we greet the guest,'" she intoned daringly. "Or is that verse peculiar to Center Munch?"

"If you must," said Nipp. Little Daffy angled the basket and shifted the napkin so Dorothy could see inside better.

"Take two, they're small, and you're a big girl," said Little Daffy, and Dorothy obliged. Then Nipp instructed the jury to file out to a private chamber.

"I wouldn't go far," said Nipp, "if you want to be present at the declaration of the verdict. I have a feeling this isn't going to take a long time. We'll convene again in an hour and I'll let you know if a decision has been reached."

9.

They walked enough apart from the crowds to be able to talk. "This trial is a wholesale farrago of justice," said Mr. Boss. "Not that I care much for justice, one way or the other. But even so. Your offer of defense, Brrr, hasn't amounted to much. She's dead meat, our little Giddy Girl Gale. Cooked and sliced and served on a party platter."

"I think so too," said Little Daffy. "Which is why I think we need to be ready to liberate her if things get ugly."

"I doubt they could get any uglier," said the Lion. The mob would have no trouble wrestling Dorothy up on the scaffold, but they'd never get his big neck in a noose. They'd think of something else for him. The mind went white-blank, and he didn't speak for a moment for fear a tremble in his voice would betray him. "Do you have something in mind?"

"Just be on your toes. I mean that literally."

Hardly fifteen minutes into the break, a bell began to ring, and the crowd surged to reassemble at Neale House. But the doors to the hall remained closed. The crowd murmured, and Brrr picked up a frisson of something different. Funny how news has a vibration in the air all its own. Something had happened. Something was happening. He shouldn't have been surprised to see, when the door finally did open, that it wasn't Nipp who emerged from the formal entrance but La Mombey herself.

The crowd broke into a cheer, rousing at first but subduing at the expression of their Eminence. A tall and striking woman, in this light she appeared more silvery blond and mature. Not unlike, Brrr thought, Dobbius's portraits of the Kanraki, those mythical spirits of the ravines of Mount Runcible. He half expected La Mombey to open her painted lips and lead them in a reprise of the Munchkinlander anthem.

Mr. Boss must have been imagining the same. Sotto voce, he began to warble a few lines.

" 'Munchkinland, its truncheon lands on all who dare drop by . . .' "

"Shhh," said his wife.

"Gentle patriots," La Mombey addressed them. "Lord Nipp will call the proceedings to order momentarily.

I beg your leave to address you on a matter of urgency in the meanwhile. It is my sad duty to tell you that our investigators have learned of disturbing developments. Word has come to the committees at Colwen Grounds that a new offensive against Munchkinland is soon to be launched. Not from the Scalps, where our noble Glikkun friends are holding the mountain passes as only they could do. Nor from Restwater, at least not that we can glean. No, the Emerald City is said to be commissioning new battalions to make skirmishes across the slopes of the Madeleines in Gillikin into the Wend Fallows of Munchkinland. The Wend Fallows are scrubby and inhospitable marches, but there is little in the terrain that could slow an army determined to cross it. Put frankly, our spies conclude that the aim of the Emerald City, after these several years of stalemate, is to up the ante. The enemy intends to press for a full surrender of the government at Colwen Grounds and Bright Lettins by engaging us on a second front."

She raised a staff and a surge of gluey white light pulsed from it. Brrr had forgotten that La Mombey was a sorceress of sorts. He could detect no evidence that a charm had been cast, except the charm of pyrotechnic dazzle, but the crowd oohed and ahhed, and people in the back began to applaud. "We will not let this happen," she said more fiercely. "In the defense of our homeland, today I declare a conscription of all Animals who originate outside our borders, including those born here whose parents or grandparents emigrated from Loyal Oz during the Animal Adverse laws. We gave you and your families succor when times were hard on you; we know you will stand with us and defend us when times are hard on us. Consequently, since yesterday I have secured the bridges and gates of Bright Lettins with a spell to help you Animals avoid the temptation to flee your duties. Links of lightning, I suppose, designed to deter any deserters. A little aversion therapy, we could call it. Following the close of this trial, Neale House will become the center for enlistment and assignment for the Animal Army of Munchkinland. May I suggest that mothers and their young among us right now be impounded for release until their husbands and fathers and mates come to ransom them. Since so many eligible male Animals seem to have had prior engagements today. For their valor in service, let us chant, hoorah!"

"Hoorah," shouted everyone except the Animals.

Brrr said, "What's the word for the tendency to be in the wrong place at the wrong time, all the time?"

"Fate's foolery," said Mr. Boss cheerily enough. "Give me one of those biscuits, wife. A surge in war fever always makes me peckish."

He fished in the basket and came up with two confections and a piece of paper. " 'Dorothy, take these two,' " he read. "Oh, don't tell me, you poisoned the others? I don't think I'm hungry anymore." He put them back.

"Nonsense, don't be silly," she said but could explain no further, as La Mombey had swooped away and the doors to the hall were opening.

When the crowd was reassembled in the broad chamber, quieter than ever, Lord Nipp emerged, and then the barristers. The Owl looked terrified. No wonder. However the verdict went, Temper Bailey would probably end up in an Animal line of defense trying to hold the Wend Fallows. Me too, if I'm not careful, Brrr thought.

The trapdoor opened and Dorothy began to climb up, but nerves, it seemed, were finally getting to her. She paused on the ladder, half into the hall, and swayed. Maybe she'd caught sight of the scaffold out the windows at the rear of the room. The Chimpanzees hurried forward and put a gloved hand under each of her armpits and more or less hauled her out. "Oh, my," she said. "I sure hope it's not my time of the month."

"Nothing good ever happens to that girl," said Mr. Boss.

"The judgment is called forth," said Lord Nipp, and the jury proceeded into the room. The foreman handed a twist of paper to the magistrate. Then followed a bit of symbolism derived from older systems of jurisprudence in Munchkinland, Brrr guessed. Lord Nipp put the paper inside one half of an empty, hinged wooden ball and clapped the ball closed to make a full sphere. The judgment of Dorothy was imprisoned inside it. Next Nipp withdrew from under his table a round cage of metal bars, like a birdcage, that spun on a central axis. Through a hinged door he popped the wooden ball, and then latched the door and spun the cage.

"Oh don't, it makes me dizzy," said Dorothy. "And Lord knows I'm dizzy enough already."

"You're telling me," whispered Mr. Boss.

"It reminds me of falling in the elevator, down in the dark, spinning around and about," said Dorothy. She put her hands out as if to steady herself. The crowd in the hall began to murmur a low note, holding the drone throughout the building and beyond it. The ball clacked against the bars of the cage, making erratic syncopation against the dark hummed note. "I don't feel quite myself," said Dorothy. "But then I think that's customary in Oz."

The rotating cage slowed down and stopped. Lord Nipp opened the door and removed the ball. "Let justice be served," he said. Then he unscrewed the two halves of the ball and took out the verdict. There's no element of chance to this gesture, thought Brrr. In an older time perhaps more than a single ball danced and battered against others. But time eliminates alternatives until there's only one eventuality, sooner or later.

Maybe that was the point.

"The opinion of the jury," said Lord Nipp, glancing up from the folded paper, "accords with my own. I have no need to amend it. The court of Bright Lettins finds the miscreant Dorothy Gale guilty of all charges. The magistrate of this court concurs. She shall be put to death to defend the honor of Munchkinland."

Dorothy swooned and nearly fell into the open trapdoor. Little Daffy was on her feet and at Dorothy's side before anyone else could move. "I'm an apothecaire, and I was Matron's Assistant at the Respite of Incurables in the EC. Before the troubles," she added. She felt Dorothy's pulse and put her hand on Dorothy's head. "Wouldn't it be just our luck if the murderess dies of a heart attack before she can be put to death? Just like what was suggested of Nessarose Thropp. Ironical in the extreme." To the Chimpanzees who had rushed forward to help, Little Daffy barked, "Move aside, Monkey boys, she needs air if she's to survive long enough to be killed."

"Clear the front of the room," cried Nipp. Temper Bailey obliged by flying through the open window.

Little Daffy motioned to Brrr to approach. "We're losing her. Quick, quick. Mr. Boss, Lord Nipp—Dame Fegg! In the name of justice! Air at once. I've left my apothecaire's satchel with my colleague just below the scaffold. We must get her on the Lion's back; he can rush her there." The magistrate and the barrister helped drape the insensate defendant on Brrr's back.

Little Daffy slapped her husband's rump and said, "Up, you too," and Mr. Boss scrambled right onto Dorothy's spine, his bowlegs splayed out on either side of her, clamping her in place. "To make sure she doesn't fall," said Little Daffy. "A hand up, please. Your Lordship, arrange that a vial of smelling salts be brought to the scaffold. It's of utmost urgency. If we're not careful, she just might slip away from us."

Then, to Brrr, "Off, you," and pointed her finger. Finally Brrr understood her scheme. He hoped he wasn't too old to clear the windowsill, and in fact he scraped his loins rather badly in the effort. He emitted more of a yowl than a roar. The Munchkins in the alley scattered in terror as Brrr, Little Daffy, Mr. Boss, and the unconscious captive bolted into their midst. His heart pounding, Brrr tossed Munchkins aside like ninepins, and passed the scaffold, its ligature looped to a peg and swaying in the force of his rush. He careered around the edge of the crowd. Whatever shocking charm La Mombey might have set upon the bridge across the Munchkin River, to keep Animals from leaving before conscription, he would push through it. The charm couldn't hurt half as much as his scraped underside already hurt. So what if links of lightning might neuter him: execution by firing squad would accomplish the same thing.

The plunge through rings of blue lightning was like being raked by sticks of fire on all inches of his body. It singed his whiskers and softened his claws, and the dewclaws dropped out and never grew back. The sizzle did give a measure of extra bounce to the curl of his mane, he could feel it through the torment. He'd make a prettier corpse in a moment or two.

Little Daffy and Mr. Boss seemed unfazed by the charmed barrier. They sat like human clamps upon their human saddle, who had not been revived by the scorching light.

Four or five miles beyond the city limits, on the west side of the Munchkin River, the Lion paused under a stand of quoxwood trees. Dorothy fell with a heavy clump off his back. "Is she dead?" he asked.

"No," said Little Daffy. "But I don't expect the effects of my poppified pastries to wear off for a few hours."

By the time Dorothy began to come around, they were a dozen miles north of Bright Lettins. Village lights to one side and another suggested happy settlements, but the Dorothy Gale Rescue Brigade hunkered down in a cart shed aside a field of lettuces. They ate the rest of the pastries and quite a bit of lettuce, and drank from a bottle of plonk that a farmer had hidden inexpertly beneath some burlap sacking.

"I hate your new hairdo," said Mr. Boss to Brrr. "Makes you look more dandified than ever. Hey, how did it feel to bust through that charm? You carried it off like a pro."

"It tickled," said Brrr, "the way being jabbed with red-hot pitchforks soaked in brine tickles." He had never thought to get a compliment from the dwarf. It was almost worth the unending agony under his pelt, as if he'd survived an attempt at the skinning of his hide. Taxidermy while you wait.

Dorothy began to stir. Her first intelligible words were, "Now that we're alone, I can ask. Where is Liir?"

"Hidden in the outback somewhere," said Brrr. "With wife and child."

"I must still be hallucinating. Wife?"

"He's older than you," said the Lion. "Remember that."

"So am I, now," said Dorothy, dizzily. But a bit of prairie reserve crept into the pitch of her voice and the upward jerk of her spine. "Why did you rescue me?" she continued, when whatever passed for coherence in her had returned.

"I did it because I don't like bullies," said Brrr, "and they were bullies to their boots, everyone except Temper Bailey."

"I did it because I don't think you're guilty," said Little Daffy. "I *was* there in Center Munch, no lie, and I was about the age you are now. I *do* remember your arrival. Everyone hated Nessarose. It was liberation. You were a Hero of the Nation. It's political expediency to name you a villain now. Bald opportunism. You were being brought down only to drum up a patriotic fervor just before the Eminence announced another front is about to open in the war. Which means it isn't going all that well for Munchkinland, I should guess. Really, do they think we are *morons?*"

"Evidently, the answer is yes," said the Lion. "And you know, of course, their tactic will work just fine. They'll find a way to make Dorothy's escape from execution play into their war fever somehow."

"As for me," said Mr. Boss, "why did I help? Well, I hardly knew what we were doing until we did it. But in a deeper sense, why did I come to Bright Lettins at all?

Because I wondered if your return to Oz was caused by the collapse of the Clock of the Time Dragon."

They all looked at him as if his thinking had, perhaps, collapsed.

"You two remember," he said to the Lion and the Munchkinlander. "Rain suggested it. Liir's child," he explained to Dorothy. "One of the last things the Clock showed us was an earthquake. After it fell down that slope near the Sleeve of Ghastille. Near as I can tell, that happened just about the same time as the earthquake in the Scalps. Maybe the Clock's insidious magic brought Dorothy back, against her will."

"Are you showing solidarity with something besides the Clock?" asked Little Daffy. "Senility hits at last."

The dwarf grunted. "Least we could do is stand by her, since she never bought the ticket to come."

"And I have no return ticket," added Dorothy. "I don't suppose there are any more of those pastries left? They leave a kick, but my, they are tasty."

V

At St. Prowd's

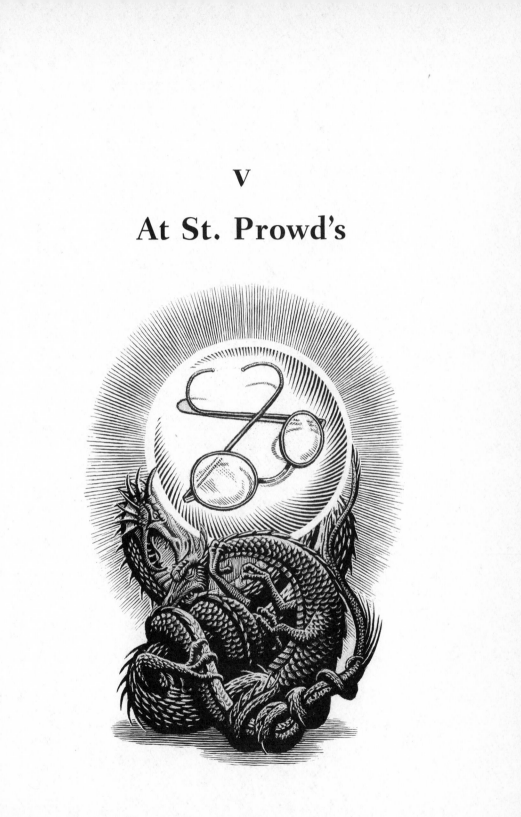

1.

Rain didn't count the days or the hours in a day.
She didn't count the items in the collections she
made, neither of pinecones nor grey stones. Feathers
ranging from the length of a human fingernail to that
of a folded umbrella, in colors from pale white to coal
and all the stations between. Animal bones—antlers, a
bat wing, a femur someone had whittled partway into a
flute and then abandoned. It was strange and triangular on one end and no one could identify the creature it
must have come from.

She cataloged clouds but didn't count the varieties;
she noticed separate weathers but didn't tally up the
sorts. She gathered a bevy of small lake seashells like
babies of her precious large one, or like its toys. The tin
cup of arrowheads was her favorite. She knew each one

by heft and design, by adze stroke and lichen stain. She didn't know how many she had.

She didn't look as closely at family matters. The incidents, the backgrounds, the causes-and-consequences, the self-delusions presented as potted biographies. To the extent she was aware of them—her relatives— they seemed like bundled, ambulatory atmospheres. But she'd picked up the art of pretending to listen. It seemed to calm them all down, and who knows, maybe she learned something. She didn't count the lessons, if there were any.

In two years the family had managed, among them, to build a little home. It had been hard going at the outset. Not much more than a lean-to dug into the side of a hill. More cave than cottage. When they'd survived the first winter, Nor had made her way overland to the nearest settlement—some two weeks away by foot—and come back to Nether How with a sack of square-head nails. Useful enough, but since the art of construction wasn't one of Liir's strengths, everyone was grateful for the help of a trio of hunters heading west to hunt skark. They'd stopped to water their horses at Five Lakes, and by the time they'd left ten days later, they had framed up a tidy cottage on the stone foundation Liir had been carting into place for a year. It remained only for him to finish it. He got the roof shingled just in time, though that second winter the house had to double as a shed. (Candle had managed to befriend a goat and some wild chickens.) He and Nor worked all winter fitting the floor and walls with planking while Candle foraged in the woods for edible roots and bark and for seedpods to begin a lakeland farm.

"What does it take to grow a farm?" Liir asked his wife once. An old joke.

"A family," she'd answered. Not so funny, but true. They all worked, husband and wife and sister and, to the extent they could get her attention, daughter.

In the luff of the Great Kells, which loomed over them to the west, the winter was warmer than they'd expected. Snow, to be sure, but many of the storms seemed to slide overhead, holding their worst until they'd moved farther east. Or maybe the site itself was magical. Long ago on a solitary trek Liir had discovered the isolated district he called Five Lakes. He'd had a certain vision right here, on the hummock of land where he'd now built their home. He told Candle and Nor about it one winter evening, after Rain had settled down.

That's what they did, to see their way through the winters: tell their lives, as honestly as they could. Rain heard these tales as she heard the fire crackle. Pretty sounds, but no way to assemble them.

"It's hard to remember for sure," said her father through his patchy, unconvincing beard. "Maybe I've filled in parts of it to make more sense. But what I remember—what I think I remember—is that as I was lying on the ground in a spasm of regret, I seemed to detach from myself, to float above my restless body. I could see myself below, half awake, turning and tossing. I became aware of a movement on the side of the hill, not far from this home, though I don't know where precisely. I saw an old man forming ghostily in the uprights of autumn saplings. He was stumbling in from somewhere, like a figure in fog taking definition as he neared. Or like the way a poaching egg goes from translucent to solid. He seemed lost, but not in that frantic manner of the very old. Just unsure of his location. He peered at the water with interest, and around at the land. But though he emerged from nowhere in a magical way, he didn't see me, either on the ground or in the air. As he filled in, I saw he had in his arms a big book. Maybe it was the Grimmerie, but I suppose there are other big books in Oz. He nodded, as if approving where he'd washed up, and turned to the north."

"I've always believed you can see the past," said Candle. "I think he couldn't notice you because you weren't there yet. What you saw had happened much earlier."

Nor grunted. "I remember hearing my mother and Elphaba talking about where the Grimmerie came from. My mother said that one day an old man had come to the door of Kiamo Ko, long before Elphaba arrived, before I was born probably, and taken a bite to eat. He said the book was a great weight to carry, and with Sarima's permission he would leave it behind. It would be collected in time. My mother put it in some attic where Auntie Witch found it years later."

Liir replied, "That weird apprehension of witnessing something past has only come over me once or twice, and a good thing too. I don't miss it."

"If we live long enough," said his half-sister, "we all end up seeing the past. That's all we can see."

"I can see the present," said Candle. Perhaps her skill was related to women's intuition, but of a steelier sort. Tonight her understanding was humble. "I can see that somebody's little girl is only feigning sleep. She's listening to every word we say."

In two years and some, Candle had learned how to be a mother. A mother to a reckless, feckless, one-off of a child—but what child isn't?

Listening wasn't quite what Rain was doing, but hearing—letting the sounds trickle by—well, yes.

Caught out, she sat up in her trundle cot that, day-times, slid under her parents' higher bedstead. "I can't sleep tonight."

"Too much talk of magic," said Nor.

"Tell me about the time you flew Elphaba's broom-stick," said Rain. She had noticed that grown-ups liked to be asked to speak.

"Pfaah, magic, a set of poison hopes," said Nor.

Candle said, "No more talk about magic. You need your sleep, Rain. We're going to try to rush another wild sheep into the fold tomorrow, spancel it and dock its tail, and you make the best sheepdog I have. Come now. Lay down." But Rain wheedled and whined until the grown-ups relented. The next telling was Nor's.

"I was about your age, Rain," said Nor, "and living at Kiamo Ko, a castle way north of here. Elphaba had come to live with us already, along with your father, who was younger than I."

"I still am," said Liir.

"I suppose Elphaba must have arrived at Kiamo Ko with that broom, but I don't know if she understood its powers. I had taken it out to a barn to clean up after our guests, and I felt it twitch in my hands, to pulse with life. Like a garter snake when you grab it, but not wriggly. It's hard to explain. I decided to ride it like a hobbyhorse, but when I threw my leg over it, it rose in the air."

Rain's eye was cool and flat but her face was bright. "Don't glamourize danger," said Liir. "I've ridden it in my time, too, Rain, and it's no carnival ride of carved wooden stallions accompanied by tinny music. I was attacked on the broom by flying dragons and I nearly lost my life."

But the attack had brought him to the ministrations of Candle, and *that* had brought Rain into the world, into their lives, so he stopped complaining.

"I want to fly," said Rain. "I want to fly, and to see."

"You touch that broom without permission, you'll get a walloping you never knew I was capable of," said Liir.

"And I'll thwack you too," said Candle, who was so tenderhearted she didn't set traps for the field mice that ravaged her seed stock.

They all looked overhead; they couldn't help it. In the apex of the ceiling, above the loft, Liir had closed in a triangular space by hammering up a ceiling three boards wide. He had boxed in the broom. If you didn't know it was there you would never guess. As for the Grimmerie, he had planned to encase it in fieldstone next to the chimney stack, adjacent the bread oven. But worries about having to flee suddenly, leaving it where it might be found, had scuttled that strategy. Thus, the Grimmerie was wrapped in an old army satchel of Liir's and kept on top of the dish cupboard. Ready to go at a moment's notice. Everyone was forbidden to touch it.

2.

So of course Rain wanted to get the Grimmerie. Any number of times she pulled over a stool and settled her hands on the dark blue canvas sacking. But it wasn't worrying about punishment from her parents that stopped her. Their cautions didn't figure. It was the memory of what had happened with the dragons on the lake. *To Call Winter upon Water.* And that was merely one page. What good might be done through the agency of a single powerful page? What good, and what evil?

She wasn't afraid of doing good or of resisting evil. She was merely afraid she might not be able to tell the difference.

Still, how it called her! If Candle could sometimes tell the present, if Liir had once or twice been able to tell the past, Rain felt she could tell the hunger of the Grimmerie. A hunger to be read. The book had an active desire to be cracked open and have its messages delivered. The furnace's lust for tinder.

They rarely left her alone in the cottage, those adults. *Her* people? She found the concept hard to take in. At any rate, the next group of people. More people to add to her collection of people. It seemed she would rotate through an endless set of temporary arrangements. She hadn't forgotten the Lion, the dwarf, and the Munchkinlander herbalist lady. Or Murthy and Puggles and other warm cloudy presences without names, those who had lived belowstairs with her at Mockbeggar Hall and taken care of her scrapes and ailments.

Back then she had run about like a chipmunk, unnoticed unless she was about to trespass on some formal affair of Lady Glinda's, in which case she'd be boxed about the ears or distracted with a boiled sweet. Here at Nether How, this scrappily forested hill hummocked up between two isolated mountain lakes, she was always under someone's watchful eye. If the three adults had to go off somewhere, either Oziandra Rain had to traipse along or she was left under the care of Iskinaary.

"They love you because you belong to them," he hissed at her once. "They can't help it. But I think you're trouble heating up on a slow flame. I've got my eye on you."

"I never done nothing to you," she replied, dropping the stone in her palm.

Sheep, companionable enough, roamed their neighborhood, keeping the ground cover cropped. Once a
year the three adults managed to shear a few of them.
How best to prepare the wool? There were tricks to it
some traveler would eventually share, but in the meantime the family kept warm enough. None of them ate
meat as a first choice, but if a lamb was found with a
broken neck and it couldn't thrive, they killed it out of
mercy and Candle thanked some deity or other for its
spirit and its chops. Liir and Nor wouldn't join in the
prayer. And Iskinaary refused to come to table if there
was flesh upon it.

"One day I'll break my neck, and then you'll have a
conundrum on your hands," he told them.

"Not such a hard choice," said Rain. "Chestnut
stuffing or bread?"

"And to think your grandmother was a celebrated
activist in defense of Animals. You should be ashamed
of yourself."

The lake was mad with fish, so they ate fish, which
Tay caught for them. They sometimes discussed
whether there was any such thing as a Fish, an opinionated cousin of the presumably nonsentient variety.
Iskinaary, who liked fish as much as he disliked flesh,
agreed to put his head under the water and try to speak
to them. But there was no reason to suspect that Fish

would speak the same language as air-breathing creatures. Since he could never manage to start a reasonable conversation among equals, the Goose always gave up and allowed himself a snack.

Still fascinated by letters and words, Rain had begun to work out languages in Oz. She collected languages, the idea of them anyway. There seemed to be a primary tongue that she had spoken since birth. For lack of another term it was called Ozish, though to a child it seemed effortless as breathing. But there were other languages. Qua'ati, of course, which she'd picked up in Qhoyre—Candle spoke it well, and Liir, haltingly. And variations of birdsong that Iskinaary seemed capable of using. Rain couldn't tell if the language was universal among the airborne or specific to certain species, Goose subtly different from Duck or Swallow. But she was too proud to ask Iskinaary.

Nor told her that the Arjikis had a language of their own, though it shared a grammar with Ozish. The Scrow and the Ugubezi and Yunamata each had different language systems. The trolls in the Glikkus spoke a dialect of Ozish that sounded like sneezing, and who knows what tribes in the unexplored far west of Oz might be able to demonstrate yet more cryptic tongues? Rain's aunt had heard that an isolated clan of Draffe people lived near Kvon Altar in the arid southwest of the Vinkus. "Draffe people? Part Draffe, part human?" wondered Rain, but Nor told her there had been no successful interspecies mating as far as she knew, and the term *Draffe* probably just meant the people were gangly and thin, the way Munchkinlanders were squat and short.

Still, Rain began to wonder about Nor and Brrr. A woman and a Lion. If they ever reunited, would they have children? Could the Grimmerie make it possible? Rain might get a kind of cousin who was part human girl and part Lion cub boy. She couldn't quite see how it would work out, but she hoped it could happen. The Lion part might eat Iskinaary by accident. That would be fun.

"I know what you're thinking," said the Goose.

"You do not."

He craned his neck and trained one beady eye at her. She tried not to rear backward. "Well, you're right," he admitted, "but I know it isn't nice."

"It's nice to me," she told him.

Then, toward the end of the third summer at Nether How, a trapper came through, an isolated Scrow who had been drummed out of his clan for some unmentioned reason. Maybe for being antisocial. Rain collected him; he was her first Scrow. His name was Agroya. He stayed a few days and helped the grown-ups shore up a terrace wall behind which Candle was trying to establish a stand of mountain rice. In halting phrases he brought news of the world beyond Nether How.

3.

Rain didn't count years any more than days. She hardly knew how to understand Agroya when he said it was now the fourth year into the war between Loyal Oz and Munchkinland.

He told them about the conscription of Animals in Munchkinland and how the second front of the war—the battle of the Madeleines—was faring. (Not well for either army, a tidal sweeping of forces back and forth, with heavy loss of life on both sides.) Nor flinched at this and wondered if her husband might have been drafted to serve in the Munchkinland army.

"Brrr? Hah. He'll have slipped through *that* duty," said Liir consolingly. "They didn't call him the Cowardly Lion for nothing."

Nor didn't speak to Liir for some time after this. Maybe, thought Liir ruefully, his half-sister had never entirely forgiven him—or his mother—for sweeping into the lives of her parents, unsettling everything, forever.

"How do you know so much about the progress of the war?" Candle asked Agroya. "Out in this wilderness, so far from the battle lines?"

In his halting way he replied, "I possess little else to pay for the goods of your table. I carry news in my mind. I traffic in it. A useful coin."

"Tell us more, then," said Liir. "What about Lady Glinda?"

But Agroya had never heard of Glinda, which made everything else he said a little suspect. "I don't go to cities," he admitted. "Tribal life among the Scrow is life in grasslands. Moving, camping, moving, always. Following the herds."

"Is Shem Ottokos still the chieftain of the Scrow?" asked Liir.

Agroya spat but admitted as much. Ottokos must have been the one to exile him, Liir guessed. Then Liir regretted having asked the question, because Agroya turned and squinted at him. "So you're Liir? The one who helped our queen through her final passage?"

Liir sat ramrod straight, unwilling to confirm his identity, and Candle picked up on his hesitation, but Agroya saw through their silence. He said, "I was in disgrace that time, in chains in a tent, but I heard what you did."

"I never did," interjected Nor. "This is news to me. Tell me."

"Princess Nastoya was stuck between life and death, unable to move because of a disguise locked upon her, and together you two brought the disguise off." Agroya pointed at Candle. "You played some stringed instrument so well you make dead relics to sing, and you"—now he pointed to Liir—"you had a charm of remembering; you helped our Nastoya leave behind her disguise as a human, and die as an Elephant. This is legend with our people."

"How droll," said Nor to their guest. Ever leery of pomposity. "I hope you sell little pictures of it to passing travelers."

"And she talked to you before she died," said Agroya to Candle.

"Oh, did she?" said Liir to his wife. He'd been away up until the last moment. "You never mentioned this."

"She awakened, as the dying sometimes do," the visitor reminded Candle. "She told you about your child."

Candle, apologetically: "I was pregnant, very pregnant."

After sending Rain out on a fool's errand, and Iskinaary to keep her at bay, Liir returned to the subject. "What did Nastoya say?"

Agroya helped himself to a handful of walnut meats. "She said that she saw the promise and trouble your child will bring."

"Oh, that," said Candle. "What child isn't full of promise and trouble?"

"Our princess said that we Scrow will watch for your child and help her if she needs help. Nastoya pledged us to this."

"Wasn't that sweet," said Candle. "And then she died."

"I'm no longer a full brother to my tribe," he continued, "but in honor of my ancestors and my former queen, I must ask if your daughter needs the help we promised to give."

"Oh, not today, thanks," said Candle. "How kind of you to remember."

The fluting formality of her voice made sense to Liir: Candle had become wary. She'd seen the danger too. "Let me get you some cakes to take on your way," he said.

They loaded Agroya up with as much as they could spare. Nor agreed to escort him well beyond the northern lake. As soon as they were gone, Liir asked Iskinaary to rush Rain away to the southern lake, five hundred yards to the south, ostensibly to find owl pellets to add to her collection.

Then Liir rounded on Candle, but good. He was incensed that Princess Nastoya's dying comments had never come up before. Candle pooh-poohed his sensitivity. "What did her comments mean anyway?

Nothing that any dying old matron wouldn't say to any pregnant young woman."

"The trouble that Rain would bring—did Nastoya's mention of that decide you to leave Rain behind when you slipped away from Apple Press Farm?"

At this Candle turned pale—in a Quadling it looked like fever—and she was unable to speak for some moments. When she regained her voice, she spoke in an unfamiliar register. Colder, acerbic. She said, "This isn't about Rain, at its heart. Is it? You're not even angry about what Nastoya said or not, or whether I told you before. Are you. Are you. You're still angry about what I've never said about Trism."

"Wide of the mark," snapped Liir. But damn her, she was right. So Candle could still see the present. Her talent had seemed submerged as they'd gotten older.

Yes, he was cross about her never having mentioned Nastoya's dying comments. But Candle was accurate that he was still harboring a wound about his old friend and lover, Trism. Another of the stories they didn't rehearse in front of Rain.

Oh, Trism.

And it happened, all of an instant, in his mind again. Like seeing the past. This time his own.

Trism had come to Apple Press Farm that same dreadful season, while Liir was away, while Nastoya was in the orchard trying to die, while Candle was readying to give birth. Liir had never found out exactly what happened. Hunted by EC soldiers who'd once been colleagues, beautiful Trism had either taunted Candle with the knowledge of Liir's affection for him or, just as possibly, fallen for Candle in Liir's absence.

Maybe their mutual passion for Liir, their mutual worry about his safety, had brought Candle and Trism together. It wouldn't be the first time such a thing had happened. But Candle had never spoken about it, and Trism had disappeared from Liir's life.

By the time Liir had returned, to find the ailing Princess Nastoya and a contingent of Scrow in residence at Apple Press Farm, Trism was gone. After Liir and Candle had helped Nastoya shuck her disguise as a human being and die as an Elephant, Liir had accompanied her corpse back over the highland route known as Kumbricia's Pass. Returning only a few days later, he'd found that Candle had fled. The new baby, hardly a day old, lay wrapped up in cloths and hidden for him to find.

Of course Candle knew he was nearing; she knew that kind of thing. She'd left a goat so he could have milk for the child. He'd always assumed that she'd abandoned the child for fear that Trism might have been trailed by assassins in order to discover Liir's hideaway. But now he wondered if she left infant Rain because Nastoya had said their daughter would bring promise and trouble. Candle's apprehension of their daughter had always been different from his. Just as loving, but more stony and matter-of-fact.

He knew what happened next. Eventually she'd made her way back to the mauntery. Word had arrived there that Trism had been beaten—well, tortured was the uglier but more honest word. Presumably Trism hadn't been able to reveal Liir's whereabouts because he didn't know them. And whether Trism, the top dragon mesmerist in the arsenal of the Emerald City, had even survived . . . there was no way to tell.

What *had* survived—maybe all that had survived of Trism—was Liir's sense of him. A catalog of impressions that arose from time to time, unbidden and often upsetting. From the sandy smell of his sandy hair to the locked grip of his muscles as they had wrestled in sensuous aggression—unwelcome nostalgia. Trism lived in Liir's heart like a full suit of clothes in a wardrobe, dress habillards maybe, hollow and real at once. The involuntary memory of the best of Trism's glinting virtues sometimes kicked up unquietable spasms of longing. To this day Liir had endured them in solitude, even as his beloved Candle sat across from him at the hearth.

Candle herself might dream of Trism, too, with dread or with desire. Liir didn't know. She and Liir never talked of it. She'd refused to speak of Trism when Liir, baby in arms, met up with her again. To protect Liir's good impression of his friend?—to keep Trism's romance of Candle to herself? You could go around and around about it, but unless Trism showed up again and filled in the blanks, Liir couldn't know.

Candle wasn't telling.

And Liir and Candle had had more urgent things to deal with than the perils of shifting affections. They had a daughter born green as bottleglass.

Green, and with few obvious virtues. On her mother's side, the girl was a bona fide peasant. Before she met Liir, Candle had been an itinerant Quadling, easily mattressed like all of her clan. Abandoned at the mauntery by an uncle who had wearied of her.

On Liir's side, Rain descended from a line, if not noble, then at least notorious. One of her ancestors had been the Eminent Thropp, de facto governor of Munchkinland before secession. Her grandmother had been the divisive Wicked Witch of the West, no less. Who knew what license or limitation descended through that bloodline?

Liir had no reason to lord it over Candle, or anyone else. He knew himself to be anything but polished.

He'd grown up without the attention of Elphaba or, most of the time, her affection. *Deprived childhood, Your Honor!* He hadn't made things better for himself by going AWOL from the army under the command of Cherrystone. Another bad career move: he'd helped Trism destroy the EC's stable of flying dragons being used to foment unrest among tribes in the west. *Tally it up for us, my good man:* at the time of Rain's birth, Liir'd been no more than a ragamuffin ne'er-do-well being hunted down in case he might lead them to the Grimmerie.

Under these circumstances, to be presented with an iridescently verdant child even harder to hide than the famous and dangerous tome . . . what a lot of laughs, this life. *I beg your mercy.*

By the time he'd caught up with Candle again, after a series of misadventures with the Scrow, the infant was almost too big to carry in his arms. For Rain's own protection, he'd drawn a hood upon her face and told passersby that she was afflicted with a sensitivity to light. What had this done to a child, for all those months to hear through burlap the sounds of human voices but rarely to see the face of anyone but her worried and stupid father?

What had he done to Rain, in order to preserve her life?

After he'd met up again with Candle at the mauntery, they wandered the landscape. Seeking a way to keep Rain from being smothered, literally and metaphorically. They had no plans, just kept moving.

One day, in some nameless hamlet, they'd stopped to barter for bread and milk and wine in return for doing fieldwork till sunset. On the far side of a sullen patch of finger potatoes, Candle straightened with her hand on her lower back and turned around with a cry. Set in a potato basket at the end of a hoed row, the baby was sitting up. Either she'd clawed her burlap caul off by herself or the fox at basket's edge had pulled it away with its teeth.

"Easy," said Liir to Candle, "easy. I haven't known foxes to be vicious."

"Clearly," remarked the Fox, training his eyes on the green child, "you haven't taken into account what recreational foxhunting by hounds and human brutes does to a Fox's native sense of cordiality."

"The light, please, it hurts her eyes," began Liir.

"The dark hurts her far more." The Fox sat down to look at the child, and the child looked back unblinkingly. Liir and Candle inched forward, gripping each other's hands. "I never met that green firebrand out in the west, that one with the broom, but I heard tell of her. And I imagine she looked like this."

"I suspect so," said Candle, honestly enough. "I never met her either."

"Your kit will have fights on her hands," said the Fox. "I suppose you're suitably traumatized over that."

"Oh, very," said Liir, "and then some."

The Fox laughed. "I like her. She doesn't seem afraid of me."

"She's seen very few creatures other than us," said Candle.

"And I thought it was my native charm. Some consider me rather good-looking, but I'll leave my social life out of it. She might benefit from a little protective coloring. Have you thought of that?"

Liir had, but Shem Ottokos of the Scrow hadn't managed the job.

"You know what I mean? The green frog in the algae, the striped chipmunk upon the striped stone? But put a green frog in the middle of a snowy meadow and you don't have a green frog for very long. I'm thinking you'll want to afford this child a little protection."

"We'd be less than sensible if we didn't," said Liir.

The Fox sat for a long time without speaking. His eyes and the eyes of the girl—almost a toddler now, had they let her toddle—didn't break their hold. Finally the Fox said, "I believe I can offer advice."

"What do you have in mind?" asked Candle.

"Though you're correct that while she's a child she needs the most protection, in your panic you're just about killing her. Daily. Now, I happen to know a Serpent with a talent for sorcery. I've seen him do wonders with a poor albino hedgehog who begged abjectly enough. . . ."

Liir and Candle walked a few steps away to discuss the proposal while the Fox kept a watch on Rain. The idea of a Serpent seemed alarming, and the whole concept of disguise could get dicey when it backfired—hadn't they seen Princess Nastoya struggle at trying to shuck her disguise off? But the child was suffocating in her life, no doubt about that. And anyway, Candle and Liir together had managed to bring the human disguise off Nastoya when the time was right. Liir hadn't inherited any of his mother's talent at sorcery, but he did possess that occasional capacity for deep memory. And Candle could cast a certain charm of knowing with the practice of her music—she had done it for Liir and for Nastoya alike. So between them, Candle and Liir had the goods to help their child reveal herself when the time was right. Didn't they? No small authority in the matter, being her parents.

So they had the Fox engage the Serpent, and the Serpent came at once.

They began to regret their decision when he arrived, for the Serpent looked menacing to them. But as he himself pointed out, what oily emerald Serpent doesn't seem menacing to human eyes? The very argument for cloaking Rain's green skin.

"I believe in certain laboratories they call it protective chromatization," said the Serpent, each syllable sliding out with an almost slatternly emphasis. "You are wise to consider it, but she'll need more help than camouflage. A very sluggy caterpillar can dress itself up as a butterfly, but that does it little good if the transformation occurs in a glade locked tight with the webs of poisonous spiders."

"All due deference, and so on," Liir said, "we're only asking for the charm, if you care to give it. We'll figure out on our own how to raise her safely."

"Perhaps you're right to resist my counsel. I am among those fathers who sometimes eat the eggs in the nest. I'll restrict myself to the question of disguise and leave you to fail with your daughter on your own schedule."

They discussed for a time where Rain might most safely be brought up. Candle, though paler than some, had the Quadling ruddiness. At best Quadlings were second-class citizens in the Emerald City, when they bothered to try to settle there. Winkies from any tribe were considered barbarians. And Liir, despite his Vinkus father and his green-skinned mother, had skin

color that betrayed Elphaba's Munchkinlander ances-
try, an easily pocked and sunburnt pinky-cream. So
the sheer fact of population figures—Gillikinese and
Munchkinlanders far outnumbering other ethnicities
and races in Oz—meant that the choice for Rain was
clear. If she could be pale, she'd have a wider range of
places to hide without being noticed.

The Fox sat with Liir and Candle in the stifling sun,
as the distance wavered with heat and insects. He reas-
sured them the Serpent was a good sort. A short way
off, under a tree heavy with persimmons, the Serpent
writhed around Rain. Sometimes he rose erect on his
ribs, hissing; sometimes he wreathed around her on the
ground. Still hissing.

When he was done, they saw he'd shed his own skin
too. He was now the color of library paste, like a worm
unused to sunlight. "Call it sympathy," he told them,
when they gaped. "Call it catharsis. When one of us
changes, we are all changed."

And so was Rain changed. An ugly, ordinary, safely
bleached child sleeping in her wraps, unaware of what
had gone on, but comfortable in the nest of crushed
grass and the pulp of overripe fruit through which the
Serpent had slithered.

Neither Fox nor Serpent would take payment, nor
would they tell their names. "She has a future you

don't like, you'd seek us out and sue us," said the Fox. "There are no guarantees so there is no fee. We help because you needed help. The transaction is done."

"I will wrinkle myself back toward green," said the Serpent, "but unless I am mistaken your daughter will find herself set for some time to come. Remember what I said about the butterfly, though, and consider how you can best protect your tadpole. She is still green inside, and if she is related to the Witch they will be looking for her. No child can thrive if it is predestined to be a pariah. I think of this sometimes, consolingly, when I'm about to gobble my own unborn young."

"You could save them yourself," said Candle, a little late. "Why don't you change *their* colors?"

"I see you take my point," he said. "A young serpent, even if she wears a coat done up like wrapping paper at Lurlinemas, can never pass as anything but a serpent."

With that the Fox and the Serpent left them. Three days later, for no good reason, the family was stopped on the road by a drunk and disorderly band of Munchkinlander militants. Released after questioning, Liir and Candle were spooked enough to feel the truth of the Serpent's words. They were all still targets, no matter how disguised. Liir had flown against the Emperor of Oz recently enough to be tagged as an enemy of the state. If he had made it so easily into Munchkinland, so could the Emperor's agents. For the baby's safety, then, because Mockbeggar Hall was not far off, they decided that Liir should approach Lady Glinda and ask her to raise Elphaba's granddaughter until such time as it might be safe for her to emerge.

All this behind them. Family stories never told. The long years of hiding out without their daughter at the abandoned chapel in the hills above the Sleeve of Ghastille. Hoping perhaps the Emperor might be successful at confiscating that bloody Grimmerie and so lift part of the reason for their going to ground. Hoping that Rain was growing up happy and blameless. Learning to live without her, their primary satisfaction being to speculate on her safety.

Then, with Rain's unexpected arrival in the company of the Cowardly Lion, the dwarf and his Munchkinlander mistress, Liir and Candle had taken up the welcome and exhausting job of worrying about their daughter more specifically but not more daily than they'd been doing already. And the resentments that they'd been able to ignore at the birth of their daughter, twelve years ago, began to seem current again. Maybe even to hurt more, this time.

"The promise and trouble your child will bring." Nastoya had said that to Candle, and she'd never told

Liir. About that, about Trism—about herself, deep down. A cold scorch Liir felt in his gut.

In Nether How, now, standing at the table. Unable to sit down. Looking away from Candle to hold from quivering with anger.

As years pass, and the abundance of the future is depleted, the crux of old mistakes and the cost of old choices are ever recalibrated. Resentment, the interest in umbrage derived from being wronged, is computed minute by minute, savagely, however you try to ignore it.

The pall clouded the household like smoke due to a blocked flue.

Liir and Candle didn't quite make up. Some fights between couples don't so much roil to a climax as settle somehow in an unnegotiated standoff. Neither "affable truce" nor "benefit-of-the-doubt stalemate" quite describes it. Liir and Candle kept to their tasks and to their promises, spoken and unspoken, to each other. They doubted that Rain ever noticed the formalizing silence that threatened to codify as policy between them.

Nor and Iskinaary, not ones to make common cause, fell to discussing the change in the household mood.

They weren't privy to the unspoken complaints. But something needed to be done.

Eventually the Goose thought up an idea, and Nor proposed it: they might pack up some bedrolls before the summer came to a close and make the trek partway up the nearest of the Great Kells where they could harvest a stash of wild ruby tomatoes. Dried, they lasted a year, and augmented any cold winter dish with a flavor of summer.

The family set out. It wasn't a successful trip, too cold and blustery for so early in the fall. When they arrived at the trove they found some mountain greedyguts had already ravaged the plot. They came home sore, weary, empty-handed, and quieter than before. Iskinaary and Nor, walking behind, shrugged at each other. Well, we tried.

Rain of course seemed to notice nothing, just kept on. She was collecting acorns and hazelnuts. They rattled in her pockets when she skipped ahead.

The family returned to Nether How at the Five Lakes, to the sentry house, as they called it, because from the front door they could see the nearest northerly lake and from the opposite door they could glimpse the southern one. They found that their home had been ransacked in their absence. They figured Agroya as the culprit. Probably he'd circled back after Nor had said good-bye to him. He'd hung out on one of the hills above the lake, waiting for a day when the lack of smoke from a breakfast fire announced the absence of tenants. Four pewter spoons that Little Daffy and Mr. Boss had given them were missing, and a sack of flour and another of salt. Liir's best skinning knife, and his only razor.

The broom was still incarcerated in the ceiling, they assumed, since they saw no sign of boards having been prised off and replaced. Candle's domingon hung on the wall. Half out of its sack, the Grimmerie lay on the table in full view. It must not have appealed to the thief.

Still, whether or not the Grimmerie had been recognized, someone knew it was there. It could be described for someone else to identify. Someone knew that Rain was there. More had been stolen from them than spoons and a razor, flour and salt.

4.

Why does the day with the brightest blue sky come tagged with a hint of foreboding? Maybe it's only the ordinary knowledge of transience—all comes to dust, to rot, to rust, to the moth. That sort of thing. Or maybe it's that beauty itself is invisible to mortal eyes

unless it's accompanied by some sickly sweet eschato-
logical stink.

The uneasiness they felt after the discovery of the
Grimmerie by some stranger only grew by the day.
Whoever had looked at it may have known what it was
but been scared to take it. Or may have seen something
uncanny in it, and fled. If the thief was Agroya—well,
as he'd told them, he trafficked in news. The word was
out, or would be soon. Too soon.

Iskinaary took it upon himself to do some reconnaissance work. Loyal as he was to Liir, he had a healthy respect for his own neck, too. He didn't want to end up as a
platter of Goose-breast unless there were no alternatives.

He came winging back in the middle of a spectacular
afternoon. Rain was collecting milkweed pods from a
scrap of meadow near the north lake. The women were
cording wool. Liir heard Iskinaary clear his throat in
the southern dooryard, and he came out into the light,
into the aroma of piney resin. Sunlight steeping on
dropped brown needles.

At the Goose's expression, Liir said, "Let me guess.
You saw a bug who had lost a leg in battle, and you
know the end times have arrived."

"Don't make fun of me till you hear what I have to
say," snapped Iskinaary, trying to catch his breath. "All
right then. About ten miles to the south of First Lake,

I came upon a band of trolls—Glikkuns, I suppose—
who had made common cause with an extended family
of tree elves."

Liir raised an eyebrow.

"I know, it sounds preposterous. Neither Glikkuns
nor elves like society other than their own. The Glikkuns are suspicious of all talking Animals and wouldn't
speak to me, but elves chatter inanely. They told me
what they were doing."

"Coming here to rape and pillage, I presume."

"No. And of course I didn't let on there was a home-
stead here. But I heard that some of the trolls are becoming unhappy over the alliance they made with La
Mombey and the Munchkinlanders. They're beginning
to think their ruler, Sakkali Oafish, was hasty, and that
the Glikkus will become a plunderpot of Munchkinland much as Munchkinland felt itself to be a plunderpot of the EC. Ripe for despoiling and primed for
heavy taxation, et cetera. And of course the emeralds
in the Scalps, controlled by the trolls for time out of
mind, would go far toward helping Munchkinland pay
for the armies they've been maintaining. So this breakaway band of trolls wants none of it. They're scouting
out other mining possibilities in the Vinkus."

"I doubt they'll find much here," said Liir, "but
then, a stone looks pretty much like a rock to me.

Maybe we've been harvesting potatoes in fields of gold nuggets, and I never noticed."

"You're missing the point. *Trolls* with *elves*? Listen—"

"I agree, an unlikely alliance. I only ever met one elf, a sort of gibbertyflibbet named Jibbidee. I don't suppose he was among them?"

"I didn't ask for their identification papers. *Will* you listen? The elves said that the second front of the war—the one opened up in the Madeleines—has disturbed their natural habitat. The Animal army of the Munchkinlanders has been particularly destructive. So some of the elves are looking west to see if it's safe to settle around here. They're traveling with the Glikkuns because you can always trust a troll in a fight."

"What's in it for the Glikkuns?"

"Nothing more than food, it seems. The Glikkuns are cow people; if they're not down in their emerald mines they're tending their cattle. They don't know how to make anything to eat except for cheese and curds and yogurt. Foraging in the forest is beyond their ken, and it's what tree elves do best. And all elves love to cook. I'd have thought this was common knowledge."

"I never got any formal schooling," said Liir. "But whether elves are natural gourmands hardly seems something for you to be gabbling about, all out of breath. Do you want some water?"

"I heard a troll addressing one of the elves as I was getting ready to leave. He said a heavy bounty had been put upon the discovery of a certain book of magic lost a few years back but almost certain to be hidden, uncorrupted, somewhere in the outback of Oz. A magic book might extend the variety of their menus. He was only joking, I think, but if marginalized populations like itinerant elves and disaffected Glikkuns know to be on the lookout for a book like the Grimmerie, I would say our recent kindness to that Scrow robber, Agroya, was a mistake."

Liir was inclined to discount anything overheard between Glikkuns and tree elves. Still, he had to agree that the hemorrhaging of public funds due to the cost of this unwinnable war could only revive the fervor to find the Grimmerie. A fervor both parties would share. The book could supply a crucial advantage to whichever side got access to its unparalleled supply of spells. "I hope you don't think we need to pack up and become traveling musicians or something like that," said Liir. "I've come to consider Nether How a blissful place. Relatively speaking."

"You're *not listening,* are you. Your enemies have finally *added it up.* The tree elves and Glikkuns know that the book is expected to be found with a green-skinned girl the age of Rain. The powers that be remember the Conference of the Birds a decade ago, in which you and I both flew, cawing out 'Elphaba lives!' over the Emerald City. Only they don't read it as political theater anymore. They think it was prophecy. Or that's what they say. Maybe when your honey boy Trism was set upon by the Emperor's soldiers, they beat out of him word of the green-skinned daughter."

"He wasn't here when she was born—" began Liir, but stopped. Candle hadn't said when Trism was or wasn't at Apple Press Farm. Maybe Trism had seen little green Rain even before Liir had taken her into his own arms.

"It doesn't matter how they know," said Iskinaary. "It could have been some oracle, it could have been some Wood Thrush squealing in exchange for clemency. What matters is that they've put it together. The conjunction in your household of a twelve-year-old girl and the Grimmerie is, I fear, a dangerous giveway."

"If I could read the book, I might find a spell to make it invisible," said Liir. "But I can't read it."

"Have you let Rain try?"

"I wouldn't dare."

"You don't trust her. Nice father."

"I don't know what damage the book might do to her. I certainly couldn't risk it."

"Well, what do you propose we do?"

Not for the first time, Liir wondered just what he'd done to deserve the Goose's loyalty. Iskinaary could take wing any day he liked. But he lived without family or flock, dogging Liir's years like a retainer. "We'll wait until my sister and my wife wake up, and we'll talk it over with them."

"They won't ask my opinion," said the Goose, "but I'll give it anyway. Birds beware roosting in the same nest for more than a season. It may be time—"

Rain was hurrying around the house, Tay at her heels as usual, so Iskinaary stopped. "You're a whippoor-will in a hurry," said the Goose.

"Some tree elves are bathing down on the shore of the south lake. I haven't seen a tree elf since I lived at Mockbeggar, and then only once, from far off. These ones are singing some song and their voices come over the water like crinkly paper music. Don't you hear it?"

The Goose and the man exchanged glances. Once more needing to be the heavy, the Anvil of the Law, Liir said as mildly as he could, "I don't think you better go there, sweetie."

"Oh, I'll just—"

"He said *no*," snapped the Goose, and dove at the girl's legs. And maybe that's why he stays around, thought Liir. He's willing to provide that bite of discipline I can't manage.

5.

It was summer, they needed no fire. They kept Rain indoors and quiet while the elves were in the neighborhood. "Sort out your collections," said Liir. "No, you can't bring a sack of rocks with you, or a cup of acorns. Take your favorite out of each collection and leave the rest behind. We'll come back and get them another time. Hush your crying. We're trying to draw no attention to ourselves. To keep still, like little mice under the eyes of a hawk."

As far as the family knew, the tree elves and the renegade trolls never did take the measure of the hearthhold at Nether How. But after a full day of discussion and two days of preparation, the family was ready to leave their cottage home.

Heavy hearts, heavy tread, but very light luggage. They took little with them. The broom they would trust to the eaves, but they couldn't leave the book. Maybe they'd come across Mr. Boss and somehow persuade him to take the Grimmerie back. Holding it from all those avaricious and willing readers of magic was taking its toll.

They started their trek on foot. They'd span the Vinkus River and then the Gillikin River before they'd need to say their good-byes.

Crossing the Vinkus looked problematic until they met a boatman. He charged punitively to steer his small vessel across the waters pummeling down from the slopes of the Kells, but he delivered them safely. On the other side, they found that the crescent of land between the Vinkus and the quieter Gillikin River was now under cultivation. Perhaps, Liir guessed, Loyal Oz was trying to make a go of supplying its own needs of wheat, corn, barley. A few grousing laborers disabused Liir of any notion of success, though. The storms that blew high over Nether How settled down here, and the snow came early and stayed deep.

At a crossroads of sorts on this undulating river plain, wagon carts rolling by from six or eight different directions, in and out as if along spokes of a wheel, the family members made their good-byes. Briskly, to the point. In a sense, they all followed Rain's lead, her brusqueness steadying the adults, helping them avoid long faces and soggy remarks.

"You are a child of Oz," said Liir to his daughter. "Your mother is Quadling, your grandmother was a Munchkinlander, and your grandfather from the Vinkus. You can go anywhere in Oz. You can be home anywhere."

Liir turned north toward Kiamo Ko. The Grimmerie was under his arm. Iskinaary hustled like a civil servant self-importantly at his side. Candle—resentful but understanding of their strategy—walked a few steps ahead. Liir could see her try to control the shaking of her shoulders. He thought, Anyone who can be home anywhere really has no home at all.

6.

So, some days later, on an early autumn afternoon of high winds and intermittent squalls, with her aunt Nor at one side lurching under a luggage bundle, and Tay scampering at her heels, Rain came into the Gillikinese city of Shiz.

7.

"Why do you think your child will thrive at St. Prowd's?"

In her time Nor Tigelaar had faced insurrectionists and collaborationists and war profiteers. She'd endured abduction and prison and self-mutilation. She'd sold herself in sex not for cash but for military information that might come in handy to the resistance, and in so doing she'd come across a rum variety of human types. She didn't think, however, she had ever seen anyone like the headmaster or his sister, who both sat before her with hands clasped identically in midair about six inches above their laps. As if they were afraid they might absentmindedly begin a duet of self-abuse in their own receiving chamber.

"I am not a widely traveled woman, Proctor Clapp—"

"Please, call me Gadfry," said the brother. He flickered a smile so weak it might have been a tooth-ache; then his face lapsed into the well-scrubbed prize calabash it most nearly resembled. His wiry hair was squared off in the back like a box hedge.

"Gadfry," said Nor, trying to swallow her distaste. She hoped this school strategy wasn't a mistake. "I have come in from the family home in the mountains to find a place for my girl. Her father died in an earthquake, you see, and I haven't the wits to know how to teach her. We live far afield, out in the Great Kells, but we know St. Prowd's comes with the highest recommendations."

"Well yes naturally, but what makes you think that your little scioness will thrive under our particular scholarly regimen?"

What did he want to hear? "She hasn't had the best preparation, admittedly." Nor worked the edges of her shawl. "In certain families in the western heights, the academic education of girls isn't considered essential, or even useful. But I—that is, my poor husband and I—wanted the best for her."

The sister, Miss Ironish Clapp, unfolded a hand. "St. Prowd's certainly counts itself among the best seminaries, but in this rough climate I'm afraid that the funds to support unprepared scholarship students simply don't exist."

Oh, thought Nor, is that all it takes? "Perhaps I misrepresented our hopes for Miss Rainary. I should have spoken more carefully: my dead husband and I wanted the very best for our daughter that *money could buy.*"

Miss Ironish brought her fingernails in to graze her pink pink palm. Her eyes did not narrow nor her breathing hasten when she said, "And how costs have risen, what with the scarcity of food in wartime."

"I'm sure you can prepare me a bill for the first year that we can settle before I leave," said Nor.

"Of course, Dame Ko," said Gadfry Clapp. "That is my sister's purview. But a child untutored in the basics may take longer to finish our course of studies than someone who has enjoyed a responsible formation. You should budget for a number of years."

"We will scrutinize her for her strengths," said Miss Ironish. "If she has any, that is."

"Oh, she is a powerful enough child, you'll see," said Nor. "Not wilfull," she added. "Nor unpleasant."

"I can't say that she presents well," admitted Miss Ironish. "A St. Prowd's girl is meant to have a certain. Ahem. Flair."

They all turned and looked through the tall narrow windows that divided the proctor's parlor from the waiting room. The oak mullions hung with panes of old green glass seized up with the vertical moraines of age. Beyond them, Rain sat hunched on a chair with her fingers in her mouth. The bow that Nor had purchased from a milliner had the exhausted appearance of a fox that has been run down by hounds.

"We rely on your good offices to perk her up," said Nor.

"But how did you choose St. Prowd's?" asked the proctor. A coquette primping for compliments.

Exhaustively Nor had prepared for this grilling; she was ready. "We considered a few places. The Home for Little Misses in Ticknor Circus seemed promising, but theirs is a horsey set, mostly from the Pertha Hills families. A bit close-minded. The Boxtable Institute seems to be in the grip of a raging ague and a quarantine made an interview out of the question. I realize that Madame

Teastane's Female Academy in the Emerald City comes very highly regarded, but one worries about the safety of a child left in their charges."

"Safety?" Miss Ironish spoke as if it was a word in a foreign tongue, a word she had not come across before.

"Well, so much nearer the front."

"Not that much nearer, as the dragon flies."

"There's near and there is nearer," explained Nor. "Given a chance to attack one of Oz's two great cities, the Munchkinlanders won't hesitate to storm the Emerald City. I couldn't take the chance. I am surprised any parent could."

"Well, we hate to win by default." Miss Ironish, Nor saw, was possessed of that skill of finding a way to take umbrage at any remark whatsoever.

It was time to go on the offense. "I chose St. Prowd's for its traditions of excellence in the rearing of proper young men and women. I thought you might defend its record against your competition. I can examine the alternatives if this is proving a waste of your—"

"Oh, there is no competition, not seriously," said Proctor Gadfry. "We're almost within shouting distance of the great colleges of Shiz—not that our students are inclined to raise their voices in any unseemly display. I am sure you know the history of St. Prowd's. We opened our doors in the third year of the reign of

Ozma the Librarian, as you could guess from the magnificent carvings in the lintel. They were thought to be from the school of Arcavius, but we have documentation on file more or less proving the master did them himself."

Nor hadn't noticed the carvings and she didn't turn to look. "It's a beautiful building in a magnificent setting," she said, indicating the narrow and sunless street on which Founder's Hall fronted.

"Magnus St. Prowd was a unionist theologician whose work paved the way for the famous Debate on the Souls of Animals held at Three Queens College. Uncommonly prosperous for a bishop, he left his home to the causes of education—this was once a bishop's palace—and he endowed the school to serve as a feeder pool for young students of unionism. As the times have become more secular, we've striven to retain as many of the customs of prayer and obedience as seem sensible."

"Though we strive for a jolly nondenominational middle road that occasionally strikes me as lunatic," remarked Miss Ironish, a rare instance, so far, of her appearing to disagree with her brother.

"I'm sure it's difficult to strike the perfect balance between piety and populism, but I'm equally confident you manage it." Nor was eager to get away before Rain did something to disqualify herself.

"Where did *you* train, Dame Ko?" asked Proctor Gadfry.

"You wouldn't have heard of it. A very small local parish school in the Great Kells."

"Ah, the godforsaken lands," said Miss Ironish.

"Not godforsaken, merely godforgotten," said Nor with a pretense at merriment. "But before we settle up, may I enquire about the size and makeup of the student body this year?"

"We began as a school for boys, of course," said the proctor. "We opened to girls during the reign of Ozma the Scarcely Beloved."

Miss Ironish put a gentle fist to her breast. "Kept hermetically distant from one another, of course. The girls lodged in the dormitory, with the boys in the annex above the stables."

"In these sorry times, though," said Proctor Gadfry, "the boys are all called to train for the army. So we've had to make arrangements to house them out of town. In a junior military camp. For drilling in the use of firearms and rapiers and such musical instruments as are required in marching bands."

"The boys are kept *intensely* busy, so the girls here in town no longer mingle, even socially, with the boys in camp. St. Prowd's Military Center, we're calling it, though we don't know if this is a permanent arrangement or if we will contract after the war is over."

"Because I know mothers worry, I find it consoling, these days, that no boys are housed on this campus to pester any of our St. Prowd's girls," said the brother.

"Not that *you* worry overmuch," said the sister to Nor. They both glanced again at Rain, who was slumping in her chair and showing scant devotion to the art of posture.

"And there are other girls her age?" asked Nor.

"We have about forty girls this year, from a little younger than Miss Rainary to a few years older. Some five or eight will finish next spring and proceed to Shiz University if they are lucky enough to secure a place. About eight have done very well on their O levels, but Z levels is where distinctions come out."

Forty girls. Rain ought to be safe enough hidden in a bevy of forty girl students roughly her own age.

"How will we reach you in case there are problems?" asked Proctor Gadfry as his sister set about to draw up a bill.

"I shall take rooms at a small house of residence when I am in town," said Nor. "Once I have settled myself, I'll post you the address. But I will be unavailable much of the time, so I must trust that in a crisis you will treat Rainary as one of your own."

"Upon that much you can rely," said Proctor Gadfry.

"That much, and much more," said Miss Ironish, blotting the paper and folding it demurely before handing it to Nor so she could open it again. Sweet Lurline. What a lucky thing that Nor's former employer, that old lascivious ogre, had died leaving a small sack of gold and mettanite florins ripe for the plucking. Keeping the sack under the table so the Clapp siblings couldn't see how much she had, she withdrew six coins and set them in a shiny line along the table.

"I forgot the food tax," said Miss Ironish flatly, and a seventh coin came out to join the others.

"Miss Rainary is now a St. Prowd's girl," said Proctor Gadfry, standing and extending his hand to Nor. "She has come a long way already, and she has a long way to go."

"I will find her a room and examine her," said Miss Ironish. At Nor's expression, she said, "I mean for what she knows, so we decide in what classroom to place her."

"She is hard to place," murmured Nor. They all looked at Rain once again, who didn't notice them rising. She had taken Tay into her lap and seemed to be whispering to it.

"Oh, goodness, of course there are no *pets*," said Miss Ironish.

Keeping her eyes upon Rain, Nor fingered an eighth coin and laid it slap upon the table. She didn't know which coin it was, but she tucked her purse back into her sleeve and left the room without comment. She made sure the door had closed behind her, sealing the Clapp family inside, before she spoke.

"You may be happy here or you may not," she said. "None of us knows where and when happiness happens. But I think you will be safe. We intend to head for Kiamo Ko, in the Kells, to see if a more private life might be had so far away."

"How long do I have to stay here." Presented as a statement.

Nor didn't want to lie. Since Rain so often refused human contact, Nor put her hand on Tay's scalp. Its bristles felt warm and papery. "Someone will come for you."

From the end of the street she looked back at Founder's Hall. It was a severe limestone box in the symmetrical mode, with narrow, watery windows set in deep recesses. Like nine icy tombstones sunk into the facade. Not so much as a single curl of carven ornament on the architrave or the capitals of the pillars holding up the portico.

The ribbon that Nor had bought for Rain to pretty her up for her new friends now seemed less a present than a blow. The heart-shaped locket, lacquered redder than yewberries, hung on a chain around the girl's neck and was hidden behind the yoke of her shift.

A silly sentimental thing picked up at a jeweler for an outrageous sum. The kind of thing Nor imagined a girl might like, though she would not have done so, and Rain had accepted it without comment. Nor hoped it might mean something to the girl one day, when and if she ever learned what a heart was.

Though maybe being an isolate already would help the girl not to suffer so much in the company of her peers. Oh, Rain, she thought. I had myself sewn so I could never have children to mourn, and you wandered into my life anyway.

8.

"Let us not start with disapproval," said Miss Ironish.

"But there's no light," said Rain. No, Rainary. She was trying to remember.

"You'll be here at night mostly. All rooms are dark at night."

"Not if there's a moon."

"You'll be too tired to stay awake mooning over the moon. It's too bad that there is no extra bed downstairs but your mother paid no attention to the registration deadlines. You're lucky we're accommodating you at all. Call it charity on our part."

"There's no light. And no window."

Miss Ironish seemed not to hear. "You have more catching up to do than any girl we have ever admitted. And believe me we have entertained some real losers in our time."

Rain reached out her hands. She could touch the sloping beams on either side. This wasn't a room. It was a coffin the shape of a tent. And it smelled of wood-mold; she could see the blotched rot where rain must come through the slates.

"You'll want to watch these protruding nails," said Miss Ironish. "They will rake your scalp if you sit up too fast. Breakfast is at five. There will be a bell, struck once. If you don't hear it, you miss breakfast. You won't miss it more than twice, I guarantee that."

Rain put her small carpetbag down. She thought about the stone in it, the bone, the shell, the feather.

"You can hang your garments on that pair of hooks—I can tell you didn't arrive with many. That's proper humility, and I applaud it. I believe we shall get along very well, Miss Rainary."

"What should I do now?"

"You can spend the evening settling in."

"Can I get something to eat?"

"Your board doesn't vest until breakfast tomorrow. However, I am not a monster. I shall send up a girl with a tray. Including water for your creature. What is it, anyway?"

"A rice otter. Its name is Tay."

"I do not think it will be happy here."

Rain thought better than to reply with the first thing that came to her mind. *Who could?* See, she was learning already. "Where is a lamp?"

"We did not budget for a lamp."

"How can I study and catch up on my learning without a lamp?"

"Very well. I shall begin to keep a ledger and write down all your demands so that your mother can reimburse the academy when she comes on Visitation Day."

"When is that? And a book too, if you have one."

"Visitation Day is the month after Lurlinemas. Some eleven, twelve weeks away. As for your reading selections, I shall pick out a volume from my private library of devotional literature. How well do you read?"

"I don't know."

"If you can derive any grace and benefit from what I send up for you, I will be surprised."

Me too, thought Rain. But anything to read was better than nothing.

Miss Ironish retired down the dusty wooden steps—not down one flight but several, as an attic filled with battered furniture separated the aerie from the dormitories in which the other girls slept. As she went she sang something quite cheerfully in a minor key. Rain took out her shifts, her petticoat, and the new pair of pale leather shoes that laced up the sides. A little light lanced through chinks in the roofing tiles, which meant, she suspected, that chill and wind and snow would sift through, too.

When she heard steps again, she went to the door to greet the girl. Mounting to the landing, hauling a lamp and a plate upon a tray, stumped a funny-looking kid with gappy teeth and freckles, and a weedy head of close-cropped ash-brown curls. "Here you be, then, Miss Rainary," she said. "All's you could hope for in the penthouse suite."

"It's not a lot. Is that supper?"

"Likewise it's very nice to meet you," said the girl pointedly.

Rain tried to sort this out, and made a second attempt. "My name is Rainary."

"I know, Miss Rainary. And my name is Scarly. Them's biscuits and some hunks of cheese hid under the serviette, if you please. I also tucked in two gingery scones when Cook weren't looking."

Rain took the tray. Tay, who liked cheese, made off with the lot of it. "Oooh, you gots your own private rat," said Scarly. "That'll help some, up here."

"Would you," said Rain, trying, trying to be normal, "would you like a scone?"

"I gets my own after cleanup time. When dinner's done."

"Will we be in studies together?"

"Miss Rainary, I en't a student. I'm the scullery maid."

Dim memories of Mockbeggar Hall. "I was a scullery maid once."

"Hoo no! Really?"

But Rain had been told not to speak of her past, ever. Already she was breaking rules. She tried to correct her mistake. "No. I just wondered what it might be like."

"It *might* be like a whole lot of fun. But it's not. Now I have to go down. There's the tables to lay. They gets roast crinklebreast of the fields tonight." Scarly put her hands in her apron pocket. "Miss, I brought you a few extra rags to stick in those cracks. That one near the chimney stack is the worst of the lot. It'll help."

"How do you know?"

"This is usually my room."

"Why do they put me here?"

"Not to feel special."

"I don't understand."

"School begun two weeks ago. You're late. The one thing Proctor Gadfry Clapp and Miss Ironish Clapp and the others agree on is that St. Prowd's students shouldn't feel special about nothing but being students of St. Prowd's. The rich ones gets their fancy cloaks locked up and their allowances locked up too. The smart ones gets to learn enough other languages to make their heads spin."

"What about the poor ones?"

"They en't admitted most often. And you, I don't know if you're rich or smart, but I do know you're late. So you got put in my room. Perbably you'll shift out after they get a better sense of how humble you are."

"Oh, I think I'm pretty humble."

"That's the right train to take." Scarly laughed. "Oh, I almost forgot your book." She pulled it from behind the bib of her apron and scowled at the silvery foil words stamped on the spine.

"What book is it? What does it say?"

"Miss Rainary, I already told you," said the maid. "I'm not a student here. I can't read. Pretty curly letters though, en't you impressed?"

Rain took the book. She could hardly make out the title due to the flourishes of display type. "I think it says *Read Me and Die,*" she said.

"You're a right card! We'll like having you around." Apparently Scarly thought Rain had made a joke. Hah! Her first joke, and she didn't even get it herself.

When the maid was halfway down the top flight, Rain hurried to the door. "But, Miss Scarly, where will you stay tonight?" she asked.

"It's only Scarly, no miss about it. I'll doss down in the boys' dormitory 'cross the way," came the reply. "It's empty of boys but haunted, say all the girls."

"Haunted with what?"

"All the boys they wish was there!" She chortled to herself down both flights. She must be a bit dim, thought Rain.

The title of the book turned out to be *Reach Me Each Day*. It was a collection of prayers in tiny cramped print. Rain still couldn't read well enough to be inspired by it. She did try. She ended up staring at the letters and imagining them to say something more juicy, and she fell asleep with Tay on her pillow. Tay's warm odor helped mask the reek of mildew.

She missed the breakfast bell, not only that morning but for eight mornings more.

9.

There were six instructors. Proctor Clapp supervised them all. At whim he would strike the iron bell in the hall, and only then could the teachers stop at the current topic and proceed to the next. Perhaps in his study he suffered narcolepsy for hours on end, for some days they would spend all morning on a single matter— the number line, or the Chronologies of Ozmas, or Primary Divinity, or dictation and diction—before the bell finally sounded.

Rain (*Miss Rainary, Miss Rainary, Miss Rainary*) was in a class with girls apparently three years younger and six years smarter than she was. They were young enough to adore tattling on her.

"Madame Shenshen, Miss Rainary doesn't even know how to do her algorhythmics."

"Madame Shenshen, Miss Rainary didn't finish her tallies so I can't check my work against hers."

"Madame Shenshen, I was paired with Miss Rainary for Spellification yesterday. Today may I have a partner who actually knows something?"

Madame Shenshen was a taurine woman who drenched herself in essence of floxflower to disguise the symptoms of a powerful digestive ailment. She was impatient with Rain up to a point, but however hard she might try, for the promotion of Rain's humility, Madame Shenshen couldn't disguise her admiration of Rain's swift progress. "For someone so evidently abandoned to the winds of chance," she claimed once, clasping her hands like a smithy, "you are proving yourself worthy of the opportunities St. Prowd's supplies you, Miss Rainary Ko. Bravo. Except this word, *admonition,* is spelled incorrectly. Please, if you will, tonight prepare me a page on which you spell it correctly three hundred times."

Rain could not yet count that high, but Miss Scarly was clever at figures and worked it out. Sort of. When Rain arrived the next day with five hundred *admonitions,* she was punished for showing off.

The girls were noisy at breakfast and lunch and sat in silence at dinner while Proctor Clapp or Miss Ironish read aloud from *Meditations of the Divine Emperor,* a slim volume bound in ivory kid that was all the stir in the bookstalls that season. Rain knew this for herself because once a week they went for promenades along the Suicide Canal or into Pfenix Park, taking care not to step on the dead pigeons. Inevitably they passed a book cart or a storefront, and *Meditations* was everywhere, in stacks and stacks.

Popular, or maybe not, as the stacks seldom seemed to shrink.

Rain wondered when the other girls were going to sort themselves out in her mind as individuals, or if they would. Unlike stones and pinecones, they never stayed still long enough for her to collect them. Perhaps because Rain had met Scarly first, she thought the maid was the most interesting of the bunch. Rain wasn't well used to launching conversations, while Scarly was trained to keep her lips closed unless spoken to. It seemed a losing proposition in terms of friendship, except that Scarly could communicate more in a saucy expression tossed in Rain's direction than the Divine Emperor seemed to be able to do in fifteen pages of discourse about his own divinity.

The reading was coming along. On the one hand, every now and then Rain regretted mastering the skill at last. She had imagined that books would have more to offer. What Miss Ironish supplied from the locked case of volumes in the front hall seemed a steady dribble of hectoring. Though very pious hectoring.

On the other hand, she saw that Shiz was full of writing in a way that the Chancel of the Ladyfish above the Sleeve of Ghastille hadn't been, nor the cottage at Nether How. Rain's least dreadful moment of the week was the walk from Ticknor Circus along Regent's Parade, next to whichever sour-faced student had pulled the short straw and gotten stuck with the *new girl*. It was a promenade of courteously brief literature! Statements applied all over the place, some in letters a foot high.

GENTLY USED GARMENTS. *PLEXODIE'S FAMOUS HARMONIA CAFÉ.* SHIZ CONSTABULARY. *PORTER'S LODGE PLS. KNOCK.*

And sandwich boards on the paving stones! LATEST WAR NEWS WITH EVERY BEER advertised near the door of the Cock and Pumpkins. *HAPPY HOURS ADD UP TO HAPPY DAZE*: that one outside the Peach and Kidneys. And her favorite, a sign over a shop down some uneven steps, almost below ground, on a mews off Railway Square: *SKURVY BASTARD'S* EMPORIUM *OF LOST AND BROKEN* ITEMS. She loved to read that one. She thought she'd like to quit St. Prowd's and go to school under the tutelage of Skurvy Bastard.

By Lurlinemas she had proceeded to the fourth primer, the one with the stories of Little Handy Mandy, a somewhat moronic child with kleptomania—she couldn't keep her fingers out of anything. She seemed preternaturally prone to trouble. Rain had used to like to steal things—was she as dull as Handy Mandy? The little girls laughed until their eyes streamed with tears. Rain said, "Madame Shenshen, I think I have finished with Handy Mandy."

"Too much for you?" said Madame Shenshen. "I'm not surprised. I believe you're ready to move up, once the Overseers have come and gone. Congratulations. I'll miss you. If you ever get a yen to look back in on Handy Mandy or on me, you know where to find me."

The Board of Overseers came for dinner at Lurlinemas, so the quality of the food was expected to improve appreciably. "Our best Dixxi House service, and if you break a plate I'll break your neck," instructed Miss Ironish. "Stand behind your chairs until the Senior Overseer is seated, and then follow his every move. If he picks up a spoon to sample the broth, you do the same. If he finds the dinner roll not to his liking, you do the same. If he leaves half his chop or asks for more peas, you do the same. If he writes his name in the custard with the end of his spoon, you are to do the same. Are there any questions? Miss Rainary, are you attending?"

"Yes, Miss Ironish."

"If the Senior Overseer puts his napkin upon his lap, Miss Rainary?"

"I will do the same."

"If he tucks it in at his collar?"

"I will do the same."

"Very well. Miss Ghistly, do you understand? Miss Mauna, Miss Igilvy? Miss bon Schirm?"

"Yes, Miss Ironish."

Rain didn't remember having celebrated Lurline-mas before. Maybe back at Mockbeggar Hall? She couldn't work out how a festival day centering around some miracle of Lurline, the fairy goddess who had founded Oz, now honored the providence of the anonymous deity everyone called the Unnamed God. Or UG.

Happily, on Lurlinemas the girls got maple syrup for their oatmeal sludge at breakfast, which almost mitigated the tedium of extra hours of prayers to the UG and a new devotional chant to the UG's Divine Presence, Shell, Emperor of Oz.

Rain thought the maple syrup more divine than the Emperor, though she had learned not to give voice to such a sentiment.

At the service, candles were brought out, and little square bells the size of petits fours. The Senior Overseer, a stooped and mild old man prinked out in a plaid vest and a pince-nez, with sore skin that peeled in birch bark curls, read aloud the text and also the instructions for the ceremony, apparently not silencing himself for italics.

"For his charity to our holy blessed homeland, may the Divine Emperor be raised up. Ring bell three times. For his purity as an example to the fallen citizens of the Unnamed God, may the Divine Emperor be raised up. Ring bell two times and bow to the sky." The Senior Overseer couldn't work out how to bow to the sky, so keeping his eyes trained to the page he just waggled two fingers toward the ceiling.

Rain could see Scarly and her maties standing in mobcaps and fresh pinafores at the back of Meeting. A small sound escaped from Rain at the sight of Scarly's comic twirl of her hands, imitating the Overseer. Miss Ironish glanced across the room at her and grimaced. Oh hell, thought Rain, a miracle at Lurlinemas. I think I may have just laughed out loud.

She almost did it again, right then, at the thought of it. And at the thought that *Oh hell* was a little bit of Mr. Boss in her still. That was a nice thought, under the circumstances.

The meal was the best food that Rain could ever remember seeing. Suspended in an iron ring, a shallow bowl of clear broth hovered about five inches behind each plate. The chops were jacketed with crispy crackling fat. Pickled beets and orrory root with a dollop of tamorna marmade on top. The aromas were subtle and strong.

The Senior Overseer, sunk in conversation with Proctor Gadfry Clapp on one side and Miss Ironish Clapp on the other, seemed to find the siblings so amusing that he kept pausing with his spoon in midair and pursing his lips in surprise at whatever they were saying. More than fifty spoons hovered when his spoon did, and though Rain slid her eyes left and right she didn't see a single brown splash of broth. Finally the Clapps concluded the long story with which they were harrying the Overseer. He roared with artificial gusto and tucked into his meal before they could start up again. He used the crinkleknife to trim the savory fat off his chop, and then put down the knife to pick up the smaller of the forks, and smiled ferociously at the nearly translucent curl, and then he removed it to a side plate.

The students, the teachers, and several other visiting overseers did the same. Not the breath of a sigh, not a whimper. No hint of anguish. Miss Ironish looked prepared to explode with pride at the manners on display. Discreetly, of course.

When the Overseer had danced the tines of his fork through his peas without eating any, and busily mashed his orrory root so he could take precisely one spoonful, and broken his dinner roll into tiny crumbs on his plate and then dropped his napkin upon the whole wasted mess of it, all the girls followed his lead. The smaller girls were beginning quietly to cry, but they were sitting at the far end of the tables and the Senior Overseer apparently wasn't keen of sight.

"There's pudding to come, of course," said Miss Ironish.

"First, let us have a gander at the finest of St. Prowd's," said the Senior Overseer. He hauled himself to his feet, his knuckles steadying himself on the linen.

Rain stood and put her knuckles on the tabletop. She wasn't being bold, neither did she realize she was alone in the gesture, because she was sitting at a corner of a table near the front and from this angle most of the room was behind her.

"Oh my, a volunteer," said the Overseer. He could see her. "May I ask you, what do you hope the Fairy Queen Lurline and her constant companion, Preenella, will bring you tonight in their magic basket?"

That was a mouthful but Rain was a quick study. "May I ask you, sir, what you hope the Fairy Queen Lurline and her constant Preenella will bring you in their basket? Magic basket?"

Miss Ironish's eyes were flashing and Proctor Clapp's mouth was open.

But the Senior Overseer just laughed. "Fair enough, young lady. I would like to see peace descend upon our fair land." Looking at her kindly enough, he waited. "Have you anything to add?"

"Have *you* anything to add?" asked Rain.

"Is this surliness or is she an idiot savant?" the Overseer asked Proctor Clapp in a stage whisper, and they all heard the Proctor's reply, "Just an idiot, I'm afraid."

"Nonsense," said the Overseer. "Come, tell me. What is your name?"

"What is your name?" asked Rain.

"I am Lord Manning. Now tell me your name."

At last an instruction that was not a question. But Rain remembered she was to bring no special attention upon herself, and she had blundered badly. "I am a new student this year, Lord Manning, who doesn't know her manners yet," she tried.

"I have already confirmed *that*," said the Senior Overseer, and to the proctor, "What's the girl's name, damn it?"

"Miss Rainary Ko, if you please, sir," said the proctor.

"Miss Rainary Ko! Are you always so insolent, or are you trying to be amusing?"

By now Rain had figured out her mistake, and she didn't return the question to the Overseer. "For Lurlinemas in my basket, if I got a basket from the Fairy Queen Lurline, I would like permission to room with the other girls, Lord Manning."

"What do you mean?" he roared. It wasn't clear if he was amused or offended by all this, but perhaps that was the result of the pearlfruit sherry which he had downed in lieu of dining, and which the girls hadn't imitated as they hadn't been served sherry. Only tall beakers of water, which they'd sipped sparingly so as not to need the loo before dismissal. "Wherever do you room now? On the rooftop?"

"Just under it, sir."

"I don't understand. Miss Ironish! Explain this child to me!" He didn't look at the proctor or his sister. He leaned even farther out above his plate to peer at Rain, the poor girl who wanted nothing but to remain invisible to the world. His plaid ascot had come loose from his collar and a dangling edge of it trailed through the flame of the tabletop candle. In a second his vest was alight. "Oh! Mighty forces!" he cried, and took his water glass and doused himself with water.

First Rain, and then thirty-nine other girls, picked up their beakers of water and doused themselves, though a couple of the very younger girls doused each other and got away with it.

Miss Ironish fainted dead away in her chair. And so there was nothing else for her brother to do but to pick up his beaker of water and toss it in the face of his sister.

That was Rain's last night in her aerie above the girls' dormitory in Founder's Hall. After Miss Ironish had recovered and the Overseers had departed—jollity masking a bitter rage on the part of the Clapps and impatience on the part of Lord Manning—Rain was ordered to collect her things.

"We will not toss you out on the street," said Miss Ironish. "But until further notice you will house yourself in the boys' dormitory across the schoolyard. Scarly will show you the way."

This is how Rain came to be exiled to the haunted dormitory where, a few months later, the ghost first appeared.

10.

She loved her new arrangement. For one thing, though again on the top floor, she now had a window. The plastered ceiling was high, and no nails poked through. While Rain had hoped and longed to be a girl swimming in dailiness with the other girls, she had little capacity for gloominess, as far as she knew, and she didn't feel lonely to be so alone.

Also, although Scarly now had relocated to the main building to take up her old room, paradoxically Rain saw her more often. The maid had greater liberty to roam the premises of the annex than any of the students. As long as Scarly carried a tray or a bucket or a lamp, she could come and go up the stairs to Rain's attic without being stopped. Usefully, the unused boys' dormitory was built above the storerooms and the stables, and the four maids were kept to a pretty clip, dashing back and forth all day. At nighttime when Scarly finished her final chores she could wander across the courtyard as if to count the clean sheets for the laundry or leave the morning list for the milk and eggs man. Then she could stand at the base of the steep winding staircase that rose two full flights and call out, "Hoo hoo!" as if she were an owl, or an Owl.

Rain's room was so far back under the eaves that she couldn't always hear Scarly. But Tay usually did. Tay would go sniffing and scraping at the closed door until Rain pulled on some socks and a tatty knitted houserobe and came inching out to meet her.

"Is the others being beastly to you?" asked Scarly, the first time she came to visit.

"Not really. At the start they were cross because Miss Ironish dumped the crawberry trifle in the horse trough behind the stables, but then the Lurlinemas baskets arrived anyway. All the girls had treats and presents enough to please them." Rain had gotten no such basket, but she hadn't expected to, and she imagined that Scarly had been similarly deprived. "Did you ever see a ghost here?" she asked, to change the subject.

"En't no such thing as ghosts."

"I hear some spooky-spooky noises at night."

"Doves in the joists. They can't sleep with them bats in the belvedere coming and going all night."

"Shall we get down to it?"

"Right, Miss."

Rain had decided to teach Scarly to read. They worked for almost an hour in the lamplight. From a classroom Scarly had pinched a slate and a slice of chalk, and Rain formed letters first while the maid copied them below. "Put more of a foot on that *L* or it will be mistaken for an *I*."

Scarly labored with her tongue in the corner of her mouth. She was tired enough when she arrived and she could rarely work for long, but she came back every second or third night. Since there was no extra coal for the stove in Rain's chamber, they sat huddled under a single coverlet like a giant slug with two heads. Tay liked to bask in the lamplight and bat at the scratching chalk the way a cat might.

One evening Scarly yawned and said, "I en't the strength to do any more nasty vowels. Let's just sit here and keep cozy for a moment till I get ready to run back through the cold to my room." It was midwinter now, and the schoolyard between the annex and Founder's Hall was hip deep in snow. "Tell me about your home."

Rain liked Scarly as well as she imagined she could ever like anyone, but she still wanted to hew to the instructions that her aunt and her parents had given her. *Avoid making idle conversation that might endanger anyone.* Rain didn't believe she knew how to tell stories, anyway, and neither did she want to lie. "I'm good at forgetting all that," she said, which was truthful enough. "Tell me about yours instead. Have you got two parents?"

"Sure enough, man and wife, live in a hamlet that en't got no name. A half hour on foot from Brox Hall, on the train line."

"How did you get all the way here?"

"They had nine other mouths to feed, din't they, so since my mouth was less sassy than some, they figured to put me to work in the city."

"You have nine brothers and sisters?" Rain almost saw shooting stars.

"No, six of 'em, plus Grandmaw, that gormless old witch, and the goat and the milk-cow. The chickens don't count as they feed themselves with grubs and such."

Rain wasn't sure how to frame the next question. "Do you miss them much?"

"I see 'em once a year, don't I?" She tightened her lips and bobbed her chin in affirmation. "That's more than my maties belowstairs, most of 'em, and also Cook, who has three sons in the army and thinks they must all be dead as dinner."

"Are they older or younger, your brothers and sisters?"

"Oh, all sorts. How about you?"

"I have Tay," said Rain.

"Anyone coming to see you on Visitation Day?"

She caught herself from saying *my aunt.* "I don't know. I haven't had any"—what was the word?—"correspondence."

"I'm sure your maw will come. They all do. The girls expect it."

"The girls are all sleeping in warm dormitories too."

"I'm warm enough." They giggled over nothing. Tay curled tighter, not so much a coil of greenish otter but a congealed heap of fur. Tay hadn't cared for the winter in the Five Lakes and liked it even less in Shiz. All at once it perked up its ears, bowed points, and raised its head in a motion so fast they didn't even see a blur.

"It hears something," whispered Rain.

"What?"

"The ghost!"

They both tried to scare themselves more by making terrified faces, with huge eggy eyes showing white around the irises, with mouths dropped open. Then it stopped being fun and Scarly said, "I better go. You'll be okay with the ghost on your own?"

"I have Tay."

"Tay the Attack Otter." Scarly got up and impulsively threw her arms around Rain from behind. "Really, you'll be all right, Miss Rainary?"

"Honestly, Scarly. You don't believe in ghosts, re-member?"

The maid swore she didn't believe in ghosts, but she left the annex in double time. Rain settled back in the blanket. It held in some of the maid's warmth long enough for her to get to sleep. She didn't dream of ghosts, though when she woke up once in the frosty moonlight she noticed that Tay was still sitting with an erect spine and a needle-sharp attentiveness. Probably a new family of mice, she thought.

11.

Visitation Day arrived at last. Since Rain had no call-ers, she helped Miss Ironish pour tea and squeeze lemons. "You're a very good child, Miss Rainary," said Miss Ironish during a lull. "Madame Shenshen speaks highly of you, and Madame Chortlebush seems to be warming up. Slowly."

"Madame Chortlebush is a fine lecturer."

"I do hope you aren't becoming attached inappro-priately." Miss Ironish saw impending doom in every situation. "It's not correct to focus your attentions upon a single individual, Miss Rainary. These little *tendresses* can begin to happen in a school setting, but they must be strictly nipped in the bud. Using the Secateurs of Personal Government. Do you remember my lecture on the imaginary Secateurs we each have in our employ?"

Rain wasn't paying much attention. "Do you have family to visit on Visitation Day, Miss Ironish?"

"The impertinence, Miss Rainary! My brother, Proctor Gadfry Clapp, is all the family one needs." She arranged the lace cuffs of her sleeves for the thousandth time. "I would like to abolish Visitation Day as a distraction, but I am afraid we would have a revolution on our hands. I'm sorry, of course, that you haven't heard from your mother. I trust no harm has come to her."

Rain bobbed a slight curtsey. She had found that when she wasn't sure what to say, a curtsey often smoothed over the silence. But today Miss Ironish said, "That's common of you, Miss Rainary. A curtsey in this situation is what I would expect the parlor maid to drop. Don't sell yourself short. Your mother may not have bothered to write or call, but still, you aren't a member of the staff. You're of finer stock than that. Despite your bullish awkwardness, good breeding will out. And if Madame Chortlebush and Madame Shenshen are right, you'll be able to do solid academic work one day. So don't pander."

"Yes, Miss Ironish." Rain stifled the urge to curtsey five or six times in a row.

At dinner Rain sat near Miss Mope, with her one-legged father in his narrow oiled beard, and Miss Igilvy, whose parents were so grizzled and birdlike their daughter must have been hatched from an egg. Above the chatter of schoolgirls, the talk was of the war.

"Fleecing us with taxes. Draining us dry," asserted Father Mope.

"We defend all of Oz, and yet do the godless tribes of the Vinkus contribute anything in manpower or strategic thinking? I'm merely asking," replied Father Igilvy.

"You wouldn't want strategic thinking from the Yunamata. They can't think far enough to build their houses with stone walls!"

The laughter was brisk and quickly over. "And yet we're defending them, too," said Mope. "And the Scrow, and I suppose those Arjiki clans in the Great Kells. They have more savvy than some of those other Winkies."

"Oh yes," said ancient Mother Igilvy, patting her daughter on the head as if she were a loaf of bread warm from the oven. "I went out to the West once, you know, and met some Arjiki royalty."

"You never told me that, Mother," chirped her equally ancient husband.

"Of course I did."

"How divinely fascinating," said Mope. "Did you write up your sentiments for the papers, or retail your anecdotes to Ladies' Clubs?"

"Indeed. And I remember quite well telling about one castle high in the mountains. It was the place where that Witch was brought down, do you remember?"

Rain began to chew exceedingly quietly so as not to miss a syllable.

"The Arjiki family who had lived there had long ago been slaughtered by the Wizard's forces, I came to understand. The place—Kirami something, Kirami Ko, I think—was crawling with flying monkeys who did their best to put on a full cream tea. I'm afraid monkeys are shambolic by nature. We were taken all over the shabby place. It was built as a waterworks, you know."

"Miss Rainary's surname is Ko," said Miss Igilvy. "Pass the gravy boat?"

"I never knew that," said Miss Igilvy's father to her mother. "A waterworks. I never."

"Of course you did, you old phony. You sat in the front row at each and every presentation I gave."

"I was napping with my eyes open. Why a water-works, so high in the mountain? Was the building put up on a river suitable for a waterwheel of some sort?"

"No, nothing of the sort. Don't you remember? I had bright illuminatums, surely you recall! I had painted them myself, on vellum from Plutney & Blood's."

"When the house lights go low I tend to go low too."

"I was led to believe that a giant reservoir, a lake of sorts, might lurk underneath the mountain, deep down, and that the castle of Kirami Ko was originally intended as the housing for a great artesianal device. A screw of some sort that would sink down oh for yonks, and pull up water in the way screws can manage to do."

"That's the hugest helping of nonsense I ever heard," said Mope affably. "The Vinkus River that cascades from the heights carries all the water the Kells could possibly provide. And every drop debouches into Restwater. The notion of drilling for more water when Restwater just sits there—the Wizard or whatever Ozma initiated that plan couldn't be so idiotic."

"Well, don't rely on my memory," said Mother Igilvy. "But perhaps it wasn't the Wizard's plan after all. Maybe the Arjiki tribe thought it all up so as to be self-sufficient from the Emerald City, just like those truncated Munchkinlanders."

"Is there any more gravy at that end?" asked Miss Igilvy.

"I never understood how the Wicked Witch of the West was killed by a bucket of water, as the legend has it," said Mope.

"Oh, I've worked that out," said Mother Igilvy. "I have concluded the bucket must have been filled to the brim with several gallons of Kellswater. It's a drearily lifeless and poisonous liquor, you know. Everyone says so."

"But what would she be doing with a bucket of Kellswater at the ready?" asked Mope.

"Dear husband, you eat any more popovers and gravy and you'll rip a stitch. My good sir, the Witch obviously had stashed away a dousing of Kellswater as a prophylactic against an attacker. But it was used against her by that Doromeo."

"Dorothy," said Miss Igilvy firmly.

"Did you hear she has come back, and has been put on trial in Munchkinland? Condemned to death," said Mope.

"The Munchkinlanders are a cruel, cruel people," said Mother Igilvy with satisfaction. "They deserve the pummeling we're giving them."

"Perhaps not quite the pummeling we advertise," said Mope in a quieter voice. "Miss Plumbago, what do you hear from your grandfather, that distinguished General Cherrystone?"

Rain swiveled her head; she couldn't help it. Miss Plumbago was General Cherrystone's *granddaughter*? How—how *enwreathed* life could manage to be. But just then Proctor Clapp got up to address the diners, and Father Igilvy fell asleep before the popovers and gravy were even removed from the table.

Rain knew they had been talking about Kiamo Ko, about her own grandmother, Elphaba Thropp. It made her feel dizzy. Hiding in plain sight. As soon as Proctor Clapp had finished, Rain excused herself, though no one noticed, and headed back to her room across the yard. The stables were filled with horses of the visitors, and out in the back street the ostlers and chauffeurs were having a smoke around a brazier and rubbing their hands to keep warm. She liked the sound of that commotion, she liked the smell of the horses. And the rising heat of their bodies warmed the annex right up to her room. She changed her clothes and took Tay in her arms and lay back on her bed, knowing she would not sleep easily tonight. Not with pictures in her head of some murdered Dorothy, some murdered grandmother, some castle she had never seen with a cellar shaped like a shaft and a giant screw plunging down, down, down, into the heart of the earth. And then she heard a noise as of someone coming through her wardrobe. It did not sound like a ghost, so she got up to see what it was.

12.

In the pearl-blue gloom of midnight she couldn't tell if it was a girl or a boy. But Tay was usually skittish and aggressive around boys, she'd noticed, and now it seemed only calm and alert, not hostile. "Miss bon Schirm?" ventured Rain, naming one of the taller girls. "Did your parents fail to come on Visitation Day too?"

But it wasn't Miss bon Schirm.

"You scared me half to death. Come out of there."

A boy emerged. Three, four inches taller than Rain, though his hair was raked every which way, and maybe if it were properly combed he'd be closer to her height. The face was wary, urgent, perhaps clever—it was hard to tell in this light, and besides, Rain didn't trust her estimations of people's characters. Yet. She wondered, in fact, if she ever would. Perhaps now was a good time to start. Was he about to strike her?

But there was Tay, attentive, curious, but hardly rearing to attack. A pretty good barometer.

"What were you doing in there?"

He held out the large shiny shell she had carried with her from nearly as far back as she could remember. "What is this?"

"Mine." She took it from him. His hands were shaking a little. "Did you come here to steal my things?"

"No. Of course not. You haven't got much."

"So I'm told. Are you going to hurt me?"

"Why would I do that?"

"You hid in my cupboard and were going to jump out."

"When I heard you coming up I hurried in there. I was waiting until you went to sleep, and then I was going to slip away. I didn't want to scare you."

"But what were you doing here in the first place?"

"Looking for something to eat."

Rain shrugged. "Nothing to eat here. Pretty obviously. Unless you like books." She took a closer look. "Are you very hungry? Are you starving? You don't look in the pink of health."

"I'm not stuffed and groaning, that's for certain. My stomach rumbles like caves collapsing."

She bit her lip and thought she should probably feel his forehead, but she didn't care for touching people. "Are you ill?"

"Look, I'll just go. I'm sorry for this rude surprise. I didn't know anyone was living in this building."

She was putting it together as best she could. "But you were hiding from someone."

"Just putting the shell farther back on its shelf. For safety," he said, reaching his hand. She didn't give the shell back.

"Oh, that's thoughtful. Do you ever break into anyone's room and just, oh, knit? Or nip into someone's house and just polish the wainscoting? You aren't making any sense."

"You're uncommonly calm. I'm glad for that. If you had screamed I would have gotten in terrible trouble. I'll leave now. If you don't say a word about this I will be a little bit safer."

Tay inched forward and sniffed at the boy's very wet boots, which were open at the toe and heel and, now Rain thought of it, smelled dreadful. Then Tay wreathed itself around the boy's ankle for a moment and looked up at Rain. She made herself do the improbable and reached out and put her palm to his forehead.

"Am I hot?"

She considered the answer to that, but while she had known how to be quiet her whole life, she had never quite learned how to lie. "I don't know. I never felt someone's forehead before."

"Feeling your own doesn't work. You can't feel yourself sick."

"Is that true?" She tried it. She just felt like herself. But what did herself feel like? She had never thought to ask.

"Do *you* know what yourself feels like?" she asked him.

"Oh, now that's the question," he replied, and buckled at the knees.

"I didn't intend such a powerful question," she commented. Then she realized he had passed out on the coverlet that she and Scarly sometimes huddled under.

She didn't know what to do, so she did nothing. She wasn't allowed to leave her room after ninth bell, not until morning bell except to visit the privy. And there was nothing useful in the privy.

She remembered that the stables were full of guest horses. She told Tay to stay put while she hustled into a waist-length wool coat and hurried down both flights of stairs. The horses in their stalls nickered and wheezed, and shuffled at the sound of her, and she was glad for their noise and warmth. Various coachmen still lingered, smoking cheap tobacco rolled in old newsprint, and husbanding pints of ale that Proctor Clapp had sneaked out to them when his sister wasn't looking. The ale had made the men jolly. They chattered on as Rain went quickly through the few satchels that had been lobbed into the shadows just inside the stable doors.

"*My* lady, she's a right dab of codswallop, she is. She pays me but a penny farthing for the trip from Plaid Acres to Shiz, and then she's late for the school supper because she's got to stop and buy new gowns in that fancified silk depot over to Pennikin Lane!"

A small quarter of cheese. Better than nothing.

"My lady's got yours beat in the mud with a beetroot up her arse. Mine's so cheap she thinks I don't merit the privacy of a loo with a closed door, so she stops before any town center at the last possible shrine to Lurlina and makes me take a dump behind it! Says it saves her a fee and helps stamp out paganism at the same time."

Oooh, a hunk of bread. Pretty hard, but maybe if she held it over her candle?

"The old gov'nor en't so bad. He's a secret royalist, though. He prays for the Emperor every night like he's told to do—he prays that the Emperor passes away peaceful in his sleep, and that some miracle return the Ozma line to the throne. He was born under an Ozma and he wants to die under one, he says. I tells him to his face, he's gonna die under a lake narwhal, the missus keep putting on the pounds like she's doing."

"You don't say that, you buggery liar!"

"I says it in my heart, like a prayer."

A lot of laughter outside. In the last satchel, a trove—a mince pie, almost fresh by the smell of it, and two carrots and an apple, probably for the horse, and a small porcelain flagon of something liquid. She nicked it all, neat as Handy Mandy, and a rather nicely woven pink blanket that was thrown over a mare, and she scurried up the stairs. No one heard her. One of the ostlers was saying, "Give over some of that Baum's Liquid Hoof Dressing, my pretty piebald is sorer than sandpaper on a sow's behind."

The intruder couldn't wake, no matter how gently or roughly she rocked his shoulder. He couldn't sample her terrific haul. It would be more stale in the morning. Damn. But she put the pink horse's blanket on him, over the coverlet, and to keep herself warm she dressed herself in as many layers as she could. Thanks to Miss Ironish her wardrobe was fuller than it had been. She was grateful for the stiff wool stockings and the promenading cape.

Round about midnight a brawl started among the carriage attendants. Maybe someone had discovered his flask was missing. She didn't mind. She sat with Tay in her lap—Tay kept her warm too—and maybe she dozed and maybe she didn't, but after a while the morning came anyway.

He looked more bruised in the morning, but perhaps that was just the coloration of another ethnic group in Oz that Rain hadn't previously collected. He sat up and said, "If I was full I would need the privy," and she answered, "Well, eat up some of this and sooner or later." She gave him a carrot that he chomped at quicker than a horse might. Then he followed it down with a sip from the flagon, which made him wince, and then a long gulp, which made him blush scarlet and pass out again.

Breakfast bell. If she didn't show up someone might come looking—it had happened before. She didn't bother to straighten her clothes or change them, as there was no time. She grabbed Scarly's slate and scratched on it DO NOT LEAVE, and she propped it up against her chair leg so he would see it if he woke. "Don't let him go, Tay," she told the otter, who normally spent the day in the room anyway, under restrictions of the siblings Clapp.

After breakfast. "Your attire, Miss Rainary," said Madame Chortlebush.

"There was a new leak in the annex," said Rain. "I shall have to use free period to launder my other gowns."

Later, Madame Chortlebush said, "I do not believe you are minding the lesson as you ought, Miss Rainary. Are you distraught because your mother couldn't see her way to attending Visitation Day?"

Rain opened her mouth. Then she thought, I am quietly lying to my teacher by pretending nothing is wrong. And I lied about my clothes without even thinking about it. So what's the difference if I lie upon careful consideration?

She didn't know if there was a difference but she had to answer the question. "Yes," she said to her teacher. As she spoke she realized that accidentally she was telling the truth. Effortlessly, she had learned to miss people a little bit. She didn't know her Auntie Nor very well, but without saying it in so many words to herself, she had hoped to be surprised by a visit from her pretend mother anyway.

Oh well, she thought. I have a boy in my room, and none of the other girls have *that*.

"Come here. You need a good squeeze," said Madame Chortlebush, who rather liked to give good squeezes.

"I think my frock is too wrinkled already," said Rain, but her teacher wouldn't relent, so Rain succumbed. Then at her desk she tried harder at her sums so as to throw off suspicion and not give the game away.

Because she had planted the story of ruined clothes in the morning, at luncheon she was released from the chore of healthful stretching in the basement game room, it being too cold to promenade. She plowed across the new snow in the yard and entered the annex. The last of the carriages had left after breakfast. The building felt quiet. All too quiet, in fact.

She hurried up the stairs, two at a time, ripping the hem in her skirt when her heel caught upon it, but she couldn't stop.

Tay was at the desk in the window in usual fashion, taking what warmth there was. The horse blanket was folded up and laid upon Rain's bed. At first she thought the boy was gone. Then she saw that he had found the ladder in the hallway and had propped it up in the alcove where she kept her clothes, which now really *were* rucked up and unpresentable. In the ceiling of the alcove, which she had never seen before because that corner was so dark, he had found a hatch of some sort, a trapdoor. And he had lifted the hinged hatch about a foot, and was standing on the ladder in a pool of unearthly light that had never before come into any room she had occupied. He looked magical. The light made his scruffy mousy curls seem pale and almost translucent. His arms were plump and hard.

She could tell he wasn't looking into the schoolyard, but in the other direction. He wouldn't have seen her coming. She didn't want to frighten him and cause him to fall. She walked up softly and put her hand on his calf, to announce her presence. Startled, he nearly kicked her teeth out. She should have guessed. A fellow citizen of Oz who didn't like to be touched.

"You nearly scared the knickers off me," he said.

"Scootch over, I'm coming up," she replied. He inched to one side, and there was just enough room for her to fit her feet on the rungs and join him.

She had never seen the city of Shiz from anywhere but gutter level, as her own window in the annex looked onto the cloistered schoolyard with its ivied walls. This high up, she saw a confusion of roofs in the bright cold glare of a winter noontime. Gables and domes—that was St. Florix, surely?—and crenellations, were they, and clock towers. And stone steeples. And scholars' towers poking from the colleges. "That dark one with the pointy windows is Three Queens Library," said the boy. "And do you see the one with the gold escutcheons high up, under the gutters? That's the Doddery at Crage Hall, I think."

"It's like a field planted with toys." She couldn't stop her voice from sounding breathy and girly, but, hell, it was beautiful.

"And the weather vanes. You can make out the nearer ones. I see a werewolf over there. Can you see it?"

"The one on the little pointy bit of roof?"

"No, that's a Queen Ant, for some reason. To the left, above the mansard roof with the pattern in the tiles."

"It looks more like a were-pig than a were-wolf."

He laughed at that, which made her feel they were standing too close. But there was no choice if they wanted to survey Shiz from this height; the hatch was only so wide. Their shoulders were touching, and the only warm thing. The wind was fierce. "Look, a goose," he told her.

"Iskinaary," she said, before she could stop herself.

"What's that?"

"The Quadling word for *goose*." There, another lie. She was getting good at it.

The bells in one of the nearby towers rang the half. "I better pretend to be organizing my clothes or I'll catch it, but good," she said. She was reluctant to leave the airy world above Shiz, the spires and slopes and ravines topping the city's close-built architecture. But she risked being tossed out of St. Prowd's altogether if she was discovered this deep in the breaking of rules.

He descended after she did, replacing the hatch. Her room suddenly felt musty. Small. Inappropriate for entertaining a visitor. He seemed too close, now that they had touched shoulders. "Get me down my dresses, will you, I have to press one of them and look more presentable for afternoon classes."

He handed her a gravely ugly frock, the color of mushy peas, a single broad ribbon sewn down the left thigh panel its only decoration. She had never thought about clothes and their decoration before. She had never thought about thinking about it, either. She was under a spell of multiple reflections and it felt too much for her. "Isn't there anything nicer?" she snapped, as if she were a Pertha Hills dame in a high street establishment, and he the clerk.

"I don't care about clothes," he said, which was something of a relief. "How about this green one?"

"With the pucker in the bib? That one? It'll do. Hand it here."

She grabbed her change of clothes. She didn't have time to do much but flatten out the skirts with her hand and twist the ties so they lay straight. She tried to think of what to say to him to make sure he stayed. She pulled the wrinkled garment she had slept in over her head. She'd already tossed it to the floor when she heard him gasp. She turned to him, questioningly, in nothing but her smalls and the red heart locket. He said, "Please—I'll wait in the hall if you like."

"Why?"

He couldn't find a word for it, and finally blurted, "Courtesy, I guess." By then she'd already slipped the replacement over her head and was wriggling her arms into its scratchy sleeves. "Never mind," he said when she emerged looking at him in total bewilderment.

"Are you going to tell me who you are, and why you're here?"

"You can call me Tip. I suppose. I'm guessing you haven't reported me to the governors of this establishment?"

"I haven't said anything to any of the girls or the teachers, if that's what you mean. But why shouldn't I?"

"I'm keeping out of sight, if I can."

"Well, I hope no one saw your stupid head popping out of St. Prowd's roof just now."

"No one but cinder pigeons, I bet."

"Look. I only have a few more moments, and then I'm away again until dinnertime. I'll try to bring you back some real food if I can manage. But you have to tell me—"

"Actually I don't have to tell you anything. And I don't need your food. Though I'm glad you are nice enough not to have ratted on me. I'll be gone by the time you get back, and I won't steal anything, I promise, not even that shiny shell you have. Cor, but that's a bit of wonderful."

"Don't go. You're not well."

"What are you, an infant doctor?"

"I have a cousin who is an apothecaire and I picked up a few things. You're liable to frostbite in this weather, or the racking congestibles."

"That sounds serious." He was mocking her.

"Don't go," she said. "Really. Not yet. Maybe to-morrow, but not today. You owe me that much. I risked getting discovered as a thief last night to find you food and drink."

"Plenty powerful lemon barley you provided, too. All right. I'll stay till you get back, but I'm not promising much beyond that." He picked up the book that Scarly had been struggling through. "*The Were-pig of Dirstan Straw*," he read. "Oh, that's where you got the were-pig from."

"Of course. You get everything from books."

13.

His name was Tip; she knew that much, and knowing his name saw her through the rest of the endless day. She managed to brush past Scarly in the buttery and whisper for an extra few rolls to sneak to her room, which was forbidden under pain of expulsion. The maid contrived to deposit a tea towel with rolls and even a beet-and-ham pasty into Rain's lap. Scarly's faintly raised eyebrow made Rain feel cheap somehow. Still, she couldn't risk giving Tip's presence away to the maid. In the interest of keeping her position secure,

Scarly might feel more beholden to her employers than Rain felt to her teachers.

After dinner and prayers she returned to find that Tip had spent the afternoon taking apart a small iron stove he'd found in some boys' dormitory below. Piece by piece he had hauled it upstairs and reassembled it. "It kept me warm, all those steps," he said. "And there's a handsome little stash of coal in the cellar beyond the stable doors, too, so you can be set for a while." For the venting of smoke he'd jerry-rigged a snake of cylindrical tin piping up through the hatch, which was now open three inches. The cold air flooding in defeated the effect of the warming fire. But the atmosphere was improved, anyway. He was proud of his work.

He wouldn't tell her much about where he'd come from or why he was hiding. He admitted he'd been wandering the country outside Shiz during the summer and had come across the military camp of St. Prowd's boys. One afternoon he'd befriended a few of them doing an exercise in bivouac, and they'd told him about this vacated dormitory in town. It hadn't been hard to find. He hadn't heard Scarly or Rain come or go; the stable walls were thick with horse shawls, and the hay stacked everywhere probably served as extra insulation.

"But what have you been doing during the day-time?" asked Rain.

He cadged food from the stalls on market day, which was easy enough, he told her. But when it grew too cold for outdoor market he was having a harder time of it. For a couple of weeks he'd worked as a kitchen boy in Deckens College, but he'd been caught trying to leave the larder with brisket in his shirtsleeves and been dismissed. Pickings had grown harder as the cold deepened. He'd taken to siphoning oats out of the feedbags of carriage horses, but the mash he could make of them was pretty indigestible. When his space downstairs had been invaded by the arrival of guests for what he'd learned was called Visitation Day, he'd had no choice but to scarper up the stairs just around the turn at the landing. He'd heard Rain come in from the schoolyard side and start up the steps. He'd panicked and kept ahead of her, sprinting, arriving at the top level before she did. Without knowing it, Rain had cornered him by going right to the room he had found at the top of the stairs.

"But where are you *from*? Have you no home? No family? Why are you hiding?"

"Where are you from?" he countered, as if he could tell by her expression that she was as guarded as he. And while she could lie about some things, to people who didn't figure much, she found she couldn't lie to Tip. Neither could she break her oath to her family and put those people in jeopardy by saying anything about them. So she said nothing.

She did, however, admit that he could call her Rain.

He spent the night on the floor beside her bed, under the horse blanket.

He slept very hard. He didn't hear her get up and turn the coals and, finding no ember willing to catch again, remove the venting pipe and close the hatch, for warmth. When she went back to bed she saw that Tay had moved from her mattress to the crook in Tip's elbow. Just for an instant she wished she were Tay, but that seemed such utter nonsense that she threw herself back onto her bed again so hard she banged into the wall and hurt her nose. Neither Tip nor Tay stirred to ask her if she was all right.

Before breakfast bell, Scarly appeared with a tea towel covering four hot scones, and so the brief time in which it was just the two of them, just Tip and Rain—well, and Tay—was already over. Rain tried not to resent Scarly standing there with her dropped jaw. Tip sat up and made to cover himself with the blanket, but since he wasn't undressed there wasn't much point. "Miss Rainary," said Scarly, "en't you cooked yourself up a pottage of mischief somehow, and no mistake."

Rain took the scones and handed them to Tip. "Well, now you're ruined too, for feeding the intruder, and I'll say so if you squeal on us, Scarly. So it's best to keep your mouth closed until we decide what we're going to do."

"We?" said Scarly. "Which *we* is that, I wonder?"

Rain wasn't quite sure, but it felt a nice word to say.

All too easily Scarly became a conspirator with special duties in menu augmentation. Tip was no fool. Well-cooked, plentiful if simple fare, delivered almost hot from the griddle, was more appealing than cold scraps that the rats had gotten to first. Snowy alleys and college kitchen yards had lost their lustre.

Tip settled into Rain's room, sometimes reading there all hours if the weather was beastly, or pacing the city streets for news and exercise if the day was relatively fine. Once in a while he came back late, slipping in from the service lane through the stables. The hinges were so old that one of them had snapped, permitting a door to be angled just so, allowing to slip through any boy narrowed enough by hunger.

Once Rain asked, "What are you hunting for?"

"News, that's all."

"News of your family? Is that it?"

But he wouldn't talk about his family, and neither would she. A silent compromise they'd never discussed, and usually she remembered not to raise the subject.

This time he relented, up to a point. "I want to hear about the war."

Rain had no interest in the war. She hardly remembered the time of the dragons on Restwater, except as an imprecise excitement that she sometimes believed she was imagining. The war had been going on as long as she could recall. It wasn't a real thing in any useful way; it was just a condition of existence, like the forward lunge of time, and the ring of deadly sands that circled all of Oz, and the fact that cats hunted mice. "All the war news sounds made up," she complained. "I never saw a cannon dragged through any country lane. I never heard a gunshot from the classroom window. If there was once more ample food to be had, it was before I was able to get used to it. I hardly believe that peace and war are opposites. I think to most people they're the same thing."

"You've put your finger on a huge problem, right there," he said. "But if you're crossing the Wend Hardings on foot, which is the only way to cross them, and if you come across a contingent of various Animals of different sizes and abilities and temperaments who, despite their natural hostilities and exhaustion, are training together to hold the line against professional soldiers—well, then." He sighed, hardly willing to sum it up. "You see more than you'd like. Battle readiness seems a bundle of small disagreements trying to aim in a common direction against a common, larger disagreement."

She had studied a little geographics under Madame Chortlebush. "Are you telling me you came from Munchkinland?"

"I'm not telling you anything. We're talking about the war, and how people talk about it in Shiz."

She tried not to pry. Too much. "How *do* people talk about it in Shiz?"

"You know as well as I do. You live here. You've lived here longer."

"Yes, but." Since he had given something away, inadvertent or not, she allowed the tiniest scrap of herself. "I'm not from here, either. So I'm not sure what I hear. Anyway, girls in school don't talk about the war. They talk about their teachers and about boys." She regarded Tip not in fondness but in appraisal. "They'd eat you alive." At that comment he didn't blush; he blanched. Rain hurried on. "War just seems to crest and crest until a checkmate is reached, and then it stays like that forever. Getting staler and staler. Nobody ever winning."

"Until one side or the other manages a breakthrough strategy."

"Like what?"

"Oh. Forcing the other side into bankruptcy. Or negotiating a pact with some useful third party, say. For instance, if Loyal Oz could persuade the trolls to switch their allegiance, the EC Messiars would be able to invade Munchkinland through the Scalps. Those trolls are pretty fearsome in battle."

"Why don't they then? It sounds pretty basic."

"Because the trolls under Sakkali Oafish have a deep-seated grudge against Loyal Oz dating back to a rout of Glikkuns called the Massacre at Traum, which happened north of here. They wouldn't unite with the Emerald City if there were only one troll left alive. They're proud like that."

"So if that strategy won't work, what else might?"

"Maybe the Emperor will die, and the pressure to continue this endless war will lift."

"Isn't the Emperor divine? He can't die."

"I suppose time will tell. Or one side will discover a new weapon that's stronger than what their enemy has."

"Like what kind of weapon?" said Rain, as innocently as she could.

"Beats me. A great big cannon that can shoot a thousand arrows all at the same time? A poison someone can sneak into the food rations of the army cooks? An important book of magic spells that contains secrets no one has managed to unlock yet?"

"None of them sounds very likely," said Rain.

"Who knows. The word in Shiz, since you asked, is about all these things."

"And the word in Munchkinland?"

"Some of those same ideas. Being hoped for, anyway."

She saw a chink. "But what are the other ideas in Munchkinland, that you don't hear in Shiz?"

Maybe because he wouldn't answer questions about his family, he felt obliged to answer her now. "Flying dragons would be a good idea. They were used once before by the EC, but in an attack by anarchists the Emerald City lost their stable of dragons and their expertise."

"Dragons in Munchkinland. Imagine."

"Few have heard of such a thing. And I'm not saying there are. Just that a lot depends on the fact that there might be. One day."

"Are you a spy? Aren't you a bit young to be a spy!"

"We're all spies when we're young, aren't we?" She didn't think he was being evasive. She knew what he meant. She agreed with him.

"Tell me what you find out, when you find out anything of interest," she said. "Promise me that, Tip."

"Spies never make promises," he said, but now he was teasing her.

14.

He wasn't going to stay there forever. That much was clear. Rain just didn't understand what conditions would prompt his departure.

She lay awake at night sometimes when Tip was asleep, out of sight, his head on the floor a foot below her head. She could hear him breathing, a faint whine in his nose that never sounded when he spoke. A distilled aroma of sour raspberries on his breath, even from this short but crucial distance. She was becoming aware of the distance between human creatures at the same time she was becoming aware of their capacity to be entwined sympathetically. Perhaps, she thought, this is perhaps how it usually goes, but since she'd never been given to reflection, it seemed as if everything was breaking anew upon her at once.

Tip's interests in current events made her listen more carefully to what the teachers said when they thought the girls were learning off rubrics of spelling or rehearsing acceptable dinner party remarks in their heads.

"Cutting the salary again, according to the magnificent Gadfry," murmured Madame Shenshen to Madame Ginspoil one day in study hall.

"We shall be living on bread and water like the miserable armies," replied Madame Ginspoil, helping herself to a pink marzipan pig secreted in her beaded purse. Rain thought: *Armies. Miserable. Bread and water.* She would tell Tip.

"It'll be better though in the spring, which isn't far off," said Madame Shenshen. "Everyone says there will be a new push to bring down that General Jinjuria."

"She seems a right smart tartlet, to hold our army at bay all this time. If she's captured, she can be dragged here and made to tutor stupid young girls," seethed Madame Ginspoil. "Quite the suitable punishment. She can live on bread and water for what she has cost Loyal Oz in comforts."

"The cost of war is in human lives, you mean, surely."

"Oh, bother, of course, *that.* It goes without saying. But I have chilblains, what with the reduction of coal allotments for our quarters. Chilblains, I tell you. I have refused to knit balaclavas for the troops this year. If they can't win the stupid war after all this time, they'll have no comfort from me. Miss Rainary, are you eavesdropping upon your elders and betters?"

Rain loved to have things to tell Tip. He puzzled over them as if he were a military strategist, but Rain took this to be largely boredom. It seemed almost everyone was more interested in the progress of the war than she was.

"Does your grandfather write you letters?" Rain once asked of Miss Plumbago.

"Grandfather Cherrystone? No," snapped Miss Plumbago. "You'd think he might. After all, he taught me to read. But he's apparently too busy to write letters or send me little bank cheques."

He's besieged at Haugaard's Keep still, thought Rain, and ventured her conclusion to Tip, who thanked her for trying but seemed to know this already.

No, it couldn't last forever. In a couple of weeks, Madame Streetflye told them, it would be time for Rain's class to take up Butter and Eggs. Most of the girls giggled and blushed. Rain didn't have a clue until Scarly filled her in. Butter and Eggs was the Pertha Hills softsoap way of talking about Human Sexual Techniques: Practical Clarifications. Rain guessed that once she sat through that class, she could no longer allow herself to share a room with a boy. Neither, probably, would she want to, if she read accurately Scarly's repertoire of expressions. Primarily scowl and disgust. What would Tip do then?

The way it happened was this. Lord Manning, the Senior Overseer, had stopped to pay an unexpected call, which was his right and privilege. All might have gone horribly wrong, since Tip was just passing through the stables when Miss Ironish rushed in unexpectedly to give some instructions to Lord Manning's coachman. Tip was caught between Miss Ironish entering the annex from the schoolyard side and the coachman arriving from the service entrance. Luckily, Miss Ironish took Tip for the coachman's boy. She handed over some papers folded inside a clasped sleeve of leather, school accounts or an inventory of students or something. "Store these in Lord Manning's pouch, young man." Tip brought them to the horseman, who in return told Tip to ask the Cook for a few extra apples. The horses had been ridden hard on such urgent business.

Suddenly, on this risky morning, Tip became a fixture in the backstairs without anyone quite having twigged to his lack of specific sponsorship.

"Bring your man this carroty cream crumble, you," said Cook, who by and large liked men, her several husbands ample proof of that.

"Tell your Cook this may be the best cream crumble in Shiz," said the coachman back.

"Tell your fellow to tell me something I don't know."

Lord Manning had had enough of hysterics. Having delivered his sorry news to Gadfry Clapp, he was in no mood to stay for a cold school luncheon. The proctor sat in marmoreal paralysis in his study, but Miss Ironish followed Lord Manning right into the ablutorium and out again, hissing at him. (The teachers kept their doors open a crack to catch the drama.)

"I am not the Emperor of Oz, Miss Ironish," snapped Lord Manning. "I do not order a thousand men to march to war. I scarcely order starch for my collars. I am merely implementing the diktat come directly from the Emerald City. Now *will* you spare me your tongue?"

"Would you leave us without a man in the establishment? Lord Manning! I could not hold my head up with the parents of our girls, if they learned we had left them unprotected!"

"I am confident in your professional skills, Miss Ironish. You are perfectly capable of fending off any attempt at assault or rapine."

"I shall close the school."

"You have no authority to close the school. Please do not give my headache a headache, Miss Ironish."

"Without a male in residence, I will not answer to the consequences."

By now Lord Manning had reached the kitchen, and he barreled through the yard as if he owned the place, heading for the stables. He caught sight of Tip munching a bacon butty courtesy of Cook, and he said, "This boy, he's old enough to be some help, I'll warrant."

"You would take the seventeenth proctor of St. Prowd's and send him to battle, and leave a strapping stable boy in charge of the protection of schoolgirls? Lord Manning, have you abdicated your senses?"

For an instant Lord Manning appeared to reconsider. But then he swiveled upon his boot heel and he poked a finger almost up one of Miss Ironish's flared nostrils. "Our charge is the protection of children, Miss Ironish. Don't you dare forget it. This boy isn't old enough to be a soldier, but he *is* old enough and strong enough for lifting down the trunks from the box room and for chasing away beggars from the kitchen yard. He will be your factotum, and that's the end of it. Boy, what is your name?"

Tip, according to Scarly who told Rain all about this later, was so startled that he leaped to his feet and answered without hesitation. "Pit."

"Was your family too poor to give you a last name?" snarled Lord Manning.

"Well, yes, sir," he answered, "I mean, in a manner of speaking, as I'm an orphan. All they left me was my name."

Lord Manning blew out air between his teeth and buttoned his overcoat. As he beetled toward the kitchen door, he called over his shoulder, "You will be Miss Ironish's right hand when she needs you, Pit. We'll settle details of a salary allowance later, but for now housing and meals, the usual, and so on. Is that clear."

The Senior Overseer didn't wait for an answer. He ignored the uninterrupted flow of Miss Ironish's protests. His carriage left with purpose.

The room slowly quietened down. Miss Ironish dried her face in a tea towel and said to Cook, "A cup of lemon tea to strengthen Proctor Gadfry, if you please, Cook." And to Tip, she added, "Your employer left you behind in a school of young ladies. He must be mad. Straighten your shoulders and look at me when I talk to you. We'll discuss your obligations this afternoon. For now . . ." But she couldn't take the measure of her new situation yet, and fled the kitchen.

Scarly came to Rain's room that night to fill her in on the details, but Rain had heard a good deal already through the gossip. Proctor Gadfry had taken to his bed; Scarly had spent much of the day attending him with hot compresses and yeasty correctives. Tip was installed in a kitchen nook behind the wall stove, a corner that had been previously used for storing the butter churn and the lesser china. He had his own bed. The room was windowless but decent warm, said Scarly with more pride than envy.

Come evening, he couldn't sneak out to Rain's room the way Scarly could. Cook, who missed her sons, marshaled Tip's company for her own maternal needs. Besides, she was a guardian of the students' virtue, so she took to sleeping on a cot in the kitchen. She put it across the door to his cubby so he would have to climb over her to get out at night. In the case of loo emergencies she supplied him with a basin for night waste and a plate to cover it from flies. From Rain, therefore, he was pinned good and proper, but not entirely from Scarly, who during the day had reason enough to pass through the kitchen. At night she brought news of Pit to Rain in the Annex.

"*Pit?*" asked Rain, incredulous.

"It was the first thing he could think of. He didn't want to say his real name, for his own reasons. The easiest thing was to turn his name backward, he said. Tip. Pit. Do you get it?" Scarly was very proud of getting it herself. Now that the stranger boy had been safely pegged into the class system of the household, which she could understand, the maid was eager to get back to studying the secret lessons that Rain had offered to resume.

Rain had her own scholastic travails to deal with. Despite the upheaval to the management of St. Prowd's Academy, the session called Butter and Eggs proceeded on schedule. Miss Ironish, who customarily spoke to girls at great length about Feminine Virtue, this year marched to the doorway of the classroom and without bothering to enter said shortly, "Girls, the most important thing to know about Feminine Virtue is that you're going to need a hell of a lot of it. Carry on, Madame Streetflye."

Rain thought the mechanics of sex less compelling than, say, the way a bird learns to fly from a nest, or a snake contorts to shed its skin. She couldn't imagine herself ever wanting to descend to what Madame Street-flye called the Happy Hello or to shiver with the Special Sneeze that sometimes followed. Despite all the rude information, she couldn't picture how the experience was actually managed. But there was so much she didn't know, and she would learn in time. People changed, sometimes more than you expect, she told herself.

For instance, she'd never imagined herself getting along with a bunch of children her own age. The one thing that hadn't happened in all her peripatetic youth, she saw now, was having access to other kids. Adults had been such a mystery that she'd paid them no mind, but children might have provided something of a support circle. You don't have to collect kids; they just clump of their own accord. Like rice otters or phant-omescent spiders.

Now she had Tip, a best friend; and Scarly, who was a little miffed at being demoted to second position; and even Miss Igilvy wasn't quite as damp as the others. Miss Plumbago was a rotter, though.

Still, Rain missed the few weeks of sharing a room with Tip, back in the paradise days before she'd heard of the Happy Hello. They'd never so much as touched hands after that one time their shoulders had brushed together on the ladder to the hatch. But they'd been closer without touching, without words, than all these girls who hugged and squealed and whispered and paraded about with their arms around one another's waists.

At least she imagined that she and Tip had been closer. There was no way to know.

15.

One afternoon, when Proctor Gadfry had been gone for a while and things were settling down into the new arrangement, the sky suddenly brightened with a sideways, vermouthy light. The air grew tinny. Ropes of clouds divided in parallel lengths, like carded wool. Since there'd been almost two weeks of cold rains, everyone went mad for a promenade.

In the old days the teachers had been considered competent enough to escort young ladies on their excursions, but with Proctor Gadfry gone for a soldier (pity the poor army), Miss Ironish had become more skittish. Or perhaps Shiz was considered marginally less safe this year than last. Who knew? So Tip, the school's jack of all trades, was enlisted to accompany Madame Chortlebush and eleven girls from Rain's section on their brisk stroll through the streets of Shiz.

Madame Chortlebush took a dim view of Miss Ironish's precautions but she tried to toe the line. "You walk first, Pit, and check for anything that might threaten us. Fissures in the paving stones, wild beasts lurking behind lampposts, bands of crazy Munchkinlanders determined to kidnap us in broad daylight and take us hostage. We shall follow behind, marching in pairs and screaming for our lives."

Ten girls chose their partners so quickly that Rain had to team with Madame Chortlebush. This didn't bother Rain as she still had little to say to her fellow students. And Madame Chortlebush did seem to enjoy Rain's company so.

Pit, Pit. Rain was trying to memorize his new name the way she had successfully learned to call herself Rainary. It was funny to see him kitted out in a somewhat ill-fitting school uniform found in the boys' clothes press. Marching along in knickerbockers and thick stockings, and a stupid jaunty scarf knotted around his neck. *Pit, Pit.* "Miss Ironish's aide-de-camp while her brother is occupied in military matters," murmured Madame Chortlebush to some friend on the street while the girls had been required to stop and gawp at the famous pleated marble dome of St. Florix. "Not my type, our Pit, but he has pretty legs for a boy."

They had their lemon barleys at a café in Railway Square. Then they crowded onto a trestle bridge to watch the noon train for the Pertha Hills inch thrillingly beneath them, thickening the bright day with coal smoke and steam. When the air cleared and the girls were brushing smuts from their clothes and hair, Rain saw Scarly enter the plaza. She looked all around, frantically, until she spotted the school group descending the wrought-iron staircase at the other side of the tracks.

"Madame Chortlebush," she cried, and waved. The teacher halted the girls on the pavement before Blackhole's, the place where university students bought and sold their old textbooks. Scarly caught up with them there.

"Important news, Miss Ironish bade me find you at once," Scarly said between gasped breaths. The news must be dreadful indeed, for what had been a bright sunny day an hour ago had gone glowery as they crossed the bridge, and the clouds that had pestered the region for two weeks were rushing back as if for a return engagement.

Scarly handed an envelope embossed with the St. Prowd's emblem.

"I can't imagine what is so important it couldn't wait," said Madame Chortlebush to Rain, while the other girls preened for the benefit of the young men from Three Queens or Ozma Towers brisking in and out of Black-hole's. Madame Chortlebush ripped the envelope open with all the finesse of a hawk eviscerating a ferret.

Then those massive ankles, clad in boots like iron socks, twisted and buckled. The considerable weight of Madame Chortlebush fell upon Rain, who could barely keep from collapsing. Tip ran to help, and he and Scarly and Rain lowered the teacher to the pavement. A clerk outside Blackhole's, covering the books on a pushcart in front in the event of rain, hurried over, too.

"She's had news of some sort," explained Scarly.

The clerk didn't have to abide by the niceties of St. Prowd's. He glanced at the folded sheet and said, "Quite quite dreadful. Her brother on the mountain front has taken a bullet."

"Taken it where?" said Scarly, though Rain could guess, and by the look on his face, Tip could too.

"Taken it to hell, I suspect. Look, we can't have fainting ladies on the pavement in front of the shop. Business is poorly enough as it is. I'll whistle for a carriage over to Railway Square, and you can get her back to St. Prowd's, if that's where she goes."

Someone came out with smelling salts. A passing student who studied magic tried to cast a charm of cheer, which made everyone's noses dribble for a few moments but produced no other discernible effect. The clerk returned with the hired carriage. Wordless and shaken, Madame Chortlebush was helped aboard, and Scarly clambered in after her to see her home.

"Mind the girls are safe, will you, Pit, there's a good lad," murmured Madame Chortlebush through her tears as the landau bounced off.

It would have been easy enough for Tip to lead the girls back at a clip, since after months of pilfering and loitering he knew the streets of Shiz well. The skies, though, chose to open just then, with renewed vigor after the morning of sunny respite.

"What'll I do?" he asked Rain, as the troupe of twelve huddled under an awning, pushing the elderly and indigent out into the downpour where they belonged.

"I saw a charabanc of some sort stationed at Railway Square," she said. "If it's still free, I bet we could all squeeze in."

Tip ran for it. The girls continued to squeal or feel faint or profess to be quite vexed indeed. The omnibus was less capacious than it had looked, and instead of four horses for which it had been designed, its shaft and harnesses were fitted to two world-weary donkeys.

"I can take ten of you, no more," said the driver, a thin mean man with toothbrush mustachios and a sorry case of pinkeye.

"Surely you can manage eleven?" said Tip. "There are eleven girls, and this isn't a downpour but a deluge."

"I'll take ten, or none. It ought to be six, but as these young ladies are all asparagus stalks I'll make an exception. I'll make four exceptions. But I won't kill my beasts for you lot. It's always the last young miss who hobbles the enterprise. Call it superstition, them's my terms."

Tip looked out of ideas. "It's all right," said Rain. "I'll walk."

So off went the driver, promising to deliver the scholars to the front door of St. Prowd's within half an hour. Rain and Tip stood a foot or two from each other, soaking but hardly chilled, looking and feeling clueless.

Rain said, "It's not going to let up for a while, by the looks of it. If we're going to get in trouble anyway, let's duck into that shop around the corner. SKURVY BASTARD'S."

They found it was closed and the storefront for lease. But the one past the newsagent's, which said BROKEN THINGS OF NO USE TO ANYONE BUT YOU, looked open.

"I suppose it doesn't matter if I'm fired, as I never applied for the job in the first place," agreed Tip at last, and they splashed through the gauze of rain and stamped through the puddles, and hurtled down the slick stone steps into the basement shop.

It was empty of customers, but at the sound of the bell on the door the proprietor emerged through a curtain of strung grommets, washers, nuts, and crimped watch springs. It was a male Bear, thinner than a Bear ought to be. A Bear brought down by hunger and stooped, maybe arthritic too, with age. He wore a shaggy bathrobe and had a muffler wrapped around his throat.

"Well, that's a nice pair of water rats the gutter has splashed down my steps this time," he said, not unkindly. "How may I be of service?"

"We're ducking the rain, actually," said Tip.

"Ducks like rain, but I take your point. Be my guest. If you find something of interest, sing out. In the meantime, don't mind me; I'll settle myself here and read the racing forms."

In time their eyes became accustomed to the gloom. "Of course, Loyal Oz wouldn't dare race talking Animals now," said the Bear. "These are antique forms. I just like to see if I can find any of my relatives. It makes me happy to see them referred to in print. I found one reference to my old auntie Groyleen, who I thought had perished in the skirmishes following the Mayonnaise Affair. She must be dead by now, of course, but in the form she was handicapped at seven to one, not bad for an old dame as she must have been even then. Don't mind me, I'm mumbling."

They wandered about. The ceiling was low, and many of the items were tall, so the high bookcases or old apothecaire's cabinets or postal boxes or discarded card catalogs, grouped back to back, built a series of chambers and secret vaults. It reminded Rain of something, but she couldn't think what. "Look, a set of wizard's globes," said Tip. "They must have had their ether extinguished or they'd be valuable. Valuable and dangerous."

Rain thought, but she didn't ask, How do you know what they are? "Here's a set of illuminatums," she said, reading the cover. "*Views of Barbaric Ugabu, with Discreet Commentary by a Missionary.*" She wasn't too old yet to stop being proud of how well she could read.

"Your wares comes from all over," said Tip to the Bear.

"So do my clients," he replied.

"And this is a stuffed scissor bird. I think they're extinct now."

"Well, that one is extinct, anyway."

The Bear shuffled to his feet and poured himself a cup of tea. "You're standing on a flying carpet," he said.

"Is that so?" asked Tip and Rain at once.

"Assuredly so. Full of flies."

Oh, but the place was musty. In one alcove a number of old tiktok contrivances stood in various stages of evisceration for spare parts. "The tiktok revolution never quite happened, no matter what the Tin Woodman said," commented the Bear. "Who needs a rebellion in labor when honest laborers are hunting for a job? I'm speaking of humans, of course; most of the Animal workforce migrated to Munchkinland during the Wizard's reign. If they could afford the punishing fees to process their applications."

Rain guessed that the Bear wasn't one of them. "You're doing all right," she said, unargumentatively.

"I'm one of the luckier ones," he replied. "I suffer a sort of amnesia, you see, and I am happiest among artifacts and antiques. Times gone by are more comforting. I don't understand these days."

"Not many do," murmured Tip.

They came across a creature made of skarkbone ribs and hooks. Some of it must be missing, for it was impossible to imagine how it might have stayed erect.

In another corner, more or less intact, was a carved wooden man, quite tall, with an enormous porcelain pumpkin balanced on skinny shoulders. "That one arrived with an actual pumpkin head," said the Bear, watching them over the tops of his spectacles. "Too many mice were making a home in his brains, though, and the pumpkin rotted. As my skull has done too. So when I came across that dreadful piece of porcelain I couldn't resist sticking it on top of the wooden man, in memory of whatever weird individual that tiktok thing once was. Jack Pumpkinhead, a certain rural type."

"It can't be tiktok without gears and sprockets and flywheels, can it?" asked Rain, remembering what she had seen of the Clock of the Time Dragon.

"There's more than one way to animate a life story," remarked the Bear.

Next to the pumpkin head stood a squat little copper beast on casters. A perfectly round copper cranium perched atop its round body. After scraping with their fingernails, they could make out the words SMITH AND TINKER'S MECHANICAL MAN on a plate corroded with green blisters. Under that an additional plate had been added, in engraver's boilerplate: PROP OF M MORRIBLE, CRAGE HALL.

He'd been messed with quite a bit. Snippers or loppers of some sort had opened his upper chest. Inside lay the dusty fragments of oraculum vials as well as coils and batteries disfigured with mouse droppings. When Rain stood back to get a look at the whole of him, for he was short and overshadowed by the others, she almost blushed. Part of the abdominal plate had come away, and a five-inch screw to which a couple of nuts were attached hung down obscenely between what you might call his legs.

"Look, we can do a Butter and Eggs lesson," she said. Before she remembered that Tip had not been in the class, she'd cupped the rusty ribbed metal piece in her hand and tilted it forward.

"Clever girl," said Tip as Rain's action wore through a weak bit of the sheathing, and the screw came off in her palm.

"Don't break the merchandise," called the Bear mildly, but he was only responding to the creak of old metal. At his desk behind his stacks of junk he was now shuffling through ancient newsfolds and reading aloud predictions of long dead weather.

Rain's manipulation had unstuck some narrow compartment in the tiktok creature's undercarriage. A rusty drawer with thin black metal edges shot forward and fell on the floor. "We should leave before I bring down the house," said Rain. "I'm a right danger."

Tip knelt and fingered the dark recess. "Something's wedged in here," he said.

He worried out a narrow packet of black cloth. "Treasure," said Rain, realizing that she knew the word but not, in fact, what might qualify as treasure in anyone else's mind other than hers. She thought of that tiny perfect inch-high horse on its single curlicue leg, carved in miniature into a stone at the Chancel of the Ladyfish. The horse like a question mark. Why hadn't she taken that as something to collect?

"Now what've we here," murmured Tip, unfolding the cloth.

Not too much—nothing like treasure according to Rain. A small rusted dirk with black stains streaked upon the blade. A set of skeleton keys. Some scraps of pink thread that might once have been rose petals? And a bit of vellum, about five inches square, folded into eight or twelve sections.

It was too dark to look at it right here. Besides, they both felt responsible. They brought it to the counter and told the Bear what had happened.

"Well, let's see what you've got there," he said, putting aside the bits and bobs, and with his shaking paws he tenderly unfolded the parchment. "Looks to me like an old map," he said. "Sadly, *not* a treasure map, as children would like. Let's have a peep."

He adjusted his spectacles. "Hmmm. Seems to be a standard issue map out of some department of government ordinances. Maybe about the time of Ozma Glamouranda? To judge by the typography? But let me find my magnifying lens." After a search he located the instrument on top of a pile of about forty children's novels, a matched set that made a column halfway to the ceiling beams. "Now. We shall see what we shall see."

"What if we bring the light closer?" asked Tip.

"My gentle friend, you are the very light of intelligence yourself. Bring the lamp. On a day this gloomy we need all the light we can find."

A second look at the map showed it clearly to be Oz before the secession of Munchkinland. The EC wasn't even called the Emerald City yet. It was an sobscure hamlet assigned the name of Nubbly Meadows. However, the general outlines of the counties of Oz seemed more or less correct. Gillikin and Munchkinland sported the greatest number of towns marked out, and the Quadling Country was represented by a single graphic smear simulating a coarse picture of marshland. The Vinkus was called "Winkie Country" and in ink someone had scrawled below, "Utter wildness, don't bother." On the left-hand margin, beyond the ring of deserts indicated by a profusion of mechanically applied dots, that same hand had written "water?" and a printer's hand-stamp of a whorled shell appeared like a messy thumbprint.

"That's nice," said Tip, pointing to the picture.

"You always liked my shell," said Rain, remembering now that he had been cradling it the night she had discovered him in her wardrobe.

Near Center Munch, in Munchkinland, Rain thought at first she spied another shell, one standing on its tip. Or maybe not. Anyway, some kind of squiggly funnel, appended by hand in quick slashes of brownish ink, with an exclamation point beside it. The punctuation mark was underlined thrice.

"This is an admirable little map," concluded the Bear. He ran his paw over the Great Gillikin Forest. "I hail from up this way, long ago. Look, does that tiny line read 'Here there be Bears'? I feel positively anointed with a personal history. Somewhere in that thicket of identical trees I imagine Ursaless, the Queen of the Northern Bears, holding court, as it was back in my day. No," he said, "I'm afraid you may not buy this thing. It has put me in mind of my past, and that happens all too seldom. If you come back tomorrow I won't remember you were here today, and if you find this map on top of a chest of drawers I'll probably sell it to you. Happily. But tonight I'm going to look at this and dream of my home, and better days long gone."

The rain was still pelting down, but the drops were less forceful, less like hail. "We should go," said Rain. They made their good-byes to the Bear, who already seemed to have forgotten them a little. As they went up the steps Tip took her hand for a moment.

"Why do you like shells?" she asked, the first thing that came to her mind in the panic of being touched on purpose.

"I like anything that is home to a secret life," he said. "I always liked nests, and eggs, and the discarded skins of snakes, and shells, and chrysalises."

"We should have bought you that flying carpet," she said. "Full of flies."

The joke wasn't any funnier the second time than the first, and Tip let her hand go. They walked back to St. Prowd's in silence to find that the girls had not been hijacked for ransom, Tip was not in line for a prison sentence or a dismissal, and Madame Chortlebush had departed already for her family home, to comfort her grieving parents.

If Miss Ironish noticed that Rain had been out alone with a boy, she chose to muscle her disapproval down. More likely, thought Rain, she doesn't really care what happens to any child whose parents don't bother to show up during Visitation Day.

But then, come to think of it, Tip himself had shown up on Visitation Day. A fairly acceptable substitution, under the circumstances.

16.

Rain thought, it's almost as if Tip and I got too close, that day in the storm, in the shop of the absentminded Bear. But he grabbed my hand, not I his. Now he seems . . . aloof. Unmoored. Like one of those floating islands that had occasionally drifted by on Restwater and, catching in some eddy invisible from shore, gently spun in place for a couple of months. Out of reach. Tip was in perfect sight, all aspects of him, just . . . just further out.

For a mean moment she thought that he might be taking up with Scarly in the kitchens, a nearer and maybe more approachable friend. But that kind of thinking was solid St. Prowd's girl attitude. Why shouldn't he chum around with Scarly if he liked her, and she was right there, shuttling between Miss Ironish and Cook? Why should it bother Rain?

She attended to her lessons the best she could. She did better and better at them. The weather brightened.

She was finishing her first full year with something that approximated honors. Astounding, given the paucity of her primary schooling. Miss Ironish remarked, "You've gone from preverbal to canny in record time," though it didn't entirely sound like a compliment.

Soon the school was abuzz with plans for the annual festival of Scandal, a city-wide hullaballoo dating to pre-Wizardic days but suppressed during his realm, due to excessive merriment and mild bawd. At recess older girls nattered to the newbies about it. A King and Queen of Scandal were elected from among the most smoldering of college students at Shiz. Comic pillorings of local magistrates and fellows at college were promised, as well as mock public punishments of random attractive passersby, administered with sprayed water or cushiony paddles. Food stalls everywhere. When the sun went down, candles would be lit in colored lanterns, magicking up the leafed-out tree boughs of Railway Square and Ticknor Circus. Music to dance by, to thrill by, to ignore. And the girls would be allowed to attend for a while, even to wander about, always under the hawkish eyes of their teachers of course.

The closer the day arrived, the less Rain was sure she wanted to attend. She hardly understood frivolity. The way everyone laughed when a bird shat once on Madame Chard's hat—but then even Madame

Chard laughed. Rain had thought it was neither funny nor not-funny. Women wear hats, birds excrete. The comedy of it seemed impoverished. Therefore, the idea of manufactured hilarity, having a good time by design or intention—well, bizarre. If not impossible or counterintuitive.

Still, she supposed, since she couldn't grasp the concept, perhaps that was good enough reason to agree to attend. Something new to learn. She could always beg off early and sneak away. Ever since the day of the rainstorm she seemed to have a special dispensation for roaming by herself, as if she alone of all the St. Prowd's girls was homely enough not to need close supervision on the street. She looked at herself in the mirror. She seemed merely to exist, neither prettier than an umbrella rack or a potted palm, nor less pretty.

Tip met her in a hallway between lessons; he was carrying a valise to Miss Ironish's study. "Are you going to lark about tomorrow at that silly festival?" she asked him.

"I'll have to wait to get my instructions for the day," he said. "Miss Ironish may be going to see her brother, who has been given a few days off from his training exercises. He is hoping for a pass to the Emerald City for some rest and recovery. I may be required to accompany her as a chaperone."

Rain's regret must have showed on her face before she could mask it. Tip said, "I'd rather skive off with you and see what's going on in the town centre."

"If I see our friend the Northern Bear, I'll give him your regards," she said airily.

"Pit," said Madame Chard from her doorway, "what *are* you doing loafing about in the hall? Miss Rainary, your books await you. We're at Lesson Seventeenish. Making the Least of Fractions."

The next day Rain's fears proved reliable; Miss Ironish did commandeer Tip's company for her excursion. They would travel by the rail line, recently completed, between Shiz and the Emerald City. It would cut their travel time in half, and they would return in under a week. Madame Skinkle would serve as proctress-pro-tem. "Honor her as you would myself," advised Miss Ironish before alighting the carriage that would take her to Railway Square. Since none of the girls particularly honored Miss Ironish, the instruction seemed easy enough to follow.

Rain saw that Scarly was also traveling in attendance of Miss Ironish. "I hope you all have a very fine time," Rain muttered as the carriage pulled away.

"What's that, Miss Rainary?" asked Miss Igilvy.

"Nothing at all. Are you going to the silly affair in town?"

"Yes," said Miss Igilvy. "Shall we be chums, after all? I'm going to wear my dotted morpheline with the lace trim. What will you wear?"

"Clothes, I suspect." That was intended to put Miss Igilvy off, but it didn't work. Rain was saddled with Miss Igilvy half the afternoon and into the evening. But she wasn't so bad. Out of some sour mood, Rain even took her into the shop. The Northern Bear didn't recognize Rain, and when she found the folded map tossed aside on top of an overstuffed and listing book-case, she took it to the counter. "Would you sell me this?" she asked.

The Bear looked at it and named a modest price. Rain hesitated. But the Bear would never miss it. Another theft. She handed over a guilty coin.

"That kind of dive is what Miss Ironish would have us pass by," said Miss Igilvy as they left. "Miss Rain-ary, we're skirting the main events. It's getting dark enough, they'll have lit the trees. I can hear the music. Enough of antique tiktokery and old maps. We're now, and here."

The festival seemed to Rain overloud and feverish, sort of desperate. A fiddler and three country dancers made a ruckus in the square, and barmaids from local establishments were going about with tankards of ale or barleywater. Miss Igilvy and Rain caught up with a couple of the girls who were about to commence to one of the colleges in the fall. "It's so different this year," complained a droll young woman whose name Rain had never learned. "I can't put my finger on it."

"It's a lack of men, you moron," said her mate. "Look about you. Even the college boys are in short supply. They've been pulled for military duty. If you've come to the party hoping to snag a snog, I believe you'll be sorely disappointed."

The whole town seemed to have turned into an extension of the experience of life at St. Prowd's—that is, without the distraction of lessons. Rain found it taxing and crude. "I think I'll go back," she said to Miss Igilvy. "Can I safely attach you to these graduates?"

"Shhh, the Lord Mayor is going to speak."

The Lord Mayor of Shiz looked quite a bit like the Senior Overseer of St. Prowd's. But what a girth of belly!

"There is a reason to celebrate on every given day," he said, once the crowd had quietened down. "We shouldn't go about the business of beating our breasts because of the hardships placed upon us by the war. And yet, as we dance and sing and feast and frolic, we should be mindful of our soldiers called up to duty. And we must remember, as all living and sentient creatures do, that the life we have today may be utterly changed by tomorrow.

"Change approaches as inevitably as the seasons. I urge you not to succumb to the rumors of threat to Shiz that abound this week, but savor every moment the Unnamed God confers upon you. What will happen next week, next season, next year, we will take in its turn. Meanwhile, in the shadow of the hallowed buildings of this ancient university, let us know ourselves to be alive. Whether we are the next generation to study peaceably in this haven or we are the final generation, let us study what we can. Learn what we can. Deliver what we have to whomever comes after, whether they sit in rubble and ashes or strut in finery upon the streets during Scandal Day."

He had to blow his nose, and his wife led him off the stage. No one had the slightest idea what he was talking about.

Madame Chard, the next day, offered a little enlightenment. "I went into a pub—only to visit the conveniences," she admitted, "and the talk I heard there would have cured your bacon, believe me. In wartime all kinds of nonsense circulates, and we know from history that the enemy will use rumors to terrify the brave patriots at home. Still, you young ladies are old enough to take in what is being said, I believe, if you promise not to frighten the younger girls with the news. It's being whispered that Shiz has been selected as a new target by the Munchkinlanders. No one knows how an attack will come, as of course our brave army is holding the Munchkinlanders off in the Madeleines."

"Holding them off?" asked Miss Igivly. "I thought we were invading them." Miss Igilvy isn't as frivolous as she seems, thought Rain.

"Tactics, strategies; ours not to question the military mind," replied Madame Chard. "But spies among us may be targeting Shiz for special attack. Perhaps localized explosions to frighten the populace. We shall stand firm. We shall not be moved."

By the time Miss Ironish returned home a few days later, many of the girls *had* been moved. Their families had swum up out of nowhere to collect their precious daughters. Graduation was held in the dining hall, since the chapel was too large and would have pointed up the thinning of the ranks.

Rain avoided Scarly and Tip, both, trying not to be obvious about it. But the third evening after they had returned, Scarly showed up in Rain's room and pressed her to talk to Tip.

"I have nothing special to say to him," said Rain.

"He needs to talk to you," she replied. "Don't ask me why."

Well, that's something, thought Rain, so the next day, in as casual a manner as she could, she found a way to sidle up to him in the buttery pantry as she was helping to clear the luncheon things away. "Yoo hoo," she said, sounding brittle even to herself. "I have a present for you."

His eyebrows raised at the sight of the map. "You weaseled this out of the Bear? How could you do that?"

"I weaseled nothing. He told us we could come back and buy it later. Why are you so huffy?"

"Never mind. I'm just—surprised."

She felt horrible and couldn't say why. "Well, you wanted to see me," she continued, all Ironish.

He shared the news about a suspected attack upon Shiz. It was all the word in the Emerald City, he said. "Yes, I'm aware of that," she replied. "I'm not blind to the fact that the school population has been cut in half. But why do you think it should concern me?"

"Well, I shouldn't want you to be caught in an attack," he said, as if bemused she should have to ask.

"Don't worry over *me*. You have yourself to think about."

"Isn't there a way to contact your mother? She won't want you left here in danger, surely?"

"I think it's all blather. Madame Streetflye flutters, 'Speculation! designed—to, to . . . intimidate us!' Tip, life seems the same to me as ever, if just that little bit more tedious."

"I don't know. In the EC they're murmuring that the enemy has gotten its hands on some profoundly dangerous and powerful book of magic. If La Mombey, who is something of a sorceress, actually has it in her possession, and can decode it, there's no telling what havoc may be unleashed upon us."

"A book of magic?" Rain felt light-headed. "Where was it found? What is it called? How long have they had it?"

"I can't answer any of those things. For all I know this is only one of your rumors, as you would have it. Designed to give a psychological upper hand to the Munchkinlanders. But that's what they're saying on every street corner of the EC. Proctor Clapp was devastated at the prospects; his sister says he's quite shattered by his experiences and may never be the same."

"Those aren't rumors," said Rain. "I must leave—I must leave tonight. Can you help me get out?"

"What are you talking about?"

"I've changed my mind. I mean about the threat of empty rumors. If the Grimmerie has been acquired by anyone—by either of the antagonists—"

"Yes, that's the name of it. The Grimmerie. How did you know?"

"Never mind. The danger is real. And I must go. I can't say why, nor where. I must go. And you must go, too. Get out of Shiz."

"You care that much about me?" His tone half taunting, half skeptical.

"If they've got the Grimmerie, they won't hesitate to use it. Everyone tells me so. The war is bleeding both countries dry, and whoever has a fiercer weapon will punish their enemy with it. You're in danger here if the Munchkinlanders have actually found the book. You have to go."

"What about Madame Chard?" asked Tip. "Or Miss Ironish? Or Miss Igilvy, or Scarly? Or the others?"

"They're all in danger, but I can't spend a week convincing them. I'll tell Miss Ironish right now, and she'll have to use her powers as proctress to decide what to do with the information. But no matter what happens, I'm leaving tonight. You should too."

"I have no place to go," he said.

"Use the map I gave you and find one," she couldn't help snapping.

Miss Ironish saw her into the study. She had aged in the year since Rain had arrived. Her eyes were sunk into dark sockets and her skin had become crepey. "Miss Rainary, I have only a moment for you. I am not in the habit of having private interviews with my girls unless I call for them."

"Thank you for seeing me, Miss Ironish." Rain explained her concerns—that she believed the threat to Shiz wasn't propaganda designed to scare the citizens of the city, but was real.

"If our enemy has acquired a weapon that might turn the tide of the war in their favor," said Miss Ironish, "I doubt they'd bother to use it on our fair city. Symbolic of achievement though we may be, we are still only a provincial capital. The Emperor of Oz rules from the Emerald City and that's where the war will be lost, should we lose it. And we could never lose it; Oz is too vast to be governed by the little people of the east."

"I don't know which city is more deserving of attack," said Rain. "Maybe because Shiz is the college town of Oz, Munchkinlanders feel it would be a more terrible blow to crush it. Or maybe they intend to, like, practice their new technique of assault here? And frighten the EC into submission? So Loyal Oz might sue for peace? To preserve the palace and the administration buildings from devastation?"

"Govern yourself. Panic is a folly, Miss Rainary. I'm impressed though by your colorful language."

"I don't care. I just want you to know that the threat is real, and you should do everything you can to protect yourself, your teachers, Cook, the maids, the girls. It is your duty."

"I will not be told my duty by a student." Eyes blazing, Miss Ironish stood up. "I will not honor you by asking you on what basis you draw your conclusions. You are criminally impertinent. I shall consider your punishment. Miss Rainary, you are dismissed."

Rain stood there, wringing her hands.

"Get out of my study, I said."

That night Miss Ironish saw to it that the wonky stable door, which Tip had foolishly repaired as part of his chores, was bolted tightly. Then she locked the door to the annex, sealing Rain inside. "I may open the door in time for your breakfast, such as it is these days," shrilled Miss Ironish through the door, "or I may not. Think upon your disgrace, Miss Rainary."

Rain wasn't sharply surprised, once the lights had gone out all over the school, to hear footsteps on the stairs. Tip arrived with a small satchel of clothes on his back.

"I saw her storming about like a maniac," he said. "Muttering your name. And since you said you were leaving, I hid downstairs before she locked you in. I know mere locks won't hold you."

"I hardly know how I am going to get out," said Rain, though she had packed a few clothes herself, and some rolls she had smuggled from dinner. She left behind the single rock, the feather, the acorn, the arrowhead. She had packed the large pink shell, though.

"Isn't it obvious how you're going to leave?"

It wasn't, until he pointed a finger skyward.

He went up the ladder first. Remembering the time their shoulders had grazed, she waited until he had clambered out of the hatch. She lifted Tay through, and then followed. She had never looked over the roofs of Shiz at night. It was beautiful, but less distinct than she might have imagined. Maybe people were darkening their windows or conserving their oil, as month by month the prices of staples had continued to rise. She could make out the famous dome of St. Florix most easily, a dark perfect mound against a velvet sky that, as it rose, became pinned in place with frozen stars.

"Up is easy," whispered Tip. "Down is tricky." But they made it quickly enough across the leads, monkeying themselves groundward via rain gutters and downspouts and old dead ivy whose thick espaliered limbs had never been carved away from the back of the stables.

Once at the street level, Rain said, "Which way are you going?"

He answered, without catching her eye, "Which way are you going?"

Rain hesitated, then pointed west.

"Then I'm going that way too."

17.

She argued furiously with him for half the night. She didn't need a chaperone. She wasn't scared to be on her own anymore. In fact, she said, she'd *never* been scared to be on her own.

He countered by saying that since he hadn't applied for a job at St. Prowd's he didn't have to apply for permission to leave. He happened to be walking on the road from Shiz at the same hour and in the same direction she was going. What was wrong with that?

Often she sunk into black silences. She wasn't used to arguing. She'd lived in her own world so much, she'd never had to apologize for it, nor explain. So a traveling partner her own age—even one she liked when she wasn't arguing with him—was going to be a burden of sorts.

"You know," she said, "if I have gotten older since we met, so have you. And while you might be young enough not to have been called up to service during this round of inductions, if you stand still in a public place like Shiz you'll be old enough to be fingered the next time, certainly."

"You're certain about a lot of things of which you have no notion."

"Explain," she said. "Prove me wrong, then."

But he changed the subject. "Where are you going? Off to find your mother?"

"In a matter of speaking," she said, for she hadn't entirely lost her habit of reticence, even though St. Prowd's, and indeed the bricked walls of Shiz, were now several hours behind them.

The moon had risen. Tonight it looked without character. Just a disc cut out of paper and fastened with sticky string to the sky. A smell of arugula and basil pushed up from small cottage farms sunk a few feet below the high road. The wind was rousing but warm. No one was about except anonymous animals scrabbling in the hedgerows. Once they heard the low of a pained cow that some unreliable farmhand had forgotten to milk. Tip was unhappy about that cow and wanted to scurry off to help her, and Rain said, "Go ahead, do that good deed, but I must keep on the road as long as my legs will carry me," so he left the cow in her misery and kept pace with Rain.

Gillikin west of Shiz.

"Where are you going?" he asked.

She didn't answer, but when they came to a crossroads where a stone gave several choices—a boon, this moonlit night!—the fifth of five choices said simply THE WEST. That road looked the most desperate, and she struck out along that one, though the striking was slowing down some, and eventually they stopped to sleep a little. They burrowed under a hedgerow, mightily irritating some birds and some sort of family reunion of mice. Was it only a dream that they were talking to her? "If you're headed for the Kells, you've chosen well enough. But once you reach the Gillikin River follow it to your left until the mountains come in sight. You will have crossed into the Vinkus by then, and be near enough to ask directions to Kiamo Ko."

She woke before Tip did. His hand was on her breast, and he slept with his mouth open. Tay dozed greenly between them, closer to both than they could dare be to each other. She hadn't heard Tip breathing in his sleep for what seemed like such a long time. She began to cry for no reason she could name. Tay stirred and licked Rain's tears off her face with its sandpaper tongue.

Once there had been a mouseskin in a field. It had been on her finger. She had wanted to be a mouse. She had wanted to be something other than what she was. She had had so many chances, and she had passed so many of them by.

I must have become what Madame Chortlebush calls a teenmonster, crying for nothing, and feeling my life is over. She warned us about this, thought Rain.

"Wake up, it's not morning but it's light enough to walk," she said to Tip, but she didn't move, for she didn't want his hand to slip away an instant sooner than it needed to.

He woke and shuddered and seemed not to notice he had been touching her. He shuffled to the other side of the hedge and let loose a long confident stream of pee, standing up. She turned her head away and softly smiled to herself, and couldn't say why.

The road grew rougher, less traveled; and while there were farmers about, with carts and animals, no one paid the young walkers much mind. Well, Rain hardly looked like a St. Prowd's girl, having slept in her best dress, which was never very good to start with. And Tip had left behind the penitential uniform that Miss Ironish had insisted he wear. They looked like brother and sister traipsing along, since they were too young still to be—to be anything else.

She tried to make small talk, as they called it, but it was too small for Tip, and she soon gave up. Tay capered after them almost as a dog might, and sometimes allowed itself to be carried on the shoulders of one or the other. They bought the cheapest food at any crossroad farmstand they passed, always taking care to follow signs for THE WEST, which by late in the day had begun to be called GILLIKIN R. With an attempt at good humor Tip referenced the map once or twice, but its markings were archaic, and Rain was happier when he put it away.

"Why aren't you heading toward your own home?" Rain asked once.

"Why aren't you minding your own business?" he replied.

So they walked, and ate, and sang a little bit—that was neutral enough—and slept again. Longer this time, for they had spent a whole day on shank's mare. The next day Rain had blisters and the friends had to slow down. The day after that Tip had grown his own blisters, worse than hers, and they paused on the banks of a river they had found. They didn't know if it was the Gillikin already or a tributary, but if they turned left at the water's edge and kept walking west, they would either see the great mountains sooner or later on the horizon, or they would see their river merge with a larger one. That is, assuming the mice in the hedgerow were correct. But how could mice know where Rain wanted to go?

A series of bluffs and strands ran down to the water's edge, which was frantic with fish life and seemed some sort of bird paradise as well. Tay dove away from them for the water, and for a moment Rain thought she might have lost her rice otter forever, but after a half hour's frolic Tay returned, its hair slicked back and some sort of weed in its teeth, a very happy look on its face.

Rain and Tip found a kind of cave with a little ledge in front of it, almost a front porch with a river view. A single room, not too deep, nothing scary asleep inside but for a few bats in the ceiling. What could be better? Tay brought them some fish, and Tip, who'd come equipped with a flintstone, struck up a small fire. Whatever fish it was, he baked it wrapped in whatever greens. It was the best meal Rain had ever eaten.

She didn't remember falling asleep, but she was suddenly sitting bolt awake. The bats were screeching in pitches too high to hear; they were saying something like "Oh!" and "No!" and "Blow!" Tip was gone, and Tay was asleep in some richly enviable dream. Rain leapt to her feet, her senses as alert as an animal's, and cried out, not even in words.

The fire had gone down and she stepped in the embers in her haste, because she had heard Tip moan, perhaps. She fell to her hands and knees and looked over the edge of the bluff. Tip lay six or eight feet below, on his chest.

She remembered someone called Zackers, but not what or where about him. "Tip?" she called.

The moon was lowering at this hour but there was enough light still for her to see an animal of some sort, an overgrown grite perhaps, and a partner or mate behind it, growling and tensing to jump.

She reached for the first thing her hand fell upon, the shell, and she almost threw it, but something stopped her. "Blow!" said the bats. She put the broken tip to her lips and puffed up her cheeks and forced air through the aperture as if it were a trumpetina.

The sound screeched like ogre's fingernails on an ogre's slate, and any remaining bats in the cave fled the premises permanently. But so did the grites. Then Rain slithered down to crouch beside Tip and check to see how hurt he was.

Not very, it turned out. He wouldn't admit until the next morning that he had gotten up in the middle of the night to pee off the edge of their cliff-porch, and misjudged. So, maybe not so hot to be a boy, thought Rain, but she didn't say so.

She remembered the Clock crashing down a slope the time her forgotten companions had come across the Ivory Tiger in the poppy fields. That earthquake. And the other time, when the Clock slid off into Kellswater, up to its gills in fatal water. Now Tip himself was hurt from a fall. To aim high—to risk the prospect—well, there was no assurance of safety. Ever. As the world turned, it kept sloping itself into new treacheries. To live at all meant to risk falling at every step.

He couldn't walk just yet; his ankle or his shin was bruised. He could hardly name the location of the pain, and Rain couldn't tell. She wished Little Daffy were here. "A day's rest won't hurt," she said.

"You are in such a hurry, can't stop to help relieve an unmilked cow. So you should go on without me," he taunted her.

She didn't reply, just went scavenging for breakfast.

Later. "You saved my life, you know. Those over-grown grites were a nasty branch of the grite family. They were all ready to jump. I couldn't have fended them off for long, or gotten away. After all this, to be eaten by beasts in the wild! A certain mythic justice, probably, but no fun for me."

"After all this?" said Rain. And now, since she had saved his life, he more or less had to tell her something. Otherwise he'd have died and she wouldn't even have known a thing about him, really.

"I know you were a fairly useless butler to Miss Ironish," she declared.

"A studied ineffectuality," he protested. "Kept me from being pestered for ever more boring chores."

This is what he told her. He had come to Shiz from Munchkinland a year or so before he had met her in St. Prowd's. He was an orphan but had escaped from the house of the person who had both raised him and imprisoned him. "A single woman," said Tip. "A powerful and important woman, who had dozens of minions at her beck and call. I never knew why she paid attention to me, but she kept me closest of all, under her eye and in her chambers. I couldn't bear it. All the time the ministers of war came and went, and I had to crouch on a stool behind her formal chair."

"She sounds very important indeed," said Rain politely. "A charwoman at some fine hotel, perhaps?"

"Don't make fun of me."

"Don't make a fool of me. I just saved your life, remember?"

So he told her. "I was in the household of the infamous Mombey, who serves as Eminence of Munchkinland, and who directs the war of defense against the mongrel Ozians."

"Mongrel Ozians?" Rain had to laugh. She was quite a mongrel herself, part Quadling, part Arjiki, part Munchkinlander.

"*They* invaded Munchkinland," Tip reminded her, but then he shook his head. "Oh, but that's only part of why I left. I couldn't bear the endless posturing. The Emperor of Oz may be a demiurge or whatever he has named himself, but La Mombey herself is a sorceress of no mean skill."

"Do you think she has found the Grimmerie?" asked Rain.

"All I know is that she has had her people looking for it," said Tip sadly. "For the book, and for the descendants of the Wicked Witch of the West, for in their hands the book would reveal its secrets most quickly, and Mombey is in urgent need of some sort of surge in the attempt to beat back the Ozians. Whether she got the book first or the Emperor's men did, I can't tell; but if it's truly in the custody of one or the other of those adversaries, things will change before long."

"Yes, they will," said Rain. She told him who she was, and that she was heading for Kiamo Ko to see if her parents were still alive, since they had had the Grimmerie last. Then, because Tip clearly hated divulging secrets of his past as much as she did, she kissed him on the mouth so there would be no more talking for a while.

She collected the kisses one by one by one, but she didn't count them.

VI

God's Great-Niece

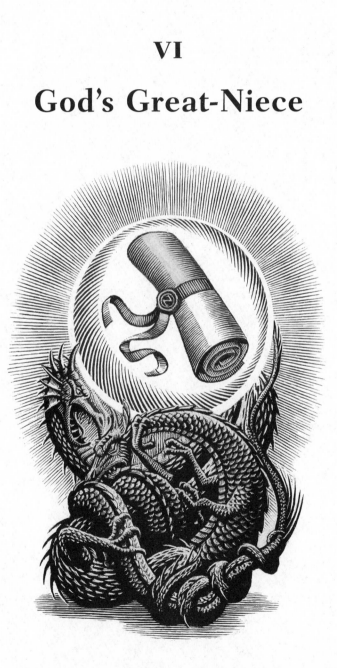

1.

A good season to walk. Later—and not all that much later—Rain would look upon the six weeks it took them to find their way to Kiamo Ko as the happiest period of her young life.

They forded the Gillikin River easily enough, swimming when they had to, wading the rest of the way. When they reached the Vinkus River, a more treacherous waterspill channeled between obdurate yellow cliffs, they feared they'd been stopped. Spent days walking first north and then south along its banks, becoming desperate. Tay responded to their anxiety and made a whimpering sound but wouldn't plunge into the water until they were ready to forge ahead too.

Finally, at a stretch where the river widened and slowed, they came across a beaver dam. How the colony had managed to build against such force was hardly short of miraculous, thought Tip. Rain, less inclined to consider anything miraculous, remarked that if they could interview a talking Beaver they might learn a good deal.

Such a moment presented itself once they were almost across. What had looked like detritus caught up against the brackwork of fortifications on the far side turned out to be a lodge. And, "Hullo there, don't step too hard or you'll bring down the ceiling on my mother-in-law," said a Beaver, turning a fish over in her paws and eyeing them with wariness and courtesy alike.

She introduced herself as Luliaba. The lodge was empty at this hour except for her aging mother-in-law, who wanted to be put to the sea in a coracle and allowed to sail to her doom, but she was too beloved by the clan and so they had locked her in her room, the better to cherish her.

"Put to sea?" said Rain, to whom the phrase seemed excessive.

"Term we have, in Beaver lore," said Luliaba companionably. "The mortal goal of our species is to build a dam big enough to flood all of Oz, as legend says once happened. Then all the rivers would flow together, making the mythical sea of story and song, and on the other side of that misty rainbow all the Beavers who've gone before will be having a fish fry, and waiting for us there. She's anxious to git going, y'see. She's been learning off new marinade recipes that have come in fashion since her lollymama and lollypapa died, and she's afraid she'll go soft in the noggin and forgit them before she gets there. The dear."

"She thinks all that, she's already soft," said Rain, for whom the mystery of the silent animal had more potency than that of the chattering classes.

"The notion of a world of water, it always makes me feel ill," said Tip. "But tell us how you came to build this magnificent barricade."

"I'm chief engineer on this job site," said Luliaba. "And I don't mind saying that the sweet accident of co-incidence is the best foundation upon which to build. Two big ole stag-head oaks, uprooted upriver upmonth, floated into view one morning pretty as you please, and lodged for a while against some rocks you can't see. About a third of the way out. Before they could work their way free, we'd established the underwater salients, using cedar logs we had stripped and at the ready. Cedar don't rot under water like some woods, you know. By sunset the first day we'd begun the breakwater to slow the pressure moving against the twiggy firmament. Come a couple more days, we'd already completed the

initial span. Your basic herringbone. Long since sub-
sumed by upgrades done by artisan builders, of course.
But the essentials we git all in place on day one."

"Let me out!" cried the mother-in-law from below.

"Can we bring her something, maybe? A present?"
asked Tip. "In exchange for your letting us cross over?"

"Bring me a gun!" cried the mother-in-law. "I'll
shoot my way out, or shoot my brains out if that don't
work!"

"A tasty flank of otter would be awful welcome."
Luliaba leered at Tay.

"We'll be going now," said Rain.

"Take me with!" came from inside the lodge. "I'll
be good! I won't foul the nest any more than I can
help it!"

"If we come back this way, we'll try to bring you a
little coracle," called Tip, looking at Rain and shrugging.

"Not too little! I'm not the glass of fashion and the
mirror of form I was in my springwater days!"

The travelers headed up the bank. Tip kept Tay
safe in his arms. "You're awfully sweet to a talky old
Beaver," said Rain. "Do you really mean you'd bring
her a boat?"

"Well, if the opportunity presented itself."

"Why are you so nice?"

"You make me nice. I'm pleased this all happened—that I ended up bursting out of your wardrobe instead of, say, Miss Ironish's. Or Miss Igilvy's."

"Or Scarly's?" She could risk making that almost-joke now that they had put so many miles between themselves and St. Prowd's.

"Or Scarly's." He was sound and firm, and didn't rise to the ribbing. "It's just as Luliaba said. The sweet accident of coincidence is the best foundation on which to build. I might have gone in any direction once I escaped from Colwen Grounds. I might have gone to the Emerald City to throw myself on the mercy of the Emperor."

"Smart move, avoiding that. For a deity, he isn't widely known for his mercy."

"Even ending up at Shiz, I might have found some sort of position at one of the colleges. Or hired out for that Bear, to help him in his shop in exchange for a mattress. I might even have come to St. Prowd's before you'd been moved out to the annex. Really!—doesn't coincidence hurt the sense of reason? What's the likelihood that I'd have escaped the court of La Mombey, where I'd already heard of the Grimmerie, only to stumble across you, who seem to be one of its closest relatives?"

"We don't do probability theory until third year at St. Prowd's, but I'd guess about ozillion to one." She trained her eyes on the tall grasses to select the best path across the plateau rising west of the Vinkus River. Butterflies hung like slow confetti as far as the eye could see. "The chances are so slim, in fact"—she paused as the thought consolidated—"that it might make me wonder if La Mombey had charmed you to find me."

"Well." He was taken aback by that. No easy riposte to offer. Finally he shrugged and said, "If she did, we have something to thank her for at last. But you'd expect she'd also have charmed me to kidnap you and take you back to her, so that even if she didn't have the Grimmerie, she'd have you in custody. Then if the Emperor's men found the book first, at least they wouldn't have you, too."

"Maybe she did charm you to do that," said Rain, though she didn't really believe it. "You just haven't gotten around to it yet."

"If she did, then you cast a stronger charm upon me," he said.

"Stop that. You sound like one of the silly schoolgirls on the second floor."

They walked in sunlight, in shadow, speaking and not speaking. The hours were long and their feet hurt, and their stomachs rumbled like thunder. They postponed fretting about what they would find at Kiamo Ko; it couldn't be helped from this distance, not yet.

Gradually the sentinel mountains emerged from heat haze, to supervise their progress. First filmy banks, easily mistaken for a low storm front on the horizon; then icy translucencies; then, too soon—all too soon— the silhoutte of Oz's natural ramparts. The Great Kells.

Foot ahead of foot, step step step. They were in little need of omens. They trusted to the charm of chance. Why not? It had done them no harm so far.

2.

From the east the Kells rose, wrinkled solidity, and scored to two-thirds of their height by innumerable aromatic conifers. Few low valleys, but as Rain and Tip climbed they kept finding pockets of higher pastureland. Hung tarns. Sudden upland meadows where Arjiki tribespeople had been settled forever.

Like the chancel above the Sleeve of Ghastille, these villages were often invisible to climbers until the last few steps, and then the settlements would appear as if sprinkled there by the wind. The huts were made of stone and the roofs of thatch and grass, bundled in bristly fagots and weighed down by rocks tied into place. The first village on Knobblehead Pike was Fanarra, said the villagers, pointing to it and naming it. Tip and Rain could understand little else but the mountain courtesy that gestured, "Come, eat. Here, sleep. Blanket." They treated Tip and Rain as a married couple, bedding them close, which Rain didn't mind and Tip didn't seem to either, as far as Rain could determine. Upon leaving the village they noticed other couples not much older than they were. They saw an infant in a sling who wailed every time the teenage mother hit it.

"That isn't right," murmured Tip as they passed.

"Send it down the everlasting sea in a little coracle, it'll be fine," said Rain. Tip didn't talk to her for a while after that.

Fanarra led, another day's steep hike, to Upper Fanarra, where the welcome was equally warm. Someone slaughtered a young goat and it was roasted at night, and the whole village celebrated. Tip sang a Munchkinlander spinniel that was intended to be comic, but the villagers closed their eyes and listened with painful care as if it were a voice from the beyond.

> Silly me tender, silly me sweet,
> Tickle me under the bandstand.
> Handle me merciful, handle me neat
> And I'll tickle you under the waistband.

"I think Tip is tipsy," said Rain that night, so he tickled her.

The villagers of Upper Fanarra responded eagerly to the mention of Kiamo Ko, and by wheeling motions they suggested it wasn't a day or two farther on, three at most. Coming up for late summer now, thought Rain. Probably autumn arrived earlier in the high hills. Rain and Tip needed to warm themselves around a breakfast campfire for a few moments before starting out.

"I'm still thinking about that little baby," Tip confessed. "I wish we had taken it with us."

"We can't even hold our liquor, can we," said Rain, "how are we going to hold a baby?"

"Not for us," he said. "I just mean, to save it from that poor exhausted mother."

"We're not old enough for a child. We're children still."

"How old are you?" he asked her.

"Somewhere between school and college."

"No, really."

"I don't know. I've grown used to ignoring the question. By the standards of the students at St. Prowd's, I seemed to be about thirteen from some points of view, and fifteen from others. But perhaps I'm eleven, and quick for my age. How old are you?"

He shook his head. "Another way we are made for each other. I can tell even less clearly than you can. I just tramp on and on and I feel as if I never change much. I've been a boy since I was born."

He had raised the subject, but now he seemed to regret it; there was tension in his face, and he walked ahead for a while. She let him go, looking at his stride, the easy throb of his lengthening hair against the straps of his rucksack. She knew what it was to have a broken childhood. It was easier to understand Tip, she now saw, than it had been to figure out the girls of St. Prowd's. That wasn't their fault, of course; perhaps she'd been supercilious to them. Too late now.

She caught up to him. "Tell me about La Mombey, then."

That eased the invisible rack of distress on his shoulders. "She's a mighty dangerous woman to have as a landlady," was all he would say at first, but he relented. "She's got scented oil instead of blood, I think; she slithers inside her clothes."

"Do you mean that really, or are you prettifying through language?"

He laughed. "I'm not sure. Sometimes you say something to be pretty and it turns out to be pretty accurate. I guess I mean she's a mystery even to me, and I've lived with her my whole life."

"Well," she said, "are you her son, then?"

"I am not." Said firmly.

"If you don't know who your parents are, how can you be so sure?"

"For a good many years Mombey was a ferocious old hag, like someone you'd see grubbing for coins in the street outside the opera. She had bristles on her chin, and her back was bent double. She couldn't walk but for sticks and my shoulder; I was her ambulatory cane. Since she was unable to move without me, I went everywhere with her and I saw everything."

"So she's too old to be your mother, you're saying."

"Yes. I suppose she could be my great-great-great-grandmother. But who cares?"

"What is she doing without you now you've run away?"

"Oh, I'm talking about long ago, before she was named Eminence of Munchkinland. You wouldn't recognize her by the description I've just given. I hardly can remember it myself."

"What happened? She found a spa and took the waters?"

"No. But she dragged me on a long journey over the sands to one of the duchy principalities, I think it was Ev—"

Rain stopped in her tracks. "No one can cross the deadly sands."

"You believe that?"

"Everyone believes it—isn't it true?"

"Oh, well, if everyone believes it." He was mocking her. "And lunch pails grow on trees, too, you know, in some parts of Oz. And even the little bunnies have their own Bunnytown."

"Don't make fun of me. I only had one year of schooling, and we concentrated on the life and times of Handy Mandy, a child burglar."

"Well, I have had no schooling but whatever I picked up at Mombey's hip. And those so-called deadly sands aren't impossible to cross. They're only deadly if you're stupid enough not to pack properly. Though, to be fair, Mombey may have made it easier because of some spell or other. We had a sand sledge and pressed on through windstorms a week in duration, and when we arrived Mombey presented herself to some second-rate duchess who served us vile sandwiches on alabaster plates. The duchess knew a secret for changing the shape of her head and her body, and performed it for us as a kind of afternoon entertainment. Like charades. Or putting on a tableau vivant. There was only a screen at the end of the room, and she showed us that there were no trapdoors or hidden chambers in which a bevy of beautiful women could wait their turn to pretend to be the duchess. Her magic was limited to that one party trick, but she did enjoy demonstrating it. Her beauty made Mombey look even more hideous by comparison."

"So . . . ?"

"So when we left, we returned via a lengthy tour of other places where Mombey had private audiences with various potentates, and I watched the sledge. Eventually we reemerged in northern Gillikin, making landfall someplace near Mount Runcible. Mombey drove the vehicle into a gulley, so we had to catch the train heading south from the Pertha Hills. And on the train old Mombey went off to use the powder room, and she powdered herself pretty damn pretty, because I didn't recognize her when she came back."

"Had she bought the charm, do you think?"

"I didn't ask. Later I wondered if the duchess of Ev woke up on her fainting couch the morning after we said good-bye to find herself dead. But La Mombey has never looked back, and presents herself effectively. Shortly after that, she managed to become elevated to Eminence of Munchkinland, due to some odd distant relationship to old Pastorius."

Rain didn't know ancient Oz history and didn't much care, but Tip had never talked so much about his past before. She didn't want to cut him off. She let him go on about Pastorius and how he was married to the last reigning Ozma, called Ozma the Bilious, who died of an accidental poisoning involving rat extermination pellets. Pastorius was to serve as Ozma Regent until his daughter grew up, but then the Wizard of Oz arrived in his famous balloon, blah blah, blah blah, and that was the end of Pastorius.

"And the baby?" said Rain, thinking of the Arjiki baby in the papoose.

"You really have wandered a far foreign strand, haven't you? Old crones and cronies cherish the legend that the baby is nestled in some cradle underground, waiting to reemerge in Oz's darkest hour. The second coming of Ozma, they call it. Since the first coming was a bit of a blunder."

"Well, that's old folks. What about anyone else?"

"The Wizard of Oz wasn't known for sentimentality. Anyone who could send that Dorothy and her minions out to slaughter your grandmother in her retirement castle would just as easily have ground up a little of that rat poison into the baby's formula and let the infant have her fatal teat. Poor mite."

"Hey, watch your mouth. One of those so-called minions is Brrr, my defender."

"I'm your defender now," he told her.

"And I'm yours," she sallied back at him. "So I'm advising you, as your counsel, to watch your mouth before I hit you."

They were only teasing, but Tay became upset at the tone of their voices, and chattered in a scolding, magpie way. So they softened their tones, and held hands to pull each other up over the rocky way.

3.

They came into the hamlet of Red Windmill when the sun had just set. The mountains were dark cutouts above them, while the sky to the west retained its paleness, as if it rose so high it became scarce of air. One of the shepherds in the village could speak enough Ozish to tell them that the castle of Kiamo Ko was only a short distance along, but the climb was difficult at any hour and impossible by dark. Rain and Tip could be there in time for morning coffee, though, if they set out at sunrise.

Finally—because she could distract herself no longer with interviewing Tip on all subjects that came to mind—Rain had to think about what they might find. The village translator wouldn't understand the questions she asked, perhaps on purpose. He said it would be safe for Rain to go and see for herself. Now good night, and leave the cups from the mint tea on the small carpet outside the door.

Tip was gentle and held her through the night, as her panic grew and then subsided. Surely Candle and Liir were there, and safe. Maybe the theft of the Grimmerie was only a rumor designed to strike fear and confusion into the military opposition. Or maybe her parents had fled, and left a note for her. Or fled and left no note at all, and there would be nothing but a hatchet on the floor and dark patches where the blood had dried to char.

Or maybe Candle and Liir—my parents, practice that!—would be waiting, a fork luncheon slapped out upon some sideboard, like St. Prowd's on Visitation Day. After all, Candle had been able to see the present, somehow. Maybe Candle knew that her daughter was restless tonight in the village below the castle walls of Kiamo Ko.

Maybe her mother knew she was sleeping with her arms around Tip. Maybe she knew that Rain had finally understood that the one missing detail in the lectures about Butter and Eggs is that the basic effects become more gratifying the more clothes you remove.

She didn't know if she slept. She must have. She must have dreamed that a little white rat poked its head out of the sack of millet in the corner of the storeroom where she and Tip had been made comfortable, and that the white rat had said, "Everything changes you, and you change everything." But she must be awake now, for Tip was saying "And you're going to dawdle, today of all days?"

She gulped a spoonful of some hot tea made of roasted straw and scarab chitin, and couldn't wait any longer. She curtseyed as Scarly had used to do, back in that lost life when Scarly had been her only friend. Then Rain and Tip hurried out of Red Windmill, past the decrepit mill that stood sun-bleached of red and any other color and, since devoid now of sails, neutered in the buffeting winds. The travelers began the final ascent on a track wide enough for a cart, though only a pair of skark could have the strength to pull a cart up a slope this severe.

A condensation on the weeds of a local skip, a damp glisten upon the sunny side of boulders. Melted sugar on cobbles. Rain and Tip couldn't speak to each other even if they wanted, the climb that arduous. They scrabbled around the brutal finials of standing stones lurking at a corner of the mountain, and then Kiamo Ko loomed above them. It wasn't at the peak of Knob-blehead Pike, not even close, but it crowned its own calf of hill with an air of mold and decay one could smell from here.

A moat of sorts, dry now, and a drawbridge of sorts, permanently down. Not much by way of defenses, if anyone could get this far, thought Rain. All of the timbers but two had rotted into the moat's ravine, so Tip and Rain held hands and balanced each other like street performers as they trod across the breach and tiptoed into the castle courtyard through gates of iron oak and jasper warped permanently open.

Four flying monkeys stood in some sort of ceremonial arrangement, two on each side. Lances crossed to make a triangular passage underneath. "I thought they were figures of myth," whispered Tip. Other flying monkeys were less elegantly disported about the sloping cobbled yard leading past sheds, stables, gardemangers, collapsed greenhouses, and ornamental stone pergolas. Beyond loomed the central castle keep and its several wings and dependences.

A broad flight of outdoor steps led to a door opened to the light and air, and the sound of horrible singing filtered out from some room deep inside.

"You'll have to hurry, they've begun already," said one of the monkeys, lowering his rip-edged staff to scratch his behind.

Rain and Tip walked up the steps to the front door, neither hurrying nor dawdling, as if they knew they were expected, as if they knew themselves what to expect. The entrance hall was huge and barren, almost

a second courtyard, roofed with a groined ceiling.
A steep staircase without benefit of balustrade rose
against several of the walls of the irregularly shaped
space. The music drew Rain and Tip along the ground
level though, farther in. Through three or four succes-
sive chambers, each a few steps above the previous one.
As if the castle itself had continued climbing the hill
before deciding to rest.

The chambers were sparsely furnished, if at all; a
rickety spindle here, an occasional table with a broken
clock upon it. But the baseboards were lined with wild-
flowers stuffed in every conceivable receptacle: milk
jugs and butter churns, washing buckets and chamber
pots, tin pails and rubber boots.

They paused at the last door, and then went into a
room more like a chapel than anything else, because
the narrow tall windows were filled with colored glass
set in lead fretwork. Two dozen congregants turned at
the sound of their arrival. Neither Candle nor Liir was
among them. The first one to speak was the Lion. No,
not speech—but a howl such as Rain had never heard
before and hoped never to hear again.

He paced toward Rain and looked her forehead
to foot as if he was worried he was conjuring her up.
His mane was in disarray, his spectacles blotched with
tears. Transfigured by distress, and Rain was a little
frightened of him. She said softly, "I en't grown up that

much, have I? It's Rain, Brrr." Then she was running her hands through his mane, and he nuzzling her hip, smearing her tunic with damp. He only wept, and she said, "It's Rain, it's Rain," and looked over his great trembling head at Tip and shrugged her shoulders to say, What? What did you expect, a fanfare? Then she noticed the coffin in its shadows on a bier made of sawhorses.

After the fuss over their arrival had died down, the Goose had to continue with the ceremony of funerary rites. Rain sat them out, feeling incapable of taking up the study of new grief. Tip, in her stead, who ought to have been freed of strong emotion in this matter, attended and witnessed and wept on Rain's behalf. Some older girl was singing a song that made no sense at all.

Nor was dead, Auntie Nor. She was dead and laid to rest in a coffin milled from starsnap pine. She was dead and never to walk again, never again to sit up and in that affectless manner look around at the treacherous world and its chaotically foolish citizens. She was dead and had stopped steaming and had begun to reek, and the flowers on the coffin were meant to cancel as much of the smell as possible. She was dead of grief, or dead of pain, or dead by the unsweet accident of coincidence. She was dead from pitching off a cliff just as Tip had done, though she didn't fall six feet but sixty. The fatal tumble, thought Rain. It was always about to happen to someone. Ilianora Tigelaar was dead now and would be dead tomorrow and all the tomorrows too numberless to name. All that was best of her had been carried away in Lurline's golden chariot, and the leftovers needed to be hurried off somewhere before the mourners succumbed to retching from the odor.

By lunchtime the pyre had begun to consume the coffin, by evening the coffin had been burned to ash. No one looked at what remained. The flying monkeys would sit watch all night to make sure the ice griffons didn't come down to snatch charred bones to crack in their wicked beaks. The monkeys were used to this, practicing the same rituals when the day of final flight arrived for one of their own. They considered it an honor to stand guard. Tip brought them cups of lemonade but kept his eyes trained away from the bonfire that hissled in the orchard beyond the castle walls.

It was easy enough for Rain to hear the bare structure of the incidents that had led to her aunt's death, but it was hard to understand them. Iskinaary filled her in with what he knew.

The raid had occurred before dawn some eight, ten weeks earlier. The Lion and his companions hadn't yet arrived in Kiamo Ko—they were still a couple of weeks out. They might have made the difference. Even a cowardly Lion can throw his weight around sometimes. As it was, panicked monkeys launched themselves airborne, shrieking. Liir had been manhandled out of his bed, and the nearby Grimmerie snatched up and satcheled. He'd been identified as Liir Ko, only child of Elphaba Thropp, the Wicked Witch of the West who had once lived as a hermit in this very place. He'd been hog-tied and roped over the flanks of a mountain skark, and the five men in black hoods and gloves rode off with him. They hadn't been Arjikis. If they were Munchkinlanders, they were among the taller type who couldn't be distinguished from Gillikinese by height. Maybe they were abductors hired by La Mombey. No one could venture a guess.

Though Candle had screamed to be taken too, the dawn intruders had tossed her aside. They had no interest in her. They thought her weak in the mind. Probably a Quadling woman held no interest for them. Candle had bundled herself in goatskin boots and raced after them on foot, and though her pursuit proved fanciful and vain, she kept at it for a few days.

Upon returning, she had pleaded with Nor to break the pledge under which she'd been bound—bound by Liir and Candle themselves—to conceal from them where Nor had hidden Rain. Originally they hadn't wanted to know, for fear that just such an ambush might happen at last, and that Liir or Candle might reveal their daughter's whereabouts if they were beaten to the margins of death for it. Liir had made Nor promise never to tell them. Never.

Rain could work out Nor's motives in resisting Candle's entreaties. Back at the crossroads between Nether How and St. Prowd's, Nor wouldn't have been hard persuaded to carry out the task laid upon her. She had understood. She who'd been kidnapped about the age Rain had been when entering St. Prowd's—she who'd tried to live with the knowledge that her own mother, her aunts, her full-blood brother had all been slaughtered by Commander Cherrystone, as he was then—she who'd been incarcerated in Southstairs Prison deep in the bowels below the Emerald City—she understood full well what crimes mortals might commit in the name of some advantage or other. She had promised not to reveal Rain's whereabouts until the girl would have reached the age of maturity.

No matter how Candle railed and wept, Iskinaary continued, Nor couldn't go back on her word. She reminded Candle that if Liir's abductors killed him in their attempt to get him to decode the deadly book for them, they would need Rain even more desperately.

They would hunt for her even more diligently. They would stop at nothing. Nor knew such men. She had sewn herself up with a rough needle and a coarse thread soaked in vinegar. She afforded the world no child of her loins to maim and abuse, and she wouldn't let Rain escape from her womb, either.

The Lion took up the story.

After his long absence from his wife, he'd arrived at Kiamo Ko from Munchkinland in time to see that the reunion was for naught. Under the relentless pleading and hectoring of Candle, Nor had gone mad, said Brrr, his paws in his mane and his back sore from the heaving of his sobs. His wife's fragile hold on anything like hope had given out. She took to wandering out of the castle to avoid Candle's weeping rages, to avoid the Lion's own overtures and condolences. Whether Nor slipped or whether she threw herself, unable to bear the unreadable future, no one could venture a sound opinion.

Maybe the mountain merely shuddered, as it had been doing for some time now. With a kind of mercy only the wild world knows, maybe the hillside had buckled, no longer willing to give fair purchase to a soul in such torment. The tremors that had begun with the great quake—the one that had toppled the east wing, where Sarima had once held her apartments—

had continued reverberating on and off ever since. The residents of Kiamo Ko had almost become used to them.

"I shouldn't have left her in order to rescue Dorothy," Brrr muttered in a voice Rain had to strain to hear. "We took our sweet months on a switchback journey in case we were being followed—we went to the Chancel of the Ladyfish first, to see if your kin had returned there, or had left word under the stone with the question-mark horse. When we found nothing, we decided to come here, hoping to find Candle and Liir. It was his boyhood home, after all. In any event, we thought this castle might be a safe hole to hide Dorothy in. But I never guessed Ilianora would come back here too. The very site of her childhood trauma, the abduction and the murders—and now it happens all over again. No wonder she couldn't bear it."

At the death of Nor a few days earlier, Brrr continued, Candle had been unable to contain herself. She had bundled some nuts and sandwiches in a cloth and said good-bye to the travelers who had arrived shortly after Liir's abduction—Brrr, and Little Daffy and Mr. Boss, with that big horsey farmgirl in tow. Candle had left on foot. She intended to go to Nether How and tear the ceiling apart with her fingernails, if she had to. She would pull down the witch's broom if it hadn't already been found and stolen by the same brigands who had stolen her husband. She would climb to the top of the house and jump off. She would teach herself to fly on that broom or die. She would dare the broom to fail her.

She would find Liir before he went farther from her than he'd already drifted.

Rain and Tip might almost have passed Candle on the trail, Iskinaary implied, but the Quadling woman was traveling by night.

Impossible, said Rain's face, now knowing the pitilessness of the landscape.

No, it was true, assured the Goose. Candle had the benefit of a lamp-lark that she had charmed with her music and petitioned to accompany her. "A lamp-lark can shine like a small beacon in the night if it's singing to a mate. Trust our Candle to play her domingon to sound like something of which the lamp-lark approved." Candle also took an uncharacteristically tame mountain goat who would allow a saddle on her.

The Arjiki period of mourning for Nor had begun while Candle's mount was passing out of sight. It was over now, just as Brrr and Little Daffy and Mr. Boss finished filling Rain and Tip in on the news.

The girl they called Dorothy sat a little way off on a milking stool, listening gravely, wrinkling her nose at the stench of roasted death stealing in on the updraft. An old woman nobody had yet introduced to Rain sat next to her.

4.

So her father was gone, who knew where. Her mother was equally gone. Her aunt Nor was gone even further. The small family that Rain had inherited late in her childhood was scattered. As a social unit families have only a limited tenure, though it's the rare soul who comprehends this while still a child. Rain was that soul.

All that was left to her was the Lion.

More than Little Daffy and Mr. Boss, the Lion stood for Rain. For her, beside her. His great lined face had turned to her finally, as if it had taken effort to slough off grief and register who Rain really was.

This upright young woman able to look him in the eye—what a sharply direct look it was, too. Loving and unflinching, the native opposite of how she had seemed several years ago. Living with her parents, then boarding at school, Brrr now learned, had straightened her out. Life had given her language. He was impressed and a little intimidated—but from the distance that a new grief imposes.

While all Rain could see, looking back at the Lion both fondly and clinically, was a creature sodden with sorrow. Shocked, and barked at into something nearing old age. His very whiskers trembled with palsy.

Tip tried to help her take measure of their situation, their resources. Laughably pregnable, this castle of Kiamo Ko. No place to stay if Rain wanted to be safe. How had Candle and Liir ever thought they could protect themselves here? Brrr, who hadn't seen Liir since parting from him in the Disappointments and turning toward Munchkinland to rescue Dorothy, couldn't answer. "I told you, it was his home, once upon a time," the Lion insisted. "He grew up here. The first time I ever saw him was in this very court yard, when the Witch's flying monkeys had carried Dorothy and me up the slopes and dumped us onto the cobbles. You know, my left rear ankle has never been the same. I've always had to favor it."

Rain could tell, even in his bereavement, that the Cowardly Lion was trying to encourage her, to cheer her up. It didn't help. Perhaps one day she would look back and it would help then.

She was growing up, to be able to conceive of a "one day" and a "looking back."

"But that it was his *home*? So what?" Rain had no sentimentality about places. "His home is built on the edge of a chasm during earthquake season, and he feels safe so he stays there? Because it's, it's *home?*"

"No place like it," said Brrr. "Don't be withering, it's not becoming."

Rain didn't get it. She asked Mr. Boss and his wife what they thought, but they seemed not to be taking the full measure of the tragedy. They slept a lot. Maybe scaling a mountain this steep was harder on their little legs than on Brrr's or Dorothy's.

Of Dorothy, Rain was dubious. The foreigner seemed spooked to be here in the Witch's castle; she didn't like to be left alone. At first Rain was afraid that Dorothy was going to make a play for Tip, and it would be the Scarly thing all over again, but Dorothy seemed oblivious to Tip's sweetness. "I just keep thinking about Toto," she said. "I wonder if he's still hunting for me somewhere, out in this blasted hideous world you cretins inhabit."

"You've gone sassy, you have," said Mr. Boss.

"Being convicted of double murder and condemned to death has helped erode some of my native midwestern taciturnity."

"I think your little dog probably met up with some great big dog," said Mr. Boss, "who is a lot more fun to hang out with than you."

"How dare you make fun of me in my distress. I'd like to find a pack of those great big dogs and introduce them to your behind."

"They're doing this for your benefit, you know," said Brrr to Rain, but she wasn't sure she believed him.

She walked with Tip out of the castle again, in the direction from which they'd approached. Away from the smoldering embers. She cried, but turned her head away from his shoulder, not wanting to shame herself that much. Tip knew better than to ask why she was crying. It wasn't really the death of her aunt, or the splintered lives her parents were living in defense of her, who had never asked to be defended. It was the whole pitfall of it, the stress and mercilessness of incident. She felt she was living on a stage controlled by tiktok machinery, and the Time Dragon dreaming her life was prone to nightmares.

Tip seemed to know all this without saying a word. He was the only article of faith that stood between her and the edge of the cliff, which looked eager to buckle if only she gave it half a chance.

She didn't sleep much, in the small room to which the senior flying monkey had showed her. Tay crowded her pillow, shivering. Apparently the rice otter didn't take to mountain air. Tip slept nearby, but apart, on a pallet outside her door. She could hear his breathing when he finally fell off to sleep. That was the first comfort afforded her since they'd arrived.

In the morning, she was all business. "Who is that old woman at the window?" she asked Iskinaary.

"Her name is Cattery Spunge, but she's called Nanny," said the Goose. "She's already passed through her second childhood and she's in her second adolescence now, and has decided to be sprightly again after spending a generation in bed."

"What's she doing here?"

"She raised your grandmother Elphaba, and she lived here with Liir until he was about fourteen. She's been retired for about forty-five years but she's considering looking for a new position as governess or possibly manager of a granary or something."

"Hello, Nanny," said Rain, approaching her.

The woman turned and put down her bowl of frumenty. Rain had never seen anyone so old. Her cheeks and neck were wrinkled like a piece of vellum scrunched and only partly reopened. "Elphie?" said Nanny.

"No. My name is Rain."

The old woman said, "My cataracts are puddings. I'd like to dig them out with sugar tongs. My, but you do look like Elphaba. Are you sure?"

"I just arrived."

"Well, I've been expecting you for a long time."

Rain wasn't certain that she had convinced Nanny who she was, but she decided it didn't matter. "You are the only one who knew Nor when she was a child."

"Yes, that I did."

"What was she like?"

"She was the first one to ride the broom, you know. Elphaba told me. She was bright and peppy and full of beans."

"But how could she ride that broom? She didn't have an ounce of magic in her."

"I'd have said so too. But who is to say that magic follows our expectations. Give me your hand, child."

"Are you going to read my palm?"

"With *my* eyes? I can't even see your fingers, let alone your lifelines. No, I just want to warm up my own hands. The young have so much fire in them."

"Do you have any idea where my father might be?"

"Oh, my dear, Frex went off to the Quadling lands to bring faith to the noble heathen, don't you know."

"My father," she said. "I'm talking about Liir. Liir Ko."

"Liir Thropp, you mean," she said. "Elphaba's boy. When the soldiers came and kidnapped the family, and little Nor among them, Elphaba was out somewhere. Shopping, or raising mayhem. Or conducting lessons in sedition. I don't want to talk about that part. Liir followed them and got kidnapped too, but then they let him go because they didn't know who he was. They thought he was a kitchen boy. Well, he always was grubby, I'll give them that. They'd have saved themselves a lot of bother if they'd kept him when they had him."

"That was then," she said. "What about this time? Did you hear them arrive, did they say anything that would give you a clue about where they were taking him?"

"I've always been a very sound sleeper. It's my best talent." She took out a few teeth and cleaned them with her thumb, and then reinserted them. "Popcorn kernels, you know; the old gums can't take it anymore."

"What do you think?"

"I think," said Nanny, "that there is nothing more I would like right now than to tell you what you want to know. But I can't. So the next best thing I would like is to have a nap in this sunlight. I feel the winter chill something fierce, you know. If when I wake I find I've remembered anything further, I'll call for you. What did you say your name was?"

"Rain."

"I don't think so." She squinted at the bright summer sun. "Snow, perhaps, or hail; it's too cold for rain at this time of year." She pulled a tippet about her shoulders and almost immediately began to snore.

Rain continued her circuit, stopping to press Iskinaary for his opinions. "Why didn't you go with him?
You're supposed to be his familiar, aren't you?"

"Only a witch has a familiar, and he's not a witch."

"That's no answer, and you know it."

Iskinaary refused to budge on the matter, but Rain
pestered. "It doesn't make sense. You've always stayed
by his side. You could have followed him from a height
and seen where he was being taken. I can't believe you
failed him at this point in your long friendship, if that's
what you call it."

She goaded him further until finally he hissed, "If
you must know, I wanted to go with him, but he yelled
at me to stay behind and take care of Candle. So I followed his word though it broke my heart."

"You're a big fat liar. You didn't follow his word
at all, or you'd be traveling with my mother down to
Nether How, to get that broom. You broke your promise to him. You are as cowardly as the Lion."

"I resent that," called the Lion, who wasn't listening
although certain phrases do carry.

"Save it for the magistrate." Iskinaary drew himself
up to his full height. His cheeks were sunken in a way
they had not been before, but his eye was steely menace
still. "Candle told me to stay here because you were

likely to show up. She has that talent. She sensed your approaching."

"And so she left," said Rain, without mercy, for what mercy had her mother ever shown her? "A talent for lighting out just when I show up. Don't think I haven't noticed."

"She wanted to protect you. She said you were more important than she was."

"I doubt you believe that," said Rain.

"I never said I believe it."

The senior flying monkey, Rain learned, was called Chistery. He was so stooped that his chin nearly touched his knees. He was devoted to Nanny and agreed with her that Rain had something of Elphaba about her. "Frankly, when I first saw you, I thought you were Elphaba returning."

"As I understand it, Elphaba was green."

"So I've heard. But flying monkeys are color-blind, so I wasn't going by your pallor. You do have something of Elphaba about you. I can't quite name what it is."

"The talent of being in the wrong place almost all the time?"

"Maybe, Rain, a feeling for magic. Have you ever tried it?"

"Don't be absurd."

"Or maybe it's your air of disdain. Elphaba was strong in that department."

Perhaps to distract the disconsolate group, Dorothy told Rain and Tip about her day in court. The subject of her trial and her conviction bore heavily on her. At lunch one day, Dorothy turned to Nanny and said, "You were present, Nanny. You were here when Elphaba disappeared. The day her skirts went up in flames and I threw the bucket of water on her. I ran weeping away when I saw her disappear, but you came rushing up the stairs as I went down."

"Oh yes, I used to have very good knees. An attractive domestic, according to certain opinions posted anonymously to me."

"What did you see when you got there? You never would say. You came down the turret stairs and locked the door, and said she was dead, but whatever happened? I don't remember a funeral such as the one we had for Nor."

"The times were different, the standards were different, and I was on my own. After all these years you can't hold me to lapses in decorum. Who are you, anyway? Are you a tax collector, asking all these nosy questions? I tithed to my eyeteeth and anyway I never earned a penny. I never stole that golden garter. Melena gave it me. Everything I did, I did for love of Melena

Thropp, my lovely Melena with the powdery skin and the lavender nosegays. Sue me."

"I'm Dorothy," said Dorothy. Her voice was taking on a peevish edge. "Dorothy Gale, from Kansas."

"Oooh she's smart," said Nanny to the rest of the table. "Wants us to know her name and address so when we read it in the columns we'll go oooh la la. I'm not impressed. Pass the port."

Little Daffy handed down a pitcher of well water and poured it for Nanny. She took a big gulp of it and said, "Yum, smackers," and fell asleep in her chair. Chistery came around to wipe her lips and to wheel her away, which wasn't easy, since his chin hardly came up to the seat of her chair. But his long arms, crooked with bone spurs, could still reach up to the chair's handles, so off they went.

"But what happened to Elphaba?" asked Rain. Perhaps cruelly, she added, "Look, we know what happened to Nor. We saw it. What happened to the Witch?"

The Lion left the table without asking to be excused, uncommon rudeness for him, but no one blamed him.

"That's the big question, isn't it," said Dorothy. "What really happened to the Witch?"

After her first reunion with the Lion, Rain noticed that he was keeping to himself. He had taken to sleeping in the very larder, Chistery whispered, that old Nanny had locked Liir and the Lion in when the Witch was hounding Dorothy up the stairs to her tower, and thence to the parapet over the gorge. "If I had only lived up to my name," Rain heard the Lion mutter once, to himself or maybe to Tay, who was hunting for something along the baseboards under the flour bins.

"What do you mean?" she couldn't help asking.

"If I'd been as cowardly as they called me, ever since the Massacre at Traum, I'd never have accompanied that foreign agitatrix, Dorothy, out this way. The first time, I mean. I'd have gone on to a long and sorry life as the confirmed bachelor I was really cut out to be."

Meaning, Rain supposed, what? That he regretted the consequences caused by the death of the Witch? That he regretted having fallen in love with Nor, a human woman? Could he really wish that he hadn't ever met her, to avoid this suffering now? Rain knew herself to be young, untried by any suffering that really counted. (Rain was still alive, after all, and though her parents were dispersed and endangered, she wasn't stretched out upon a stone floor with her chin in her paws.) But even were something to happen to Tip, she thought, she couldn't imagine wishing she had never met him.

Maybe she just didn't know Tip well enough yet. Maybe you have to earn the kind of grief that the Lion was exhibiting. Though privately, and perhaps this was callous of her, she also wondered if Brrr was putting it on just a bit thick.

Still, he had the benefit of knowing what Kiamo Ko had been like with his common-law wife in the next room, for a few days anyway, of fatal reunion, and now—where was she? Where was she really? Where did the dead go?

Where had Elphaba gone?

5.

It took Rain two or three days to realize that Chistery and the other flying monkeys were deferring to her, as if she were the owner of the castle now. "I'm not Elphaba," she reminded Chistery, after he came down from Nanny's room where he had been discreetly changing her bedding.

"Don't I know it," he told her, but nicely.

"And I'm not my father."

"You're quite a bit like your father, you know."

"I don't know. I don't know him at all."

"See, that's what he always said about his mother too. Disavowal of family resemblances; it's a family trait."

"Chistery," she said, "what are we going to do?"

"Rain," he answered, "don't you see? It's up to you."

"I'm a child, for the love of Ozma!"

"And I'm a flying monkey. I wasn't born either to fly or to talk, but your grandmother Elphaba brought both capacities out of me. I am the patriarch in a line of creatures that wouldn't exist without your family's interference. Now I can't fly from here to the washtub, but I *will* use my tongue to give you my mind. You have to figure out on your own how to use your talents."

She pouted at him. "That sounds like the motto of every improving sermon made by any teacher at St. Prowd's. You could lecture there."

"Don't mock me. How could I decide for you what should be done next? I've lived fifty years on this estate and I'm not trained at situational analysis."

He handed her the sheets and nodded with his chin toward where she should bring them. "Child of woe," he added, "don't you see? You're in charge now. Nor is dead and the Lion is incapacitated. Liir is gone and Candle is gone and dear old Nanny is feeling fitter than usual but she's not ready yet to lead a cavalry charge. Tip seems sensible enough but he's not family. And the little people seem to think they've come to a holiday resort." He snorted. "They could make up their own bed of a morning, in my humble."

"I'm sorry," she said. "I'm tired too."

"I'm sure you are. Get over it. There's work to be done."

"May I go up to what used to be the Witch's room?"

"I told you. It's your castle now. You can go where you want."

So after lunch, Tip and Rain, with Tay at their heels, followed Chistery's directions and found the staircase leading up to what used to be the Witch's room, at the top of the curving stairs in the southeast tower.

The flying monkeys, who lived mostly in the outbuildings but took care of basic housekeeping, had by all appearances done little more than dust in here once or twice a year. The room looked as if it were being kept as a kind of installation of a Witch's offices, or possibly a memorial chamber to bring faint tears to any pilgrims able to brave the journey. Though so far no one had ever shown up.

The room was broad and circular, wide enough in circumference to hold a dance competition if the furniture were cleared out. In the center of the room the floor was level, but on several sides, up a few steps, a sort of mezzanine or gallery stretched, lowest underneath the room's one great east-facing window, higher on the other side. Perhaps originally this had been an armory, and these stone flats designed for the laying out of lances. Clearly, Elphaba had used the chamber to study arcana derived from her twin interests in natural history and matters numinous.

A huge stupa of a beehive collapsing in on itself—it must have held five thousand bees. (What a song they sang; they must have driven the Witch mad, thought Rain.) A deceased crocodrilos pickled in brine still hung on chains from a rafter. Some wag, maybe a monkey, had put game dice in its eye sockets, so it peered out at Rain and Tip with a pair of singletons. A flat file revealed sixty or seventy bat skeletons, all different. On a stiff board they found a full mouth of wolf's teeth, uppers and lowers, laced in by wire and labeled from front to back in a script that had faded illegible. Several umbrellas had been left opened to dry, and had dried well enough by now that their fabric had given way, leaving only ribs and tatters. On one umbrella, spiders had built webs between every one of the struts. It was creepy and wonderful at once, and reminded Rain of her thirst for a spiderworld, long ago.

The great window was like a web through which to peer at Oz.

Collections, thought Rain. My shell belongs here.

Maybe Chistery is right. Maybe I do have something of my grandmother in me. For as long ago as I can remember, I've listened better to the animals than to any person. Though I have no magic in me, and I cannot tell what they are saying.

"Here's a ball of glass, somewhat mirrored, I think," said Tip, rubbing dust off with a rag. It stood on a table in the center of the room. "I doubt it's an ornamental gazing ball. She doesn't seem to have gone in for interior decoration of that sort."

"I'm not sure I want to look at it," said Rain. "I've never liked looking at myself."

"That makes two of us. But we've come to see what is here. Don't you think we should try?"

She moved around the room, learning things with her fingers and her nose as much as with her eyes. He waited, slumped against a stand-up desk, arms folded.

Rain scowled, not at him but in the act of walking her thoughts along. "Both my parents have their own weirdness—maybe that's what drew them together. My mother can see the present, she said. I thought she meant she could tell when I was about to snitch a scone from the larder at Nether How. But what mother can't tell that? Now I think she meant something else. She had—she has—some capacity to understand the present. It probably only affects those she loves or cares about. She could tell, if my father was away hunting for a week, that he was almost home. Is that just intuition, or is it a special kind of seeing?"

He waited. He knew she was talking mostly to herself.

"And my father? He didn't speak about it much, but my mother told me. Once or twice he could see the past. He saw an image of his parents—Elphaba and Fiyero—together. More than once—like a vision. He thought it was just his imagination, that he was trying to invent a relationship between them, to convince himself who his forebears were. But he could see a little more than that, my mother told me. She told me about what happened just before I was born, when Liir had brought the dried faces of human beings—"

"Don't," said Tip, wincing.

"Is that any harder to consider than a dried crocodrilos?"

"Actually, yes."

"Liir had brought them to the farm where I would soon be born. He hung them in the trees, and my mother played the domingon. He saw that they had histories, that they could speak if they were charmed to do so, and my mother laid the spell upon them to come into the present and recite the—the beauty of their lives, I guess she said. And that testimony of soundness, of themself-ness, helped lift the disguise of a human off of old Princess Nastoya of the Scrow, and she died as she had wished to go, as the Elephant she was behind her disguise."

"Maybe your mother's singing—your father's memory—called forth the lost Elphaba into you. While you were in the womb."

"Maybe you believe in tooth fairies? Or time dragons?"

"So *don't* you want to peer in the ball? What if you have some scrap of the talent in your eyes that your parents do? That your grandmother did?"

"I can't bear to see the present, if it involves my father being tortured. I can't. I can't bear to see the past, in case it involves him having been murdered. I can't bear to see my mother fleeing this house of disaster. I prefer my disguise of blindness a little longer."

He asked in a low voice, "Can you bear to see yourself unveiled? Or me?"

She looked abruptly at him in case he was tending sexy. But he meant it truer, deeper than that. "I don't know," she finally answered. "What if I do have a talent, and it is neither Liir's nor Candle's, but my own? What if I can see the future? I don't think I want to know."

"Can you live without knowing?"

She almost laughed. "I have lived without knowing most of my life. Isn't that what we're all so good at? That's the easy part."

So they didn't look in the gazing ball, either of them, Rain by conviction and Tip out of deference.

Instead Tip opened the shutters on one side of the wide window. Facing east, away from the wind off Knobble-head Pike, the window showed a view of the valley they had walked up from. They could see the ruined stump of Red Windmill, and the valley where Upper Fanarra lay hidden. Through a dip in the mountainous horizon, probably harboring the track of their arrival, they could see where the plain of the Vinkus River must begin. And somewhere down there the beaver dam, with the mother-in-law of Luliaba waiting for them to return with a coracle to float her to her future.

Before leaving, they made a halfhearted search for accoutrements of magic, but they could only picture tchotchkes from a pantomime about Sweet Lurline and Preenella, her *aide-de-sorcière*. What were they expecting to locate? Magic wands? They found a bristling bunch of cattails, which magically still had their fur, but that was all the magic in them. What else might they wish for? Some faded pamphlet of practical magic, to help summon up a nice flank of terch or garmot instead of endless salads? A corked vial of smelling salts that might revive the Cowardly Lion into something of his usual growly but steadfast self? They found none of that. The only magic thing they were sure of was the crystal sphere on its stand of carven dragons in the middle of the room, and that much magic was too much. They would have to make their way without it.

In the welter of so much animal zoologics, they almost forgot Tay. They couldn't find the otter at first, and then Tip laughed and pointed. Tay had leaped up somehow and landed on the back of the airborne crocodrilos. The green rice otter was swaying back and forth, defying gravity, having a modest little carnival ride for itself.

"Come here, you nutcase," said Rain, and Tay obliged.

"It's trying out what flying on a broom might be like," said Tip. "You should try it someday too. If your mother returns with that broom."

If Chistery is right, and it's up to me to take charge, she thought, then I have to decide what to do.

She called a council that evening, after Nanny had gone to bed. Of the flying monkeys only Chistery sat in. Brrr was cajoled and then browbeaten to leave his larder, and the Munchkinlander and the dwarf bestirred themselves to climb onto the edge of a sideboard so they could see better. Rain took one side of the circular table, Tip opposite her. Dorothy and Iskinaary perched on stools, completing the round. Eight of them.

Tay played with a dust mouse under the big table. A broom only goes so far.

They seemed a small and enervated group, too wasted in strength to mount much of a campaign. That couldn't matter. There was no one else, even if all they did was think.

"We can't stay here like this," Rain said. "Not for the threat to us—the threat is everywhere now. We can't stay because to stay is to let more of the worse things happen. To stay is to give up."

"We *have* given up," said Mr. Boss, linking hands with Little Daffy.

"We haven't. Have we?" asked his wife. "Well, we've given up the Clock, yes, there's that. But we haven't given up on each other."

"That's the point," said Rain. "We haven't given up on my father, surely? Or defending one side or the other against a fiercer attack than has yet been seen?"

"Wait a minute. Which side are you intending to defend?" asked Little Daffy, waving her bonnet for attention.

"Either side," said Rain.

"That's insane. You're insane," said Mr. Boss. "She's insane," he told his wife.

"Listen to her a moment," said Brrr, from his lethargy.

Rain spoke as slowly as she could, working her way like a tightrope artist across her thoughts, feeling them an instant before walking the words out. "Mr. Boss. You never showed any allegiance either to Loyal Oz or to Munchkinland. What difference does it matter to you who we defend?"

"If I showed no allegiance to either, why defend either?" he shot back. "Waste of effort. I showed loyalty to the Clock, because my job was to keep it in tiktokety trim as a house and harbor for the Grimmerie."

"And the Clock is drowned, so that burden is lifted from you. Meanwhile the book is stolen and about to do damage, serious damage, by whatever faction nabbed it. Isn't that part of your job?"

"I quit. I was to mind the book when it was handed to me, to keep it safe. But my employer scarpered on me, leaving me holding the goods. Anyway, I gave the book to Liir. His problem now."

"But that's my point. The book isn't safe. It's on the loose, in the wrong hands—whoever hands it is in are the wrong hands. We can't excuse ourselves from the need to stop it harming anyone—on either side— the damage could be immense."

"After you finish St. Prowd's," said Chistery, "go to law school."

"There won't be a St. Prowd's if Mombey has the book and can torture my father into decoding it for her.

If he's able. Or maybe being so powerful Mombey can decipher some of it herself."

"You could read it," said Tip to Rain. "You told me."

"Yes, well," said Rain, "I was only learning to read back then. Not having a history of other writing to complicate me, I managed. Lucky guesses."

"It's in her blood," said Chistery, pointing at Rain. "Elphaba could read it at once, I'm told. She used it to help give me language."

"You're right about one thing," said the dwarf to Rain. "I never took up with political or religious clans. Never cared to. But I suppose since my wife is a Munchkinlander and our children will be part Munchkin—"

"Not to spring any surprises on you, darling, but I'm so far beyond the changes that I'm more of a dwarf than you are," said Little Daffy.

"Our symbolic children," he said to her. "The children of your hometown in Center Munch. You've professed a love for your besmirched land. You've persuaded me to join you wherever you are. If you're on that side, so I am."

"I love you too, ducks. Though what Munchkinland has become, a shame. A bloody shame."

The Lion turned his head this way and that as if not quite believing what he heard. The dwarf and Little Daffy were holding hands.

Tip said, "Well, I've been all over Loyal Oz and renegade Munchkinland, and it seems to me that no people own the land they live on. The land owns them. The land feeds them by growing them their wheat and such, in the Corn Basket of Munchkinland, or growing them their meadows for the grazing of livestock, in the agricultural patches of Gillikin. Or growing them their emeralds in the mines in the Glikkus, or their wind-swept pampas or steppes in the wide grasslands west of here, which I've never seen, but which support the horse cultures of the Scrow and other tribes."

"Bollocks. Natural geography may be hospitable—or not—but human history claims geography," argued the Lion. "Love for nature is a hobby for the mentally unfit. History trumps geography. And thus you can't blame the Munchkinlanders for defending themselves, however cruel it makes them."

Dorothy hadn't spoken so far. She drummed one hand on the tabletop and put the other hand on her hip. None of them of course had ever seen the Auntie Em about whom she complained, but Rain guessed that Dorothy looked quite a bit like old Auntie Em right about now.

"I've seen a fair amount of Oz, too, you know," she said, "and as far as I'm concerned loving any part of it without loving the whole thing is a load of fresh ripe hooey. Not that I'm especially enamored of any of Oz on this trip, mind you. But I have a treasury of song in my heart and I can summon up affection for anything with just a little concentration. Would you like me to sing?"

"No," they all said.

"Too bad," she replied, and stood up.

She got out about four lines.

> O beautiful for spacious skies,
> For amber waves of grain,
> For purple mountain majesties
> Above the fruited plain. . . .

Little Daffy was already in tears. Mr. Boss was rolling his eyes heavenward and plugging his ears. Iskinaary murmured to Rain, "What rainbow is she *from?*"

"Let her go on," said Tip, who had no authority here, but they obeyed him as a matter of courtesy. He was a guest, after all.

> America! America!
> God shed his grace on thee,
> And crown thy good with brotherhood
> From sea to shining sea!

"There's that sea thing again, it makes me want to heave," said Brrr.

"Good is always crowned, isn't it?" said Little Daffy. "The argument for royalty."

"What's amerika? Part of that game the beauty boys used to play, shamerika?" asked Mr. Boss.

"It's another name for Kansas," said Dorothy.

"I thought you hated Kansas," said the Goose.

"Let me have my say, if you're ready for it. Or I'll sing the next verse."

"We're ready, we're ready."

"Everyone has a right to love the land that gives them the things they need to live," said Dorothy. "It gives them beauty to look at, and food to eat, and neighbors to bicker with and then eventually to marry. But I think, now I've seen a bit more of America and a lot more of Oz, that your own devotion to your familiar homeland should inspire you to allow other people to embrace their homelands as beautiful, too. That's what the song says. That's why I sang it. You can't see the shining sea from the purple mountains—"

"I should hope not," said the Lion. "You'd just cave."

Rain said, "I don't know about the mountain and sea business. But I suppose we're saying something of the same thing. It's more important to try to stop what may be about to happen, whichever way it goes—because it's all worthwhile to someone. The beaver dam is worth something to the beavers, the—the shell to the lake creature that built it—the roost to the hen, the swamp to the marshstalker. Nether How to my father."

"And this place to me," said Chistery, "though Kiamo Ko could do with a bit more in the way of central heating."

"Are we going to decide what to do, though?" asked Rain. "That's why we've come here to sit together for a few moments."

Iskinaary said, "Well, Chistery is too old to fly anyplace."

"Speak for yourself," replied the flying monkey, but admitted he had obligations to Nanny that would keep him from leaving his highland home.

"Are we to break up into groups? One to the Emerald City, one to Colwen Grounds, and try to intercept the Grimmerie somehow?" asked Iskinaary. "I'm sorry, Rain, but I'm not quite getting your drift."

"I don't have a plan yet. We're working on it together."

"I am *not* going back to Munchkinland, thank you very much," said Dorothy. "Don't forget there's an order of execution on my head."

"My countryfolk *were* beastly to you," agreed Little Daffy. "But don't be harsh on them, dear. They're under so much stress, invaded by Loyal Oz. Now, as to schemes. Personally, *I* have precious little interest in ever visiting the Emerald City again. Who would ever give *me* the time of day there, if the sons of the EC and Gillikin are dying in battle against my countrymen?"

"Against the Animals," corrected the Lion. "But point taken. Sentiment is fine over a round table, but once you decide to come down from this high peak, you have to make a choice one way or the other. That's the human condition.

"I know," he added. "And I'm a Lion. Same difference."

"We'll sleep on it," said Rain.

Once again she was asleep and then she heard a voice, but she could hardly tell what it was saying. She half-woke, and rolled over in the moonlight to see if there was a mole, or maybe a goldfish come up from the fishwell in the basements. The only thing she saw was the iridescent shell, its usual gleam even brighter against the gloom of a mountain night in late summer.

She picked her way over Tip, careful not to disturb him, and hardly knowing what she intended, she retraced the steps she'd taken earlier in the day and walked up the stairs to Elphaba's chamber.

Snaggle-toothed autumn was loping in. A jackal moon was assembling its features in the sky. Rain had heard that the constellation appeared only once in a generation or so. It didn't last long, but while it lasted, peasants and mill laborers alike considered it a time of peril and possibility.

Without Tip to watch her, she had a different kind of courage. She creaked open the shutters of the Witch's great window, both sides, and the moon stepped through spiderweb fretwork into the chamber.

A patter at her heels made her turn. Tay had appeared from nowhere. It must have sensed her moving at night. She smiled at it—and almost could have sworn it smiled back. Though a creature of the wild has no smile we can recognize.

"Look in the glass," said Tay.

"You can't talk," she said, not alarmed; she realized she was sleepwalking.

"I know," said Tay. "I'm sorry. Look in the glass."

Because this was not a nightmare, and because a calm had lit upon her, she wasn't scared to look. She rubbed the surface of the globe and huffed upon it to make it shiny. The moonlight helped, one sphere to another. Tay leapt to the table and entwined, almost snakelike, around the carved legs of the stand.

The initial sense was of flatness—more like peering through a porthole than into a fishbowl. She remembered staring at a page in the Grimmerie once, when a glassy circlet had shown an unidentified figure gesturing at her. Trying to make a landfall of some message or other. She left that memory behind, and leaned closer.

At first she saw nothing, just shifting smudges. Clouds seen from below the surface of a lake, as if you were a fish. Or it might be clouds seen from above, she thought, if you were a kind of creature who wasn't tethered by gravity to the time and place in which you were born, and if you could approach from anywhere, see anything.

The mothy batting pulled apart, like the spun sugarbrittle sold at Scandal Day. She began to focus.

It took a moment to realize she was examining something of what Dorothy had been warbling about. The mountains of Oz stood up first—not as in a map, flattened out and drawn, but built up in miniature, as if in pastry-dough. From a great distance mountains show earliest; they are the first face of a world. She could see Oz the way Dorothy had said to see it in a song, all at once: Mount Runcible to the north, poking up like a king-hill, uncrowded and pompous; and the Great Kells in their scimitar curve, bending to the left and then angling to the right, toward the south, softening. She could see that the Quadling Kells and the Wend Hardings were just smaller cousins of the Great Kells, and that the Madeleines and the Cloth Hills were second cousins who had moved out of town to get a little room. And the Scalps, up in the Glikkus, were the high bishops of the whole affair, in their emerald crowns, although of course she couldn't see the emeralds.

The picture shifted. An angle of moonlight picked up the silver that shines on water, and then she could see the eight or ten queenly lakes of Oz drawn out as neatly as Madame Chortlebush could have done on a map. The long silvered leaf of Restwater at the center, the birthing pool of all of Oz; and bootblack deadly Kellswater not far off. Spottily, here and there, the turquoise lakes that depended on mountain runoff for their bounty: Lake Chorge in Gillikin, Mossmere and Illswater in Munchkinland, and a shifting lake in the Thousand Year Grasslands at the far west of the Kells. The moving lake that she'd heard came and went at its own choice, drawing thousands of prairie beasts like magnets back and forth to its iron will.

Another shift of the snout of the jackal moon, pointing out the forests of Oz. A lot of Oz was woods, from the snarl of northern wilderness, the Great Gillikin Forest, to virtually every slope and vale in regions mountainous or gentle. And see, the rustling abundance of the eastern Corn Basket, a neatly governed patchwork cousin to the wild grasses of the west. Look how the marshes of Quadling Country are the damp wet footing for the tall pines of the Great Gillikin Forest fifteen hundred miles to the north.

She peered for the slopes below Kiamo Ko, to see if the Five Lakes around Nether How came to view. Reluctantly, like shy fish, they winked up at her. But this was a dream, and like all dreams it had some conditions. One of them is that she couldn't push for more than it would give. She couldn't screw her focus tighter, or by force of desire pull the world into greater resolution. Though she thought she could even find the kindly hillock of Nether How itself, she couldn't make it any clearer. She couldn't see the house. She couldn't see her mother. She just couldn't see her mother.

Neither could she see anyone, she realized, not human or Animal or animal. From the height of an angel, there seemed to be no sign of occupation of this vast textured complexity. Not even a city—not even the Emerald City, which she might have expected to spy blooming in the center of Oz like a big throbbing bee stinging the living organism, or sucking the bloom of its sweetness.

Then, even in her dreaminess, her mind remembered the map she and Tip had found in the shop in Shiz on that rainy afternoon. She remembered the story of Tip and his trip to Ev, out of Oz across the deadly sands, and of the stamp of the shell on the left edge of the map, beyond the Outer Vinkus. She rose on tiptoe to see beyond the sands north of Mount Runcible, and south of Quadling Country. She torqued her face to try to peer beyond the sands west of the Thousand Year Grasslands. But the jackal moon wouldn't loan its light through the glass at so oblique an angle. She could only see what it would show her.

As if she had done the world wrong by being curious, the picture of Oz began to shrink, sinking deeper in. But then she realized the dioramic glimpse was no less particular, just smaller, just sized differently. It took up a modest segment of the globed glass, like no more than a scrap of colored apple peel plastered on an ornament from Lurlinemas, leaving the rest unknown, unfounded. So much unknown.

The clouds began to move in. She guessed her dream was about over, and she wondered if she needed to walk back downstairs or if she could just drift, too, like the clouds, and let the dream wake her in her bed when it wanted. But the clouds swirled some, and cleared, and she looked again just in case.

All she saw was her own face. That face she hardly ever dared scrutinize. She identified the Quadling cheekbones from Candle, the stiff, thick, flowing dark hair from Liir. Oh, what a dream this was! For she saw herself green, green, if you could believe it.

She laughed at the gifts of sight and blindness, and turned to go.

"Did you see?" asked the crocodrilos, rolling its eyes into a pair of sixes.

"Oh, I saw."

"What did you see?" asked the ghosts of bees, crawling out of the hive and standing in a ceremonial line as if she were the new Lord Mayor of Kiamo Ko.

"I saw the hills and waters of Oz, the growth and wetness and dryness of it."

"What else did you see?" asked the smile of the wolf teeth.

"I saw no sign of any crying child smacked too often by a tired mother, or any old Dame Beaver wanting release from her daughter-in-law. I saw no kidnapped father, and no mother gone AWOL."

"Just because you didn't see them doesn't mean they aren't there," said the phantom of a dog named Killyjoy, who had been sniffing at something dirty and interesting in a bottom drawer that he couldn't scratch open.

"What else didn't you see?" asked the spiders in a chorus of shrill, pinched voices.

"I didn't see the edge beyond Oz."

"Just because you didn't see it doesn't mean it isn't there," said Killyjoy.

"I know," said Rain. "That's one thing I know."

"What else didn't you see?" asked the drawer of bat skeletons, in an uncoordinated recitation that took Rain a while to decipher.

"I didn't see the woman who brought you all here," said Rain.

"Just because you don't see her doesn't mean she isn't there," said Killyjoy, wagging his ghost tail and panting over his extended ghost tongue.

"What else didn't you see?" asked any number of crows—she couldn't tell if they were ghosts or maybe living crows, not in this light—who appeared to perch on the top of the wardrobe and crowd each other, so that every now and then one would tumble off the near edge and then flap back and shove till someone else tumbled off the far edge.

"I didn't see you when I was here earlier," said Rain. "You'd have scared me off, I think."

"Oh, we're nice enough," said the crows, but then they all flew away.

"Is there anything else you saw, or didn't see?" asked Tay, who now seemed to be the master of ceremonies of this dream.

"No," said Rain. "Not that I can name tonight."

"Well, then, I guess we're done."

"Oh, there is one thing," she said to Tay, as the room settled, the wolf teeth stopped chattering, the crocodrilos stopped its swaying, the phantom dog and bees dissolved and the spiders curled up into little circles, like handbags for lady mice attending a mouse opera. "I didn't see if you are male or female. I have never known."

"Does it matter?" asked Tay.

She didn't answer. They left the room and walked downstairs. This was still a dream. The dwarf was asleep at the kitchen table with the end of his beard in a round of soft cheese Chistery had been saving for breakfast, and the Lion seemed to be knitting in his sleep, making his paws go back and forth. Little Daffy was nowhere to be seen, though there was a smell of baking in the air. Tip was invisible too, but she stepped over where she knew he would be in the morning when she awoke, and settled down with her back to him, looking at the shell. Tay went instantly to sleep.

She thought the dream was over, and maybe it was. Maybe she was awake now. She picked up the shell and remembered what someone had said to her. She couldn't remember who it was. That insane birdwoman in the tree, that's who it was. No? Doesn't matter.

Listen to what it is telling you.

She put it to her ear for the thousandth time and tried to make out a sound beyond the hush. It was fruitless, as usual, after such a noisy night of cryptic dream messages. She fell asleep that way, and when the shell dropped from her cheek an hour later and another fragment of its tip snipped off, she didn't even hear it.

In the morning there was a note from Tip on the table, pinned in place under the shell.

La Mombey may not be the one to have taken the Grimmerie, and your father. Then again, she might be. I will find out. I know we can't bring Dorothy back to Munchkinland. I am the only one who can get in safely. Mombey will punish me but not torment me—though I am not her son, I am her only family. She will forgive me and I will learn what is to be learned.
Don't worry about my leaving by night. The jackal moon has lit up the path like torches. I will be safe.
And I will come back to you.
  Love, Tip

6.

They had beaten him at first, chained him naked and whipped him in the hot sunlight filtering through the canopy of a dunderhead pine. Riverines of blood drained down his calves and made carmine socks over his heels and arches. The dripping resin from sap stung in his wounds. They weren't as merciless as they might have been. When he loosed his bowels upon his calves they realized that they'd gone too far, and then someone had the sloppy job of cleaning him up because he couldn't move his spine. They were gentler after that. Apparently they didn't want him to die en route.

They were careful to conceal their destination.

Five of them. Men of few words, quick movements, each one of them athletically taut—sleek and trained. Professional abductors. Once they reached the base of the Kells they slaughtered the skark, for target practice as far as Liir could tell, or to alarm him. They continued on horseback. Liir had never been much of a rider; with his hands tied behind his back he was in constant danger of falling off and being dragged to death. Clever, one of them figured out a way to harness Liir's shoulders loosely to the horse's bridle, so he would have to fall forward if he blacked out from loss of blood.

"Just waiting to bleed, weren't you," was the only phrase he heard at first. "Just saving it up for us to wring it out of you. Some are like that." But the speaker was hushed, perhaps so as not to give away an accent of origin.

They avoided farmsteads. If they had to venture into villages they waited until dusk, when they stuffed Liir's mouth with rags and hooded his head so he couldn't see where they were going. But in the open country, night or day, they left his head bare, and he could tell they were continuing east, picking their way into Gillikin. But how far? If to the Emerald City, they'd need to turn south soon enough. If all the way to Munchkinland, sooner or later they'd meet up with the battle lines of the soldiers of Loyal Oz. They'd have to find a way to break through somehow. Any chance to escape would come in a moment of panic and confusion.

But his kidnappers were seasoned soldiers.

Not any older than Liir was, but hardened in a different way. How can I feel that I belong to a different species, he wondered, not for the first time in his life.

He could intuit no chink of friendship, imagine no possibility of cozening up to his captors. They steeled themselves against that. They didn't drink. They didn't joke with one another, even. Most of their days were spent in silence.

Though he'd never been one to consider weeping a weakness, Liir didn't weep. The contusion on his brow from when he had slipped and fallen against a boulder, unable to stop himself because of his yoked arms— that was a badge of honor. The ache in his thighs from riding, the split lip from that mailed hand across his face—he could taste the blood two or three times a day, as the wound kept reopening with the jolting in the saddle—he treasured these, in a way. Tokens, medallions of his love for his daughter. If the soldiers had him, they might soften their hunt for *her*. His job since the day Rain had been born had been to keep her as safe as he could.

In some ways, though, he wasn't functioning well. He couldn't eat much because of his lip, not to mention the lost teeth in the back. (They'd pulled a couple for fun, to see if he would read the Grimmerie for them, and there had been so much pus and pain he couldn't talk for two days. At least the sacrificed teeth were in the back, so if he ever had to bite a hand he could at least try. And he still had his beautiful smile, ha-ha.)

His grip on *now* and *then* began to soften. The heat brought on mild slips of focus. At times he thought he was being captured by Cherrystone's men, following that time he'd been stationed in Quadling Country, in Qhoyre. After he'd helped torch the bridge at Bengda, with Ansonby and Burny and the other fellows. After he'd seen the Quadling parents, their own backs sporting wings of fire, slinging their daughter into the water, hoping she might clear the burning oil on the river, hoping she might survive somehow. He wept for that little girl now. He would never know if she had made it, or if he had succeeded in fulfilling his military mission and murdering her and her parents. He deserved to be caught at last, though Cherrystone would be clapping him on the back, rum chap, for a campaign carried out successfully. Liir would make Prime Menacier if he could be forgiven for skedaddling.

Daughters. The girl should have been able to fly above the flaming waters. But who could teach daughters to fly? Parents were by definition earthbound, grub eaters, feet in their own coffins, by dint of being parents.

He once thought he was crossing the Disappointments on horseback, Trism on a mount just behind him. It was dawn, a rimefrost was on the ground, but however Liir twisted, he couldn't catch sight of his lover.

Other times Liir thought he'd reached the sanctuary of Nether How. The men on horseback around him seemed to shimmer and disappear, and the horses too, and Liir, the scourge of Oz, was continuing alone, on foot. He wanted to sleep against a hill, he wanted to fall into the falling leaves. To melt away the soil as he might melt away a snowbank. To sink into a grave he had burned for himself. But as he lay there in the dappled grass among the sheep droppings, he began to elevate out of his body—maybe he was dying—and he saw an old codger materialize in the trees and look about with a curious or perhaps a guilty expression. He carried the Grimmerie with him. He consulted the book for a moment, closed it decisively, and headed north.

This time Liir shouted out, "You have no right to plant that danger here! Take it back! We don't want it!"

But the horsemen reemerged and cuffed him silent. He was on a horse, being taken somewhere by men to whom he'd never been properly introduced.

He noticed the jackal moon, sooner or later, and remembered the last time he'd seen it. That was just before he met Candle and fell in love with her, before he met Trism and fell in love with him. The jackal moon was no friend to love. Fall under its spell and look what happens. Your wife never forgives you for giving her a child who must be hidden to survive. Your boyfriend never returns. You have your life, that scrappy thing you keep dragging after you as long as you can. Less visible than the weightless shadow you also drag but oh, so much heavier. You have your hopes for your daughter. You have little else.

Except the damn book.

He turned his head from the jackal moon, unwilling to meet its eye. Cutting it in society. You've already had your truck with me. I'm not going to scombre in the snowdrifts for you like a poodle. Look elsewhere, jackal. Hunt up some other jerk. I want no more love and no more regret than the investments I've already made.

It was a better day. Maybe more protein in the diet, or his blood was slowly replenishing itself. He was more alert. He realized that by now they must have passed any turnoff to the Emerald City. They'd been weeks on the road, no? They were approaching a range of low hills spiked with the scorched trunks of scrub pine. Maybe torched to reduce coverage for snipers. The Madeleines, probably. So he worked it out. They were coming up near the border between Gillikin and Munchkinland, where the second army of the Emerald City was said to be in fierce hostilities with an Animal contingent roped up by the Munchkinlanders. Though he could read no sign of activity at the moment. Were they going to try to make a run for it, cross the breach of wasteland?

Or maybe hostilities had been concluded, miraculously. It could happen. Wars stop eventually, don't they? If not in our own lifetimes, surely peace hies into sight for our children?

Around midafternoon on a day of dry, hurrying winds that whipped the first leaves of autumn around the horses' hooves, the captors stopped. An outcropping of feldspar trusset, sparkling with mica, big enough to be a landmark.

"The cart is supposed to be here," said the captain.

"It en't here."

"You'll have to go find one."

His colleague cursed, but two of them took off and returned next morning with a cart and several donkeys looking dubious.

"They're not talking Animals, are they?" asked the chief abductor. "Fled over the border to escape the war, and passing as stupid beasts?"

"They tell me they're not," replied his colleague. For that, the donkeys were whipped with a riding crop to see if they would cry out in Ozish, but they only haw-heed as they bucked.

"All right," said the captain to Liir. "You have a choice now."

"I prefer two choices, if you're offering," said Liir.

"You can open that book of charms and find a way to make us all invisible until we get across the border."

"You wouldn't trust me with that book," said Liir. "If I could read it at all, I would turn you into shoes or ships or sealing wax."

"If we don't arrive within the next few days, the word will go out to take in your wife," said the captain.

"We left her there as an encouragement to you to co-operate, but if you try to escape, the vengeance will be swift."

"So. That's one choice," said Liir.

"The other one is to ingest a little potion we've had supplied for us. It will put on you a disguise that will help us smuggle you over the border."

"A disguise," said Liir.

"The trouble is, there's no telling how long it will last," said the captain. "It'll probably work itself off in a few days."

"Do I get to know what it is?"

"You'll be an Animal. You'll appear to be dead. We'll be seeking a mercy crossing to bring you to burial in the land you fought for. The EC brass are cruel but not inhuman; the armies exchange their dead every few days."

"I'm not sure I can adequately play a dead Animal. I haven't had academy training."

"You'll learn on the job. What'll it be?"

"I don't believe I could be much good to La Mombey if I remained a dead Animal for very long. So I'll risk the disguise, and I'll go that way across the border. If the sentries don't believe you and they kill me, well, I'll be dead already, won't I? So presumably it won't hurt a great deal more."

"I would try the book if I were you," said the captain.

"You've been so kind with advice along the way," said Liir. "But I can't read that book. All your labors will be for naught in the end, I'm afraid."

"We've had our job, and it's almost done. Put the book in its casing, and lie on top of it in the cart. I'm afraid you're going to have to take off your clothes. You'd look a bit rare splitting out of your tunic and leggings."

"Oh, I'm going to be something larger than a bread box?"

"Hurry up."

He did as he was told. The air felt good on his skin. They let him pee as a human, and then helped him climb into the cart. Nakedness among men might once have bothered him for all sorts of reasons, but it didn't bother him now. He was going to his death in a tumbrel, humble as a deposed king.

The captain cradled Liir's head in his gloved hand and forced the vial to his lips; he was like a child being given medicine. Elphaba had never given him medicine, though. It had been Sarima, or Nor, or Nanny. Elphaba hadn't noticed if he was ever sick or dead. The feel of the captain's strong hand on his scalp and the plug of the silvery flask at his still bruised lips felt almost tender. He could see only fans of golden leaves against the autumnal blue sky. The world was waving him out, cheerily enough. He closed his eyes not to betray his sense of final calm.

"For all our sakes, may this be a safe crossing," said the captain. The last thing Liir heard. Behind his eyelids, the sun began to blacken in segments, and sound peeled back like a rind, exposing the silence within it.

Above the cart, an old Eagle watched with a steady eye. He saw the donkeys struck with cudgels, he saw the naked man curled like an overgrown embryo. He saw poison administered. He didn't know this was intended as a temporary death, a coup de théâtre. He hadn't been able to hear well; hearing he left for his friend the Hawk, who was nowhere near.

When the cart moved, the Eagle waited a while and then made a short circling flight, keeping to a height. He didn't want to be seen paying his last respects. Liir would have preferred this final indignity to be private, he knew. Liir was like that.

Kynot watched as his old friend, the boy-broomist, began to tremble in his death, and thicken. Liir's lifeless body didn't so much disappear as become bloated with something that looked fungal, growing from his limbs, spine, buttocks. The swellings emerged pale, like new mushrooms after an overnight downpour, but blackened as they enlarged. The wounds on Liir's back disappeared, and that was a mercy, even to an Eagle who abhors sentiment of any variety.

He waited only to see what shape Liir would take in death, in case the information was ever useful to him. One never knew. By the time the Eagle was ready to fly away on his unsteady wings—he was good only for short hauls with longish rests, these days—he recognized Liir as the corpse of a small Black Elephant. The soldiers must have known that was the aim of the liquor, as they pulled from their supplies a silly sort of mash-up of harness and brocade and arranged it on Liir's back like a crumpled howdah, ruined in battle. Then they took on the aspect of mourning, and raised a periwinkle standard, the sign of request for safe passage.

Go in peace, or something like that, thought Kynot, and flew away.

7.

"If Tip has been brave enough to go look for the Grimmerie in Munchkinland," said Rain, "I'm going to the Emerald City and present myself to the great and powerful Emperor of Oz. If he has the Grimmerie, he can keep it. But if he has my father, I want him back."

Chistery had only been acquainted with Rain for a week, but he knew her well enough not to doubt her. "Suicidal, but I'll pack you a satchel," he said.

"Wait a minute," said Iskinaary. "Your parents have spent their whole lives keeping you out of the way of trouble. They've lived and, who knows, they'll die for it. And you're identifying some adolescent martyr impulse in that flat breast of yours? Squelch it, darling, or I'll squelch it for you."

"I'm going," said Rain. "How much good has choosing to be fugitive done anyone? No one has ever stood up to Shell, at least not since the Conference of the Birds. That political gesture should have been only a beginning. Discussion comes next. I'll bargain with him if I have to."

"Hi-ho, I don't think we can be of use in this particular venture," said Mr. Boss.

"We're going," said Little Daffy. "At least as far as the gates of the Emerald City, anyway."

"Isn't marriage bliss?" he replied, and went to ready his kit.

"Well, it's a fool's errand, and I suppose I'm fool enough to qualify. I'm coming too, then," said the

Goose, but Rain said, "Think again. If you didn't go with my father when he was kidnapped, you can bloody well stay here. When my mother comes back with the broom, you need to tell her where we are."

"Chistery can do that," said the Goose.

"Chistery can't fly on his old wings. If my mother has the broom and can learn to fly it, she'll have to catch up to us soon enough. You can accompany her, if you want to accompany someone. And if she doesn't come back, but something else happens. . . ." She meant, *if Tip returns for me*, and they all knew what she meant though she didn't put it into words. ". . . you can come let me know."

There was sense in what she said, but Iskinaary didn't like being bossed around by a schoolgirl. He hissed and rushed at her legs. She batted him away absentmindedly as if she couldn't bother to feel the pinches.

She was furious at Tip, and fury made a useful source of energy. She'd never known. It was almost fun until she realized that the fury was partly a disguise for raw fear. How *could* he keep safe? In some ways Tip was more innocent than she was. However hobbled a childhood she'd had, she'd learned to be more wary than he had.

One final time she mounted the steps to the Witch's chambers. She looked around to see if there was some scrap of something bewitched she might take as a souvenir, in case she never came back. In a wild sense, this was her ancestral home, though she'd never seen it before, and by the looks of things the castle wouldn't survive the next earthquake. She might never see it again.

She couldn't find anything worth saving. The dead scraps of beast bored her now. She intended to live among the living for a while longer, so she wanted no huffle yet with bones and bits. "You're enough for me, Tay," she said to the otter.

For reasons she couldn't name, she went up to the gazing globe. It came off the stand easily enough. She held the world in her hands, if it was still the world. "I don't care," she told it, "don't show me another glimpse more, it's too much." But she looked again. Was she seeing herself, cold and heartless at last? The face in the globe looked green and leering, mocking. Almost daring her to manage this mayhem. She hurtled the glass bubble out the window so widely that she never heard a crash.

From under a bench she pulled a few baskets. One of them revealed a substantial collection of deer antlers; she left them there. Another had desiccated bits of moss, or that's what it looked like now; she didn't want to know. A third had a scatter of spare buttons. Imagine the Witch sewing on her own buttons! Rain clattered the lot all over the floor and left the room with the basket, which was the right size.

She didn't look back to see if the crocodrilos was rolling its dice at her. She didn't care.

On the way downstairs she passed a children's dormitory and went in. Underneath one of the beds was a grey stuffed mouse. Rain put it on her finger for a moment, then slipped it in her pocket.

Next level down, she stopped to peek in at Nanny, who now slept in a library off the reception rooms. Nanny was awake, awake enough, and sat up happily among her pillows when Rain came forward.

"My Elphie, give Nanny a kiss," she said.

"I'm not Elphaba, Nanny, I never was."

"That's a duck. No, I suppose you're not, or not today. When is she expected back? Off larking I suppose?"

"I suppose." But Rain had never mastered lying and she didn't want to lie to Nanny as she left her behind. "She's not coming back, Nanny. She's gone."

"Oh, she's a tricky one, she is," said Nanny. "Don't you fret."

"I'm leaving now, too," said Rain.

"If you see her, tell her to hurry herself up. I can't be doing about the oven any more or I'll set myself on fire, the way she did."

"Nanny." Rain tried one final time. "What did you come upon when you got to the parapet? The day Dorothy threw the bucket of water at her? You were the first one up the stairs, and you never let anyone else see."

"No, I didn't, did I," said Nanny. "I was a smarty-puss, I was."

"But—but what? What was there? What did you do with her body?"

"Little girl," said Nanny, "you don't need to worry your head about that. I did the right and proper thing, to save that Liir any more grief. Adults know what to do. What to do, and what to say, and while I haven't always been the most honest woman in my life, I'm telling you the truth now."

Rain leaned forward and grasped Nanny's hands.

"And the truth is this. What I did is *none of your business.*"

Rain almost hit her.

"Was that you throwing Elphie's globe out the window, or has that air-bubble Glinda been floating around in her private pfenix again? Never a moment's peace around here. Child, let me confess something to you."

Was this it? "Yes, Nanny."

"I stole a lot in my time. Garters, beads, a considerable amount of cash. A pretty little green glass bottle, once. It did me some good. You have to learn to take what you need. But don't tell anyone I said so."

The original Handy Mandy, thought Rain. "I've stolen a bit already. Good-bye, Nanny."

"Good-bye, dear," said Nanny. "Good-bye, Rain. Yes, I see it now. You're not Elphaba, are you? But you'll do."

They left before dinner, to make it at least to Red Windmill, maybe even to push on to Upper Fanarra. Since the skies were cloudless, the jackal moon would be usefully glary. Dorothy and the Cowardly Lion, the dwarf and the Munchkinlander, Rain and Tay. On the stony path again.

Iskinaary and Chistery waved from a wobbly wooden porch that looked about to become unglued from the side of a turret. A raft of flying monkeys tossed their jaw-edged spears into the air as a salute. They clattered into the dry moat and blunted, which would give the monkeys a lot of work to do over the long winter, repointing all those blades.

———

At Upper Fanarra they paused long enough for Rain to scour the weaving collective and single out the tired teenage mother who'd kept smacking her child. Rain offered the babykin the small stuffed mouse she'd found in the vacant dormitory in Kiamo Ko. The infant grinned and gummed it at once. "Tell the mother," said Rain to a factotum of the clan who could translate, "the mouse is from Tip. From me, a promise that if she keeps hitting that child I'll come back and wallop the crap out of *her*. I'm not as nice as Tip."

Easier going down than up, though hard on the calves. It only took about five days for them to get to the dam where they could cross the Vinkus River. Once again most of the Beavers were out foraging, but Luliaba was still hanging about, minding the mother-in-law.

"Let her go," said Rain.

"It's none of your concern," said Luliaba.

"The little girl said let her go," said Mr. Boss, baring his teeth.

"I could take you in a bite fight, mister buster," replied the Beaver, baring her own.

"Let her go," said Little Daffy.

"I keep her locked up for her own good. She's a menace to herself."

They all looked at Brrr, but he didn't speak. Since the death of Nor he chose his moments more carefully.

Dorothy said, "Let her go, or I'll sing."

"Sing away!" called the mother-in-law inside her prison. "She hates that. I do it all day to annoy her."

Dorothy began that song about plain fruits and majestic purples. The others joined in as best as they could. They sang it twice, three times, four, until Luliaba said, "Stop! I give up. You win. I can't take that kind of malarkey. What kind of a patriotic song is it that doesn't even mention Beaver dams? *That's* what makes our nation great. Come on out, you old bitch. Your constant carping has set you free at last. What your son will say when he gets home I don't want to think."

"He'll thank you for it," said the old Beaver, emerging and blinking and twitching her white nose. "He never liked me neither. So, who's the little dolly who was leading that anthem?"

They all pointed at Dorothy. The Beaver mother-in-law said, "Most disgusting song I ever heard, but it did the trick. You're a sweetheart."

"Here's your coracle," said Rain, handing her the button basket.

"I hope it floats, but where I'm going, it doesn't really matter," she replied, climbing in and rocking it a little. "Hmmm. Sound bottom, near as I can make out. Push me off, honeybunches, and let me go find my sweet Lurline and give her a little love nip on her holy ankle."

As she rocked away on the vicious water, they heard her begin to sing.

> O beautiful, to make escape
> And leave this world behind.
> Had I to stay another day
> I'd lose my fucking mind. . . .

Over the roar of the water they couldn't hear any more after that, and were grateful for it.

8.

The corpse of the Black Elephant was hauled through the porte cochere of Colwen Grounds and around to the back. Here the ground sloped away, allowing access to some whitewashed stables, clean to clinical standards. All had gone according to plan so far. Various Munchkinlanders helped drag the cart into a stall with a bricked barrel vault ceiling, also white. They kept this place in fine fettle, but that was what Munchkinlanders were like.

Its formal name was Parliament House, though since no parliament had ever been convened everyone still called it Colwen Grounds. The ancestral home of the Thropp family, the place old Nanny had started out in domestic service as Cattery Spunge, late of the spindlemills. Back when she was young Nanny. Or young enough. When she'd been engaged to help raise Melena Thropp, the randy and irresponsible mother of Elphaba, Nessarose, and Shell, now Emperor of Oz.

No one from the Thropp line was here to see Liir return to his birthright at last. And maybe for the best. The humiliation of being a prisoner. What would Liir's ancestor Eminence, Peerless Thropp, have made of this?

Taking it for a genuine corpse, the palace staff began to prepare the pyre. But La Mombey herself descended into the basements—they'd never known her to do that before—and required the corpse to be rolled over. The book in its sack wasn't appreciably squished, and she grabbed it with both hands.

"Shall we continue our preparations to burn the corpse?" asked the grounds overseer.

Mombey said, "Do you smell the stench of death?"

"I don't know what the stench of death is for a Black Elephant."

"Believe me, you'd know if you smelled it. Hold the torches. It might pull through."

"Can I take that for you, Your Highness?" asked her handmaid.

Mombey said, "Jellia Jamb, I can carry my own books to school, thank you very much. Don't you ever touch this one." She took the book in her arms and stalked away with it. The handmaid shrugged and made a face at the farm overseer. You never knew what Mombey was going to say or do; she was a different woman every hour of the day.

Not so different from the rest of the race of women, though, thought the overseer.

9.

At this point in the early autumn, the waters of the Gillikin River had fallen. Fording the great broad flat was almost a picnic. They were ahead of the seasonal rains by two or three weeks, maybe.

It felt good to be going somewhere again. Maybe I'm just a wanderbug, thought Rain. Everyone I care about most in the world is off and in trouble, and I'm noodling along on the road as if it's my job.

Tay looked at her almost as if it could read her mind, accusatorily. *Everyone you most care about? Hello?*

Well, not everyone, she thought. Come here, you. And she carried Tay a stretch.

She remembered the marking stone that had shown a fork in the road, but she wasn't sure that she had crossed the Gillikin River at the same place where she and Tip had done those weeks ago. Still, after they passed through a couple of fairly prosperous town centers and some dustier cousins, too, they came to a sarcen on which directions were painted, with arrows. Sitting on top of the stone was an Owl.

"Which way now?" asked Dorothy to the Owl.

"Depends, I suppose, on where you want to go."

"Out of Oz, and the sooner the better," said Dorothy, and then she recognized the voice. "Why, it's Temper Bailey. What are you doing here?"

"Relocated after my professional humiliation."

Little Daffy said, "Oh, that was a rigged case if ever I saw one. You never should have taken it on."

"I was required under pain of caging."

"And you're now a Loyal Ozian?" asked Dorothy. "Have you no patriotism toward Munchkinland?"

"None."

That seemed to be that. "Well, we're headed toward the Emerald City," said Rain.

"If you stay on this road, you're too far north. You'll eventually end up in Shiz."

"No, thank you," said Rain. "I might be tempted to kidnap Miss Plumbago and hold her for ransom until I get my father back, and I don't want to stoop to their tactics."

"Then turn around and find the crossroads in the village you just quit. Take the left road out of town, the one by the ironmonger. That'll bring you to a high road that joins up with the Yellow Brick Road."

"You've done me a service again, as you did once before," said Dorothy. "Will you come with us to the Emerald City?"

The Owl scuffled his talons. "You're going there again? Are you in complete *denial*? You've picked the wrong support group with this lot. Or what, are you going to ask the Wizard to grant you your heart's desire?"

Dorothy took no offense. "Well, I've come to see you have a point. Concentrating on getting your own heart's desire is myopic at best. Or just plain selfish. But there isn't any Wizard anymore, is there? He hasn't made a comeback?"

"Of course not. I was just testing to see if you'd regained any more of your marbles. I don't think you did your cause any good, by the way. Being so scatty."

"I don't imagine you've seen Toto? My little dog?"

"Never met the chap, and have no interest."

Dorothy crossed her arms. "Temper Bailey, are you sorry you took my case?"

"Sorry doesn't begin to cover it. I've lost my home and my family, and my professional reputation. I haven't been eating well and my pellets are punky. If I'd known you would be coming this way I would have hid in a roasting pan somewhere with a gooseberry in my mouth and a twig of rosemary up my ass."

"So you won't join our merry band?" asked Rain.

"You losers?" The Owl hooted. "Dorothy's gathering another pilgrimage to storm the gates of the Emerald City? In the fine tradition of the Wizard, the Emperor's going to grant you all your hearts' desires? Forget it. Besides, I thought the Lion already got his medal for courage."

"Get out of our way," said Little Daffy.

"You have no way," said Temper Bailey.

Mr. Boss stooped down and picked up a stone.

"Stop," said the Lion. His voice buzzed with catarrh; he hadn't spoken in days. "He couldn't help what happened. The Owl was set up just as mercilessly as Dorothy was."

"If you should come across a Goose called Iski-naary—" began Rain, but Temper Bailey had taken wing.

"If he's such a crabbycakes, can we even trust his directions?" wondered Little Daffy. "Maybe he's flying off to alert the authorities we're coming."

"Cheeky twit-owl. I should have popped him one," muttered the dwarf.

"We're walking into trouble any way we go," said Rain. "We can't stop now. Let's press on. Surely we'll find another shortcut through to the Yellow Brick Road. If we accidentally detour to Shiz, well, maybe some good will come of it. Maybe we'll find they've taken my father there instead of to the Emerald City, for some reason. We can always take the train, or follow the Shiz Road to the EC. If we need to."

"You're still so young," said the dwarf. "The world is so big, and you always think you're going to walk right down the middle of it."

10.

The first thing to return was a sense of smell.

Oh, it was rich. A sense like none he'd ever had before. Confounding, complex, an appreciation of distinctions changing instant by instant. A symphonic approach to odor. Aromas were not separate after all, nor settled. They changed in relation to one another, varying as quickly as the shadows under a young summer tree in a high wind.

He could tell the separate ages of the wood from different pieces of furniture and from the doorframes; he could even tell it was furniture and doorframes before he opened his eyes. He knew about the mothballs in the third drawer down (he could count with his nose) and the relative moments of death of the generations of moths that had immolated themselves around the globe of an oil lamp overhead. He could tell colors too.

Time to open his eyes.

He was lying on his side. He couldn't remember how he'd gotten here, or whether he'd always been an Elephant. He did remember he was a he, but his name took a little while to return. He couldn't lift his head and he wasn't either uncomfortable or alarmed at the situation. He reached to scratch a patch of dry skin, and the mobility of his nose surprised and delighted him, but he drifted off to sleep again before he could question why he might be surprised.

Then again, it's always somewhat surprising to wake up and be alive again.

A doctor of some sort was shining a light in his eyes.

"He's going to come around soon enough," said the doctor. "Ready to have a drink, little fella?" The doctor pushed a cart with a bucket of well water too rich in the riskier algae, but fresh this hour, and Liir drank it gratefully by suctioning it through his trunk and then spraying it into his mouth, which had gone dry as bones and felt in need of a good gingerscotch gargle.

"Can you speak?" asked the doctor, a little man who was standing on a stool. A Munchkinlander physician.

Liir thought he might be able to, but didn't answer. He needed to remember more before he spoke.

The next time the door opened, a woman came through it. She was taller than the physician by double, with a head of flaxen-rose hair and a stern and loving expression. "They have said you're making progress, Liir Thropp," she told him. "I am La Mombey Impeccata, the Eminence of Munchkinland. I should like you to sit up now and pull yourself together."

He thought about it, and then heaved himself over by rolling back and forth like an old dog. Under the low table on which he rested, the newly installed supports made of tree trunks creaked, and sawdust sifted onto the slate floor beneath the table.

"You ought to be coming out of your stupor now. I calibrated the semblance of death to last only so long. Can you hear me?"

He couldn't remember why there might be a reason to hesitate, but he erred on the side of caution. He could smell high intention in her pheromones, and duplicity, and mastery, superscribed with patchouli and underlit by garlic chive.

"I need your help and I need it quickly. I have the power of life and death over your wife and your daughter."

He could smell the lie, but knew it lay soon enough to the possible truth to be important to consider.

"Nothing has been done to you that you cannot out-live, and much good will come your way if you cooper-ate. We are within striking distance of the conclusion of this sorry war. The quicker you decide to help, the fewer people will fall. The fewer Animals will die. As I have made you a Black Elephant, I can keep you that way, or I can have you shot like the skark you saw my men take down. It's your choice. Every moment you delay your return to full consciousness and due dili-gence is a moment that soldiers put their lives on the line, waiting for you. And a moment nearer to the forced repatriation of your daughter, who is after all, going back a generation or three, a frond of Munchkinland, just as you are yourself. Have you any questions?"

He had a few questions, but he didn't ask them of her.

She turned to leave. He could smell her dress whispering comments of straw brushing along the slate. The soap that had not been rinsed out well four washings ago. He could smell her anger and her cunning. What he couldn't smell—and, if he'd ever really been a human man, he didn't recall having been able to smell it then, either—was the lure of power, the attractiveness of it. He seemed bereft of a certain lust for strength and dominance. He didn't think the lack had pestered him much.

Unless its absence had put his family in danger all too often. There was that.

At the door, she said, "I know about you. Not as much as I will, not as much as I'd like, but enough. I know you have hesitations and you also have capacities. I know you admire the Elephant as a creature and you consider hiding inside. I know about Princess Nastoya and your campaign years ago to release her from her spell. Who do you think she first turned to, all those decades past, for a charm to give her the guise of a human being? Mombey Impeccata, at her service. I am the foremost master of forms and shapes in all of Oz.

Go up against me, Liir, and you will see what form and shape of vengeance that I take against you."

He closed his eyes. He had already died as a human being, and in fact it hadn't seemed a noticeable effort. If the time came to die as an Elephant, maybe he would come across Princess Nastoya in the Afterlife. Maybe after all this time he might meet up with Elphaba Thropp again, his so-called mother. He could give her a piece of his mind. He could give her a great thumping with his trunk for being such a bitch.

He smelled time passing as he slept, and learned as he slept to smell it in minutes and hours as well as in warmths and darknesses.

Then he was stronger, and more Liir, more aware of himself as the old Liir inside the Elephant skin, though a changed Liir in ways he still couldn't smell. There's a reason we live in time. We are too small a flask, even as an Elephant, to tolerate too much knowing. Instead, truth must drip through us as through a pipette, to allow only moments of apprehension. Moments diffuse and miniature enough to be survived.

The door opened again. Now that he was more aware of hearing, he tried before turning his head to hear who it might be. The little physician? The maid, Jellia Jamb?

Or La Mombey herself? If La Mombey, could he smell her as a blonde, or as a Quadling with that plaited dark hair like Candle? Or as a chestnut-coiffed karyatid with lilacs and turquoises in her headpiece?

He didn't believe what he smelled, so he rolled over and turned his head. His eyes were the least strong of his senses so far, but he strained to focus as well as he might.

The man stood at the door, light glaring around him. The Elephant's eyes stung for a moment, and so tears stood, but they were tears of ocular pain and adjustment, not of emotion. Not on Liir's part, though maybe on Trism's. "Is it you, or is it another of her tricks?" asked the Elephant's old lover.

Liir might have asked the same, if Mombey had used a semblance of Trism to trick Liir into a confidence, but his nose was strong enough to tell this was Trism, no disguise. He remembered the smell of every follicle root, every breath, every fold and crevice, every secretion and hesitation. The sight and the knowledge took Liir's breath away, but when it came back, his voice came back with it.

"It is I," he said, "more or less. Rather more, I should guess. I mean, I'd actually gotten wiry since I last saw you, up until recently when I seem to have put on a few pounds."

Trism closed the door. He came across the room, but stood outside the range of Liir's waving trunk, which was raking in ten years' worth of nasal history, satisfying the longing Liir had so long denied himself the right to feel.

"Why are you here?" asked the Elephant.

Trism drew himself up. He'd gone thicker. A barrel cage for a chest instead of a butter churn. Still, he'd maintained his military trim, a strong stomach and tight waist, and his bearing was all that the Emerald City home guard had taught him years ago.

But he was working for the enemy.

Depending on who *was* the enemy.

Trism answered quickly enough. "I came over, I fled Loyal Oz after—after you know what."

"I don't entirely know what."

"After we torched the dragon stables in the Emerald City, and we fled by night," he said. "After we became lovers for a moment. After I followed you to that farm—"

"Apple Press Farm."

"I remember its name. You weren't there. After all that."

All that might have happened with or against Candle, all that she had never told Liir about, never spoken about.

After all this time, though, here stood Trism. If Candle had preserved her feelings for Trism as her own secret, Liir found he had uncovered new reserves of patience to let those feelings remain unknown. Perhaps another skill of Elephants that we so-called humans would be wiser if we could learn.

"You left, under whatever circumstances," said Liir. He hadn't moved off the table since he'd been put there, and he was rolling in his excrement, that which the helpers had not been able to reach to scrape away. There was so much of interest to smell in manure, but in any case, Trism didn't seem offended.

Liir tried to work his huge pie-plate front hooves to the floor, to close the gap that Trism still maintained.

"You left," said Liir, "and you went over."

"They were always looking for you. As soon as they'd figured out who you were. You were behind the flight of the Birds, and the Emperor sorted that out easily. And of course Cherrystone knew what the Emperor knew. They put us together soon enough, you and me, and they had me followed, hoping I'd lead them to you. They thought I couldn't resist your charms enough to save your skin."

"I was never very supple, but I seem to have side-stepped them a good many years running."

"Yes, and sidestepped me."

"I didn't know where you'd gone, Trism."

"And you had a wife. You told me about Candle but you never told me about a wife. You had a wife and a child on the way."

Liir supposed Trism had a point. "If it makes any difference to you, I didn't know she was my wife at first. Though that's a bit of a story to explain."

"I remember. *She* told me once. You think I have ever forgotten a scrap about you? A single blessed word?"

No, Liir didn't think that, not any longer. He could smell that it was true. "But why did you come *here*? If I could go underground in Oz for ten or fifteen years, why didn't you?"

"Can you fathom what they did to me, looking for you?" Trism didn't know which of Liir's Elephant eyes to look into; you couldn't look into both at once. Then Trism turned around and raked up his tunic and dropped his leggings to his knees, and bent over the sideboard with its medicines and the scrub brushes. His behind was still high and beautiful, if puckered on the flanks of it, and Liir reached forward and caressed it with his nose, traced its cleavage. But then, as Trism rolled a little onto his right side, Liir saw that his mate was not baring himself for mortification or attention. The skin on the forward side, from the second rib down to his left calf, was vitrified pink, hairless as a boiled ham.

"Cherrystone did this," said Trism, and pushed Liir's attentive nose away and dressed himself. "Under the Emperor of Oz, your uncle Shell Thropp, Cherrystone did this to me. *Cherrystone.* Do you think I would stay in Oz where I could be caught again? Slowly peeled away with hot knives? Until I had decided to seek you out and lead them to you, betray you to protect myself from being shaved like a carrot? I'm lucky this is all they took off."

"You did that for me," said Liir.

"Don't look for satisfaction. None of us knows why we did what we did back then. I know why I'm doing what I'm doing now. And I'm here to ask you to listen to Mombey's request, and help us."

Liir listened. His ears were big enough now to hear anything.

"Your uncle, taking a leaf out of the old tricks of one of his predecessors, the Wizard of Oz, has been launching an attack on the Animal armies, which have been pushed entirely out of the Madeleines into the Wend Fallows. Another foothold in Munchkinland, see. Shell has ordered the construction of small-scale aerial balloons filled with light gas. He's sending them over the hills to explode upon impact as they descend. The panic is immense and the Animals are close to scattering, or worse yet, surrendering. If we lose the Wend Fallows, the EC Messiars will be in Colwen Grounds in a matter of days, and it's all over."

"Frankly, I'm surprised the Animals didn't scatter at the first chance."

"Many of them remember their parents having to flee Loyal Oz a generation ago, under the Wizard's Animal Adverse laws. They harbor an old grievance, and when Animals fight, they fight fiercer than humans. But few creatures, human or Animal, will fight to the death to defend the honor of a dead generation. So the strictest of Mombey's human commanders are in charge of the Animals, and the Animal conscripts receive a more merciless punishment for going AWOL than I did."

"The Animals are an army of prisoners, effectively."

"Indentured mercenaries. But without pay. You said it. And when those prisoners finally panic and break loose, the bedlam will not be believed. We're in the final days of this war, one way or another."

"So why have you brought me here?"

"It wasn't my idea. Mombey brought you, to read the book to us."

"I still don't understand. How are you involved, then?"

"You remember my original training in the Emerald City? Your mother long ago had given the Wizard of Oz a page from the Grimmerie, *On the Proper Training and Handling of Dragons.* I was the chief dragon-master. I trained those dragons who attacked you years ago, the ones we later slaughtered before we fled."

"I remember. Trism the cute dragon mesmerist."

"When I left Loyal Oz, I carried with me the secrets of the trade. It's hard enough to secure a dragon's egg and raise it to life, and keep it alive—dragons don't like Oz. Oz is too wet and full of life for them. Dragons are desert creatures. But a few years ago Cherrystone got his hands on a clutch of eggs and managed to raise them to maturity. The creatures were to be used in the attack on Haugaard's Keep."

"I heard about that," said Liir, though he didn't understand that his daughter had been partly responsible for slowing the attack. "Do you remember Brrr, the so-called Cowardly Lion? He told me what he knew about that campaign. He was in the vicinity when it happened."

"I never met that Lion."

"The dragons were destroyed, I understand."

"Not all of them. One of them escaped, and it was found tending its wounds on the banks of Illswater in the south of Munchkinland. It was captured by

Mombey's people, brought north, and stabled not far from here. It yielded a clutch of eggs a short time later. They came to term."

"With no male to fertilize them? Capable dragon."

"There is much we don't know about dragons." Trism still had that I'm-older-than-you tone, Liir noticed.

"So you've raised the baby dragons up, you traitor dragonmaster."

"I have indeed," he said. "And not a moment too soon. They're ready to go. But Mombey knows this is her last chance. She can't risk their failure. The dragons have to do the job right."

"She's not one for letting things slide? Just my luck."

"She's been smart about keeping the Munchkinlanders focused and fired up. That show trial of Dorothy happened in the nick of time, as interest was flagging and recruitment was off, what with the endless stalemate. The arrival of Dorothy and the attention paid to her trial helped Mombey corral her first battalion of Animals in a single week."

"The conscription of Animals was promoted as defense, but really she needed to open a new front in the war. I see."

"Yes. General Jinjuria had lured Cherrystone in Haugaard's Keep but forgot to figure in the cost of keeping him under siege there. She can't knock him out of Haugaard's Keep; it's said to be so well fortified that he has imported a barge full of dancing girls and a craps game that goes on all night. He's running a fucking resort there on Restwater. He keeps Jinjuria guessing and occupied. And she can't rush what's left of her forces up to the Fallows. Something's got to give, and soon."

"So you'll use the dragons to attack Haugaard's Keep."

"If you can help, we'll use the dragons to attack the Emerald City."

He had said it. Liir turned his head and looked at Trism with the other eye, to see if his first eye had missed something. "There are civilians in the Emerald City."

"There are civilians in both armies, too. At least they were civilians before they were drafted. Look, if we can strike against the Emerald City hard enough, we might be able to pull Cherrystone and his floating vacationers out of Haugaard's Keep; they would be recalled to defend the Emperor. Munchkinland could retake Restwater and offer a truce. How many civilians' lives will have been saved then?"

"A lot of ifs, I suppose."

"With your great schnoz, can you smell possibility in this plan?"

It was a shame to say that he could. So he didn't say it. He just looked at Trism. They had both grown old enough to have learned how to ignore the needs of individual lives for the purported good of the lives of nations.

Trism knew him still; he saw what Liir was thinking; he threw himself against where Liir's arms would be if Liir had had arms; Liir wrapped the shattered stranger in his trunk and held his best beloved tight.

11.

Perhaps they ought to have followed Temper Bailey's advice, because the track they chose to wander along faltered and lost itself in a small but confounding wood. The leaves were beginning to change, the lavender of pearlfruit and the red of red maple and the gold of golden maple. The tarnishy tang of fox musk under the jealous snout of the jackal moon, who wanted to be down there with them—it was all a glorious adventure. But they were lost and doing no one much good.

"We'll find our way out tomorrow," said Dorothy. "I think there's some song about that. There ought to be."

The next morning they woke up even more lost. A bank of fog canted from the warmish earth into the chilling air, rather thicker than what they might have expected at this time of year. It wasn't only visibility that gave out, but also sound. Stifled. A clammy tightness seemed to filter through the lower branches, as if the air was congested. Any leaves much above head level dissolved into a pale ruddy glow.

"You stay close to me, Tay," said Rain.

"Shall we sing to keep up our nerve?" asked Dorothy. No one bothered to reply.

Then Brrr paused and said, "I know what this is. Or I think I do."

He had spoken so seldom recently that they were all surprised. They waited for him to continue.

"I saw this once before, this trick of atmospherics. When I was hardly more than a cub. I think this is the Ozmists. But what are they doing so far south? We can't have wandered off course so badly that we missed Shiz and entered the Great Gillikin Forest? That's where they live, as I understood it."

"Not a chance," said Mr. Boss, who of them all had traveled the widest in Oz, and for the longest time. "We'd've had to cross the rail line to the Pertha Hills, and we never did. So we're still west of the forest and west of Shiz. Though whether we're heading south still or have veered some other way I can't say in this swamp of wet tissues. Anyhow, I never heard of any *Ozmists*. Who are they? The essence of royalists gone to ground, literally, and their appetite for the crown seeping up?"

Brrr spoke with more urgency than he'd shown for weeks. From this new danger, a new capacity for governance. "Listen. If something comes over us— everyone—*listen carefully*. You must not ask them any questions if you don't have something to tell them in return."

"But Ozmists," demanded Rain. "We don't know about them."

"They're particles of ghosts, I think," hurried the Lion, "ghosts who can't congeal into anything like the individuals they once were. Fragments of rotted leaves in a puddle never coalesce into living leaves again. Listen, once I saw a friend lose his way in life by forgetting to give them news. You see, the Ozmists exist—it's not living, but it is existing, I guess—for their future. *Their* future, which is our present. They hunger to learn what they couldn't know in life—and they might answer a question if we chose to ask it. But our question can't be about *now*, for they are dead and don't know *now. Now* is what they're hungry for. Our question must be about something in the past that they might have knowledge of—this is important, pay attention! Or you'll pay too steep a price."

They heard the tremor in his voice; it was their old Lion, forceful and worried for them, herding them together. They gathered into a circle, and even as he spoke a cloud of sparks seemed to shimmer with its own fulguration, an orgy of lightning bugs packed into a space the size of a stable.

"Hang on," said Brrr. His voice sounded far away to them though he was right there; they were all right there.

They hung more than stood in a void not like the world. For a while they couldn't see their feet or paws or hands, just their profiles, like dolmens rendered flat and brooding by soft weather.

Then the Ozmists greeted their audience, just as the Lion remembered it, in one voice, though indistinctly. The way a single head can have a thousand overlapping shadowy profiles if a thousand candles are placed about it. *Barter*, chuntered the Ozmists.

The companions waited for Brrr to answer for them. Would he have the courage? It took a moment. Or a week.

"I know about barter," replied Brrr. "What do you want to know?"

Is Ozma returned to the throne of Oz?

"She is not," said the Lion.

"Not as far as we know," said Little Daffy. "I mean, we haven't had news of the Emerald City"—she heard the Lion fake a cough and she amended her statement in time—"not the Emerald City, of course; but we know that Munchkinland is fighting strong to remain independent, holding the line at Haugaard's Keep, holding the line at the Madeleines, keeping faith with the Glikkuns to the north, and sweeping the poison sand off their thresholds at the desert back door."

The Ozmists seemed to take a few moments to absorb this considerable punch of news. *Where is Ozma?* they answered.

"It's our turn to ask a question," said Brrr. Rain tugged at his mane to quiet him, but he wouldn't be silenced. "Where is Nor?"

"No, Brrr, don't," whispered Mr. Boss. "Don't do that." But the question had been asked.

The Lion waited as the lights spiraled, not unlike the waltz of corpuscles that sometimes trickle across the surface of the eye.

"Where is Nor?" asked Brrr again, more firmly still. "I know how this works. I've been here before. We've answered your question. Now you answer ours. You can't hold out on us."

There is nothing of Nor here, came the reply.

"She isn't dead? But of course she's dead," murmured Little Daffy.

We consist only of the appetites that would not die, the Ozmists churned. *There was nothing of her left that wanted to know more. This is how it is with some deaths. We know little more about where her spirit is than we know about the lives of the living. We are caught in the middle by our lust for answers. We are the part of Oz's past that cannot give up its hope for the present. That is all.*

"Since you ask about Ozma," said Rain, "then it follows that she isn't there with you. But perhaps Ozma, like Nor, has passed into nothingness. She was only an infant when she was killed. She could have no appetite for the present; she was too young to know the difference between past and present and time to come."

She never passed through us, said the Ozmists. *It is believed here that she has not died.*

"She'd be a thousand and eighty," said Little Daffy wonderingly.

"No one is that old, except Nanny," said Rain.

"Baby Ozma might have taken an omnibus to hell. You Ozmists aren't the only filter to the Other Side," said Dorothy staunchly, in that bullishly public voice she sometimes had.

If there could be said to be a pause in a hissle of ghostly fragments, there was a pause.

"What happened to my parents, then?" asked Dorothy. "If you're so comprehensive? They died at sea, in a boat going to the old country. It sunk, and that was that. Where are they? What did they want to know about me? I don't believe you have a thing to say about it."

The Ozmists had nothing to say about it. Neither, noticed Brrr, did they pester Dorothy for news. Perhaps they didn't want to know about the Other Side that Dorothy hailed from. Even ghosts have their limits of tolerance.

"Tell us about Elphaba," said Rain.

Barter, said the Ozmists, a sense of relief in their voices.

"The head of St. Prowd's, Proctor Gadfry, has gone for a soldier."

That's of no significance to us.

"It is to him, and it's his history," said Rain. "Unless he's died and is with you now, it's as significant as anything else. The history of this war hinges on what every single person alive chooses to do or not to do. Now tell me about Elphaba."

Still they resisted. Clangingly, silent-noisily, dark-lightly.

Rain said, "Okay, my great-uncle Shell is Throne Minister of Oz. He is Elphaba's brother. That's current events, up to the minute. But we can't find out what happened to Elphaba Thropp, my grandmother, once Dorothy threw a pail of mucky water at her. She's been dead and gone almost twenty years, I'm told. Why is there no evidence of it?"

When the Ozmists spoke, they were cautious, even a little apologetic.

In all of history, of most human lives, there is no proof of passage, they said, *neither coming in nor going out. Don't be offended if someone you love has left no trace. That doesn't mean they were absent in their own time.*

"So you're going to be coy about it too?" asked Rain. "Figures. Useless phantoms."

You think that someone with the capacity of El-phaba Thropp would let us gossip about her, even if she were here in our midst? In life she paid no attention to the rules of the game. In death she'd not suddenly go corporate.

"So she's not dead? Or is she?" asked Rain. But this they wouldn't answer.

You strayed at the stand of four beeches, several miles back, they said, relenting.

"I don't remember four beeches," said the Lion.

We've been moving while we've been congregating. Ghosts can't keep still. You won't find the beeches again. But keep the stream on your left and you'll soon be on the right track.

"And what track is that?" asked Dorothy.

To the future, they said, wistfully. *And, you? With the shell?*

"Yes," said Rain.

Blow it once, they said.

She did. It had almost no sound in this cloaking paleness, but the Ozmists took on a glow like that of lights in water, a wetter look. A blueness, as of heat lightning.

If you need us, blow the horn for us, they said. *We will come if we can.*

"Why would you do that? I've given nothing to you. It's all about barter, isn't it?

You give news even when you don't open your mouth. What you've given to us is for us to know. It is enough. There is no balance due.

"Hey, what about Toto?" Dorothy thought to call out. "Is he a phantom dog now, romping about with you?" But the Ozmists were lifting and would not reply.

The world they left behind—the commonplace world of now—felt a little more tightly pulled together, as in a blackout between scenes of a theatrical piece stagehands rush on and plump the pillows. Each glowing rotting leaf on its trembling stem stood out to be counted.

Rain looked, noticed. She did not count them.

"Really, we got precious little out of that but a chill," said Little Daffy, rubbing her forearms. "Anyone for a pastry, to get the juices flowing again?"

12.

The Black Elephant had regained the native strength that elephant musculature and armature allow. He was standing on all four legs in the sunlight outside, being washed with buckets of water and scrubbed toward ecstasy with long-handled brooms. The sun smelled of everything in the entire cosmos. His eyes were closed and the water was paradise, was better than air in his lungs and beetles in his bowels. But his ears heard the commotion when a boy was escorted into the yard. The newcomer was tied and bound and laid on the back of two yoked Wolves running in tandem.

Liir didn't think he was intended to see this miscreant's arrival, but the Wolves were thirsty for water after their hard run, and they made straight for the buckets from which the Elephant minders were working. And

Wolves have little regard for hierarchy even when the hierarchy is La Mombey. They let foot soldiers and garden boys and Jellia Jamb pull the lad off their backs as they slavered up the water meant for Liir's capacious backside. The Elephant trumpeted in their faces but they paid him no mind. Not the first ones to do so.

La Mombey came out on a balcony above him. Liir could smell that her face was more puckish, like the rosewater face of a maid over a counter of chocolates. Younger, fuller. He could smell the pink in her cheeks, augmented by powdered sugar mixed with dust of sun-dried and pummeled red grape that had come into season four and a half weeks ago, on the sunnier side of some slope fed by iron-rich aquifers. Oh, to have a nose.

"You dare to come back?" shouted Mombey. "Or you are fool enough to be entrapped? Answer me, don't make me stand here waiting."

The boy—half boy, half man, like the rest of us, thought Liir, forgetting for a moment he was actually an Elephant—rolled onto his knees and stood up with an enviable elasticity. Ah, to be young, too. Though maybe the lad had been treated relatively better than Liir had. The boy dusted himself off and said to the Wolves, "You did your job and you managed to avoid eating me. Fellows, my commendations."

"Answer me," bellowed Mombey.

"I went on a bit of a walkabout," called the arriviste. "I'm sorry I didn't tell you, and I hope I haven't made trouble. I was on my way back to accept my sentence already when your Wolves recognized me and insisted on ushering me home. Find a prison deep enough for me, a chore too hard to survive, and I'll endure it for as long as I can. I've learned I have no place out there without you, and I accept my punishment as the price of what I've learned."

A stinking bouquet of lies, and Liir almost tromboned his laughter at them; but he noted Mombey's caught breath, and he thought, She loves him so much she is unwilling to believe he might be lying. Smart as she is, she can't see a lie from this kid.

"You had me frantic," said Mombey. "I thought you'd been kidnapped so someone could barter with me for your release."

"Who would kidnap your boot boy?" His voice was innocent but scornful. "Would *you* kidnap someone just to get advantage?"

"You shall pay for your mistakes," she said, but her voice was full of joy; no revised countenance could disguise that. "Sir Fedric, Sir Cyrillac, you have done your duty well. A year's liberation from the effort of the war for you and all your kin."

"We are a randy pair," said Fedric, and Cyrillac nodded. "We are related to every Wolf in your army."

"Then a year's liberation for you and your wives and cubs, and let that be enough."

"Thank you, Your Eminence," said Fedric, and Cyrillac added, "We are not of a monogamous bent, and we have between us married every female we know and sired every cub younger than we are."

"It's the wolf in us," said Sir Fedric, modestly and without shame.

"Then a year's liberation for you two alone, and if you make any other conditions, a year's incarceration for dragging this conversation out."

The Wolves nodded and skulked away like dogs that have been scolded.

"Tip, come up here," said Mombey. "Come into the house and let me see that you are all right."

"Hi, Tip," whispered Jellia Jamb, waving one hand and biting a nail on the other.

Liir's nose followed the boy as he made his progress to a flight of stone steps on which the servants were spreading spittlegreek and lavender to dry upon an oilcloth. Liir could smell that Tip had the brush of Rain on his lips. For the safety of the boy, in whom he could smell no honesty but no menace either, and for the safety of his daughter, Liir held his tongue, but his nose was primed for more salient information. Had he come across this lad once before? Liir's nose had a better memory than his brain.

As Tip was succumbing to Mombey's embrace, Trism appeared from around the conservatory. He noticed—for he was no fool—the rapt attention that Liir the Elephant was paying to this reunion. Before Trism could say anything, though, before the yard could clear, an Owl flew down from the corner of the building and landed clumsily on the drying lavender, clouding the air with the scent of old ladies' water closets.

"Abysmally bad timing," said Mombey to the Owl. "I'll take no report out here in the open."

"As you wish, my liegitrice," said the Owl. A more obsequious creature Liir had never met, either as Elephant or man.

But he heard what the Owl said before the final shutter was pulled. Liir's nose might be more magnificent but his ears were also as large as palmetto fans. "I found her on a road west of Shiz, but I lost her in a sudden and puzzling fog. When it lifted, I studied the road to which I had directed them, where your spidery agents were waiting to apprehend them. But somehow the travelers slipped through the unseasonable weather, and I lost—"

"Indeed you did," Mombey said, and there was a sound of something not quite a whip, not quite a mousetrap, but something iron and deadly. Liir heard no more from the Owl after that.

When the yard had cleared, and the maids put away their brushes, and Liir had come to accept that no one would scratch his rump again today in the way that gave him joy, he turned to look at Trism, who had remained.

"Tip?" said Liir.

"Her factotum," said Trism.

"Her son, it must be."

"No one knows. He was lost and he is back. This means she will move immediately into action. The dragons are ready. The only hold against our striking earlier was whether she might inadvertently be putting him in danger, not knowing his whereabouts. If the boy is back, and secured, any remaining prohibition against an attack has been lifted. You'll be propositioned tonight. Mark my words."

"Propositioned. Hmmm."

"They'll ask you to confirm that the spells I'm trying to cast through the arcane language of that solitary page of the Grimmerie are accurate. They'll ask you to examine the book and refresh the spells, refine and intensify them, with any other charm that you can find.

It's why you've been brought here. Only your mother showed any real skill with that book; everyone else has fumbled and failed with it. Even Mombey is dubious about reading it. She will promise you something real, and she'll keep her promise, if you help her bring down your uncle."

"That boy knew my daughter," said Liir.

"You must put that sort of thought aside. Perhaps you can survive long enough to be a help to your daughter again."

"I have been no help to her at all. Ever."

"Get ready for what they will ask. They'll ask only once."

"Will you love me whatever I say?"

"No. I don't promise that. I may have made my own choices, for my own reasons, but I won't love you unless you make your own choices, for your own reasons. That's the bargain of love."

A man and an Elephant, talking about love, and neither of them shamed. What a world I've come up through, said Liir to himself. Oh, what a world, what a world.

Trism knew about which he spoke. By the light of the jackal moon Mombey came into the garden behind Colwen Grounds, where Liir had been allowed to graze. She presented herself as a woman of gravity, with a furrowed brow and silvering hair, and she walked with a cane, but she hadn't gone so far as to concede to a wrinkled neck. Trism walked four feet behind her, his head down, his eyes cloaked, his hands clasped, trying to be as remote as possible in the presence of an Elephant who still loved him.

"We will launch our attack by dawn," La Mombey said. "Will you help?"

"I can tell by my sight, my smell, and my hearing that my family is not here. Beyond that, I don't know where they are," Liir replied. "Naturally, I can't help you target anyplace they might be, and they might be anywhere."

"What if I told you we know where they are? Both of them?" said La Mombey. "Your wife and your daughter? And they would be spared? What if I gave you proof? Would you help us then?"

"It doesn't matter that your proof could be false." He stood firm on his big Elephant feet. "You've also targeted places that harbor any child who is not mine, and I find no difference between them and a child who is mine."

"With your proboscis, you can't smell the difference between your own kin and someone foreign?" she said, laughing.

"With my proboscis," he said, "I can smell that there is no difference. I will not help you."

He didn't have to bother to say that he believed the skill to read the Grimmerie, just as the tendency to be born with green skin, might skip a generation, the way corrupted thumbs skipped in the northern Quadlings, or obesity in certain fruit flies. It didn't matter. He turned from Trism, who was wringing his hands; he turned from Mombey, who was drunk with elation. "Ready the fleet," she said to her dragonmaster. To Liir, she said, "You have sealed your own doom by your refusal to assist in this campaign. Count your final moments."

"Trism, no," said Liir.

"Mercy on your soul," said Trism to Liir.

"Mercy on yours," replied the Elephant, without malice, only heartache.

13.

With the advice of the Ozmists, Rain and her companions managed to avoid Shiz entirely. Unwittingly, they also sidestepped the cohort of jumbo shadowish spider-thugs Mombey had sent across the border to apprehend them. The travelers approached the capital, just another clutch of private citizens set roaming by wartime hysteria. Rain hadn't known what to expect of the EC. From a distance, it looked seven, nine, nineteen times more immense than the university city of Shiz.

Dorothy proposed that they make their way into the Emerald City via the great squared archways known as Westgate. So the companions stopped to take stock on the graveled slopes outside the city walls, where travelers arriving from the West were required to unroll their Vinkus carpets, lay out their satchels for inspection, and present papers of introduction if they had serious government business. Rain was daunted.

So were her friends. "It'll be impossible to find a kidnapped man in this canyon of towers," said Mr. Boss. "Tall buildings, begging your pardon, dwarf me." He looked dubious. He'd never dared risk bringing the Clock of the Time Dragon through any of the gates of the capital, so the EC was one district of Oz about which he was entirely ignorant.

"I've come this far, but I don't know as I'd be welcome farther, being a Munchkinlander," said Little Daffy. "Sadly, I have no state secrets to sell to the Emperor of Oz. Only curious cupcakes and the like."

Rain turned to Brrr.

"Well, I'm with you," he said. "I'm not bailing."

"But aren't you still wanted in this town?" Rain asked him.

"Yes, I had a prison sentence converted to a civilian assignment, to find the location of the Grimmerie and report it, from which I went skipping away five or six years ago. And yes, some magistrate or another might remember. But I'd venture everyone has other matters on their minds these days."

"You must be mad," said Rain. "Back then, you were one of the centerpieces of their campaign to locate the Grimmerie. You failed to bring it in. You can't risk showing your face here. You'd never get out alive."

"Nobody does," said the dwarf. "You'll have figured that out by now, sweetheart."

"I'm going alone," said Rain.

"You can't go alone," said Brrr. "We can't let you."

"I'll go with her," said Dorothy. "It's safest for me. Anyway, I remember this place. I can do the Emerald City. I'm older now, I've been to Kansas City and San Francisco. We can find our way together."

Rain turned on her. "Not on your life. I'll need to be circumspect. You couldn't be circumspect even with your mouth tied up in muslin bandages."

"You know, I used to like you people in Oz a lot more than I do now," replied Dorothy. "Time was I could just open my mouth and people would be quiet and listen. Now it's just jabber jabber jabber, shut up and sit down. Well, too bad, Rain. I'm coming with you."

"But you're *Dorothy*," said Rain. "You make a spectacle of yourself just by how you stare at things so deeply."

"It's called astigmatism and it's correctable with lenses but they got crushed in the landslide in the Glikkus. As far as I've ever heard, it's a free country, Rain. So I'm traipsing along. I'll promise not to sing and I'll go buy a shawl from one of those vendors. We'll get by just fine. I can be your big sister. You can call me Dotty."

The dwarf and the Munchkinlander looked at each another. "Dotty. It has a certain legitimacy," said Mr. Boss. Rain gave up.

Dorothy found a shrub to hide behind as she wriggled out of her skirt. She turned it inside out. The several kinds of cloth used to patch and line it were unmatched and worn. Suitably seedy. "We make do in Kansas," said Dorothy. The reversed garment helped conceal that look of dirty glamour a tourist can bear. Draped in a rough grey wool shawl, Dorothy could almost pass as a peasant milkmaid from the Disappointments—one who has somehow avoided rickets and malnutrition due to fierce inner strength.

Meanwhile, Rain had always managed to mosey along without attracting attention even though she'd been hunted her whole life long. She said to Dorothy, "You better carry the shell. I don't want Tay disappearing into the crowds," and she drew Tay up into her arms.

"Heavens, not that," agreed Dorothy. "If Tay is anything like Toto, you'll be dropping the avoirdupois chasing after him. I'd have always preferred a French poodle, frankly. Though I'd never tell Toto that to his face. It would ruin him."

Rain said good-bye to the Lion, the dwarf, and the Munchkinlander. "We'll make up a plan as we go along," she said. "Maybe Dorothy will be an asset after all."

"Maybe this time," sang Dorothy, but then restated that without musical expression.

"Rain, are you sure about this?" asked the Lion. He seemed to have shrugged off some of his distractedness following the death of Nor. The congress with the Ozmists may have set his mind at rest—whatever else might be said, Nor was no longer suffering. Anywhere. Now, Brrr could look with beaded focus and a certain concern at the girls standing before him.

Rain shrugged. "Dorothy might be able to get an audience with the Emperor. She once saw the very

Wizard of Oz himself, even though he was a recluse. Few can say they ever did that."

"Indeed," said the Lion.

"She might be able to find out if they are holding my father. She might be able to strike a bargain for his release. I'll keep my head down. I promise. We'll just look about. We'll see what we can learn, and we'll come back. Will we find you here?"

The Lion said, "Rain, when thunderheads are about to open, it's hard to say which way anyone will run. Think about it. Various thugs hunted your parents down in Apple Press Farm. You yourself had to flee from Mockbeggar Hall. Then someone found out about Nether How. Now your father is hauled away from Kiamo Ko. The only place you've ever stayed unmolested is the Chancel of the Ladyfish above the Sleeve of Ghastille. Should we get separated, remember our plan to leave messages there. Weighed down by that question mark horse-stone. All right? Agreed? But I promise you this, we won't leave here unless we have no choice."

"There is no safe place in Oz, is there," said Rain.

"There is no safety anywhere," said the Cowardly Lion.

Those to stay behind took their leave in a formal fashion, like parents departing from their scholar daughter in the reception room at St. Prowd's Academy. As the storm clouds gathered—literal, heavy rain clouds, the seasonal burst approaching at last—Rain and Dorothy and Tay turned to slip among a large group of foreigners come for market day, some plains Arjiki and some Yunamata froggy-folk. Together Dorothy and Rain passed under the massive carved transoms of Westgate. Through which so many years ago (but how many?) Dorothy and the Lion, the Tin Woodman and the Scarecrow had originally emerged after their famous interviews with the Wizard of Oz, their instructions firmly in hand: to march to the castle at Kiamo Ko and kill the Wicked Witch of the West.

Dorothy didn't remember the names of the thoroughfares that interlaced the vast city, but once they reached the knoll of a public park she identified the towers of the Palace in the distance. "*That* much hasn't changed," she promised. "It was called the Palace of the Wizard when I had my several audiences with him, and just as I was leaving Oz last time around they were talking about renaming it the Palace of the People. But it doesn't look any different. A Palace is a palace."

Rain barely listened to Dorothy's prattle. She was trying not to be daunted by the weirdness of it all. Not the buildings—what meant buildings to her, really? The statues on their plinths, the great crescents of fine houses, the iron railings and the pushcarts, the monumental stone tombs of art and commerce. Rain was more aware of the people. So many. Who could ever make a collection of so many people?

When they passed one of the market squares, it was life as Rain knew it, people squabbling for food, bargaining over prices. But the trestle tables set up under bentlebranch arbors offered small choice, and more to the point—Dorothy saw this too—the vendors and the shoppers were predominantly female. An occasional elderly bearded man in green glasses, carrying a blunderbuss; that seemed the police force and the minister and the army, the whole local patriarchy all at once. Schoolboys, to be sure, and toddler boys nearly indistinguishable from toddler girls, and genderless babies. But men the age of her father? Absent.

"We wouldn't want to start our search for your father in Southstairs, would we?" whispered Dorothy.

"The prison? I hope not," replied Rain. "Let's go directly to the Emperor. If we can't get in to see him by dint of one trick or another, you can reveal yourself as Dorothy."

"What if that doesn't cut the mustard with him?"

"You can warble him into submission. Or I'll come forward and claim the Emperor as my blood relation. What is there to lose now?"

Dorothy bit her lower lip. "As I hear it told, you've spent your whole life on the run from this man. It seems a dicey strategy to go up to him and holler a big ole Kansas howdy."

"Yeah, well, running in place hasn't gotten me very far, has it. I'm tired of skulking through my life. We're facing the music."

"Do you think your father would help the Emperor use the Grimmerie against the Munchkinlanders?"

Rain said, "Don't ask me a question like that. There are so many ways I don't know who my father is."

Dorothy was silent for a while. They made their way along a canal colonnaded with cenotaphs celebrating various Ozmas of history. A dead cow floated by, and even Tay wrinkled its nose. "The city has seen better days," said Dorothy. "I have to add, though, I don't know who my father was, either. Really. Lost at sea and all that. Makes you wonder what any of us knows about who we are."

Rain hadn't taken to Dorothy, and she didn't think she was about to start now. But she reached out and squeezed her hand. She had learned to touch people, a little, by touching Tip, and Dorothy was a stranger here. Stranger than most.

It began to sprinkle. A smell riled up from drains that had gone too long untended—the municipal workers all having been called to the eastern front, probably. The city was hard to navigate. They ended up in a place called the Burntpork district and bought a few rolls to eat, but had to give them to Tay because they were too hard. "I've come this far, and I keep losing my way," said Dorothy. "Let's try that sloping bridge over the canal; it looks as if it carries a funicular, or maybe it's an aqueduct. It's heading vaguely upslope, so it has to get us to the higher ground of the city. We make another misstep and we'll plunge into the sinkhole of Southstairs and be stuck in prison the rest of our born days."

By midafternoon, tired, they found the forecourt of the Palace, or one of them. "Is this it, then?" asked Dorothy.

"Yes, I think we're ready."

The Kansan turned to the Ozian. "You know, if we've played this wrong—if the Emperor wasn't the one behind the abduction of your father—we're in for big trouble. You know that."

"It's a risk I'm ready to take. Are you?"

"The Munchkinlanders tried and convicted me of murder," said Dorothy, "so if I'm a villain on that side of the border, I should be welcomed as a heroine here. How do I look?"

"Don't forget you killed both sisters of the Emperor."

"Yes, there is that. Perhaps I should switch my skirt around again."

But it was too late. The door of the military offices of the forecourt opened. A bleary stooped man with only one leg wheeled himself out and examined a clipboard, and then looked at the two young women standing before him.

"Miss Rainary?" he said in a dubious voice.

"Proctor Gadfry," said Rain.

"I take it you've fled Shiz like everyone else," he said. "I can offer you no succor here. You're looking for a certificate of matriculation? Go away. St. Prowd's statute of limitations has expired until after the war. Or has my tyrannical sister sent you here to pester me? I have more than enough to do than see to the mess she's made of all our hard work."

"Proctor Gadfry," said Rain. "You went to battle."

"And battled till I could battle no more," he said, flicking one wrist toward where his absent knee should be. "I'm lucky to get a sinecure here until hostilities are concluded, one way or the other. But I was expecting a coven of downscale marsh witches who want to file a protest about something that happened about twelve thousand years ago. You're not with that group?"

"I have brought someone," said Rain. "To see the Emperor."

"Hah. Go away."

"A visitor named Dorothy Gale," said Rain. "A friend of mine."

Dorothy curtseyed a little clumsily and almost lost hold of the shell, but then turned and smiled at Rain with an expression both soft and fierce. It was the use of the word *friend*. Rain dropped her eyes.

"I see," said Proctor Gadfry, sizing up the situation for how it might be used to his own advantage.

Her uncle Shell. Her great-uncle Shell. The Throne Minister of Loyal Oz until he named himself Emperor of Loyal Oz and its colonies, Ugabu and the Glikkus and Dominions Yet Unrecorded. And eventually the Emperor had declared himself divine. Quite the career path.

Hard to know exactly how to prepare to meet the Unnamed God, thought Rain. Especially when he's given himself a name and he's related to me on my father's side.

Dorothy and Rain were brought to a dressing chamber and asked to change into simpler robes. Then they were escorted into a parlor that showed no signs of being the worse for wear due to the long war. Fresh prettibell spikes arched against the burnished leather walls, and an aroma of arrowscent and pickled roses issued from braziers set in brass wall brackets. The windows were draped with lace worked over with scenes from the life of some Ozma or other. The visitors had to take off their shoes to stand on the patterned carpet, which felt like moss on its first day.

"I am Avaric bon Tenmeadows," said a gentleman with a pince-nez and a silvery whirl of mustache. "I will direct you on proper comportment for your audience with His Sacredness."

"Are we meeting His Sacredness all by itself, or are we actually meeting *him*?" asked Dorothy. "I just wanted to ask," she sidelined to Rain, who was shushing her.

"Enter with your heads covered and do not remove your veils until directed by His Sacredness. Do not speak until you are spoken to. Do not turn your back on His Sacredness—when instructed, you will leave the room by walking backward, heads covered, eyes down. Mention no subject with His Sacredness that His Sacredness does not introduce. Ask for the blessing of His Sacredness in your life past, present, and to come. Ask for the mercy of His Sacredness in considering your petitions, if you have any. You will have about ten minutes. Have you any questions?"

"Well, it reminds me what it was like with the Wizard," said Dorothy. "There must be a rule book everyone follows, generation to generation."

"All this fuss. It reminds *me* of the visiting Senior Overseer at St. Prowd's," said Rain. "I hope His Sacredness doesn't douse himself with water."

"No, not *that* party trick," agreed Dorothy. "Had enough of that one!"

"I will retire through this near door. When the far door opens, that's your sign to approach," said Avaric. "You will proceed through it. But before I go, Miss Gale, may I be permitted to make a personal remark?"

"No one's stopping you, far as I can see."

"I want to thank you for your service to our country," said Avaric. "I knew the witches of Oz, those Thropp sisters. We were well rid of them."

He clearly thought of Rain as little more than Dorothy's retainer. Fair enough, thought Rain. A few more moments of anonymity in this life—let me treasure it before it's trampled to extinction.

The far door swung wide. Obeying Avaric's instructions, the pair of visitors made their approach to His Sacredness, Shell Thropp.

He didn't sit on the throne, an impressive carved chair capped by an octagonal canopy chained to the ceiling with golden links. Rather, he squatted upon an overturned bucket. Three small tiktok creatures, narrower and more locustlike than the round brass figure Rain had once seen in that shop in Shiz, moved around in the shadows behind him, performing devotional measures with fans and also seeing to the flies, which were everywhere.

A man about fifty, maybe. He didn't wear the glorious robes of office, just a humble sort of sackcloth loin rag and a skirt. A beggar's shawl about his shoulders. His eye was keen and his form sleek despite the initial impression of poverty.

He said, "His Sacredness never knew those women very well. Nessarose Thropp, Eminence called Wicked Witch of the East. Elphaba Thropp, miscreant called Wicked Witch of the West. His Sacredness lived with them in the Quadling badlands when His Sacredness was young. His Sacredness's sister Elphaba was born with infirmities. His Sacredness's sister Nessarose was born with infirmities. His Sacredness himself was born whole and clean and is the Emperor of Oz and Demiurge of the Unnamed God."

There didn't seem to be a question yet, so they just waited.

He said, "His Sacredness sits on the bucket that was used to kill His Sacredness's sister Elphaba Thropp. It represents to His Sacredness the loss of the living water of grace. A loss that will be reclaimed once the battle for dominance with Munchkinland is completed and Restwater is permanently appropriated as the basin of water to cleanse and to nourish the suffering citizens of Oz's capital city."

Rain saw Dorothy peer at the bucket to see if she recognized it, but Dorothy just shrugged at Rain. A bucket is a bucket.

He said, "Both of the sisters of His Sacredness were removed from life by the hand or the hearthstone of Dorothy Gale, leaving the Eminenceship of Munchkinland open to question. Therefore His Sacredness offers gratitude to the visitor. She delivered unto His Sacredness the rights to Eminenceship of Munchkinland. This moral privilege underpins and sanctifies the military effort to subdue the traitorous Munchkinlander rebels. For that reason has His Sacredness deigned to extend the right to an audience with His Sacredness. His Sacredness is aware of certain Munchkinlander accusations against Dorothy. His Sacredness proposes the publication of a divine testimonial clearing Dorothy of all suspicion of malfeasance in the matter of the death of his kin. The certificate." A tiktok minion rolled forward holding a salver upon which lay a scroll bound with a green ribbon and a clump of sealing wax. Shell handed it to Dorothy.

He put his hands together in a tender way. His eyes never left Dorothy's.

He said, "His Sacredness allows that the visitors may now retreat. Go with the blessings of the Unnamed God conferred through this avatar on earth." Only now did he close his eyes, in acknowledgement of his own immortal splendor.

Rain said, "But we've come to find my father."

The chirring of the tiktok acolytes wheeled faster, as if spinning out disbelieving air from their metal lungs. A stench of hot oil spilled from some gasket with a slipped ring, maybe. Shell, her great-uncle Shell, said nothing. It was as if Rain hadn't spoken to him but perhaps to his machinery.

"We have come to barter," she said, but she wasn't sure to whom she was talking. Maybe not the man nor the tiktok-niques but to the empty throne itself behind them.

"You don't barter with God," said Shell, in a quiet voice, not deeply fussed at the breaking of protocol. Most likely he could see that his visitors were young and foolish. "Go now. I am tired and I am waging a war in my heart. Only if I win it in my heart can it be won in the land, for I am the blood of Oz itself. I am its sacredness and I am His Sacredness."

Rain felt cornered by sacredness.

She knew her great-grandfather had been a unionist missionary to the Quadlings, trying to convert them. She knew her great-aunt Nessarose had inherited his convictions and institutionalized them in Munchkinland, a theocracy overturned only when Dorothy arrived the first time. She knew her great-uncle Shell was divine, or divine enough.

On the other hand, of her grandmother Elphaba's convictions she knew nothing. And while Liir had expressed admiration for the courage of independent establishments of outspoken maunts like the place Little Daffy had come from, he had perpetrated in Nether How no ritual of prayer, no theological discussion. And Candle's faith was limited to herbs and intuition.

So Rain had avoided the questions of devotion, mostly. The concept of an Unnamed God was too much for her. If you're abandoned by your parents, do you hunt them down to love them more deeply, or do you learn to do without? If the Unnamed God has gone to ground leaving no forwarding address, why bother to pester him?

Still. Rain had had just enough schooling at St. Prowd's to be able to think for herself. It would take a pretty talented godhead to infuse itself in a single person as the living essence of the land—the very Ozness that made it be Oz. If this were really true, then what would happen to Oz if Shell Thropp, Emperor, happened to get a splinter in his naked heel? And die a week later of a rude infection that refused to acknowledge the divinity of the foot it blistered?

"You are too great for me to know who you really are," she admitted. "But I know something of who I am. I am the daughter of Liir. I'm told that I'm the granddaughter of Elphaba. I'm your great-niece. My name is Rain."

"She's also the rightful daughter of Munchkinland," Dorothy interrupted. "If I've got the line of succession straight, and I've been keeping track, the Eminenceship of Munchkinland descends through the female line. So the nearest female relative of the last ruling Eminence has preference. That would be my friend Rain here."

"I don't care about that," said Rain. "I only want to know if you have taken my father. Your nephew, Liir. Someone kidnapped him and made off with the Grimmerie. We have come to secure his release." She rephrased that to be more docile. "I mean, to beg for his release. Humbly."

The divine Emperor looked just a little annoyed. "I don't barter with human lives."

"You attacked Munchkinland when I was eight," said Rain. "Human lives tend to be involved in military attacks."

"His Sacredness has consternation in his heart. Go away."

Dorothy drew herself up. "Look, you. I know what I've done and not done. I have no need of your certificate of forgiveness unless I ever meet up with Toto and in all the excitement he has an accident. He's not a puppy. A convenient roll of testimonial parchment could come in handy just then."

"His Sacredness has a headache. Do go away."

"You'll have more than a headache when I get through. When I arrived first time I came in a house that smashed your first sister. Before I left I threw a bucket that splashed your second sister. Is it time for me to take care of you, too? As I was preparing for my encore, I brought down a good deal of San Francisco with me. I arrived from heaven in a gilded elevator cage right down the side of a mountain. I'm getting pretty good at this. I can bring upon your holy kingdom an entire downtown district of hearty commercial buildings. Just try me."

A pretty bold bluff, Rain thought, but it may not work on someone like Shell, who has lived in power for so long he doesn't remember what it's like to be powerless.

Dorothy clasped her hands together and prepared to break her promise not to sing. Rain motioned to her, *don't, don't.* Dorothy filled her lungs with air and, consumed with trust in the conviction of sweet melody, fixed upon her countenance an expression of mighty choral readiness. *La Belle Dame sans Merci.*

Great-uncle Shell, you're not the only one who's become deranged by power, thought Rain.

As the tiktok characters ran for cover, the door of the magnificent salon opened up, and Avaric bon Tenmeadows rushed in. "What is the meaning of this?" he cried.

Dorothy opened her mouth and began to sing about rainbow highways and raindrops and storms. Awful lot of rain in there, thought Rain. The thunderclouds broke overhead at the same instant, a tympanic accompaniment to the sound of Dorothy's voice. When she reached the end of her musical preamble and paused for breath before launching into the melody proper, the thunder roll was deteriorating and another mounding behind it to take its place. They realized that it wasn't only thunder overhead.

14.

The autumn clouds covering central Oz had screened the approach from the east of the dragons trained by Trism bon Cavalish. Maybe their arrival over the Emerald City had kindled the lightning and signaled the thunder. Or maybe it was only the meanness of the Unnamed God, allowing fire and destruction to rain upon the capital under the guise, initially, of an ordinary cloudburst.

In the sudden darkness, Rain and Dorothy ran for cover. They followed the tiktok acolytes until, one by one, the tiktokery exploded their glass gaskets due to barometric anomalies, spinning out on the marble floors, knocking over the plinths of fresh flowers. The girls didn't know if Shell was behind them, but they could hear the man named Avaric calling to someone, so perhaps he was leading the Emperor to safety.

"Don't go outside," they heard Avaric's voice yell, but Dorothy was freaked by the sound of collapsing buildings. "We'll be crushed in this damn place, a mausoleum in the making," she yelled at Rain, and grabbed her hand. "It's this way, I'm sure. I'm pretty good at directions."

"How do you get out of Oz, then?" screamed Rain, with a touch of hysteria of her own. Was her father here in this roar of tumbling stone, or was he safe somewhere else? Or, anyway, safer?

Dorothy's sense of the architecture of the palace wasn't quite what she advertised. They ran through a long, slightly bowed corridor of steep arches, like the hollowed-out chambers of a lake nautilus built on a scale for giants, and they came across Avaric approaching from the other direction. He was leading Shell by the hand. A contingent of palace apparatchiks and staff huddled behind them.

"The city is under attack," Avaric told them.

"And I'm just warming up," said Dorothy, assuming a performance pose.

"Don't!" cried Shell.

"Where is Liir?" demanded Dorothy, going up to the Emperor. "Where's that damn book? Tell us, or I'll go into a reprise."

"We haven't got him," said Avaric. "Not for lack of trying, but the enemy must have got to him first. Do you think they could unleash this havoc without his assistance? Mercy, girl; the city is falling. Don't make it worse."

Dorothy took a breath, then closed her mouth. "Well, all right then. But I'm warning you."

"We can see the buildings collapsing," said Avaric. "The Law Courts is flaming rubble. Look, there's a passage from the Palace directly to Southstairs Prison. We'll be safer from assault from the sky if we're underground, and Southstairs is nothing but underground. Come; we owe you that much, child of Liir. Come with us."

"If my father isn't in prison, I'm not going," said Rain. "I'll take my chances outside."

Avaric said, "On your own head, then. We can't wait. His Sacredness must descend to the safety of the megalithic tombs, to emerge in triumph when the aerial assault is over." He began to beetle away, and the fragments of court society that had continued to gather in the corridor flooded after him.

Shell, in his humble garments, stood his place a moment longer. "Rain Thropp," he said. "I never had daughter nor son of my own. I took many a woman but never a wife, as I couldn't find one suitable for my ambitions. His Sacredness does not have a wife."

"You'd better hurry," said Rain, as the thunder gathered again.

"Your right to the Eminenceship of Munchkinland supersedes mine," he concluded. "Your being my only living female relative also consolidates in you the right to be Throne Minister of Oz, as the historical line of Ozma is severed and dead these five decades. Should I fail to emerge for reasons of transcendence, it is your throne to accept, your scepter to grasp."

She didn't answer. She grabbed Dorothy's hand and they ran away.

The guardhouse had been hit. What had been Proctor Gadfry Clapp lay in pieces, his other limbs severed and spread out from his chest as if hunting their missing brother leg. Farther out, poorhouses had collapsed, and the corpses of men too frail to have gone for soldiers were already being laid upon the streets. Something called the Ministry of Offense was in flames. It was hard to value the relative sounds of terror: that of the thunderous clouds, from which dragons stitched down like great herons gaping underwater to gobble up terrified minchfish, or that of response from the ground, where buildings shuddered, and the trapped and the shocked and the grieving and the terrified wailed with one voice.

"We've got to get out of here," said Dorothy. "Back to Westgate, back to our friends."

But there was a child who'd been jettisoned in a tree, somehow, and Rain said, "We can't leave that infant there." Its mother in the dirt with her skirts over her face, dead, and the baby carriage on its side, wheels still spinning. "Tip wouldn't let that child loiter in branches."

They claimed the child and placed it in the arms of a woman who was rushing somewhere with a barrel of melons; she took the baby without comment and hurried away.

At the Ozma Embankment the girls came upon a bevy of ladies who had flung themselves into the water to escape the first wave of flaming parcels dropped by the dragon fleet. In their big skirts they couldn't clamber out. Dorothy and Rain yoked themselves together and pulled, but unless the women conceded to abandoning their finery to the ashen water and climbing up in their petticoats, they would remain only floating lily pads in a pond that reflected skies of lightning, gold fire, and scudding clouds. The women bowed to the urgency of the moment and allowed themselves to be rescued, and hurried off, giggling, as if public nudity were a greater scandal than the fall of the Emerald City.

Rain hadn't seen dragons since her efforts, with Lady Glinda, to call winter upon the water. She remembered the creatures with some affection, but she wasn't as inclined to admiration now. The beasts swooped from the clouds with a malice she couldn't have imagined. She didn't know if from Munchkinland her father had used the Grimmerie to focus their attack, or if the climate of storm from which they emerged had terrified them to fight harder. She couldn't tell what they carried in their claws and what they dropped, but all about the Emerald City explosions burst as large as torched trees— like trees turned into flame, a central trunk of impact from which limbs and arteries and fringed hems of fire bloomed instantaneously.

The dragons and their detonations would do more than bring down the government, if they hadn't managed that already. They would slaughter every living creature in Oz.

Only then did Rain realize that in the welter of panic she had lost track of Tay. "We have to go back," she told Dorothy.

"We can't," said Dorothy. "Tay will find us."

"Like Toto?" said Rain. "Come on."

"Tay is smarter than Toto. Not that it's hard to be smarter than Toto."

Rain was no hero, she was no saint; she knew that. It was no lost child hanging from a tree branch, no dead school administrator in pieces on the ground that pitched her mind to thinking of a solution. It was the loss of Tay, her silent companion. She couldn't bear to lose the rice otter, not when she'd lost so much else. Over and over again, the losing.

She stood on the edge of a schoolyard of some sort, amid some children's rusticated ramps and gymnasial fretwork, and she said to Dorothy, "Give me the shell." Dorothy obliged without comment, for once. Rain said, "I don't know if this will work, but it can't hurt." She lifted the shell to her lips and sounded a call as long and hard and intensely as she could.

When Rain had finished, Dorothy supported her to keep her from falling over and passing out from the effort. "The Ozmists?" asked Dorothy.

"They said they'd come if they could. And they're already dead, so how could anything harm them? The dragons have cover from the clouds; perhaps the Ozmists can provide cover from the ground."

No one hurries for history, not even ghosts. The Ozmists emerged slowly, evincing themselves more as a kind of cloaking odor at first than anything else— the laundry sweetness of freshly prepared shrouds— but they did come.

On the first day, the lower districts of Oz saw shreds of white tendril coalescing as thin filmy fountains. They appeared to emerge from the cobbles, and before long they joined to form a low canopy about four feet above the street. The air beneath was breathable, and survivors searching for water or for the bodies of their kin could safely make their way—squatting, hunched, lurching from the well to the lean-to and back again.

The maw of the high-security prison, Southstairs, open to the sky, and the Burntpork district, and the corn warehouses beyond the military garrisons near Westgate, and the taverns of the so-called Quadling Quarter—that is, the haunts of the downtrodden— were hidden first. Properties on higher ground, the Mennipin Squares, the government houses, the theater and opera circuit, remained exposed. They took their beating by the dragons, who had apparently been taught only to attack what they could see. The dragons had no power against the poor and the lowly as long as the poor remained properly invisible, which suited the poor just fine, this once.

On the second day the Ozmists strengthened. More of the Emerald City was protected, though the assaulting dragons sounded fiercer because frustrated. But people will pick themselves up and go about the next day's work, whether it be hunting for potatoes or looting in the rubble of Mirthless Neddy's Ruby Exchange. A cadre of Palace ministers stormed the doors of St. Satalin's Nook for the Criminally Insane, recognizing it as the safest spot to convene a crisis government, in case His Sacredness the Emperor of Oz proved undivinely mortal. The criminally insane, however, threw them out, saying they already had their lives under control as well as could be expected, thank you very much.

Before dawn on the third day Brrr found Rain sleeping under the steps to a bridge on the Ozma Embankment. "Why didn't you come back to us?" he said, nosing her awake.

"I knew you would brave it if I needed you," she replied to him, putting her arms around his neck. "But how did you find us?"

"Tay came and led us here," said Brrr. And there was Tay, hanging back, green as a goblin's hoard, whiskering now up to Rain's ankles.

Rain told the Lion she didn't believe her father was in the EC; the attack coming from the east must prove he and the book had been abducted by the Munchkinlanders.

"So we'll go there," said the Lion. "No?"

"Not yet. There's too much to do here."

The Lion didn't reply at first. Then he said, "Well, tell me what to do."

"I have no plan. Never did. But if Munchkinland is winning this war, their army will enter the city before long. We'll wait and greet them when they come. If the Grimmerie is important enough to La Mombey, she'll bring it with her, and she'll bring my father with it."

"Any day we wait might be a day she takes his life," said Brrr.

"Any day we wait might be—" began Rain, but she was fully awake now. Dorothy was rousing from under a greasy tarpaulin of some sort, yawning. The first work beckoned—finding breakfast for those children living under the steps on the far side of the bridge. So Rain's reticence kicked in. "Where's Little Daffy? And Mr. Boss?"

"They've come forward, despite their apprehensions. She's liberating decoctions from ruined apothecaries and administering them as best she can. And she's bossing Mr. Boss around to help her. We'll meet up with them later, if we survive the day."

"We'll survive this day," said Rain, grinning. "The Ozmists are strengthening daily, don't you think?" It was true. As the day advanced, the mist thickened. It made travel difficult but also safer in some ways, and the sound of attacks from dragons was limited to ever more circumscribed neighborhoods.

On the fourth day Candle arrived by broom, accompanied by Iskinaary and the venerable old Eagle named Kynot. She found Rain at the edge of the Ozma Fountain, rinsing the sores on what was left of the legs of a teenage pickpocket. Rain hardly looked at her, just handed her mother a roll of bandage and explained what needed to be done. Only in the evening, when Candle crowded under the bridge with Dorothy, Rain, the others, did the daughter learn what the mother had done. But Candle brought out her news slowly, cautiously.

"I remembered that Nor could learn to fly the broom as a young woman," said Candle, lying on stones, her eyes closed and one palm over her forehead, the other palm tucked into Rain's two hands. "I thought: maybe the ability to fly isn't given just to the young or to the talented, but to the needy, too. In any event, if I couldn't fly on the broom, I thought you might. I found the thing and I mastered it. Well, let me be honest. I didn't master the art of flying, but I managed it."

"You managed," murmured Rain, apprehending the feel of her mother's palm but almost asleep herself. "How did you know how to find me?"

Candle said, "But that's the intuition. The seeing the present. You may have it too, someday, if you don't have it yet."

"I can't see my own toenails," said Rain. "Too tired."

"Tomorrow we'll start in Quadling Quarter," said Little Daffy to Mr. Boss. "There's a nasty rash flushing up on the hindquarters of the squelchy-folk that I don't like the look of one bit. We'll boil up some unguent in that copper laundry tub you nicked from the kitchen yard of Fancy-Pantsie House or whatever it was called."

"Never marry a dominatrix," said Mr. Boss, and he rolled over to snore himself silly.

"Have you heard what has happened to your father?" whispered Candle, once everyone else had gone silent.

Rain tried to find in herself some capacity for knowing the present. All she could know of the present was exhaustion. "I have not," she admitted.

Her mother sat up. "Ready yourself, Rain."

"I'm never ready for this," she replied. "But tell me."

Candle spoke carefully, drawing each phrase from her mouth like a rounded stone she could set down in a line, barely touching the next. "An old friend. Saw your father. Bewitched into a foreign corpus. And die on a cart. That Eagle named Kynot. He broke with the habit. Of Birds. To stay aloof. He sent out word. To let me know. For Liir had been an honorary Bird once. Before you were born."

"What can Eagles know?" whispered the haunted child.

"Liir was born a bastard. He flew as a Bird. As an Elephant he was hauled across the border into Munch-kinland. He has died inside that skin. I'm afraid this is so, dear Rain. I cannot see it otherwise."

Rain wept a little. The tears were hard as ice. Dorothy sat up, eyes closed. Her shoulders shook just a moment, and then she sleep-hummed a tune of mourning or condolence, something that seemed to provide her some comfort. Perhaps for once her melody comforted the others, too. Though Rain didn't expect to sleep, she drifted off holding her mother's hands, dreaming of her father's hands.

The shreds and selvage of a life, her own or her father's—she couldn't tell the difference anymore.

Iskinaary kept a vigil by the bridge, his eye for Liir dry.

By the fifth day there was nothing left for the dragons to attack but the great dome of the Palace of the Emperor. It alone rose above the bank of Ozmists that had saved the City of Emeralds from annihilation. As the sole final target of the dragons, the dome suffered tremendous damage, though not as much damage as the pickpocket, the proctor, the laundress or the nursery orphan. It never collapsed upon the palace, but it remained scarred and defiant in the fog of history.

Midday, the dragons were called off. Almost immediately the Ozmists began to thin, but not to disperse. At dusk on the fifth day, La Mombey entered the Emerald City triumphant. A pack of nearly visible spider-thugs on their furry scrabbling stems surrounded her gilded sledge, which ran along the drifts of silted ash as neatly as if they were drifts of snow.

VII

To Call the Lost Forward

1.

Avaric, Margreave of Tenmeadows, was waiting in front of the Bureau of National History to meet La Mombey's conveyance. The Emperor had given him the dirty job of emcee at the armistice negotiations. At first he wore the sneer of a playground monitor. Well, the place was a shambles. No one had taken a broom to the city yet. The piazza was littered with fragments of marble Ozmas. The sound of trumpeteen and brass-flummery, though shrill, inadequately masked the muttering of the mingy crowd.

It's a loser's job to broker the conference, thought Brrr, who peered from behind a toppled column. How surprising that they didn't offer it to me.

The Lion was looking out for signs of Liir, on Rain's behalf as well as his own, but the Lion wasn't eager to be recognized by Avaric. Later, Brrr would hold his tongue when people said of the Margreave that through the truce negotiations he had comported himself with a deference to the Eminence of Munchkinland that seemed little short of concupiscent. Such is the shame of the lawyer. Avaric, they whispered, had never managed to be that fawning even before His very Sacredness, the divine Emperor of Oz.

Which comment, true or not, attached itself to Avaric for the rest of his life and made public dining at the Oak Parlor in the Florinthwaite Club a bloody pain in the arse.

La Mombey alighted in uncinched bell-curves of pure white linen dropping from the shoulder. The mob of spider-things clustered about her with the devotion of bloodhounds until she clicked her fingers, and then they rolled themselves up into bobbins and an assistant swept them into a casket. Once they were gone everyone breathed a bit more easily.

The Lion watched carefully. He'd always possessed a decent eye for detail. He saw how Hiri Furkenstael might have treated the pomp of the occasion. How a student of the School of Bertius might have handled La Mombey's bib, freely suggesting its pale mink tippets and its appliquéd off-white lozenges inscribed with sigils like letters in a foreign script.

He was memorizing the moment so he could tell his companions about it. How the pale beautiful woman appeared as a smudgy blankness, almost, among the colored leaves of those ornamental shrubs and trees that hadn't been blasted by shrapnel. Something about her so—so lambent and concealed at once. Floating amid the blur of dissolving Ozmists, or was that sentiment clouding his eye? How to put it?

But so often, before words can rise to the mind to imply the ineffable, the ineffable has effed off. From his place near the ruined Hall of Approval, the Cowardly Lion watched the impossible happen: Loyal Oz falling to the upstart Free State of Munchkinland. Words would fail him, later on.

La Mombey paused so Avaric could approach her. In rounded public tones she summoned the Emperor of Oz to join her for a discussion of the terms of peace. Then her voice dropped, and Brrr couldn't hear what else was said. After she retreated to her sledge, Avaric stood nodding and bobbing till it slid away. He turned almost at once to where Brrr was hunched behind broken stone. Apparently not hidden well enough, then.

"Sir Brrr, Namory of Oz," called Avaric. Naturally, thought Brrr, the only time my title is used in public is after the throne that conferred it has collapsed. Figures. "I see you there. I need your advice."

Brrr prowled up to the man who, once upon a time, had arranged the Lion's plea bargain and brought him into service of the Emperor's secret agencies hunting for the Grimmerie.

Avaric spoke as if they'd just fallen in step somewhere in Oz Deer Park or along the Shiz Road. "A propitious time to return to the capital. Now that the army of Animals can lay down its—teeth. But I see you didn't personally drag in the sledge of La Mombey."

"I've done enough menial toil in my day. That foursome of Tsebras managed an elegant enough job of it without me. Oh, are you implying I've arrived as part of a conquering army? *Me?* How droll. As if I was ever on the winning side. Really, you flatter me."

Brrr was glad the crowd had melted away with La Mombey's departure. No one was close by to hear Avaric reply, "You were assigned to discover the whereabouts of the Grimmerie and you never returned. It's not for me to prosecute you, but I'll remind you that you jumped probation as set by the magistrates of the Law Courts—"

"One might wonder if those resolutions have been nullified. Given that there's about to be a new administration in Oz. Anyway, the Law Courts are in recess just now. I passed what was left of them on my way here."

"Exactly so," said Avaric. "Leaving other matters aside, I need your help. I can tell by your bedraggled state that you've been out and about on the streets of the city. Tell me what you know. What building left standing might be large and dignified enough to house the teams that will work out the conditions for a cease-fire? The Palace is intact, or most of it is, but it might seem ungracious to invite La Mombey in for tea only to have the central dome collapse upon her."

The Lion thought for a moment. "Well. The People's Academy of Art and Mechanics is closed for business. That's out. The Lord Chuffrey Exposition Hall, which had such beautiful light, now has beautiful shadows. But I think the Lady's Mystique, that small theater on the edge of Goldhaven, is still standing. And what luck—I'll bet the afternoon matinee has been canceled."

"Too small, and too—theatrical. The Emperor will need room to be at some distance from La Mombey. Space around His Sacredness."

The Lion eventually suggested the Aestheticum, a circular brick coliseum of sorts, long ago roofed over for trade shows. A place where antiques vendors displayed their wares—fine art, and the more collectable of historic furniture. He had once cut something of a figure among the great and the good who ran the

Aestheticum, back when he had fancied himself a con-
noisseur. In exchange for any lingering obligation to
the Throne Minister of Oz, current or future, to the
extent that the Margreave could plead his case, the Lion
agreed to make arrangements. "Deal?" asked Avaric.

"Deal," said Brrr. "Though I suppose it would be
overmuch to request an elevation of my title?"

"To Brrr bon Coward, Lord Level of Cowardly Custard and Environs?" Avaric hadn't lost his capacity to
sneer. Brrr realized he'd gone too far.

"Well, tell me this then, because everyone's asking,"
he countered, as much to change the subject as to hear
the reply. "Shell Thropp has shown little love for the
people he ruled all these years, the people he's driven
into war and ruined. Why is he yielding to Mombey's
aerial attack? It can't be concern for massive civilian death or the destruction of the Emerald City. Can
he really have begun to fear for his own life? Isn't he
immortal?"

"He's the sort of immortal who will live eternally
after his corruptible human sleeve—his shell, as it
were—succumbs." Avaric could talk political theology
as smoothly as if he were discussing the point spread
in a wager over the gooseball playoffs. "I suppose you
know that his real name, the name given him by his
unionist minister father, is Sheltergod?"

"And my real name is Birthdaysuit—" the Lion began, but Avaric cut him off.

"The name reflects a sentiment that some spark of the Unnamed God burns within us all. His Sacredness may have determined that he received the lion's share—"

"Well, he sure got mine, because I harbor no god within me. It sounds like worms. One would need castor oil, or dipping."

"—but in the panic of La Mombey's attack, and in sure and certain fear of an insurrection by his own followers, he has been called to yield."

"Who called him? Who gets to place that call?"

"Now you're being snarky. He called himself, of course. Are we done?"

The Lion walked away. He didn't mind sashaying this time. So God talks to himself. Just like the rest of us do.

All the vendors had taken off during the first of the attacks and by now were either dead on the road amidst shreds of their favorite paintings or were lingering in some summer home waiting to hear news from the capital. The Aestheticum was boarded up. After some pounding and a couple of roars the Lion managed to raise attention at the loading dock. The

thrice-bolted door was opened by that clubfooted society hostess from Shiz, Piarsody Scallop, with whom,
however inanely, the Lion had once been paired in the
press.

"I haven't got room for another postage stamp,"
said Piarsody, but when she recognized the Lion, she
added, "especially from you," and tried to close the
door. Her clubfoot got in the way somehow, and Brrr
barreled past.

"I'm not negotiating art, either purchase or sale," he
growled.

"You're the only one in the city who's not."

He saw what she meant. The Aestheticum was
jammed to the ceilings of the mezzanine with furniture,
bibelots, treasured artworks, bolts of better tapestry,
carpets. "It's a madhouse warehouse," said Piarsody.
"People know high-end decoratives will come back,
and they stash their valuables here until the first collector sniffs that the war is truly over and moves in for the
firesale bargain. But we're stuffed to the gills. I can't
move, I can't do inventory, I can't even see well enough
to be able to tell what is good and what is better used to
build a fire to cook my lunch."

"I don't care if you burn it all and have a really big
lunch," said the Lion. "I want the center of the hall
cleared out by noon tomorrow."

"You've lost your mind. I always knew you would," said Miss Scallop. "A bit too high-strung. Back in Shiz they whispered that to me when you were in the Gents'. They will say it here, too."

"I'll help you. I can get others to help. We'll shift everything to the motherhouse of Saint Glinda across the square, assuming it's still standing. The war with Munchkinland is over, Miss Scallop, and the little buggers won."

"Don't they always?" said Piarsody Scallop.

All afternoon they sorted out antiquities. The better paintings could be hung over the railing of the mezzanine to grace the event. Some of the furniture could be packed drawer against door along the outside walls, under the balconies, slotted so thickly in place as to make a six-foot wooden henge. The rest of the stuff had to go.

Brrr roared himself into the cloisters across the square and commandeered them. The motherhouse had long been under the thumb of the Emperor, unlike the cenobitic mauntery in the Shale Shallows, and the women scurried to oblige, driven nearly mad with delight at having a part to play. The mauntery afforded plenty of space along the arcades to stash a museum's worth of antique fussiness in home decor.

When the job was almost done, Brrr happened to back into an oak chest standing on its end. The lock sprung open and the lid popped, spilling the contents on the tiles of the mauntery floor. Included were no fewer than seven sets of jeweled shoes modeled after the famous set that Lady Glinda had given to Dorothy Gale once upon a time. The Lion threw all the shoes into the well in the center of the cloister garden. Any splash they had, they'd made a long time ago.

2.

For his work helping Avaric bon Tenmeadows to set up the council for peace, Sir Brrr, Lord Low Plenipotentiary of Traum, Gillikin, was invited to sit in attendance.

"I've come up in the world," he told the meagres under the bridge. "I'm still small fry, but I could probably sneak a few of you in if you want to get a peek at history."

"Busy. Sorry," said Rain, in her new iron-hard voice.

"We have to do something useful," explained Candle to the Lion. "With Liir's death—we have no choice. It's that or die." The Goose, under the obligations of family loyalty, bobbed his head in agreement. He had never liked either Candle or Rain, but was now something of a retainer in their broken circle.

"As for me, I wouldn't come within a mile of Mombey," said Dorothy. "It was her court that convicted me of murder, remember. And even if I wanted to brandish that stupid testimonial of my character, it's probably null and void under the new regime. By the way, Brrr, you risk being imprisoned for aiding and abetting a psychopathic criminal in her notorious escape from justice." She batted her eyelashes.

But the Lion had lost too much, and gained too much, to be prey to the same worries that had bewitched him most of his life. Nor gone first, and now Liir. What else could they do to him? Really?

It was left to Avaric to plead the terms of the truce with His Sacredness who, rumor had it, was keeping comfortable in a bare cell in the prison of Southstairs. Living on water and celery, and approaching the mercy of a deeper aestheticism.

Avaric had to work to get the Emperor's attention. Either poor Shell's mind had snapped or he'd ventured further toward divinity than he may have intended. "It's a bit of a nonstarter, some conversations," Avaric said to Brrr. "But we'll get there. Those creepy Ozmists are lifting little by little—even the dead can't be bothered to haunt you forever, it appears that they have other things to do—and the dragons are camped on the Plains of Kistingame outside of the Emerald City to the north. Mombey can call them in again to move matters along if the Emperor proves unwilling to focus. On some level he knows this. He and his ministers are doing what they can to set matters right."

"What are the preconditions of surrender?" asked Brrr.

"That's confidential," said Avaric, but when the Lion pinned him down and threatened to rip off his arms with a novel dental technique, Avaric changed his mind about confidentiality.

"No, no," said Brrr. "I'm not interested in what the *Emperor* is giving up. I know what he's giving up, and what was never really his to yield, either. What I want to know is what demands he is making of Mombey."

"The niceties of military surrender are new to me, but it's my understanding His Sacredness is not in a position to make demands."

"Of course he is. He can refuse to yield unless Mombey offers something. And if *you* refuse to yield—"

"I take your point," said Avaric. "I think I may need that elbow in the future? Thank you. Is there something special that you'd like His Sacredness to request of La Mombey?"

"There is indeed," said Brrr. "I should like her to bring the corpse of Liir Thropp to the Emerald City so his family can bury him."

"Mombey has murdered Liir Thropp?"

"Apparently. Well, it stands to reason. If the EC didn't kidnap Liir from Kiamo Ko, Mombey's men did. That must be how she managed to marshal the violence of those dragons. She got to him first after all. And to the Grimmerie."

"If you had done what the court asked of you—find us the Grimmerie—Munchkinland would be suing Loyal Oz for peace instead of the other way around."

"What His Sacredness is demanding in exchange for signing the treaty of surrender," said the Cowardly Lion, "is Liir's earthy remains. Are you sure you're getting all this?"

That evening, the Lion told his companions—including Rain and Candle—that he'd negotiated the release of Liir's corpse. Although what kind of achievement, really, did it count as? The dead are no less dead whether buried at home or abroad.

Around the brazier they'd set up underneath the struts of the bridge, they talked about Liir. Thirty or forty homeless citizens of the Emerald City listened as they shared stories of the Emperor's nephew. Dorothy had known Liir for too short a time, back when he was fourteen or so. "I don't remember much about him. I think he was sweet on me for a while. But in the end I probably wasn't his type. Seems my lot in life."

Her eyes tracked the dirty hem of her dress. She'd carried a torch for him from the age of ten, thought Brrr. Poor thing.

Candle said, "I saw Kynot this afternoon. He has been very kind to me. I told him we hoped to have a pyre to burn the body, if the corpse hasn't corrupted so fully it has had to be burned already, or been buried in Munchkinland. The Eagle is calling veterans of the Conference of the Birds to attend as an honor guard."

Rain said, "I'm not sure I want to be there. Am I required?"

Her mother said, "When have we required anything of you, Rain? Except to survive? You do as you see fit."

The girl sat hollowly in the light of the fire until the fire slumped, and then she did too. The Lion tried to offer comfort, but she would have none of it. All night she lay on the ground shivering, and would take no blanket, as if trying to learn in advance what chill of the grave might be visited upon her father. Tay squirreled into her arms, half a comfort.

Three days later, a caparisoned and hooded cart was escorted by mounted guard through Munchkin

Mousehole, the southern gate of the city, and through the Oz Deer Park and along the Ozma Embankment to Saint Glinda's Square. In lieu of Candle, who had decided her place was at the side of her living daughter and not her dead husband, the Lion stood to receive Liir's Black Elephant corpse.

In a silence broken only by the rush of the wings of pigeons as they pivoted about city skies now safe again, His Sacredness the Emperor of Oz emerged through some secret egress from Southstairs. The prison governor, Chyde, carried the Ozma scepter and Avaric, Margreave of Tenmeadows, the crown.

Mombey waited on the steps of the Aestheticum. In keeping with the gravity of the day she displayed herself as aquiline of nose, cheeks of pale ice. Her straight tresses, colored steel, almost violet, were looped and fixed in place with constellations of emerald set in mettanite.

It took Brrr a moment to realize that the attendant at her side was Tip.

3.

Walking back to where his friends were camping under one end of the bridge, the Cowardly Lion didn't know if he should mention the presence of Tip.

With the arrival of her father's corpse and the need to attend to her mother, Rain already had so much on her mind. To say nothing of the work she'd taken on this week, to attend to the needy. Why that selfless labor, Brrr had no idea; Rain had hardly ever seemed conscious, before, of the sores of others—indeed, of her own sores, either. The Lion wondered if Rain's summoning the Ozmists to help had put her in a position of noticing both what those ghost-bits had done, and what they couldn't do.

So many burdens on her young back. She might not be able to tolerate the return of her friend Tip, for whom her affection had been no secret except, perhaps, to herself.

In any case, Tip would guess that Rain might be in the city as well. What else had he expected her to do after he set out to find her father and the Grimmerie? It wasn't hard algebraics. He'd be looking for Rain here, if he wanted to find her.

But if he didn't want to find her, was it doing her any good to help *her* find *him*?

In the end it was Dorothy who decided the Cowardly Lion on the matter. The Lion had walked her to a clutch of broken pipes protruding from the back of a collapsed Spangletown whorehouse. The dripping pipes were set high enough in the wall that larger creatures could wash without too much crouching, and since Dorothy still had a tendency to croon given half a chance, the Lion stood guard over her virtue, her modesty, and her critics while Dorothy sponged herself and performed a musical set for unbelieving rats and such harlots as hadn't yet fled the district.

On the way back, Dorothy said, "I've been wondering what to make of myself here in the Emerald City." The Lion, his mind on Rain, didn't take in what she meant at first. "I mean," continued Dorothy, "there seems no particular campaign to ship me out of Oz the way there was the first time. Everyone's so distracted, and who can blame them? So I've been wondering if I should just go into some line of work, and settle down here. Back a ways we passed an old sandwich board advertising the eighteenth annual comeback tour of Sillipede at the Spangletown Cabaret. Did you see it? Do you think I might look her up, if she's still alive, and maybe get some professional advice? I could perform on the boards, you know, and put a few pennies together."

The Lion shook his head and heard his wattles wuffle. "What are you on about, Dorothy? We're witnessing an historic change in government, not hosting a jobs fair for immigrants. A little perspective, if you please."

"You're not going to stick by me forever. The Tin Woodman and the Scarecrow haven't been popping up like vaudeville headliners to welcome me with a song-and-dance upon my return to Oz. Do you think I haven't noticed? Life goes on, Brrr. We move on. I have so few choices, really, if I can't get myself back home. Maybe that's what growing up means, in the end—you go out far enough in the direction of—somewhere—and you realize that you've neutered the capacity of the term *home* to mean anything."

"I never use that word."

"Neutered? Sorry."

"No. I never say *home.*" And Brrr realized it was true, and that Dorothy was right, too. We don't get an endless number of orbits away from the place where meaning first arises, that treasure-house of first experiences. What we learn, instead, is that our adventures secure us in our isolation. Experience revokes our license to return to simpler times. Sooner or later, there's no place remotely like home.

"We'll get you back to purple waves of grain and amber plain, somehow," said Brrr, though he had no ideas at the moment. What was he going to do? Go fish those knock-off slippers from the well in the mauntery motherhouse and make a mockery of Dorothy's own fond memories of enchanted travel?

They were almost back to the bridge. A mile away some strafed building was finally collapsing. The clouds of dust, even at this hour, evoked the haunting by Ozmists and made those who dozed nearest death to tremble at the sight. "We don't get too many chances, do we?" said Dorothy. "I've had more than my share, even while buildings fall around me on a regular basis."

"What do you mean?"

"I don't think we—as individuals—have much choice in our affairs, after all. Despite any fond hope for life, liberty, and the pursuit of happiness, I haven't been able to avoid Oz or to get out of Oz. I'm just a pawn. I didn't ask to be born an orphan, or to be taken on by Uncle Henry and Auntie Em. I didn't ask to annoy everyone with my soapy character. It wasn't my idea that an earthquake should punish San Francisco the week I arrived. We really can't do much about our given circumstances, can we? We may have free will but it isn't, in the end, very free. I might as easily have been born in China."

The Lion purred in agreement, though it was a wise, consoling purr. "Limited range. We get relatively few chances to make good."

"Still." Dorothy's eyes were unnaturally bright, even for her. "I suppose if we don't even have bootstraps with which to pull ourselves up, we had better become highway robbers and steal some off someone who has extra."

"Dorothy," said the Cowardly Lion, "did anyone ever tell you that you are a piece of work?"

She wasn't listening. She was staring at a small scrap of caninity barreling with businesslike dispatch along the road, away from the thud of the collapsing architecture. His nose was to the gutter and his tail wagging ferociously as if he, for one, had never doubted the nature of home or the adequate play of his own personal free will. "Toto!" cried Dorothy.

So that was home, then, thought the Lion, as the dog catapulted into Dorothy's bosom. That's as good as it gets. I have no right to deprive Rain of the possibility of reunion with Tip because I fear it might not satisfy her. Let her take her chances and make that decision herself.

"Rain," he said before they turned in for the night, "let me tell you what I saw today."

4.

She didn't know what to think about Tip arriving with Mombey. Rain needed to see him first before talking to him, to make sure that in returning to Mombey he hadn't betrayed Rain somehow, been party to her father's death. Maybe he'd been a secret envoy of Munchkinland all along.

After all—that coincidence—that he should have come to be hiding in her wardrobe! They'd talked about it, laughed and loved it. She was much older now, and it seemed suspicious.

"I'll install you in the Aestheticum," Brrr told her. "There are a dozen places to hide among the legs of all that compacted furniture. You can watch and decide what to do as you like. If you're quiet enough, you will witness history."

"I've witnessed enough history," said Rain. "But I can be quiet. That's one of my strengths, remember."

She got ready to go with Brrr the next morning. Early, before dawn. The wind off the canals was disturbing ash and dirt from where it had settled overnight, gritting the air for the day. Candle got up too and silently helped Rain dress—not that Rain needed help. Mother and daughter fussing with a face flannel, apron strings, getting in each other's way. A few feet off, Dorothy snored softly, Toto in her arms. The light in the sky a system of beveled intensities, pale, less pale. Candle said, "I don't want you to make the wrong choice, Rain."

Rain didn't look at her. "How do you know what choices I have?"

"I don't. But I know . . . I know you are going to select among what possibilities are offered you. Every parent knows this, and I know it as well as any."

"No matter how far from me you have lived."

"No matter." Candle brushed her daughter's hair. "We've lived apart, but I see what you know today, and that you don't know everything. Rain, don't. . . ." She paused.

"Don't make the mistake I made?" Rain heard her own voice, low and mean. Rain was the result of Candle's mistake. Or maybe the mistake itself. No doubt about that.

"That's not what I meant at all," said Candle. "Every choice brings wisdom in its wake. If you got to have the wisdom first, it wouldn't be a choice—just policy. What I mean is—" She turned her attention to Tay, who was now awake and grooming itself. "I mean, don't sleep with the boy."

"Oh, well, I've already had my sleep for tonight." Larky-snarky. Such kindness as Rain might have wakened with had evaporated. The dawn began to steep in the limbs of the pummeled trees. In the company of the Lion and the rice otter she took her leave, and without turning around she waved her hand over her shoulder at her mother's farewell.

Dawn over the Aestheticum. A mawkish pink. Word had apparently gotten out among the Birds. The silhouette of the shallow dome, its granite ribs and quoins picked out a pale yellow, was punctuated with sentinels of Birds. The old Eagle, Kynot, saw the Lion and the girl approach, and he swooped down to meet them with a guard of three or four.

"It's not quite the original gang," said General Kynot. "Birds don't tend to live as long as humans. But respectable enough, to see our companion off."

"Lurline love-a-chickadee, but you've grown," said a Wren to Rain. "You remembers me? Doesn't you, sweet? Quadling margin lands, when you was traveling with that Clock? It's Dosey, begging your pardon, miss."

Brrr glanced at Rain. Her face was blank. She who had always had more time for Animals was eager to see her human. "We can't stop to chat about the old times," said the Lion. "We must get in before the girl is spotted here."

"We'll be up top," said the Eagle. "If you need us, roar for us, Lion. We'll break through the high windows if we can."

Brrr pawed out the keys to the Aestheticum. Since he and Rain were the first to arrive, he gave her a quick tour. "This platform here, with the single schoolroom bench—the Emperor will come in and sit upon that. Opposite, a platform of exactly the same height but, notice, covered with that rather rare Varquisohn carpet, is where La Mombey will sit. Her throne is actually a stage prop from a community theater production of *The King of Squirreltown's Daughter,* but I don't think Mombey will object. Her ministers will be here, see, and here. While the Emperor's staff and emissaries of the counties will be installed behind that velvet rope. Do you think the jeweled beeswax candles are a little over the top? Yes, I think they are." He plucked out the emeralds, pursed his lips, and then put them back in.

Rain wandered about. All the alcoves under the balcony that ringed the whole room were piled thick and high with dusty furniture. She found a cove she could wriggle into. An old marble tomb ornament of a knight and his lady afforded some height. Rain could climb up, kneel onto the flat of the knight's stone sword laid along his breastplate and down between his knees, and peer through filigreed gewgawkery scrolling along the tops of wooden pillars. If she stayed in gloom and no further illumination was cast, she might remain unobserved and still catch most of what was going on.

She pulled open the door of a wardrobe and removed a couple of broken umbrellas, making room so she could duck inside to hide in the event of necessity. In another piece, a huge linen press, she found a bottom drawer two feet longer than she was herself, and deep enough to sleep in. She took a pillow from yet another drawer and arranged herself a bed in case this festival of political mortification went all night and she was stuck here unable to move. On a second pillow she set the shell, for safekeeping. She even found a royal chamber pot tagged with a stamped provenance: OZMA THE BILIOUS. Well, she'd use that if she had to.

"There will be pastries at the tradesmen's entrance in half an hour," said Brrr. "You can be my assistant until a certain moment, then when I give the signal, you'd better make yourself scarce."

At Brrr's side, she hung out at the door, listening to the city come alive. Horsemen tethered their steeds to stanchions of iron; vendors showed up to sell early chestnuts, stale bread, apricots, onion tarts—mushy and a little rank. Sometimes she heard what Brrr muttered to her, a who's who of contemporary Oz. The Lord Mayor of Shiz, here to represent all of Gillikin. A Scrow chieftain identifying himself as Shem Ottokos, to witness for some of the tribes of the Vinkus. "The Yunamata won't cede to him rights of representation," whispered Brrr, "but whoever knows what the Yuna-mata think about governance? They don't even use hair combs."

The delegation from the Quadling Country was late. Rain caught a lot of eye rolling. She overheard someone say, "You know the squelchyfolk.

> But the Quadlings, ah, the Quadlings,
> Slimy, stupid, curse-at-godlings . . .

They probably got lost in the big city."

Then the advance party of the victors began to assemble—the Munchkinlanders. Most of them were squat and small, like Little Daffy. Others were more rangy, with their small breasts and big pelvises, kangaroo-folk as Rain had heard it put about at street corners.

Militia in dress habillard, ministers in robes of office, a few key generals called in from the field. Brrr wondered if General Jinjuria, who had held the terrain beyond Haugaard's Keep for much of the past decade, would be arriving to witness, but she didn't show up. On reflection, the Lion realized that any conquer-ing leader who had the capacity to change her visage daily to capitalize on shifting opinions of beauty and glamour would probably be less than happy to have a

popular female general known as the Foill of Munchkinland descending to divert attention away from her
superior.

"Time to take your hiding place," he murmured to
Rain.

She looked both ways before slipping into the shadows. Everyone was busy with pots of ink and stacks of
vellum, books of legal doctrine. Arguing over seating
and who took precedence over whom. It was easy to
disappear in plain sight.

Once inside the forest of furniture, she scrabbled this
way and that to reclaim her vantage point. Memory,
which rarely came together for her, woke up a little.
This was like crawling around Lady Glinda's bedroom,
back in Mockbeggar Hall, the time they'd all been
crowded into a single room. Would Lady Glinda arrive
to witness the historic moment? Rain craned to look.
The first person to come into her line of vision, appearing a little lost, was Tip.

Rain caught her breath. It hadn't been long since
they'd seen each other, but so much had happened in
the meantime—the news of her father's having been
magicked into the form of an Animal, and of his death
in that form. The assault by dragons upon the storied
Emerald City. So Tip seemed different, in just those
few weeks. One could change that fast. What had

happened to him? What had he put himself through, and for whom? For her? Or for Mombey?

The earlier anxieties metastasized now there was so much to be lost. What if Tip had only stayed at her side until they had gotten to Kiamo Ko, where they found out that both Liir and the Grimmerie had been taken into custody? Had Tip been using her to locate her father and the book for Mombey, his admitted guardian? What if the abduction of her father hadn't yet happened? Would Tip have stolen the volume and left her that way instead of the way he did?

A cold dampness covered her skin. She'd been used. He'd been planted somehow in her cupboard to seduce her, to learn her secrets. When she'd had no more to yield, he'd left her. On the double.

She huddled behind a varnished oak column carved with volutes and wooden ivy. Tay writhed at her ankles. Rain couldn't breathe, just looking at how Tip moved cautiously into the open arena, holding himself in a new way. Stiff. Uncertain. Stronger. More supple. Or was it less supple?

Additional impedimenta were being hauled in. Some minions with fans, in case the heat grew oppressive. Some other lackeys with braziers in case of chill. Someone set up fifteen music stands and fifteen music stools, and moments later someone else came along and

ordered them taken away again. Tip circulated, his eyes
at the roof level, as if he were part of the guard detail,
making effort to fortify the premises. But he looked
goofy doing that.

The room was coming to order. There was no
chair for Tip; clearly he had no formal role here. His
pacing slowed down. Luck was playing games with
Rain and Tip both: he paused in the very quadrant of
the large hall in which Rain had hidden herself, and
he began to hunt among the furniture for someplace
to lean. He moved a few feet in under the overhang,
where a low desk gave him a perch. He was in the
next alcove to Rain's, and an arched opening allowed
her to see him through hat racks and the legs of overturned tables.

Was he honing in on her whereabouts as he might
have done at St. Prowd's? Was she a lodestone to his
compass needle, that he should pick this section of the
space to loiter? More certain than ever that something
was amiss, she knew she must back away. As soon as she
could breathe, and before she could die. But Tay slithered in the shadows and wriggled forward to wreathe
Tip's ankles the way the lake otter had been cavorting
around Rain's own, with a teasing alertness.

Tip was magnificently composed, Rain saw. His
chin never dropped to indicate he'd noticed Tay. His

eyes remained trained on the lintels of the room, the struts in the ceiling, as if flying monkeys intent on attack might be lurking in the shadows. His cheeks reddened and his breathing quickened.

The ground was shifting beneath her feet, and she must leap one way or the other.

On the basis of those involuntary clues—the beauty of how his body responded—she would leap toward hope, this time, and trust he was not Mombey's agent. If he was to give her away, let him do it now, so she would know. She couldn't live any longer without knowing one way or the other.

Tay returned to Rain, soundlessly. A furniture warehouse seemed as natural a habitat for a rice otter as a swamp, the way that green spirit moved about it.

Rain began to wriggle her way through the maze of tight spaces. Tip folded his arms across his chest, in the manner of a man hard to please but cautiously satisfied with what he saw. He backed up against the nearest pillar. He sank his right hand in the sash of his tunic, as if looking for peanuts or a key or a handkerchief. He put his left hand around the edge of the glossy polished cylinder, and Rain caught it. She was on her knees in the shadows, behind the pillar, kissing his finger-tips, moving her mouth against his soft cupped palm, which had opened to receive her chin. She grazed his fingertips again with her lips, and parted her lips to take two fingers into her mouth.

"All unauthorized service force, five minutes," bellowed Avaric. "We will clear the hall for the dignitaries."

Factotums, servants, attachés, and minor satraps scurried, sending dust motes to eddy into the light slanting down from a ring of clerestory windows just below the shallow dome. More gentlefolk and fiercefolk from Munchkinland arrived. Though the hall became fuller and warmer, the noise began to subdue itself. Would he be forced to leave, her Tip, or had he received clearance to stay? She tugged at his wrist: *come, come.* She pulled him backward into the shadows and stood to meet him face-to-face.

"I may not be seen to disappear again," he whispered.

"They know you're here, they know you haven't left," she whispered back. "Have you left? Have you left me, Tip?" But if she'd ever known anything before in her life, she knew the answer now by looking at his face. He had not left her. "Don't leave me. Don't go. How will you find me again?"

"But you gave me a map. Of course I'll find you."

He pressed his fingers against her temples, pressed a forefinger to his lips to hush her, and sidled away. But the expression on his face said *wait,* the expression on his face said *later;* it said *soon.*

He went to his post behind the dais to which La Mombey would be escorted. With a new military bearing he stood, his polished boots just a little apart, his arms folded behind his back in that gesture that signifies no need for quick access to weaponry. His hair had been cut shorter. Someone had nicked the back of his neck with a razor. After all the blood and death Rain had seen, she wanted to weep over that nick as she hadn't yet wept.

The Emperor arrived with such a lack of fanfare that at first Rain didn't even notice. Shell was more hunched than she remembered. He wore a gown of gilded brocade that made a columnar sweep from his narrow pointed beard to his bare toes. Something in his bearing made Rain feel he was naked underneath the robe. Naked and proud. But his eyes looked glazed in a different way, as if perhaps he hadn't been taking proper nourishment for some days running.

He sat at his schoolboy bench for a few moments. When the air became even grander with the puffery of incense, he removed himself to his knees. Someone hurried over with a cushion but he waved it away, and stayed on his knees, eyes closed, as La Mombey entered at last.

Rain had heard Brrr's descriptions of the Eminence of Munchkinland—the various guises—and she remembered Tip's story about how Mombey had come by the skill of transformations. La Mombey looked like—what was it? Yes—she had it—like one of those figureheads on the boats that were dragged across the lawns at Mockbeggar Hall. She might have been carved of ancient oak. Her brow was broad and her wide-set eyes the color of overripe plum. Her hair was not so much blond or carrot as a kind of livid gold, shining with metallic highlights, just as her full skirts and bodice did. She was taller than anyone else in the room.

La Mombey approached her station and curtseyed to the Emperor of Oz and bade him rise. He did. The formal statements began in a humdrum tone, low to the ground, that Rain didn't strain to interpret. She merely watched the attitudes of the two leaders, the Emperor's form sagging, nearly listing, Mombey's body cantilevered forward with unnatural strength.

Once the proceedings were under way, a steady stream of interpreters, legislators, orators, and reconciliators moved into place, speaking in the vernacular of ceremony. Men and women moved pieces of paper from ledgers to lecterns and back again. Other men and women brought tea. Someone welcomed, late, an emissary of the Nome King of Ev. Someone petitioned that the proceedings be halted until a Quadling representative arrived. Someone else petitioned that that previous petition be reproved. Then the Quadling emissary stood up and said he was already present, thank you very much. It was Heart-of-Mushroom, identifying himself as the Supreme Glaxony of Quadling Country. He wore the same loincloth he'd worn in the jungle, and nothing else.

Eventually the proceedings became humdrum enough that Tip could back up and stand down from the dais, turn to consult an honor guard posted underneath a vulgar plaster cast approximating the famous Ozma Lexitrice statue near the Law Courts Bridge. Tip then circulated the perimeter of the hall, choosing his moments carefully, until he'd returned to the edge of the nook where Rain waited for him.

All eyes were on Mombey and the Emperor. No one looked at Tip, no one saw Rain in the shadows. Even Tay seemed glued to the proceedings. Tip stepped back into the carrel, among the boxy secretaries and bureaus, the carvings, the wardrobes and linen presses. It was no longer like Lady Glinda's salon. Now it was like the crowded basement shop in Shiz. BROKEN THINGS OF NO USE TO ANYONE BUT YOU.

They didn't speak, but they mouthed words, and read each other's lips. Read the language of relief on each other's faces.

You're all right.

You're all right?

Yes, I'm all right. Now.

How did we manage?

How will we manage.

I love—

I love—

There they stuck for a moment, words failing them, until Tip leaned forward. He put his arms around her, cradling her bottom, lifted her till his face was between her breasts. Silently he stepped forward and sat her down on the statue of the knight, on the broad flat blade of the stone sword. *We mustn't,* he said. *No. It can't be.*

He climbed upon the memorial, clenching her hips with his knees. He cradled the crown of her head with his large soft capable hand; he pressed her backward so her head rested against the pommel and quillion of the marble weapon. Upon a marble homage to a forgotten soldier died in a forgotten battle at a forgotten time for a forgotten cause, he rested his form against hers. *No,* he said. *We shouldn't.*

Tay looked away.

Rain reached up her hand to her neckline. She hooked a finger around the chain and pulled at it until the locket that Nor had given her appeared. She palmed it and then slipped it into her mouth and rolled it on her tongue.

She felt for the skin at the back of his neck, where his scalp had been cut too close. *No,* mouthed his words, *we mustn't,* but his face disagreed, coming nearer to hers. He put his lips upon hers, just lightly grazing. She opened her mouth and gave him her heart.

5.

The prosecution of the surrender was being managed reasonably, with courtesy and even courtliness. The only sticking point emerged when Avaric reminded the ascending Throne Minister of Oz, La Mombey, of the Emperor's private request. "His Sacredness requires the right to bury the corpse of his nephew, Liir Thropp, who has been taken prisoner by the Munchkinlanders and whose corpse has been brought, it is understood, to the EC from Colwen Grounds."

"Oh, the bodily husk is of little use," said La Mombey, at this point barreling through the negotiations herself, because she was getting bored with the high language of deference, and wanted elevation to the throne. "When the time comes, it'll slough off soon enough."

"The Emperor agrees about the insignificance of the human body," countered Avaric, "but in deference to his family he has promised them a proper disposition of the corpse. So the formal grieving can begin."

"Oh," said La Mombey, dismissing the matter with her hand once she had understood. "The body of Liir! I see. But he's not dead. Not essentially. Whoever said he was dead? Yes, I had him drugged and enchanted, to bring him to Munchkinland, and he proved sullen and torpid as a prisoner of war. Refused to help the cause, et cetera. It's not my fault he's made no effort to reject his disguise as a Black Elephant. It's his own lack of will that causes the form to cling to him. The form will kill him if he won't slough it off. I can't help that. Hah!—more of a mouse than a man, even. In my opinion he's not man enough to *deserve* to be an Elephant. He can't carry it off. But I thought *that* was the corpse to which you were referring. True, he refused to come here with us to supervise the handover, either, so I had him drugged again, to spirit him away from my dragonmaster. Liir is not very well; he wasn't meant to harbor so long in that form, and suffering it may be the death of him, in time. But for now he's relatively alive in that shroud of an Elephant body, I'm afraid. I thought you wanted to demand his release. Wasn't that it? I got up too early, I'm not focusing."

At this Shell spoke for the first time, giving his final directive as Emperor. "He is, nonetheless, a relative, even if I never recognized him as such the few times our paths crossed. Sever him from his disguise, so I may honor my word to his kin and mine."

"A condition of the surrender agreement," intoned Avaric.

"Now? Dreadfully inconvenient. But very well. You'll have to clear the hall." Mombey waved her hand.

"You'll need his wife. It's only right and proper," said the Cowardly Lion, and he sent for Candle.

"People, I want this finished," said La Mombey. "If I'm to do what I can to return this Liir to his human form—hoping he doesn't go and die on us in the operation—I'll need to freshen up."

The room never completely emptied. Underlings hastened about, scribes made copies by hand for an orgy of signatures. Rain and Tip remained in the shadows, warm from their romancing, thrillingly shy of garments. Learning every inch of each other's forms using every measure at their disposal.

By evening most of the dignitaries had left. Under orders of the ascending Throne Minister of Oz, the great Varquisohn carpet had been shifted to the center of the vast concourse. Upon it waited some implements of her trade.

Only a dozen or two witnesses remained when La Mombey emerged from behind a screen. Brrr thought she was displaying a latent tendency to slumming. She returned not as a goddess in wings of hammered gold but as the Crone of a Thousand Years, almost Kumbricia-like in her hobbledy-hoyness. Her skirts were patched, and a bonnet sat on her head large enough to house a pair of alley cats. Rain, peering from her hideout, found Mombey smaller and more humble than expected—almost dumpy. Her shoulders were stooped as if she'd suffered rickets in childhood, and her chins seemed doughy and marmy. Around her shoulders she wore a woven shawl whose warp looked like dead ivy and whose weft was made of broken twigs.

"Mombey as she used to look in the old days," whispered Tip. "I never expected to see her like this again."

On a small black iron plate Mombey lit four coals. Into the throats of a trio of bottles of sarsaparilla or something she had plunged the feathers of a peacock. She set two keys down in a definitive way. "The Key of Material Disposition," she said fatuously, "and the Key to Everything Else." She seemed to be enjoying herself.

Rain and Tip dressed each other slowly so as not to allow a single rustle of garment. Their fingers lingering over ties, traced skin underneath the clothes as far as hands could reach. Tip sucked every button on the back of Rain's simple shift. Rain lifted the chain off her neck and put it around Tip's, where the red locket dropped behind the breastplate of his dress habillards. At last, decent, having returned to each other the disguise of their clothes, they stood, holding their hands together, all four of them knotted.

Rain couldn't help feel that lying with Tip had brought her father back to life, a little, just as Liir's lying with Candle had brought her to life, once upon a time. It was a sentiment only, but it suffused her.

Candle arrived with her domingon. Next to the sorceress Candle looked like the evening nurse. She didn't bow or make other obeisance. She merely sat on the floor and put her domingon into her lap.

She'll be a good help, thought Rain. She'd had experience drawing the human disguise off Princess Nastoya, just before I was born. Seeing the present: she can see what of Liir might still remain alive.

And she knows I'm here, thought Rain; she's like that. But she's protecting me with her silence.

Workers swung open the double doors of the loading dock and dragged the cart inside. It almost didn't clear the lintel. Upon it lay the gently steaming form of the Black Elephant. Rain's father, if word was to be believed. Alive somewhere, somehow, inside.

"Smoke and mirrors, don't nobody ever tell 'em nothing?" snorted Mombey. Her voice had lost its toney veneer; she sounded like a common hill witch taking a holiday in town. "Everyone sit down, and do as I say. This will take a little concentration. I had a nice supper but it's been quite a week and I want to make sure we get this right the first time. Are the doors barred? Light the candles, those ones there."

The Lion nodded. Avaric and the Emperor took their places on the simple bench. Rain and Tip shuddered in the shadows. The Elephant, in this musty failing light, looked like a giant delivery of coal. Tay sat on the closed eyes of the stone knight. Upon her domingon, Candle struck up a tonic plangetive.

Herbs were brought out, and a magical powder of some sort. Maybe it was just a localized pyrotechnical conceit, for drama. The vapor was scented now of violets, now of a camphorous licorice.

Rain leaned against Tip's shoulder. Everything was about to change once again. Her father would awaken. He was no longer a threat to Mombey now that the Grimmerie had been impounded. As the final condition of his uncle's surrender, he would be liberated. Rain's family would be reunited. A normalcy that Rain had never known might be waiting to punish them all.

But what would happen to Tip in all this? Mombey's chosen boy? Would there be a place to which Rain and Tip might slip away, far from the Palace of the People, far from the clasping arms of parents who had never, could never get enough of holding their arrogantly independent daughter?

But they had made her so.

Twenty fingers intertwined, pulling, twisting, pushing back. Make me hurt, thought Rain, while I can feel something, in case I die during this and fail to feel anything again.

"It's a stubborn enough spell," muttered Mombey, and she began to refresh some aspects of it, picking up a little way back for momentum.

"Perhaps he's already a bit deader than I figured," she apologized a half an hour later. "I trust this isn't going to present an insurmountable problem to His Sacredness."

"Call me Shell," said the Emperor.

"Liir is a quiet sort, but he's never been much of a team player," observed Brrr.

"Now you tell me," complained Mombey, and started once again.

Another twenty minutes and she began to get alarmed. "I'm getting interference," she complained. "Something is not right. I don't believe this lad has the nuggets needed to block me. My power is honed over a hundred years." She turned one of the keys at an angle to the other, then put it back the way it had been before.

"He's the son of a witch," said the Cowardly Lion. "Elphaba Thropp. Don't forget that."

"Never met the bitch," murmured Mombey. She began to be lost in chanting. Her hands elevated, swanning about, making patterns of the smoke that issued from the scorching coals.

"I'm losing him," she called out suddenly. "He can't hold out against me. It's not remotely possible. Let me try the book. Tip. Tip?"

Had she looked, had she noticed that Tip had wandered off into the shadows, perhaps she'd have paused. Secured the premises, sniffed Rain out as the disturbance skewing the results of her spell, sent the girl packing. The evening might have resolved in favor of a mundane result rather than as a manifestation of history's aggressive atropism. But Mombey was tired and off her mettle. She didn't look up. She just held out her hand and called him again, and Tip slipped from the shadows and came forward. He picked up the

Grimmerie from a plant stand and he set it upon her bony palm.

She put it down and expertly, without hesitation, opened it and flipped its pages. A mighty witch, La Mombey, and further empowered by her victory. The Grimmerie could no longer hold its secrets from her. The pages rattled with a noise like silver chains, like ropes of rain through gutters of carven bone.

"*To Call the Lost Forward,*" she murmured, "I know I saw you in here. Don't you betray me, after all I've been through to get you and use you."

She was talking to herself now, but every syllable quivered in the air. "I'd've stayed a common witch but for hearing about you from the foreigner. A humbug if ever I stumbled over one. I can use this book better than he might've done. Obey me!"

She found the spell and turned it upon the air so swiftly that Rain gasped. The cold memory of trying, with Lady Glinda, to call winter upon the water, back in the days when Rain herself had hardly materialized yet. In remembering how difficult that spell had been to cast, yet how natural, Rain felt it all over again. As if she too were being acted upon by the strength of the spell Mombey was casting. As if the spell the old sorceress was invoking was calling Rain's own past forward, reminding the girl of what it had meant to begin to read. The memory quickened, of how she awoke to life under the charm of the Grimmerie. She felt full of a salty disgust, an objection deep in the blood. She had done nothing but wing through her shallow days on earth like a shadow of something else, something only windborne, without initiative, without merit or aim. Her ears hurt.

"I've called the lost forward, damn it," shouted the harridan. "You can't resist me—I won't have it. I'm stronger than you, Liir Thropp! You'll come forward when I order you to!"

Watching Liir struggle to resist the spell, Tip had fallen on his hands and knees behind Mombey. She didn't notice. Maybe Tip was stricken in sympathy by something like the throes with which Rain herself felt throttled. Her skin burned leprous, her hearing raged.

"You *won't* die as an Elephant, damn it. Don't you dare. You haven't the willpower!" cried Mombey.

"Liir!" cried Candle. "Don't! Don't go!"

The pain squeezed Rain at her sides, to hold her back, but she wouldn't be held. She burst out of the hiding place. Putting the shell to her lips, she added its long plaint to the thrum and pall of the domingon accompaniment. Candle's eyes were closed against her own tears. She couldn't have been surprised by her daughter's clarion voluntary; Candle didn't lose a note in her own playing.

The shell made a gravelly tone like that of a low horn in the fog banks of a summer morning on Restwater. Some tug leaving harbor to begin its day of taxiing sheep and goods and day-trippers across the lake.

Almost at once the floorboards in the great hall creaked. For a final time the last of the Ozmists seeped forth, a thousand individual fissures of steam. They clouded the room with a powdery warm presence, a fragrance. They turned, to Brrr's astounded eyes, a different shade of white—at first lavender, he thought, but then a kind of silvery green. As if under the spell Mombey had cast they too remembered their particular origins, origins not in spirit but in spirit's organic counterparts.

Tip rolled on the floor with a thud. Before her, Rain saw him go over. She was caught between twisting toward him and turning to her father, whose Elephant form was beginning to stir for the first time. In sympathy, was it, Rain's own skin thrilled and stung, the bridge of her nose to the roots of her hair. Her fingertips and armpits and thighs all at once, as if the Ozmists were conveying some sort of airborne desiccant, a powder of ammonia or lye to vex her.

Mombey had come to a more perfervid attention. Her hat had fallen back off her head, revealing a scalp nearly as bald as a dragon's egg. "What have you done!" she cried to Rain. She crawled and lurched halfway up, on one knee, as if she couldn't rise fast enough and would have chosen to hurtle across the room to punch Rain down, if only she had maintained a more strapping form. One with more flexible joints. "What are you doing here? Where have you come from? No one gave you clearance. I never called you back!"

6.

The Elephant was rolling. Liir was rolling. The huge vertebrae were creaking as loudly as Ugabumish castenettas. The trunk swayed; the hooves scraped at the air and great swaths of black black hair, like handfuls of scorched grass, sifted through the gloom to the cart and the floor. The Elephant trumpeted, though whether it was a death throes or a calibration of mortal triumph, the Cowardly Lion couldn't say. He didn't bother to try. He was half scared to death himself.

Only the Emperor seemed unfazed. Still on his knees after all this time, still placid. He put his hands together and then he lifted back the collar of his great robe. It fell away from his neck, halfway down his arms, but stopped there. The Emperor opened his eyes and said, "Liir—Elphaba's boy. I never knew you."

As far as the Lion could tell, the noise was neither Animal nor human. The Elephant rose on his back feet, tremblingly, as if he might tumble upon La Mombey and flatten her. The Ozmists around him went iridescent emerald, like light striking a thousand whirring beetles in flight, gold and emerald, emerald and gold, the colors of Lurlinemas, the colors of pine pollen in champagne sunlight. In the dusk outside, the air was filled with the clattering of the wings of the honor guard of Birds, circling the dome, crying "Liir lives! Liir lives!"

"An ambush!" shrieked La Mombey. "A coup!" Her few guards had fallen to the floor, panicked and paralyzed, the way Tip also seemed to be, twisted, tilted onto his side, his hands between his legs. A seizure of some sort. The Elephant lifted onto one foot. His tusks fell away and his hide fell away. The bruised naked man lurked there, revealed, smaller than a newborn Elephant. Shaking off disguise, called forcefully back to live some while longer, whether he wanted to or not.

Outside, the Birds heard La Mombey shriek and swooped down upon the cordon militaire she had set around the building—the linked limbs of spider-thugs.

Every Bird settled on a target. Even Dosey the Wren was able to wrestle one spider from its partners, heft it aloft, and when she had gone as high as her wings would carry her, drop her cargo to squish against the dome of the Aestheticum.

Rain heard the pelting of the dome. She cried out to her father even as she hurried toward Tip, but the scraping pain across every inch of her form tightened into a net that drew the air from her lungs, and she fell.

7.

Rain didn't come around for seven days. In the meanwhile, the events of that evening having been deemed confidential, all of the Emerald City talked of nothing else.

In the light of the revelation of Mombey's perfidy, Loyal Oz's suit for peace had been postponed. Emissaries of both armies picked up their staffs and swords again, just in case. They didn't hold them for long, however. After a decade, war has a way of getting old. Soldiers from opposing contingents shared their bread and settled down over portable game boards. Some of the battalions entered into singing competitions organized by Dorothy, who in the fray was turning into a kind of mad mistress of ceremonies, a mascot of both sides. "What can I tell you?" she said to her friends, shrugging. "War is lunacy."

After Liir had recovered enough human muscle tone to be able to collapse upon the Varquisohn, Candle and Brrr brought him into a tent that had been readied for him just outside the doors of the Aestheticum. Little Daffy, having stocked up with unguents and palliatives of every strength and nastiness, whether useful or bogus, was waiting there. She went to work again on the patient whom she had first met as a young man attacked by dragons. Liir, young Liir, dropped out of the sky, bereft of possibility. All these years later she remembered his form, and she did her work well, slapping Mr. Boss on the wrist when he tried to help with too forceful a forearm. Her husband's quiver of talents didn't seem to include much of a bedside manner.

Candle had Rain brought in, too. She kept the lights low all night. On adjacent pallets father and daughter struggled for health, struggled against different resistances. Avaric scuttled to the edge of the tent, but Brrr wouldn't let him enter. "This is no business of yours," he said.

Later, well beyond midnight, the Emperor of Oz arrived, on his own. In the middle of the night, without a guard or an escort, without even a dog on a leash. The Lion stood up stiffly and emitted a low warning rumble, but Shell was family, like it or not, so the Lion had to let him pass.

"She is not your concern," said Candle quietly to Shell.

"She is God's great-niece," said His Sacredness. "She is my older sister's granddaughter. I can see that now."

"Go away. What you couldn't see when she was in disguise you can't see now. All human forms are disguises. And you claim to be sacred? You know nothing but the shell of people, nothing. Go away."

Liir sat up in the gloom and spoke for the first time, across the insensate body of his daughter. "Go away," he agreed. "She has nothing for you."

"She holds both the future and the past," said Shell, wringing his hands.

"No more than the rest of us," said Liir, and pitched a shoe at His Sacredness.

Near dawn, Dorothy came by the tent, exhausted from a night of revelry. Liir was asleep inside and she said again that she didn't want to bother him. She joined Brrr, who was still sitting guard outside. "Something's got to give," she said. "I can't go on like this. Here, I brought a flagon of freshwater. They're saying that Mombey has been taken into custody."

"Oh, they'll say a lot, won't they," said the Lion huskily. "Get to the point. What are they saying about that Tip?"

"Not much."

"Can you find out a little more?"

"Are you asking me to be a spy?" Dorothy smiled wanly. "Look, Brrr. I'll do what I can. A lot of the Quadling army has removed itself to the Plains of Kistingame, along with the dragons. I can go sniff around there."

"Dorothy, you think pretty highly of yourself, but even you risk trouble traipsing among an army of angry soldiers. You watch yourself. They came to conquer, and they feel themselves tricked into surrender. They'll take it out on you."

"Toto's a little nipper. He'll see me safe."

"He's dead asleep in your basket."

Iskinaary emerged from the tent, shaking his head. He'd been keeping vigil too. "I'll go with you, Dorothy. And I'll bet General Kynot can send us a couple of Falcons."

"Father Goose," said Brrr.

"Don't start," said Iskinaary.

"The truth is," said Dorothy, "I'd rather have something useful to do than sit here and wait." She twisted her hands together looking, Brrr guessed, perhaps a little bit like that Auntie Em. He remembered his theory that the young Dorothy may once have had a crush on the Witch's boy. Liir was solidly middle-aged while she was only now becoming marriageable. She'd come back to Oz too late, to a man who got away by growing up faster than she could. She's had to put up with an awful lot, our Miss Dorothy, thought the Cowardly Lion. Meeting up with Liir if she doesn't have to is one adventure I can see she'd rather avoid.

"Send word if you find anything out about Tip," said Brrr fondly. "And while I don't make the plans for this group, I'm guessing that as soon as Liir and Rain are well enough to be moved, the family will want to evacuate this tent and get out of the City. We can work out details later."

On the sixth day, Little Daffy sat back on her heels and said to the Lion, "Come, you, we're going to the Corn Exchange to try to scare up some flour wholesale so I can bake something and open up a little commercial concern of my own."

"You can manage without me," said Brrr.

"You heard me," said the Munchkinlander. "With everything still in flux I never know if the good people of the Emerald City are going to set their dogs upon a humble Munchkin farm woman plying her trade." She meant what she said. Certainly the Lion would prove a more useful defense than her dwarfish husband. But Brrr realized that she too was ready to let the Thropp family alone for a few hours, to come to what peace they might. And Dorothy thought the Lion should take himself out of the picture too.

Liir and Candle alone in the tent, Rain as catatonic upon the pallet as her father had been in his cart. Liir thought, I've given to her all the worst of my traits. If I had lost the will to live, for a time, how could I hope that she might be stronger? I've shared nothing with my daughter but my fear of inconsequence, that which has plagued me from my first days.

"In your disguise as an Animal, where did you go?" said Candle to him. The first direct remark she'd made since he'd been abducted from the castle in the west. The absence of the guardian Lion was giving her license to speak, it seemed.

Liir had thought about this. "The soldiers plying Mombey's charm of bewitchment gave me a bigger choice than they thought. They believed it was a superficial charm, and perhaps in some persons it might have been. The hide of an Elephant, the guise of one. But I remembered how Princess Nastoya had lived as a human. Despite her long concealment she never stinted from embracing the fullness of a disguise, its meaning—she learned as much as she could about how to be a human while trapped inside the human's form. Even though she wanted liberty from the disguise, in the end, so she could die an Animal. I thought perhaps she had made the wiser choice. I thought she had managed to become a human better than I, born one, had yet done. I thought I would rather die an Animal.

"A cowardly choice, perhaps," he admitted, but Candle had said nothing.

"You didn't help train the dragons to attack the city."

"No, I didn't. That was Trism."

"I know who it must have been."

They looked at opposite panels in the walls of the tent.

"In the end, Trism knew enough about dragons to do the job himself," she said. "They never needed the Grimmerie, did they. After all that. After our ruined lives. They didn't need you to read the book, nor Rain."

All the wasted time running, hiding. All the years.

"No," he admitted through his tears. "They only needed time—the time it took for Trism to experiment, over and over, with what he had learned from that one page of the Grimmerie torn out by Elphaba Thropp, those years ago, and given to the Wizard of Oz. Time to work it out. Once they'd gotten the book at last, they found—ha!—that Trism couldn't read the book. They wanted me to try but I refused. It was then I must have chosen not to come back—to stay an Elephant, let the disguise kill me. Mombey was enraged. She tried to read the book, too. I don't know how she managed the other evening, for she couldn't crack it open when she had it in her hands."

"Of course I know how she managed. Rain was there. The book obeyed her, not Mombey. The book itself brought the spell forward."

"Rain didn't do a thing."

Candle rolled her eyes. "*You* didn't do a thing. No, listen to me. You didn't do a *thing* to stop any of this. You didn't open the book to try to learn how to turn the dragons against their masters. You didn't halt the attack in which very few families in the Emerald City failed to lose a loved one. You didn't make any effort to . . . to call fire down upon the dragon hordes. You didn't move to stop an assault that pitched itself against your own daughter."

"I didn't know she was here, of course."

"Where else would she be?"

Liir thought of the girl thrown off the bridge at Bengda, the bridge he as a young soldier had set fire to. It was a bridge that had never stopped burning, and it never would. A child who had never stopped falling through the night, and she never would.

He said, "I haven't the words to answer you. The Grimmerie has brought nothing but grief to every soul who has used it. I wouldn't use it against my kind— Loyal Ozian or Munchkinlander—even if I had ceased to be my own kind."

Candle said, "That is not like you, Liir. That is vile. It is inhuman."

"I do not claim," he admitted, "to have made the human choice."

8.

When Brrr looked into the tent flaps the next morning, Rain was sitting up in the cot. "No, don't leave," she said to the Cowardly Lion. "I know already."

He shrugged. Liir got up and went out to find some facilities to use, to shave. The weather was coming in colder and they couldn't stay in a tent much longer, if Rain was to continue to recover. Candle, who after last night wasn't yet talking to her husband, left too but in a separate direction. Little Daffy and Mr. Boss sat down in the sun outside with a coffee tin to share. They counted up their earnings. Little Daffy called into the tent, "When is Dorothy going to come home and regale us with tales of her night's adventures before sacking out to sleep the morning away?"

The Lion intended to keep private his sense of Dorothy's hope to avoid seeing Liir. "She's on a mission," he replied.

"Isn't she always."

Rain said in a low voice to the Lion, "You don't have to pretend. I know. I know it all, Brrr. I know it already."

He arranged himself as he thought a stone lion in front of a library might do, with dignity and a sense of starch. "Well, everything's changed," he said, companionably enough, as if the acrobats had evacuated the arena overnight and a troupe of fire-eating tree elves had arrived to set up instead. "Not such a big surprise. Things do roll on."

"On the strength of this one accusation against Mombey, the war has been called for Loyal Oz? Who did the calling, then?"

"I have a theory, Rain," said the Lion. "Hiding in the heart of every downtrodden commoner is where the romance of the crown lives strongest. Alarming, I

know. The citizens of Oz struck with mobs and protests, days and nights of rioting, and neither army
would take up weapons against them."

"How is Tip? Brrr, I know what happened. I'm not
blind. And I think maybe I've always known. Just tell
me—how is Tip?"

He had to decide if she was working him to find out
what little he knew himself, and had heard, or if she
was confessing a knowledge beyond his. Probably the
latter. For all her youth she was proving basalt at the
bone.

"Dorothy and Iskinaary have gone to reconnoiter.
The Goose sent a report via that Wren. Tip is recovering nicely enough, that's what is said on the streets.
The Hall of Approval has been meeting right next
door, in our own Aestheticum, to try to work out the
proper course of action, but Tip isn't attending—hasn't
the strength yet."

"Where is my . . . where is my friend?" she ventured.

"They've made space in a private apartment in
Madame Teastane's Female Seminary, which is somewhere on the edge of Goldhaven."

"With attendants, I assume. An armored guard."

"Well." The Lion tried to smile. "An old chum of
yours, as I understand it. A woman from Shiz named

Miss Ironish. She's been brought in from St. Prowd's, since Madame Teastane's staff and students all fled the city weeks ago and are sitting out the troubles comfortably on the shores at Lake Chorge. Miss Ironish claims to have known Tip in a small but honorable way. Her blameless record convinced the Emperor that she was the right one for the job."

"And Mombey?"

"Ah, that's another story. Some say she's in Southstairs, secreted there for her own safety under cover of darkness. The Palace will neither confirm nor deny that rumor. Others say Mombey accidentally called her own past upon her as she called that of others, and too much corruption crept up in her blood, and she expired of extreme old age as she ought to have done a century ago. That's hard to confirm or deny either, and the Palace has its reasons for keeping the matter in doubt. They don't want to be accused by patriotic Munchkinlanders of having assassinated the Munchkinlander Eminence the minute she entered the capital."

"What do you think?"

"I think if she had the strength to change her visage just one last time, she became a woggle-bug and someone stepped on her in the rush to catch the latest newsfold."

"Or swatted her with a rolled-up newsfold."

He waited.

"I learned how to read, once upon a time," she told him. "I can read the headlines, you know."

"I suppose you can."

"The royalists will be having mighty parties."

"It's too early to tell. Though the confetti factories are probably going into overnight shifts."

She sighed. "And my great-uncle?"

"Well, it's all up in the air still, isn't it? There's the question of how ready to rule the new leader might be. As we know from Dorothy, age doesn't always constitute wisdom. And people grow up on different schedules, one from the next."

"Has Shell abdicated the throne?"

"It's still unsettled whether the Palace will accept a return to the rule of monarchy. And the question of whether the monarch wants to rule. I understand there is human choice involved."

"I don't know if there is," said Rain.

"Oh," said the Lion. "Don't give me that. I'm the Cowardly Lion, remember. There's always human choice."

She put her face to his shoulder, her greening hand upon his paw. "All right then," she said. "Enough grieving. Can you make arrangements for me to have an audience?"

"I have it on the highest authority that Tip has been waiting for you to ask."

"Who's authority is that high?"

"A little Bird told me."

9.

Miss Ironish opened the door of Madame Teastane's Female Seminary. She shooed the guards on the stoop to one side and told them if they didn't stop bristling their bayonets in her face she'd give them what for and no mistake. "Come in, Miss Rainary," she said. A new sobriety had tightened her corset. She never mentioned the change in Rain's appearance, except to mutter, "My, how you've grown."

Scarly took Rain's umbrella and put it against a hat stand.

"I believe you will be comfortable in the parents' parlor," said Miss Ironish. "Scarly will bring you a biscuit or a glass of water if you like. Please wait here and I will announce the Crown in a few moments."

"I can help myself to a glass of—"

"This is hard on everyone," said Miss Ironish sternly. "Wait."

She left the room with a backward glance rich in opprobrium. A few moments later Scarly tiptoed in with three lemon brickums and a cheese tempto congealing upon a porcelain salver. Apparently school fare didn't improve even for royalty.

"Miss Rainary," said Scarly, moving out of the sight of the crowds who haunted the paving stones, the faithful who waited outside day and night, desperate to catch a glimpse of the miracle. "Oh, Miss Rainary." She couldn't control the gasp in her voice.

"I hope it isn't too horrible," said Rain, a little coldly.

"It en't horrible," said Scarly, and she took Rain's hand. She could get nothing else out, though, and fled through the butler's pantry when she heard Miss Ironish return.

"You may arise, Miss Rainary," said Miss Ironish, and stood back against the door as Tip came through, making every effort not to twist her hands. Miss Ironish retreated and the door closed firmly though without the sound of a click.

Rain said, "Am I to call you Ozma?"

"You may call me Tip," she answered.

"I'm told that when you discovered what had happened, you fainted dead away. I thought, when I could think, 'Well, isn't that just like a girl.'"

"Not funny, Rain. Under the circumstances. How did you find out?"

Rain neither moved away nor did she come closer, and neither did Ozma Tippetarius. They stood nine feet apart on opposite margins of a sun-bleached carpet. "I suppose—I don't know—maybe I dreamed it."

"You're lying. You don't lie. Have you changed?"

"Well." She held up her green fingers. "A little."

Tip waited.

"Tay always liked you," said Rain, "and Tay didn't like men, generally."

"Was that it?"

Rain thought. "Yes, I think that was it."

"You've never even known if Tay is male or female itself, have you? Yet you claim to know how Tay can respond to me, even when a disguise is laid upon me for—for all those years I can't remember?"

"We're unlikely to make an acceptable ruling couple," said Rain. "For one thing, you're about a hundred years older than I am."

"Well, I hide it well, don't I." The tone was bitter.

"You knew it all along," said Rain.

"I didn't. Mombey kept me apart from other children. We always shifted about every few years. I'm told most childhoods feel eternal, Rain. Mine did too. I wasn't to know it was longer than anyone else's. Perhaps I wasn't smart, but grant me that. Or maybe Mombey charmed some sense of calendar out of me. It doesn't matter. We've both had our childhoods filched from us, Rain. There's that. If there's nothing else."

"There's that," Rain agreed.

They stole glances at each another, the green girl and the queen of Oz. Those forgotten called forward, against their wishes, into themselves. Rain might as well have been Elphaba at sixteen. Ozma Tippetarius had eyes the color of half-frozen water.

They could not cross the carpet to take each other in their arms. Maybe someday, but not today. More of their childhoods had to be stolen, yet, for that to happen—or maybe some of it returned to them. The charmless future would show them if, and when, and how.

VIII

Somewhere

1.

In the streets of the city they were saying that Ozma had come back. Within weeks, illustrated pamphlets in six colors became available at every vendor. One edition with bronze ink on the cover cost two farthings extra and sold out to collectors in an hour. It purported to present an entire modern history of Oz, starting with the arrival of the Wizard and the deposing of the Ozma Regent, Pastorius. The best part was a grotesquely colored section that everyone turned to first: the murder of Pastorius. Oh, the blood! Like a fountain all down the steps of the Palace of the Ozmas. Then the Wizard's vile contract with Mombey, Pale Queen of Sorcery, to secret the child away while the Wizard set up shop to hunt for the fabled Grimmerie. For which he'd come to Oz in the first place, and over which, failing to secure it, he left, disconsolate.

In one of the final panels of that section, Mombey secretly made a pact with the Ozmists, and siphoned a zephyr or so of them for pumping up the Wizard's balloon, to assure he could never return across the Deadly Sands. A lovely and theatrical conceit, if unsupportable by the testimony of witnesses, who wrote letters to the editor complaining about the rewriting of history. The liberties these artists take! Hacks, the lot of them.

Dorothy had her own section. Part III. They colorized her too highly and she looked like a Quadling afflicted with St. Skimble's Rash. With her familiar, Toto, who could speak in the funny pages (*arf arf!*), Dorothy careered around Oz like some sort of a drunken sorceress, spilling mayhem out of her basket and kicking up her sparkly heels in musical numbers that didn't translate particularly well on the page.

A nod was made to Elphaba and to Nessarose Thropp, and to Dorothy's crime spree against them. However, maybe because the Emperor was about to abdicate the Throne Ministership of Oz, his portrayal was accorded a certain respect, if only for his having served as a place holder until Ozma could be released from her spell. How quickly a history of offenses can be rewritten. Yet there was some sour truth to it: Shell Thropp may have ordered the invasion of Munchkinland, but *he* hadn't killed Pastorius. Nor had he imprisoned Ozma

Tippetarius in a spell so deep it could keep her in a near perpetual boyhood until, through trickery played by a magic mouse (a magic *mouse?*) La Mombey accidentally reversed her own spell, revealing her depraved plan for world dominance. Or Oz dominance.

The extravaganza went into seven printings in a fortnight. It didn't begin to show up wrapped around take-out fried fish for at least a month.

Little was made in print, either by the popular press or by pulpit expositories, of the material waste and psychic distress of the recent past. The dragons of Colwen Grounds, the war, the long privations, the fight for water, the death of so many on both sides of the conflict. The negotiations remained in a delicate stage. It didn't do to allow sensibilities to become inflamed with reference to abominations too recent to be forgiven—if ever they could be forgiven.

Would Ozma come to rule? How would her legitimacy be determined since eighty-five years, give or take, had passed since her birth, but she was apparently still in her minority? Had Mombey herself not unwittingly identified the girl as Ozma—by that unsavory magicking of Tip homeward from boy to girl—the metamorphosis might have gone unremarked as any other backstreet carnival trick. (The details of the transformation were too squeamish for most citizens to

imagine closely, except the depraved.) "Not Ozma!"
Mombey had cried, out of her skull. Everyone present
had heard her, and when Tip had been carried away for
medical attention, the form of a teenage girl in a lad's
dress sartorials had escaped no one's notice. (A number
of men had trouble satisfying their wives for months in
the ensuing vexation to their own makeup.)

Whether Ozma still wore the red locket on its
chain—only one person knew enough to ask that question, and she would not ask it.

Hardly anyone else alive had ever seen Tip's mother,
Ozma the Bilious. No one could comment on any
family resemblance the new Ozma might have to her
forebears except by the fading rotogravured portraits
that had remained hung, seditiously, during the reigns
of the various Throne Ministers, in houses left shabby
because their tenants could never afford redecoration.

And would Ozma Tippetarius accept the mantle?
Did she have to? Did she have a choice?

Furthermore, would Munchkinland accept *her* as a
ruler of a reunited Oz? No stalwart Munchkinlander
could forget the crunchy little fact that the Ozma clan
was Gillikinese. But it was Mombey who'd brought
Ozma Tippetarius back to the throne from Munchkinland, which gave the rebel nation a stake. Before a
month had passed some began, quietly, to call Mombey

the savior of the nation. Without an Ozma to pull the warring factions together, the fighting might have gone on a good deal longer.

It was said that at Haugaard's Keep, on Restwater, when they learned what a mess things had gotten to in the Emerald City, General Traper Cherrystone called a ceasefire and invited the Foill of Munchkinland into the Keep to discuss an end to the hostilities. No one was quite sure what happened next. The only witness was a tree elf named Jibbidee, and he wasn't talking. In the Oak Parlor of the Florinthwaite Club, bruited about over a third glass of port, thank you, retired military officers whispered the rumors. Loyal Oz's General Cherrystone had proposed to General Jinjuria that together they decline to accept the nonsense about the return of Ozma to the Emerald City, join forces, and rule as a military tribunal over Restwater themselves, setting up a protectorate over the access rights to the great lake. Jinjuria was said to have refused, whereupon Cherrystone shot her, and then took his own life.

The legal standing and even location of Lady Glinda Chuffrey of Mockbeggar Hall remained unknown.

So, too, the confused reputation of the Wicked Witch of the West. But in the rush of sentimental and even patriotic fervor that greeted the unexpected return of Ozma Tippetarius, word began to circulate that the great spell cast by La Mombey, to call the lost forward, had done more than stay Liir Thropp from his death and reveal the green skin of his daughter, Rain. It had done more than sabotage Mombey's own plan to keep Ozma Tippetarius young, hidden, dumb, and male for another hundred or two hundred years. Mombey's application of the spell from the Grimmerie, they said, had also inadvertently summoned Elphaba Thropp from—well, from wherever it was she had gone.

"As if she'd come back when asked," said Mr. Boss. "What do they think she is? A charwoman?" The accidental family—what was left of it with the death of Nor, with the departure for Nether How of a frosty Liir and an angry Candle and an eye-rolling though mute Goose—was squatting in a garden flat below a shell-shocked semidetached villa off the Shiz Road in the Northtown neighborhood. Rain had refused to follow her parents unless she had settled things in her own mind.

Until the circumstances righted themselves somehow, they'd resigned themselves to this dump for the winter. The rising damp gave them all headaches of a morning but tenacious ivy hid the worst of the damage to the building's exterior plaster. The place had views on a strip of garden that hadn't benefited from the firebombing of the dragons a few months ago. None-theless, Tay liked to climb on what remained of the shattered ornamental cherryfern.

"I can understand the rage for Elphaba. It's more convenient to have a hero waiting in the wings than to endure a blowhard standing in the spotlight," said the Lion. "Didn't Nor used to say that? Also easier on your moral comfort, for one thing, to keep waiting for redemption of one sort or another rather than work it out for yourself. Since its time hasn't arrived yet."

"Well, *that's* a matter of opinion we never asked you for," said Dorothy, who had agreed to return to the fold after Liir had made his departure. "Just for that, I think I'm going to do my warm-ups. Right here."

"I mean, look," explained the Lion. "The so-called where's-the-Witch mania has simply displaced Ozma hunger, that's all. No one alive can remember what it was like to live under blood royalty. Three genera-tions have grown up without the crown—to go back to it again just like that satisfies the appetite for resolu-tion too quickly. People *need* something to be missing. They need to crave something they don't have."

"It used to be Lurline, when I was growing up," said Little Daffy. "Lurline would come back eventually and grace us all with the spirit of better posture, or some-thing. If the Ozma vacancy has been filled, then the people on the street need a new hunger. Why shouldn't it be for that old witch?"

"This new hunger you're talking about," said the dwarf. "Better get going or we'll miss the morning rush."

They were making quite a killing with Little Daffy's Munchkinlander Munchies. Once they had set aside enough capital they were planning to fund a trip back to the Sleeve of Ghastille to harvest more of the secret ingredient.

"There's someone here at the door," called Mr. Boss as he and Little Daffy were leaving with their bakery wheelbarrow.

"It'll be for you, Dorothy. You go. I've got blisters from padding halfway across town chasing after your damn dog," said the Lion. "It doesn't know how to pee without dashing all the way to Burntpork. Dorothy, if you don't get that Toto a leash and a muzzle, I'm going to get one for you."

"You try muzzling me and watch the nation rise against you."

Dorothy came back. "For you, Brrr," she said. "They asked for *Sir Brrr*." She mimed a mean little curtsey but ruffled his mane as he went by. "Where is Rain, anyway?" she asked in general, but only a grandmother clock ticked in answer. Brrr had gone into the garden to talk to a military guard of some sort. No one else was home.

For a few days, like the other curiosity seekers who thronged the kerbstones of Great Pullman Street, Rain found herself drawn to the facade of Madame Teastane's Female Seminary. A sober building made of brick, painted in a no-nonsense black flatwash and finished in white trim, it signaled with confidence the rectitude of public office. The windows at street level remained curtained. No one came and no one went except ministers, who refused to comment. Rain saw Avaric bon Tenmeadows once, with a satchel, ducking a rotten apricot lobbed at him by someone impatient for news of the Ozma. Their queen. If queen she was.

Rain's life had been spent in hiding. Disguised with ordinariness. She now felt cursed with this glare of green upon wrists and cheeks and everywhere else— she couldn't bear to look at herself much. But as she wandered about the streets of the Emerald City like any one of the thousand paupers hoping to filch a meal, cadge a donation from some softie, work for an hour or maybe fall in love for less, she realized that no one bothered to bother her.

She hadn't needed to hide her whole life long. No one wanted to find her anyway.

The winter had come in mild, and the shrubbery of the Oz Deer Park remained in sufficient leaf to give her cover. She felt she blended in better than, say, the starving families of the Quadling Corner, who took the most menial jobs and for breakfast ate paper and leaves with mustard. She could walk along the Ozma Embankment, looking for her life. Wherever it might be.

It wasn't housed on a top floor of Madame Teastane's Female Seminary, that much was certain.

Perhaps, she thought, she would go up to Shiz. If they would have her. She was a year early but Miss Ironish had concluded that, against all odds, Rain was clever. Perhaps she could have a private tutor for a year to prepare. She didn't quite qualify as a legacy student, as her grandmother had never matriculated. But those were mere details. Miss Ironish could arrange it.

Tay scampered after Rain but she felt the creature was suffering from the lack of a campaign. Maybe she would take it back to Quadling Country and release it to its companions. Male or female, it could find what company it might. Perhaps she owed the rice otter that much.

She was circling around the ramparts of Southstairs Prison, slowly heading for home, or what passed for home, when she stopped to let a carriage go by. Two small children of the Vinkus—Arjikis, she thought, in those leggings—were splashing in the gutters. "A lion could beat a dragon any day," said one, speaking pidgin Ozish. "Could not," said the other. "Brrr could," protested the first, "now he's in charge."

That was how Rain learned that Tip had accepted the institutional role of the Ozma only provisionally, on a condition of deferred elevation. Tip had finalized a military settlement for peace by proposing for elevation to Throne Minister, as her regent, the Lord Low Plenipotentiary from Traum, Gillikin. None other than Sir Brrr. The Cowardly Lion as he once had been known. When Ozma reached her maturity, she would reconsider whether to rule.

Well well, thought Rain, Tip had only a handful of days in which to ascertain the Lion's strengths. And all he had done during that period following Nor's death was to grieve. Is that, in the end—that capacity to hurt—the most essential ingredient for a ruler?

In a ceremony of surpassing simplicity, Sheltergod Thropp, His Sacredness, turned over the accoutrements of power to the Cowardly Lion. Shell handed over two keys, a few folded documents, some receipts for personal items that had gone missing during his term in office, and one or two crowns. He wasn't sure which was more legitimate, so Brrr had them placed on a wooden hat rack in his dressing room where they wouldn't pester his mane. He hated to have his waves flattened now that he could afford to have them done again.

"You'll stay for the formal investiture?" the Lion asked Shell.

"I don't believe so, if you don't mind."

"We are recalling Lady Glinda from Munchkinland."

"I never cared much for Glinda. No, I'll just tootle along if it's all the same to you."

"But where will you go? Private life could afford little by way of satisfaction to one of your, um, background."

The former Emperor said, "There was a story my old Nanny used to tell me at darktime. A fisherman and his fishwife lived by the side of the mythical sea that shows up in so many old tales. The fisherman caught a great thumping carp, all covered in golden scales. The Fish spoke—fish can talk in stories, you know—and in return for being thrown back into the sea, it promised to give the man a wish. The man couldn't think of much to wish for—a ladle for his wife, maybe—but when he got home that night and she had a ladle, she hit him with it for having such low self-esteem as to request only a kitchen implement. Go back, she said, and ask for something better. I want a cottage, not this bucket of seaweed we sleep in. A cottage with real glass windows, and roses round the dovecote."

"Indeed," said the Lion, who had always felt skittish about stories and anyway had a country to begin running.

"You can imagine how it goes. She kept sending him back over and over. The Fish was obliging. Whatever the fishwife wanted, the fishwife got. And it was never enough. In succession, she required to be a duchess, to have a castle, to be a queen, to have a palace, to be an empress and have an empire. Why the man didn't throw *her* into the sea, I don't know. Stories don't make much sense sometimes."

"He must have loved her."

"Eventually, in the teeth of a horrible storm, lightning and thunders from all sides, she demanded to be made like the Unnamed God itself. Quaking for his life, the fisherman crawled to the sea and made the petition. The golden Fish said, 'Just go back, she's got what she wished for.' And when he went back home—"

"She wore the golden sun on her brow and the silver moon on her fanny," guessed the Lion.

"She was sitting in the bucket of seaweed again."

"She overreached herself," said the Lion. "Ah, morals."

"Or did she?" said Shell. "Perhaps the most godly thing is to be poor, after all, to give up trappings and influence."

"So." The Lion was trying to steer this interview to a close. "You're going to take up telling stories to children during Library Hour?"

Shell clasped his hands. Only now did the Lion notice they were mottled and trembling. Shell had his sister Elphaba's long nose, and a drip was forming just below the tip. High sentiment, or an aggrieved immune system? "There are rumors of caves in the Great Kells—as far as Kiamo Ko, even farther. Hermits go there to live, to hide, to die. Sometimes earthquakes come and bury them in their homes. I should be prepared for that, don't you think?"

The Lion didn't reply. He was learning to hold his opinion to himself. For a few years, until Ozma was ready, he was no more or less than Oz itself. Oz didn't have opinions. It had presence.

Plans for the installation of Brrr as Throne Minister would have involved Rain, but she couldn't bear to be close to Ozma in some public setting. Ozma—Tip—Ozma (but which one?) had the greatest power in the country, and could send for Rain at any hour of any day, for a private audience, and Rain would have come. But that message never arrived. So the thought of accepting a formal invitation to sit in a formal chair for hours a few feet away from the young monarch-in-waiting gave Rain a feeling in her chest as if her very heart was somehow suffocating in there.

But she had no heart, she'd given it away.

Her accidental family never mentioned the matter. They protested, too robustly to be convincing, that they would much rather stay home with her. They preferred cards. But when the afternoon of the Lion's elevation arrived, a scrappy sense of jubilation broke through anyway. Little Daffy and Mr. Boss celebrated by whooping it up like a couple of teenagers, drinking too much whiskey-sweet from a hip flask. Dorothy sat in the garden even though the air had turned chilly. When the time came near for the actual coronation, the four of them changed their minds, linked arms—well, Little Daffy and Mr. Boss linked arms and, at a different altitude, so did Rain and Dorothy—and they hurried through the streets to stand at the back of the crowd and watch from afar. Both the hall and the piazza in front were hung with banners of Ozian emerald, but they were interspersed with standards of red and gold. The Lion's chosen colors, perhaps. They tended to mute the patriotism of the event in a way Rain admired.

The music was atrocious, though, and way too loud.

Just before Rain slipped out of the proceedings a guard collared her and said, "*There* you are. You're requested in a reception room in Mennipin Square this evening."

Her heart skipped up some stairs. "Surely you've mistaken me for someone else."

"Not bloody likely." He grinned at her. "You don't exactly pass, you know."

She supposed she didn't. "I don't want to meet Ozma in some chaperoned chamber—" she began.

He interrupted. "Begging your pardon. I'm not representing Ozma."

She waited until she could govern her quavering voice. "I see. Then am I under arrest?"

"Only socially. Do you want an escort?"

"Are you offering to be my boyfriend?"

He blushed. "No, miss, and no offense intended. I merely meant to suggest if you didn't care to travel alone at night—there's some young ladies who wouldn't dare, you see—I was offering my services, I mean the services of my regiment. Miss."

"Well, I'm not one who is troubled by being out at night," said Rain, and took down the address. She had accepted no invitation to dance at any of the installation balls that were mounted all over the city.

With whom would she dance? Her grandmother's old broom?

She walked to the assignation more or less impervious to the explosions of colored lights that scratched themselves against the black sky over standing sections of the Palace of the People. She thought she could hear Dorothy leading a sing-along at the Lady's Mystique, but that couldn't be right. Now that the official business was over, Dorothy would be at the Lion's side. Must be one of those entertainers who impersonated her. Rain moved herself along.

Crossing a bridge over one of the nicer city canals, Rain paused for a moment to look at the pyrotechnics reflected in the water. The fireworks were like great colored spiders. For an instant she saw the Emerald City under attack again, this time by monstrous insects. But Mombey was in custody now, and her bloodhound spiders no longer hunting for Rain or the Grimmerie. The past was the past. Rain had to get out of here. She was going mad.

At first she didn't recognize the man who answered the door. Neither did he twig in to who Rain was until they had said their good evenings to each other. Their voices cued them both. Then she fell into his arms in a way she had never fallen into her father's. Puggles said, "To think I lived to see this day! You are a sight for sore eyes."

"No, I make eyes sore. Tell the truth!"

But they laughed, and she had not laughed—well, she hadn't laughed much in her life at all. Had she.

"So this is Lady Glinda's house? Why didn't they just tell me?"

"She doesn't want her circumstances to be widely known," said Puggles. "It's a temporary posting, you see. She can't be bothered to become engaged in the skeltery-heltery of social callers. Not under these conditions."

"May I ask what conditions you're being cagy about?"

"I'll leave it to her to tell you herself. She's awaiting you in the front parlor. Can you see yourself up? The double doors on the right. I can't do the stairs as well as I ought."

She was halfway up but turned and called lightly to him, "Puggles? What happened to Murthy?"

He shook his head and made some obscure pious gesture that country folk persisted in making, against all odds.

Lady Glinda sat in warm lamplight with a throw rug upon her knees.

"I should have thought you'd be kicking up your heels at the prime event," said Rain, coming in as if she'd just gone to pick up a pack of perguenays at the local newsagent.

"Oh, I've long since gotten over the taste for fuss, though I was obscenely pleased to be extended an invitation."

"A former Throne Minister of Oz, no less, taking a quiet night at home, and on such a night. You surprise me."

"Come here, my dear, and stop remonstrating. Let me look at you."

Lady Glinda's voice was still warm, but a little frail, and a tremor pestered the stem of her neck so her chin dove and rose in the tiniest of hummingbird flutters. She hadn't lost her taste for pearls, and the at-home tiara was vintage Glinda, though it looked as if it had gotten sat upon more than once. So too the spectacles that fell on a loop from Lady Glinda's neck. She'd been reading. Who knew.

Glinda put the pince-nez to her face. "So it's true. Oh, my darling, it's true."

"That I've gone native?"

Glinda nodded and patted the sofa next to her. "I had to accept it on faith, you know—that you were Liir's daughter. By the time I met you the concealing spell had already been cast. You could have been any other urchin child brought for protection to a big house and left there by a loving and canny parent who didn't know how to care for a child."

Rain said, "They dropped me off like laundry, didn't they? To be washed and dried and cared for? By a stranger."

"Now don't be like that, child. They were under extraordinary pressures. We all were, back then. Some of us still are."

"Tell me about it."

"They did the best they could. Besides, I was hardly a stranger. I had known your grandmother. We were like this." She twinned her second and third fingers together as if they might strangle each other.

"All that I might have had of them," said Rain. "Access to my mother's instincts for the present, for knowing the truth of what was happening now, here. Access to my father's occasional capacity to read the past, to tell it. And what did I get in exchange?"

"You lived," said Glinda simply. "You survived. I won't say in style, for I can see that doesn't mean a whole lot to you."

"I lived alone," said Rain. "Until General Cherrystone came to Mockbeggar Hall and put you under house arrest, I had the run of the kitchen yard and the

run of the backstairs workrooms and the ledge at the
edge of the lake from which to jump into the water.
There were people everywhere but no one was mine,
and I was no one's. I can't repair that."

"The history of a nation was happening around you.
Children don't often notice this, but it happens, most
years, to be true. For you no less than some, but no
more, either. Every child makes its peace with aban-
donment. That's called growing up, Rain."

"My first memories are of mice, and fish, and a frog
in the mud," said Rain.

"Is that anyone's fault?" replied Glinda. "And is that
so terrible, after all?"

"No one has to be so alone." She gritted her teeth.
"I pushed my hand in the pocket of ice and pulled up a
little golden fish, and saw how alone it was. It was the
first family I had, you know."

Glinda sighed. "Your hand was bare. The fish
flopped upon it, I suppose? Tickled some, maybe?"

"Yes. Just about my earliest memory, I think."

"Who do you think was holding your mittens while
you pawed about to rescue the fish?"

Rain looked at her lap.

"Who do you think put the fish back in the water
so it could swim to its own kind when the sun went
down?"

The spectacles slid off Glinda's lap into a pile of knitting on the floor.

"Who do you think walked you back across the weir and handed you over for a bath to warm you up?"

Rain said, "And you didn't even know if I was really Elphaba's granddaughter."

"And I didn't know if you were Elphaba's granddaughter."

They had tea brought in by a parlor maid. Glinda showed Rain her collection of bubbles on ormolu stands. "Don't talk to me about the present," said Glinda. "I know something about what is going on. Tell me what you've done. Where you've been since you left Mockbeggar all those years ago."

Rain obliged with brevity. Glinda paid only scant attention, taking up her knitting and counting stitches under her breath. When Rain began to talk about the Chancel of the Ladyfish above the Sleeve of Ghastille, though, Glinda began to listen more closely. "Describe that place to me," she said. "I love architecture, you know. It's one of my passions. Always was."

Rain did the best she could—the low stumped pillars, the altarpiece built lengthwise into the wall, the view from the height. The figure of the fishy goddess or whatever it was. "I never could do mythology," admitted Glinda. "The Great Morphologies of vin Tessarine totally defeated me back at Shiz. I cheated on the final, but don't tell anyone or they'll revoke my grade, which wasn't very high even with the cheating."

"I don't do mythology either," said Rain.

"It's the building I'm interested in," said Lady Glinda. "The way you describe it sited on that slope. I've always paid attention to the temples of Lurline—so many small and insignificant Lurline sightings were claimed in the Pertha Hills of my childhood. The dales are positively crusty with chapels. You can't ride the hounds without breaking your mount's leg at least once a season on some sacred stone omphalos overgrown with ivy. But what you describe doesn't sound Lurlinist to me, or if it is, it represents a watery variation of the myth of our sky-goddess and avatrice."

"The great stone woman was maternal and stern and supplied with a fishtail. Beyond that I can't say; I don't remember the details. I had just met up with my parents for the first time in memory and frankly I was distracted by the inconvenience of them."

"Well, if I had to venture an opinion at a meeting of the Crowned Heads' Book Discussion Group and Jug Band, I'd guess your parents stumbled upon the remnants of a temple built for quite a different purpose than the consolidation of religious feeling. It sounds more like a business center to me. Commerce always builds fancier temples than faith does."

"A fishmongery in the highlands?" Rain laughed. "You ought to have studied for that test a little harder."

"Well, if you go up to Shiz, you study for me, now, will you? Learn from my mistakes." Glinda laughed too. "Rain, what *will* you do?"

"I don't know."

"Do good, though, will you?" She blinked brightly at the green girl. "If not for your parents or your grand-mother, then for me?"

"I don't know what good I could do."

"None of us does. That doesn't let us off the hook."

"What will you do?" asked Rain challengingly.

Glinda sighed. "Haven't you heard?"

Rain shook her head.

"I am being sent to Southstairs. I go tomorrow."

"What for? That's impossible!"

"It's not impossible and now don't you go upsetting yourself or you'll upset me. It's quite right and proper that I pay for my mistakes. When I was at Mockbeggar Hall I unleashed the power of the Grimmerie against those dragons, and the dragons were indirectly under the supervision of Shell Thropp. I attacked the armed forces of the Throne Minister of Oz, Rain. That's just about treason. I can be pardoned, but not quickly.

Haste would not be seemly. The Lion, if he's to rule wisely and deserve the trust of the citizens of Oz, must be seen to have no favorites. Including me. Justice demands no less. I am a former Throne Minister but I'm not above making mistakes. I leave in the morning." She laughed. "I had been hoping to finish this little bed-jacket before I went, but I think I'm going to have to have the carriage stop at Brickle Lane on the way to Southstairs so I can pick up something ready-made. I don't want to arrive looking less than my best."

"But it's outrageous. Southstairs! If you go, I should go too."

"You were a child, dear. Not responsible. If you persist in objecting, you're a child still." She put out her hand so Rain could help her stand. "I mustn't keep you, dear. And I have much to attend to myself. I just so wanted to know if it was true, and now I know. Maybe Elphaba will come back one day, or maybe she won't, but in the meantime I have known you. That will see me through, I do believe."

Elphaba is not coming back, thought Rain, but she couldn't bring herself to say it. Not to an old fool like Glinda.

"Oh, Rain," said Glinda, when the girl was almost out the door. "One more thing. About Tip. You may think that a story should have a happy ending—"

"Whoever told me stories?" asked Rain. "I'm not looking for happiness. But I'm not looking for an ending either." She wouldn't talk about Tip to Glinda. She just waggled her green fingers and slipped away.

It wasn't hard for Rain to get the attention of the Cowardly Lion, though it was difficult to get a private moment. He was surrounded by staff.

"I want architects from the planning council all over that dome, do you hear me. Extra buttressing against tremors. Talk to some professor of aesthetics about the designs if you must, but I want to approve them. I don't care which college, pull a straw from a broom and make a wish. Tell the Glikkun contingent they can go to hell. No, don't tell them that; give them some chits for supper and have them come back after dark. Pursley, have you the list? I want a delegate sent to the town of Tenniken to see if you can find any contemporaries who knew a soldier named Jemmsy. Died in the Great Gillikin Forest thirty odd years ago, a member of the Wizard's army. Don't ask me why, just do it. I'm issuing a new line of medals for courage, and his relatives deserve a whole bunch of them. They can flog them in the streets for all I care."

Rain almost grinned. The rogue Lion as a functionary of the government.

"Was Rain here? Where is she? There you are, my dear. Have you come to advise me about the Glikkuns? They've refused to be party to the peace we brokered with Munchkinlanders and a nasty little situation is brewing up in the Scalps. Sakkali Oafish, the troll chieftain, wants nothing to do with me. The harridan. We go back a ways. I wouldn't be surprised if she tried to get the Nome King involved. Common cause among the trollfolk. It appears history is going to keep happening, despite our hopes for retirement. And what about the Munchkinlander problem? They're not cooperating with my proposal of extension of health benefits to the Animals who served in their army. Can we be shocked, do you think?"

"You look in clover, Brrr. If not particularly rested."

"It's the weskit, isn't it? A Rampini original. How do you like the curls?"

She shook her head.

"I was afraid so, but I've gotten used to them. It keeps the mane out of my eyes without my having to resort to a hairband. Now, about the color? I was silvering prematurely, but is this look a bit rancid?"

"You're expecting Muhlama H'aekeem to come find you here, now you're single again and, oh, by the way, the *king of the forest*. Ha!"

"Ha," he agreed, brought down a bit. "She hated authority. Did everything in her power to avoid it. She didn't come to the installation nor send a card. When did the noble old concept of tribute go out of style? Well, maybe when my term limit has expired, she'll show up again." He began to comb out his whiskers with his claws, worrying in advance.

"Brrr. Pay attention. You can't seriously be intending to put Lady Glinda in Southstairs prison?"

The assistants bustled, but more quietly, so they could eavesdrop. He roared them out of the room, but then told Rain she had understood the matter perfectly correctly. He hoped it would not be for long. Glinda would be given every courtesy possible under the circumstances, but liberty was costly, and she would have to pay. "It's for the good of the nation, Rain," he said. "I shall haul her up again just the first moment that my advisors recommend it safe to the polity to do so."

Mister Mikko, the Ape, came to the door with a few statements needing signatures, but Brrr sent him packing. "So glad to be able to put him on payroll. I owe him. Now what are we going to do about Dorothy?" he asked Rain.

"Don't look at me," said Rain "You're the Ozma Regent now."

"She hangs around the Emerald City any longer, she'll become a demagogue," said the Lion. "Either that, or a parody of herself. Like the rest of us."

"What does she want?"

"Well, I believe she wants to go home. Again. Doesn't she?"

"Last I heard. She's not insane, you know. I'd want to leave too."

"But I haven't got any ideas," said Brrr. "I'm the leader now; I don't have time to think."

"We could always try the Grimmerie," said Rain.

"Mister Mikko, bring the book from the treasury," roared Brrr. "I do so love having my whims indulged in," he admitted to Rain. "How about some chocolates?"

"You'll suffer again, Brrr. No elevation is eternal."

"Don't I know it. I'm just trying to have fun while it lasts."

So, thought Rain, an Animal as Throne Minister of Oz. After all this time. Whatever would Elphaba think of that?

Dorothy's departure from Oz was arranged so hastily that Little Daffy and Mr. Boss were absent—out of town, engaged in their harvesting expedition in the Sleeve of Ghastille. They didn't get to say farewell, or anything saltier.

Before dawn, Brrr escaped his royal guards and commandeered a hansom cab so he could make his goodbyes to Dorothy in person. He met Rain and Mister
Mikko in the insalubrious courtyard of a private atelier in the Lower Quarter, a back-neighborhood place
Mister Mikko had located where they might attract less
attention. Mister Mikko commandeered the book. An
elderly chatelaine, Miss Pfanee, opened the gate to the
few who had gathered. She curtseyed low when she saw
the Cowardly Lion among the delegation. His presence
had not been advertised. But when she caught sight
of Rain gleaming green in the predawn gaslight, she
gasped and fled and didn't come back.

Amid the wheelbarrows and compost and some
rangy geraniums put out to die but refusing, so far,
Rain settled on an old blanket and touched the Grimmerie for the first time since the pine barrens above
Mockbeggar Hall.

Mister Mikko stood on one side, almost asleep from
the strain of his new responsibilities. Dorothy knelt at
the other, Toto gnawing the edge of one of her heels.
Rain pulled back the cover. The book flew open to a
blank page—at least it began blank.

They didn't know the word for a *watermark*, but a
faint green huzzle of light seemed to radiate from the
page—so dimly at first that they thought it a refraction

cast by a drop of water balanced upon a nearby leaf. A zigzag—a *Z* escaped from the *O,* thought Rain. The edges of the image were blurred, as if they were made of the smallest bits of paper, the kind of airy nothings that fly in the light when the pages of a book are turned. Ozmists of the page, perhaps.

"It's almost Elphaba, isn't it," said Dorothy tearily.

"Nonsense," said Mister Mikko, who had taught Elphaba Thropp in the good old days, back at Shiz. "It's nothing at all like Elphaba. It's the soul of a deceased bookworm, nothing more. Let's get this over with."

"She's not coming back," said Dorothy, "and I'm not either."

Rain flipped through the pages, which were docile enough under her touch. *On the Extermination of Pests.* No! Dorothy was a hot ticket, but hardly a pest. *To Call Winter upon Water.* There it had all begun, for Rain: the beginning of a coherent memory of her own life, not just a collection of incidents. *For Tomfoolery, Its Eradication or Amplification.* Please.

Was there a spell *To Make the Heart Whole, Regardless?*

She better be careful before she mischiefed herself—or Ozma—into disaster.

She laughed when she saw the next page. *Gone with the Wind.* Well, Dorothy had arrived via a mighty big windstorm the first time, no? Maybe it was time to call it up again.

"Are you ready?" she asked Dorothy.

"Next time I want a holiday," said Dorothy, "I'm going to try overseas. The Levant, maybe. Or the Riviera. Or the Argentine pampas. Over the great ocean to meet the China people. All this gadding about Oz has confirmed in me a taste for travel."

"Overseas. Please." Rain looked up from where she was bent over the book. She knew herself well; she wasn't the type to mouth pithy sentiments suitable for crocheting. All she could think of to say was, "Dorothy, next time? Take out some travel insurance."

"Right. And I'm going to choose my fortune cookie a little more carefully next time too. Now listen. Rain." Ever tit for tat with Dorothy. "Before it's too late? Don't give up on Tip. I mean Ozma. There's so much ahead for you still. I wish—"

"Don't wish," said Rain, "don't start. Wishing only . . ."

"And about your grandmother," said Dorothy. "I don't know if—"

"I don't want to talk, I have work to do."

"I just mean," said Dorothy, smiling painfully, "there's no need for her to come back. I mean, look. Here you are."

Rain glanced around herself miserably. The Lion and Dorothy were gazing at her with watery grins. She wanted to throw a potted geranium at each one of them. "I'm going to send you on your way before you feed me any more of your nonsense," she barked.

Dorothy then turned to Brrr. "I used to like the Scarecrow best," she began.

He gruffed at her, "So did I. Now are you ready to take some advice from a Cowardly Lion? Make your way safely home. With our royal blessing. But when you get there, don't surrender, Dorothy. Never surrender."

"You didn't, did you," replied Dorothy. "Local Lion Makes Good. Well, first thing I'm going to do when I get back is find out what happened to Uncle Henry and Aunt Em, bless 'em. And if San Francisco is in as much of a mess as the Emerald City, well, I've learned something from Little Daffy about setting a bone. I'll pitch in. Singing all the way, of course." She was making fun of herself to settle her nerves. "We might've made a nice duo, Brrr, but courage called you elsewhere." They didn't speak again, but it took them a few moments to pull out of each other's grip.

Rain began to intone the spell. A small local windstorm kicked up from the cobbles. For a moment it looked like the Ozmists, once again, but it was grittier.

An updraft lifted Dorothy in the air as if she were flying high in the elevator she'd never stopped describing to anyone who would listen. All that was left of Toto, as Dorothy snatched him up, was a little pointed turd, which Mister Mikko kicked into the compost. No one had time to say good-bye to the dog. The basket in which Toto had traveled was left behind on the ground, rocking in the force of their disappearance.

Still, Tip remained in Madame Teastane's. Maybe, thought Rain, Tip is only waiting until the right moment to steal away. And then what? And then what? Crack open the Grimmerie and—and what? We'd do what? Steal from the truth and lock each other in disguises again? That could do no good.

But weeks went by, and then months. No message arrived.

When to stay any longer would be to accept paralysis as permanent, Rain readied to make her departure from the Emerald City. Once the warm weather settled in she would leave by foot. Alone. She sent word to the Cowardly Lion. He replied by messenger. Perhaps he'd experienced one too many good-byes. As casually as sharing a loaf of bread, Brrr deeded Rain the Grimmerie in its blue sack. "You're the only one who can use it," he wrote. "It's too dangerous to have in town. I don't want to know what you do with it, just don't bring it back to me. Love, Brrr."

A packet in brown paper, done up in string, slid out of the sack after the book. Rain opened it. A medal that said *COURAGE* on it. Brrr making fun of himself? The ribbon was of ivory silk with a silver thread. No doubt he'd supervised the design. She turned it over. Oooh, fancy, a bit of engraving. *RAIN,* it said. WHO KNOWS THE DIFFERENCE BETWEEN TIME PAST, PRESENT & TO COME.

The matinal hour suited her now. Ever since the day Dorothy had made it out of Oz—safely, one hoped, though if ever a girl was trouble prone it was La Gale of Kansas—Rain found that she preferred to walk the streets as night was shifting toward dawn. Perhaps at that hour a native greenness in the atmosphere hovers below the registration of our easily blinded eyes.

In any case, before dawn one weekday she put Tay in Toto's old basket and left it on the doorstep of Madame Teastane's Female Seminary. "For Tip" said her own note, "from Rain. For as long as Tay allows." Tay hadn't fussed at being left on Tip's doorstep. It was as if the rice otter knew where Tip was, and who Tip was, and what job it had to do. A small job of comfort, if green comfort was possible. Half a comfort. Who could say.

She walked to Nether How in total silence.

The next year, when the Grasstrail Train came through and delivered one of those color supplements to the gang at Kiamo Ko, Chistery borrowed Nanny's glasses and read every panel out loud to her.

"Oh my," said Nanny, and "Read that bit again, will you," and "Mercy!"

"And that's that," said Chistery when he was through.

"A load of hogswallop," said Nanny, "but affecting in its way. Is she coming back, do you think?"

"Elphaba?" said Chistery. "Now, Nanny."

"No, Rain, I mean," said Nanny. "Really, monkey-boy. I'm not moronic. She wouldn't care to stay around in the Emerald City. Do you think she's coming back here to live? This is her castle, after all. And something tells me she has that old book that has caused so much trouble."

Chistery was humbled by the correction. "I'm sorry," he said. "I have no clue about Rain's future. I thought you were asking if Elphaba was coming back."

"The very idea," said Nanny, removing the hard-boiled egg from its shell and settling down to eat the shell. "Besides," she said a few moments later, "Elphaba's already come back. I saw her last week on the stairs." But Chistery was clattering the cutlery. Having gone hard of hearing, he didn't take this in.

Candle and Liir lasted another year or so in the house at Nether How, but in the end, Candle decided to leave her husband. Rain wept and thought it was her fault. She shouldn't have come back; she shouldn't have brought her endless ache to infect the rooms of the cottage of her parents. She should be the one to go.

But Candle insisted she herself needed to light out until she could come to some understanding about how she could have been persuaded, all those years ago, to give their daughter's childhood away to someone else. She and Liir had never fought again, but nor had they spoken like lovers or even friends. It was time.

"My childhood was never yours to have, and anyway, you gave it to me the best way you could," said Rain, sniffling. She'd come to believe this.

"Liir was frightened for his life, so he was frightened for yours," said Candle of Liir. "When you were born green, he choked, and hid you away. I let it happen.

That's how it seems to me now, Little Green. Maybe I'll learn to forgive him, or to forgive myself. Maybe I'll come back then. I can only see the present, not the future."

After she was gone, Liir said, "I'm to blame for more than everything. And if I mention, Rain, that Candle left you first—when you were a newborn—it was for a good reason. To save you. She knew who you were. She had that touch. She knew you'd survive, and she left you for me to find. She had that confidence in you and that instinct to protect you too. Maybe what she's doing now—for you, for me—is no less kind. Though we can't see it yet. She does see the present, remember." He tried to disguise a wince. "I can vouch for that. On some level, as an Elephant, I was dead to her—that's probably why she couldn't see the present, see me as still alive."

"Do you think she's gone off to find the famous Trism? Now that you located him after all these years?" Rain couldn't help herself; it was easier to hurt someone else than to plumb her own griefs.

"You know," said Liir, "when I met your mother at the mauntery of Saint Glinda's in the Shale Shallows, everyone called her Candle. Candle Osqa'ami. She did herself. But I think that was a mispronunciation from the Qua'ati. Her name is nearer to Cantle. It means 'a part of a thing.' A segment, portion. Sometimes something that has broken off, a shard. A potsherd. A cantle of a statue, of a shell."

"Stop talking about it. Either she'll come back or she won't."

"You know, I've heard only a shell with a broken tip can make any music."

Iskinaary said, "I was thinking quail eggs for supper? Or a nice lake trout." Neither father nor daughter answered him. Rain went out to the front yard and looked at the hills. There was nothing to collect anymore that had meaning, nothing to count or to count on. She walked anyway, dropping fistfuls of nothing, trying to empty herself out of herself.

They buried the Grimmerie on the slope of Nether How, as close as Liir could remember to the spot where he'd seen it emerging in the arms of that ancient magician. They marked the spot by staking Elphaba's broom into the ground, thinking it would last the winter. In the spring they would haul some stones to mark the spot permanently.

When they returned in the spring, though, the broom had taken root and was starting to sprout virgin green, so they left it where it was as marker indeed.

———

Another year passed. No word came from Tip. Rain didn't want to hear news from the Emerald City or, indeed, from anywhere in Oz. She took to wandering the hills around the Five Lakes, and she ventured farther and farther upslope into the Great Kells. Though she had applied by mail and been admitted into Shiz University, she never accepted the position or the bursary and she let the matter slide.

The world seemed slowly to unpopulate, the winds to speak to her in subtle and aggressive tones that she couldn't understand.

Then one day in spring, when the afternoon had a summery clamminess to it though the mountain slopes were only starting to leaf out, she thought again about the shell that had summoned the Ozmists and, perhaps, helped trick La Mombey into giving away the location of the hidden Ozma Tippetarius. The Ozmists had only spoken of appetite for the current day, which was for them the future. One day Rain would be dead too, though she would still be curious about the future. She would be among the Ozmists herself no doubt, eager to know about the children of Ozma Tippetarius, if any could ever be born. The appetite to know ever further what might happen—it was an endless appetite, wasn't it? The story wants to go on and on. She couldn't fault the Ozmists for the permanence of their affection for life, even in death. Half dead herself, she felt that affection too, though it had no focus, no object upon which to address itself.

She took up the shell she'd stolen from Chalotin, that old Quadling seer without feet. She didn't blow it. She felt the broken tip of it—the breakage that allows it to sing. She remembered someone once saying something like "Listen to what it says to you."

She put it to her ear. That same spectacular hush, the presence of expectation, the sound of expectation. A cantle of nothing whole.

She could make no words out, of course. She had tried for years and had never heard so much as a syllable. She laid it back upon the table. The Goose, who had gone rather silent the last year, eyed her balefully. "Well?" snapped Iskinaary. "Anyone leave a message for you?"

His question provoked the answer. What was it saying to her? Nothing in words—she'd been listening to the wrong thing. It didn't speak to her through its hush. It spoke to her through its presence.

It was saying to her: I exist, so what does that say to you?

Liir took no interest in the buried Grimmerie. Instead he negotiated with a tinker to hunt out and eventually deliver to the cottage at Nether How a set of eighty pages of blank paper. Then Liir spent most of the month of Lurlinetide binding them with glue and string into a codex of sorts. After some sloppy experimentation, he managed to accumulate a pot of lampblack by scraping the soot from the chimneys of the oil lamps and grinding it with resin and the char of burnt bark. Iskinaary donated a quill, and Liir sat down to write. It seemed to make him happy while he was waiting for—well, whatever he was waiting for.

"What are you doing?" His industry made her cross.

He looked up as if from a long distance away. His eyes were green; she'd never noticed that.

"I'm writing a treatise, maybe. A letter, anyway. To send to—to Brrr. And Ozma."

She was insulted already. He was barging into her life, trying to make it better. It was less trouble to be abandoned. "About?"

"About. About, I guess—power. About governance. About the birds of no like feather who flew together, to make up the Conference of the Birds. About the maunts who decided to govern themselves by committee rather than by obedience to a superior. About Ozmists and their need to listen to the future as well as to the past. I haven't gotten it straight in my head yet."

"You're angling for a court position? As advisor to the Throne Minister?"

"I'm only angling to question the rationale of a court and a throne. The justice of it."

"Writing never helped a soul to do a thing."

"Except, maybe, to think." He went back to work.

Rain thought he was too young to be so meditative, and his patience made her impatient.

To escape the sound of his thoughts scratching along, she stayed out in cold weather and worked on building a fieldstone wall around the asparagus patch. She remembered the polished chunk in the Chancel of the Ladyfish, with that tiny inscribed creature that seemed as much feather as horse. Maybe one day she would set out on a walkabout across Oz by herself and collect that stone. Inanimate objects were somewhat less bother than people.

She was pausing from her labors late one morning, wiping sweat from her brow despite the rime on the grass and the shelves of ice cantilevering from the shores of the lakes, when she saw a twitch of movement near the broom-tree. Ever wary of some fiend or sorcerer coming by and sniffing out the Grimmerie somehow, she moved closer to check. In the shadows of the tree she startled a serpent of sorts, who proved Serpentine when he reared up, flared his striped lapels, and addressed her.

"You don't need to apply that heavy stone to me," said the Snake. "I mean you no harm."

She shifted it to her hip. "I'm afraid you've picked the wrong place to digest your breakfast. That tree is off bounds to you. It's a memorial garden of sorts."

"I'm no fool. I know what lies in this grave."

Rain didn't think he was being impertinent, but she had long ago lost the gift of a catholic sympathy. She'd grown up too much. "You'd better move along."

"I recognize you, I think. I believe I may have helped your parents degreenify you. I see the spell wore off at last. Most do." He leaned closer on one of his several dozen snake-hips. "You're doing all right, then? You made it?"

"I'm afraid I don't give interviews, Mr. Serpent."

With alacrity he wound himself around the stem of the tree to get a little more height, and then dropped his head from a branch so he could be closer to her. His eyes were acid yellow, not unkind. "Quite wise. I don't either. I find it does the likes of me no good. Everyone twists your words so."

"Are you ready to move along?"

"Are you? Oh, don't look at me like that. I'm merely a concerned citizen of Oz. Also I am a venerable if not downright ancient Serpent, and as such I suffer the affection for the young that afflicts the elderly. I can tell

what you hoard buried beneath this tree, Miss Oziandra Rainary Ko Osqa'ami Thropp. And as I keep my
ear to the ground—little joke, that—I know something
of what you've been through. What I can't guess is why
you don't use the tools at your disposal to do something
about it. And put down that granite cudgel while I'm
talking to you. It's distracting and not at all polite."

She put the boulder down but kept her hands and
her heart clenched.

"I'm merely saying. You have the richest bloodlines
for magic in all of Oz. You have the strongest instrument for change this land has ever seen. And you have
your own need to answer to. There is Tip, turned into
Ozma. You could turn, too. You could be Rain, or you
could be—well, I won't name you. But you could name
yourself. Why do you resist?"

"I think you'd better go."

"If I see no future for my own offspring, I eat them,"
said the Serpent. "If I didn't eat you when I was introduced to you as an infant, why would I sink my venomous fangs into you now? You've done much good.
You've helped complete Elphaba's work, and in a way
your father's work, too. Don't you deserve a reward?
Oh come now, don't look at me like that. What I'm
bringing up is a morally neutral proposition. You think
it is purer to be one gender or the other? That it makes

a difference? I know—no one listens to a Serpent. And I'll move along now, as promised. But think about it."

He passed through the grass. When she looked closer, she saw he'd left his skin behind. A green sheath. It could be made into a scabbard for a dirk. Before going back to the asparagus, she put her finger in the skin and tried to feel the magic of being a Serpent.

She asked her father for permission to leave.

"As if you need my permission," he said calmly, with a clumsy attempt at cheer. "But what shall I say if someone comes looking for you with a message from Ozma?"

"There's no chance of that."

"Rain," he said softly, "anyone who spent the better part of a century being prepubescent is going to need some time to figure out how to be grown up. It could happen."

"Yes. And Candle might come back. And Trism too."

He wasn't hurt. "I leave the front door unlocked for one of them and the back door unlocked for the other. They know where I am. I've cherished them both, Rain, and I do still. Whoever they are. I love both Trism and Candle. It isn't impossible for you to love both Tip and Ozma."

"What's impossible," she said, "is to know the truth inside someone else's heart if they don't tell you."

He agreed with that. "Well, *I* love you. Just in case you ever wondered. And don't forget that I've spent some brief time of my life as an Elephant. They say Elephants never forget, and as I live and breathe, I'm telling you that this is true of humans no less than Elephants. Now, listen. I'm being serious, my desperate sweetheart. What about if a message arrives for you? Where shall I say you've gone?"

She threw an arm about airily. "Oh, way up high. Over the rainbow somewhere, I guess."

2.

In her cell, Glinda woke up with a start. The lumbago was more punishing than the incarceration, but a sense of spring had filtered all the way down the open canyon roof of Southstairs, and she caught a whiff of freshness, of arrogant possibility. Her glasses had broken a year ago. She didn't need them anymore, not really. She knew who was turning the door handle of her cell. She called her name sleepily, and added, "You wicked thing. You've taken your own sweet time, of course."

3.

Elphaba's broom, planted at Nether How and fed by the magic of the Grimmerie buried beneath it, had grown into a tree of brooms. Enough to supply a small coven of witches. Too much to say that the breeze soughing through them all was, well, bewitching? On a spring day of high winds, Rain broke off a broom from the treasury tree of them.

But she waited until her father was deeply asleep one night, and Iskinaary collapsed in front of the stove like a Goose brought down by buckshot, snoring. She took her father's spade over her shoulder and went back to the tree of brooms. She said softly, "Okay, Nanny, I'm following in your footsteps," and she dug up the Grimmerie. Stole it. She left the spade below the tree so her father would know what she'd done. Then she wrapped the fierce book in an oilcloth and strapped the satchel upon her back. She began by walking west across the Kells, which took her several months. She didn't look back, not once, to see if Tip was following her.

By the autumn it was too cold to go on, and she spent the winter with a breakaway tribe of the Scrow, none of whom had ever heard of Elphaba Thropp or Ozma Tippetarius and who seemed unconcerned about Rain's skin color or, indeed, her solitary pilgrimage through the Thousand Year Grasslands. Rain taught herself a bit of Scrow and tried to tell the story of Dorothy, to amuse the clan on the long tent-bound evenings when the icy winds howled, but one of the grandmothers bit her on the wrist, a sign to stop. So she stopped.

She brought out the shell once or twice, to Animals who had learned some Ozish, to itinerants the following spring who had wandered too far to the west and were happy to get directions back to civilization. They nodded about it, unconcerned, unsurprised. One rather lumpy sand creature with an irritable disposition wouldn't talk to her at all but pointed west, west. Farther west. And then dug itself into the sand and wouldn't come out for any pleading at all.

She saw a clutch of dragon eggs in the sand once, and let them be.

Though the thought of them made her sling her leg over the broom for the first time. If she was going to hell in a handbasket, maybe she could fly there faster, get it over with.

She kept herself going by remembering the clues. The great salty marshes of Quadling Country. The huge stone wall upon which paintings of colored fish were refreshed annually, though no such fish ever existed in any lake or river of Oz. The way the berm of Ovvels was built like a quay. The image of a shell stamped in the margins on the left-hand side of a map of Oz. The way that Lady Glinda had deciphered the Chancel of the Ladyfish as a market center of some sort. Something more than a temple, more like the seat of an empire. An empire ruled by a goddess with the tail of a fish.

Listen to what the shell says to you.

The grasslands were beginning to give way to sand, but in no particular hurry, she'd noticed. There would be miles of grass, as far as she could see from the height she was learning to achieve on her broom (which was not impressive). Then sands, in belts between grasslands, until the grasslands gave out. They called it the endless sands, and she saw why. They rippled in waves and crests, static on clear days, fierce and active in the darkness, shifting and reshaping themselves on a nightly basis. There was no track across sands. They rewrote their own topography endlessly.

But then came another stretch of grassland, and beyond that, another swatch of desert. The world was not as definite as the few dots on any map would suggest.

Almost a year after her departure, she was living for a week in a temporary hut she'd built for herself somewhere to the west of Kvon Altar in the southwestern Vinkus. She'd come down with a cough of a sort, and was afraid that perhaps she was dying and might die but forget to notice, and so keep flying forever over alternating patches of wilderness. She gathered liquor from where it beaded up on the shell every night, she licked the dew collected there. Just enough to keep herself from parching. She didn't think she had much time left.

She didn't want to leave the Grimmerie lying around in the desert where some scorpion might find it and teach itself to read, as she had taught herself to read. Almost in a fever one dawn, she took the shell and nourished herself with it as best she could, and then, remembering an old life, she blew the horn once again through the broken tip.

Even Ozmists can't survive in the desert, she thought to herself, sinking into a sleep as the sun rose. The wind blew her lean-to apart but she was too removed from reality to notice. Through the vast sky the sun threatened to burn her green skin brown and mottled. Light wriggled behind her clenched eyelids like threads of blood.

Around midday, delirious with thirst, she opened her eyes. She thought she saw a figure of bones standing nearby, looking down at her. He wore a coat made of greenery. Mountain pine, fir, holly, laurel. Impossible life. The skeleton looked at her. He seemed to smile. All skeletons smile. She closed her eyes and forgot about it.

Back there.

Disturbed in the middle of a moonless night by something unseen, a cock chortily hacked at the silence in a northern barnyard. A farmer threw a soup ladle at it, threateningly. The cock subsided.

In the forest of Gurniname outside Wiccasand Turning, a stand of rare bone-oak trees, famous for their centuries of barrenness without decay, burst into bloom. The blossoms glowed, not white, but a rich velvety jade with lavender margins. A gourmand hunting for truffles discovered it, and for a while painters flocked to catch the mystery on canvas. But the effect was always too startling. It looked fake. Eventually most of the canvases were painted over. Patrons of art preferred their bone-oak blossoms white, or dead.

Kellswater at dawn. A giant Tortoise emerged from a cleft between two stone plates nearly collapsed one upon the other. She'd lived eighty of her two hundred years in private meditation, prayer and fasting, and she was on the morning side of munch-ish. The history described in the pages of this and previous volumes had escaped her, and she it. Undeterred by such scathing ignorance she moved forward on fungoidal flippers, and her rust red horny beak scratched at the air. The light leaching over the horizon snagged and pulled upon ripples of water fletching the lake. Small circles as if from invisible drops of rain puckered the surface. The Tortoise remembered. She knew the commotion was the morning activity of swarmgits upon water, and that where swarmgits could skate in buggy congress of a fine morning, a hungry carp or a lake terch wouldn't be far behind.

And—and this Kellswater. The dead lake. But she did not comment.

That's the way it looked to plants and animals. Somewhere else in Oz—the province, the town doesn't matter—a prissy and adenoidal tutor straight out of Three Queens College had taken a position to hector local schoolchildren into their letters and morals. Intending to set an early example of the mercy of discipline, he arrived in the schoolroom with a small box made of close-meshed wire. "Approach and regard," he said to the boys and girls in his thrall. "We must be wary of the natural world, learn from its habits of violence and self-interest, and tame it so it may survive. This morning upon my hearth I found an insect of a sort never known before in Oz. I studied entomology and lepidoptery under Professor Finix at Three Queens, so I claim some wide experience with bugs. I say this is an aberration of an existing species— smaller, cannier, and more cunningly hued for camouflage. Were it allowed to breed, it could chew its way through our 'Oz in endless leaf.' For our own protection I have caged it in this box. It looks faintly related to the locust of the Grasslands or to the marsh fern-hopper. It saws music from its legs, when it is happy. It isn't happy now, but we will require it to learn to be happy in a cage. And so will you—"

The youngest student, a lad who still wore double padding against accidental leakage, picked up the willow switch in the corner and cracked it upon the docent's remonstrating finger. The other students rioted. They threw books out the window and chased the teacher into the henhouse, locking him inside. He sat most of the morning blubbering. Then the students ate all their lunch at once and left the wrappings to blow about in the schoolyard, and sang songs of loyalty to anarchy as they released the cricket from its cage.

Not too much should be read into all this. It is the sometime nature of children to be wild. And in wildness, as a traveler from another land has reminded us, is the salvation of the world.

In the coolness of the evening—that evening or the next, maybe—Rain came around enough to find—she must be hallucinating—that her face was shaded from the setting sun by an umbrella.

"Very nice," she said, admiring her psychosis.

"I'd hoped you appreciated it," said a familiar voice. Iskinaary peered out from behind the upturned bowl of the fabric.

"Are *you* the angel of death? Goodness, you scared me enough in life, you're not going to accompany me across the divide, are you?"

"Very funny. Have a cracker." With his bill he secured a hard round biscuit from a little satchel slung over his neck. "Don't worry, it's not one of Little Daffy's Curious Cupcakes."

"I should be glad for one of those right about now. What are you doing here?"

"I've been following behind you for the better part of a year. Your father sent me to look for you when you didn't come back after that hard winter in the grasslands, and I heard you'd continued on. I've been waiting out of sight, a few miles back, for several months. Not wanting to be presumptuous."

"Oh, a little presumption is welcome now and then."

"You're dehydrated. Let me take that shell and fly to find some freshwater somewhere."

"There's no water here."

"You don't know where to look."

Iskinaary, if it was really he and not some irritating mirage, allowed himself to be fixed with the shell in a kind of sling, and went off for a while. When he came back, the basin of the shell slopped over with freshwater. Rain drank so quickly that she vomited most of it back up again. He didn't mind. He got her more, and she kept the second portion down more neatly.

In the morning, or the morning after that, she felt better again. "You carried that umbrella all the way from Nether How?"

"I used it too, on certain nights. My feathers are thinning and the drainage isn't what it used to be." Yes, Iskinaary was an old Goose.

"You never liked me," she said.

"I don't like you now. But I am your father's familiar, so let's put personal feelings aside. We have a ways to go, I'll warrant."

"I don't know how far I'm going to get."

"I don't know either." He smiled at her or winced, it was hard to tell the difference in any Goose, and particularly in Iskinaary. "But I think we are not very far from the edge."

"The edge," she said.

"Where you are going."

"You don't know where I am going."

"Not ultimately."

They considered this stalemate a while, and then Iskinaary relented. "Your father wasn't much of a witch, was he?"

"He wasn't much of a father either."

"But he was pretty good as a Bird, when he flew with Kynot and the Conference. He learned a little bit. He didn't learn enough."

She waited.

"The Birds have always known," said Iskinaary. "At least, some have. But Birds, and birds, keep to themselves usually. They flock with their kind. It takes the rare spirit to convince them to flock with those unlike them. Your father conducted one such campaign, in those dark days when the dragons first threatened Oz, threatened the skies for all the Birds, and the earth for all crawling creatures. Liir flew with us on his broom, as you fly now. He might have learned more from us, but he was young, and Birds, well, they don't volunteer much. It's not in their nature. They are neutral, and possessed of a certain appealing reticence."

"Some of them," admitted Rain. "Not you."

"So," Iskinaary continued, "we've known. We have always known, or anyway we've heard rumors. We could have told you what we'd heard. I could have told you. Humans are so blind, their eyes on the ground, themselves always at the center. Birds know themselves not to be at the center of anything, but at the margins of everything. The end of the map. We only live where someone's horizon sweeps someone else's. We are only noticed on the edge of things; but on the edge of things, we notice much."

"Is everything all right back there in Oz?"

"I've not followed along all these months to gossip." He seemed angry. "I'm trying to tell you to keep going."

"Well, all right then. But if I'm right, I go alone."

"You make the rules for the ground. I'll make the rules for the air."

She launched herself and didn't look behind to see if he was following. She knew he was, the rolled-up umbrella in his claws. It would be kinder if she were to carry it, but she wasn't ready to be kind.

That night, among scratchy grass, she slept and dreamed of Tip. She didn't know if it was Tip or Ozma, really; it was that kind of a dream that made her furious with need and regret and hope all at once. She awoke in the dark, clammy in a cold sweat even though it would be a warm day, she could tell. A sort of fog, as from Restwater, hung over the sedge.

She said to herself, Did my father send Iskinaary after me because a message had arrived at last?

But she wouldn't ask the Goose for fear of the answer, either way it might be spoken. She wasn't ready to know.

She found a place to squat, and after that she broke her fast with Iskinaary. More dry biscuits. Delicious. The wind, the world of shadows. The taunting stars strung on their invisible threads across the glowing velvet black. They didn't speak—not girl, not Goose, not stars.

Near dawn, she strode through the grass to the top of the near slope, to see if the air would clear, if she could catch a glimpse of the next stretch.

Beyond the slope, at bluff's edge, the ground dropped away in a returning curve, a bevel carved out by a stronger breeze. The air felt stronger, brusquer, colder, more filled with tang, almost a strange kind of vinegar in the wind.

She kept going, down that slope and up the curve of the next. The wind possessed bluster and noise she'd never heard at ground level before. Ever.

The fog had oriented itself into a composite of colored scarves through which the sun from behind her was beginning to seethe, gilding the unnatural hills.

They weren't hills of earth.

The world's edge was water; water as far as the eye could see; water from the scalloped strand out to the horizon. There was no end to it. The noise wasn't the sound of wind, after all, but of moving water that made endless avalanche against the sand, punching and pulling back. Foundries of spume and spit, and salt stinging her eyes. Thrashes of weight from side to side, streaked laterally with zinc; mettanite; emerald; lamb's wool; turquoise. The great weeping rim of the world.

She didn't wait for the Goose. She slung her leg over the broom and launched at once. A new technique for flying would be needed against this force. Later in the day, if she lasted, she might glance back and find that the Goose had anticipated her departure and was steadily keeping pace a mile or more behind. She trusted that this would be true.

She would make no plan but this: to move out into the world as a Bird might, and to perch on the edge of everything that could be known. She would circle herself with water below and with sky above. She would wait until there was no stink of Oz, no breath of it, no sight of it on any horizon no matter how high she climbed. And then she would let go of the book, let it plunge into the mythical sea.

Live life without grasping for the magic of it.

Turn back, and find out what that was like; or turn forward, and learn something new.

A mile above anything known, the Girl balanced on the wind's forward edge, as if she were a green fleck of the sea itself, flung up by the turbulent air and sent wheeling away.

FINIS

About that country there's not much left to say.
Blue sun, far off, a watery vein
in the cloud belt. The solid earth itself
unremarkable: familiar ruins
littered with standing stones our people
had lost the ability to decipher.
How deeply had we slept? Beneath the jellyfish
umbels of evergreens, each one a dream,
and the effervescent stars, strange currents
tugged at our thoughts like tapestries
unraveling into war. All spring
the nightingale perched on the green volcano's lip.
The rats had abandoned the temples.
My mind was a voyage hungering to happen.

—Todd Hearon, "Atlantis"

. . . we must learn to live a secondary life in an
   unmarked world.

—Ron MacLean, "Duck Variations"

Acknowledgments

Thank you, one and all, to the many friends and colleagues who helped one way or the other in the work of getting *Out of Oz* out on paper.

—Douglas Smith, artist, for the splendid jacket and case, section art, and maps

—David Groff, Betty Levin, Andy Newman, for their close reading and helpful remarks

—William Reiss of John Hawkins and Associates, for the same

—Cassie Jones, Liate Stehlik, Lynn Grady, and other fine people at HarperCollins: Rich Aquan, Ben Bruton, Jessica Deputato, Tavia Kowalchuk, Shawn Nicholls, Lisa Stokes, Nyamekye Waliyaya, Chelsey Emmelhainz, and Lorie Young

—the producers and creators and performers of *Wicked* the musical, at home and around the world, whose good cheer has become a constant background melody in my life

—Scott Glorioso, Lori Shelly, and Elizabeth Williams in the GM office, for managing crises from technological to overnight posting to accounting, but perhaps especially to Emily Prabhaker, for helping me compose an index and synopsis to the first three books of *The Wicked Years*, which was an invaluable map and guide as I drove the complicated story to its complicated conclusion

—Todd Hearon and Ron MacLean, for permission to quote from their work at the novel's close

—Andy and the next generation of Maguire Newmans, for all the life that cannot be found in the pages of novels

Coda

Before you close the cover of the present volume, and allow the writer to sink back into its pages, living both through and beside his characters, let's grab a last look from the promontory. The next eyes to glance over our horizon will see something else. Something new, prompting a separate issue to propose and explore.

Oz before sunrise. The ancient predawn light makes of the earth below a mystery, and of all those anonymous lives more mysteries still. The tired stars winking out, the smear of cloud dividing the midnight from pale marigold dawn. The sheet of the heavens holds the stage a moment longer, eclipsing earthbound dramas of tedium, resurrection, and despair; of individual aspiration and sacrifice; of national effort and disgrace.

A welcome amnesia, our capacity to sleep, to be lost in the dark. Today will shine its spotlights to shame and to honor us soon enough. But all in good time, my pretty. We can wait.

Oz at sunrise. What one makes out, from any height, are the outlines. The steel-cut peaks of the Great Kells, the pudding hills of the Madeleines. The textured outcroppings of Shiz, Bright Lettins, the Emerald City. Ignore the few pixilated dots of gold in the black (early risers—those with ailing relatives, or scholars late at their books, nothing more than that). We see little of human industry and ambition to chart at this hour. This is a roughed-out landscape only coming into life. A map done in smudged pencil, a first draft. Much to be filled in when light arrives. But thank you, Mr. Baum, for leaving the map where I could find it.

Watching the world wake up, dress itself in the dark, take on its daily guise, reminds me of how we fathom human character when we encounter someone at a distance, at a gallop, in the shadows. We get no more than a quick glance at the man on the street, the child in the woods, the witch at the well, the Lion among us. Our initial impression, most often, has to serve.

Still, that first crude glimpse, a clutch of raw hypotheses that can never be soundly clinched or dismissed, is often all we get before we must choose whether to lean forward or to avert our eyes. Slim evidence indeed, but put together with mere hints and echoes of what we have once read, we risk cherishing one another. Light will blind us in time, but what we learn in the dark can see us through.

To read, even in the half-dark, is also to call the lost forward.

HARPER LUXE

THE NEW LUXURY IN READING

We hope you enjoyed reading
our new, comfortable print size and found it
an experience you would like to repeat.

Well – you're in luck!

HarperLuxe offers the finest in fiction and
nonfiction books in this same larger print size and
paperback format. Light and easy to read, HarperLuxe
paperbacks are for book lovers who want to see
what they are reading without the strain.

For a full listing of titles and
new releases to come, please visit our website:

www.HarperLuxe.com